#4

# BATTLE STATION PRIME

# THE SPIRIT IN THE STONE

## AN UNOFFICIAL GRAPHIC NOVEL FOR MINECRAFTERS

## CARA J. STEVENS

### ILLUSTRATED BY SAM NEEDHAM

SKY PONY PRESS
New York

Sky Pony Press books may be purchased in bulk at special discounts for sales promotion, corporate gifts, fund-raising, or educational purposes. Special editions can also be created to specifications. For details, contact the Special Sales Department, Sky Pony Press, 307 West 36th Street, 11th Floor, New York, NY 10018 or info@skyhorsepublishing.com.



Minecraft® is a registered trademark of Notch Development AB.
The Minecraft game is copyright © Mojang AB.

Visit our website at www.skyponypress.com.

10 9 8 7 6 5 4 3 2 1

Library of Congress Cataloging-in- Publication Data is available on file.

Cover design by Brian Peterson
Cover and interior art by Sam Needham

Print ISBN: 978-1-5107-4730-2
Ebook ISBN: 978-1-5107-4741-8

Printed in the United States of America

This book is not authorized or sponsored by Microsoft Corp., Mojang AB, Notch Development AB or Scholastic Inc., or any other person or entity owning or controlling rights in the Minecraft name, trademark, or copyrights

#4

# BATTLE STATION PRIME
# THE SPIRIT IN THE STONE

# MEET THE

**PELL:** A boy with a talent for getting lost and for making the best of every situation.

**LOGAN:** Pell's best friend, who is an expert hacker and redstone programmer.

**MADDY:** Logan's very smart little sister, who has a talent for enchanting objects.

**UNCLE COLIN:** Pell's uncle, who is an excellent politician and leader.

# CHARACTERS

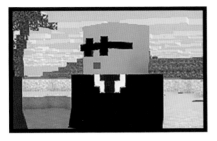

**MR. JAMES:** The leader of Battle Station Prime.

**NED:** A great chef who has a mysterious past.

**BEN FROST:** A programmer who has a talent for inventing clever solutions.

**CLOUD, ZOE, AND BROOKLYN:** Residents of Battle Station Prime.

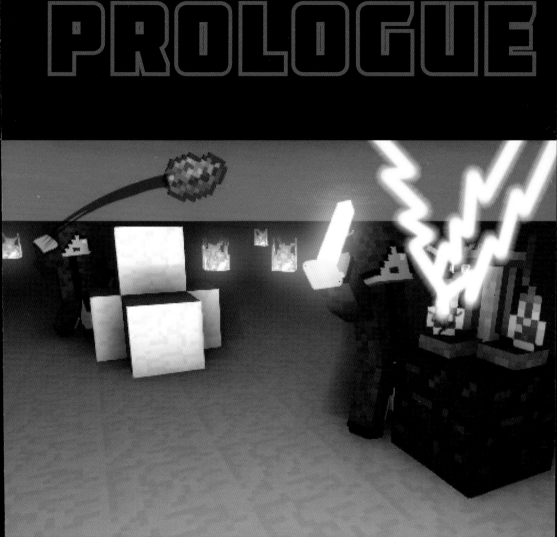

# PROLOGUE

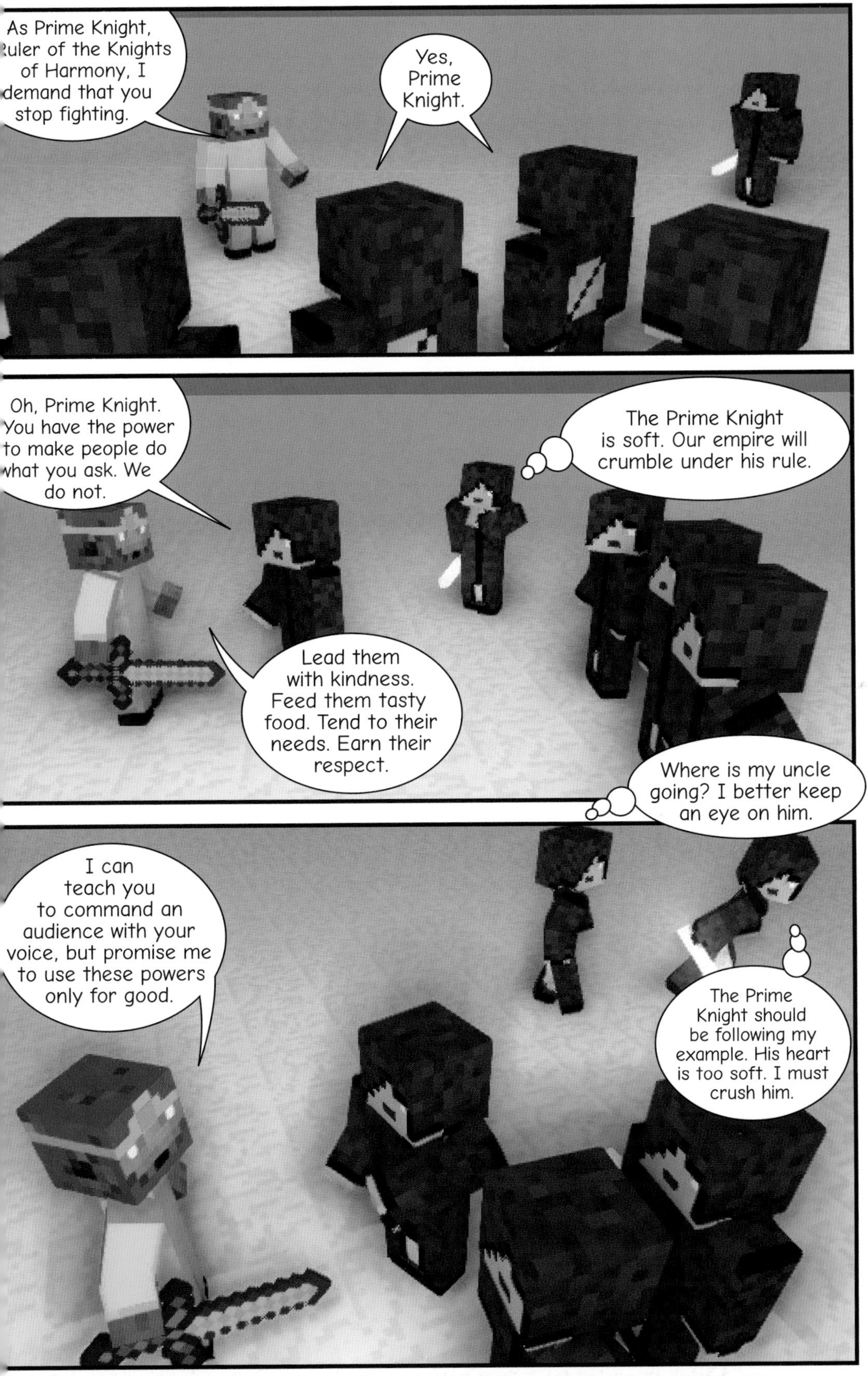
As Prime Knight, Ruler of the Knights of Harmony, I demand that you stop fighting.
Yes, Prime Knight.
Oh, Prime Knight. You have the power to make people do what you ask. We do not.
The Prime Knight is soft. Our empire will crumble under his rule.
Lead them with kindness. Feed them tasty food. Tend to their needs. Earn their respect.
Where is my uncle going? I better keep an eye on him.
I can teach you to command an audience with your voice, but promise me to use these powers only for good.
The Prime Knight should be following my example. His heart is too soft. I must crush him.

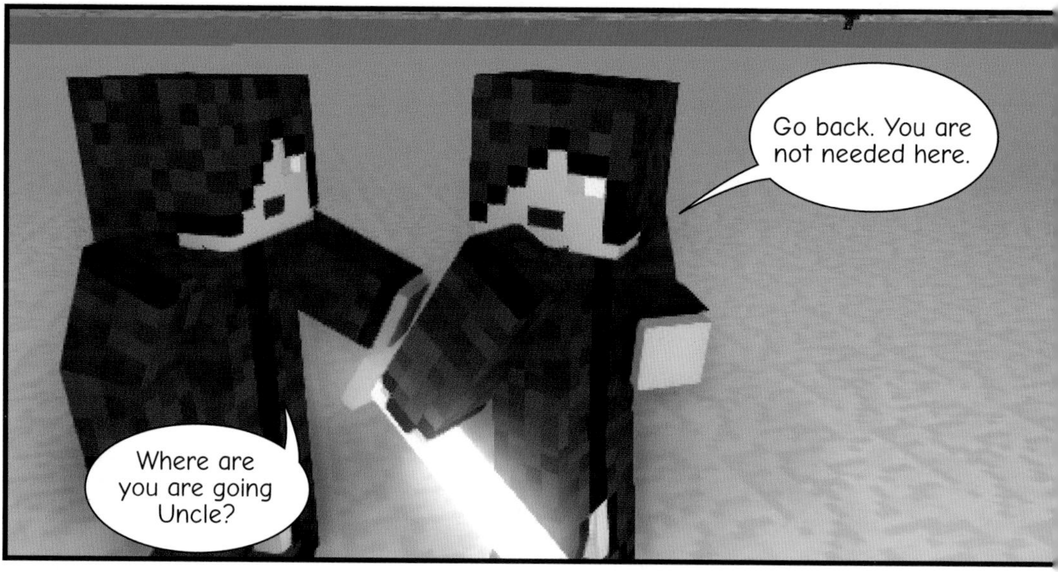
Go back. You are not needed here.
Where are you are going Uncle?

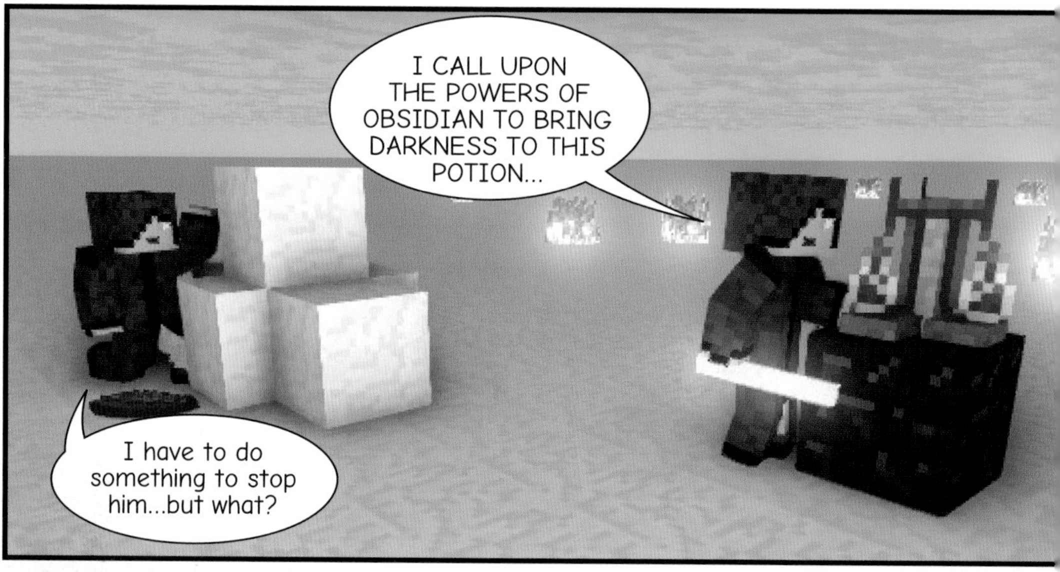
I CALL UPON THE POWERS OF OBSIDIAN TO BRING DARKNESS TO THIS POTION...
I have to do something to stop him...but what?

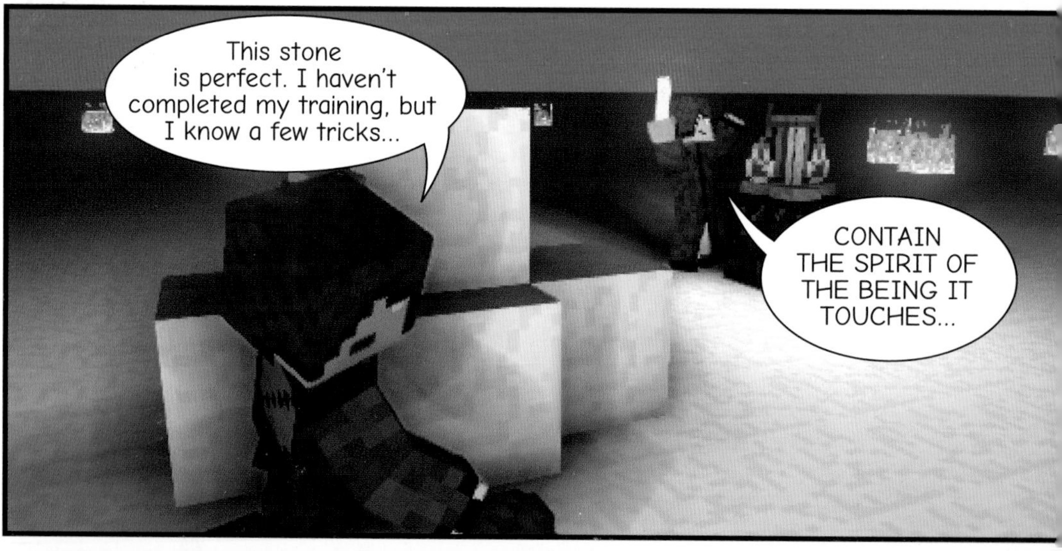
This stone is perfect. I haven't completed my training, but I know a few tricks...
CONTAIN THE SPIRIT OF THE BEING IT TOUCHES...

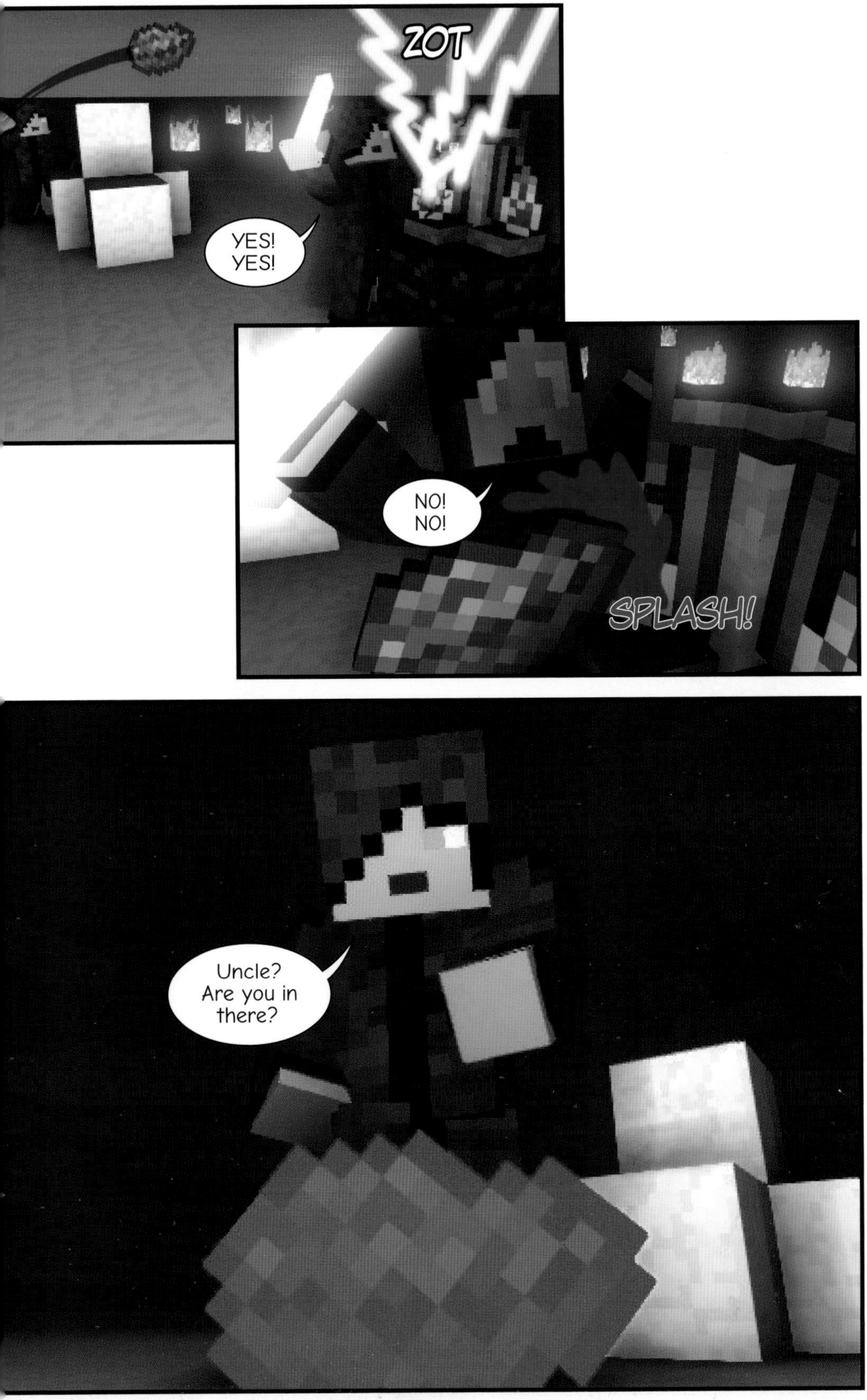
ZOT
YES! YES!
NO! NO!
SPLASH!
Uncle? Are you in there?

# CHAPTER 1

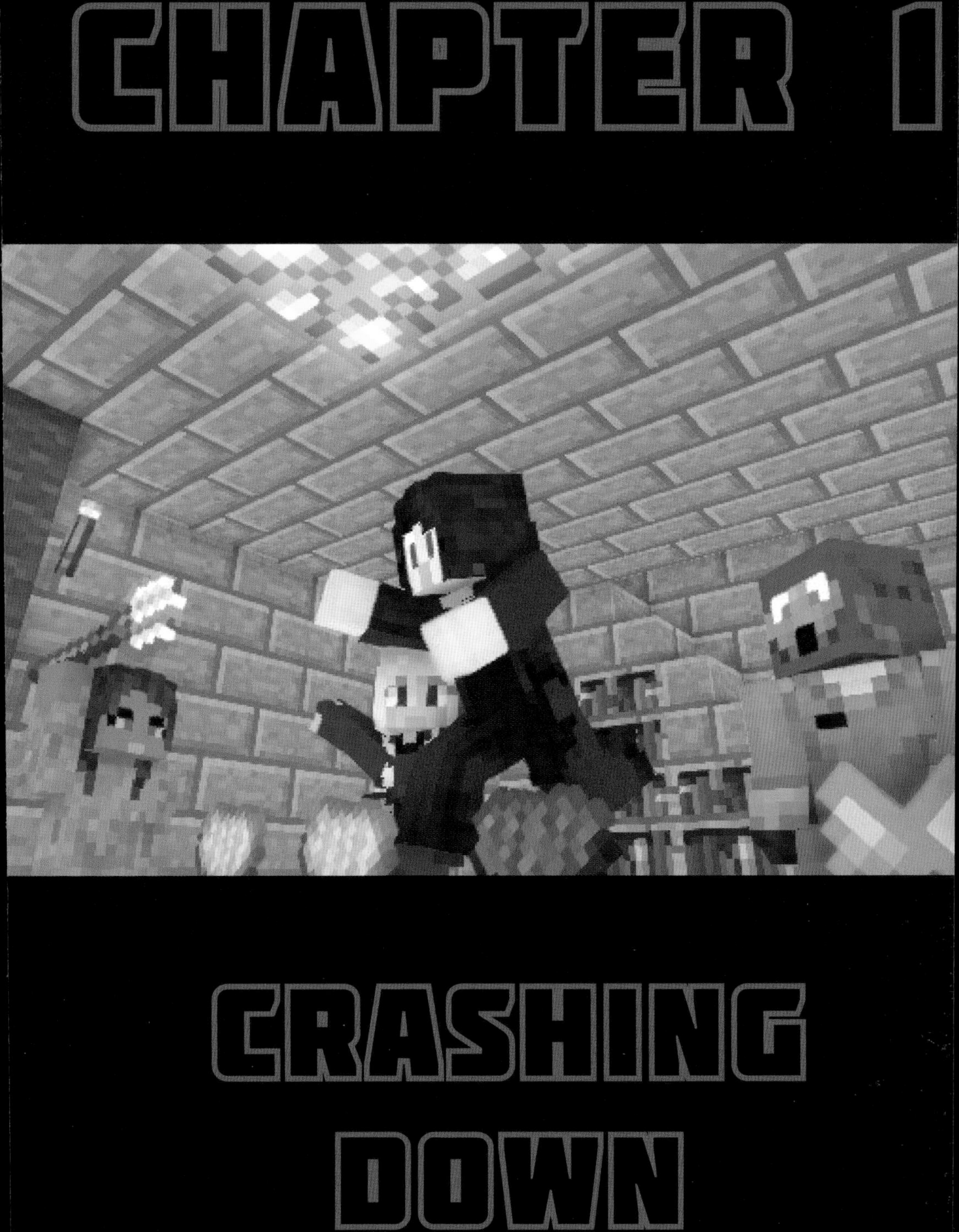

# CRASHING DOWN

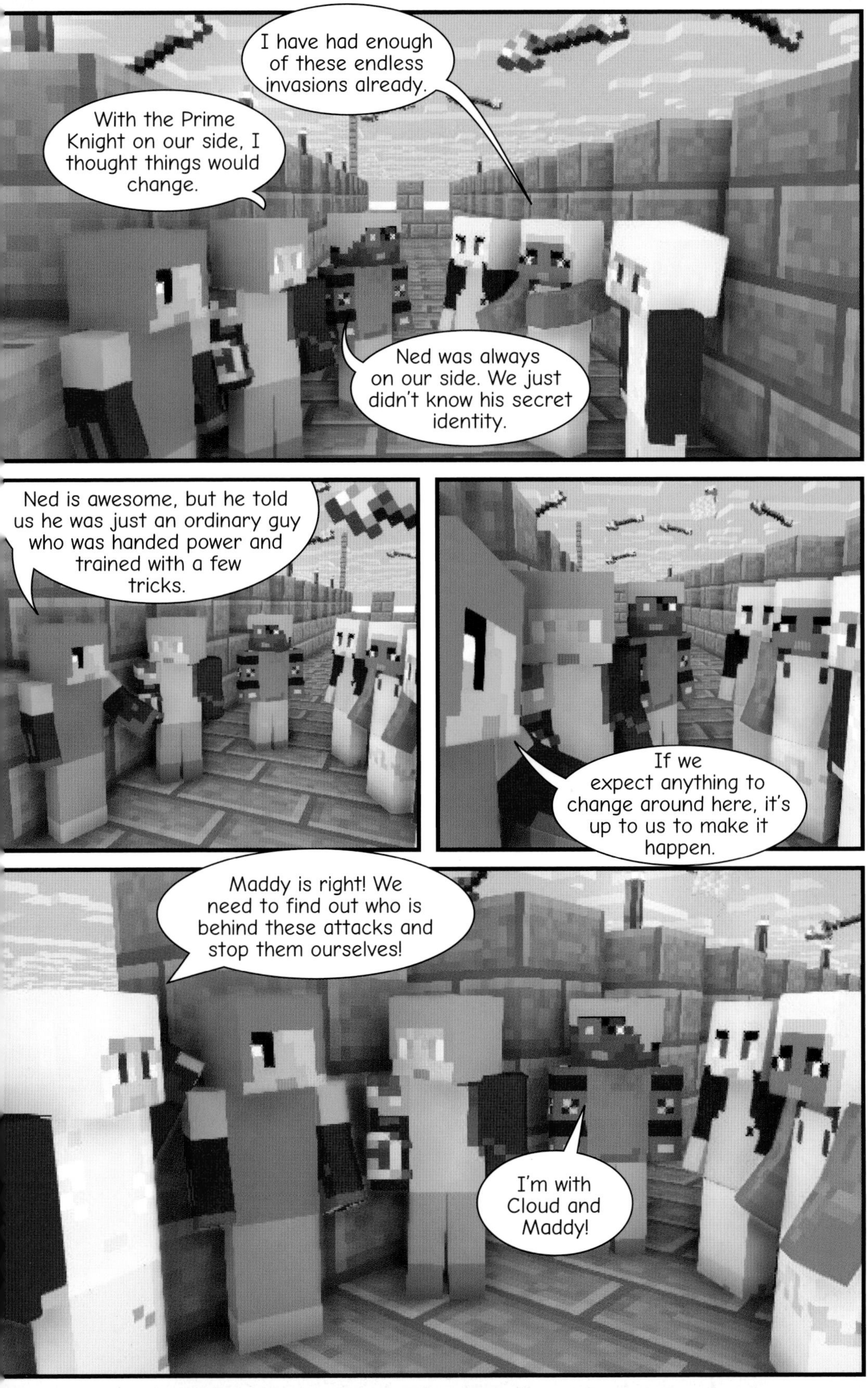
I have had enough of these endless invasions already.
With the Prime Knight on our side, I thought things would change.
Ned was always on our side. We just didn't know his secret identity.
Ned is awesome, but he told us he was just an ordinary guy who was handed power and trained with a few tricks.
If we expect anything to change around here, it's up to us to make it happen.
Maddy is right! We need to find out who is behind these attacks and stop them ourselves!
I'm with Cloud and Maddy!

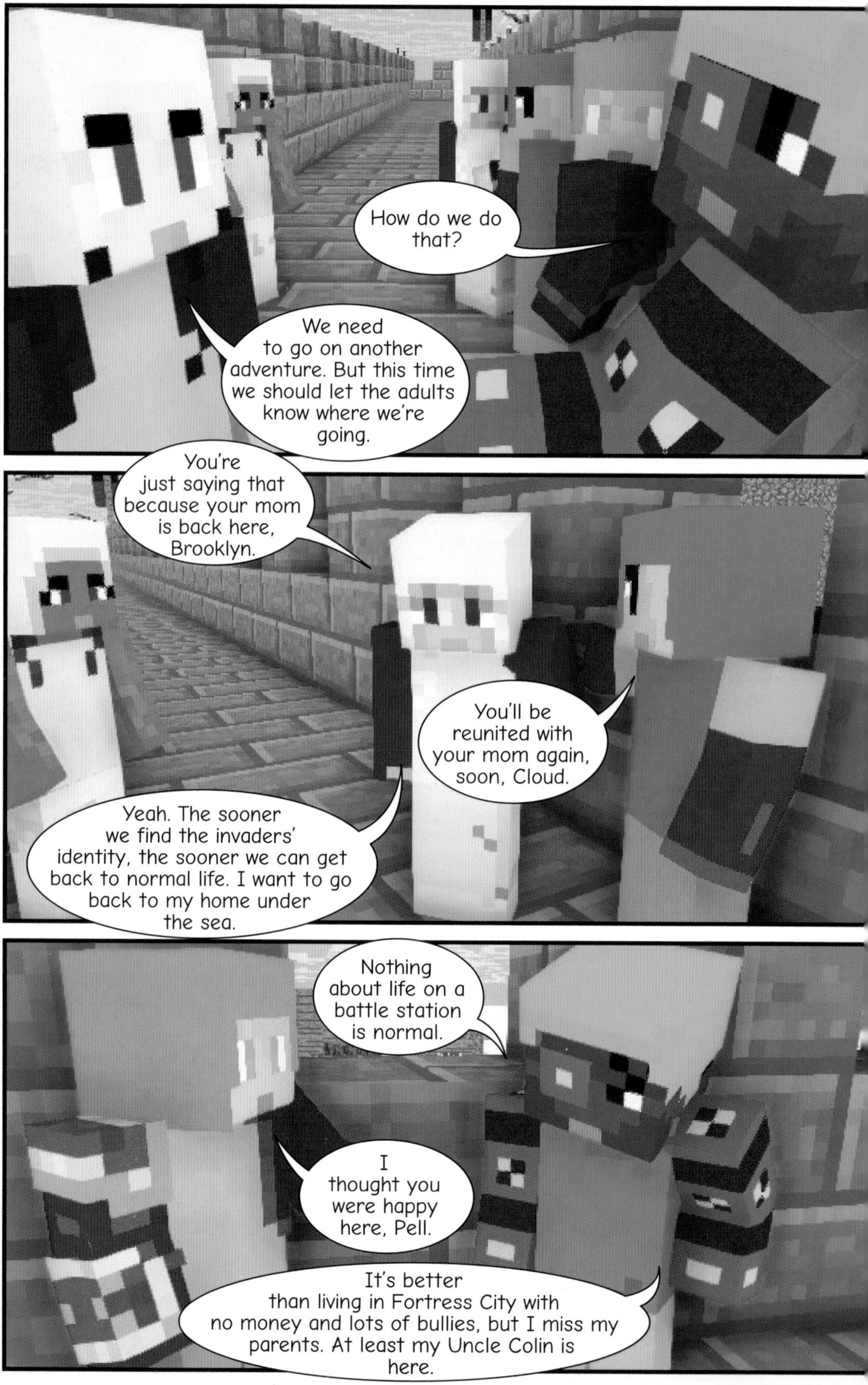
How do we do that?
We need to go on another adventure. But this time we should let the adults know where we're going.
You're just saying that because your mom is back here, Brooklyn.
You'll be reunited with your mom again, soon, Cloud.
Yeah. The sooner we find the invaders' identity, the sooner we can get back to normal life. I want to go back to my home under the sea.
Nothing about life on a battle station is normal.
I thought you were happy here, Pell.
It's better than living in Fortress City with no money and lots of bullies, but I miss my parents. At least my Uncle Colin is here.

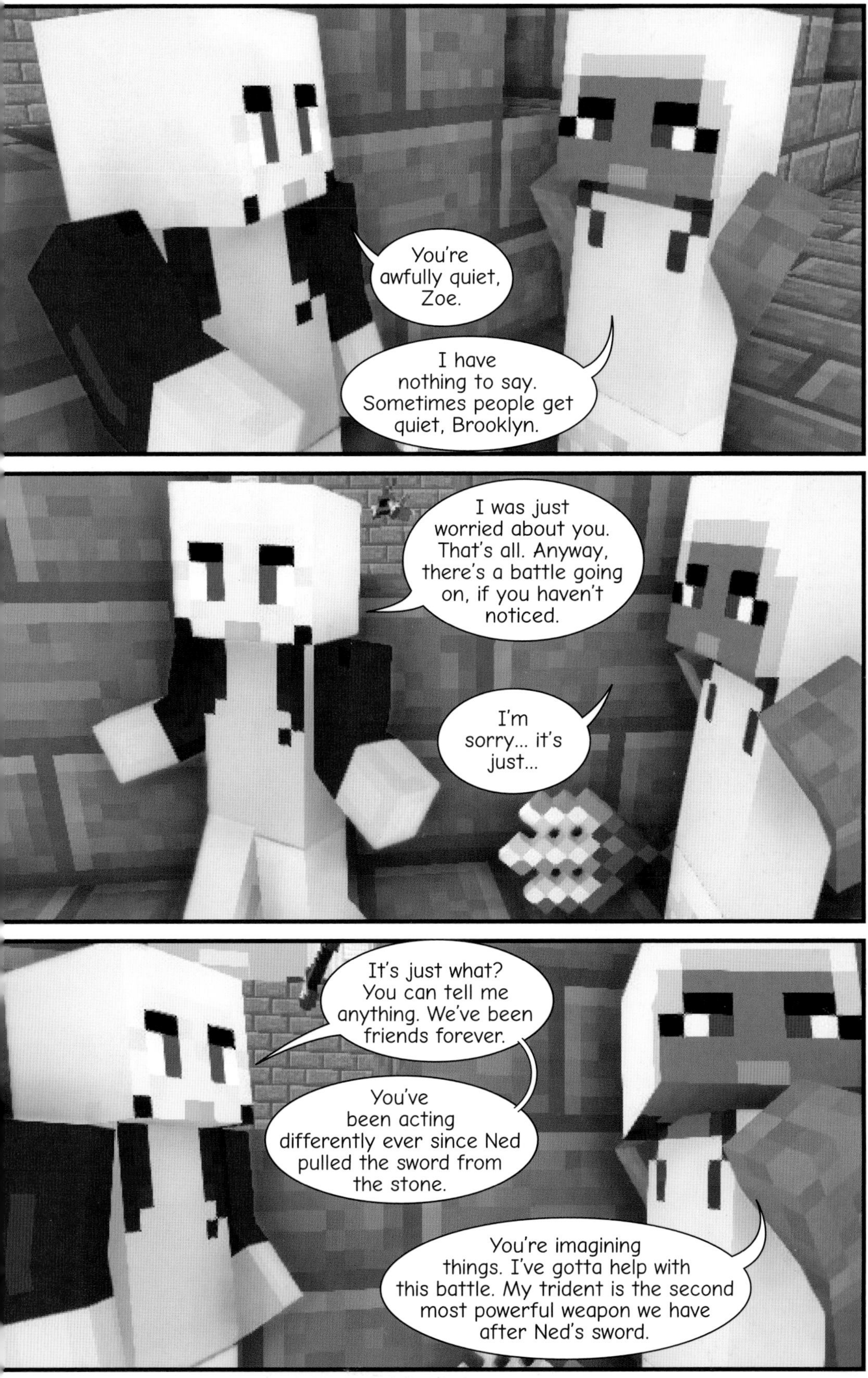
You're awfully quiet, Zoe.
I have nothing to say. Sometimes people get quiet, Brooklyn.
I was just worried about you. That's all. Anyway, there's a battle going on, if you haven't noticed.
I'm sorry... it's just...
It's just what? You can tell me anything. We've been friends forever.
You've been acting differently ever since Ned pulled the sword from the stone.
You're imagining things. I've gotta help with this battle. My trident is the second most powerful weapon we have after Ned's sword.

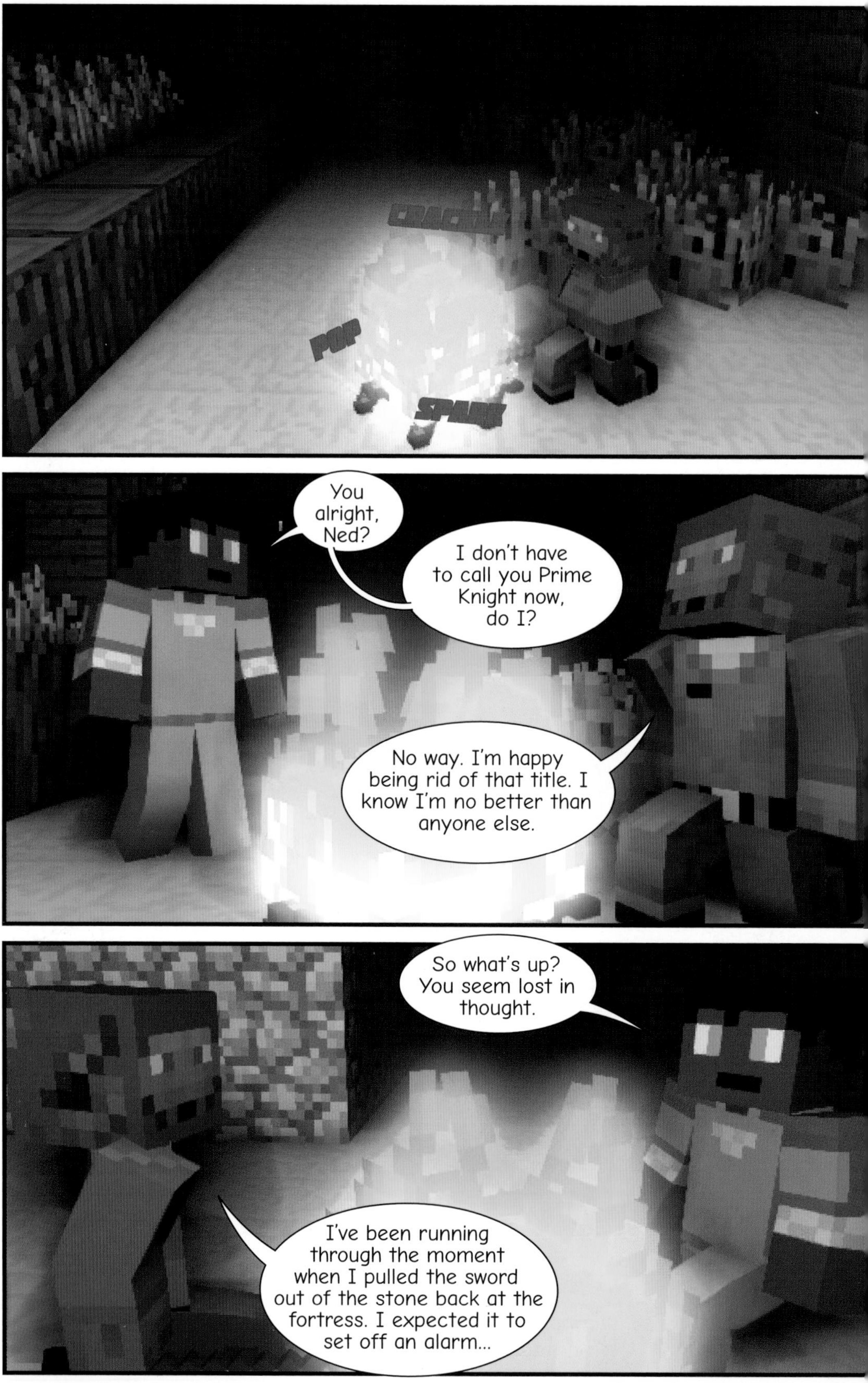
POP
SPARK
You alright, Ned?
I don't have to call you Prime Knight now, do I?
No way. I'm happy being rid of that title. I know I'm no better than anyone else.
So what's up? You seem lost in thought.
I've been running through the moment when I pulled the sword out of the stone back at the fortress. I expected it to set off an alarm...

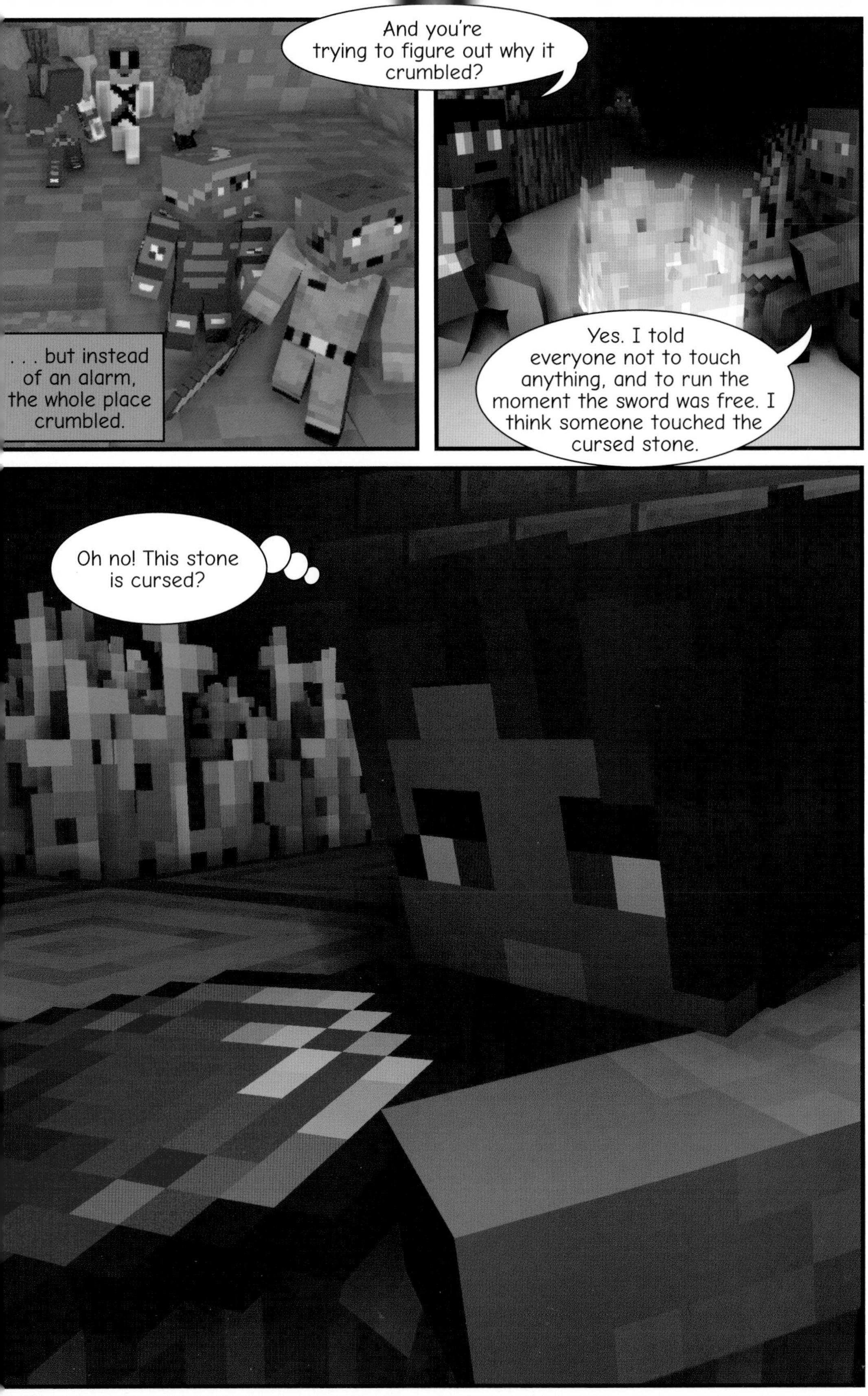
. . . but instead of an alarm, the whole place crumbled.
And you're trying to figure out why it crumbled?
Yes. I told everyone not to touch anything, and to run the moment the sword was free. I think someone touched the cursed stone.
Oh no! This stone is cursed?

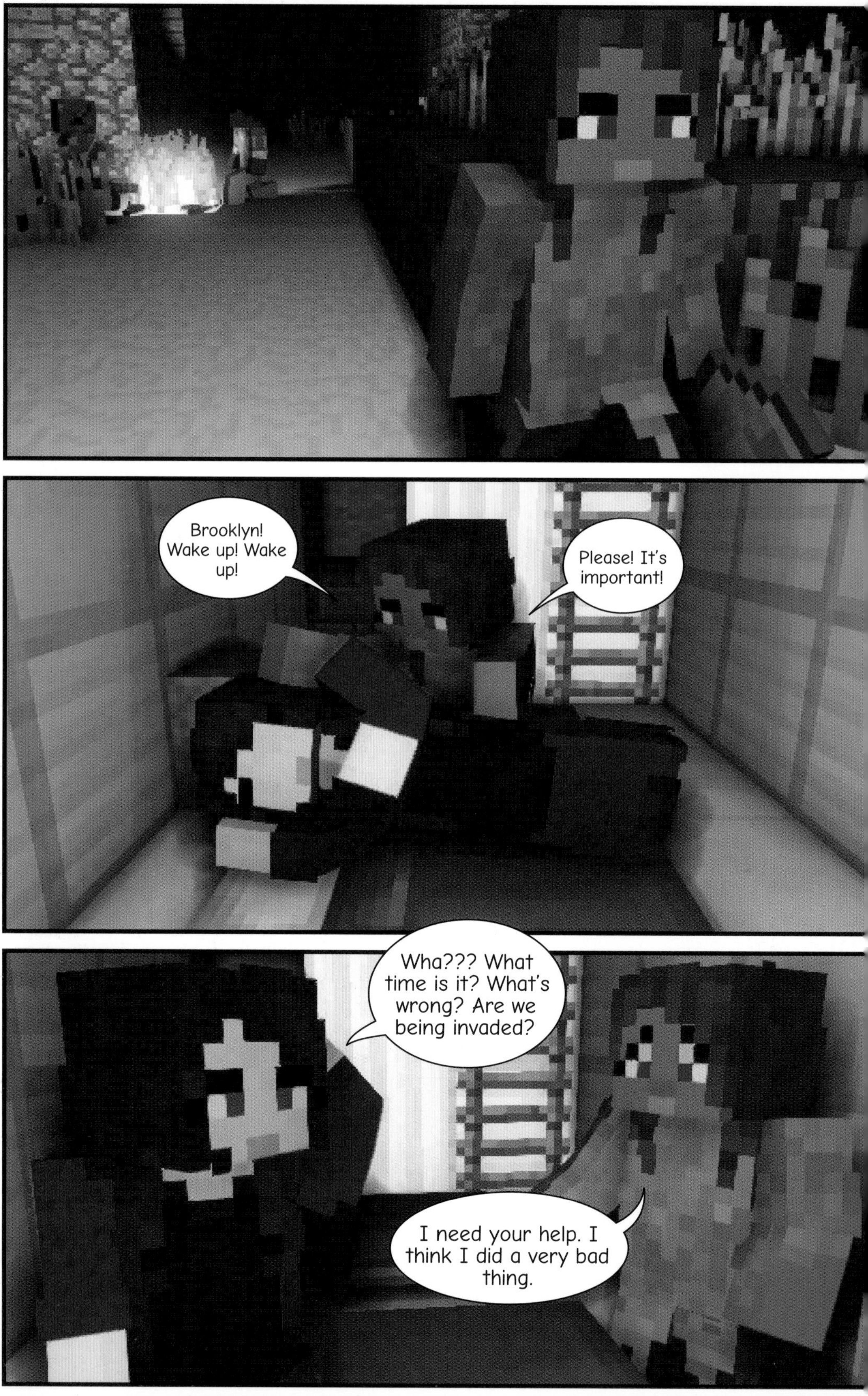
Brooklyn! Wake up! Wake up!
Please! It's important!
Wha??? What time is it? What's wrong? Are we being invaded?
I need your help. I think I did a very bad thing.

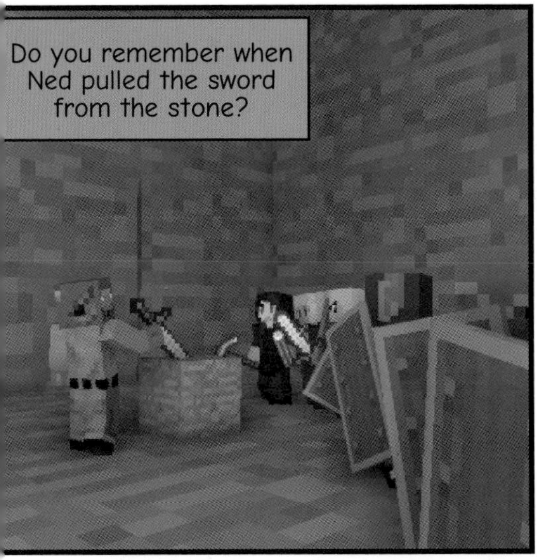
Do you remember when Ned pulled the sword from the stone?

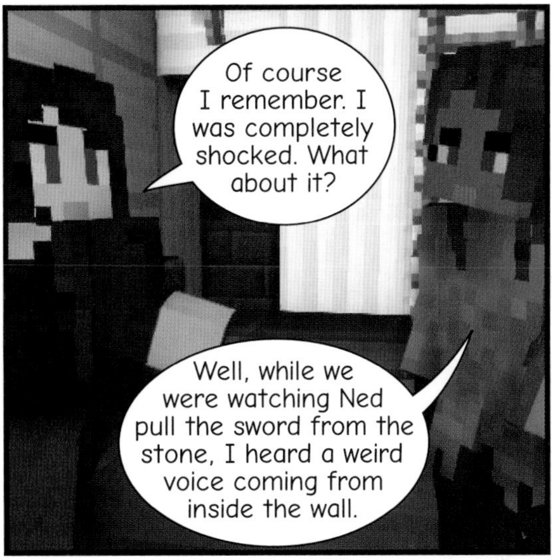
Of course I remember. I was completely shocked. What about it?
Well, while we were watching Ned pull the sword from the stone, I heard a weird voice coming from inside the wall.

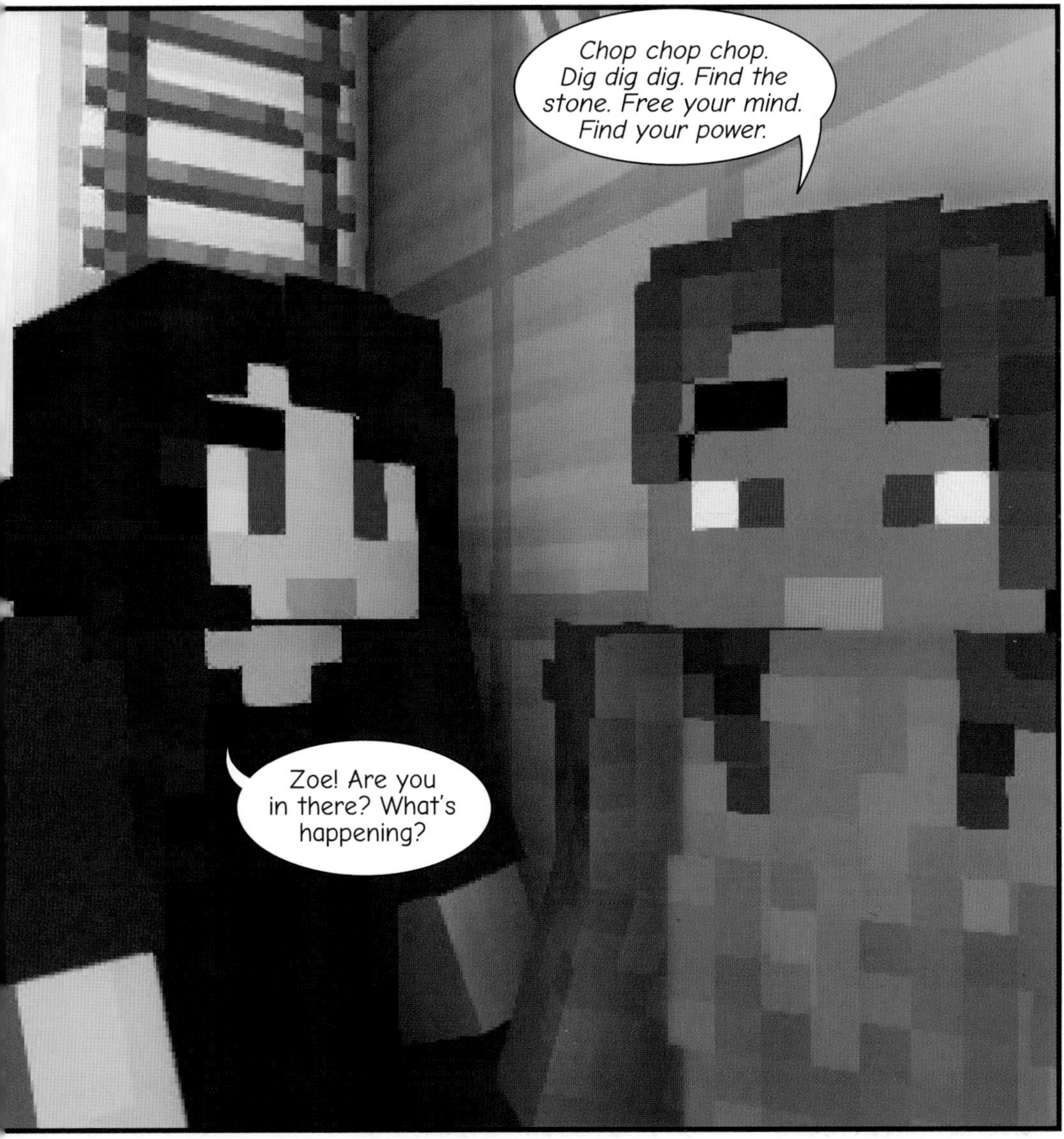
*Chop chop chop. Dig dig dig. Find the stone. Free your mind. Find your power.*
Zoe! Are you in there? What's happening?

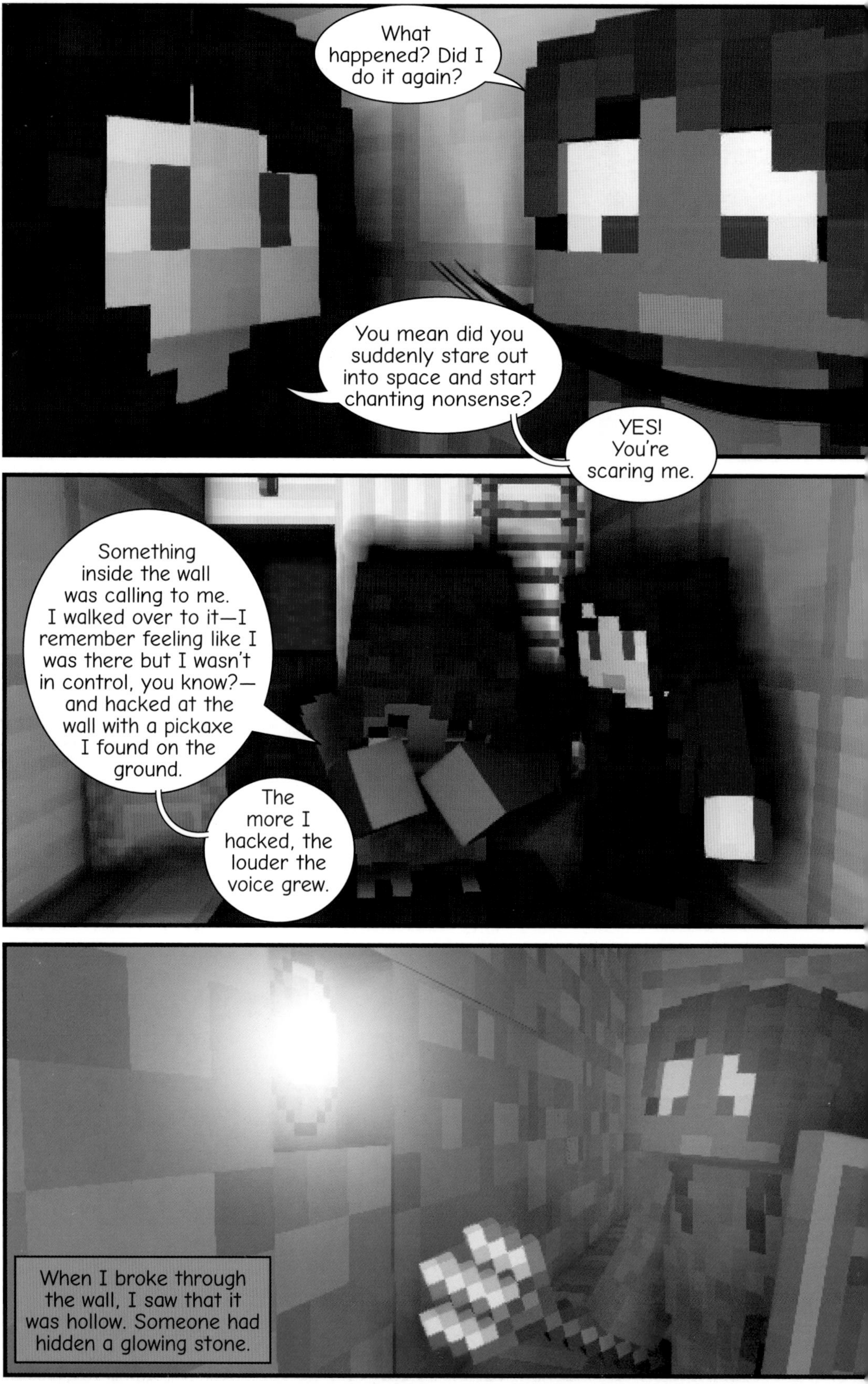
What happened? Did I do it again?
You mean did you suddenly stare out into space and start chanting nonsense?
YES! You're scaring me.
Something inside the wall was calling to me. I walked over to it—I remember feeling like I was there but I wasn't in control, you know?—and hacked at the wall with a pickaxe I found on the ground.
The more I hacked, the louder the voice grew.
When I broke through the wall, I saw that it was hollow. Someone had hidden a glowing stone.

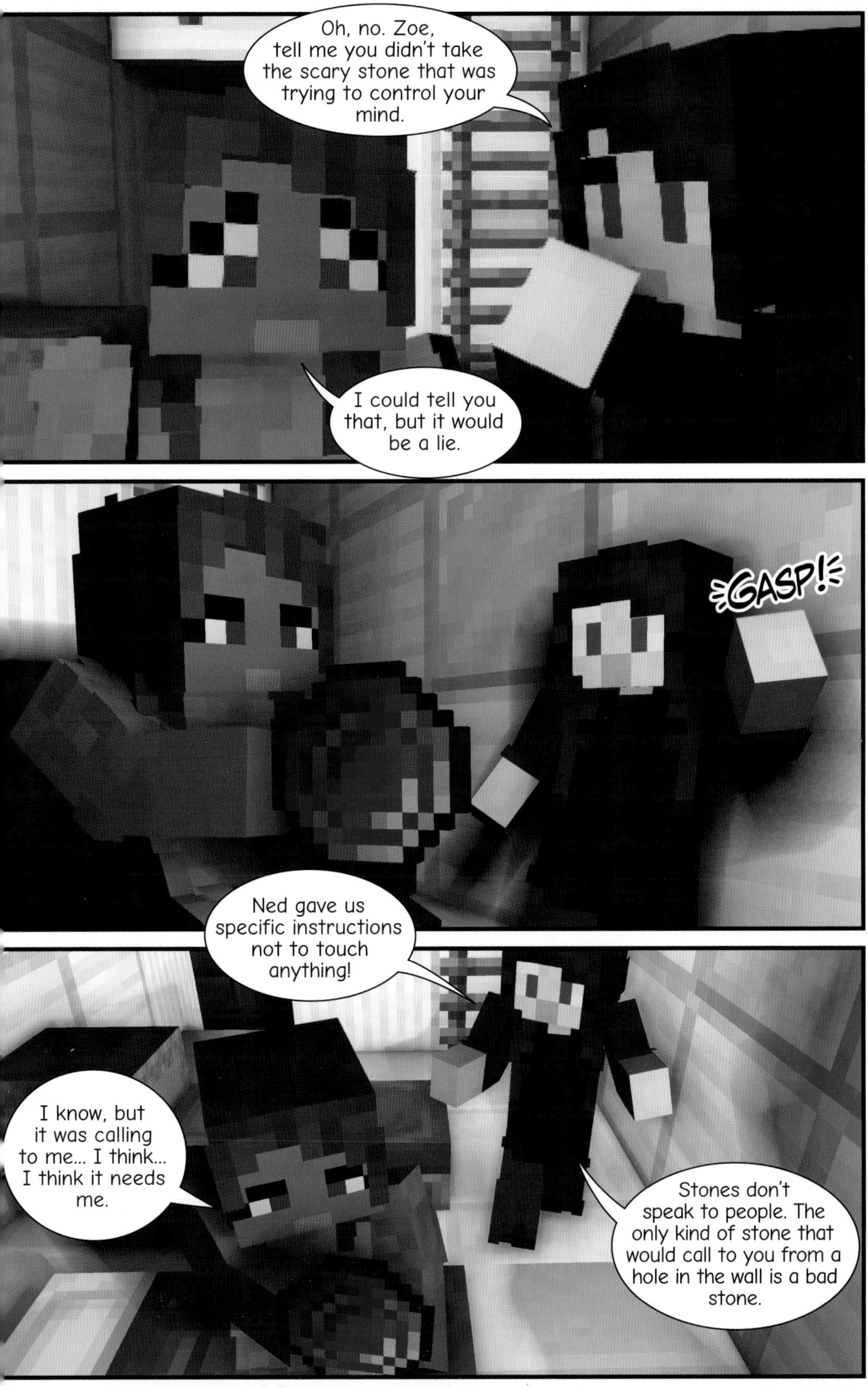
Oh, no. Zoe, tell me you didn't take the scary stone that was trying to control your mind.
I could tell you that, but it would be a lie.
GASP!
Ned gave us specific instructions not to touch anything!
I know, but it was calling to me... I think... I think it needs me.
Stones don't speak to people. The only kind of stone that would call to you from a hole in the wall is a bad stone.

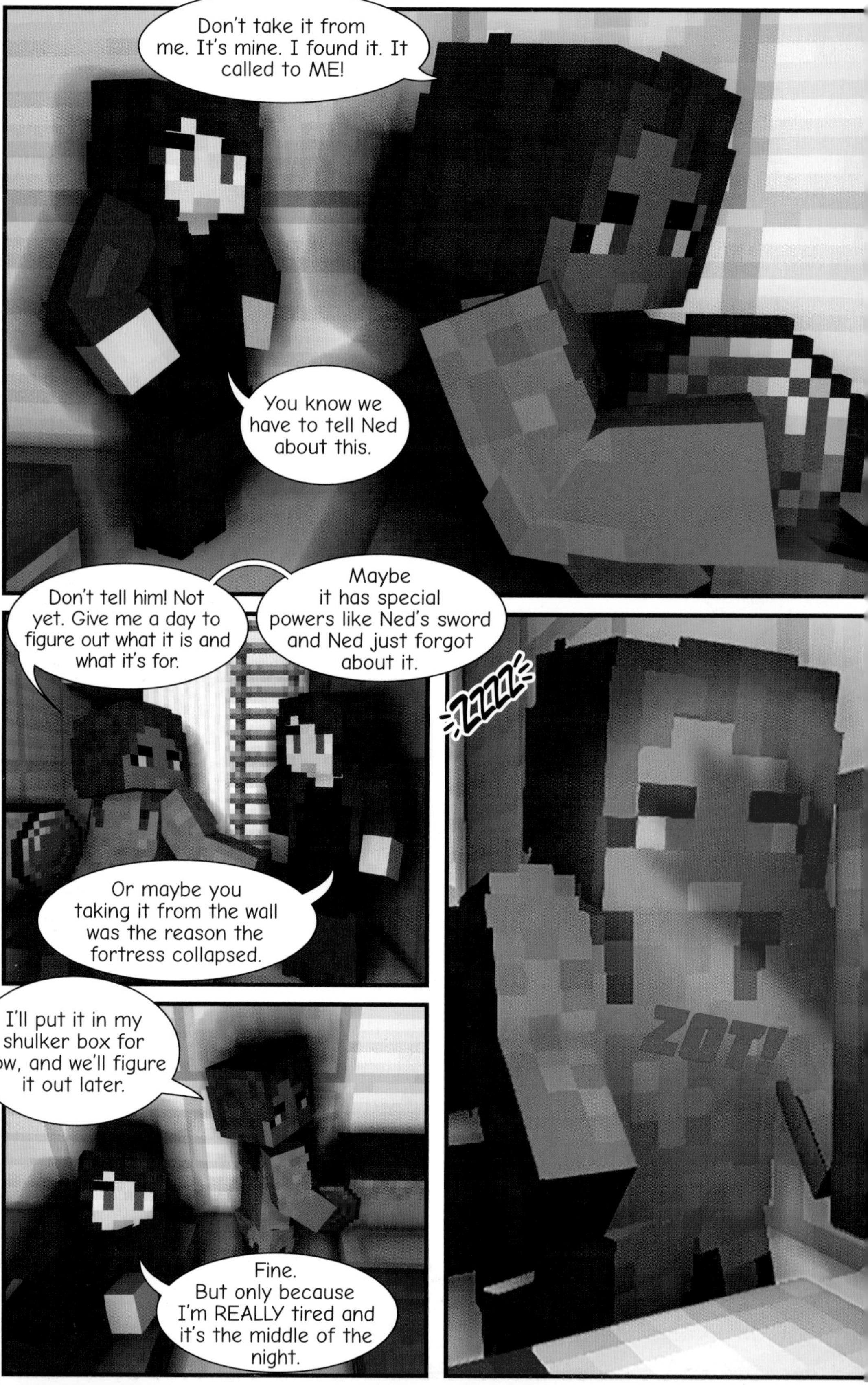
Don't take it from me. It's mine. I found it. It called to ME!
You know we have to tell Ned about this.
Don't tell him! Not yet. Give me a day to figure out what it is and what it's for.
Maybe it has special powers like Ned's sword and Ned just forgot about it.
Or maybe you taking it from the wall was the reason the fortress collapsed.
I'll put it in my shulker box for ow, and we'll figure it out later.
Fine. But only because I'm REALLY tired and it's the middle of the night.
ZZZZZ
ZOT!

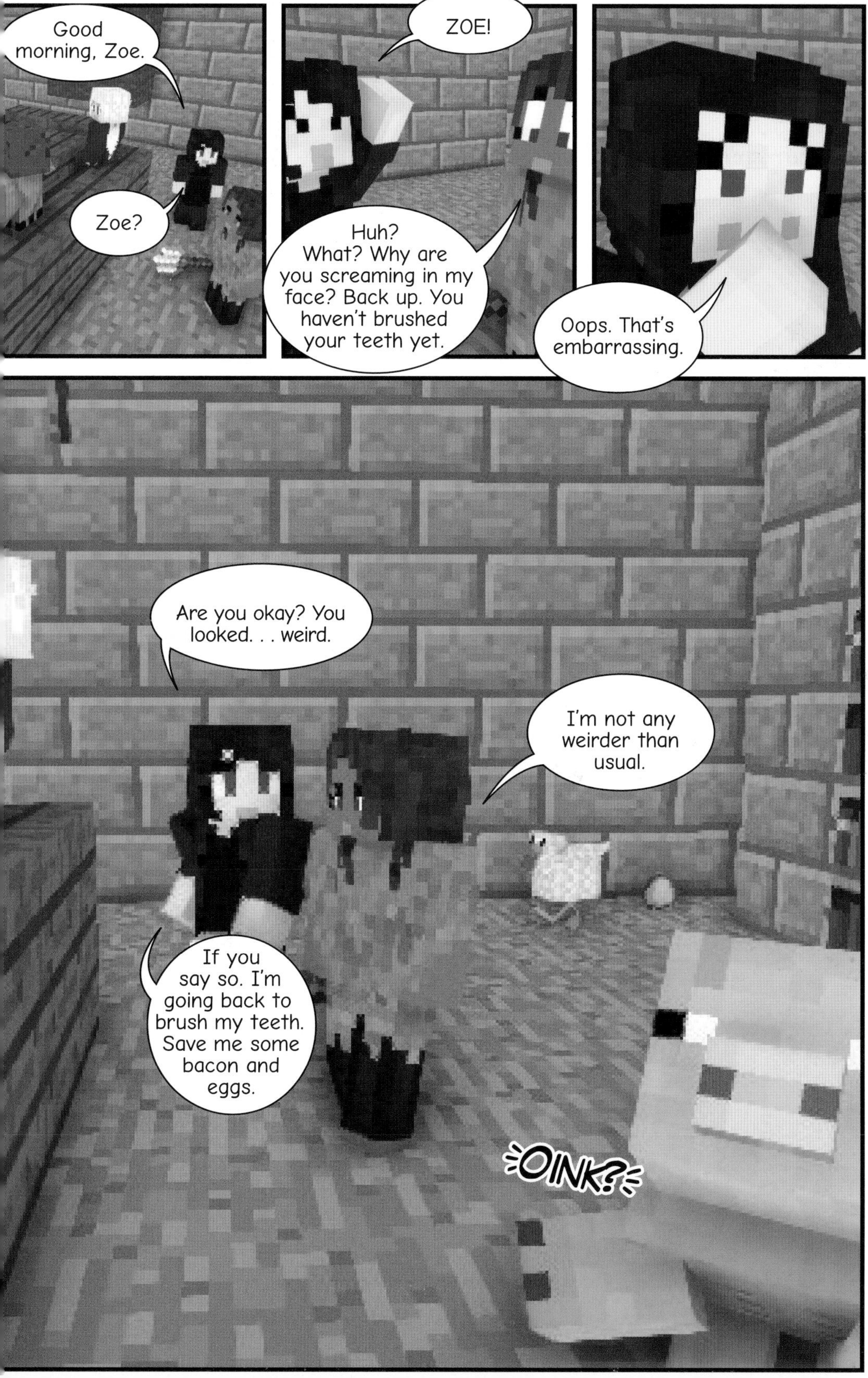
Good morning, Zoe.
Zoe?
ZOE!
Huh? What? Why are you screaming in my face? Back up. You haven't brushed your teeth yet.
Oops. That's embarrassing.
Are you okay? You looked. . . weird.
I'm not any weirder than usual.
If you say so. I'm going back to brush my teeth. Save me some bacon and eggs.
OINK?

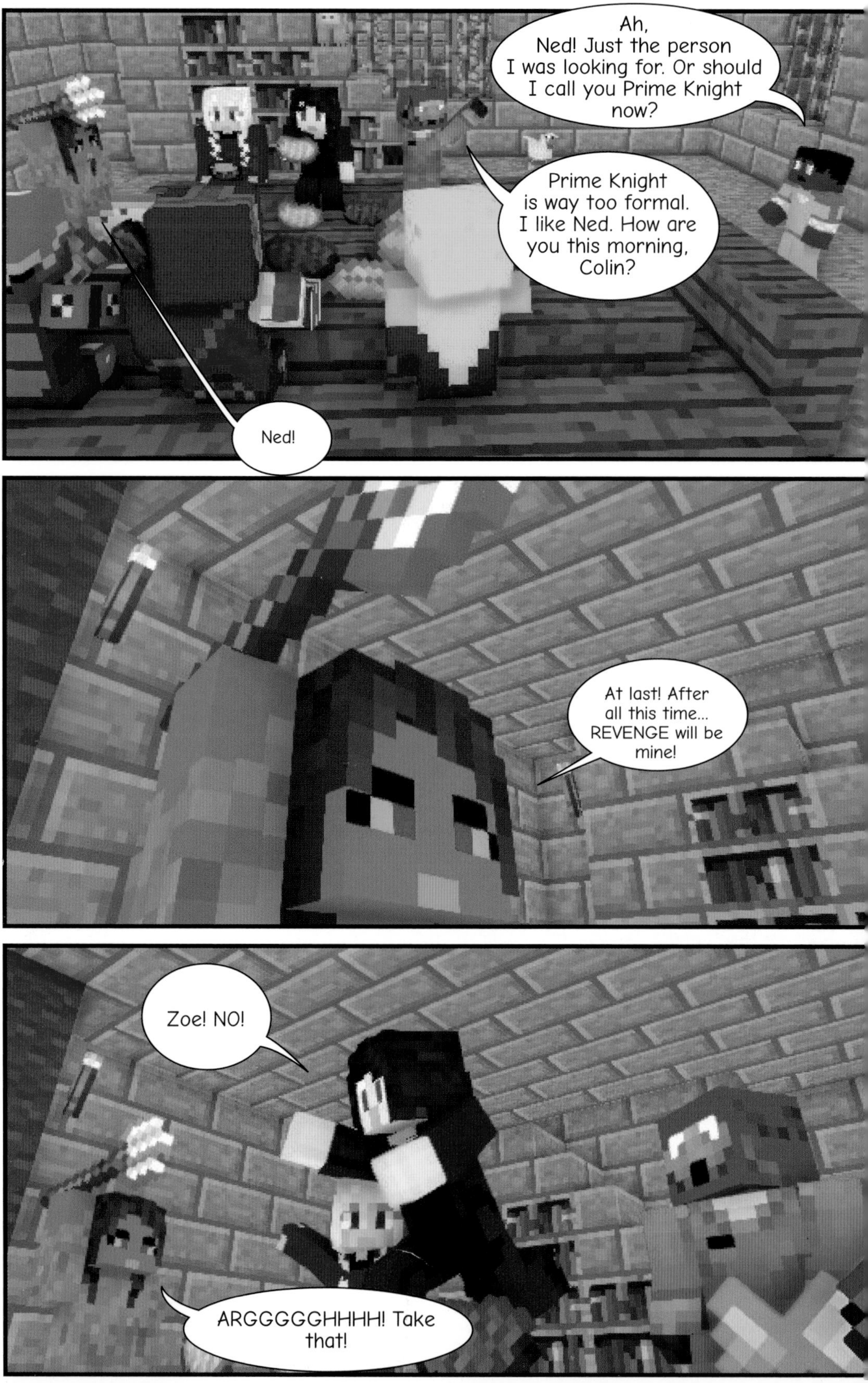
Ah,
Ned! Just the person
I was looking for. Or should
I call you Prime Knight
now?
Prime Knight
is way too formal.
I like Ned. How are
you this morning,
Colin?
Ned!
At last! After
all this time...
REVENGE will be
mine!
Zoe! NO!
ARGGGGGHHHH! Take
that!

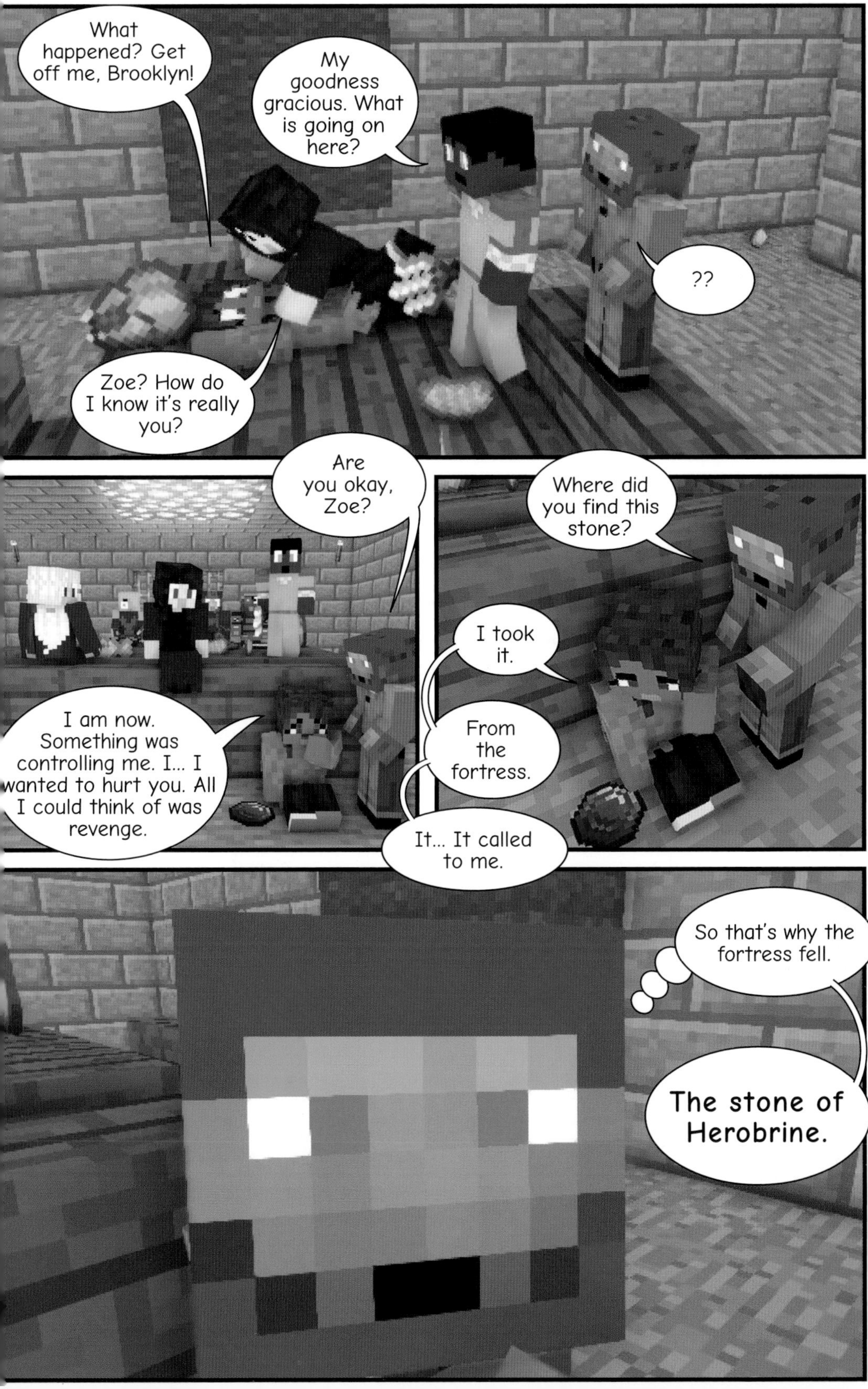
What happened? Get off me, Brooklyn!
My goodness gracious. What is going on here?
??
Zoe? How do I know it's really you?
Are you okay, Zoe?
I am now. Something was controlling me. I... I wanted to hurt you. All I could think of was revenge.
Where did you find this stone?
I took it.
From the fortress.
It... It called to me.
So that's why the fortress fell.
The stone of Herobrine.

# CHAPTER 2

# THE SPIRIT

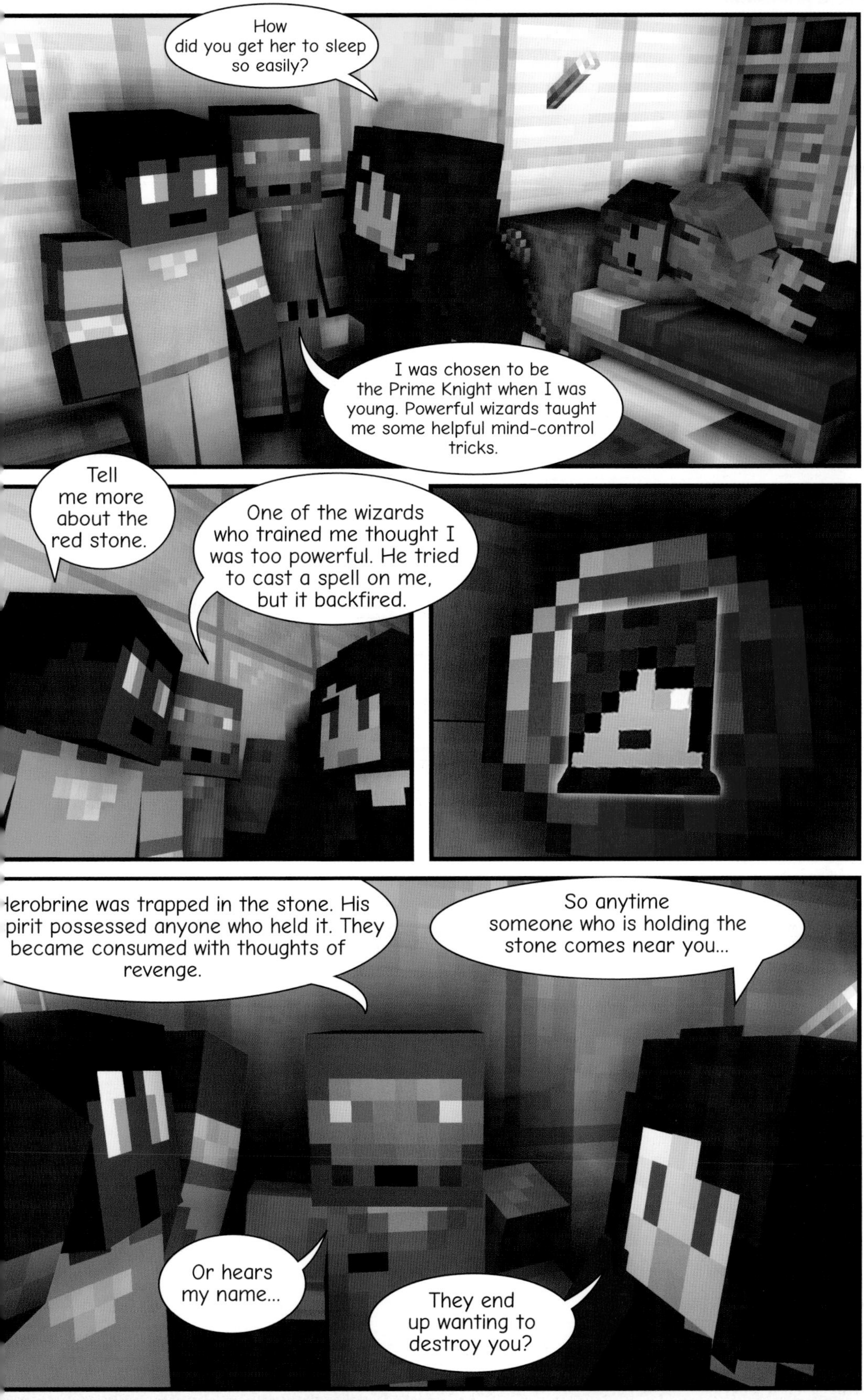
How did you get her to sleep so easily?
I was chosen to be the Prime Knight when I was young. Powerful wizards taught me some helpful mind-control tricks.
Tell me more about the red stone.
One of the wizards who trained me thought I was too powerful. He tried to cast a spell on me, but it backfired.
erobrine was trapped in the stone. His pirit possessed anyone who held it. They became consumed with thoughts of revenge.
So anytime someone who is holding the stone comes near you...
Or hears my name...
They end up wanting to destroy you?

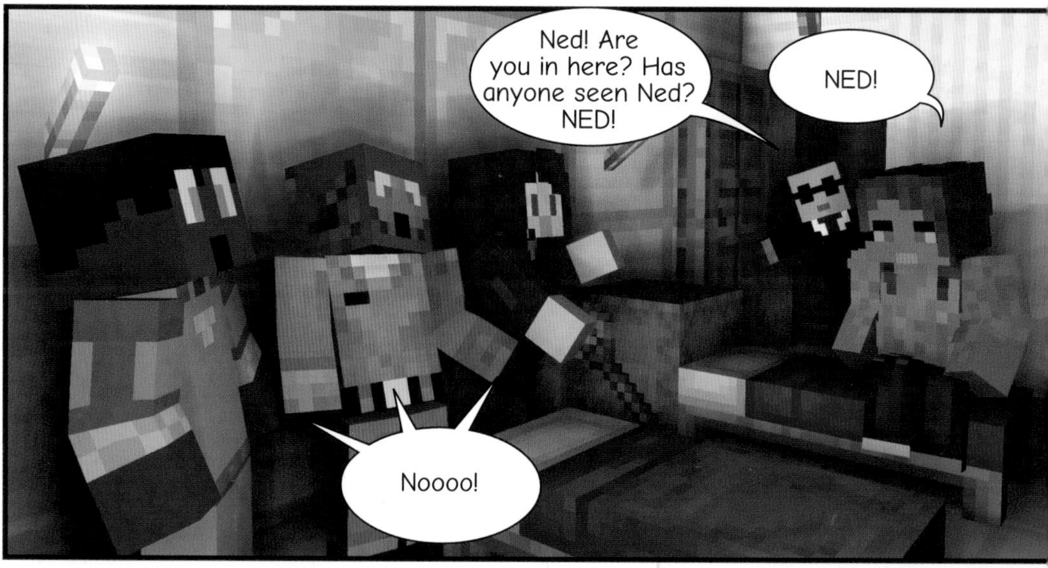
Ned! Are you in here? Has anyone seen Ned? NED!
NED!
Noooo!

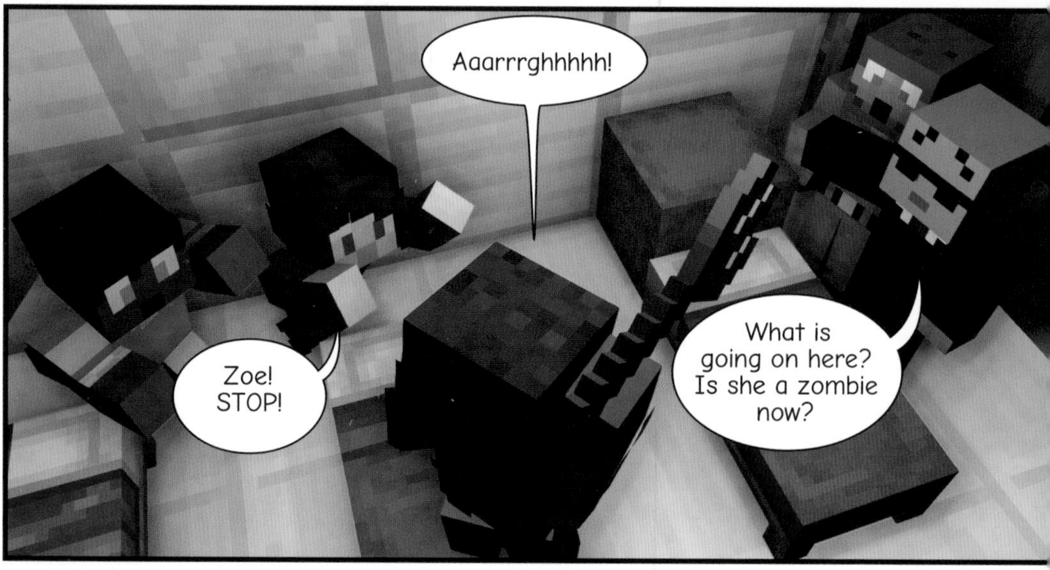
Aaarrrghhhhh!
Zoe! STOP!
What is going on here? Is she a zombie now?

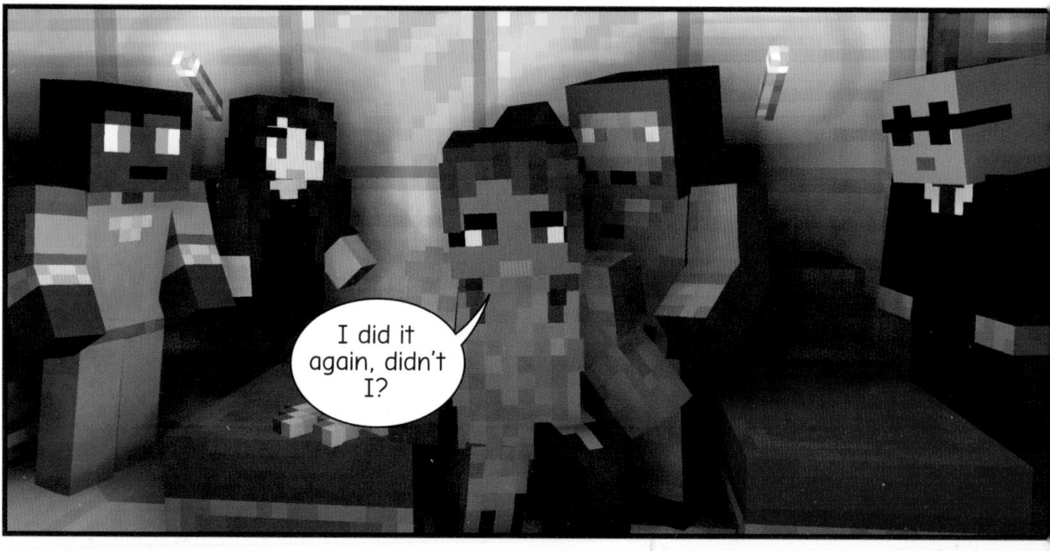
I did it again, didn't I?

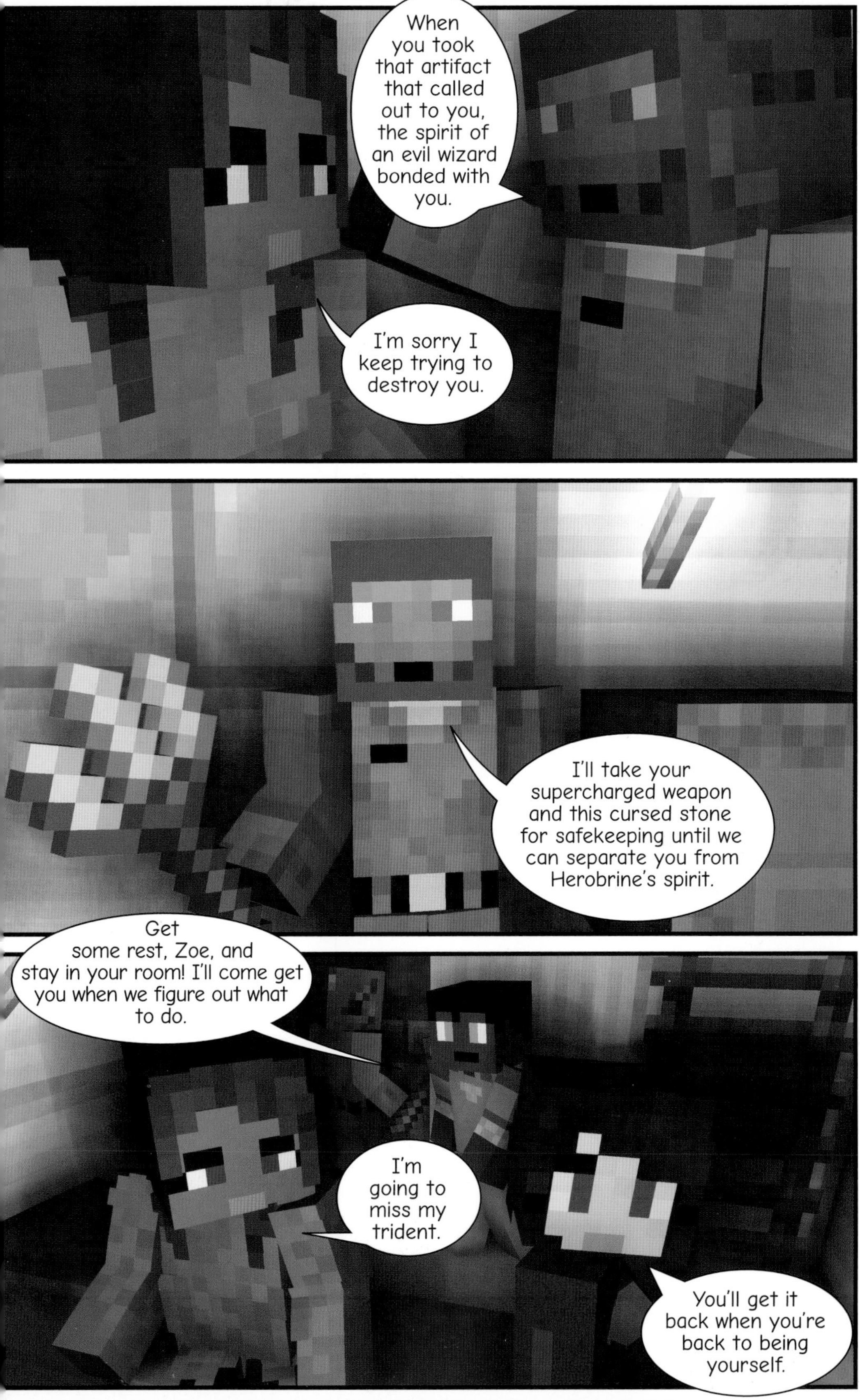
When you took that artifact that called out to you, the spirit of an evil wizard bonded with you.
I'm sorry I keep trying to destroy you.
I'll take your supercharged weapon and this cursed stone for safekeeping until we can separate you from Herobrine's spirit.
Get some rest, Zoe, and stay in your room! I'll come get you when we figure out what to do.
I'm going to miss my trident.
You'll get it back when you're back to being yourself.

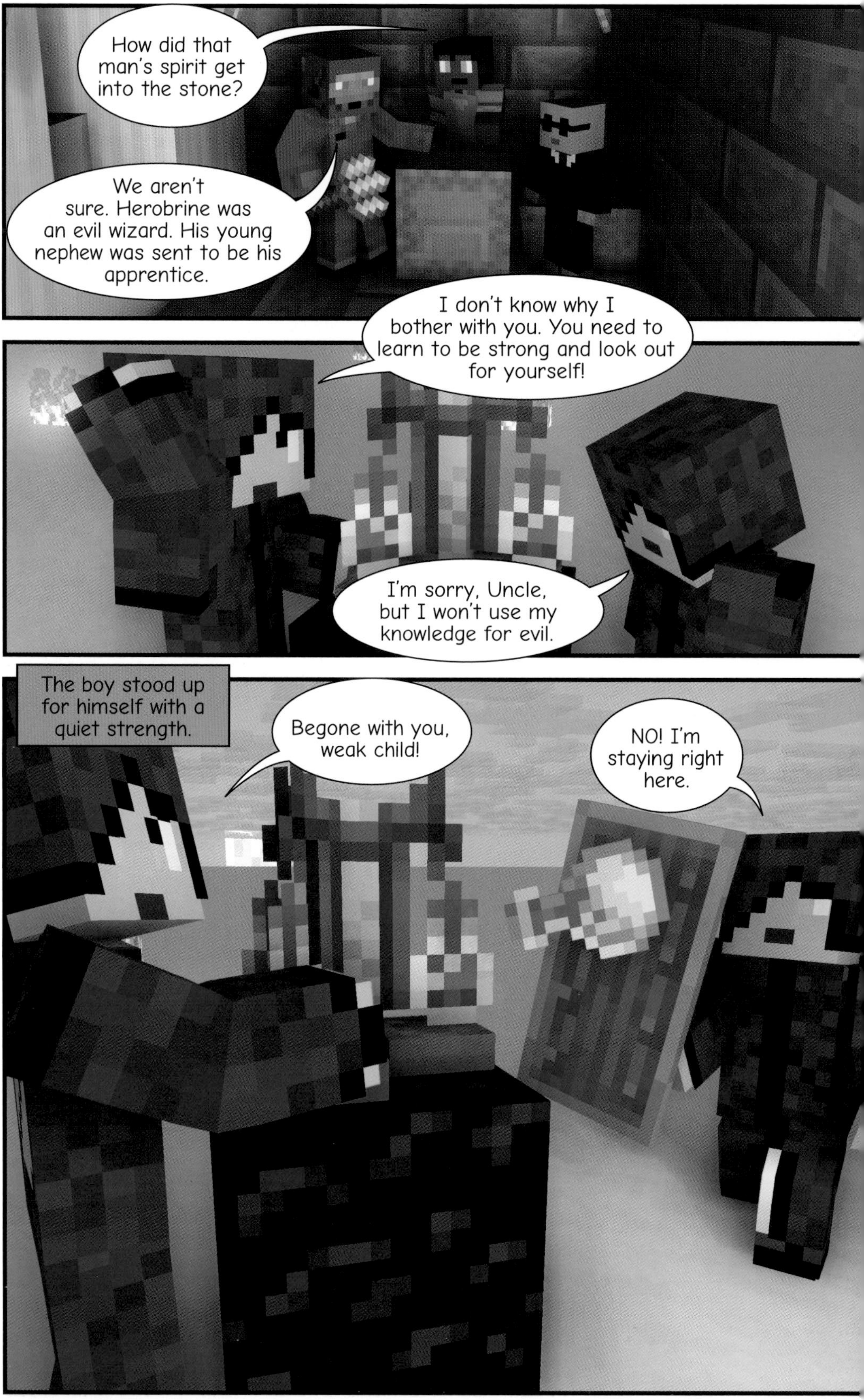
How did that man's spirit get into the stone?
We aren't sure. Herobrine was an evil wizard. His young nephew was sent to be his apprentice.
I don't know why I bother with you. You need to learn to be strong and look out for yourself!
I'm sorry, Uncle, but I won't use my knowledge for evil.
The boy stood up for himself with a quiet strength.
Begone with you, weak child!
NO! I'm staying right here.

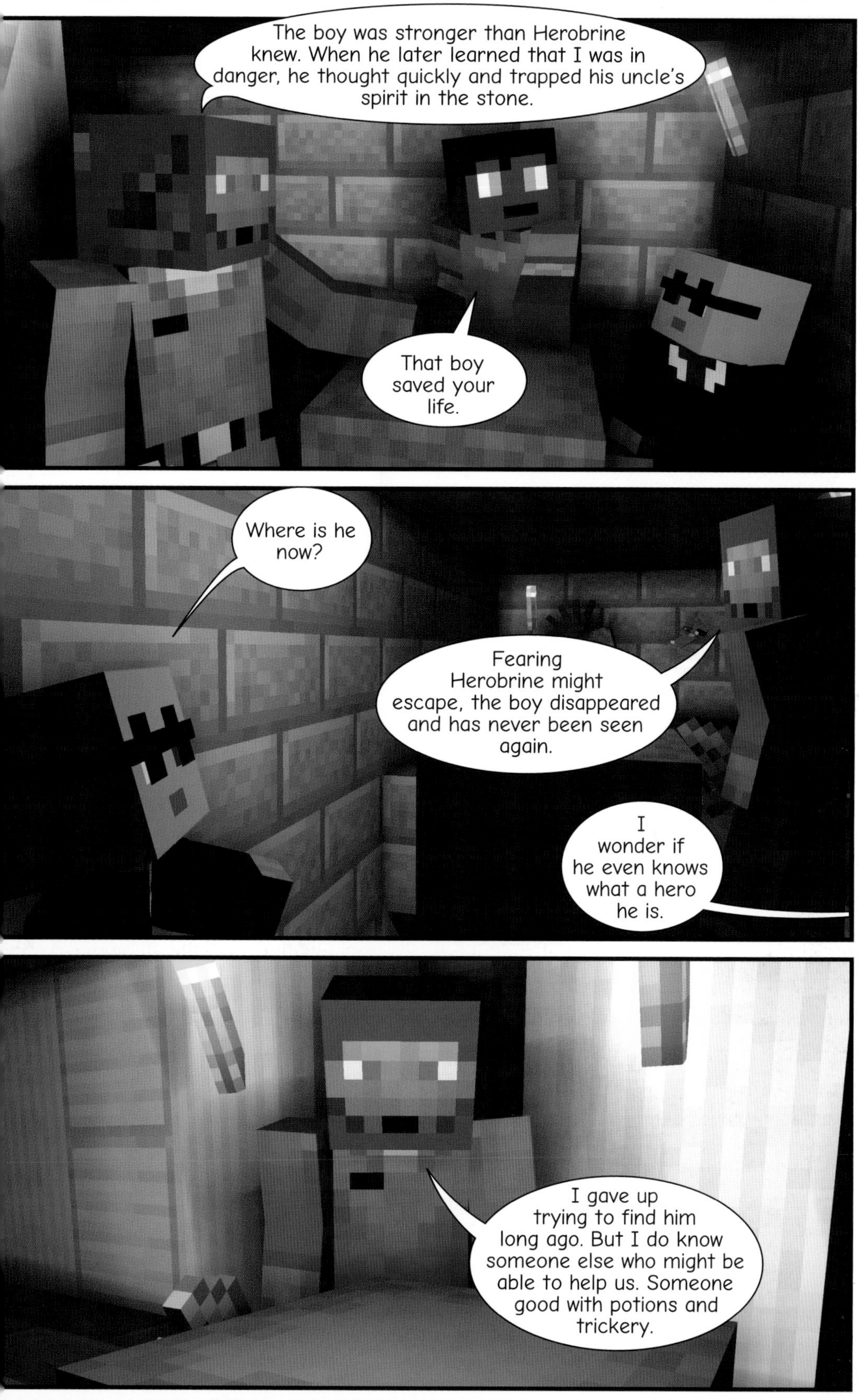
The boy was stronger than Herobrine knew. When he later learned that I was in danger, he thought quickly and trapped his uncle's spirit in the stone.
That boy saved your life.
Where is he now?
Fearing Herobrine might escape, the boy disappeared and has never been seen again.
I wonder if he even knows what a hero he is.
I gave up trying to find him long ago. But I do know someone else who might be able to help us. Someone good with potions and trickery.

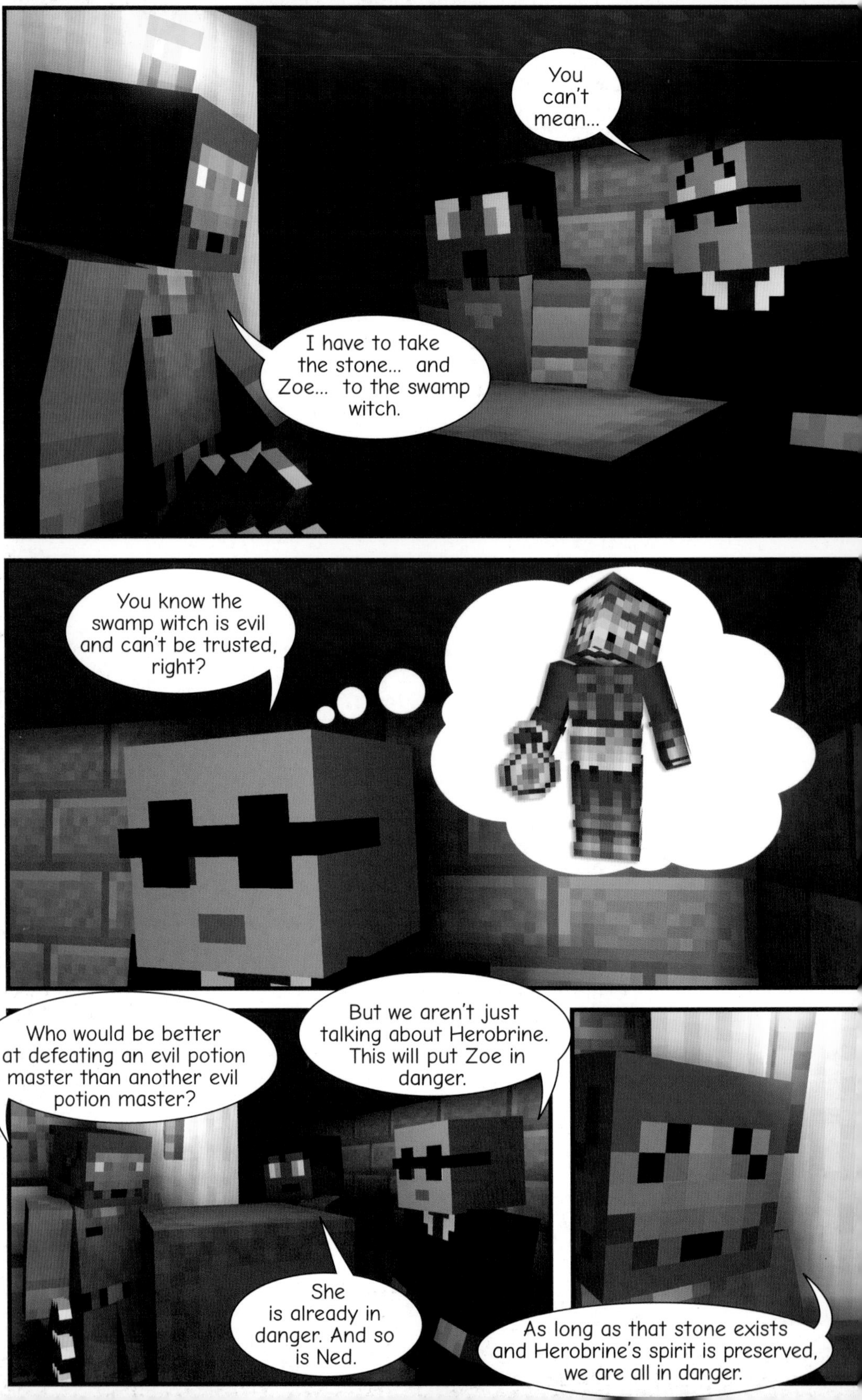

You can't mean...
I have to take the stone... and Zoe... to the swamp witch.
You know the swamp witch is evil and can't be trusted, right?
Who would be better at defeating an evil potion master than another evil potion master?
But we aren't just talking about Herobrine. This will put Zoe in danger.
She is already in danger. And so is Ned.
As long as that stone exists and Herobrine's spirit is preserved, we are all in danger.

# CHAPTER 3

# THE WITCH

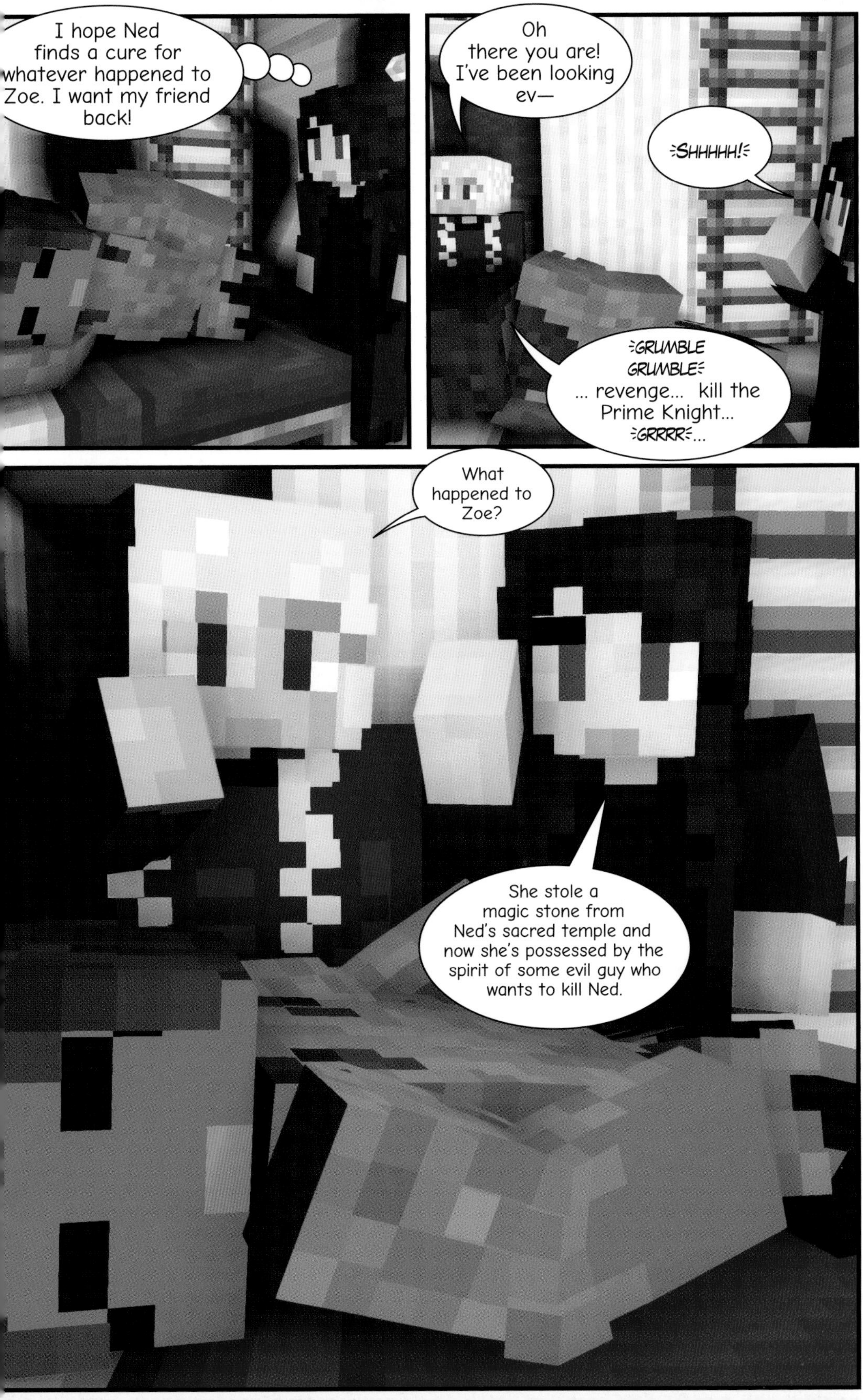
I hope Ned finds a cure for whatever happened to Zoe. I want my friend back!
Oh there you are! I've been looking ev—
SHHHHH!
GRUMBLE GRUMBLE
... revenge... kill the Prime Knight...
GRRRR...
What happened to Zoe?
She stole a magic stone from Ned's sacred temple and now she's possessed by the spirit of some evil guy who wants to kill Ned.

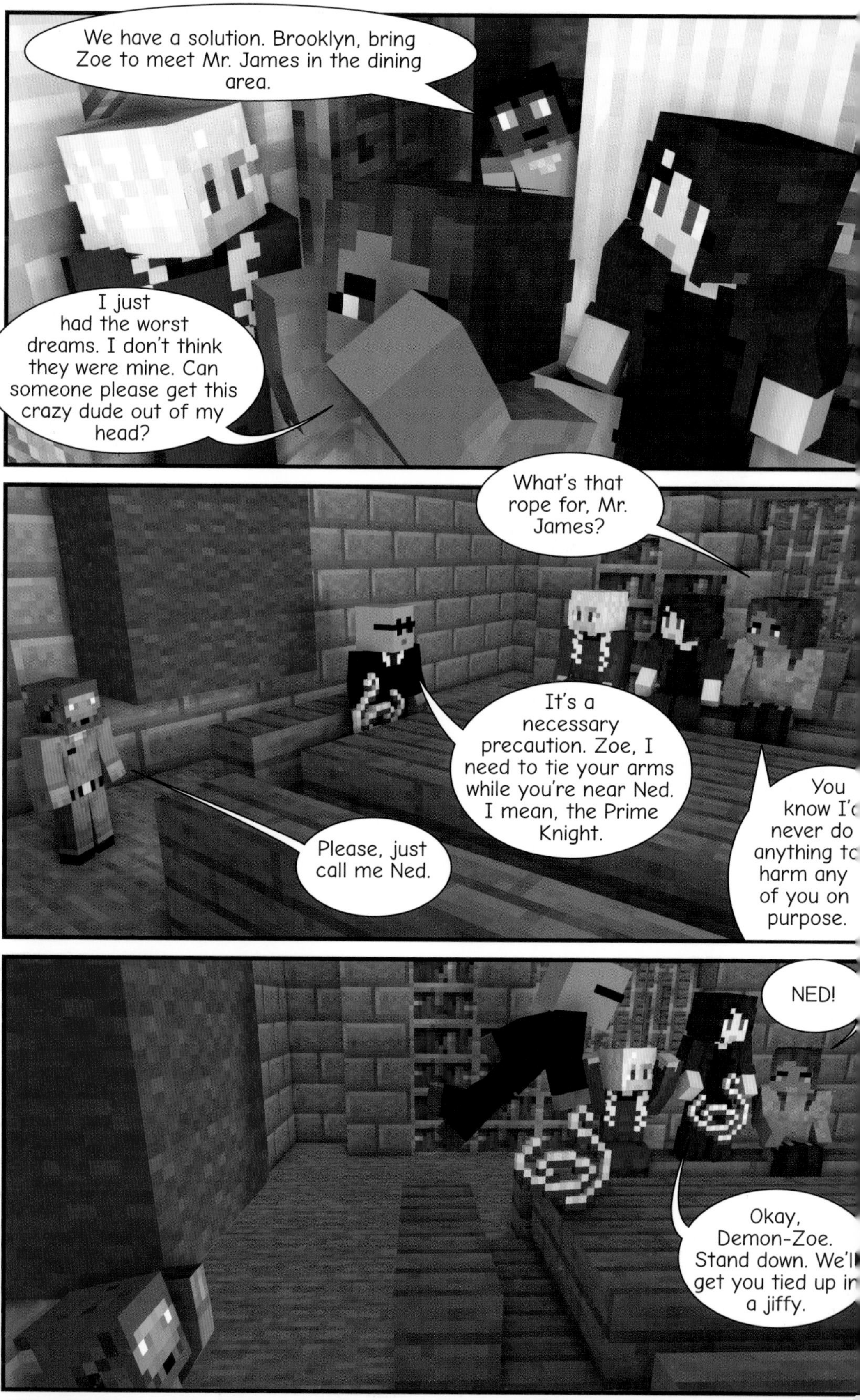
We have a solution. Brooklyn, bring Zoe to meet Mr. James in the dining area.
I just had the worst dreams. I don't think they were mine. Can someone please get this crazy dude out of my head?
What's that rope for, Mr. James?
It's a necessary precaution. Zoe, I need to tie your arms while you're near Ned. I mean, the Prime Knight.
Please, just call me Ned.
You know I'd never do anything to harm any of you on purpose.
NED!
Okay, Demon-Zoe. Stand down. We'll get you tied up in a jiffy.

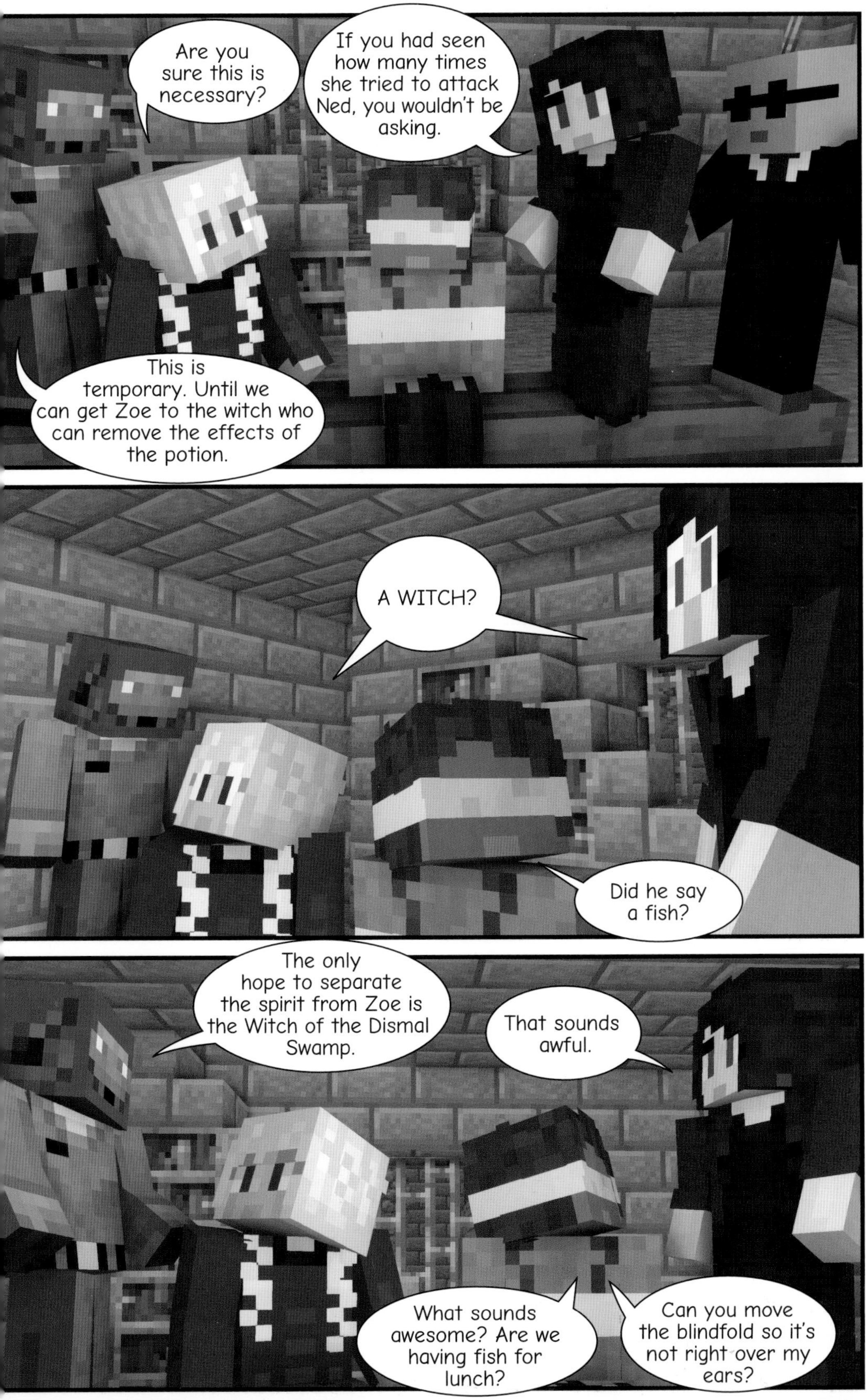
Are you sure this is necessary?
If you had seen how many times she tried to attack Ned, you wouldn't be asking.
This is temporary. Until we can get Zoe to the witch who can remove the effects of the potion.
A WITCH?
Did he say a fish?
The only hope to separate the spirit from Zoe is the Witch of the Dismal Swamp.
That sounds awful.
What sounds awesome? Are we having fish for lunch?
Can you move the blindfold so it's not right over my ears?

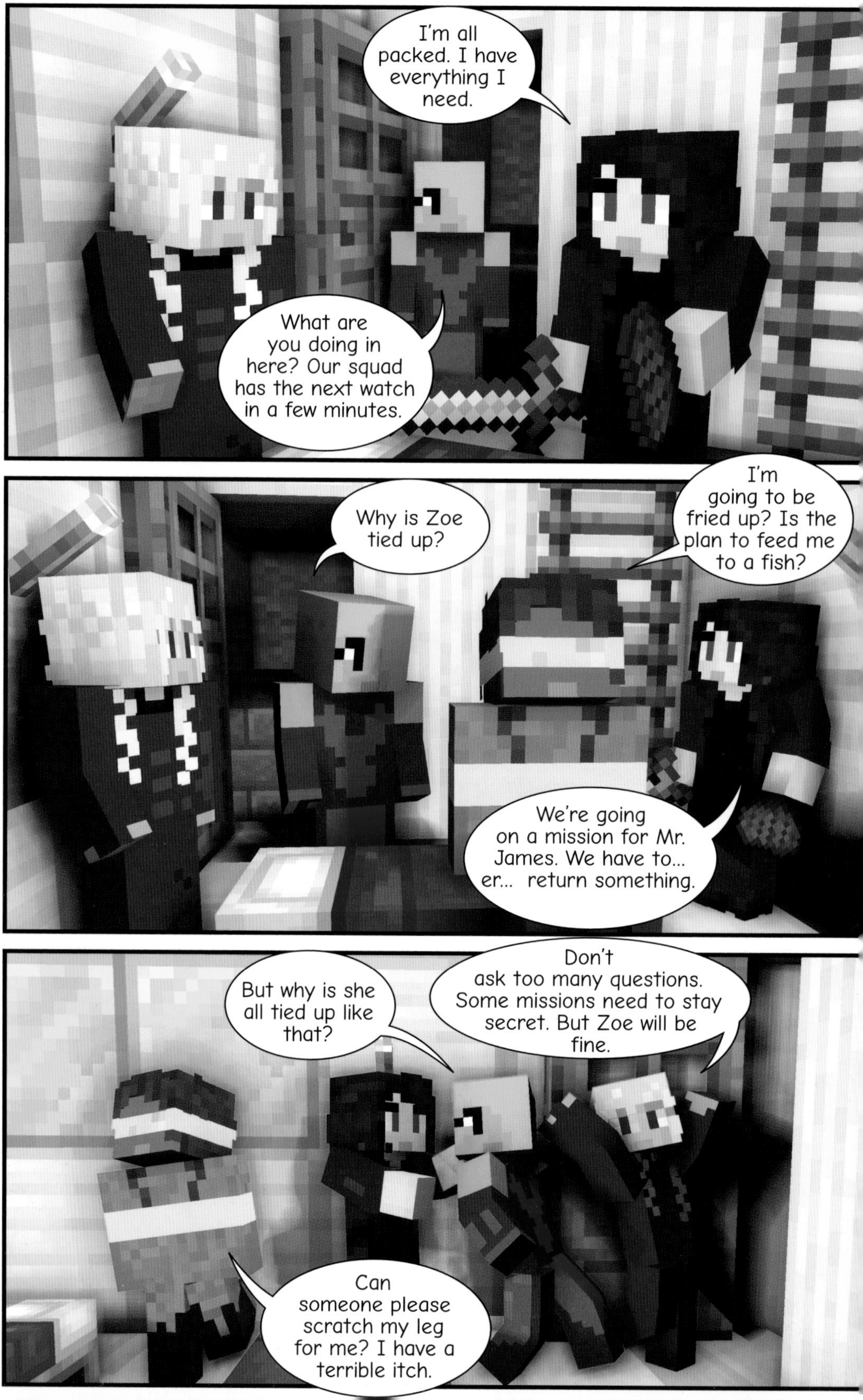
I'm all packed. I have everything I need.
What are you doing in here? Our squad has the next watch in a few minutes.
Why is Zoe tied up?
I'm going to be fried up? Is the plan to feed me to a fish?
We're going on a mission for Mr. James. We have to... er... return something.
But why is she all tied up like that?
Don't ask too many questions. Some missions need to stay secret. But Zoe will be fine.
Can someone please scratch my leg for me? I have a terrible itch.

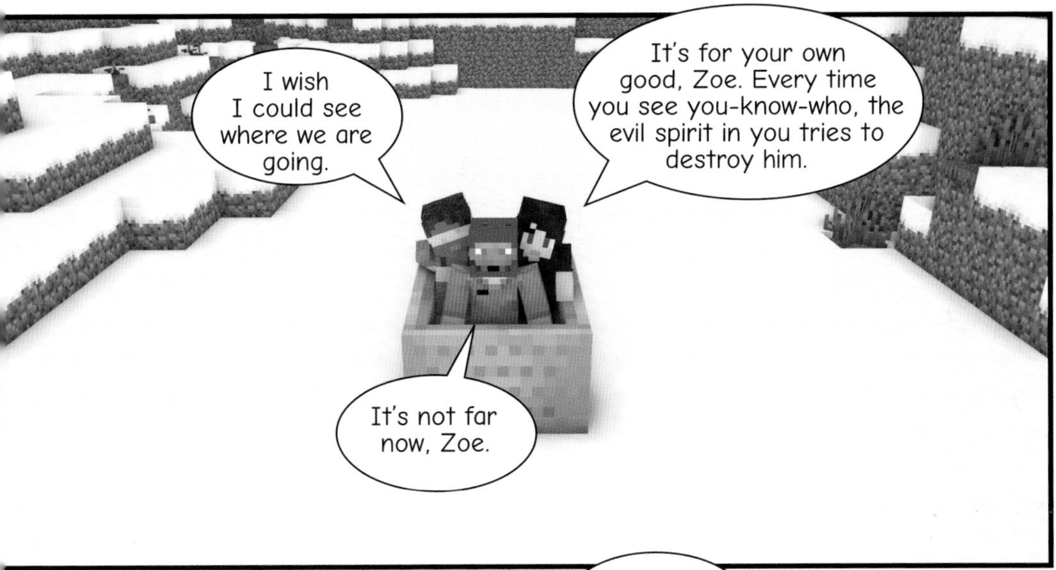
I wish I could see where we are going.
It's for your own good, Zoe. Every time you see you-know-who, the evil spirit in you tries to destroy him.
It's not far now, Zoe.

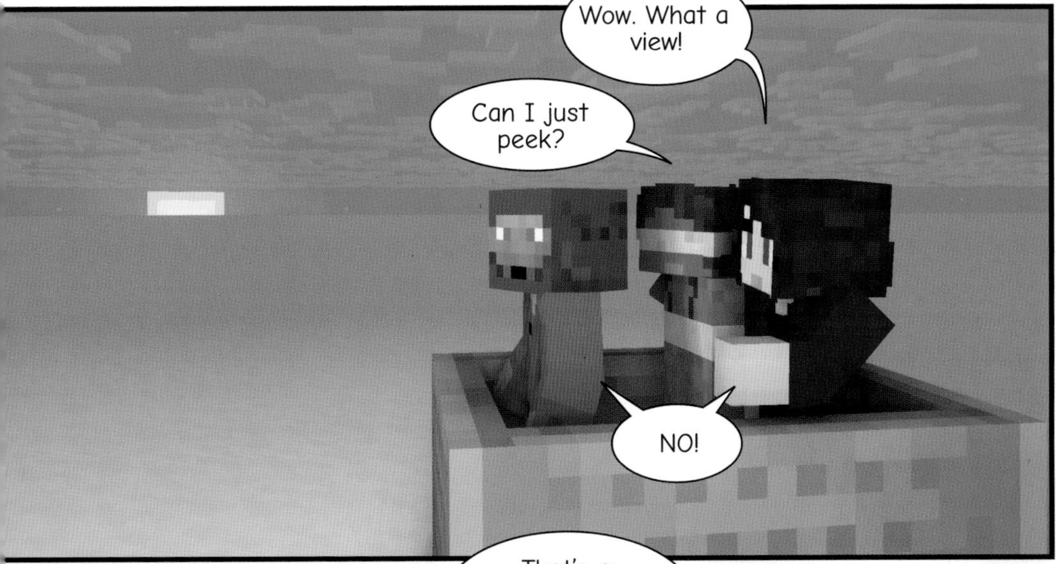
Wow. What a view!
Can I just peek?
NO!

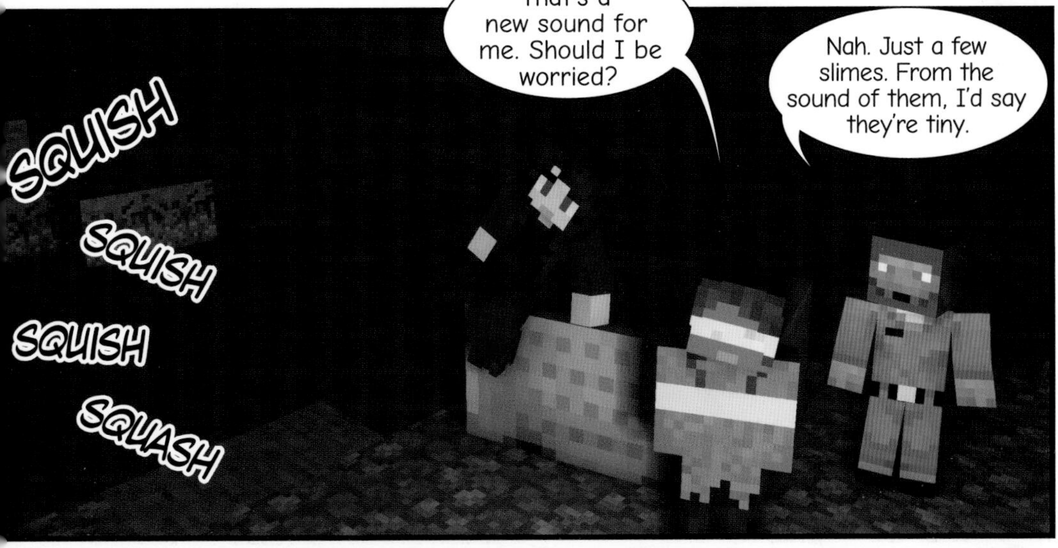
That's a new sound for me. Should I be worried?
Nah. Just a few slimes. From the sound of them, I'd say they're tiny.
SQUISH
SQUISH
SQUISH
SQUASH

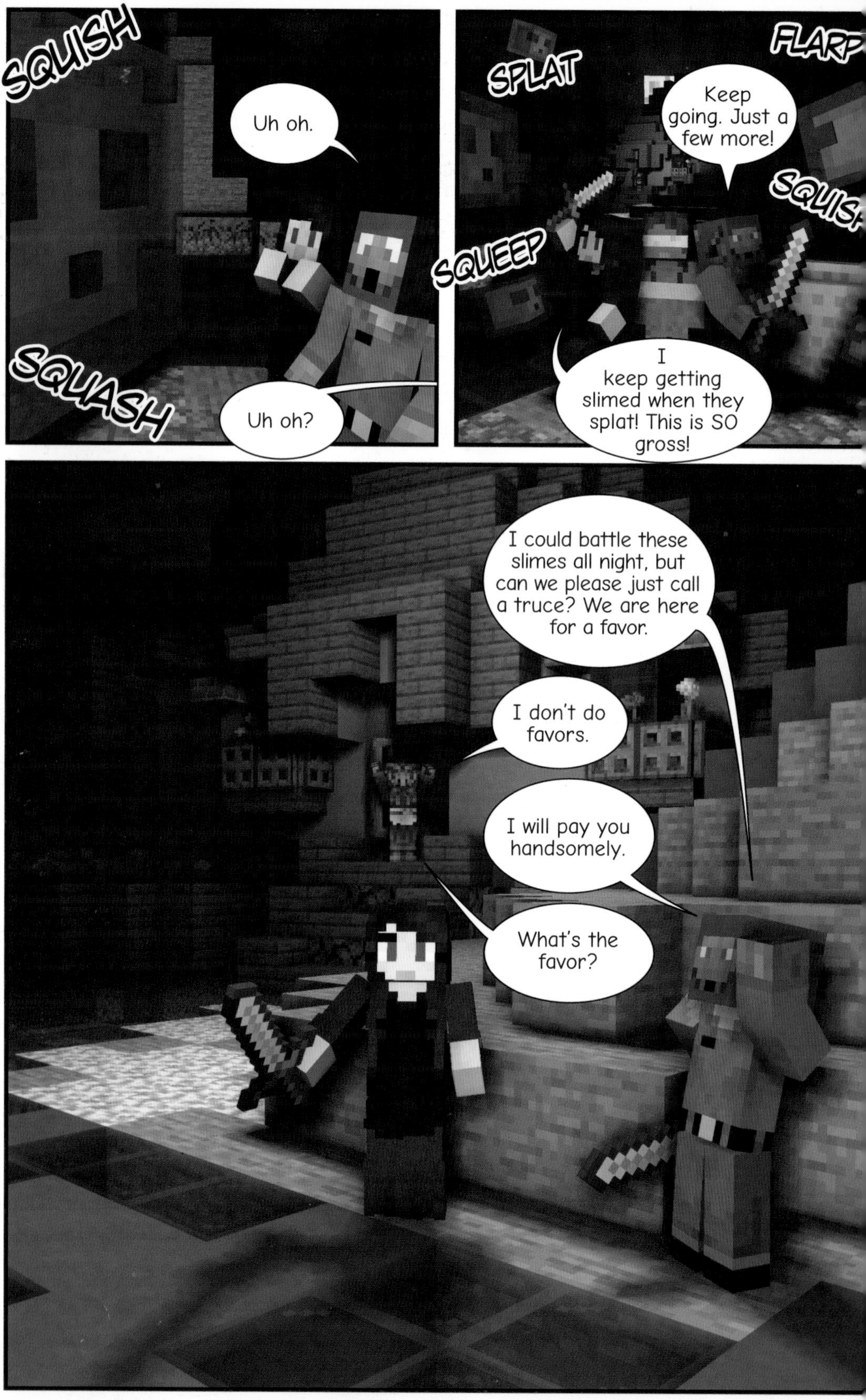
SQUISH
Uh oh.
SQUASH
Uh oh?
SPLAT
FLARP
Keep going. Just a few more!
SQUISH
SQUEEP
I keep getting slimed when they splat! This is SO gross!
I could battle these slimes all night, but can we please just call a truce? We are here for a favor.
I don't do favors.
I will pay you handsomely.
What's the favor?

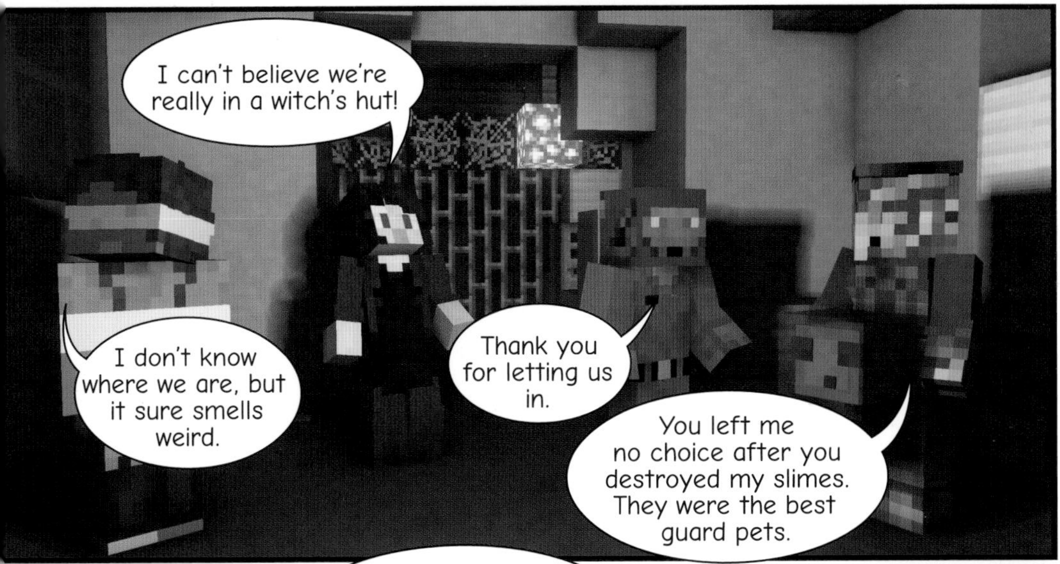

I can't believe we're really in a witch's hut!
I don't know where we are, but it sure smells weird.
Thank you for letting us in.
You left me no choice after you destroyed my slimes. They were the best guard pets.

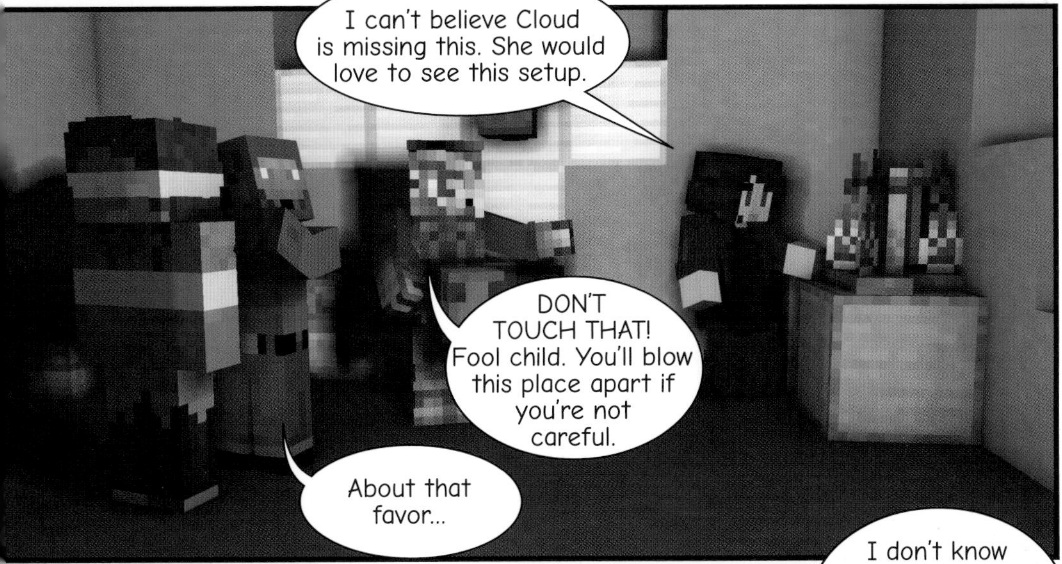

I can't believe Cloud is missing this. She would love to see this setup.
DON'T TOUCH THAT! Fool child. You'll blow this place apart if you're not careful.
About that favor...

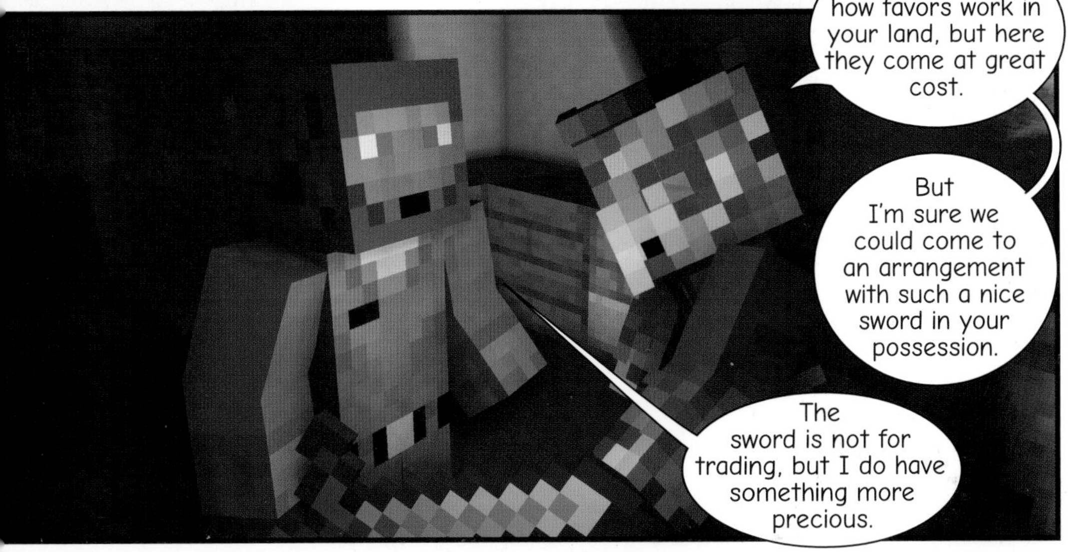

I don't know how favors work in your land, but here they come at great cost.
But I'm sure we could come to an arrangement with such a nice sword in your possession.
The sword is not for trading, but I do have something more precious.

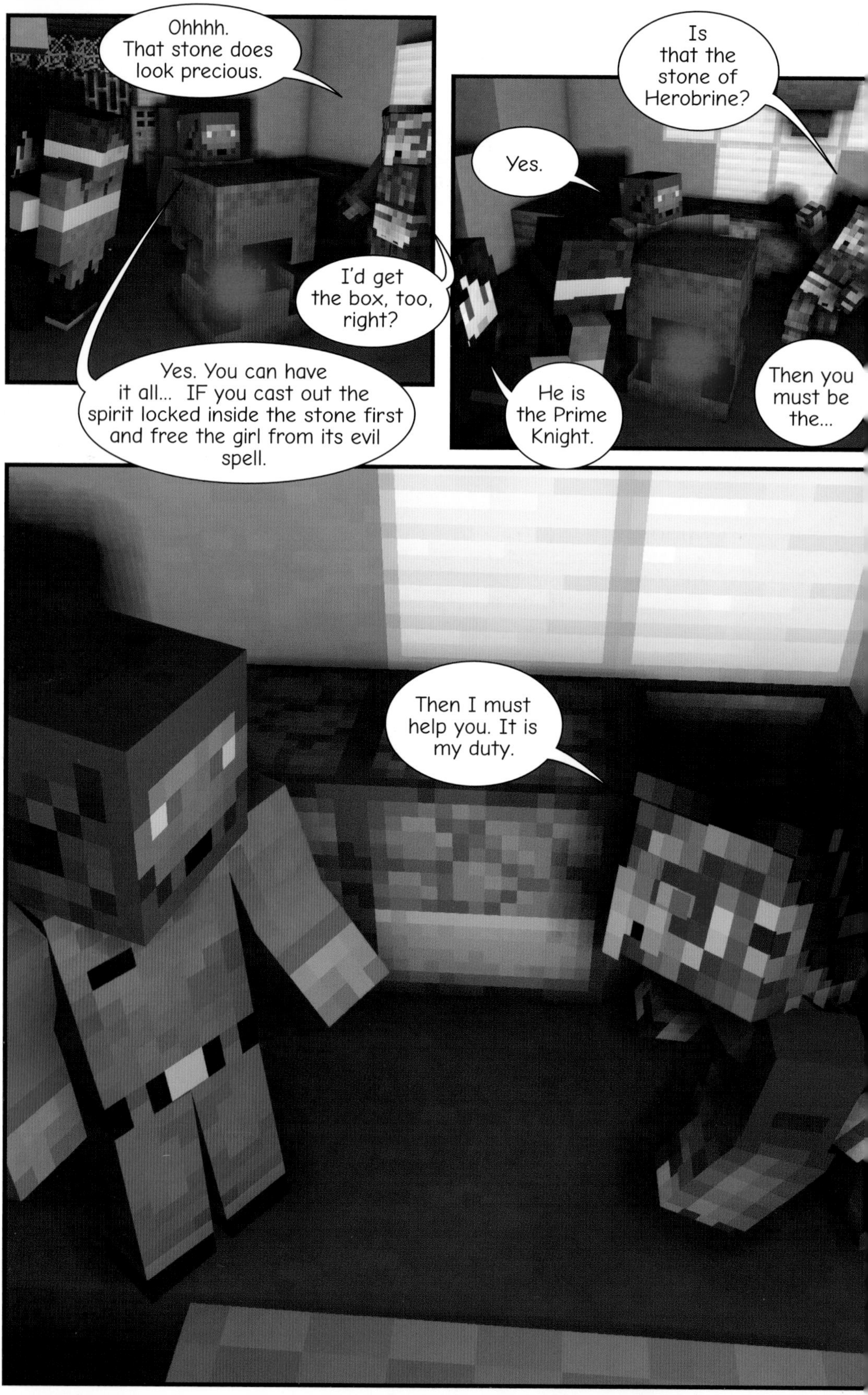
Ohhhh. That stone does look precious.
I'd get the box, too, right?
Yes. You can have it all... IF you cast out the spirit locked inside the stone first and free the girl from its evil spell.
Is that the stone of Herobrine?
Yes.
He is the Prime Knight.
Then you must be the...
Then I must help you. It is my duty.

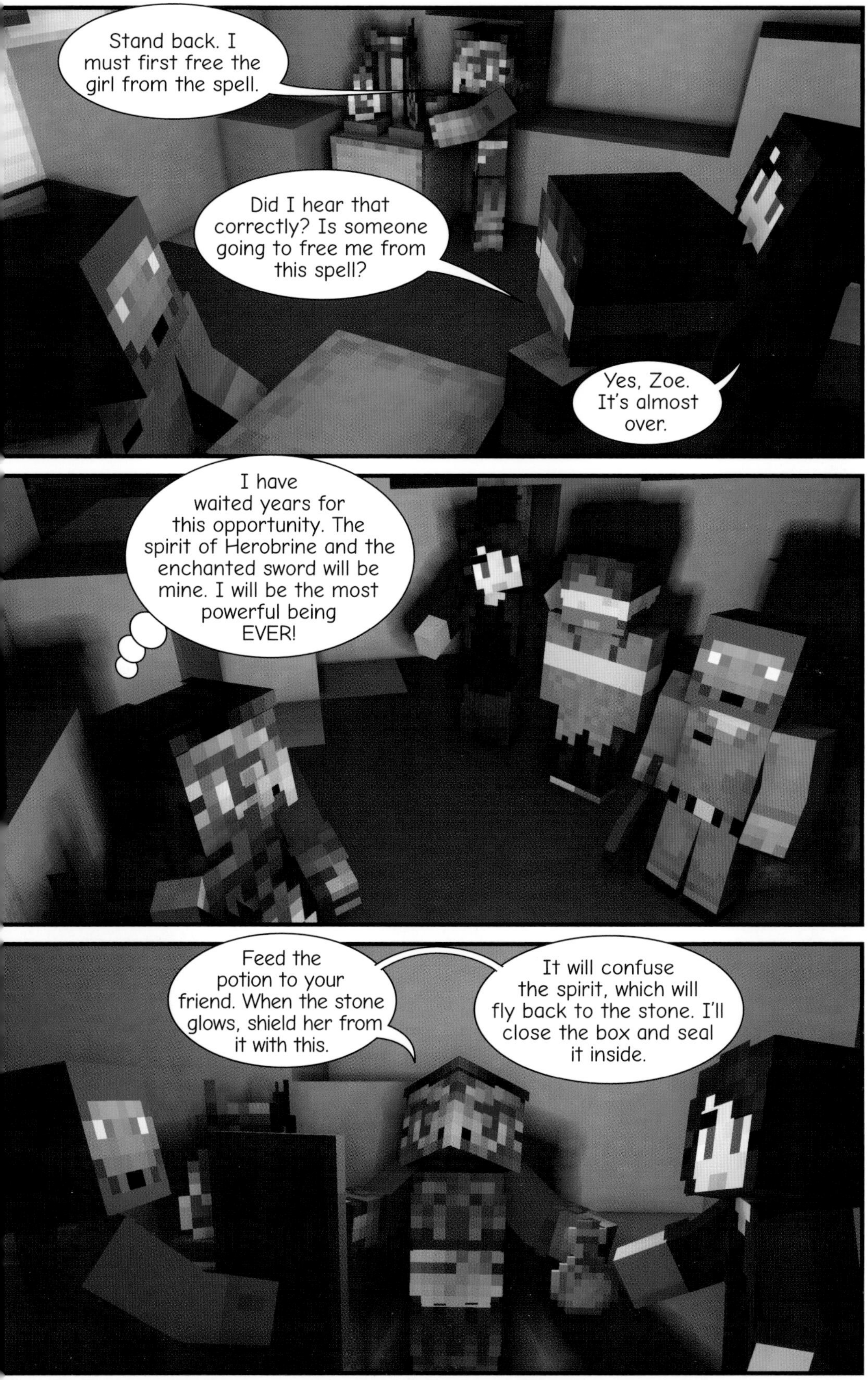
Stand back. I must first free the girl from the spell.
Did I hear that correctly? Is someone going to free me from this spell?
Yes, Zoe. It's almost over.
I have waited years for this opportunity. The spirit of Herobrine and the enchanted sword will be mine. I will be the most powerful being EVER!
Feed the potion to your friend. When the stone glows, shield her from it with this.
It will confuse the spirit, which will fly back to the stone. I'll close the box and seal it inside.

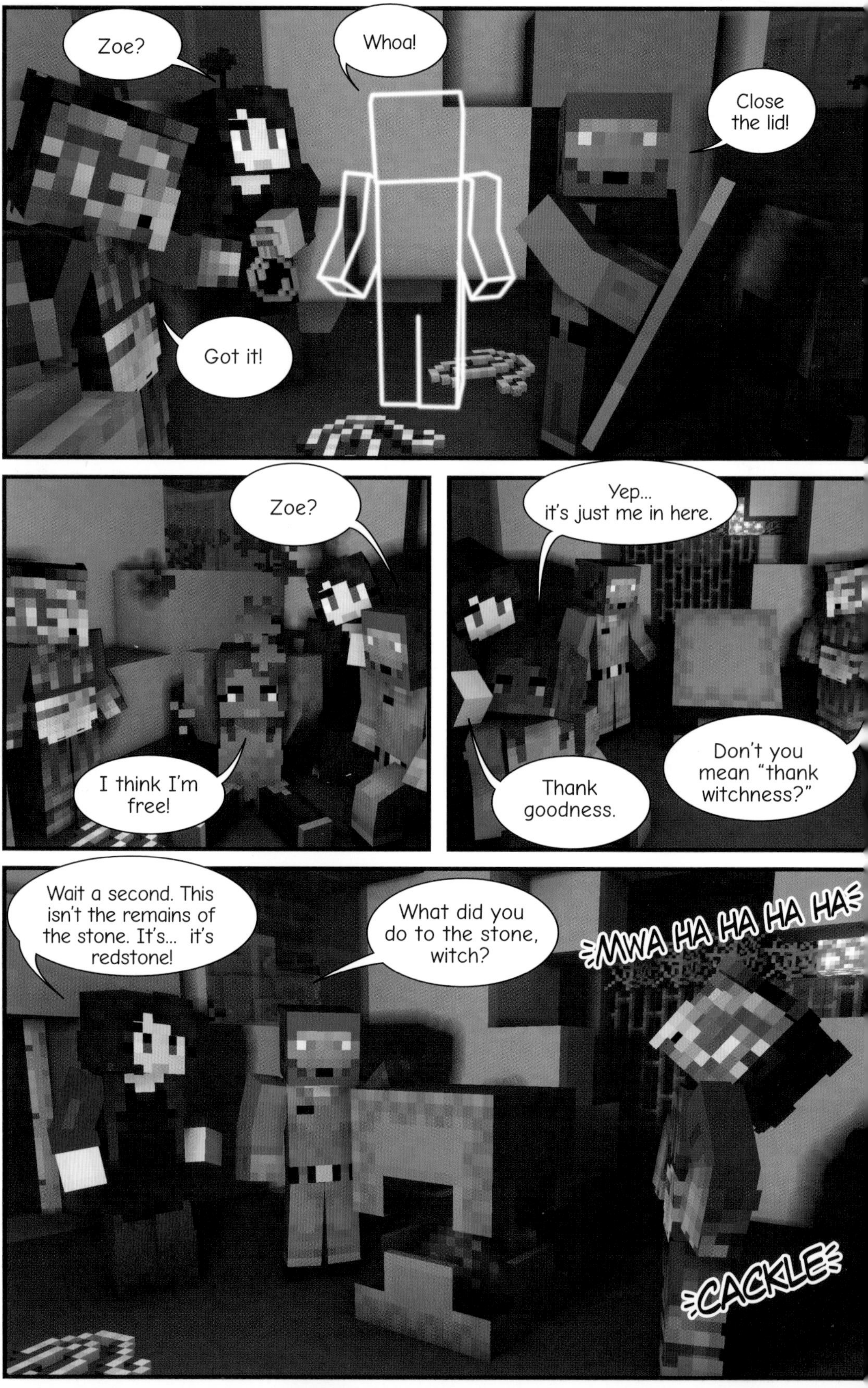
Zoe?
Whoa!
Close the lid!
Got it!
Zoe?
I think I'm free!
Yep... it's just me in here.
Thank goodness.
Don't you mean "thank witchness?"
Wait a second. This isn't the remains of the stone. It's... it's redstone!
What did you do to the stone, witch?
MWA HA HA HA HA
CACKLE

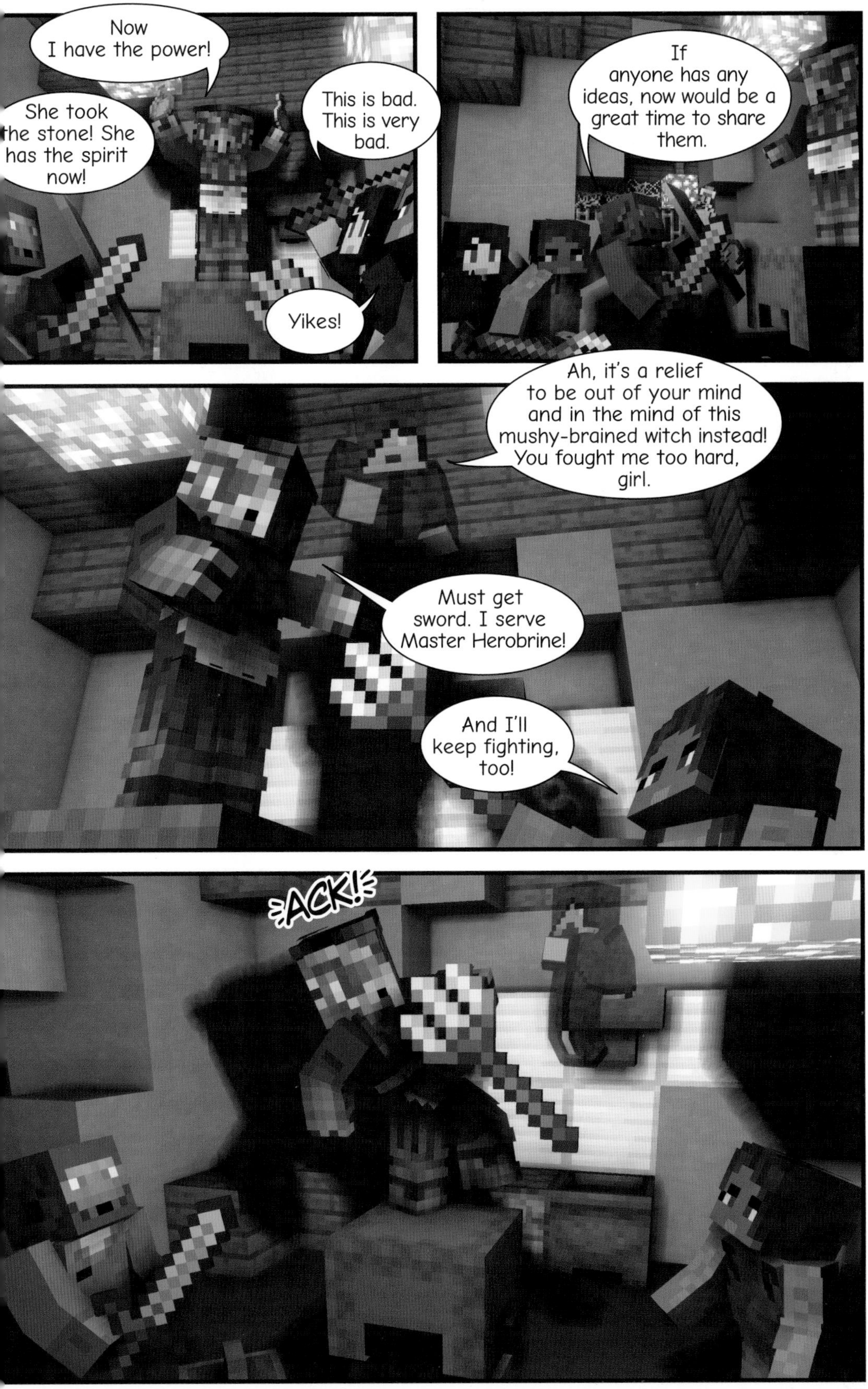
Now I have the power!
She took the stone! She has the spirit now!
This is bad. This is very bad.
Yikes!
If anyone has any ideas, now would be a great time to share them.
Ah, it's a relief to be out of your mind and in the mind of this mushy-brained witch instead! You fought me too hard, girl.
Must get sword. I serve Master Herobrine!
And I'll keep fighting, too!
ACK!

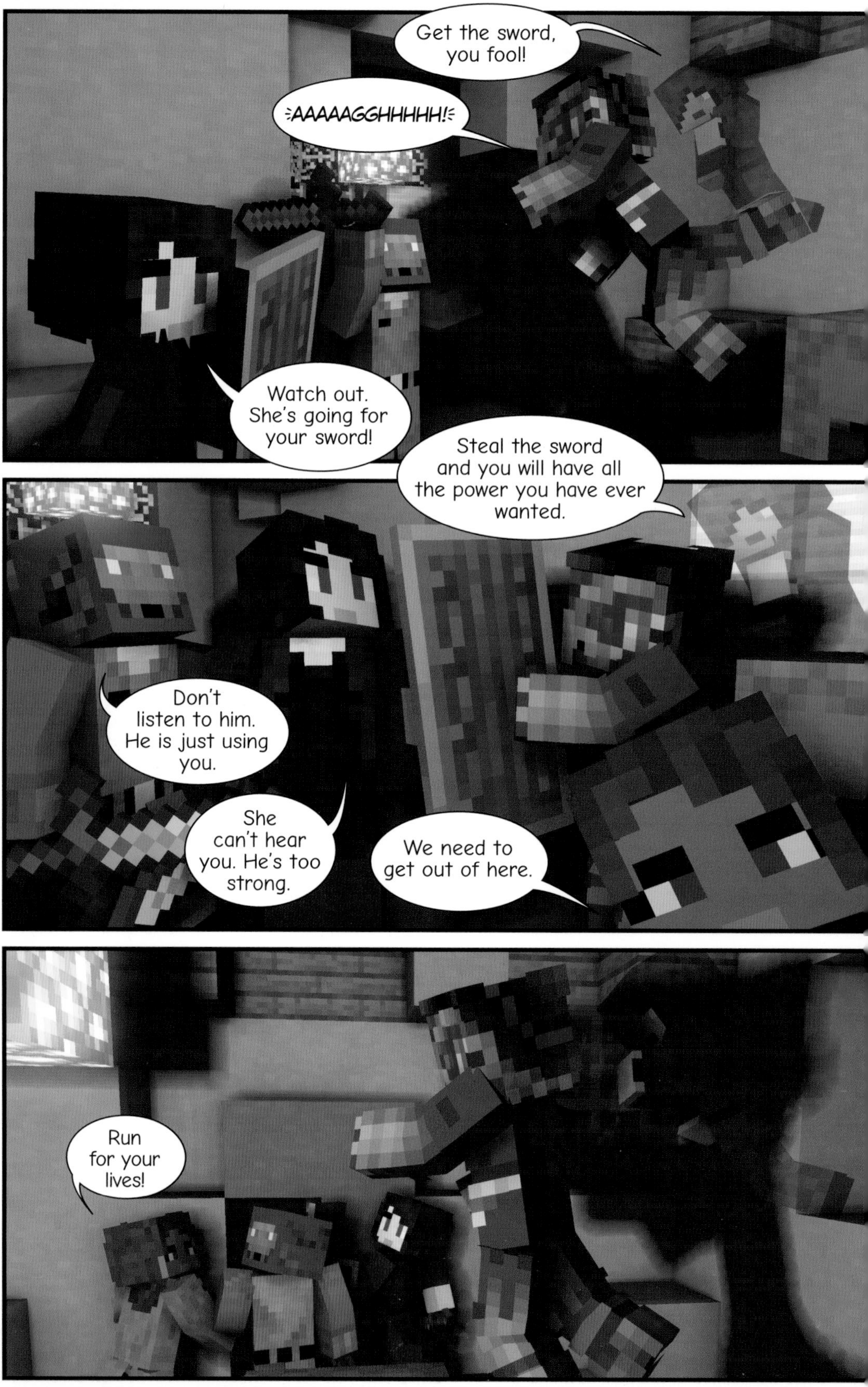
Get the sword, you fool!
AAAAAGGHHHHH!
Watch out. She's going for your sword!
Steal the sword and you will have all the power you have ever wanted.
Don't listen to him. He is just using you.
She can't hear you. He's too strong.
We need to get out of here.
Run for your lives!

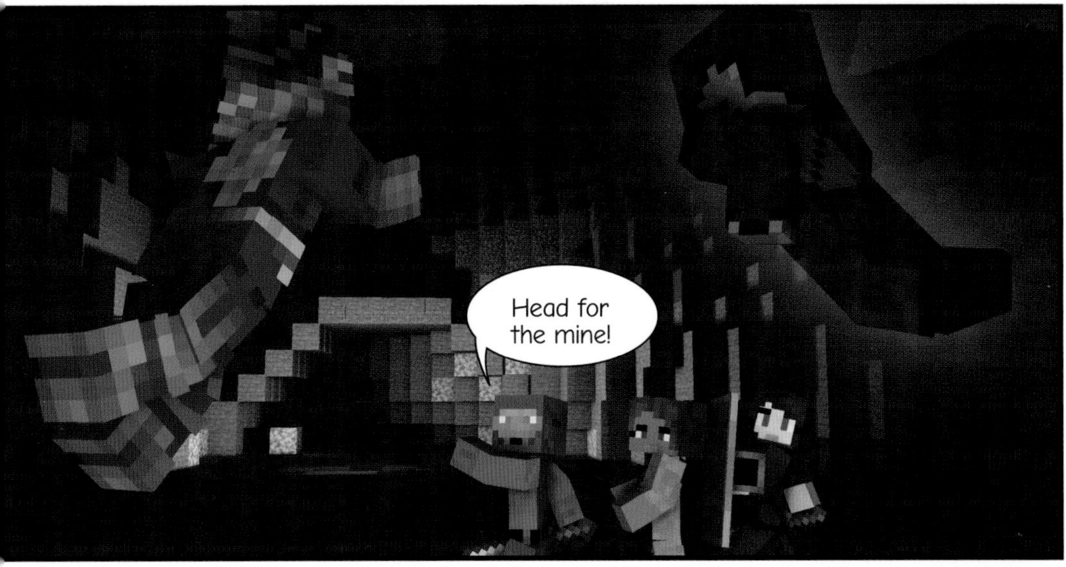
Head for the mine!

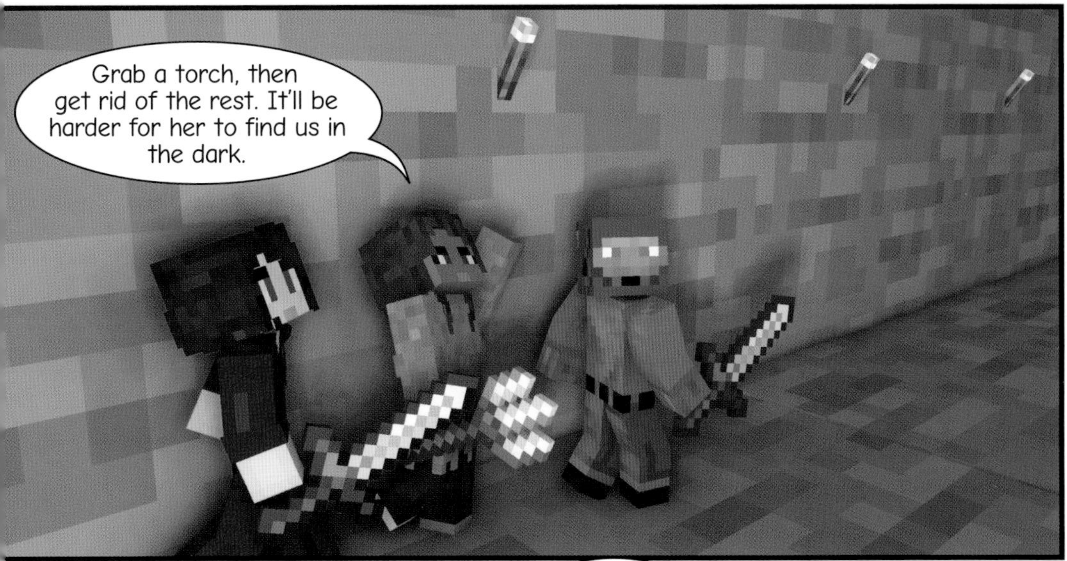
Grab a torch, then get rid of the rest. It'll be harder for her to find us in the dark.

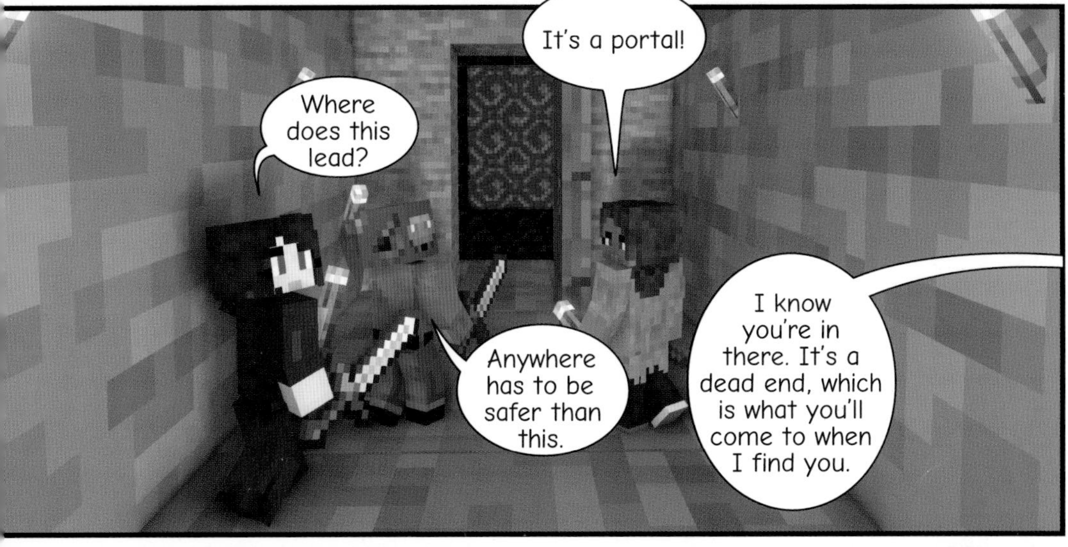
Where does this lead?
It's a portal!
Anywhere has to be safer than this.
I know you're in there. It's a dead end, which is what you'll come to when I find you.

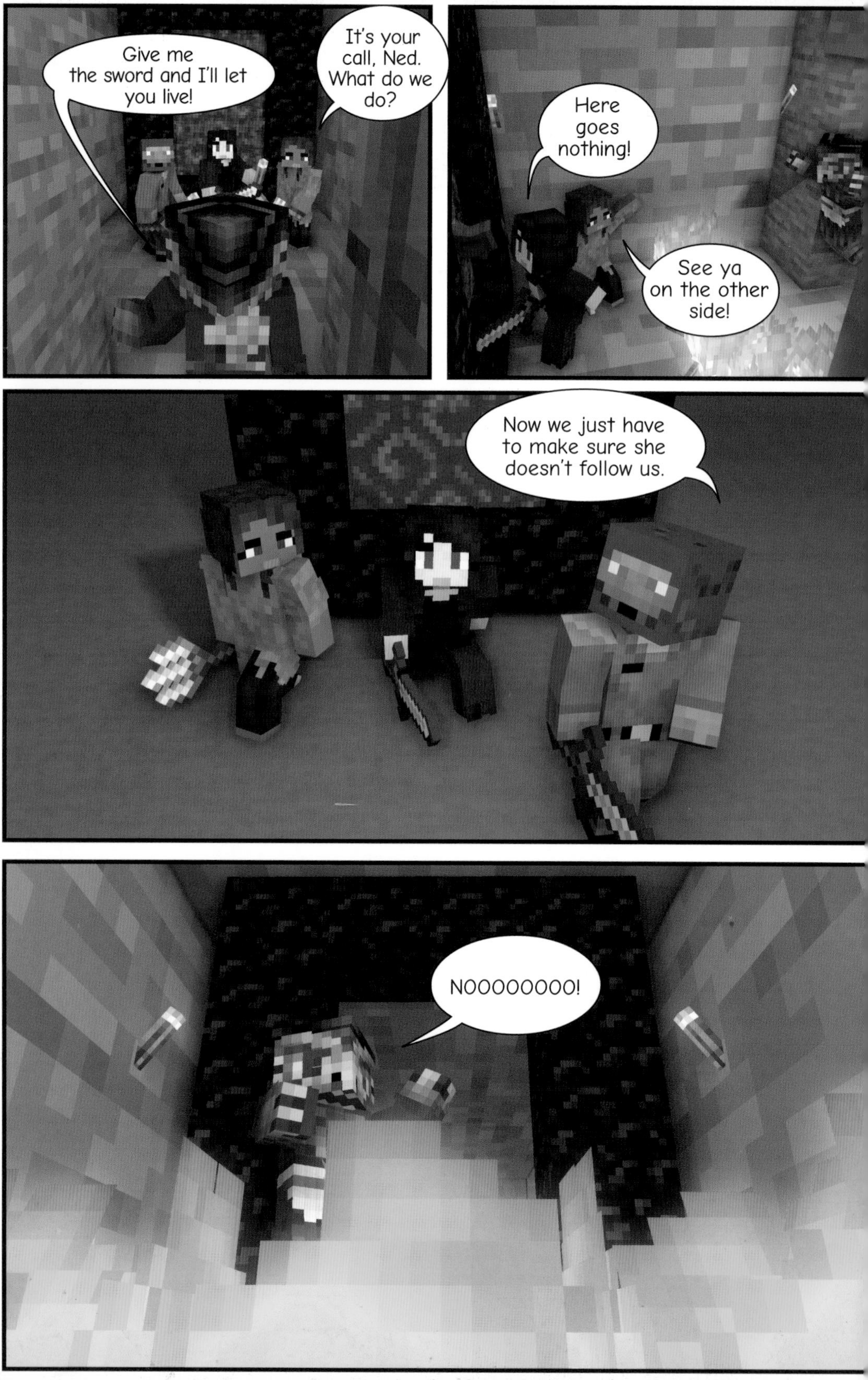
Give me the sword and I'll let you live!
It's your call, Ned. What do we do?
Here goes nothing!
See ya on the other side!
Now we just have to make sure she doesn't follow us.
NOOOOOOOO!

# CHAPTER 4

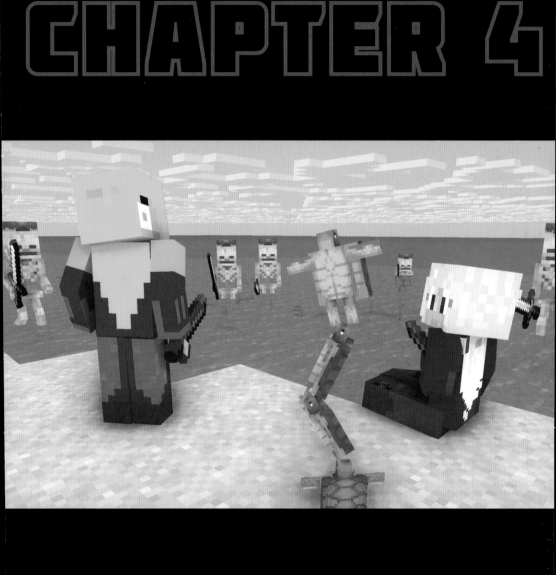

THE PAST

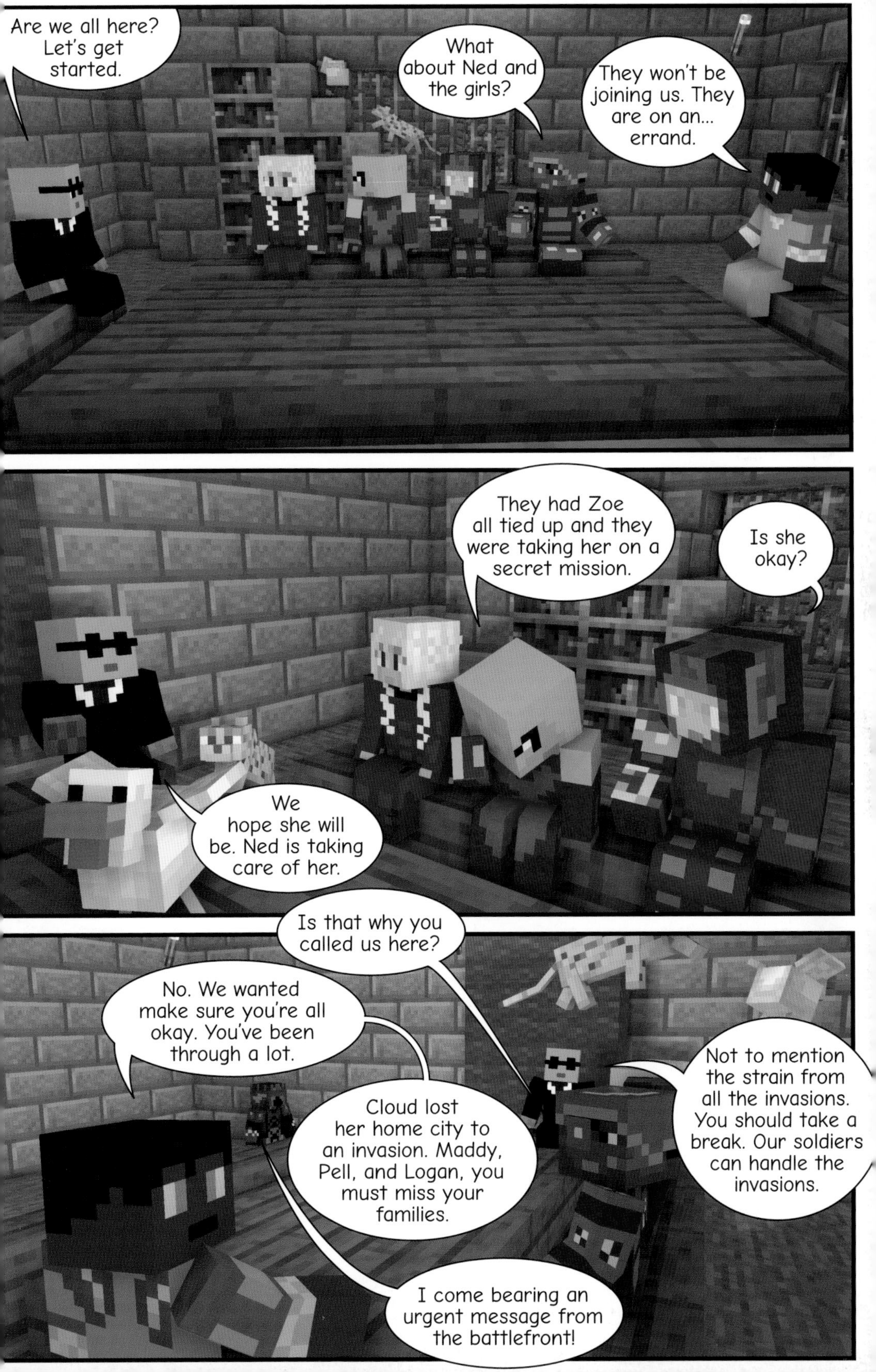
Are we all here? Let's get started.
What about Ned and the girls?
They won't be joining us. They are on an... errand.
They had Zoe all tied up and they were taking her on a secret mission.
Is she okay?
We hope she will be. Ned is taking care of her.
Is that why you called us here?
No. We wanted make sure you're all okay. You've been through a lot.
Cloud lost her home city to an invasion. Maddy, Pell, and Logan, you must miss your families.
Not to mention the strain from all the invasions. You should take a break. Our soldiers can handle the invasions.
I come bearing an urgent message from the battlefront!

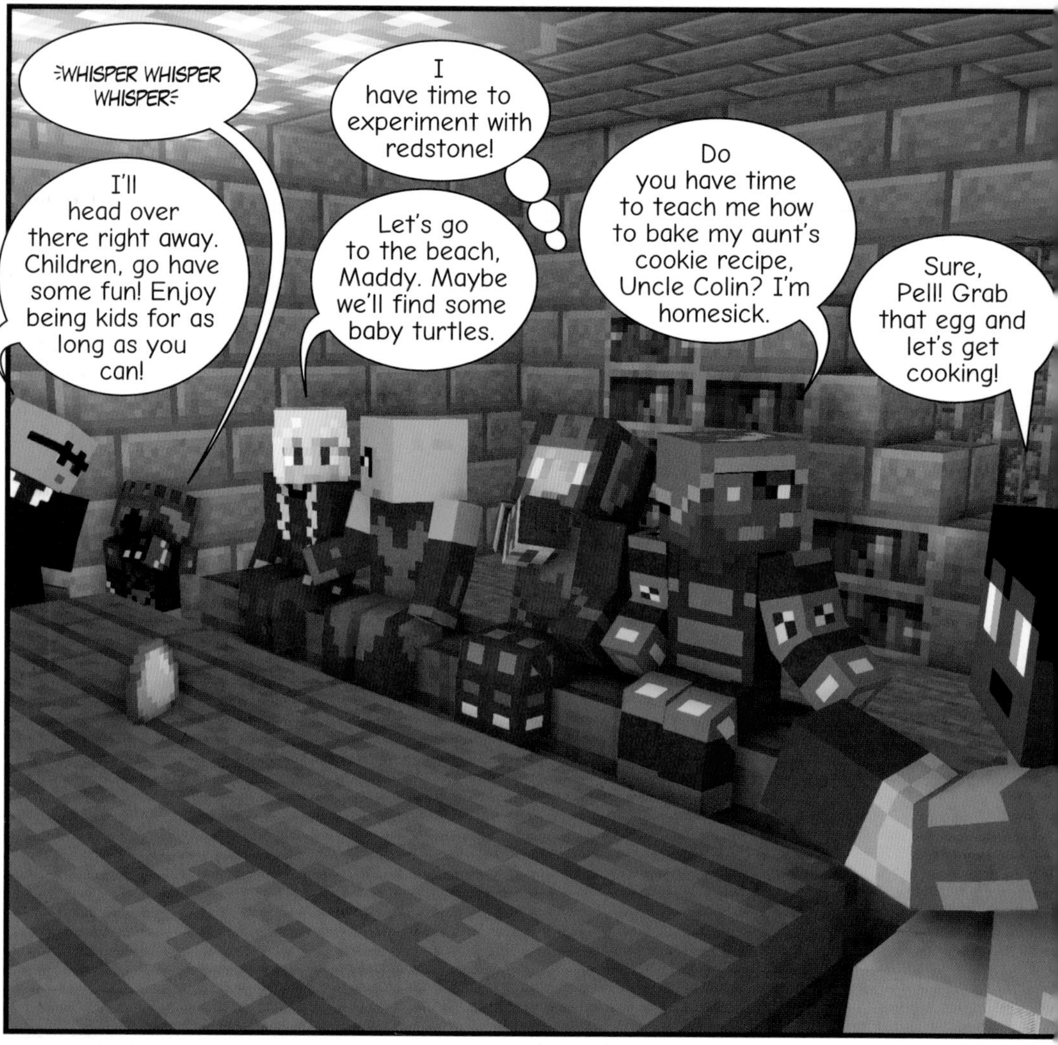
I'll head over there right away. Children, go have some fun! Enjoy being kids for as long as you can!
WHISPER WHISPER WHISPER
Let's go to the beach, Maddy. Maybe we'll find some baby turtles.
I have time to experiment with redstone!
Do you have time to teach me how to bake my aunt's cookie recipe, Uncle Colin? I'm homesick.
Sure, Pell! Grab that egg and let's get cooking!

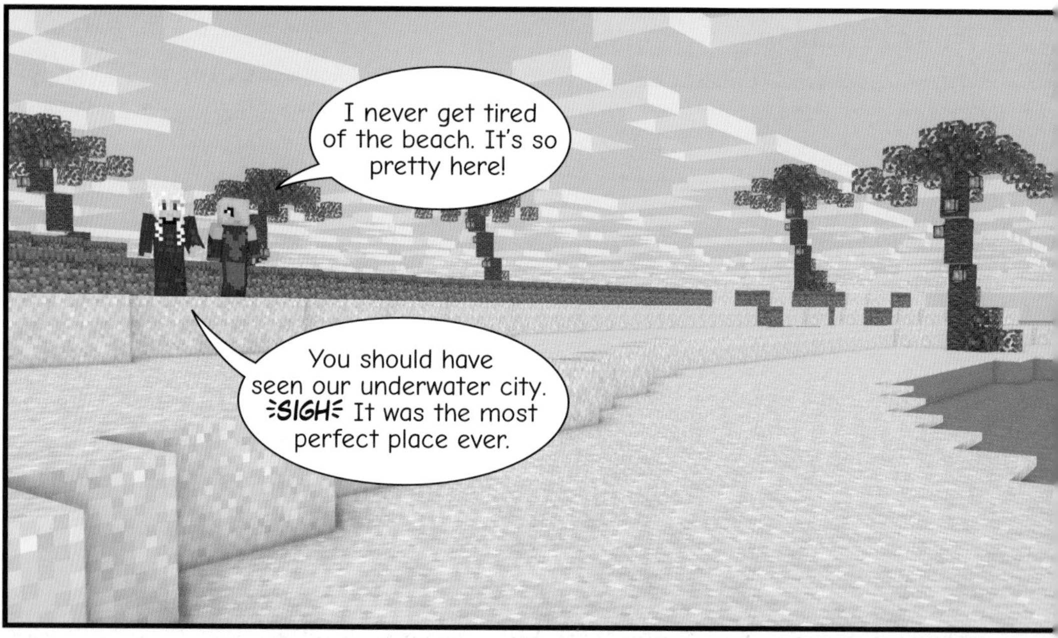
I never get tired of the beach. It's so pretty here!
You should have seen our underwater city. SIGH It was the most perfect place ever.

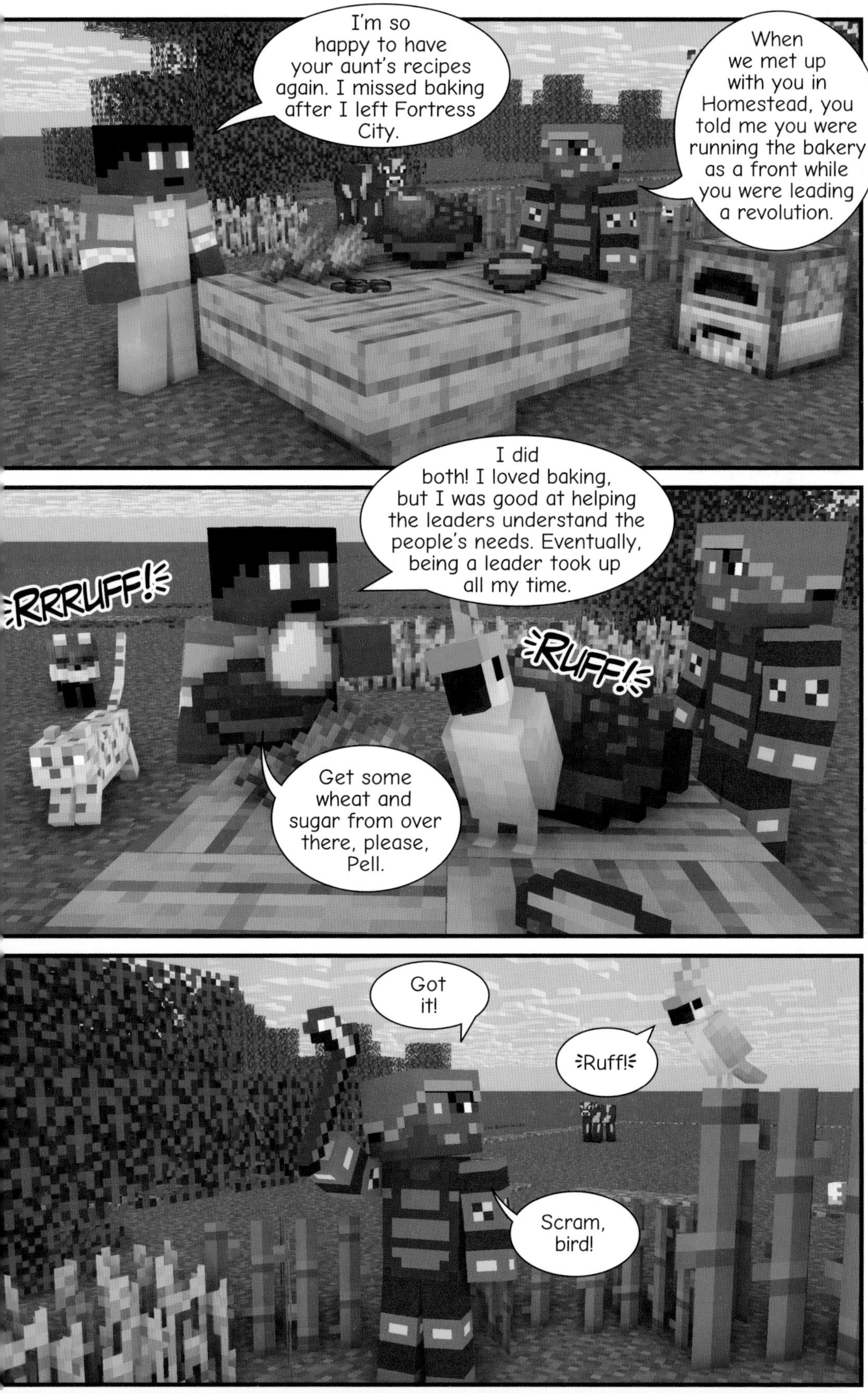
I'm so happy to have your aunt's recipes again. I missed baking after I left Fortress City.
When we met up with you in Homestead, you told me you were running the bakery as a front while you were leading a revolution.
I did both! I loved baking, but I was good at helping the leaders understand the people's needs. Eventually, being a leader took up all my time.
RRRUFF!
RUFF!
Get some wheat and sugar from over there, please, Pell.
Got it!
Ruff!
Scram, bird!

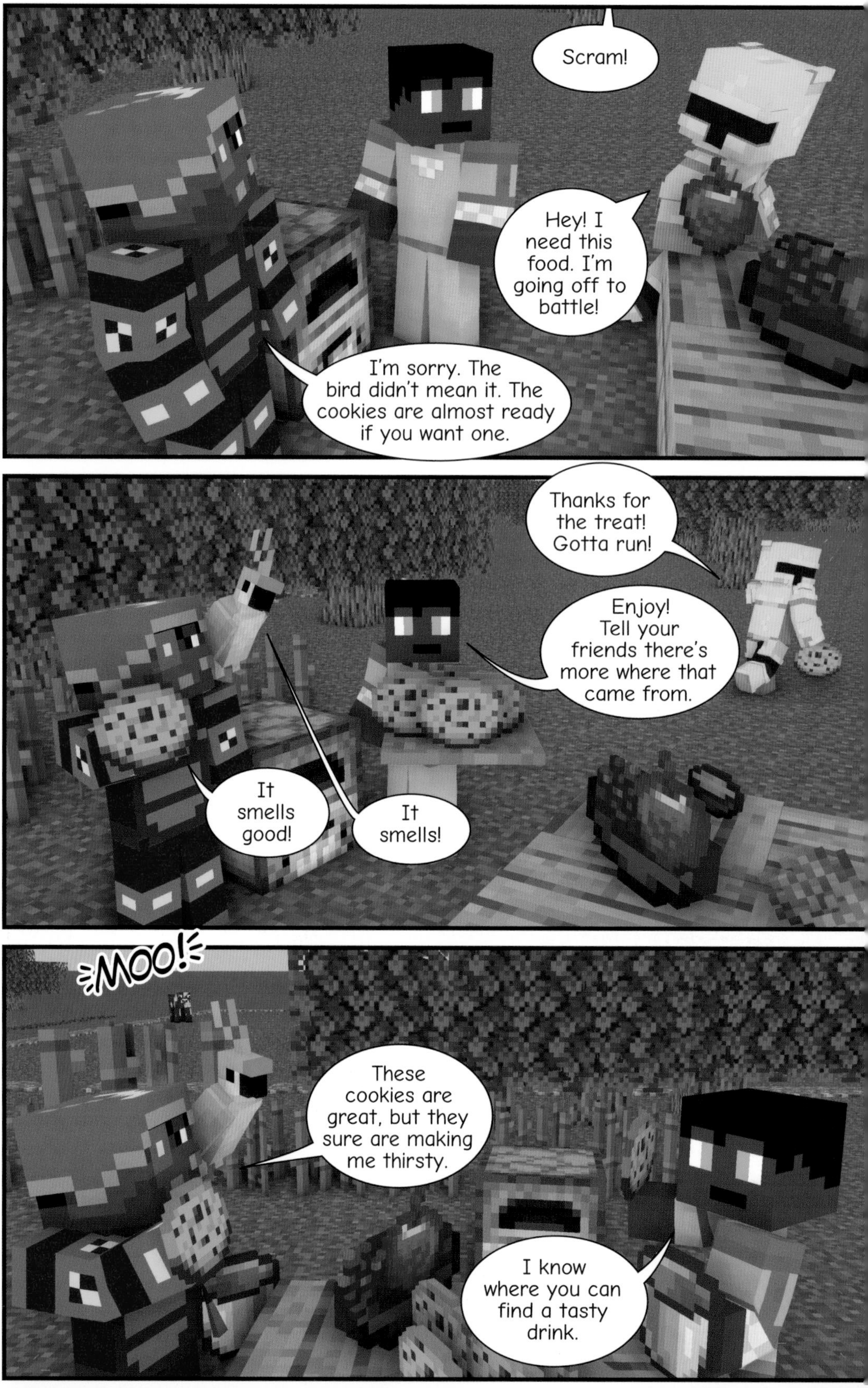
Scram!
Hey! I need this food. I'm going off to battle!
I'm sorry. The bird didn't mean it. The cookies are almost ready if you want one.
Thanks for the treat! Gotta run!
Enjoy! Tell your friends there's more where that came from.
It smells good!
It smells!
MOO!
These cookies are great, but they sure are making me thirsty.
I know where you can find a tasty drink.

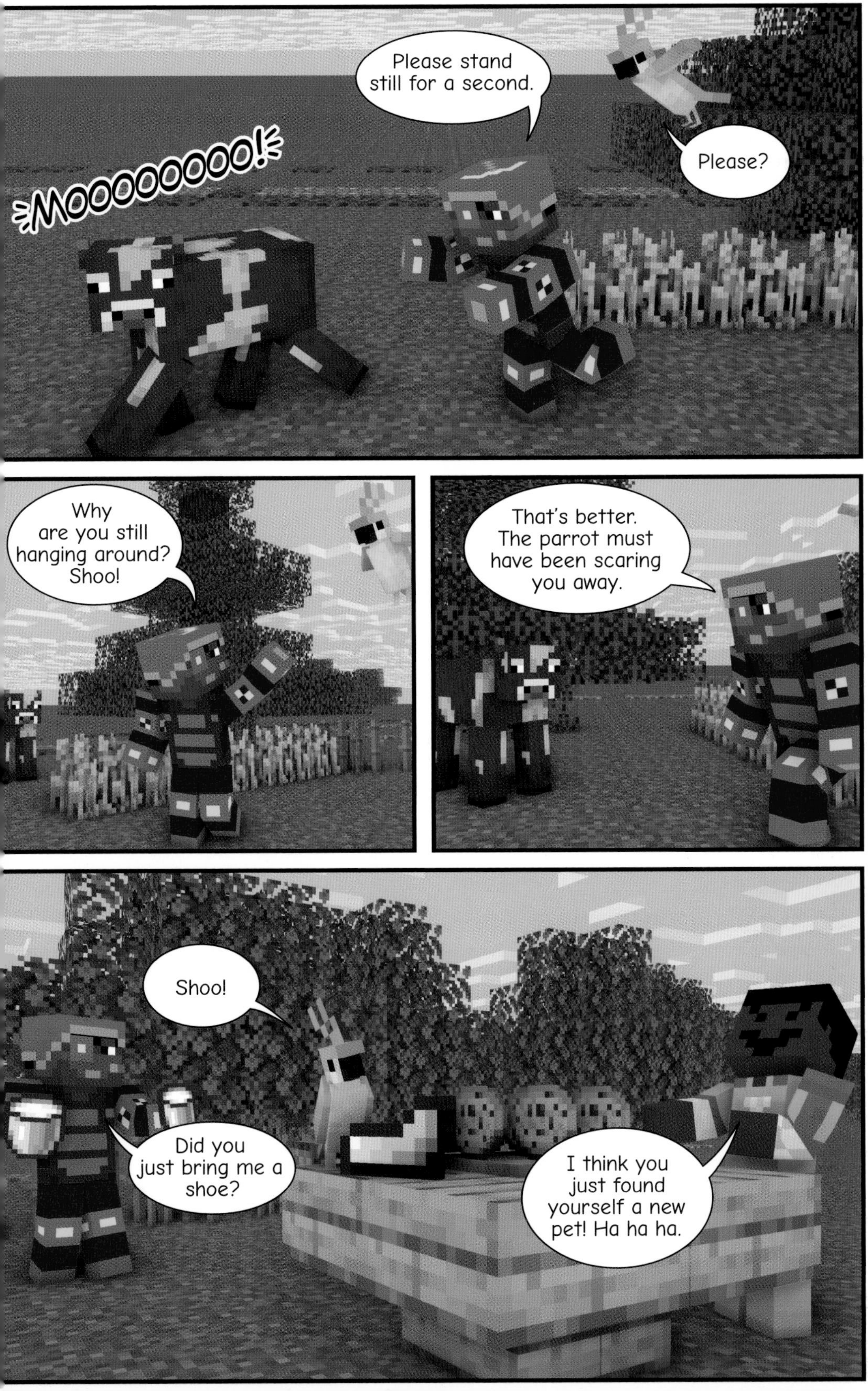
Please stand still for a second.
Please?
MOOOOOOOO!
Why are you still hanging around? Shoo!
That's better. The parrot must have been scaring you away.
Shoo!
Did you just bring me a shoe?
I think you just found yourself a new pet! Ha ha ha.

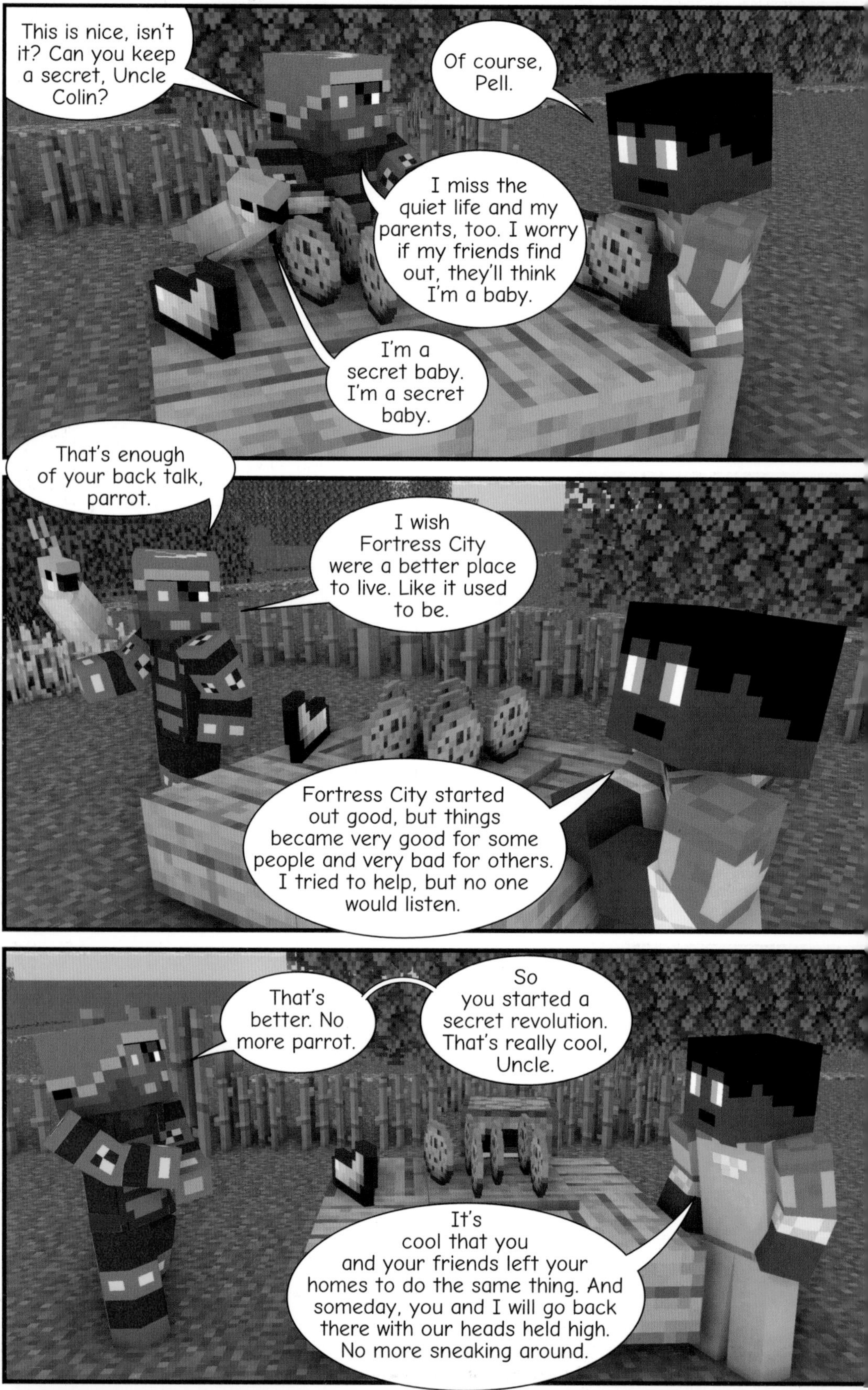
This is nice, isn't it? Can you keep a secret, Uncle Colin?
Of course, Pell.
I miss the quiet life and my parents, too. I worry if my friends find out, they'll think I'm a baby.
I'm a secret baby. I'm a secret baby.
That's enough of your back talk, parrot.
I wish Fortress City were a better place to live. Like it used to be.
Fortress City started out good, but things became very good for some people and very bad for others. I tried to help, but no one would listen.
That's better. No more parrot.
So you started a secret revolution. That's really cool, Uncle.
It's cool that you and your friends left your homes to do the same thing. And someday, you and I will go back there with our heads held high. No more sneaking around.

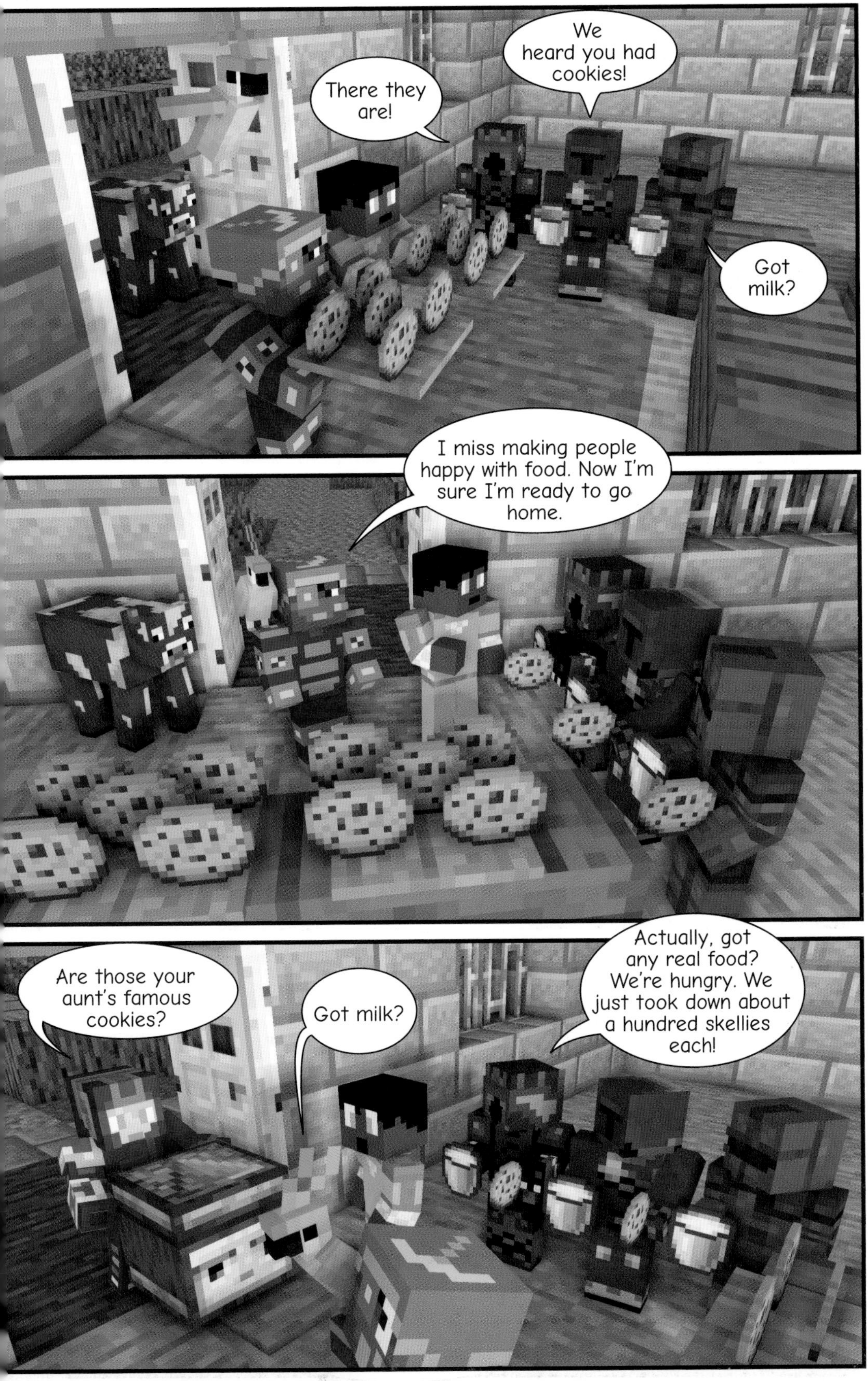
There they are!
We heard you had cookies!
Got milk?
I miss making people happy with food. Now I'm sure I'm ready to go home.
Are those your aunt's famous cookies?
Got milk?
Actually, got any real food? We're hungry. We just took down about a hundred skellies each!

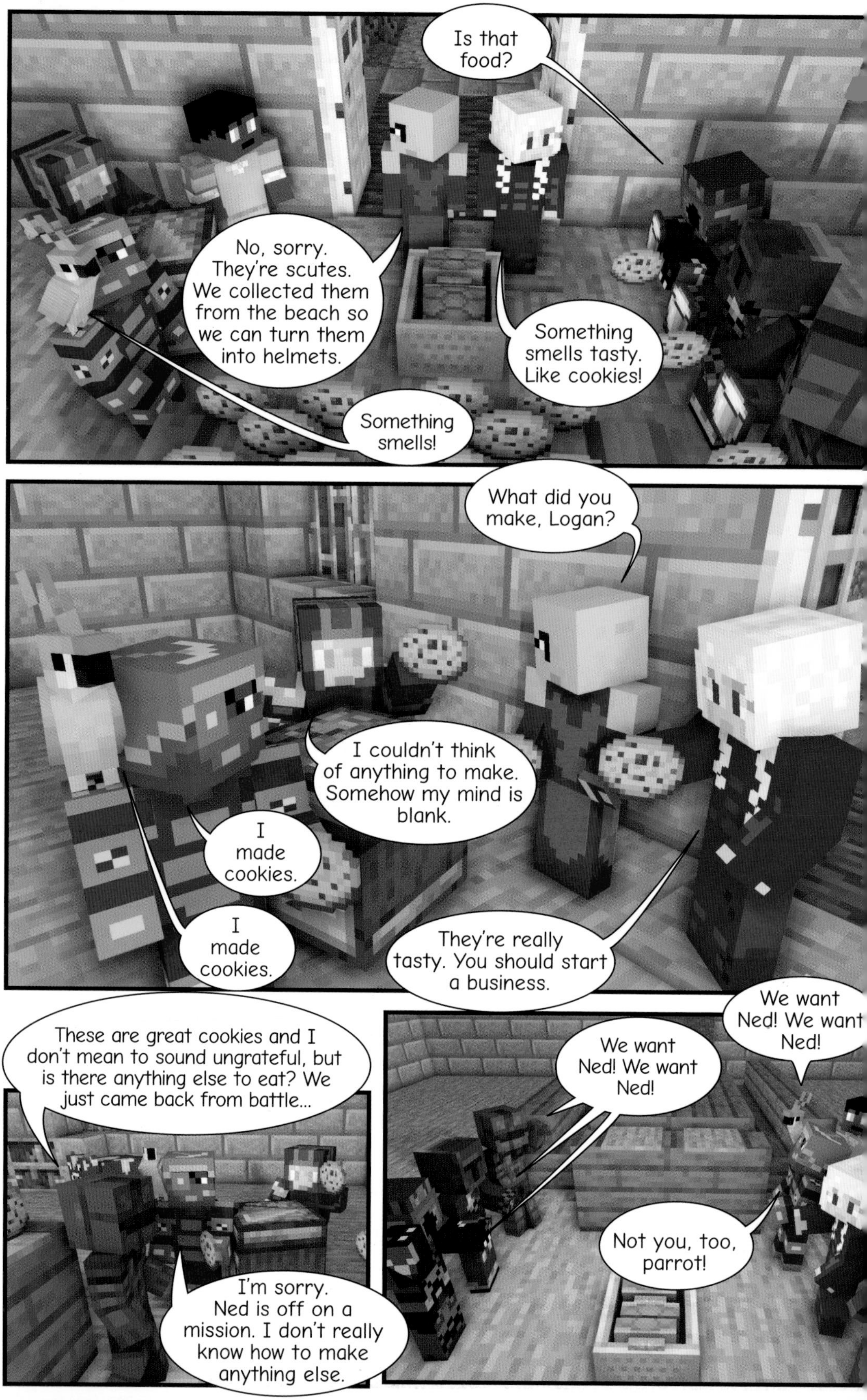
Is that food?
No, sorry. They're scutes. We collected them from the beach so we can turn them into helmets.
Something smells tasty. Like cookies!
Something smells!
What did you make, Logan?
I couldn't think of anything to make. Somehow my mind is blank.
I made cookies.
I made cookies.
They're really tasty. You should start a business.
These are great cookies and I don't mean to sound ungrateful, but is there anything else to eat? We just came back from battle...
I'm sorry. Ned is off on a mission. I don't really know how to make anything else.
We want Ned! We want Ned!
We want Ned! We want Ned!
Not you, too, parrot!

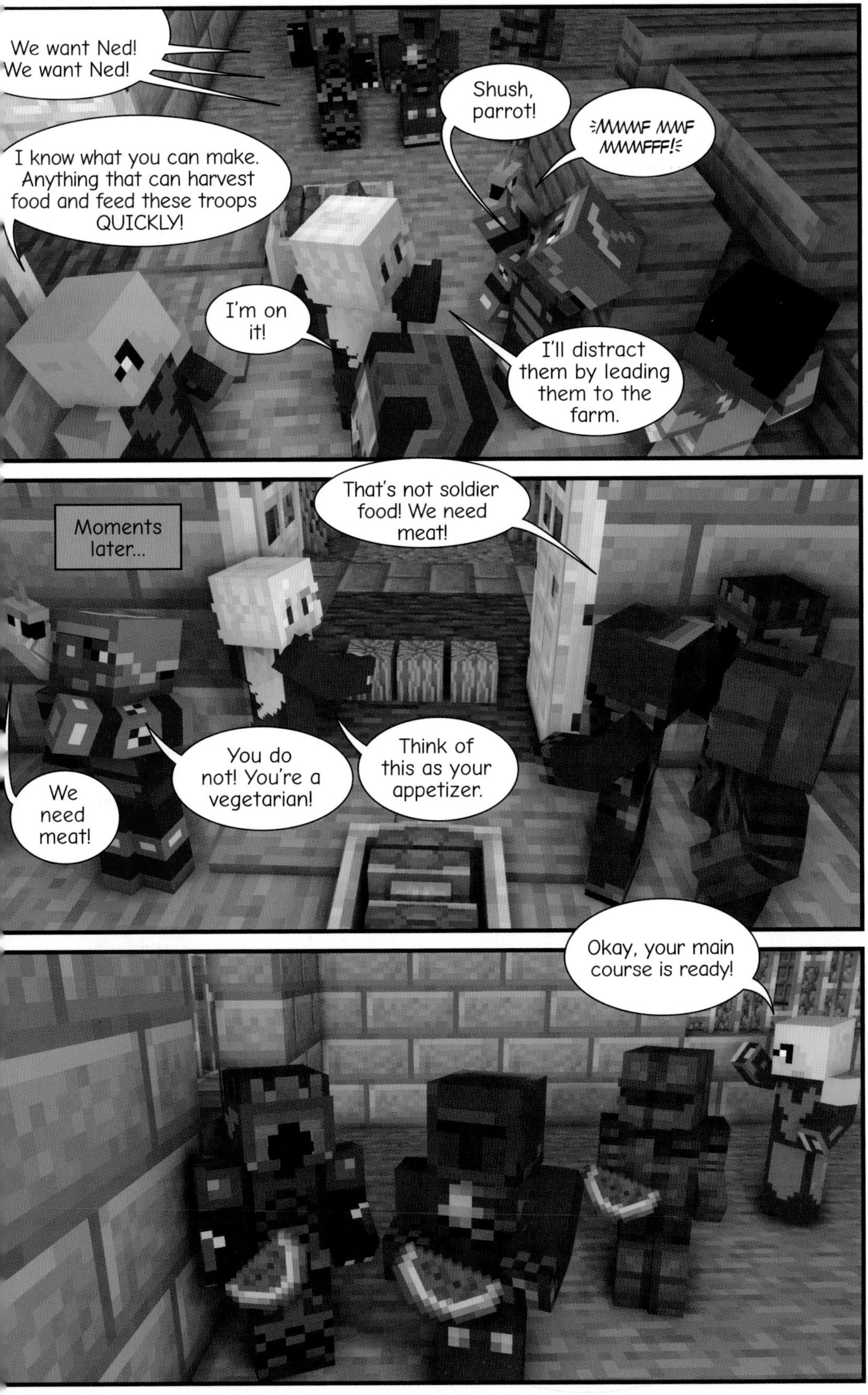
We want Ned! We want Ned!
I know what you can make. Anything that can harvest food and feed these troops QUICKLY!
Shush, parrot!
MMMF MMF MMMFFF!
I'm on it!
I'll distract them by leading them to the farm.
Moments later...
That's not soldier food! We need meat!
We need meat!
You do not! You're a vegetarian!
Think of this as your appetizer.
Okay, your main course is ready!

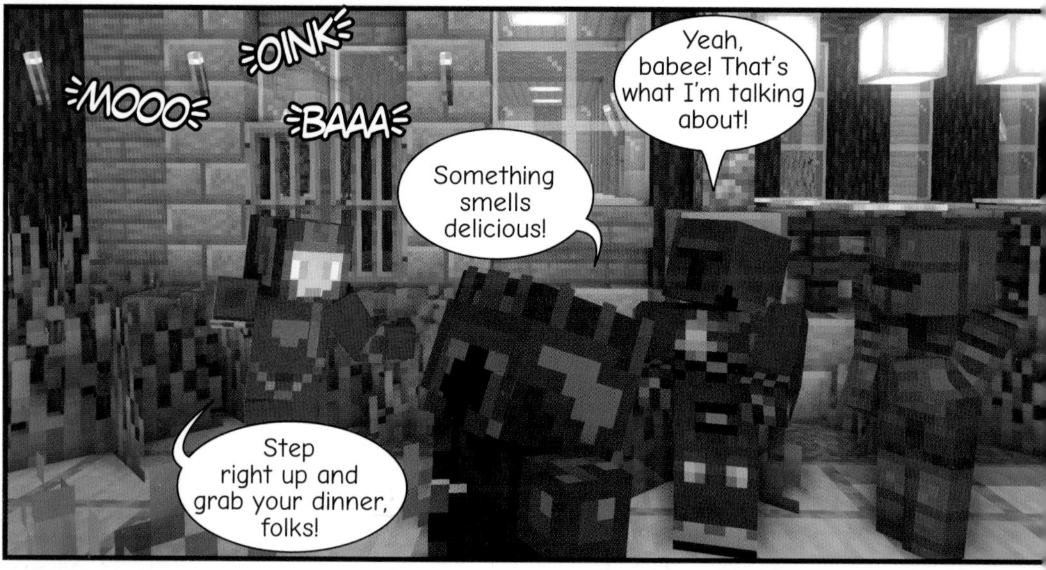
MOOO
OINK
BAAA
Something smells delicious!
Yeah, babee! That's what I'm talking about!
Step right up and grab your dinner, folks!

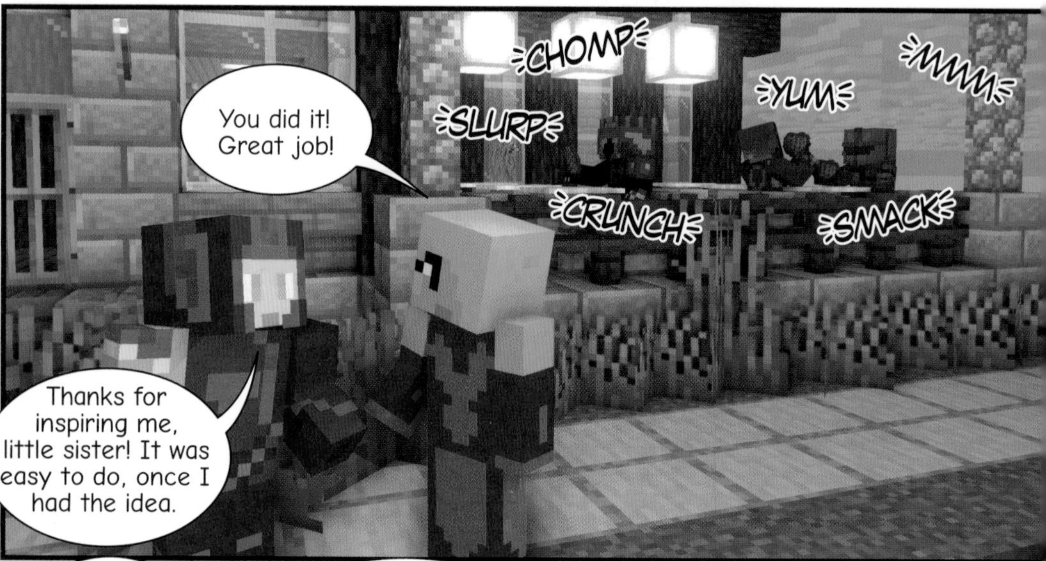
CHOMP
MMM
YUM
SLURP
You did it! Great job!
CRUNCH
SMACK
Thanks for inspiring me, little sister! It was easy to do, once I had the idea.

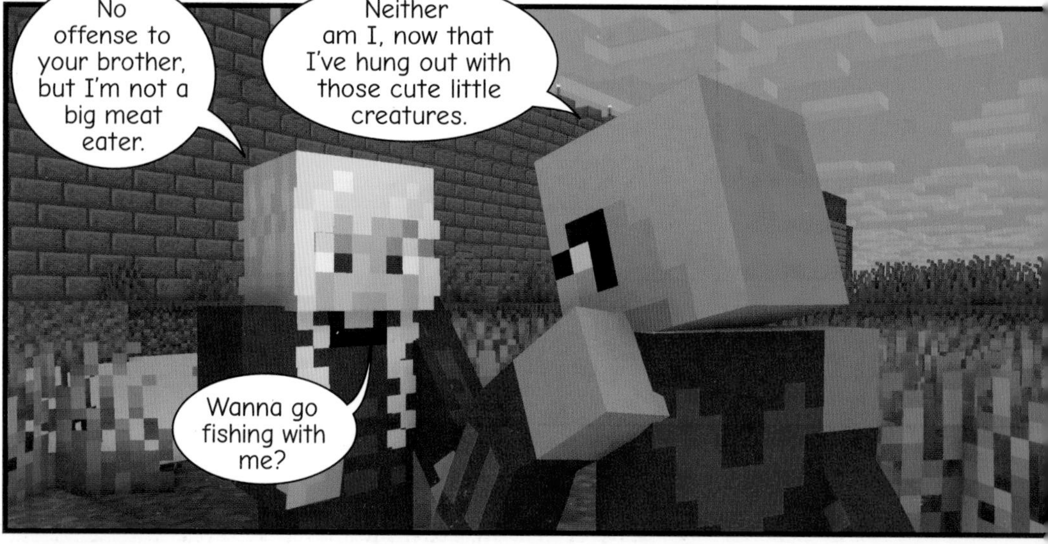
No offense to your brother, but I'm not a big meat eater.
Neither am I, now that I've hung out with those cute little creatures.
Wanna go fishing with me?

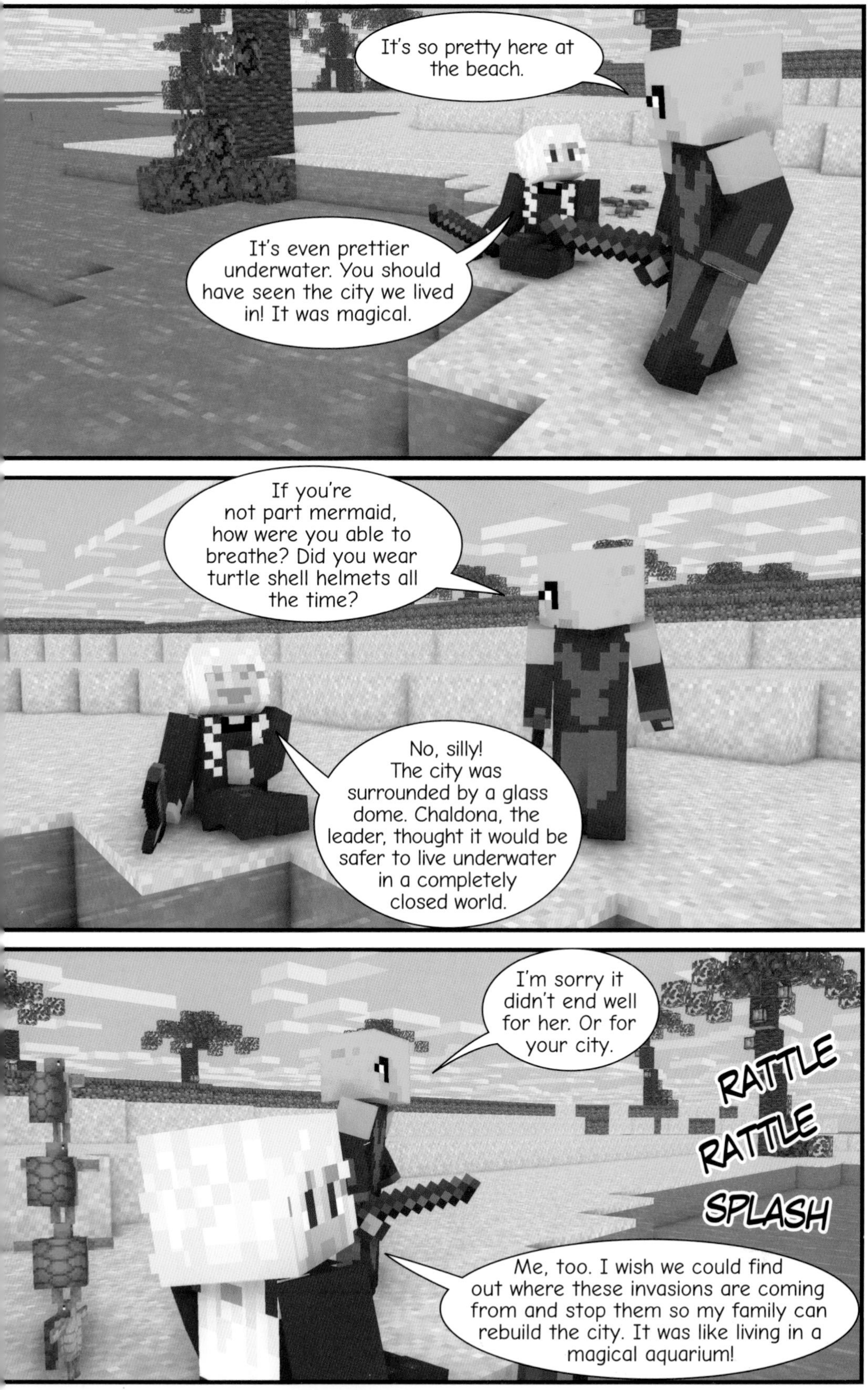

It's so pretty here at the beach.
It's even prettier underwater. You should have seen the city we lived in! It was magical.
If you're not part mermaid, how were you able to breathe? Did you wear turtle shell helmets all the time?
No, silly! The city was surrounded by a glass dome. Chaldona, the leader, thought it would be safer to live underwater in a completely closed world.
I'm sorry it didn't end well for her. Or for your city.
RATTLE
RATTLE
SPLASH
Me, too. I wish we could find out where these invasions are coming from and stop them so my family can rebuild the city. It was like living in a magical aquarium!

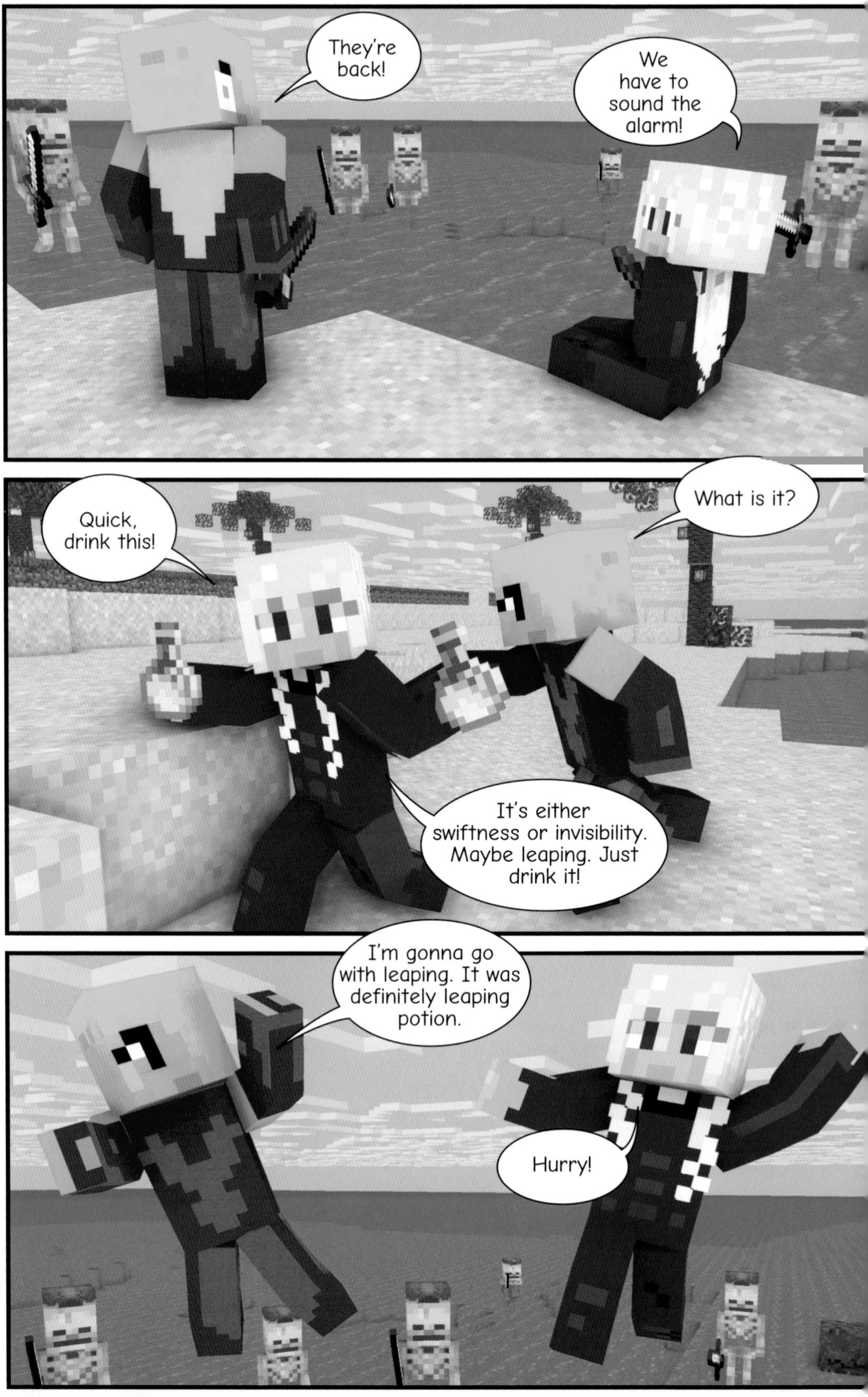
They're back!
We have to sound the alarm!
Quick, drink this!
What is it?
It's either swiftness or invisibility. Maybe leaping. Just drink it!
I'm gonna go with leaping. It was definitely leaping potion.
Hurry!

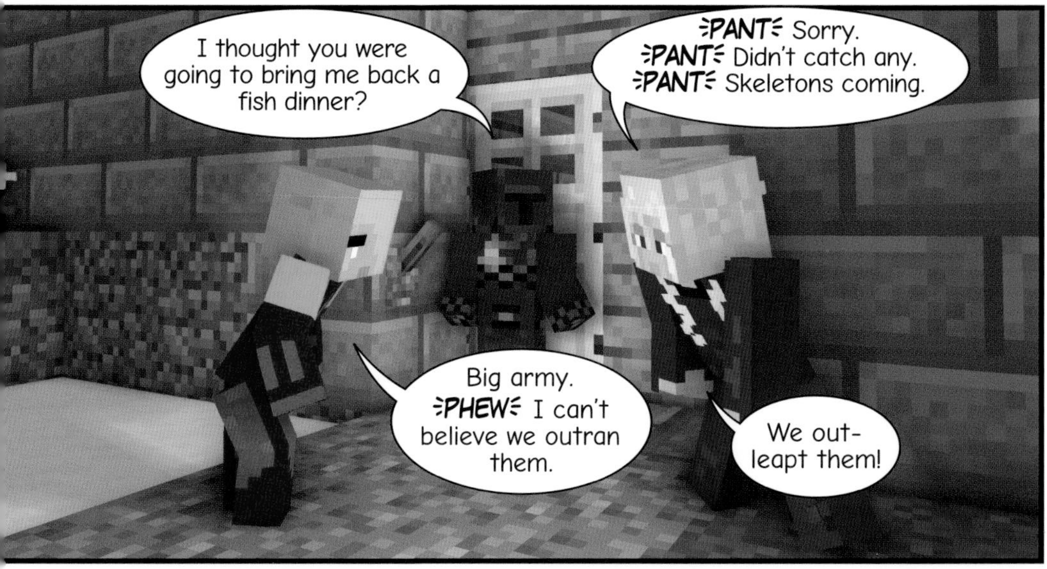
I thought you were going to bring me back a fish dinner?
PANT Sorry. PANT Didn't catch any. PANT Skeletons coming.
Big army. PHEW I can't believe we outran them.
We out-leapt them!

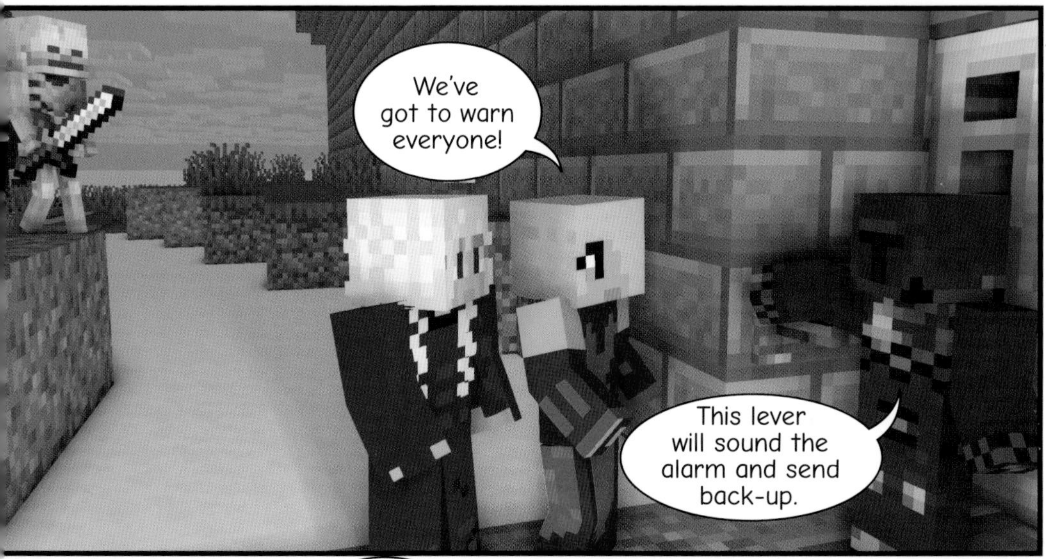
We've got to warn everyone!
This lever will sound the alarm and send back-up.

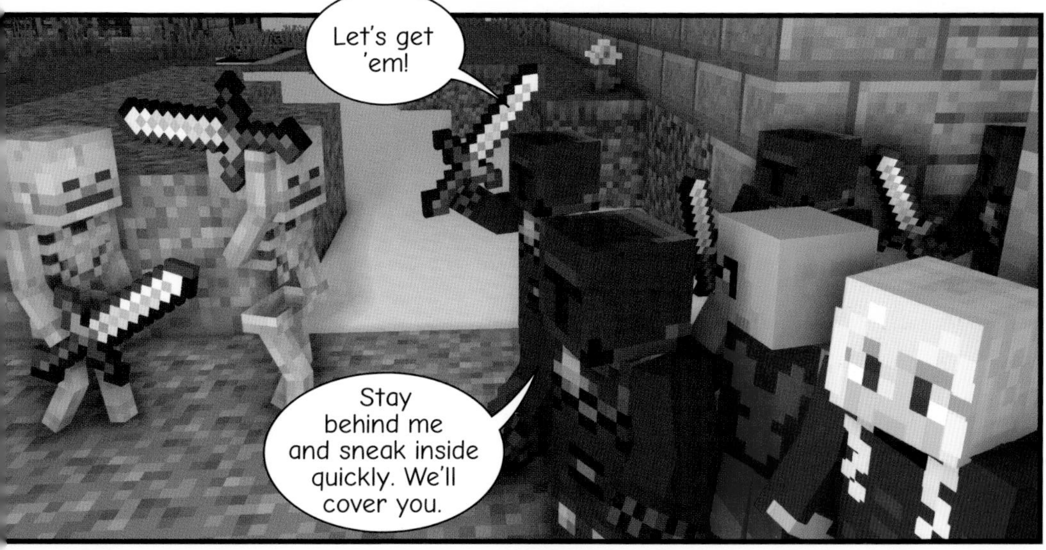
Let's get 'em!
Stay behind me and sneak inside quickly. We'll cover you.

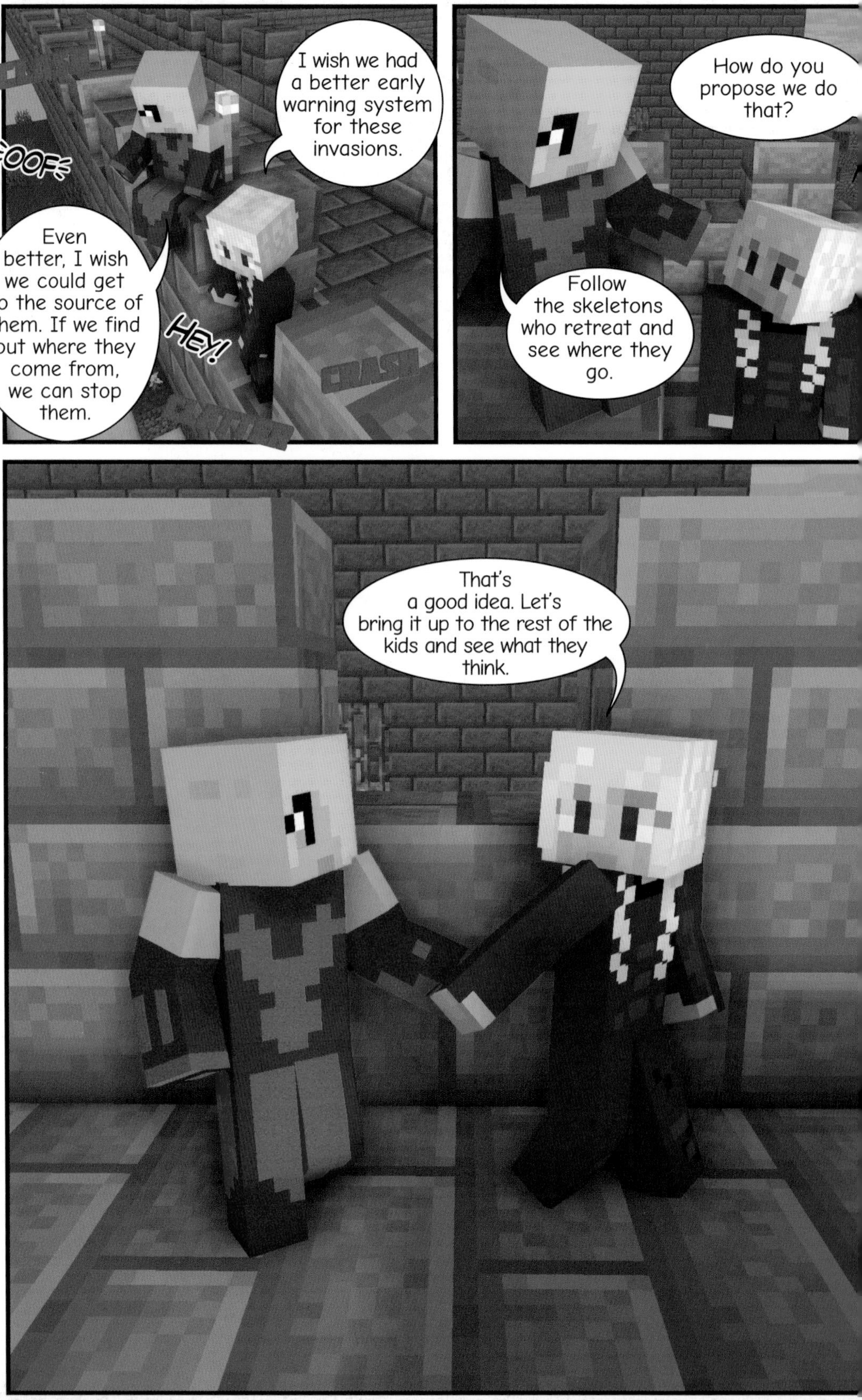
I wish we had a better early warning system for these invasions.
OOF
Even better, I wish we could get to the source of them. If we find out where they come from, we can stop them.
HEY!
CRASH
How do you propose we do that?
Follow the skeletons who retreat and see where they go.
That's a good idea. Let's bring it up to the rest of the kids and see what they think.

# CHAPTER 5

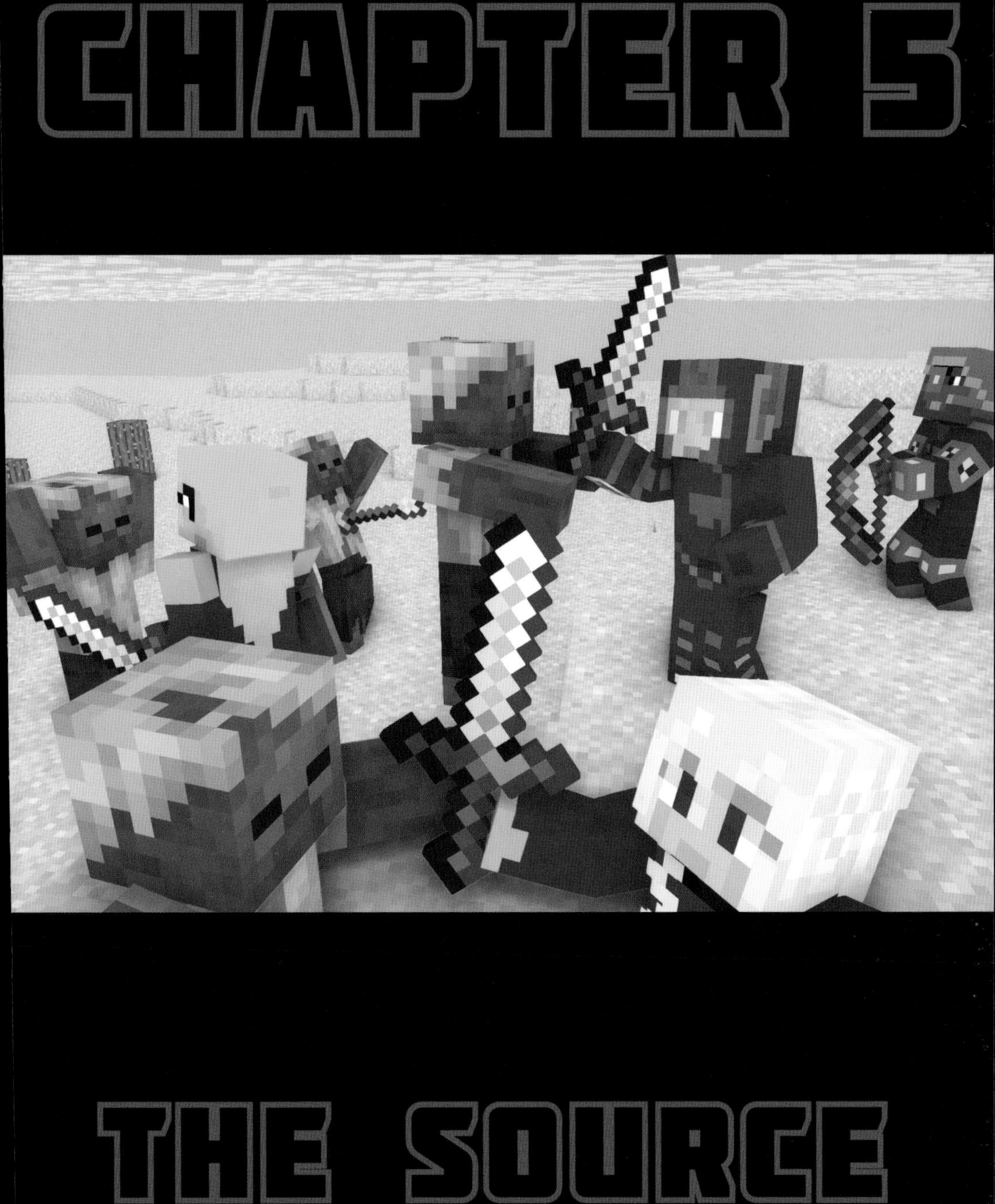

# THE SOURCE

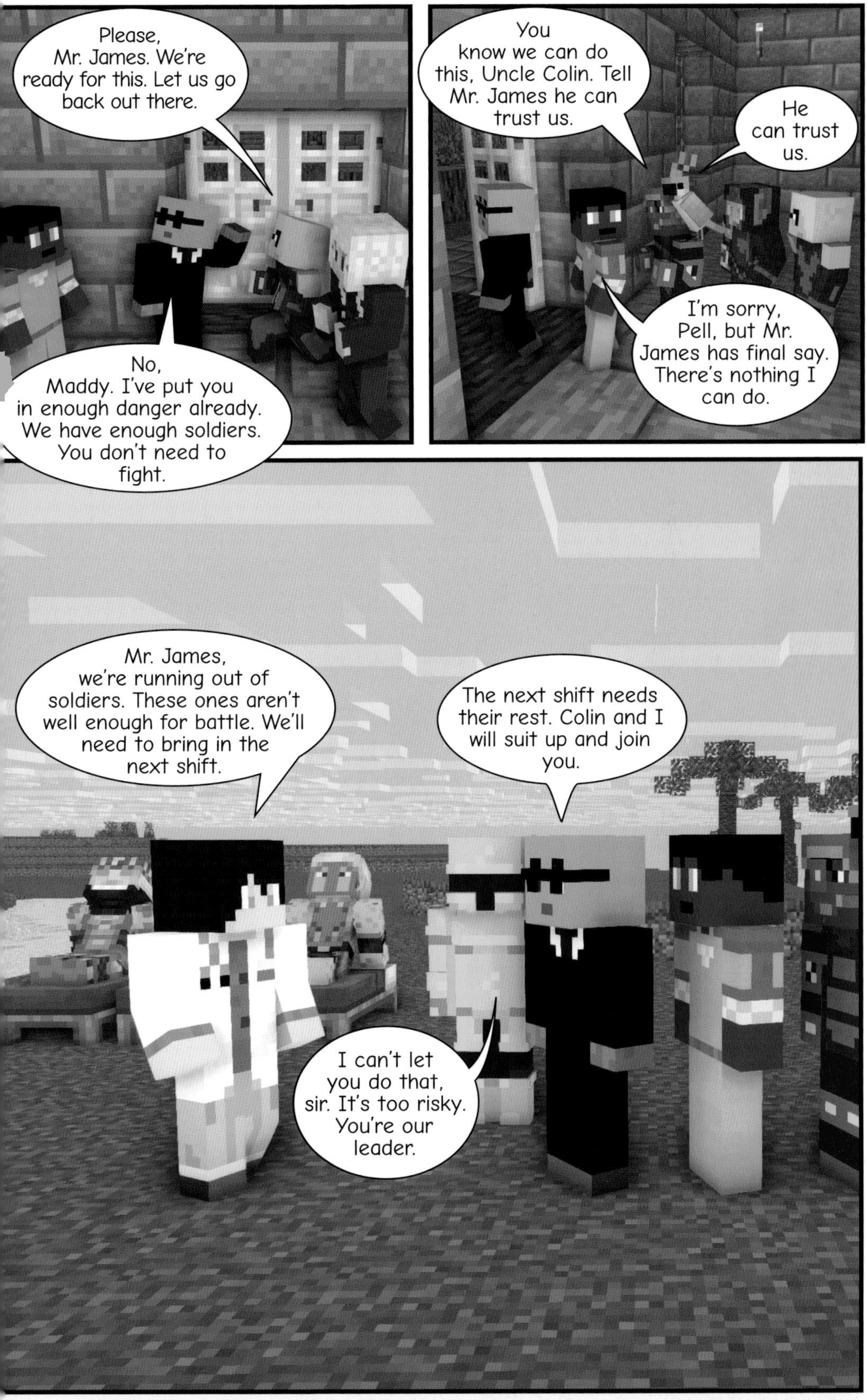
Please, Mr. James. We're ready for this. Let us go back out there.
No, Maddy. I've put you in enough danger already. We have enough soldiers. You don't need to fight.
You know we can do this, Uncle Colin. Tell Mr. James he can trust us.
He can trust us.
I'm sorry, Pell, but Mr. James has final say. There's nothing I can do.
Mr. James, we're running out of soldiers. These ones aren't well enough for battle. We'll need to bring in the next shift.
The next shift needs their rest. Colin and I will suit up and join you.
I can't let you do that, sir. It's too risky. You're our leader.

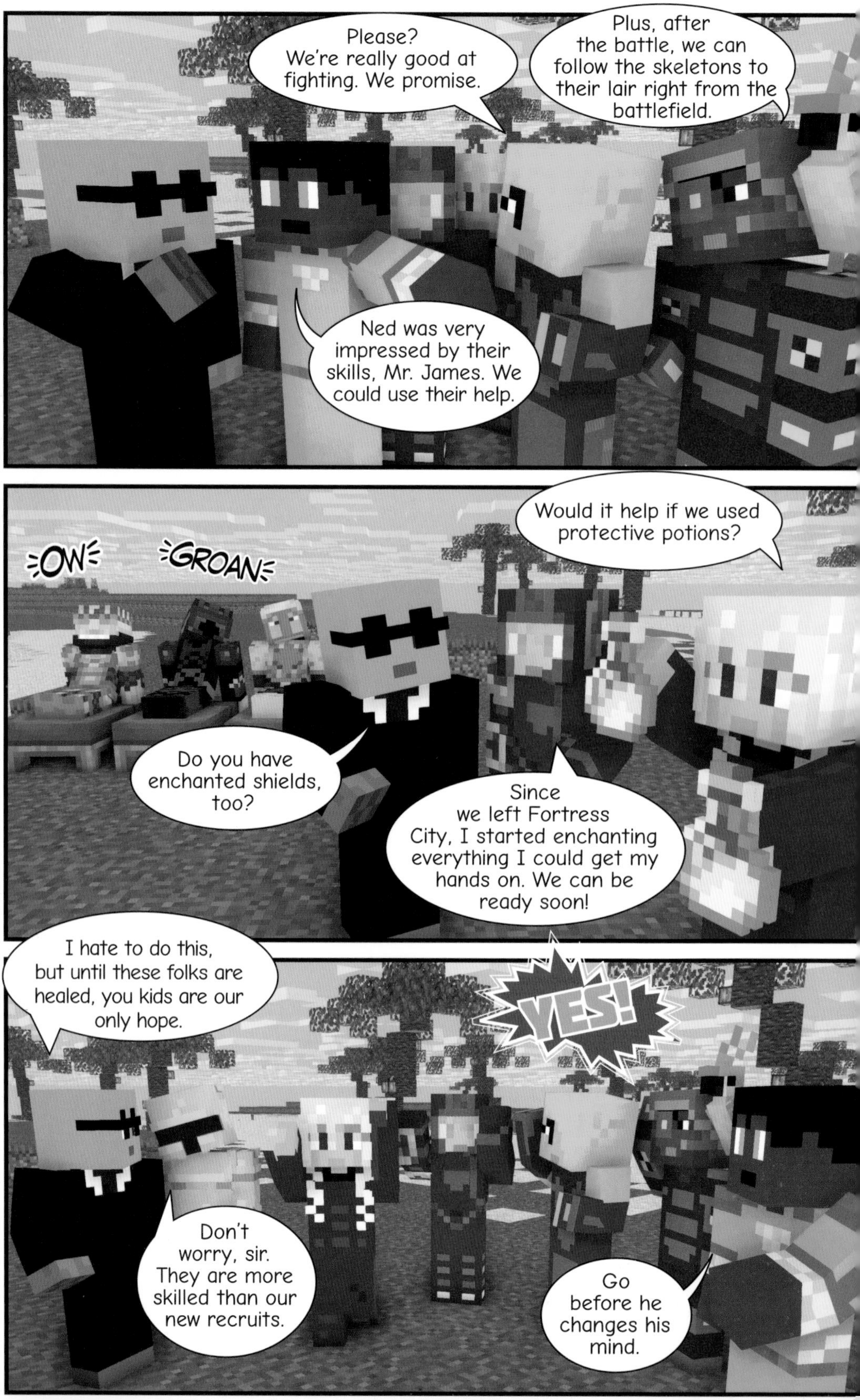
Please?
We're really good at fighting. We promise.
Plus, after the battle, we can follow the skeletons to their lair right from the battlefield.
Ned was very impressed by their skills, Mr. James. We could use their help.
OW
GROAN
Would it help if we used protective potions?
Do you have enchanted shields, too?
Since we left Fortress City, I started enchanting everything I could get my hands on. We can be ready soon!
I hate to do this, but until these folks are healed, you kids are our only hope.
YES!
Don't worry, sir. They are more skilled than our new recruits.
Go before he changes his mind.

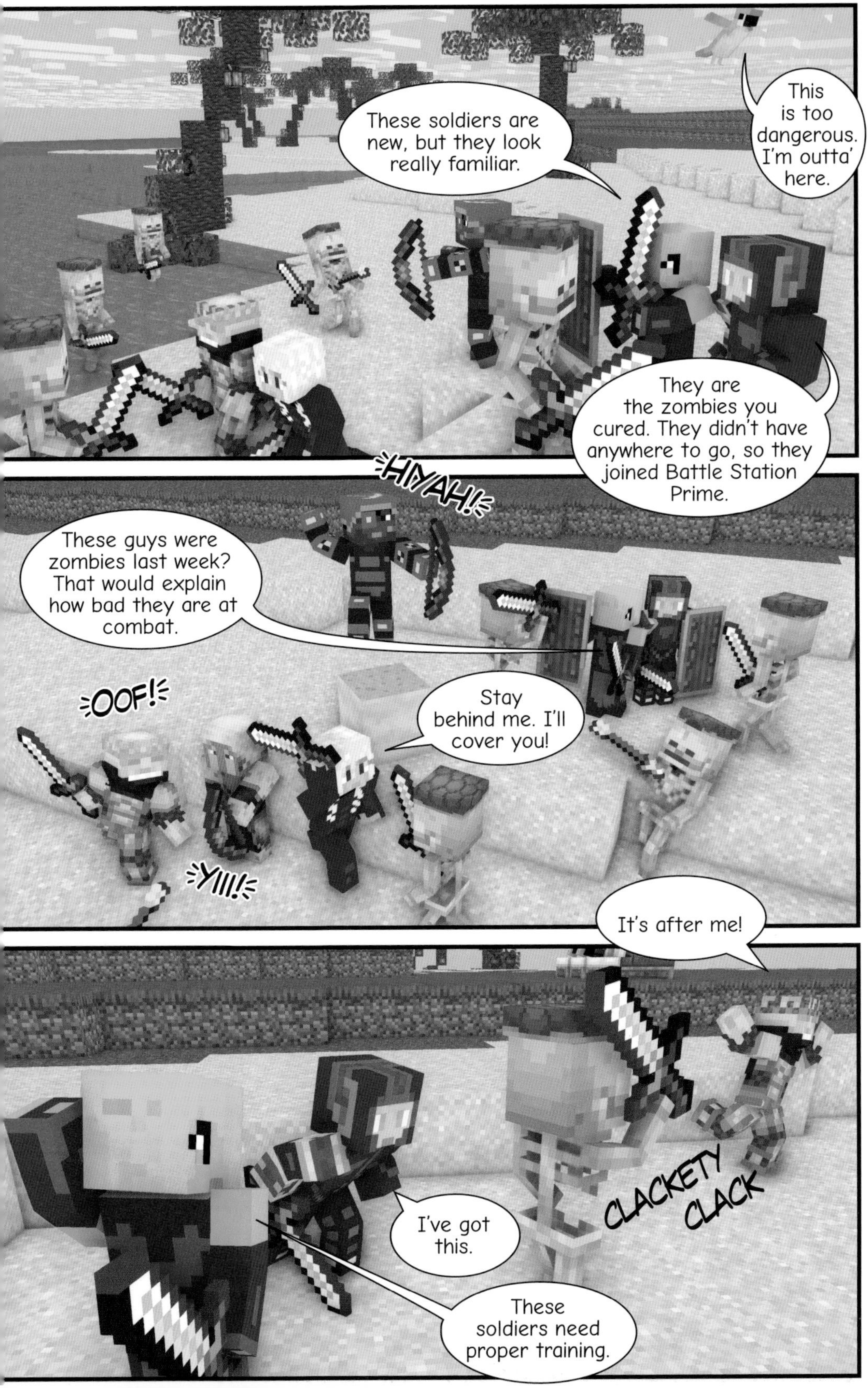
This is too dangerous. I'm outta' here.
These soldiers are new, but they look really familiar.
They are the zombies you cured. They didn't have anywhere to go, so they joined Battle Station Prime.
HIYAH!
These guys were zombies last week? That would explain how bad they are at combat.
OOF!
Stay behind me. I'll cover you!
YIII!
It's after me!
CLACKETY CLACK
I've got this.
These soldiers need proper training.

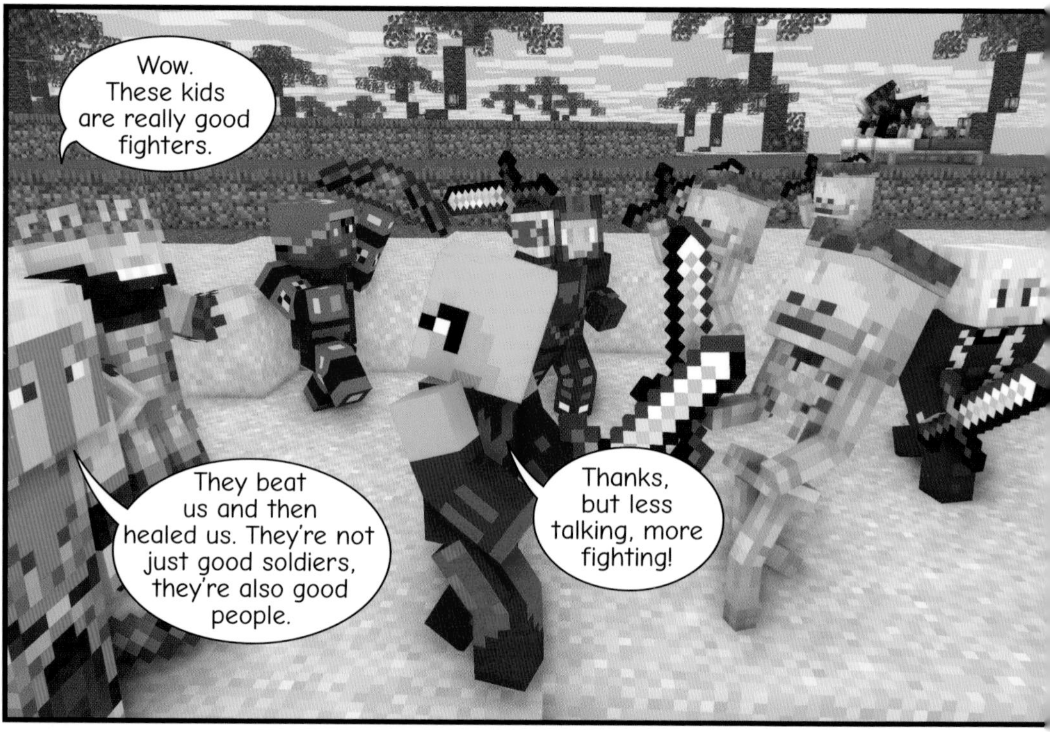
Wow. These kids are really good fighters.
They beat us and then healed us. They're not just good soldiers, they're also good people.
Thanks, but less talking, more fighting!

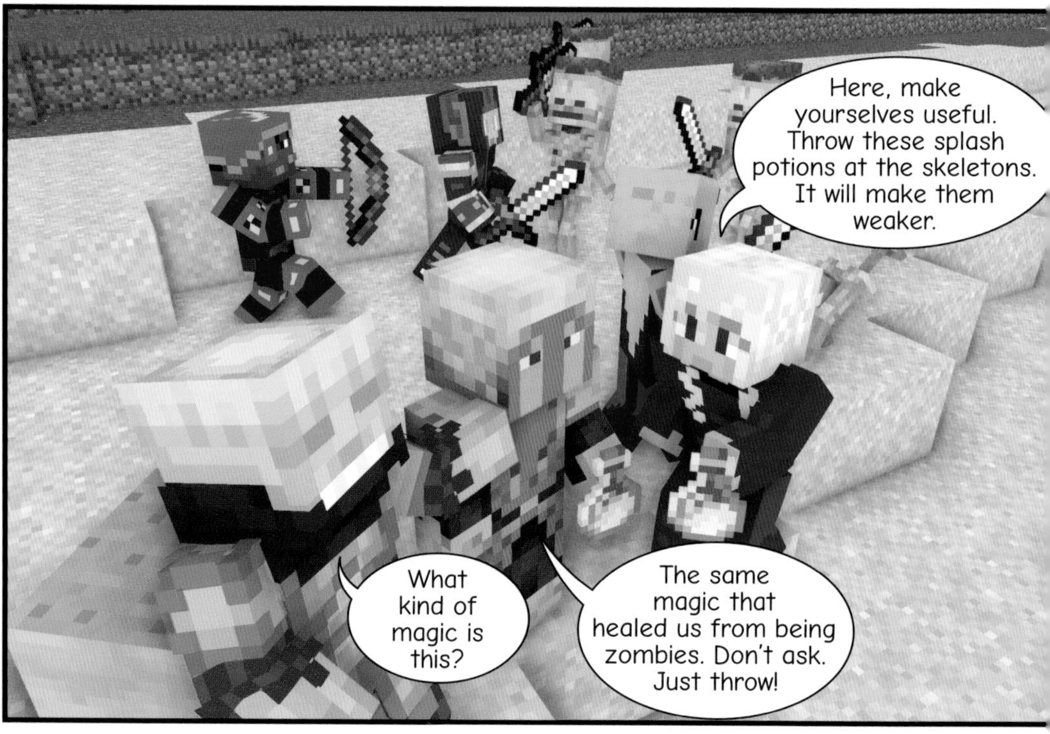
Here, make yourselves useful. Throw these splash potions at the skeletons. It will make them weaker.
What kind of magic is this?
The same magic that healed us from being zombies. Don't ask. Just throw!

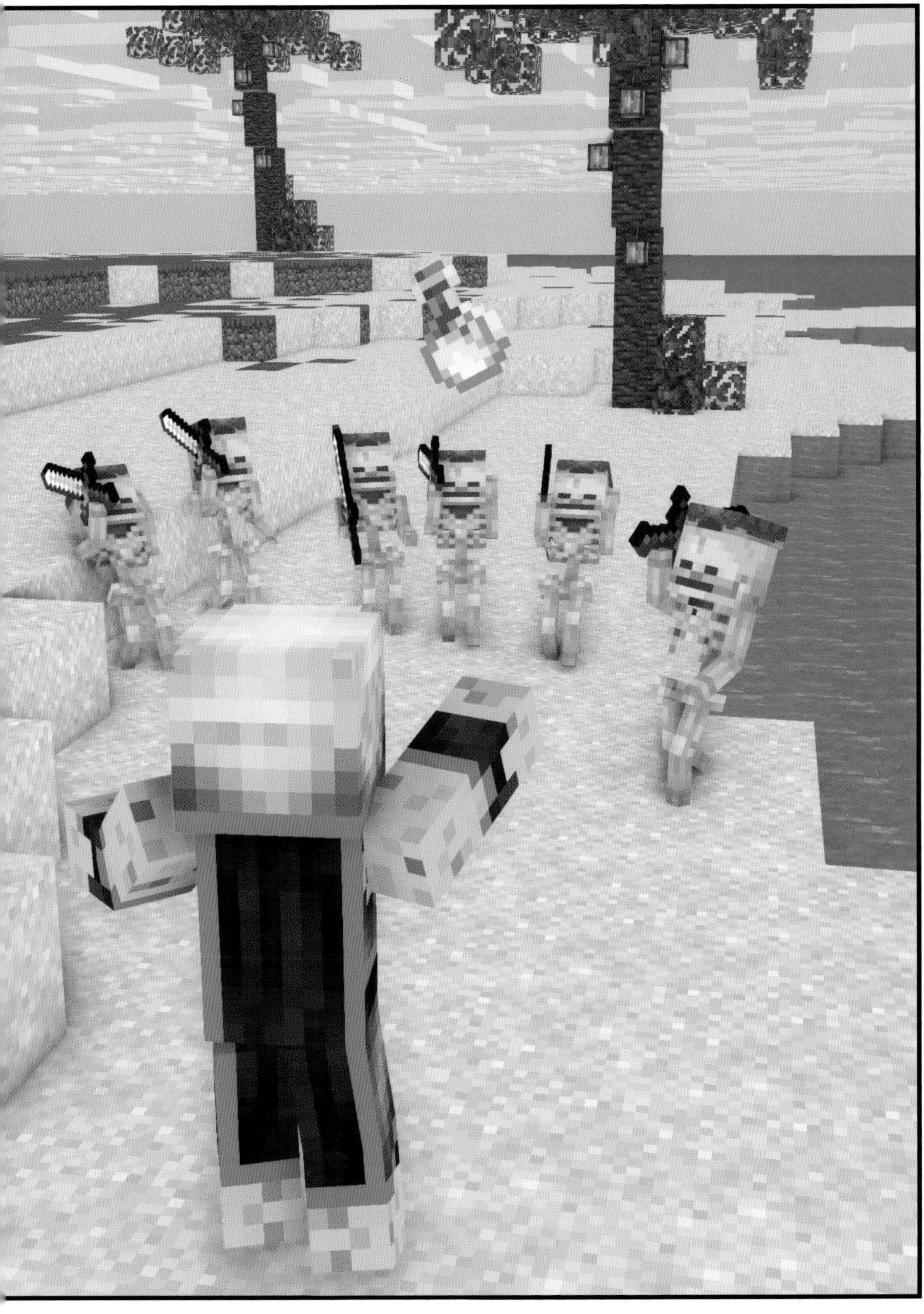

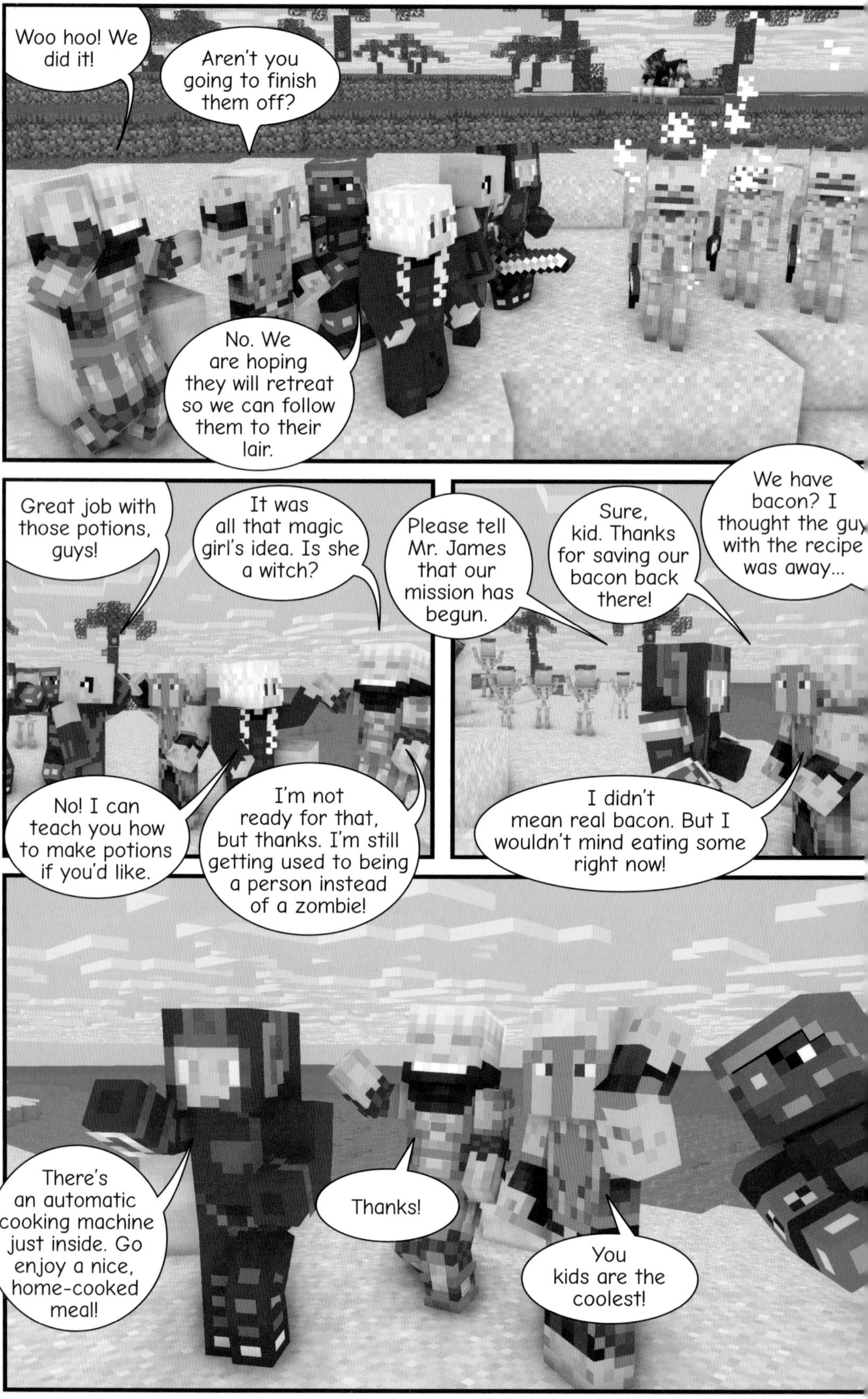

Woo hoo! We did it!
Aren't you going to finish them off?
No. We are hoping they will retreat so we can follow them to their lair.
Great job with those potions, guys!
It was all that magic girl's idea. Is she a witch?
No! I can teach you how to make potions if you'd like.
I'm not ready for that, but thanks. I'm still getting used to being a person instead of a zombie!
Please tell Mr. James that our mission has begun.
Sure, kid. Thanks for saving our bacon back there!
We have bacon? I thought the gu with the recipe was away...
I didn't mean real bacon. But I wouldn't mind eating some right now!
There's an automatic cooking machine just inside. Go enjoy a nice, home-cooked meal!
Thanks!
You kids are the coolest!

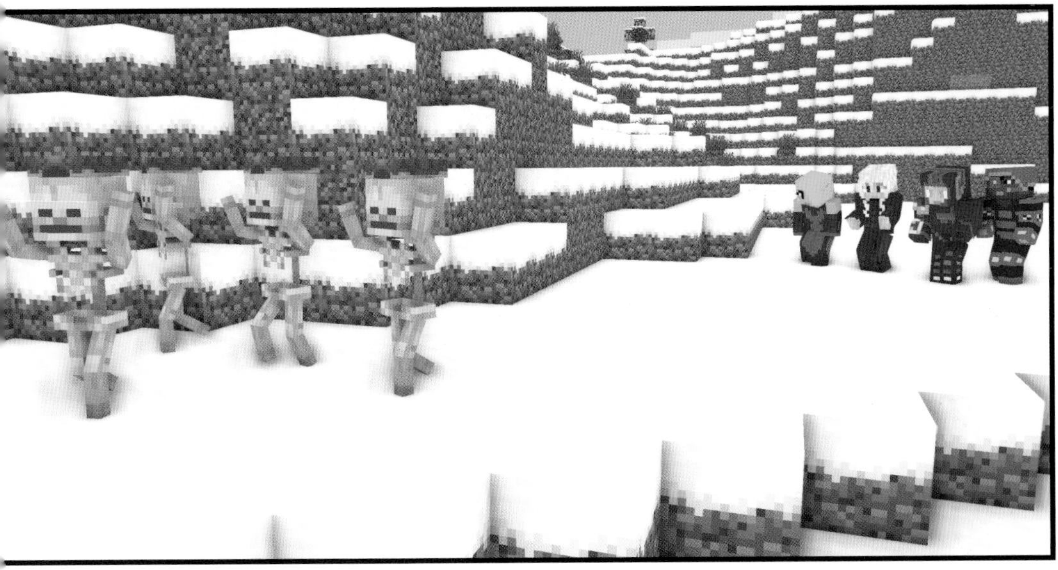

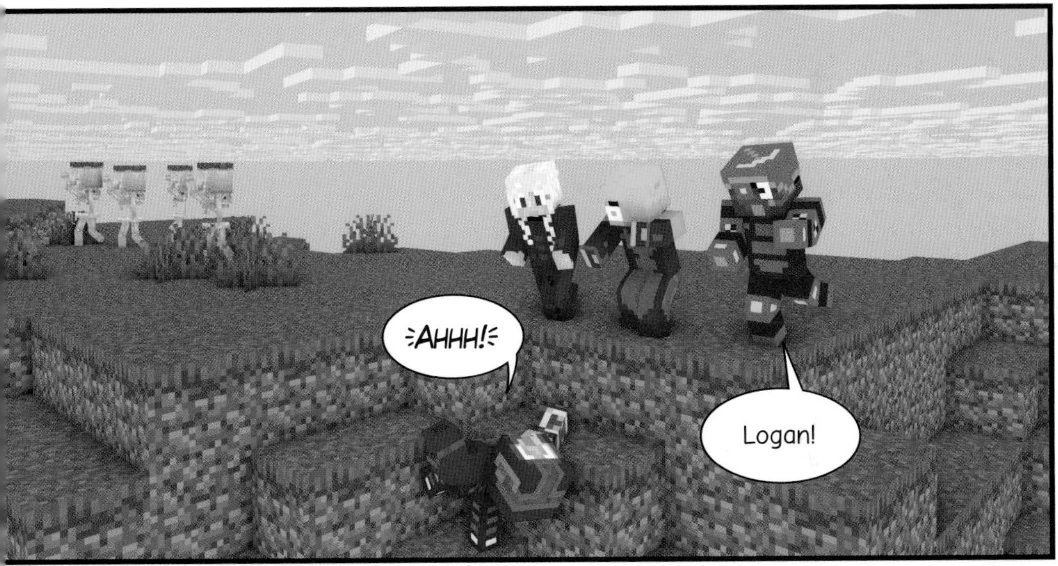
AHHH!
Logan!

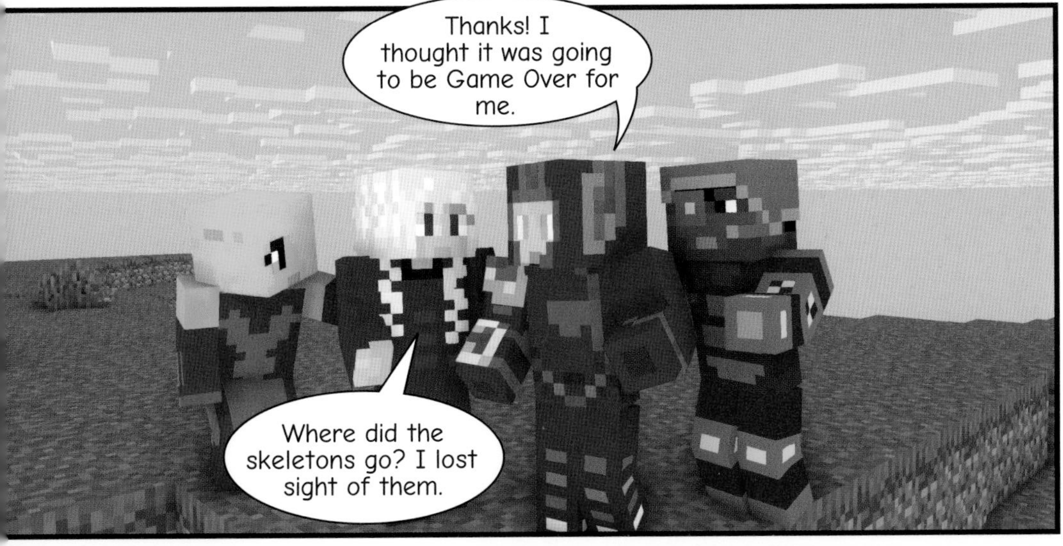
Thanks! I thought it was going to be Game Over for me.
Where did the skeletons go? I lost sight of them.

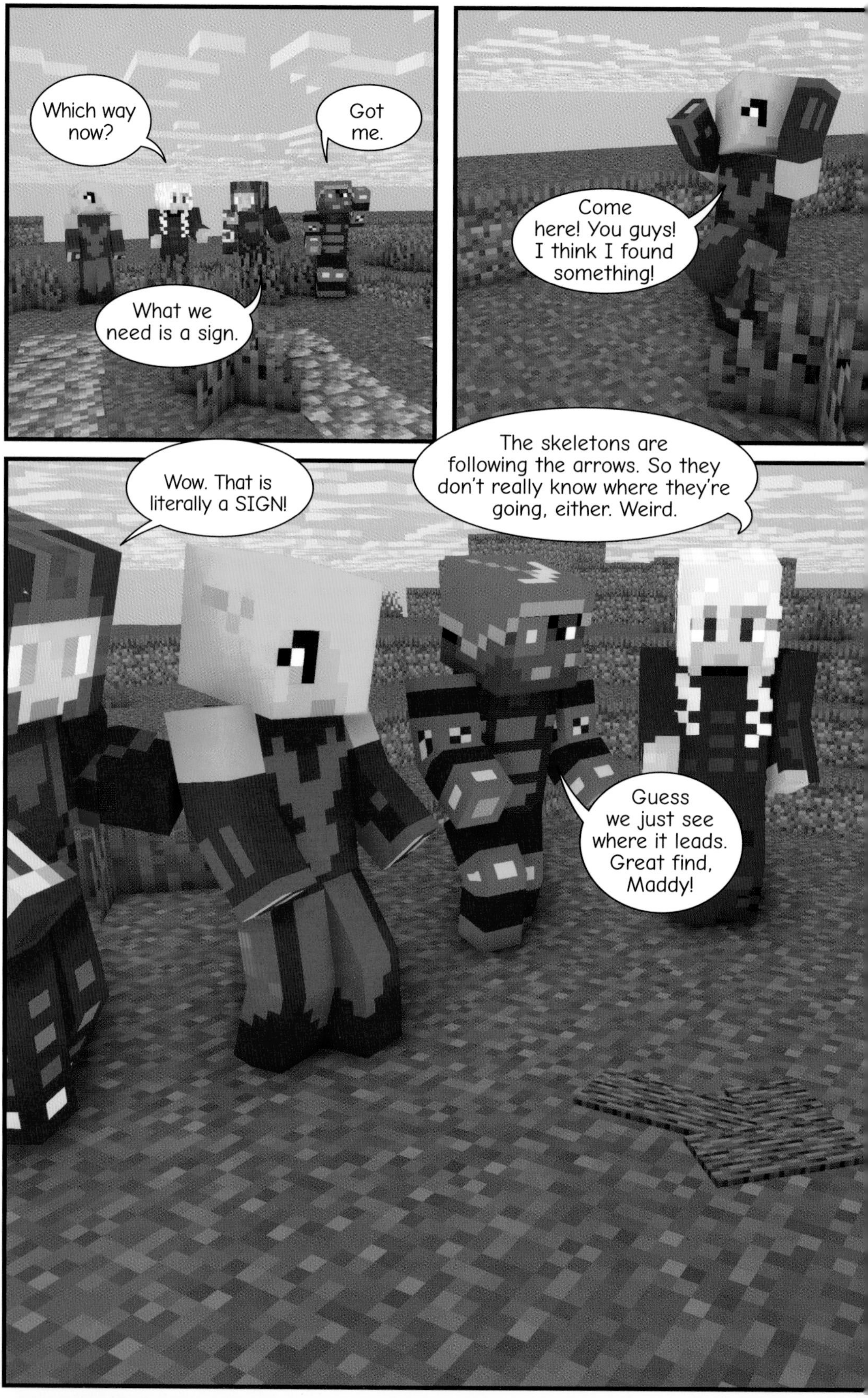
Which way now?
Got me.
What we need is a sign.
Come here! You guys! I think I found something!
Wow. That is literally a SIGN!
The skeletons are following the arrows. So they don't really know where they're going, either. Weird.
Guess we just see where it leads. Great find, Maddy!

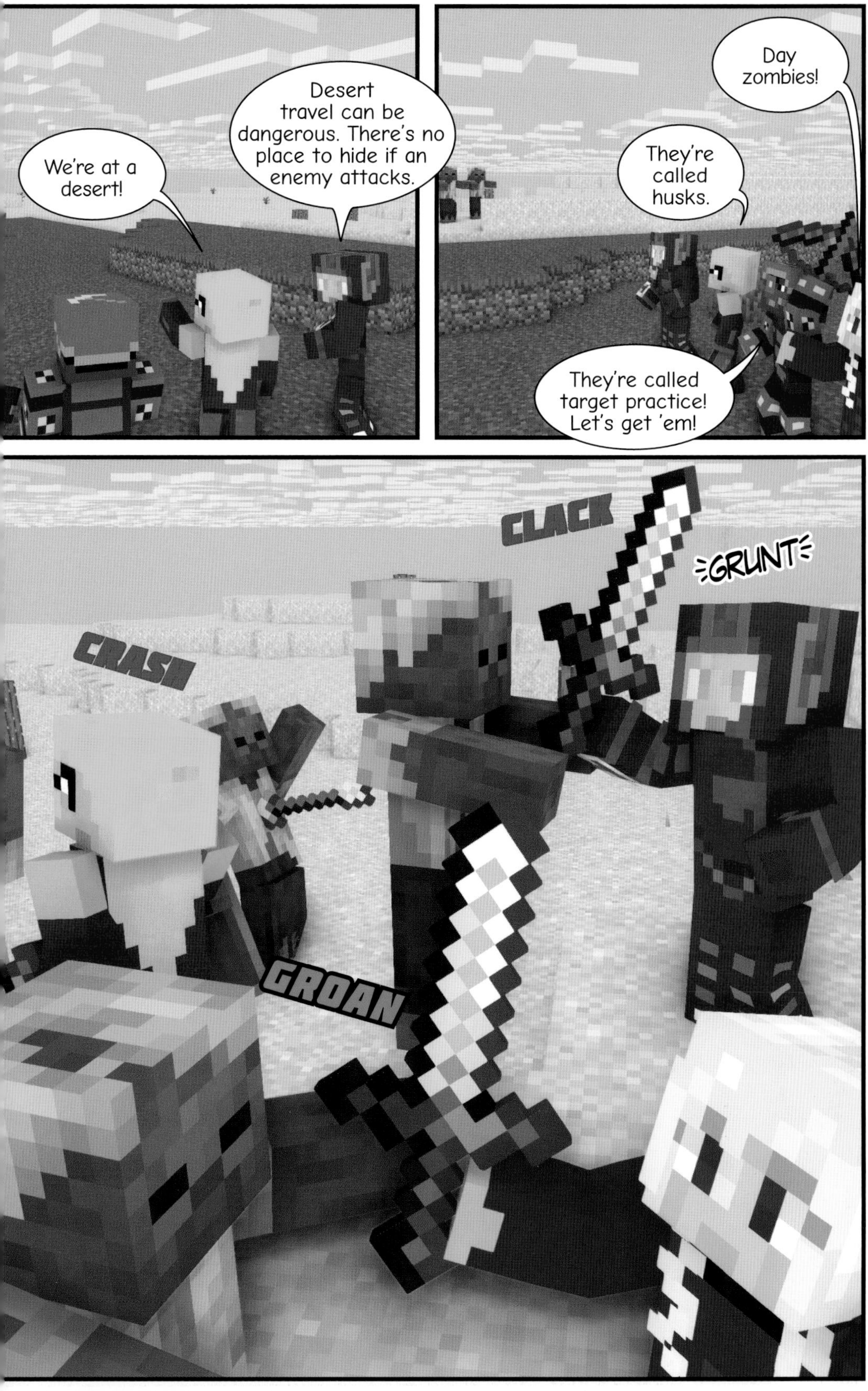
We're at a desert!
Desert travel can be dangerous. There's no place to hide if an enemy attacks.
Day zombies!
They're called husks.
They're called target practice! Let's get 'em!
CLACK
GRUNT
CRASH
GROAN

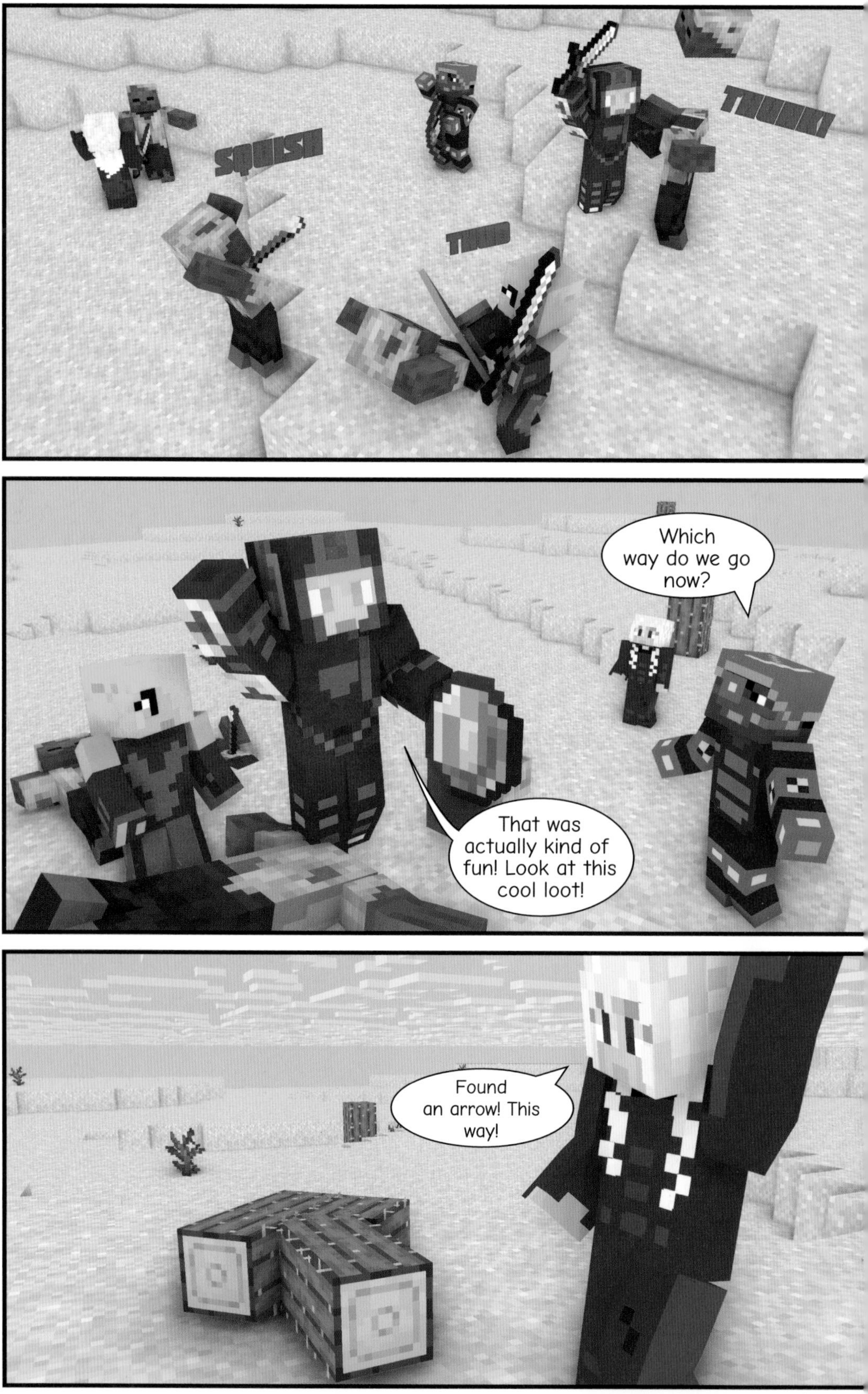
SQUISH
Which way do we go now?
That was actually kind of fun! Look at this cool loot!
Found an arrow! This way!

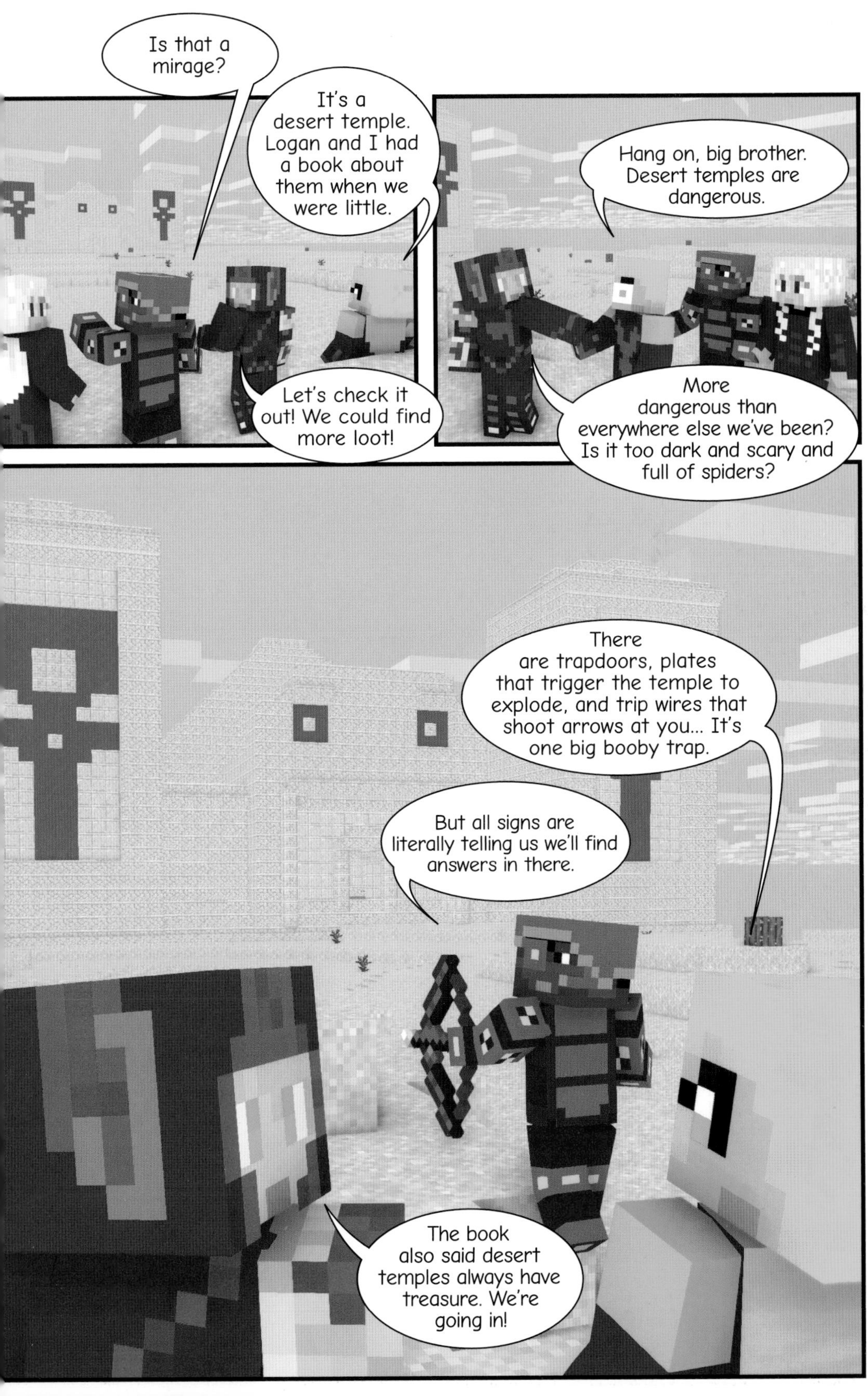
Is that a mirage?
It's a desert temple. Logan and I had a book about them when we were little.
Let's check it out! We could find more loot!
Hang on, big brother. Desert temples are dangerous.
More dangerous than everywhere else we've been? Is it too dark and scary and full of spiders?
There are trapdoors, plates that trigger the temple to explode, and trip wires that shoot arrows at you... It's one big booby trap.
But all signs are literally telling us we'll find answers in there.
The book also said desert temples always have treasure. We're going in!

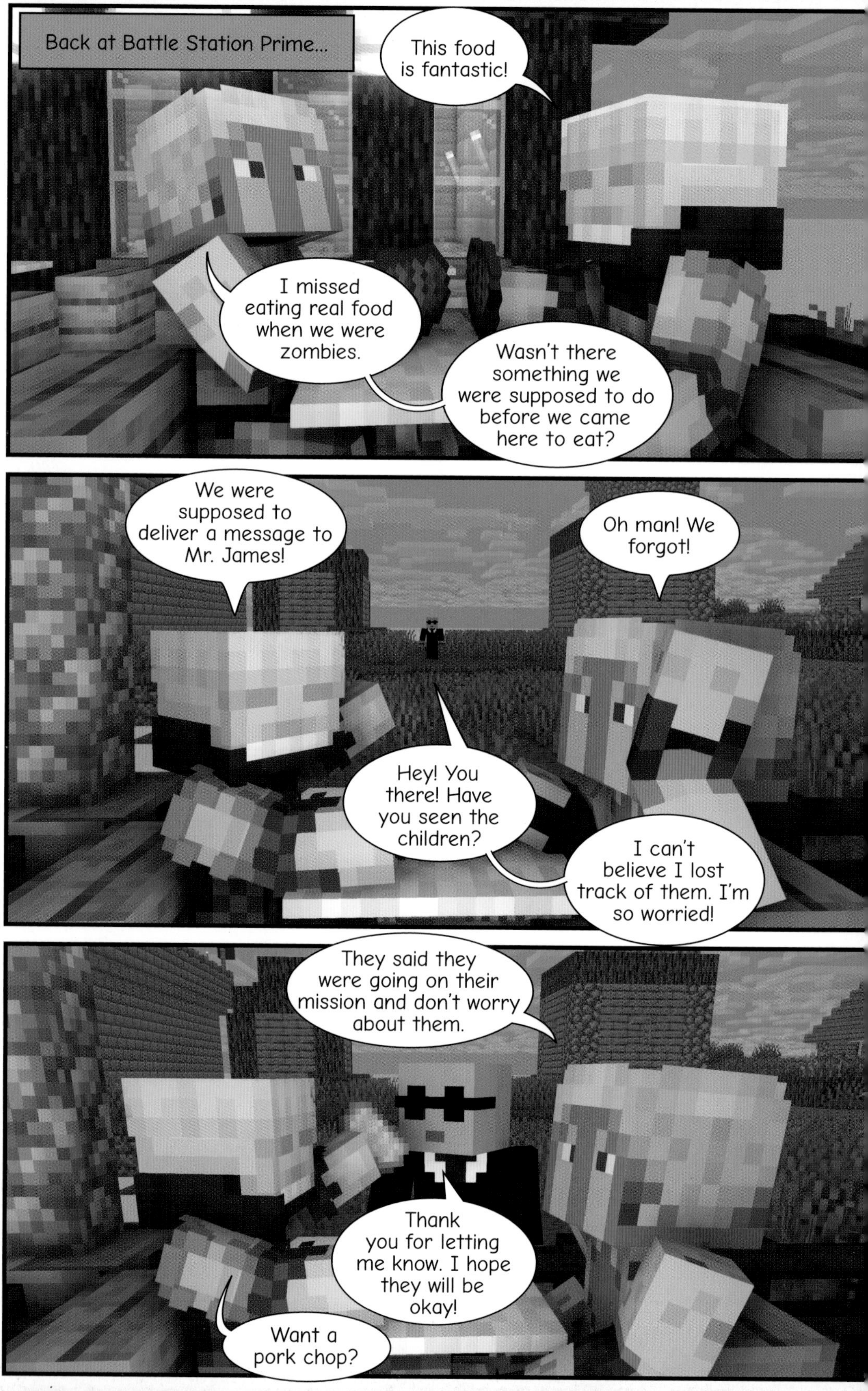

Back at Battle Station Prime...
This food is fantastic!
I missed eating real food when we were zombies.
Wasn't there something we were supposed to do before we came here to eat?
We were supposed to deliver a message to Mr. James!
Oh man! We forgot!
Hey! You there! Have you seen the children?
I can't believe I lost track of them. I'm so worried!
They said they were going on their mission and don't worry about them.
Thank you for letting me know. I hope they will be okay!
Want a pork chop?

# CHAPTER 6

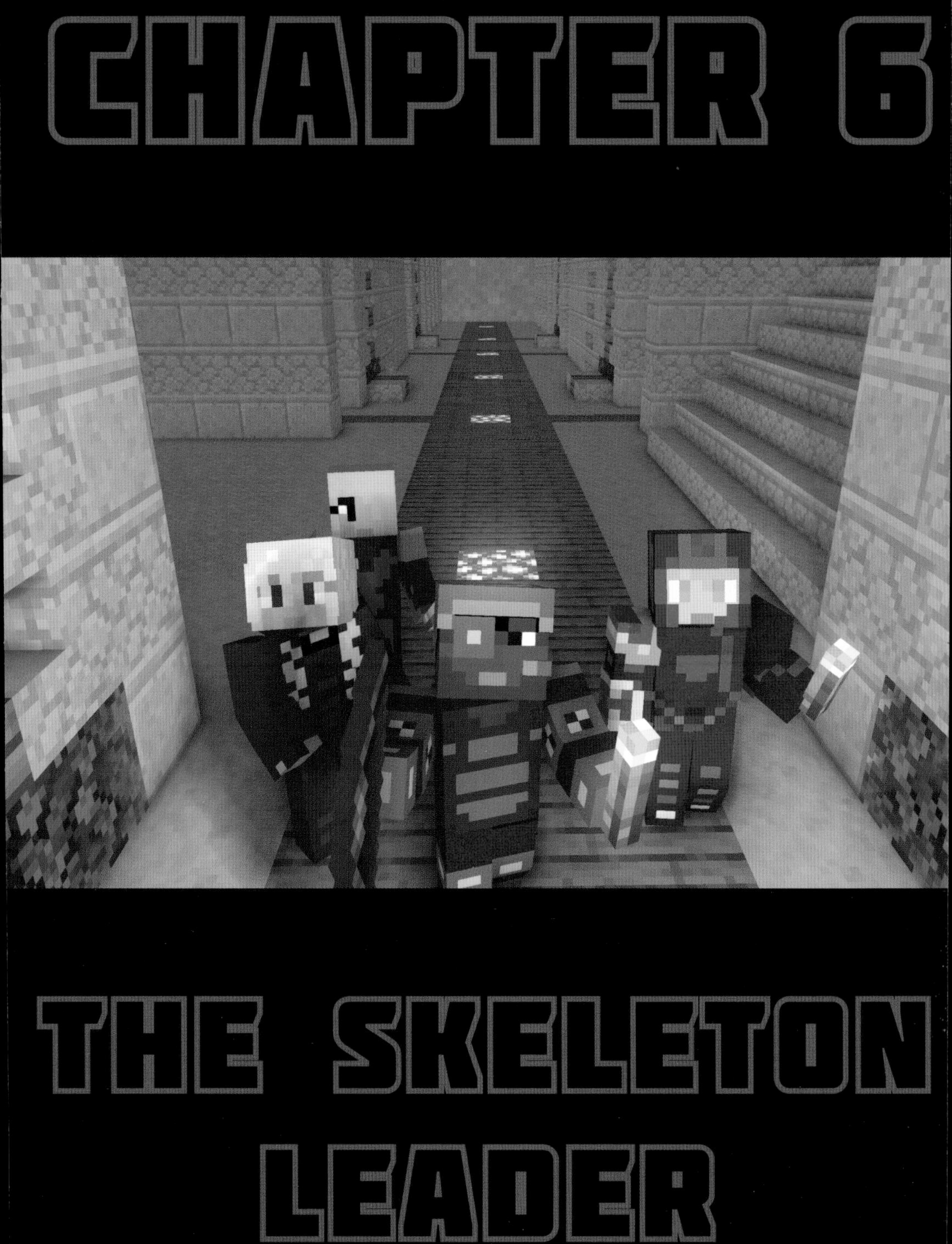

# THE SKELETON LEADER

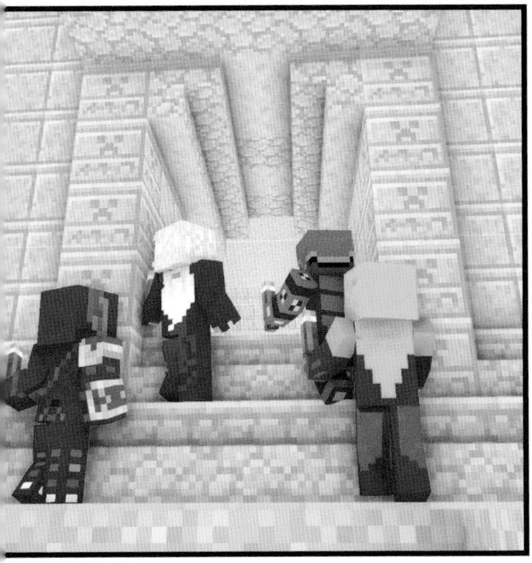

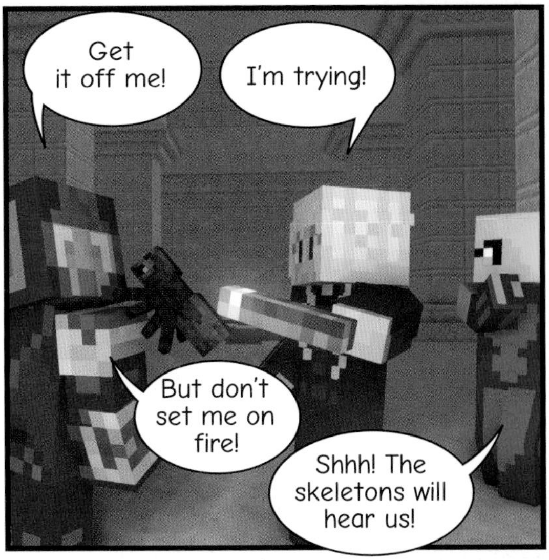

Get it off me!
I'm trying!
But don't set me on fire!
Shhh! The skeletons will hear us!


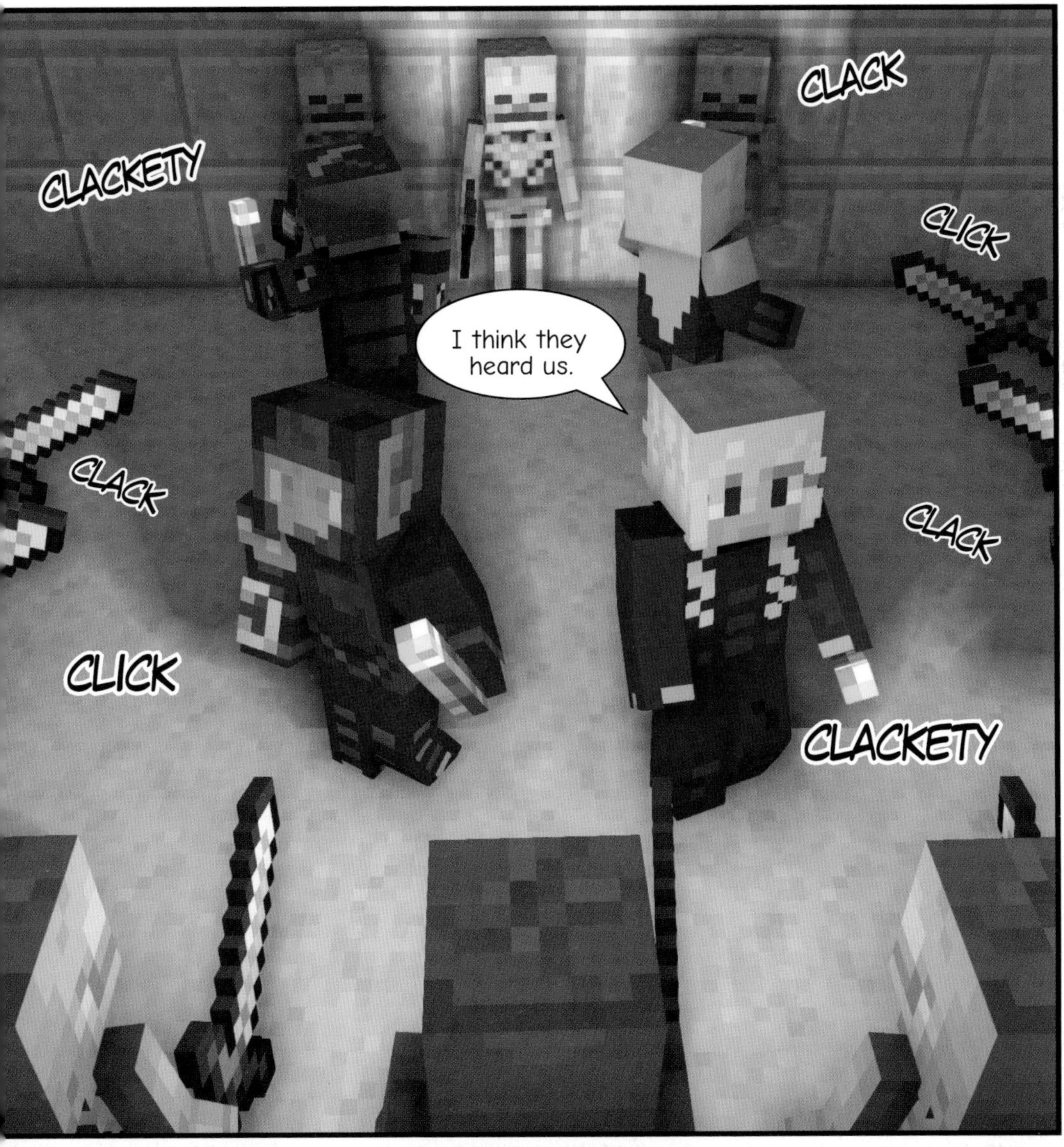

CLACKETY
CLACK
CLICK
I think they heard us.
CLACK
CLACK
CLICK
CLACKETY

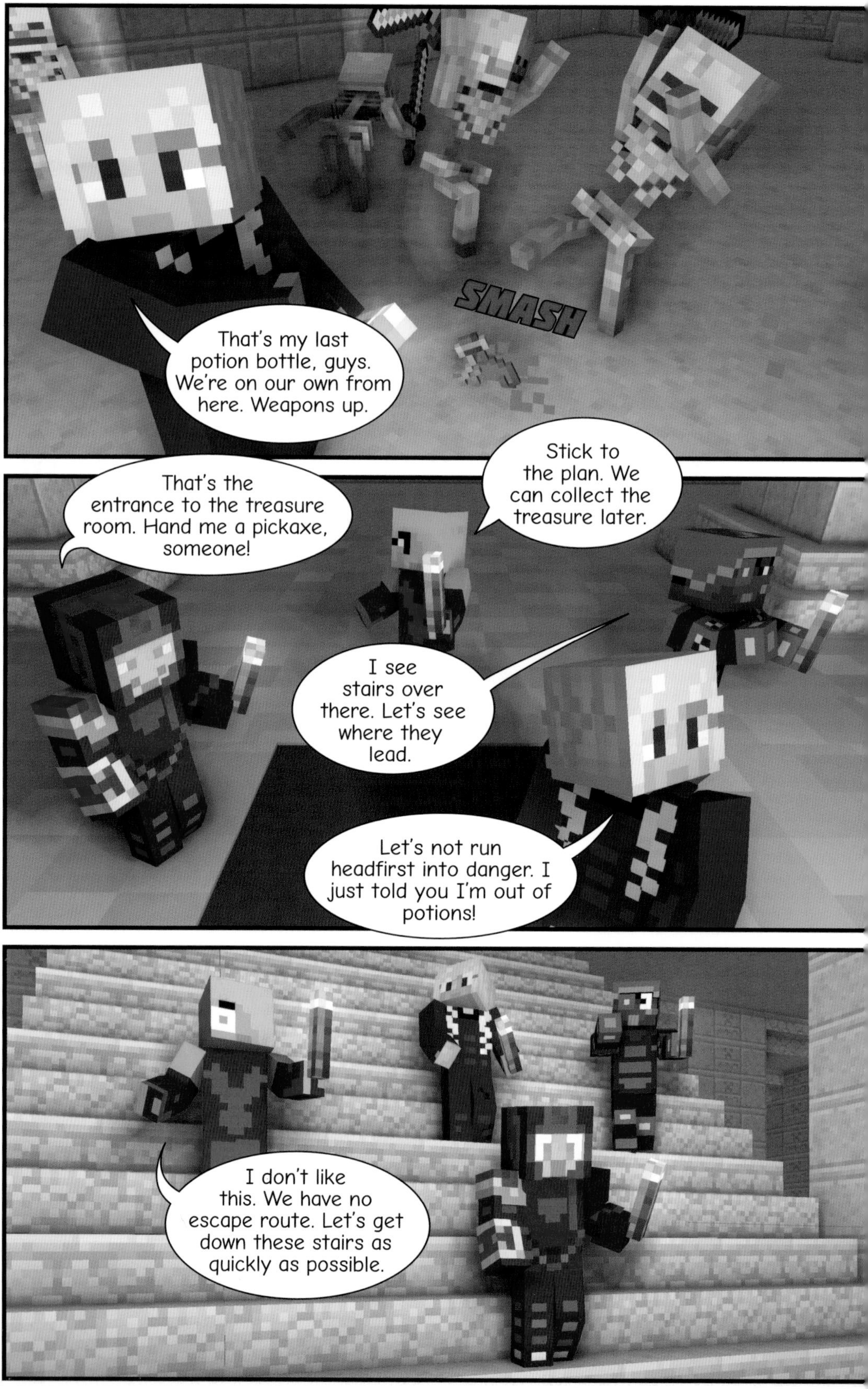
SMASH
That's my last potion bottle, guys. We're on our own from here. Weapons up.
That's the entrance to the treasure room. Hand me a pickaxe, someone!
Stick to the plan. We can collect the treasure later.
I see stairs over there. Let's see where they lead.
Let's not run headfirst into danger. I just told you I'm out of potions!
I don't like this. We have no escape route. Let's get down these stairs as quickly as possible.

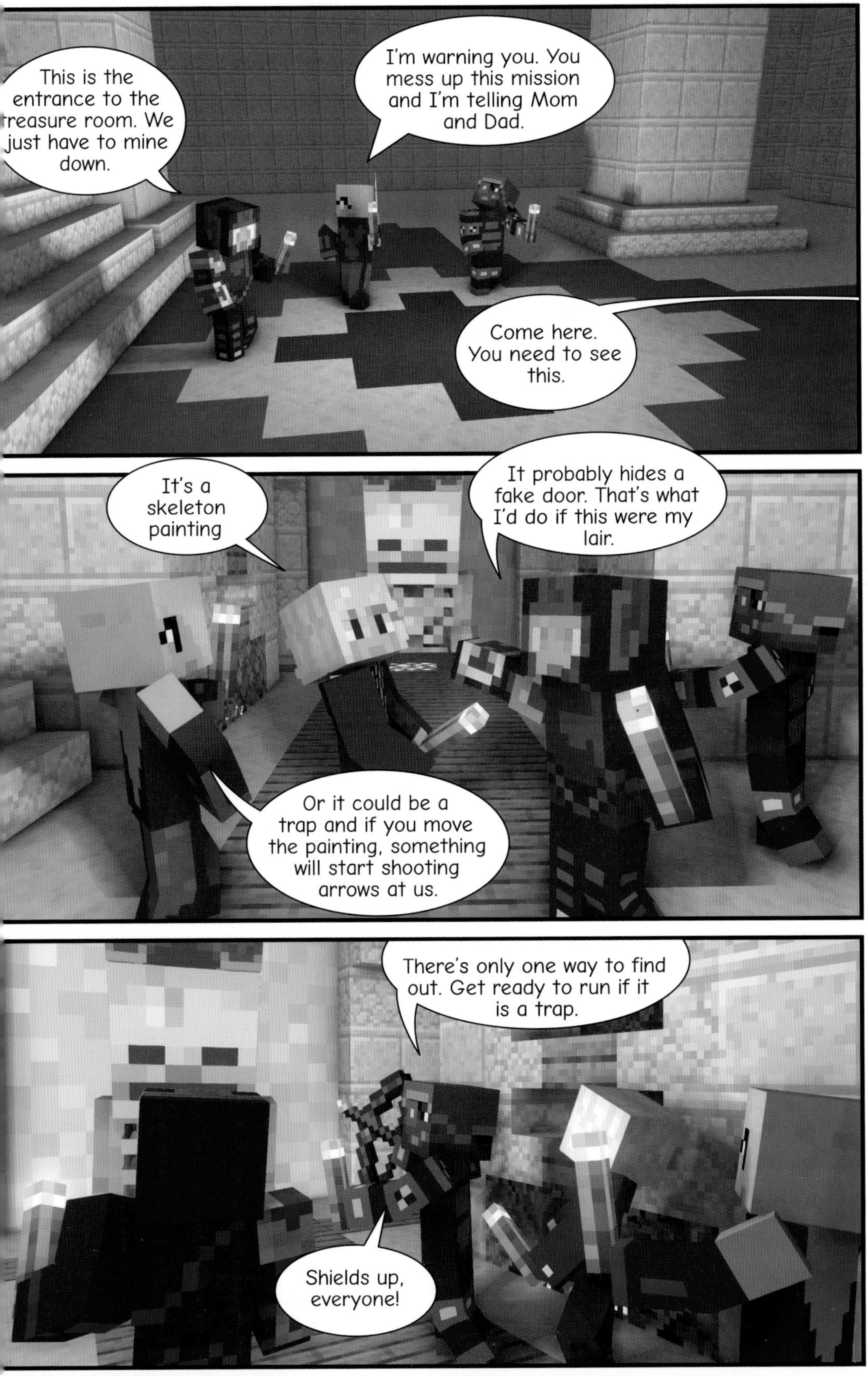
This is the entrance to the treasure room. We just have to mine down.
I'm warning you. You mess up this mission and I'm telling Mom and Dad.
Come here. You need to see this.
It's a skeleton painting
It probably hides a fake door. That's what I'd do if this were my lair.
Or it could be a trap and if you move the painting, something will start shooting arrows at us.
There's only one way to find out. Get ready to run if it is a trap.
Shields up, everyone!

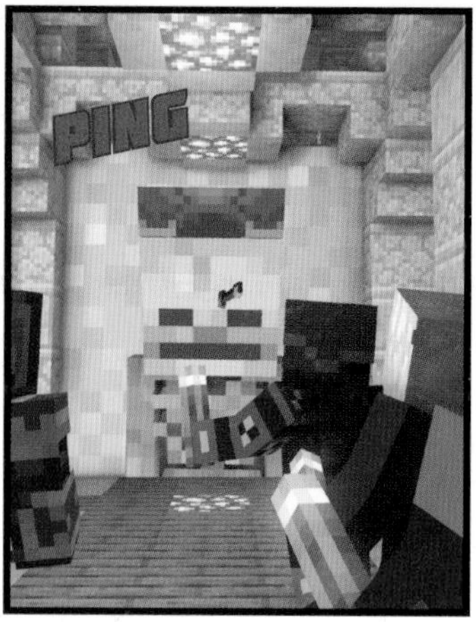
PING

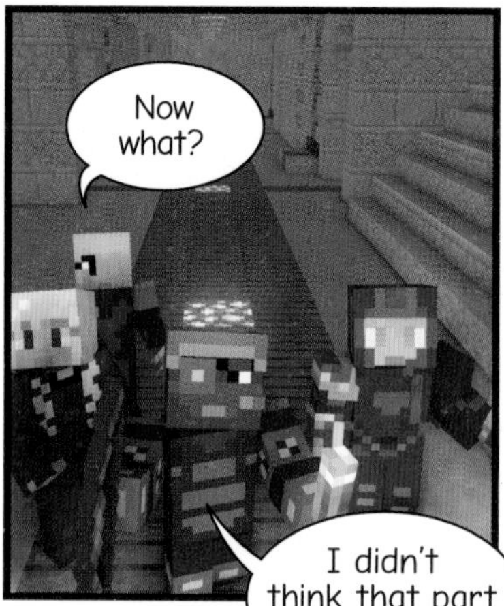
Now what?
I didn't think that part through.

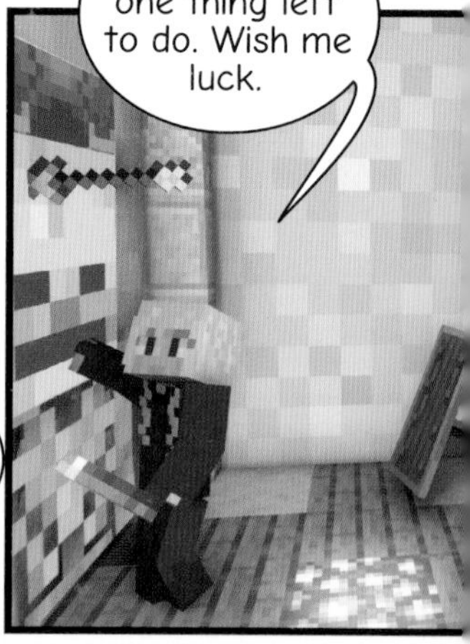
There's only one thing left to do. Wish me luck.

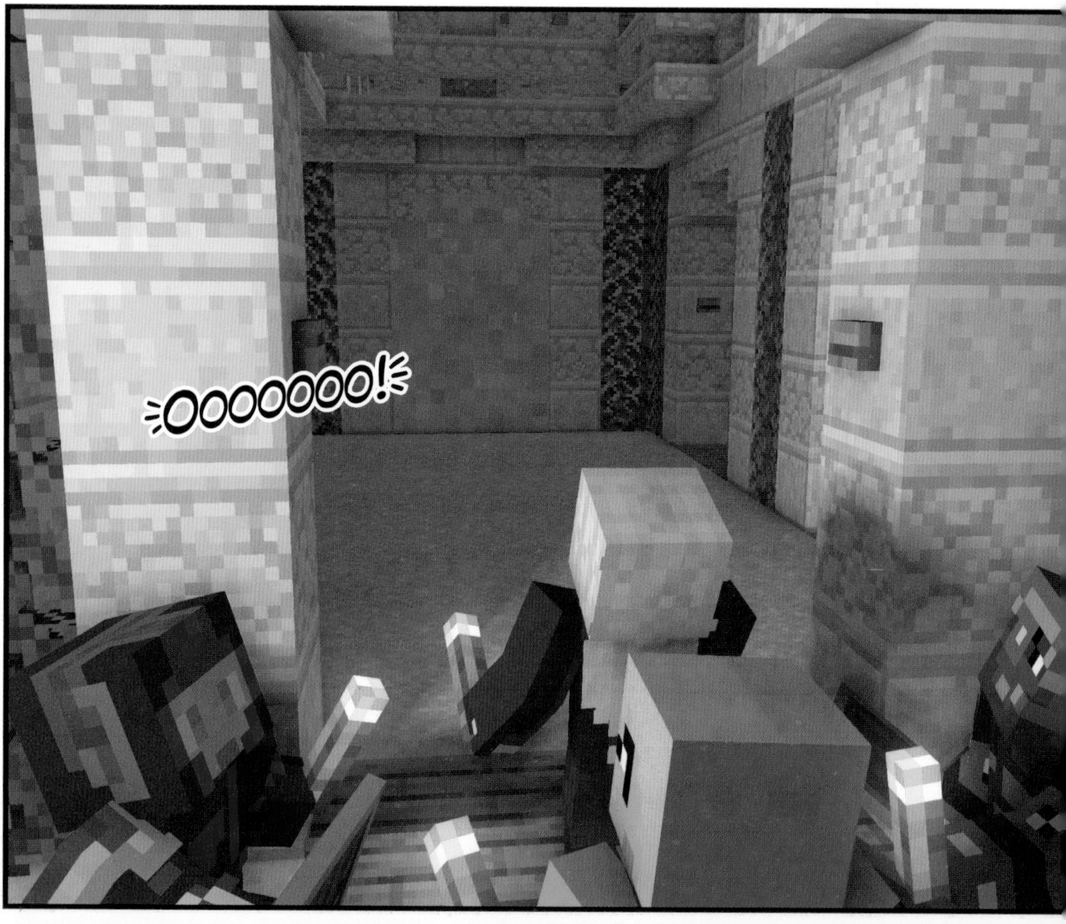
OOOOOOO!

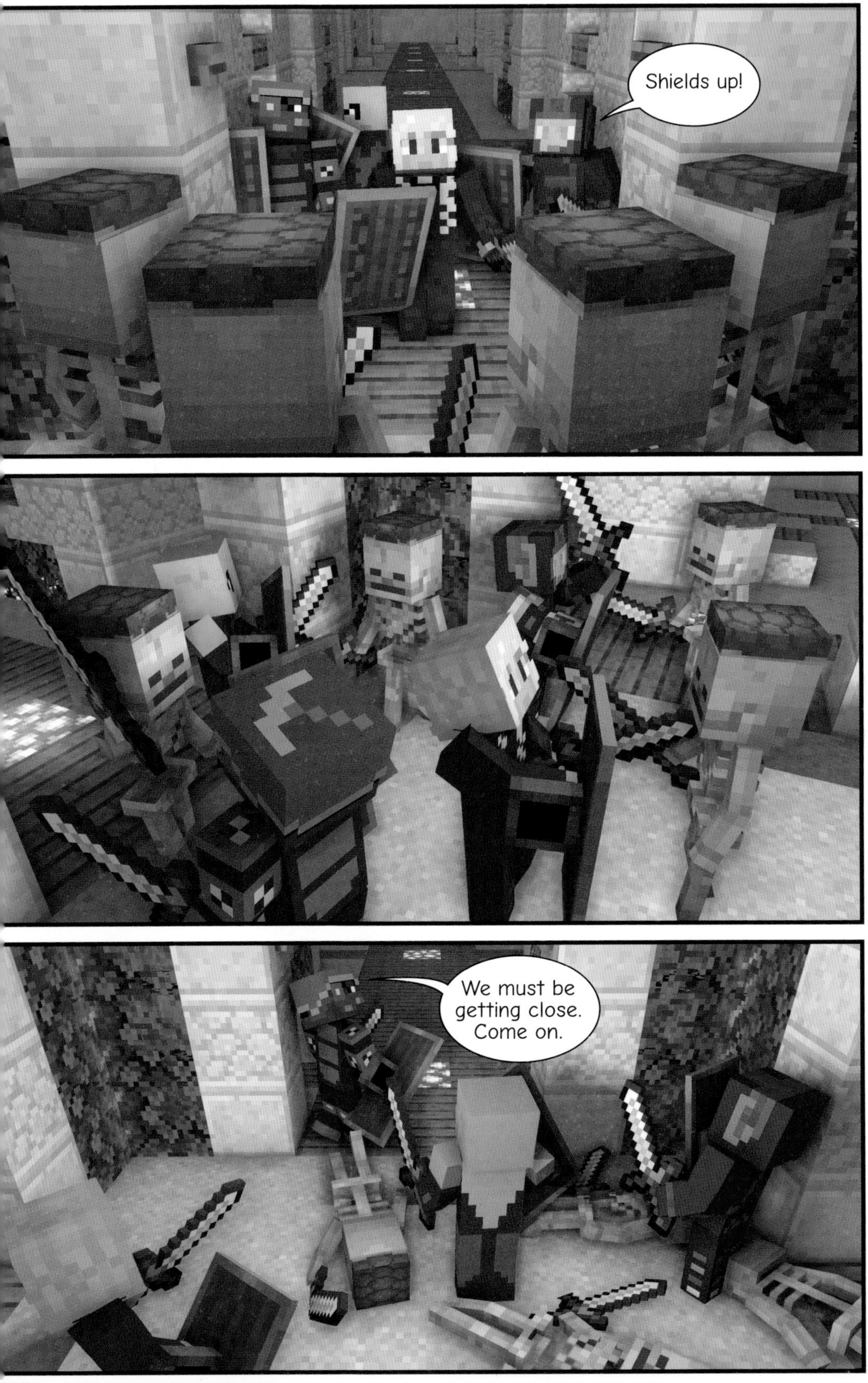
Shields up!
We must be getting close. Come on.

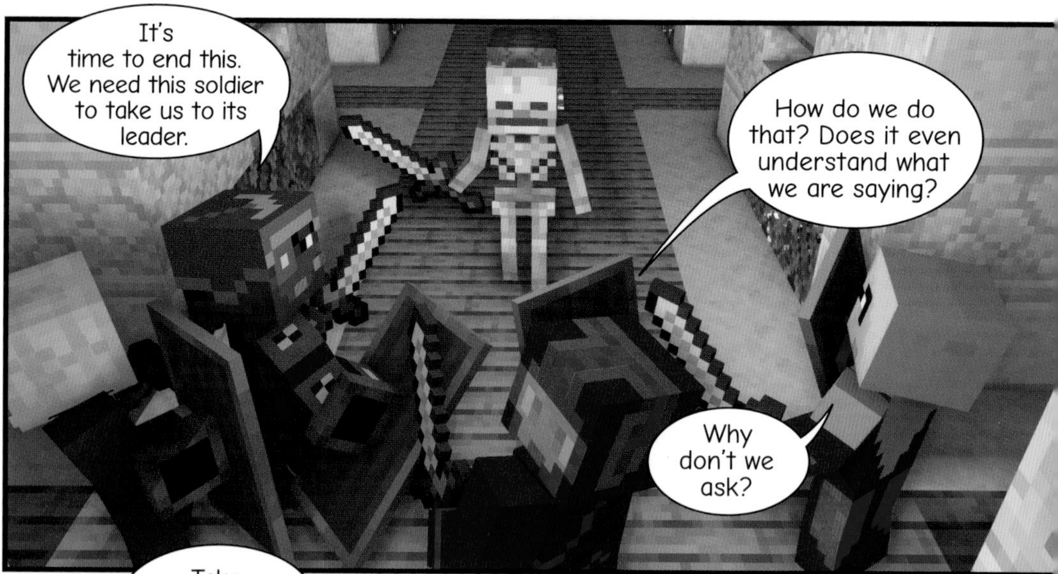
It's time to end this. We need this soldier to take us to its leader.
How do we do that? Does it even understand what we are saying?
Why don't we ask?

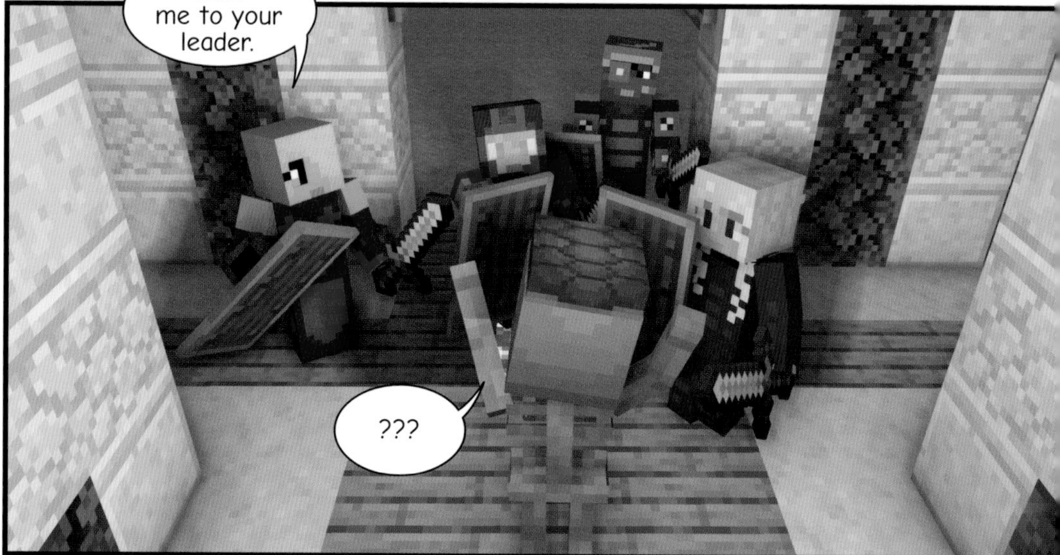
Take me to your leader.
???

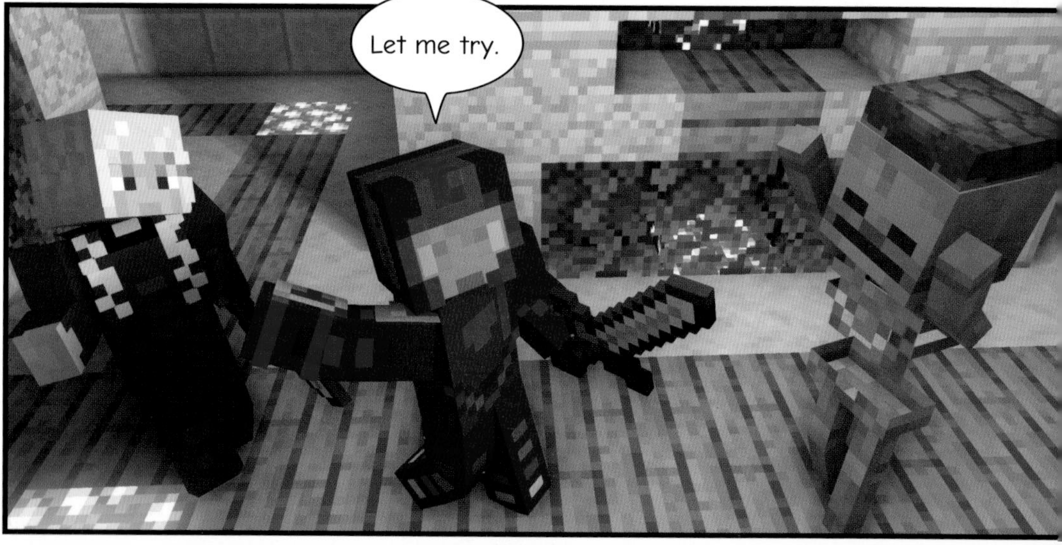
Let me try.

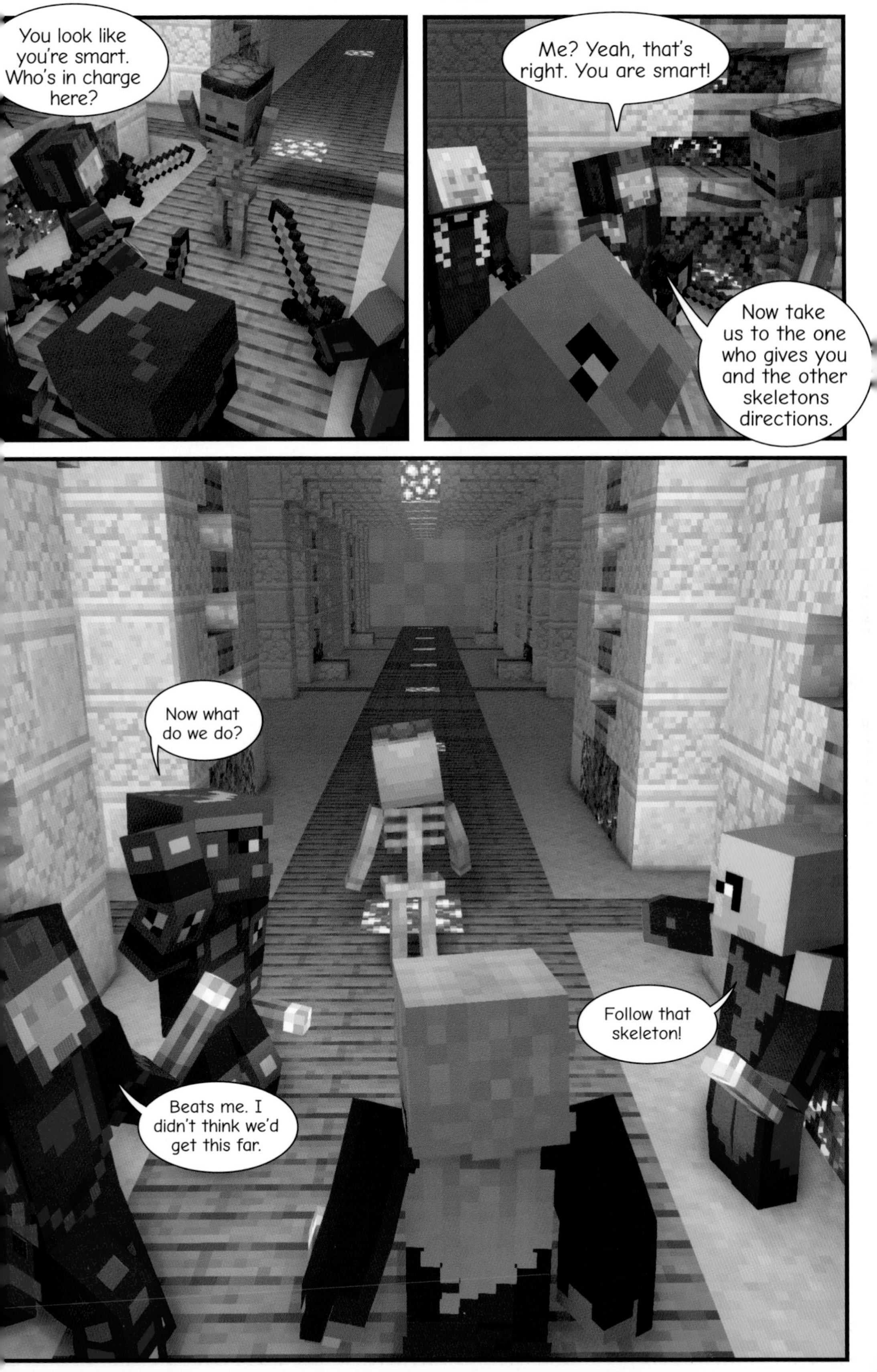
You look like you're smart. Who's in charge here?
Me? Yeah, that's right. You are smart!
Now take us to the one who gives you and the other skeletons directions.
Now what do we do?
Beats me. I didn't think we'd get this far.
Follow that skeleton!

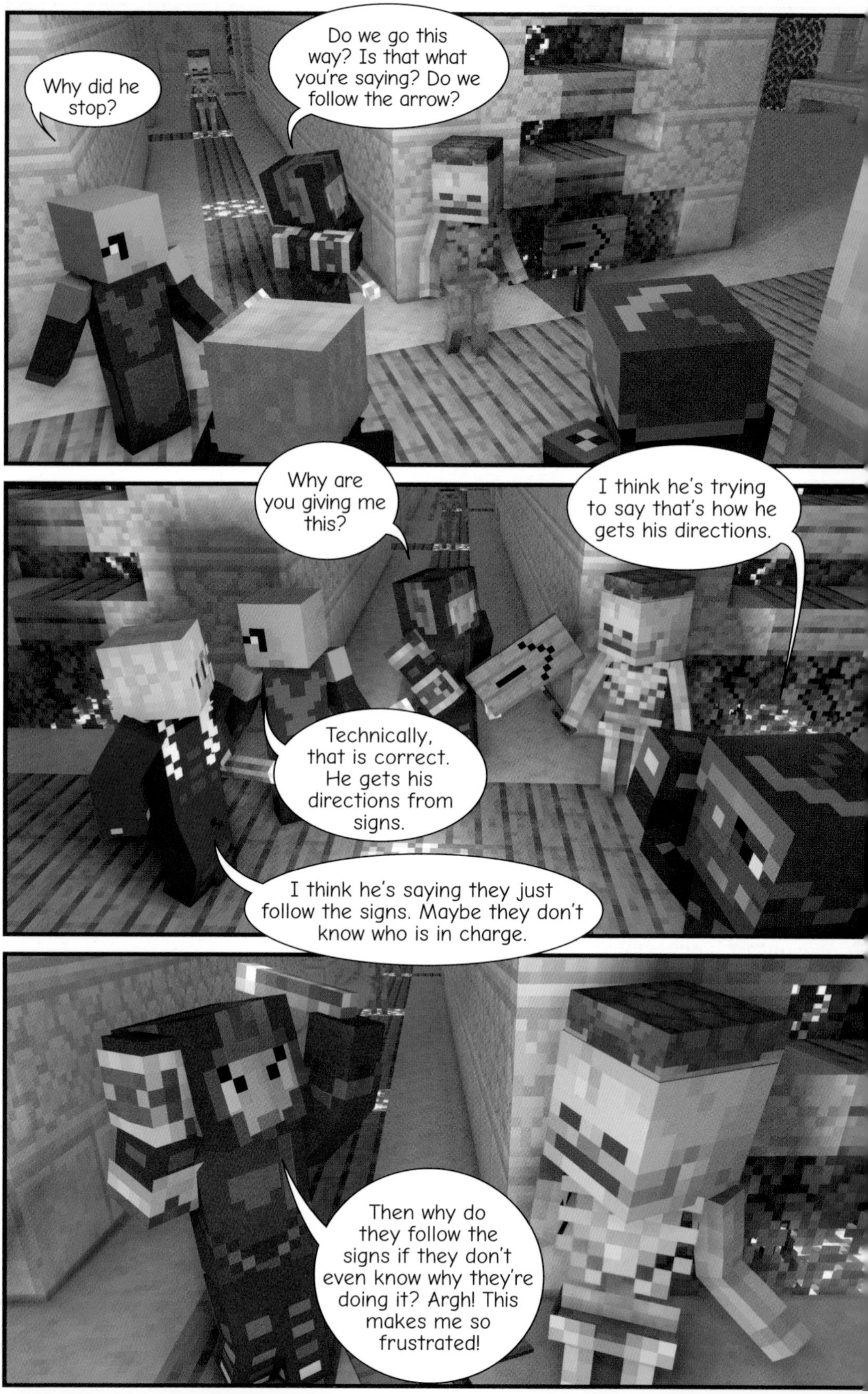
Why did he stop?
Do we go this way? Is that what you're saying? Do we follow the arrow?
Why are you giving me this?
I think he's trying to say that's how he gets his directions.
Technically, that is correct. He gets his directions from signs.
I think he's saying they just follow the signs. Maybe they don't know who is in charge.
Then why do they follow the signs if they don't even know why they're doing it? Argh! This makes me so frustrated!

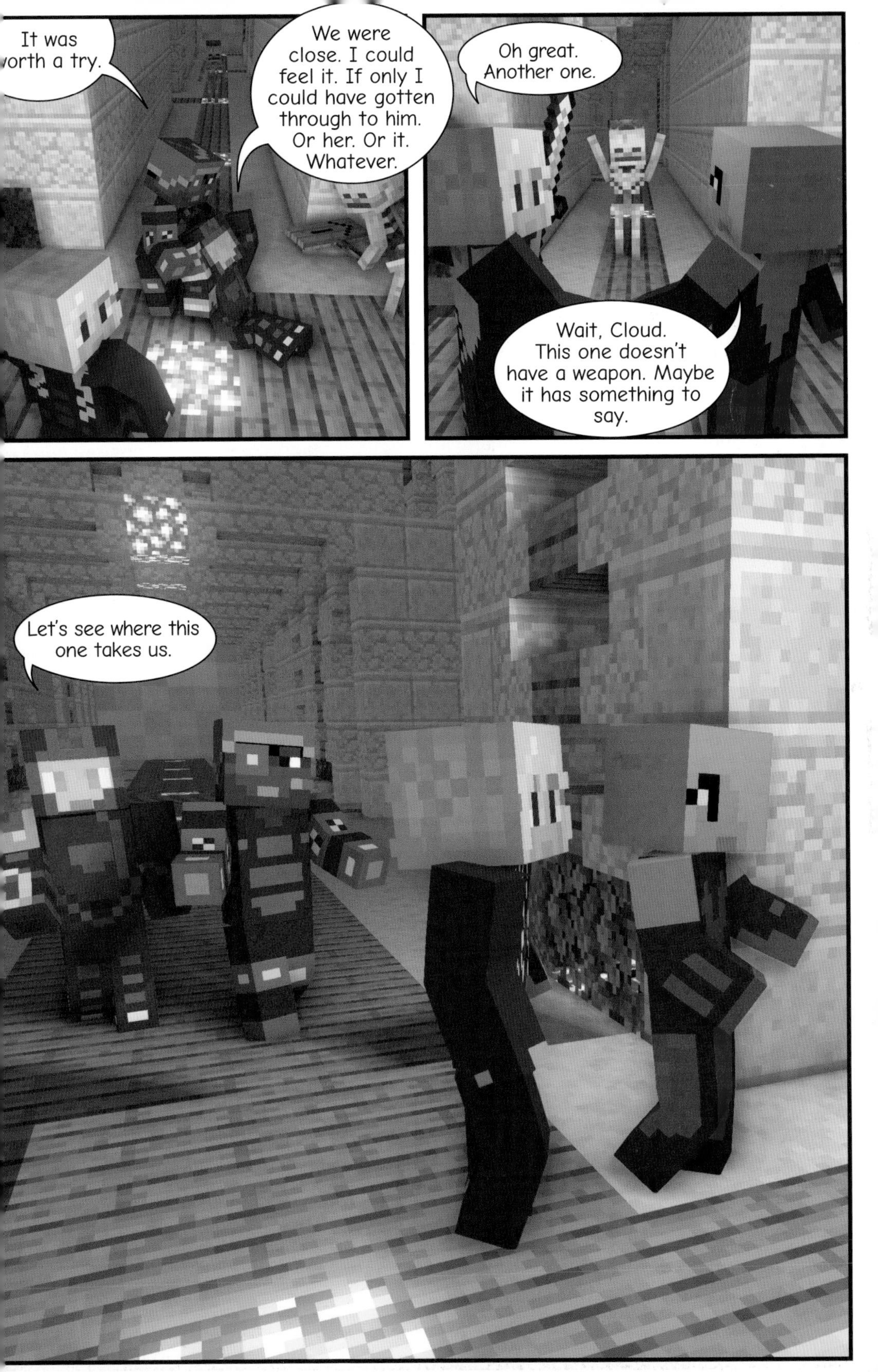
It was
worth a try.
We were close. I could feel it. If only I could have gotten through to him. Or her. Or it. Whatever.
Oh great. Another one.
Wait, Cloud. This one doesn't have a weapon. Maybe it has something to say.
Let's see where this one takes us.

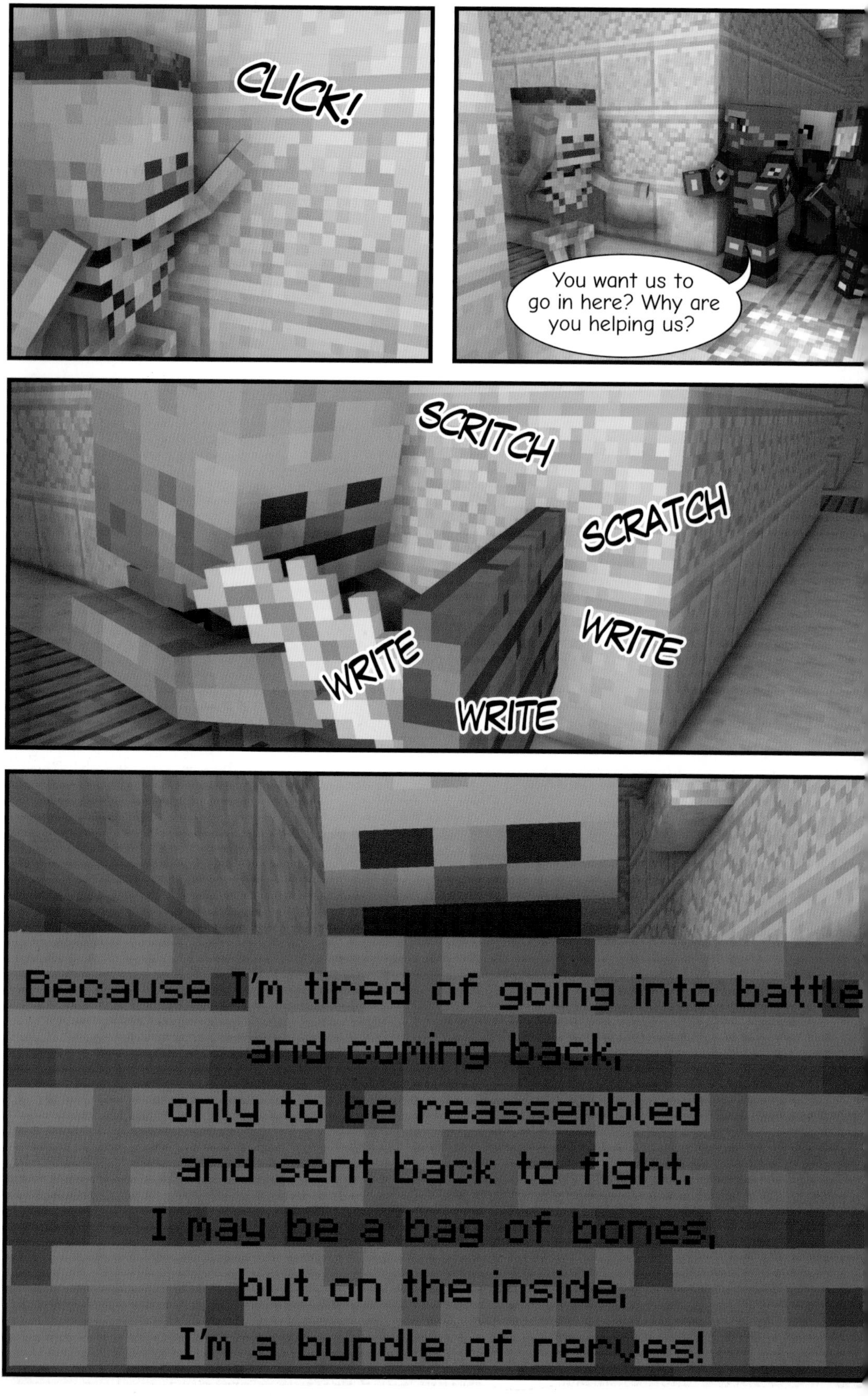
CLICK!
You want us to go in here? Why are you helping us?
SCRITCH
SCRATCH
WRITE
WRITE
WRITE
Because I'm tired of going into battle
and coming back,
only to be reassembled
and sent back to fight.
I may be a bag of bones,
but on the inside,
I'm a bundle of nerves!

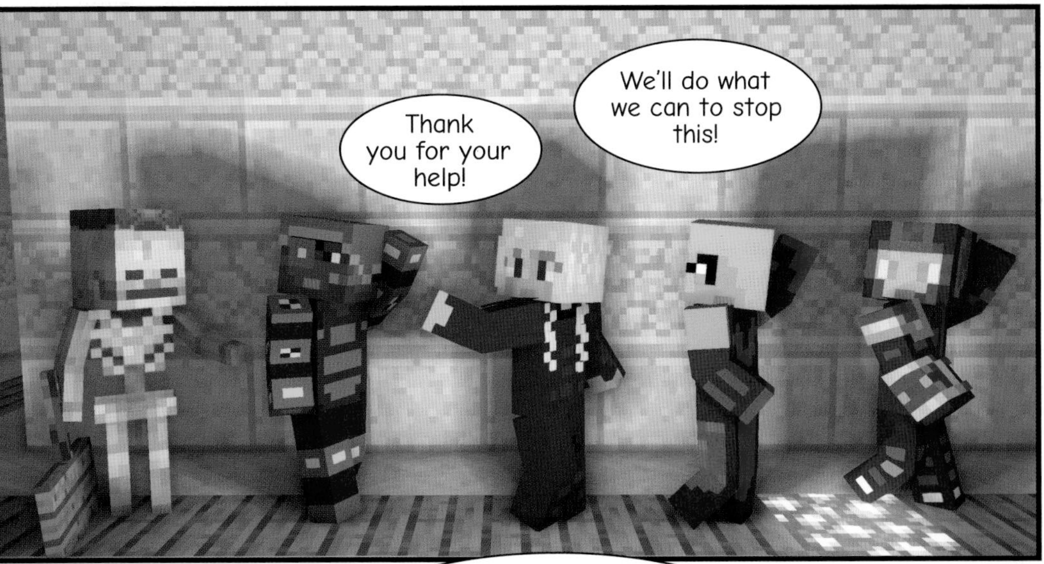
Thank you for your help!
We'll do what we can to stop this!

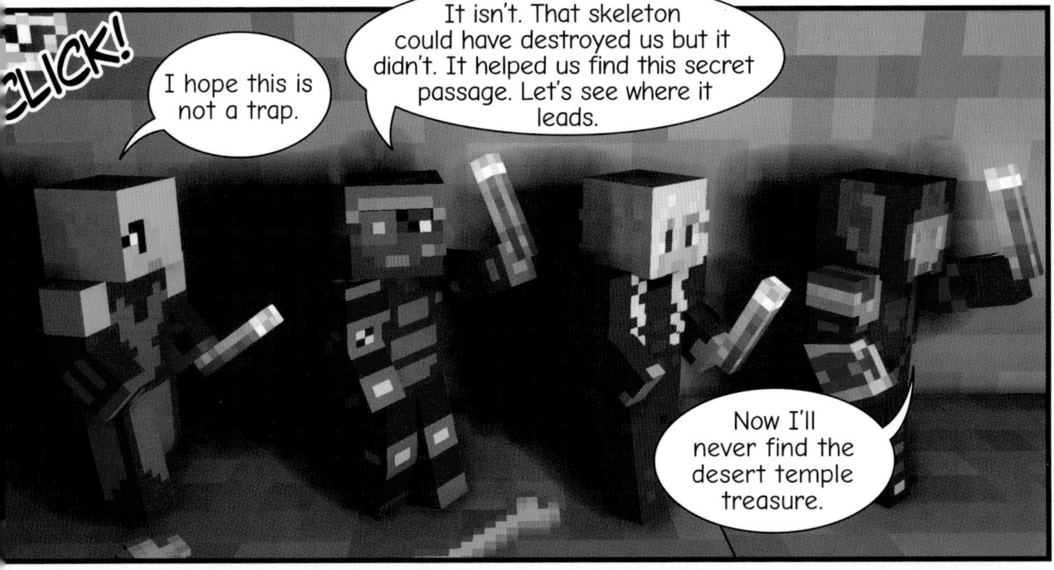
CLICK!
I hope this is not a trap.
It isn't. That skeleton could have destroyed us but it didn't. It helped us find this secret passage. Let's see where it leads.
Now I'll never find the desert temple treasure.

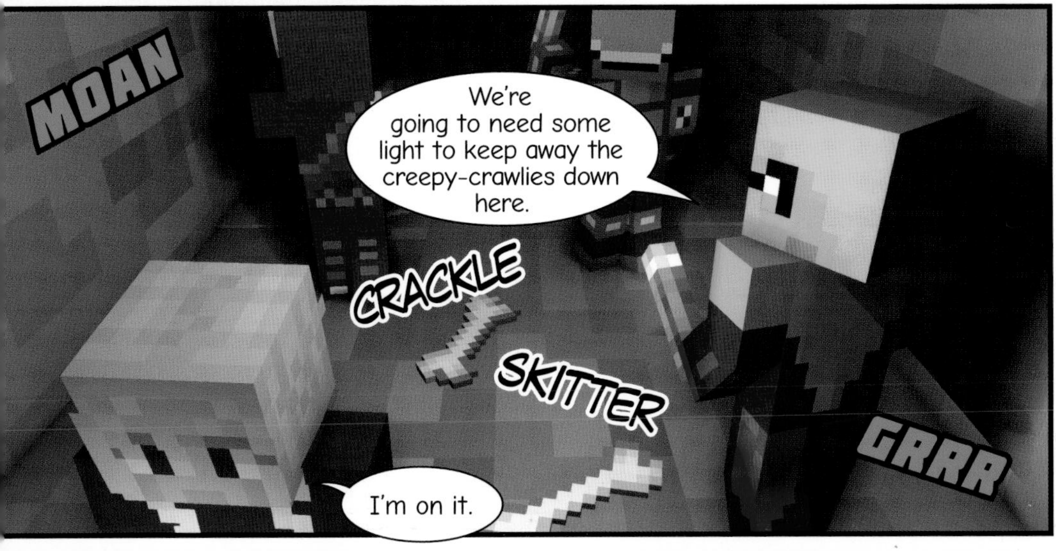
MOAN
We're going to need some light to keep away the creepy-crawlies down here.
CRACKLE
SKITTER
GRRR
I'm on it.

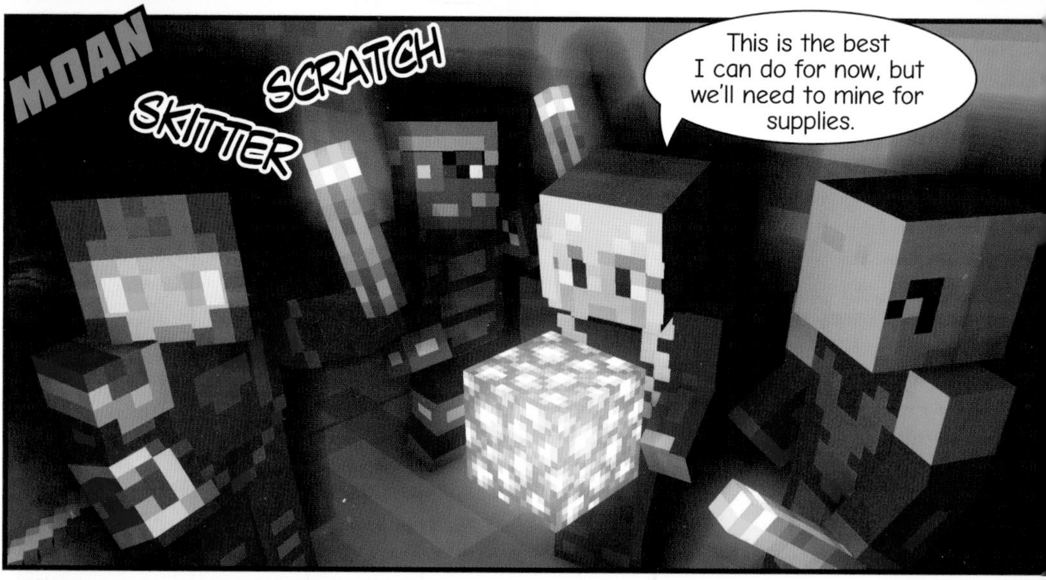
MOAN
SCRATCH
SKITTER
This is the best I can do for now, but we'll need to mine for supplies.

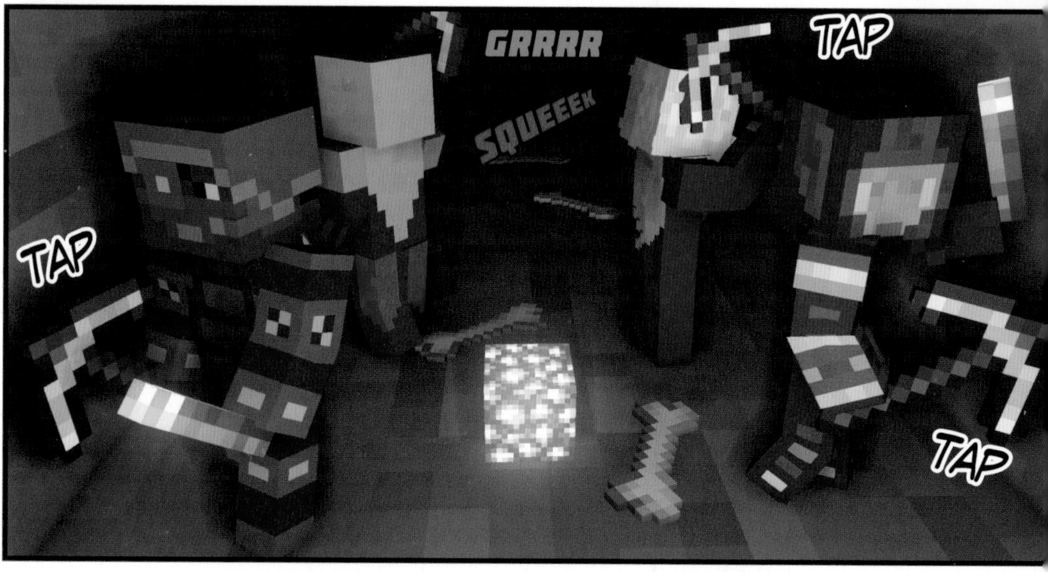
GRRRR
TAP
SQUEEEK
TAP
TAP

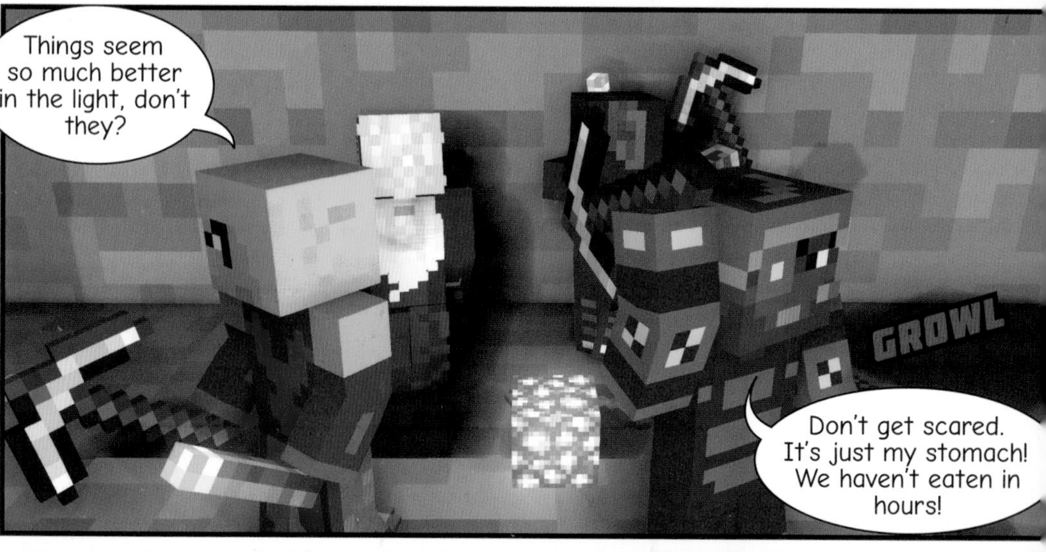
Things seem so much better in the light, don't they?
GROWL
Don't get scared. It's just my stomach! We haven't eaten in hours!

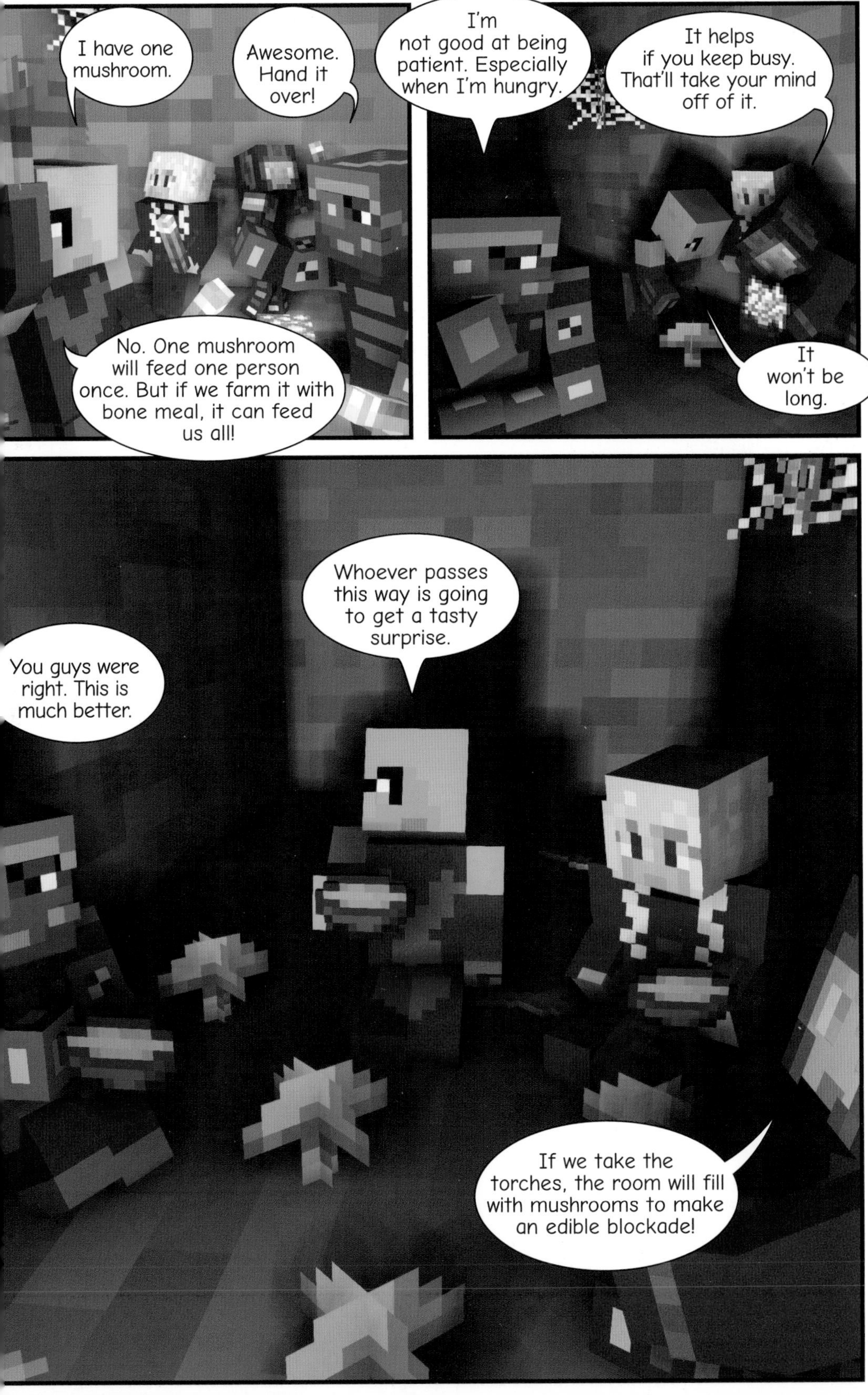
I have one mushroom.
Awesome. Hand it over!
No. One mushroom will feed one person once. But if we farm it with bone meal, it can feed us all!
I'm not good at being patient. Especially when I'm hungry.
It helps if you keep busy. That'll take your mind off of it.
It won't be long.
You guys were right. This is much better.
Whoever passes this way is going to get a tasty surprise.
If we take the torches, the room will fill with mushrooms to make an edible blockade!

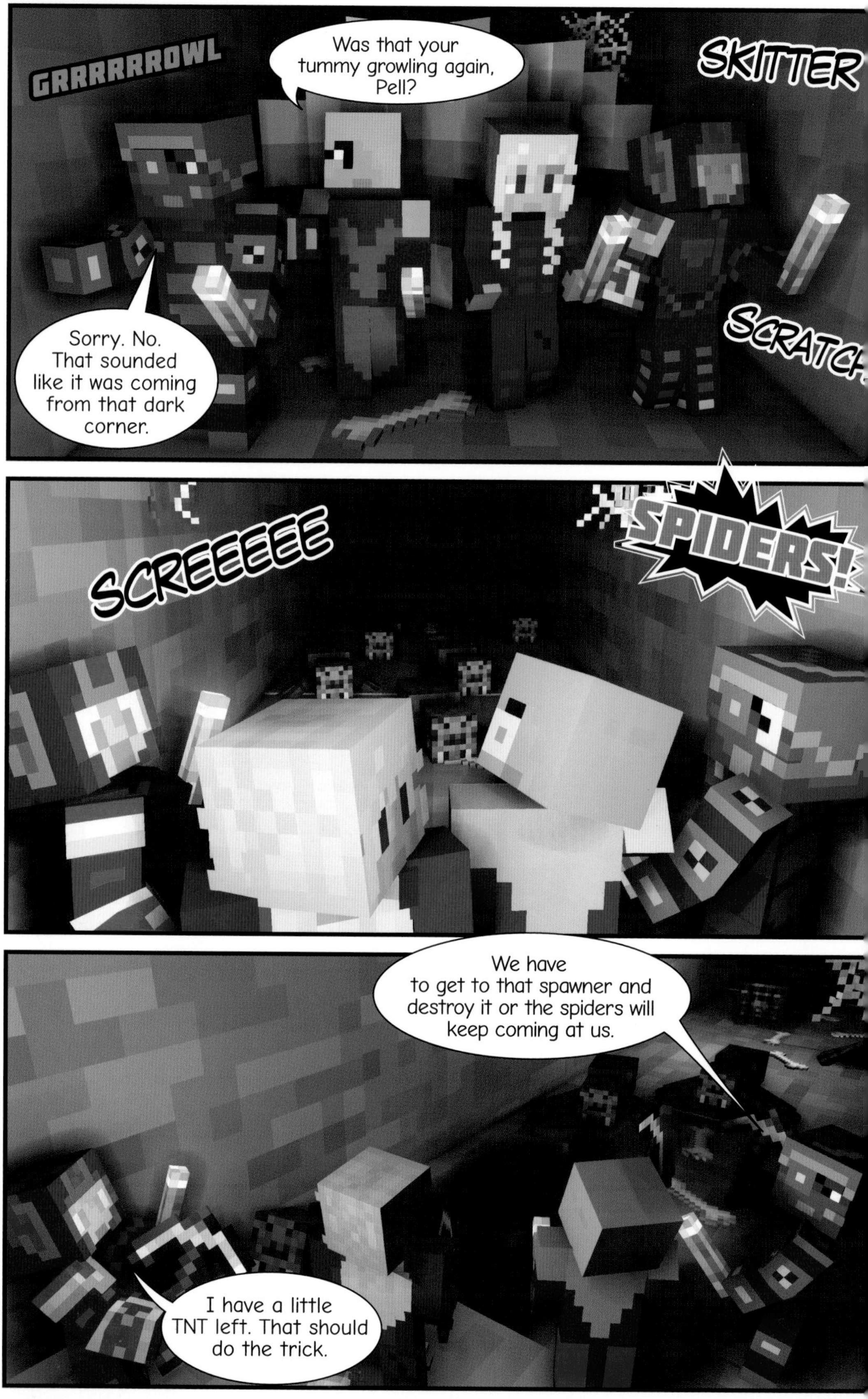
GRRRRRROWL
Was that your tummy growling again, Pell?
SKITTER
Sorry. No. That sounded like it was coming from that dark corner.
SCRATC
SCREEEEEE
SPIDERS!
We have to get to that spawner and destroy it or the spiders will keep coming at us.
I have a little TNT left. That should do the trick.

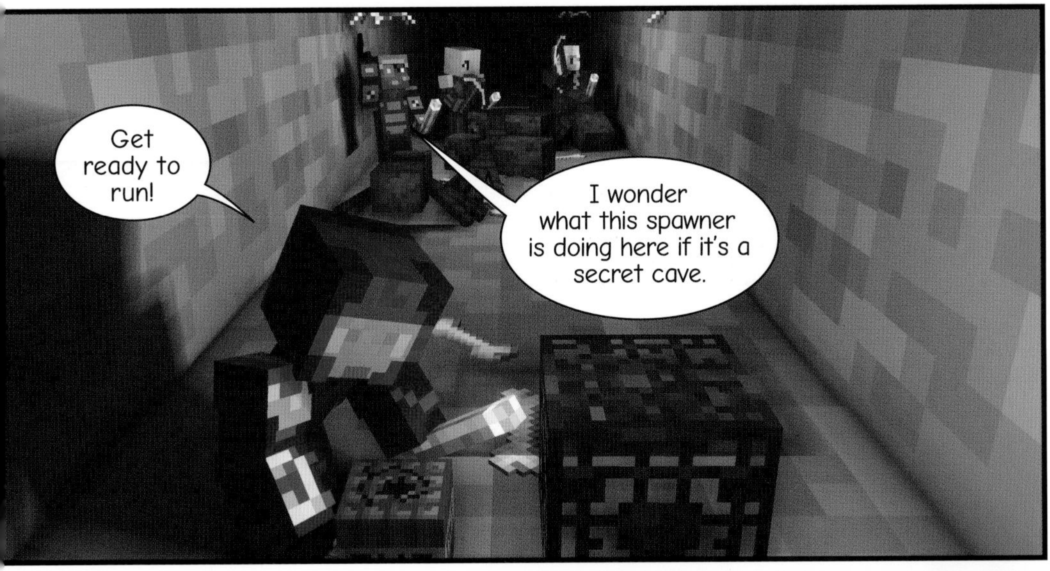
Get ready to run!
I wonder what this spawner is doing here if it's a secret cave.

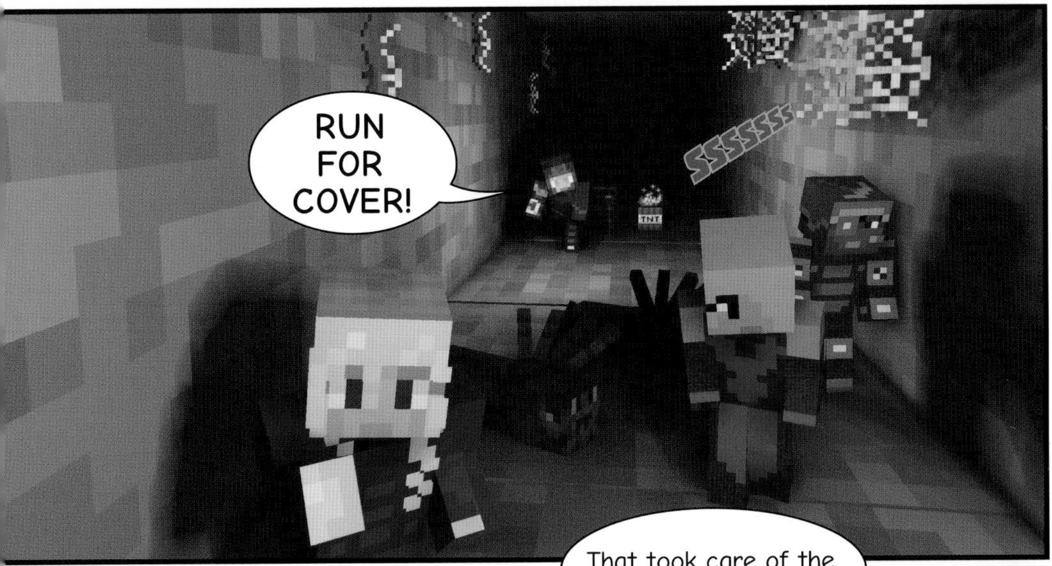
RUN FOR COVER!
SSSSSSS

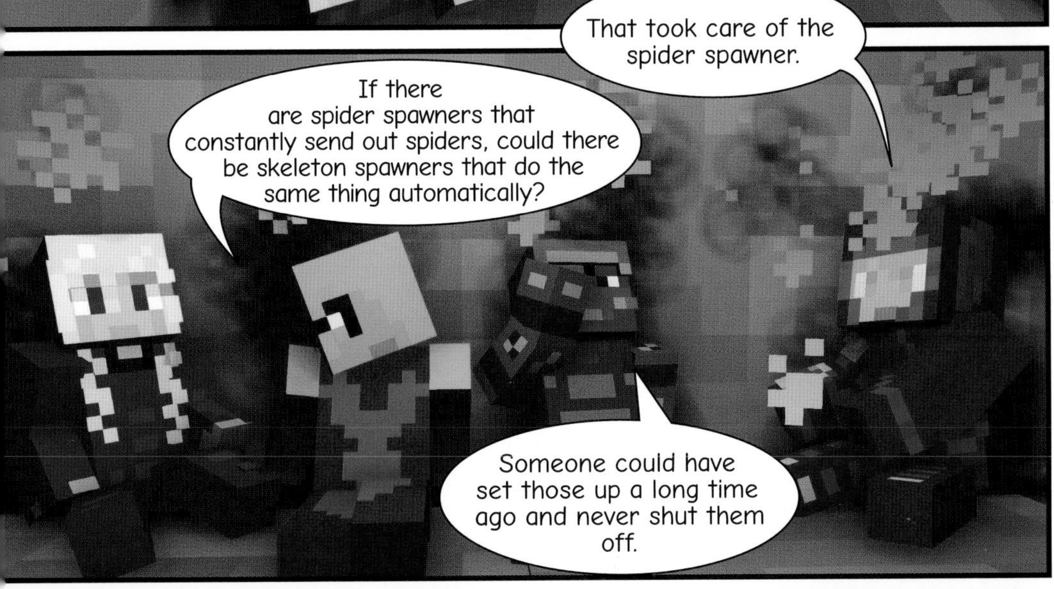
That took care of the spider spawner.
If there are spider spawners that constantly send out spiders, could there be skeleton spawners that do the same thing automatically?
Someone could have set those up a long time ago and never shut them off.

# CHAPTER 7

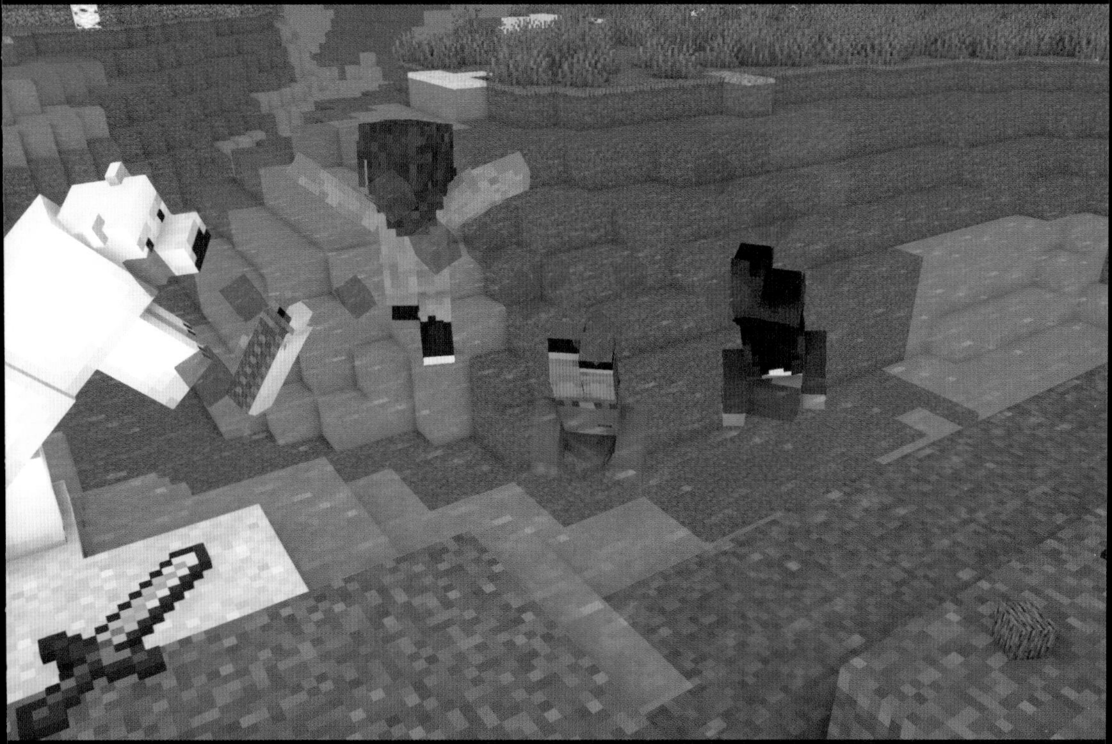

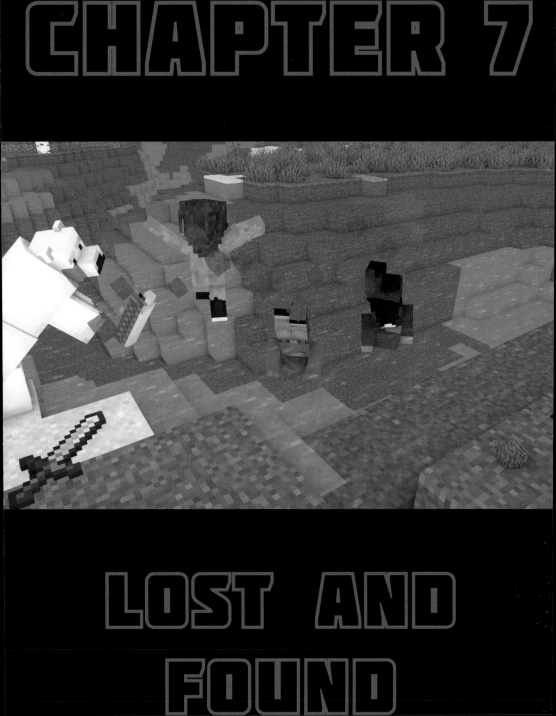

# LOST AND FOUND

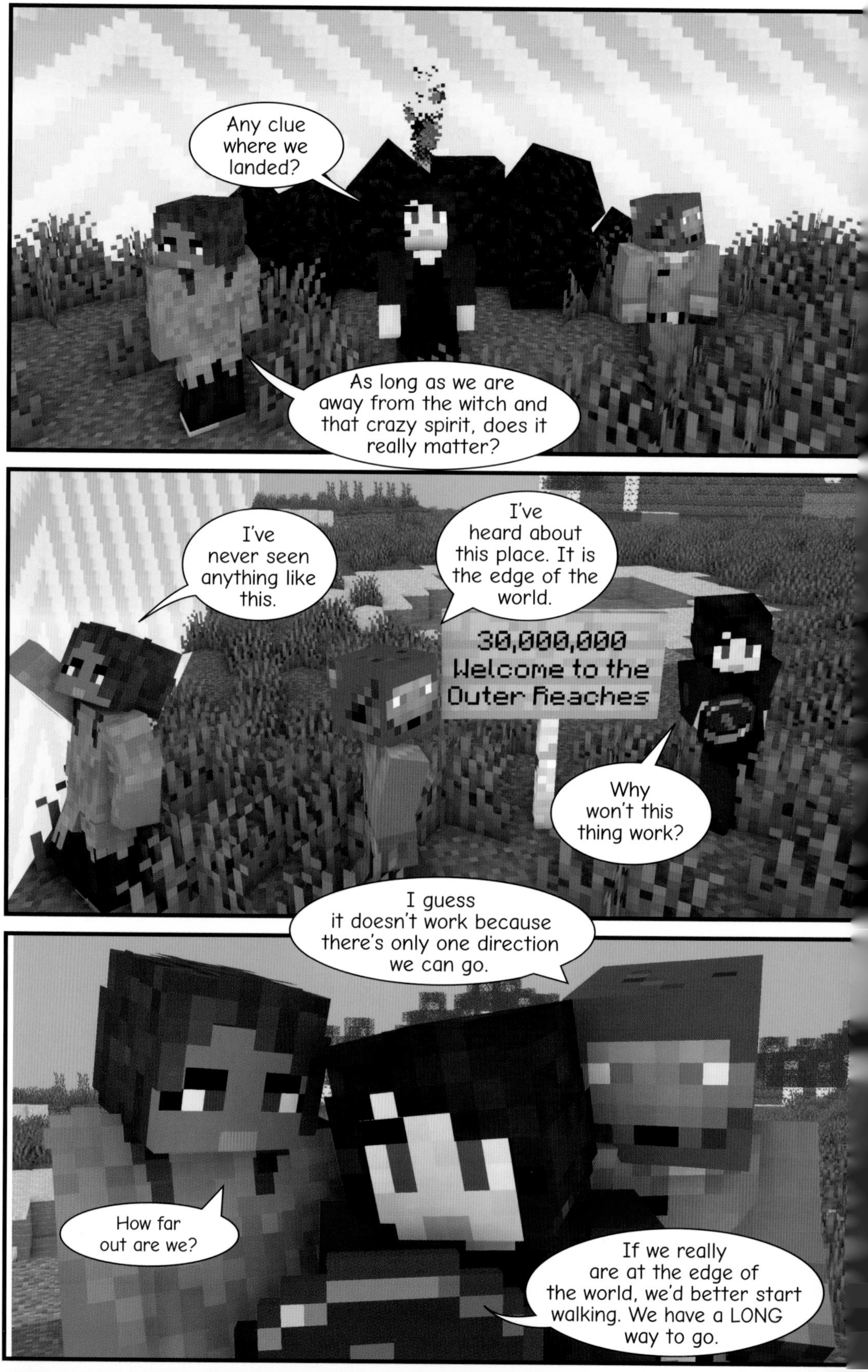
Any clue where we landed?
As long as we are away from the witch and that crazy spirit, does it really matter?
I've never seen anything like this.
I've heard about this place. It is the edge of the world.
30,000,000 Welcome to the Outer Reaches
Why won't this thing work?
I guess it doesn't work because there's only one direction we can go.
How far out are we?
If we really are at the edge of the world, we'd better start walking. We have a LONG way to go.

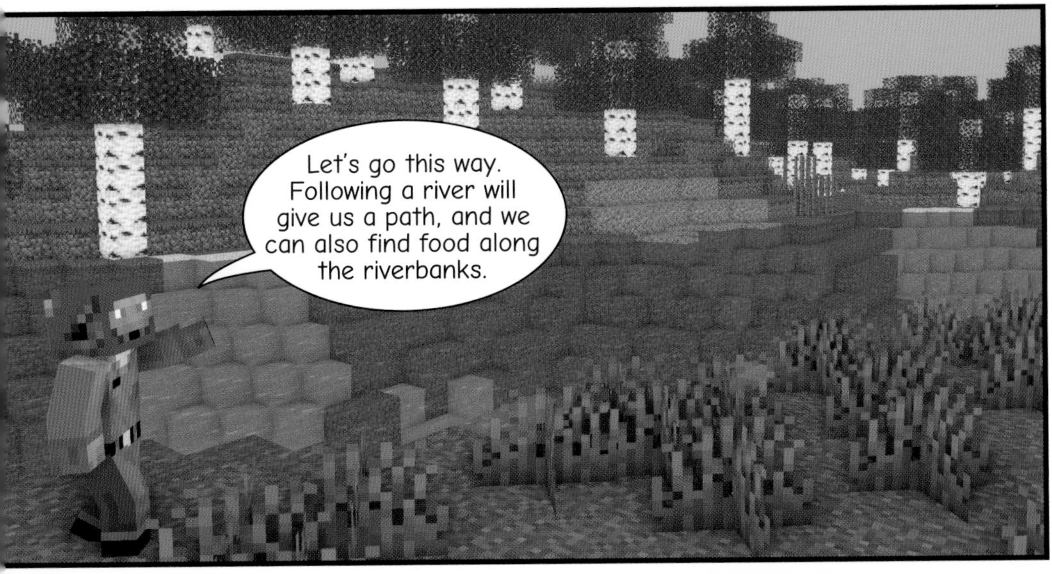
Let's go this way. Following a river will give us a path, and we can also find food along the riverbanks.

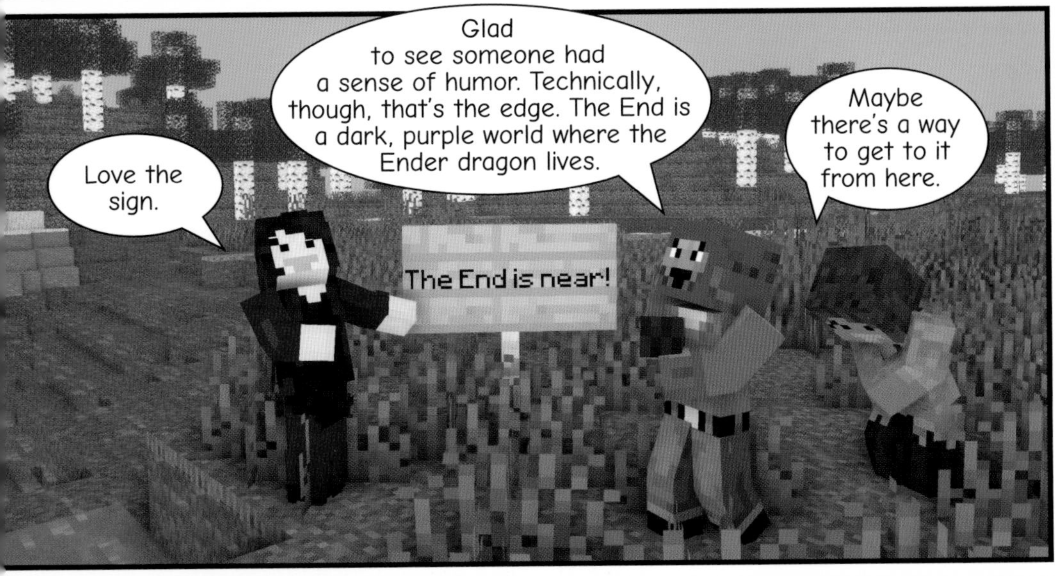
Love the sign.
The End is near!
Glad to see someone had a sense of humor. Technically, though, that's the edge. The End is a dark, purple world where the Ender dragon lives.
Maybe there's a way to get to it from here.

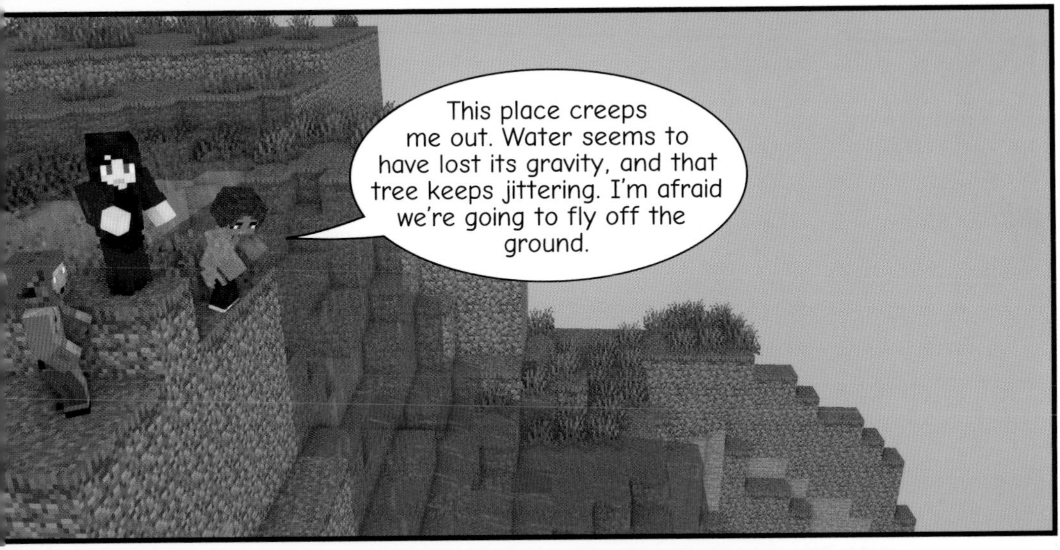
This place creeps me out. Water seems to have lost its gravity, and that tree keeps jittering. I'm afraid we're going to fly off the ground.

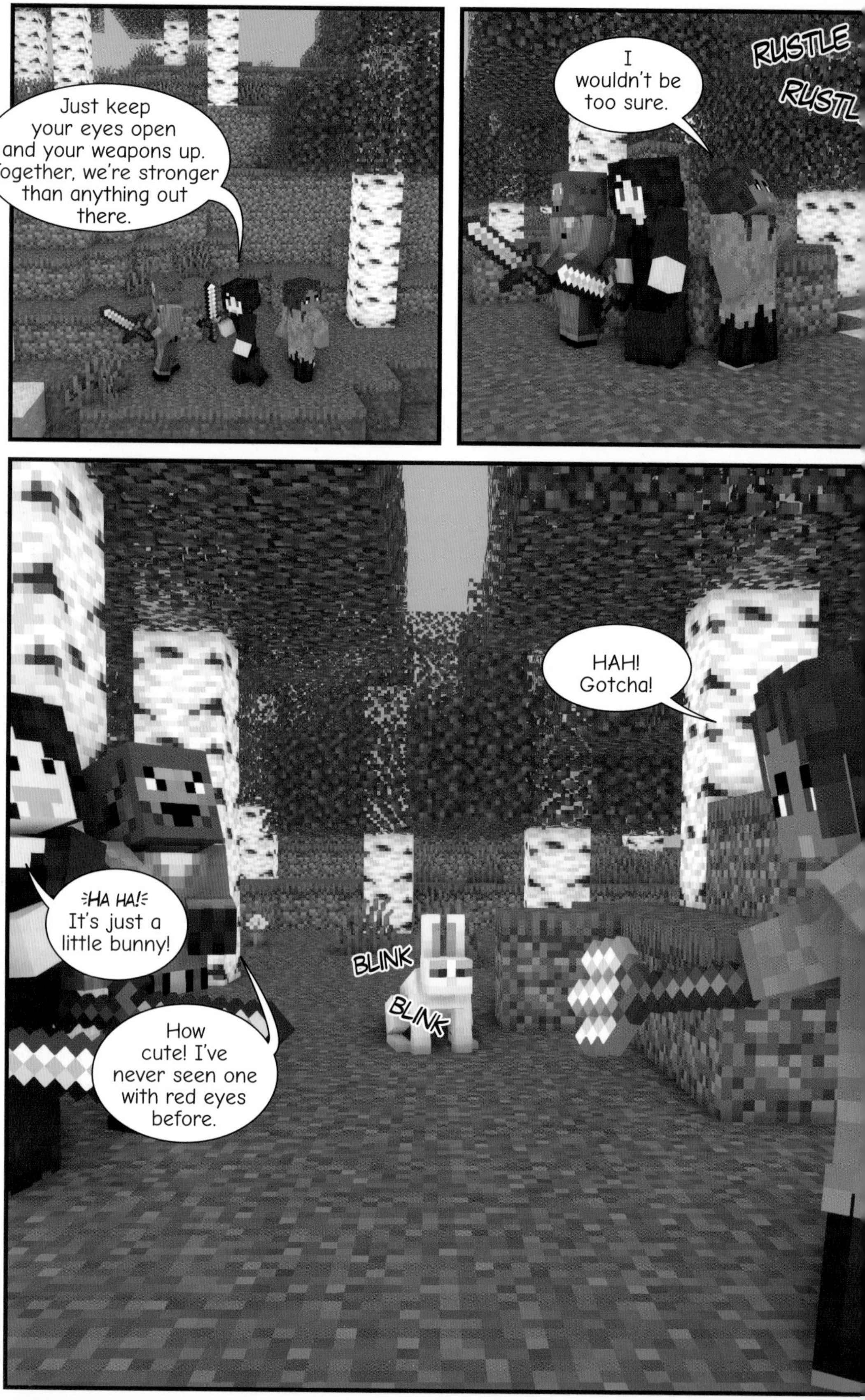
Just keep your eyes open and your weapons up. Together, we're stronger than anything out there.
I wouldn't be too sure.
RUSTLE
RUSTL
HAH! Gotcha!
HA HA! It's just a little bunny!
How cute! I've never seen one with red eyes before.
BLINK
BLINK

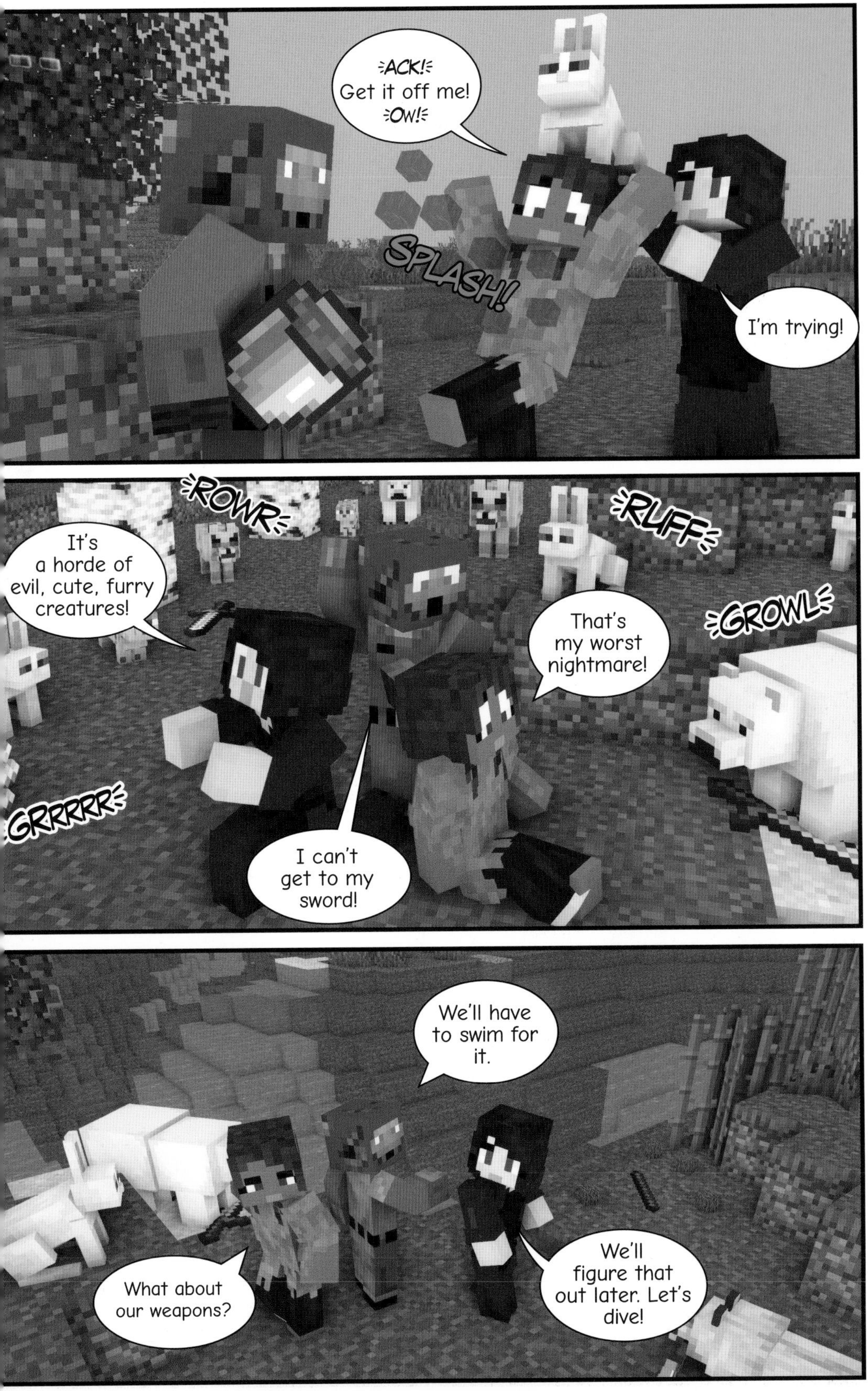
ACK!
Get it off me!
OW!
SPLASH!
I'm trying!
ROWR
RUFF
It's a horde of evil, cute, furry creatures!
GROWL
That's my worst nightmare!
GRRRRR
I can't get to my sword!
We'll have to swim for it.
What about our weapons?
We'll figure that out later. Let's dive!

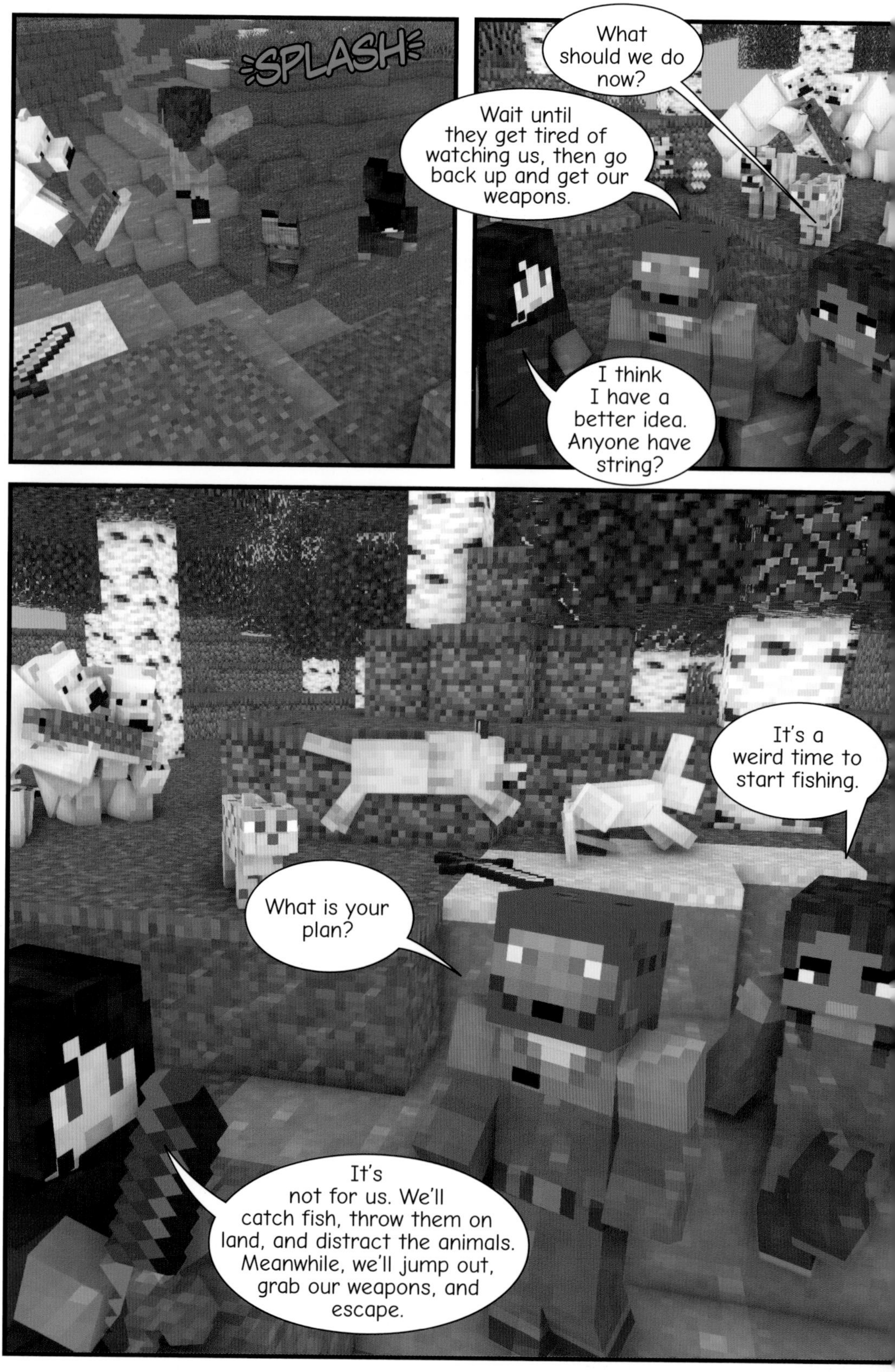
SPLASH
What should we do now?
Wait until they get tired of watching us, then go back up and get our weapons.
I think I have a better idea. Anyone have string?
It's a weird time to start fishing.
What is your plan?
It's not for us. We'll catch fish, throw them on land, and distract the animals. Meanwhile, we'll jump out, grab our weapons, and escape.

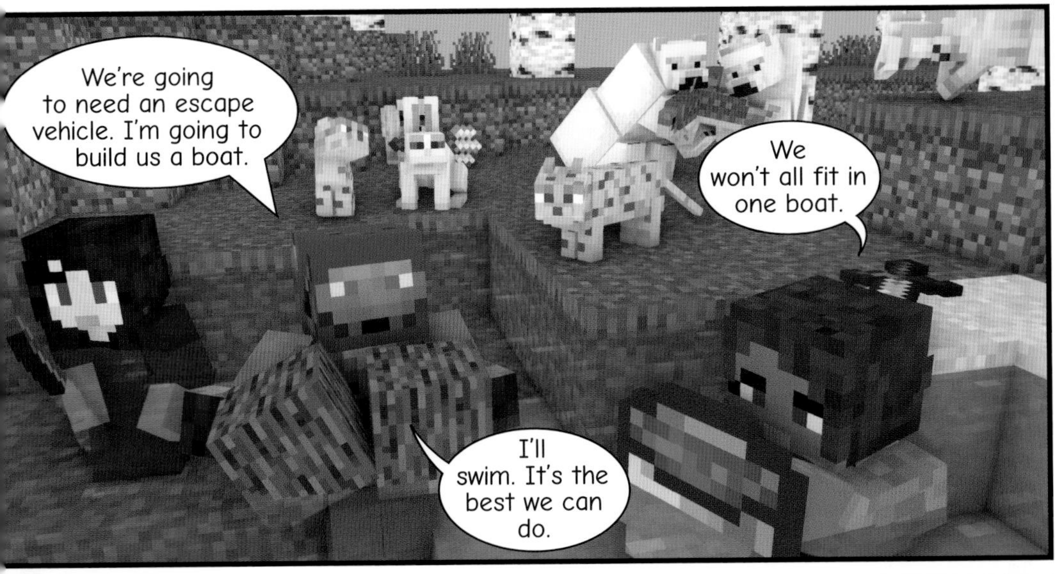
We're going to need an escape vehicle. I'm going to build us a boat.
We won't all fit in one boat.
I'll swim. It's the best we can do.

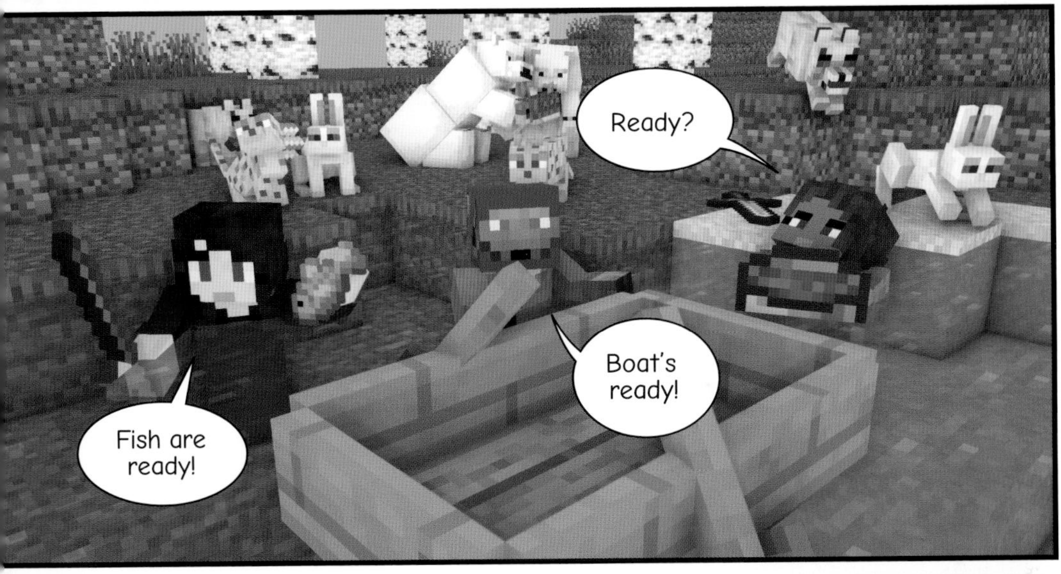
Ready?
Boat's ready!
Fish are ready!

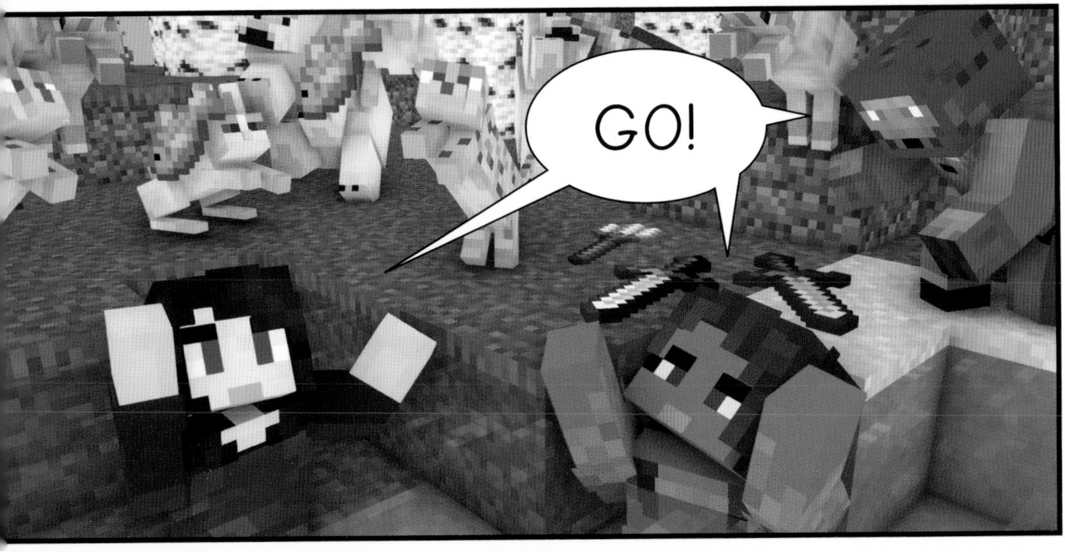
GO!

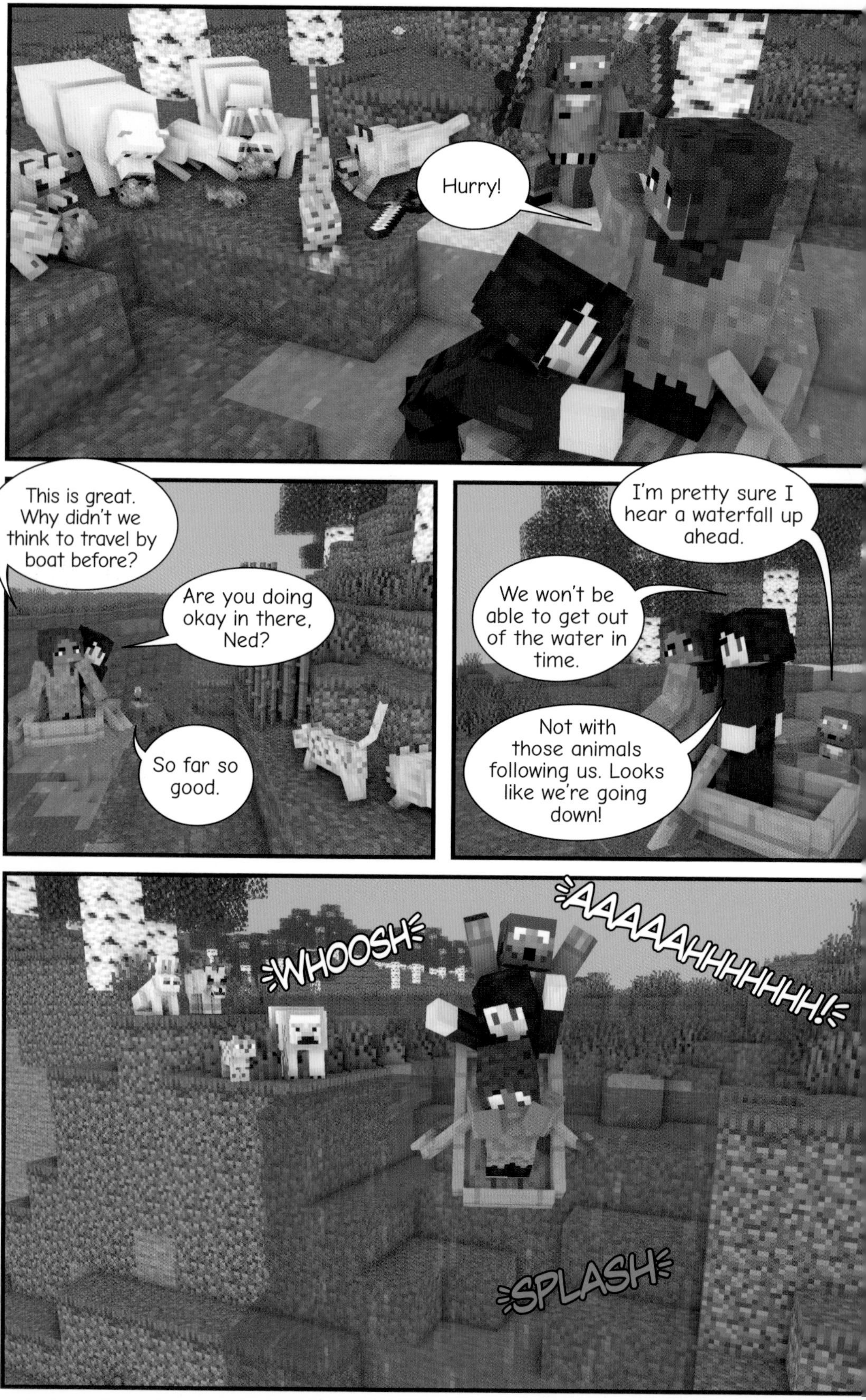
Hurry!
This is great. Why didn't we think to travel by boat before?
Are you doing okay in there, Ned?
So far so good.
I'm pretty sure I hear a waterfall up ahead.
We won't be able to get out of the water in time.
Not with those animals following us. Looks like we're going down!
WHOOSH
AAAAAHHHHHHH!
SPLASH

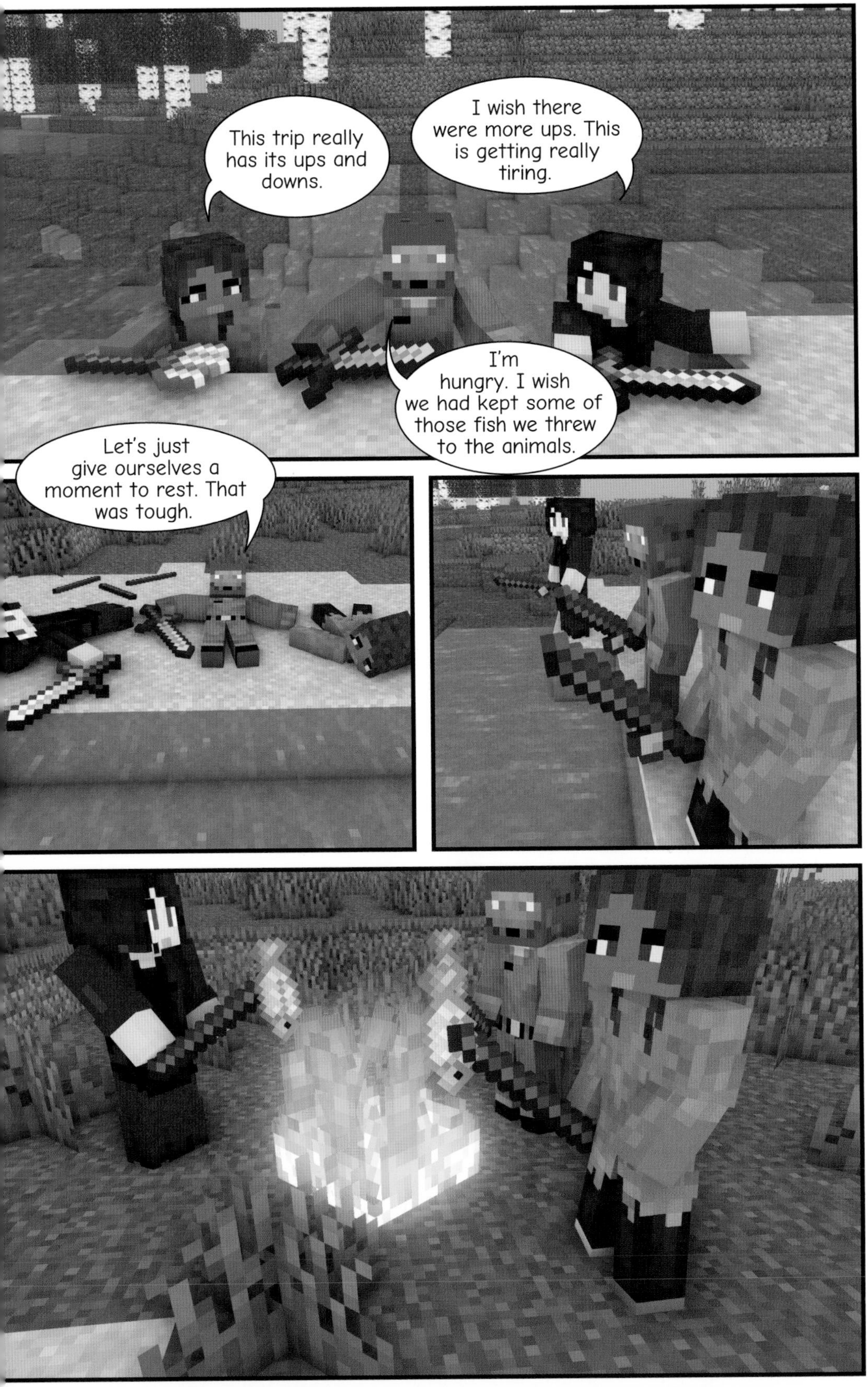
This trip really has its ups and downs.
I wish there were more ups. This is getting really tiring.
I'm hungry. I wish we had kept some of those fish we threw to the animals.
Let's just give ourselves a moment to rest. That was tough.

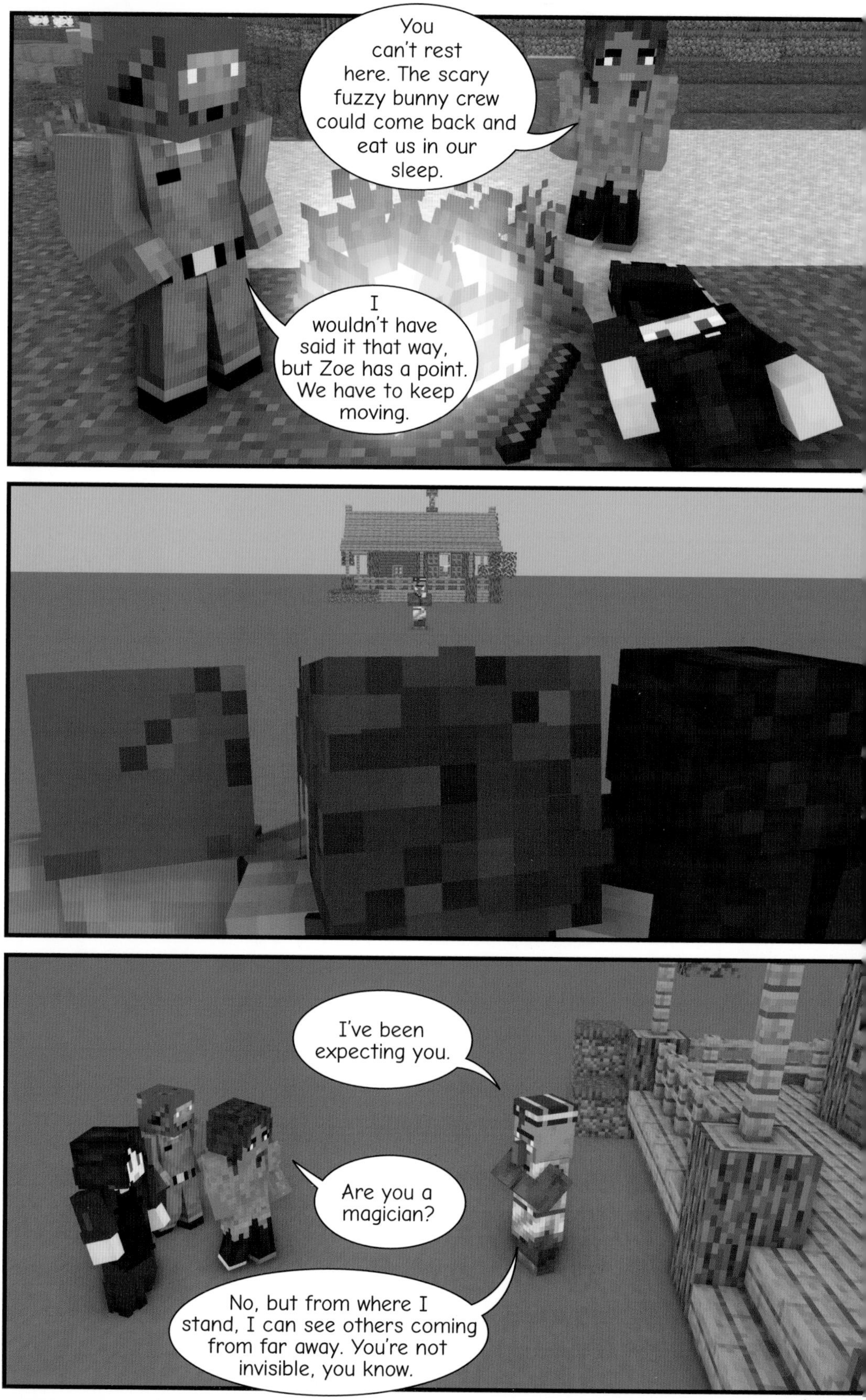
You can't rest here. The scary fuzzy bunny crew could come back and eat us in our sleep.
I wouldn't have said it that way, but Zoe has a point. We have to keep moving.
I've been expecting you.
Are you a magician?
No, but from where I stand, I can see others coming from far away. You're not invisible, you know.

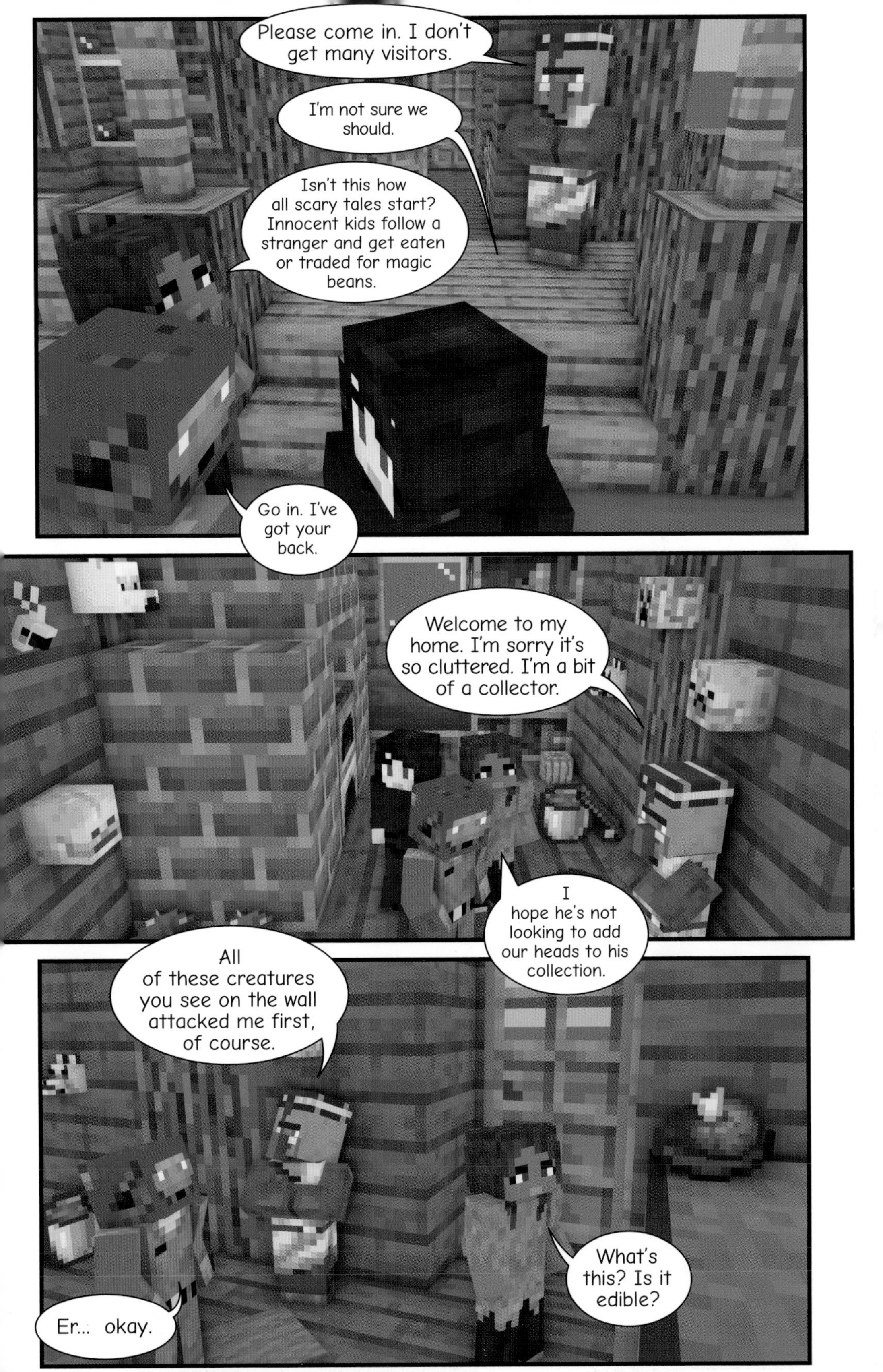
Please come in. I don't get many visitors.
I'm not sure we should.
Isn't this how all scary tales start? Innocent kids follow a stranger and get eaten or traded for magic beans.
Go in. I've got your back.
Welcome to my home. I'm sorry it's so cluttered. I'm a bit of a collector.
I hope he's not looking to add our heads to his collection.
All of these creatures you see on the wall attacked me first, of course.
Er... okay.
What's this? Is it edible?

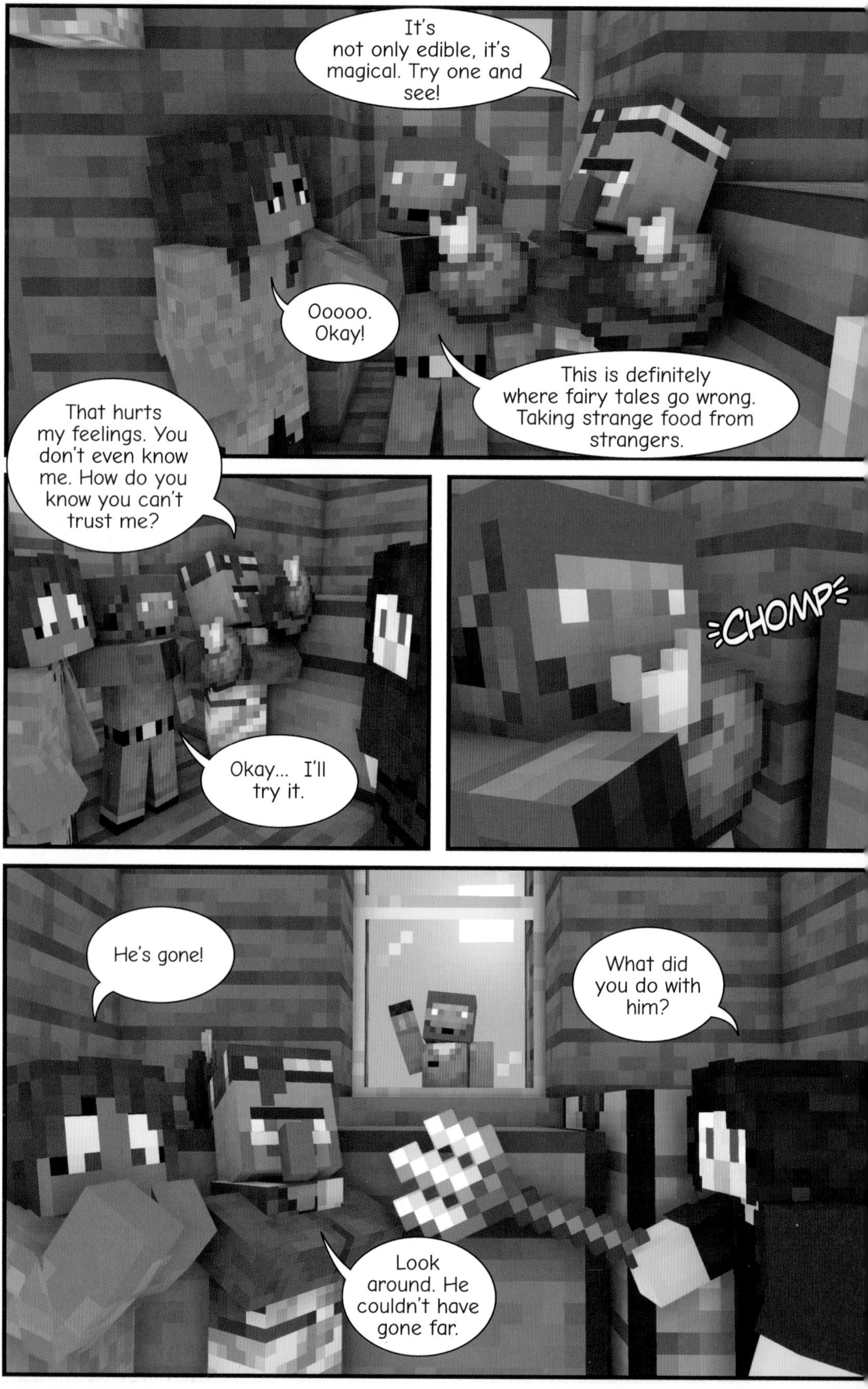
It's not only edible, it's magical. Try one and see!
Ooooo. Okay!
This is definitely where fairy tales go wrong. Taking strange food from strangers.
That hurts my feelings. You don't even know me. How do you know you can't trust me?
Okay... I'll try it.
CHOMP
He's gone!
What did you do with him?
Look around. He couldn't have gone far.

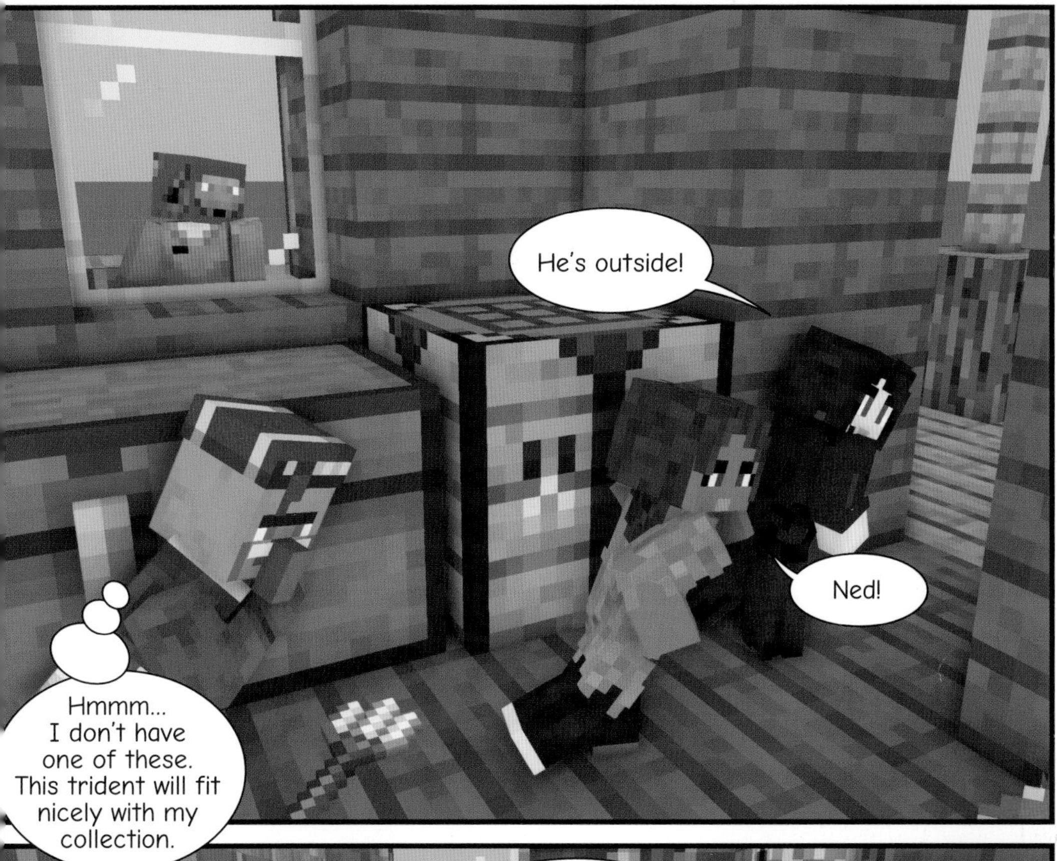
He's outside!
Ned!
Hmmm... I don't have one of these. This trident will fit nicely with my collection.

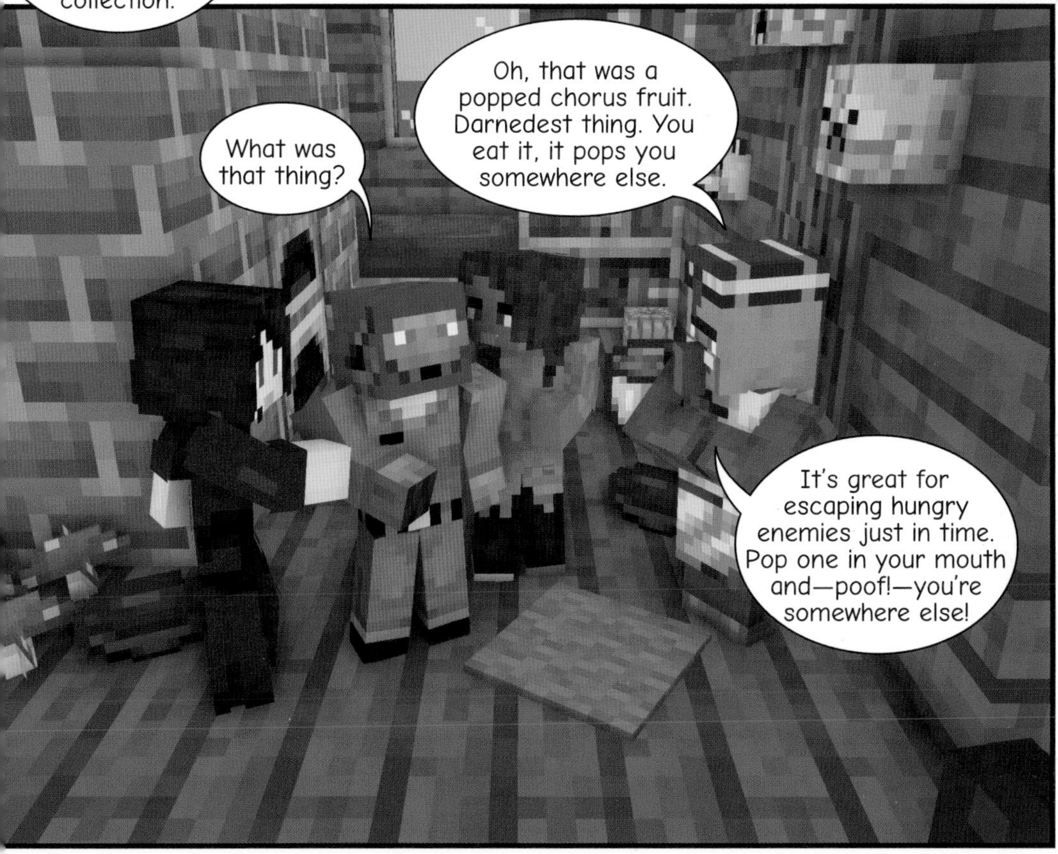
What was that thing?
Oh, that was a popped chorus fruit. Darnedest thing. You eat it, it pops you somewhere else.
It's great for escaping hungry enemies just in time. Pop one in your mouth and—poof!—you're somewhere else!

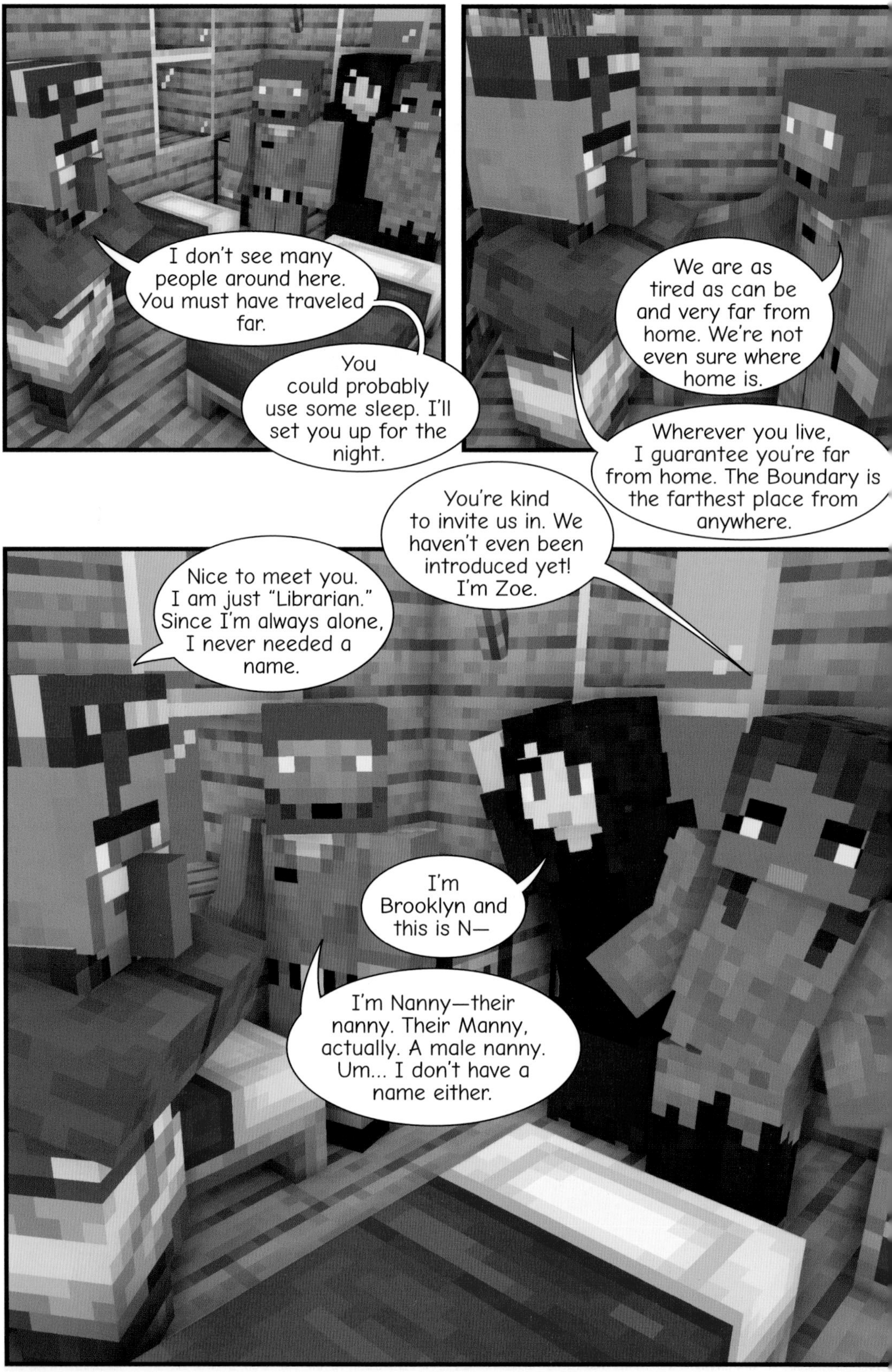
I don't see many people around here. You must have traveled far.
You could probably use some sleep. I'll set you up for the night.
We are as tired as can be and very far from home. We're not even sure where home is.
Wherever you live, I guarantee you're far from home. The Boundary is the farthest place from anywhere.
You're kind to invite us in. We haven't even been introduced yet! I'm Zoe.
Nice to meet you. I am just "Librarian." Since I'm always alone, I never needed a name.
I'm Brooklyn and this is N—
I'm Nanny—their nanny. Their Manny, actually. A male nanny. Um... I don't have a name either.

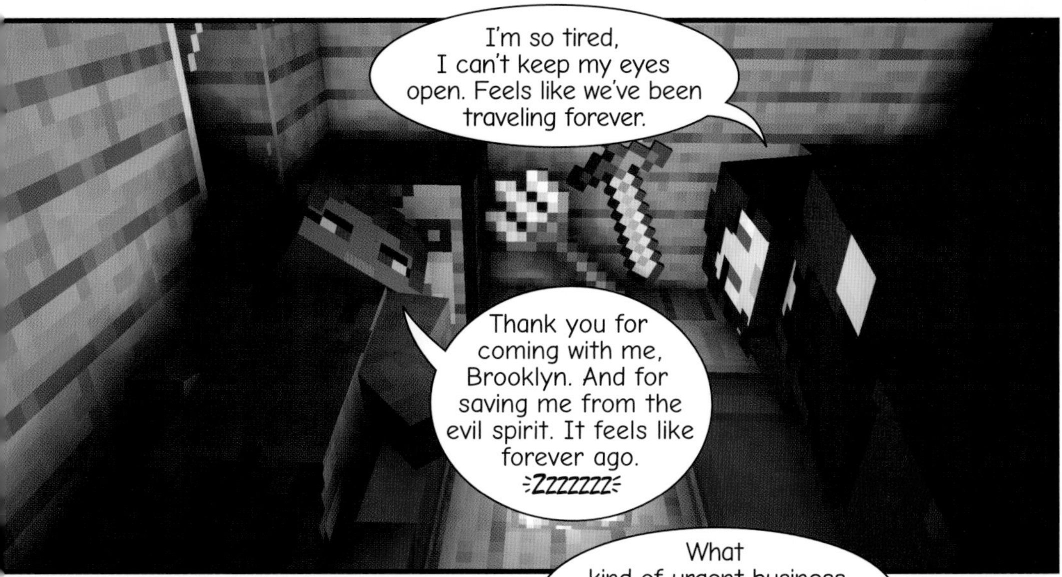
I'm so tired, I can't keep my eyes open. Feels like we've been traveling forever.
Thank you for coming with me, Brooklyn. And for saving me from the evil spirit. It feels like forever ago.
Zzzzzzz

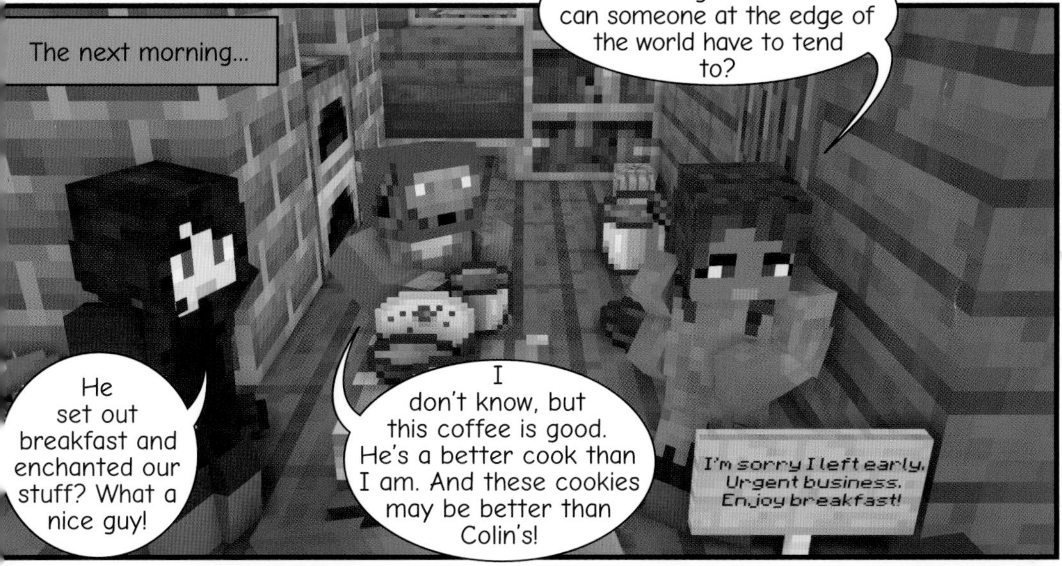
The next morning...
What kind of urgent business can someone at the edge of the world have to tend to?
He set out breakfast and enchanted our stuff? What a nice guy!
I don't know, but this coffee is good. He's a better cook than I am. And these cookies may be better than Colin's!
I'm sorry I left early. Urgent business. Enjoy breakfast!

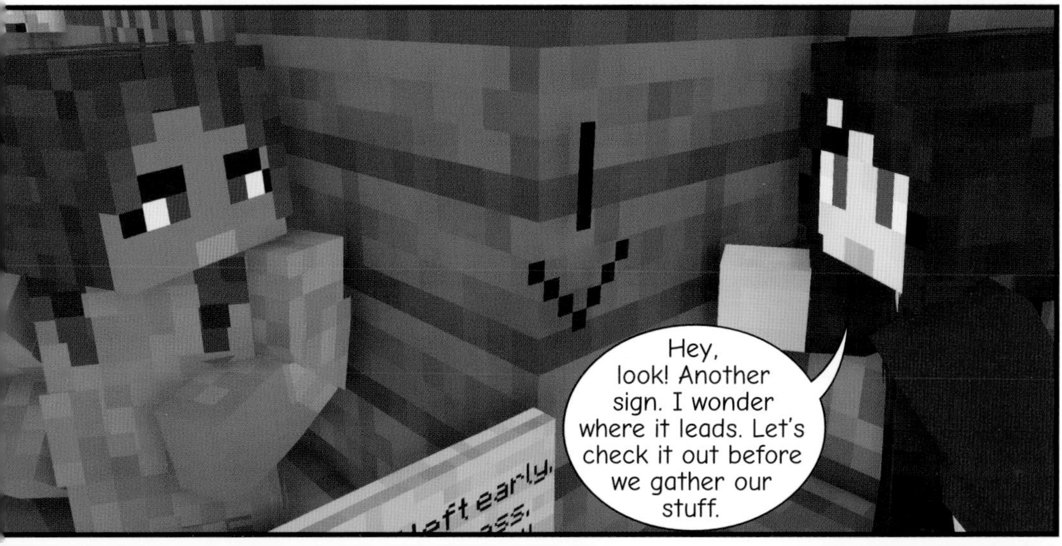
Hey, look! Another sign. I wonder where it leads. Let's check it out before we gather our stuff.

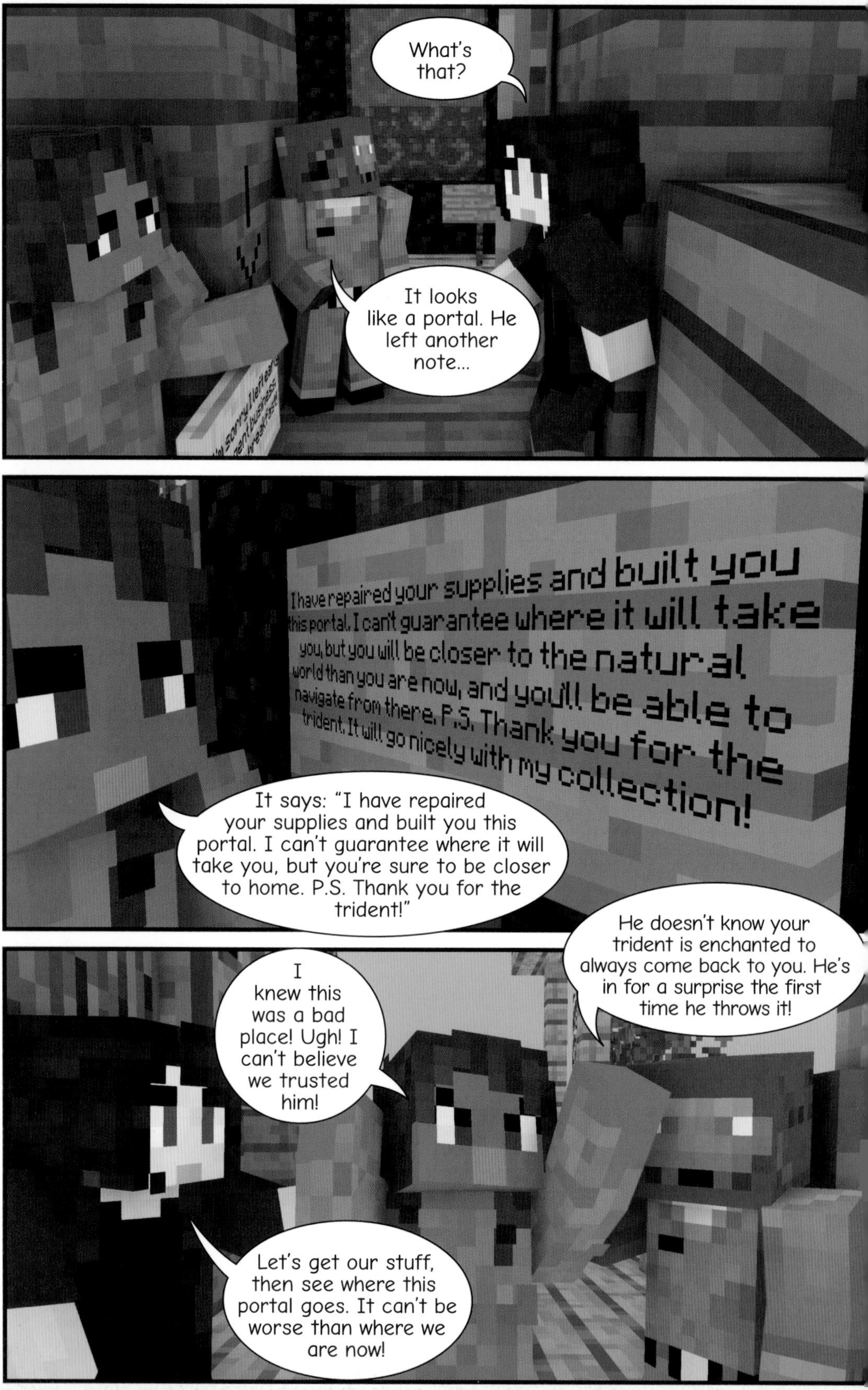
What's that?
It looks like a portal. He left another note...
I have repaired your supplies and built you this portal. I can't guarantee where it will take you, but you will be closer to the natural world than you are now, and you'll be able to navigate from there. P.S. Thank you for the trident. It will go nicely with my collection!
It says: "I have repaired your supplies and built you this portal. I can't guarantee where it will take you, but you're sure to be closer to home. P.S. Thank you for the trident!"
I knew this was a bad place! Ugh! I can't believe we trusted him!
He doesn't know your trident is enchanted to always come back to you. He's in for a surprise the first time he throws it!
Let's get our stuff, then see where this portal goes. It can't be worse than where we are now!

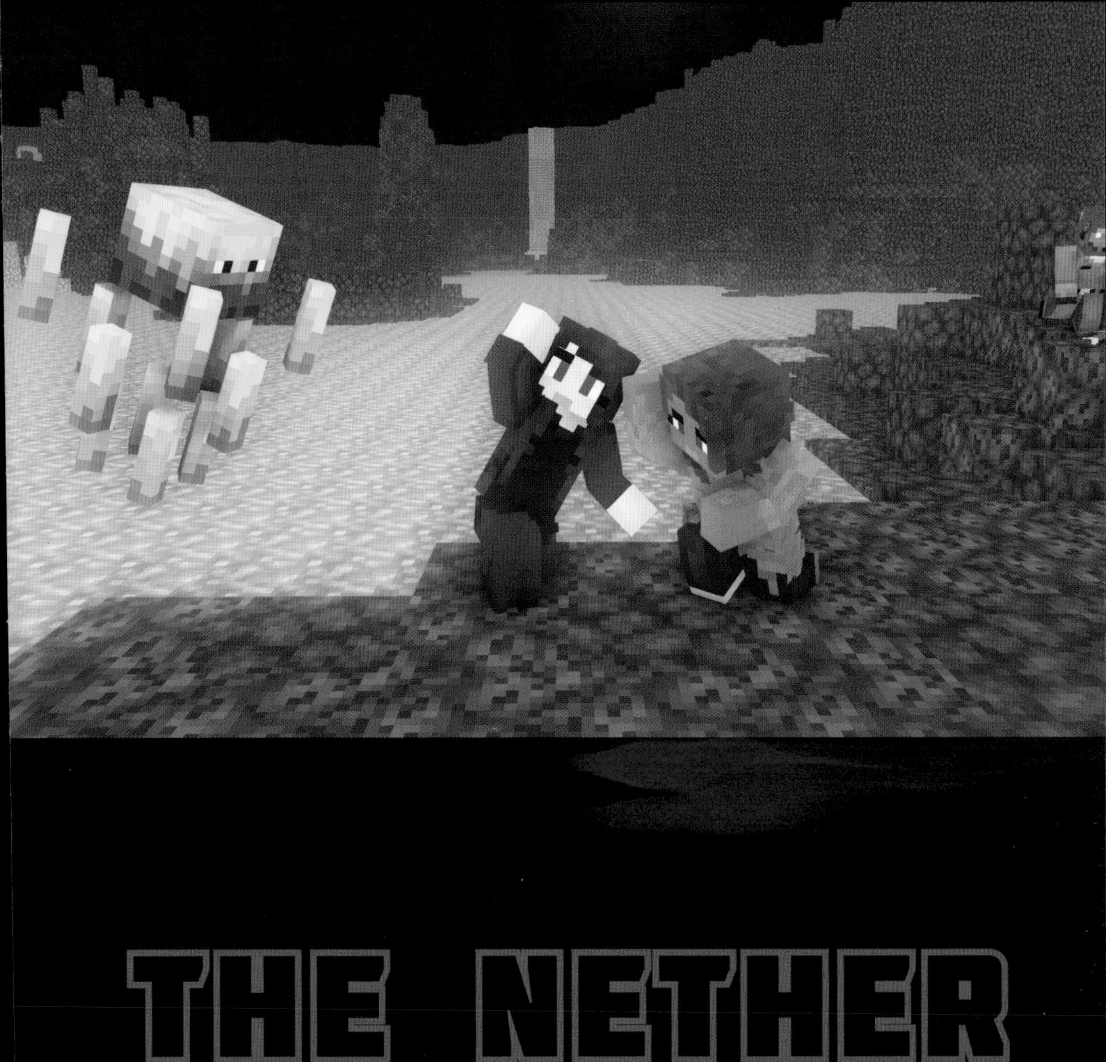

# THE NETHER

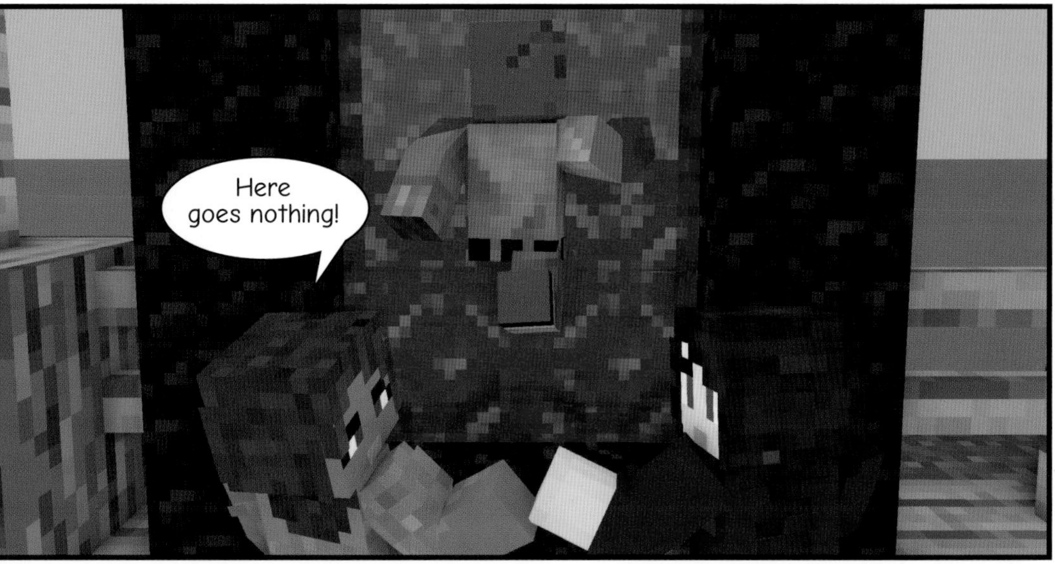
Here goes nothing!

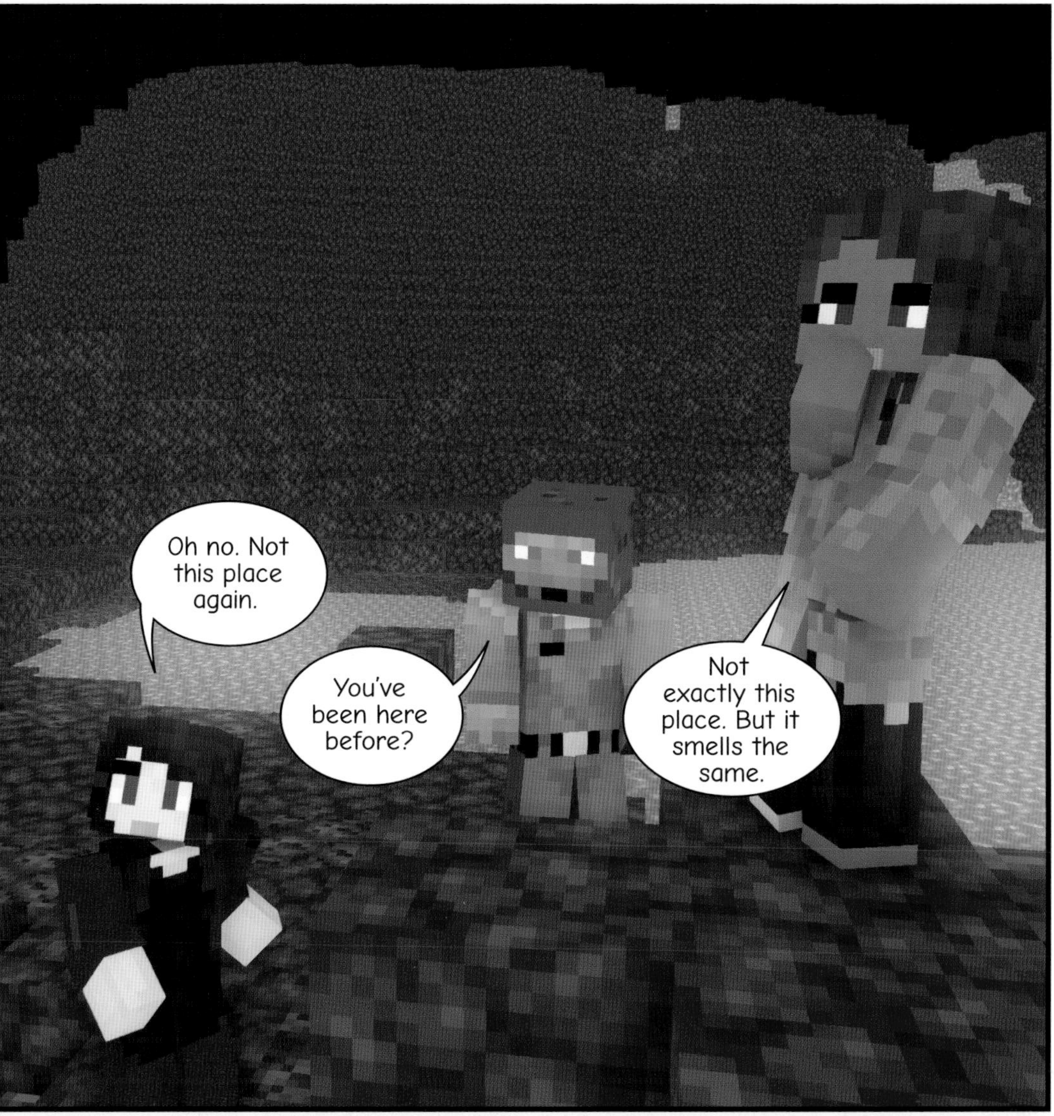
Oh no. Not this place again.
You've been here before?
Not exactly this place. But it smells the same.

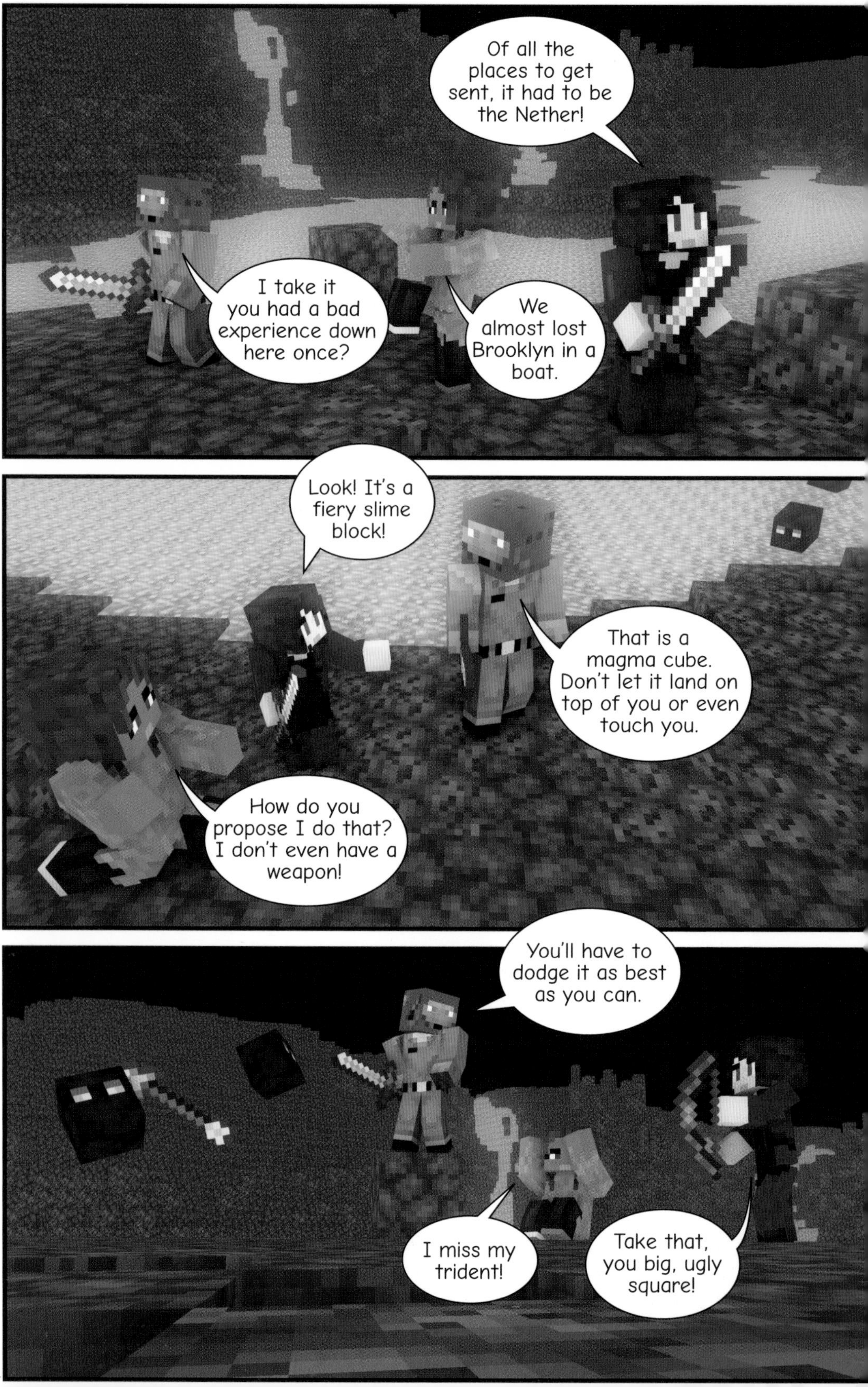
Of all the places to get sent, it had to be the Nether!
I take it you had a bad experience down here once?
We almost lost Brooklyn in a boat.
Look! It's a fiery slime block!
That is a magma cube. Don't let it land on top of you or even touch you.
How do you propose I do that? I don't even have a weapon!
You'll have to dodge it as best as you can.
I miss my trident!
Take that, you big, ugly square!

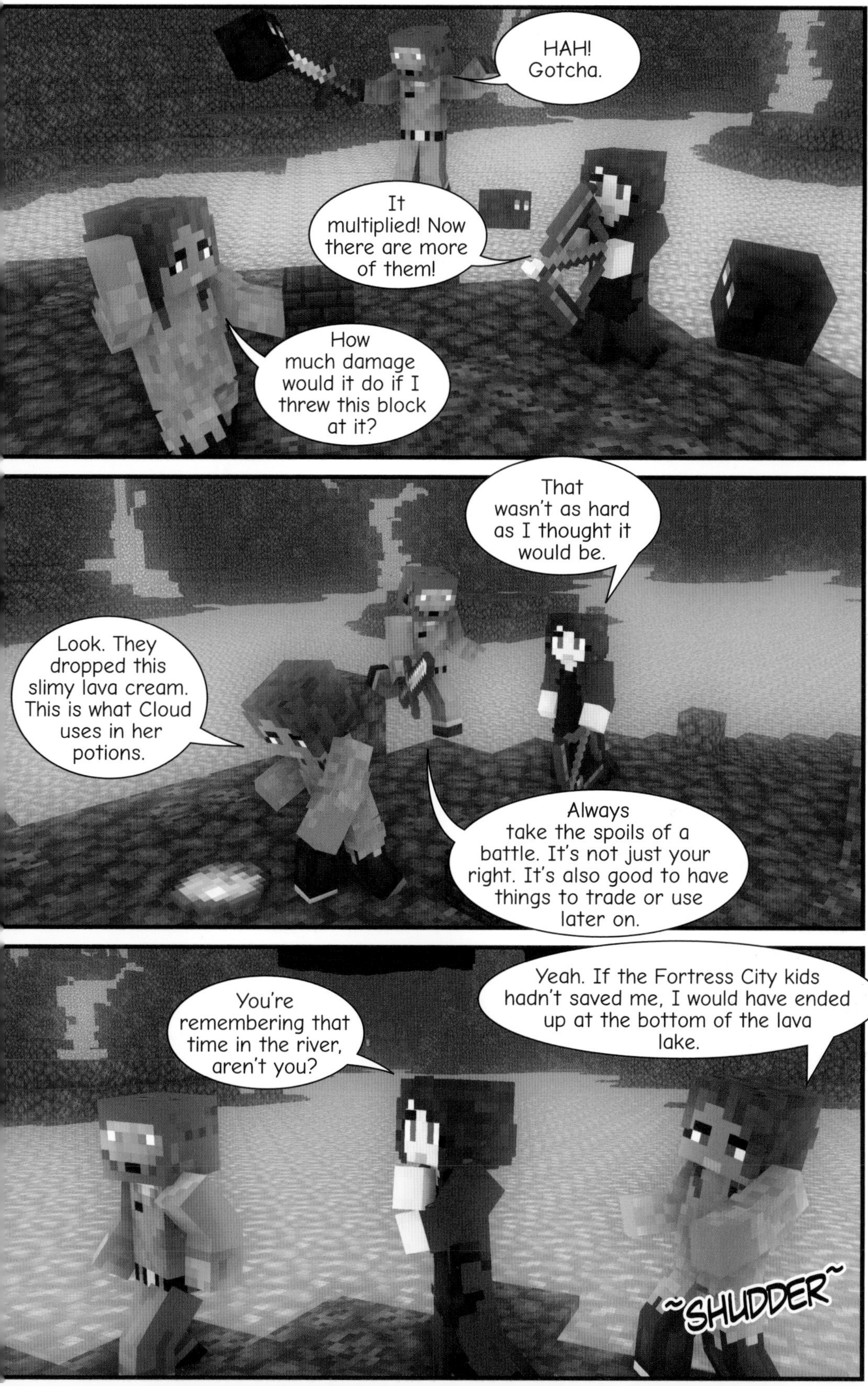
HAH! Gotcha.
It multiplied! Now there are more of them!
How much damage would it do if I threw this block at it?
That wasn't as hard as I thought it would be.
Look. They dropped this slimy lava cream. This is what Cloud uses in her potions.
Always take the spoils of a battle. It's not just your right. It's also good to have things to trade or use later on.
You're remembering that time in the river, aren't you?
Yeah. If the Fortress City kids hadn't saved me, I would have ended up at the bottom of the lava lake.
~SHUDDER~

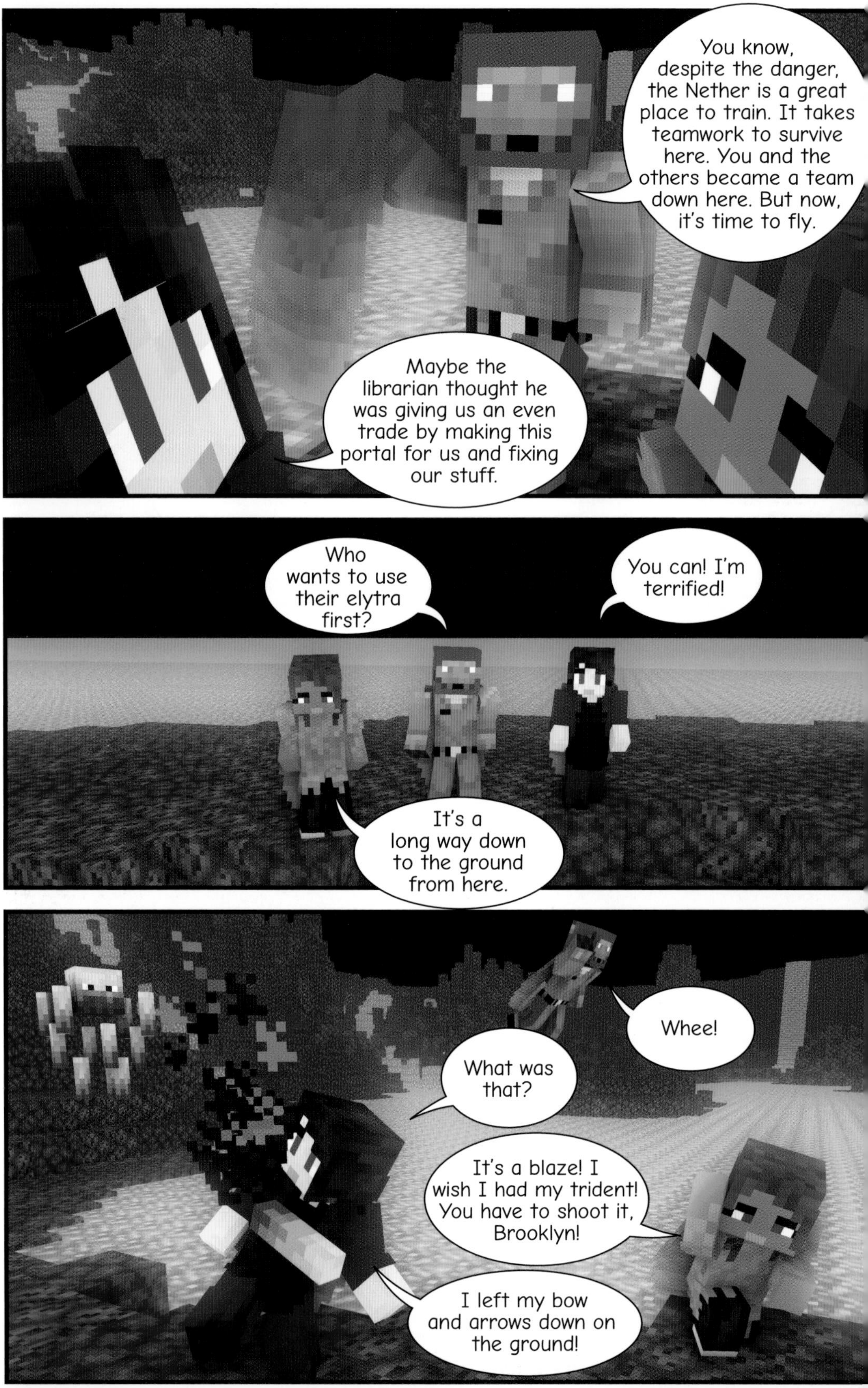
You know, despite the danger, the Nether is a great place to train. It takes teamwork to survive here. You and the others became a team down here. But now, it's time to fly.
Maybe the librarian thought he was giving us an even trade by making this portal for us and fixing our stuff.
Who wants to use their elytra first?
You can! I'm terrified!
It's a long way down to the ground from here.
Whee!
What was that?
It's a blaze! I wish I had my trident! You have to shoot it, Brooklyn!
I left my bow and arrows down on the ground!

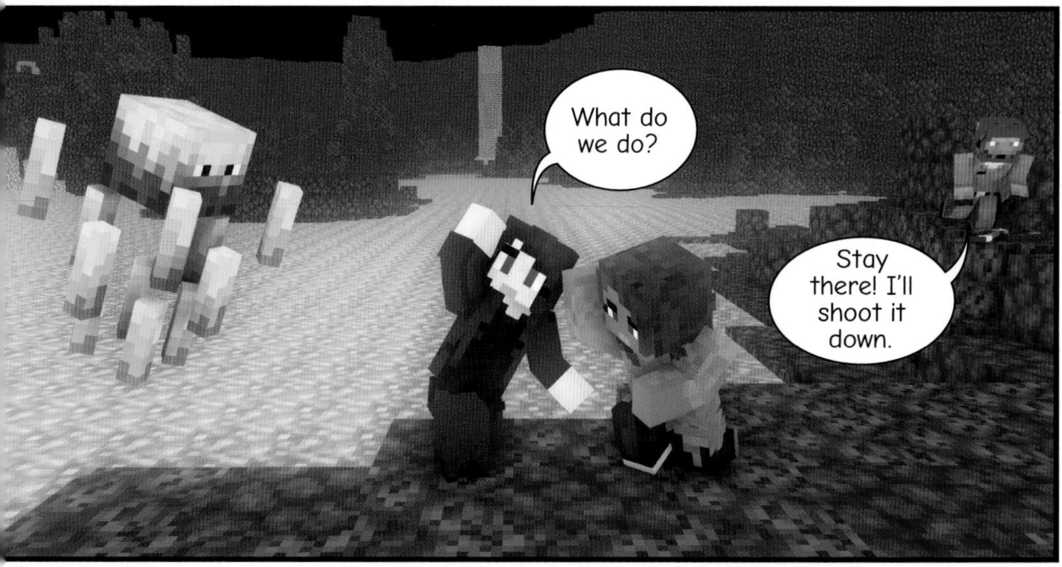
What do we do?
Stay there! I'll shoot it down.

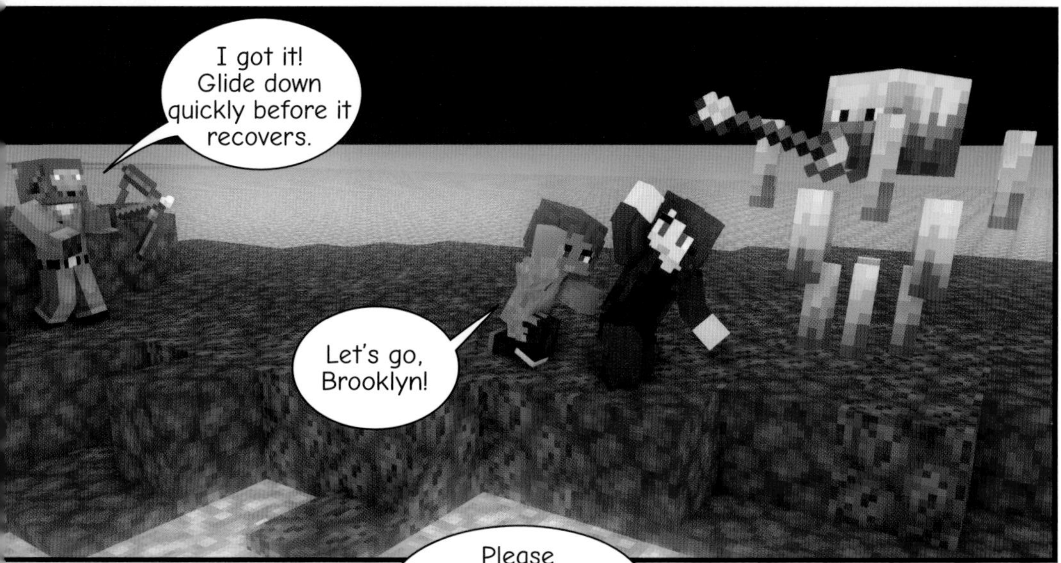
I got it! Glide down quickly before it recovers.
Let's go, Brooklyn!

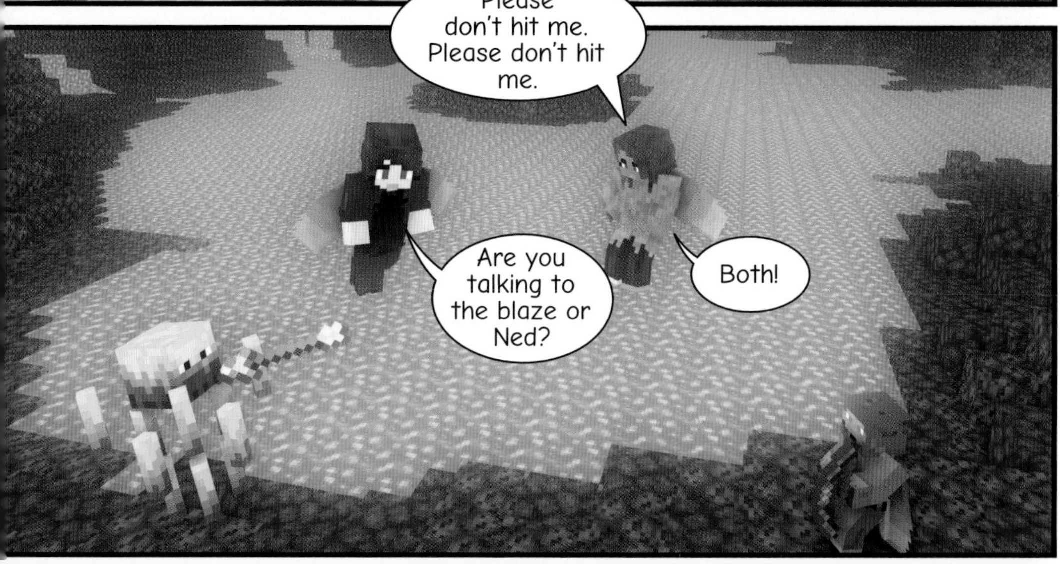
Please don't hit me. Please don't hit me.
Are you talking to the blaze or Ned?
Both!

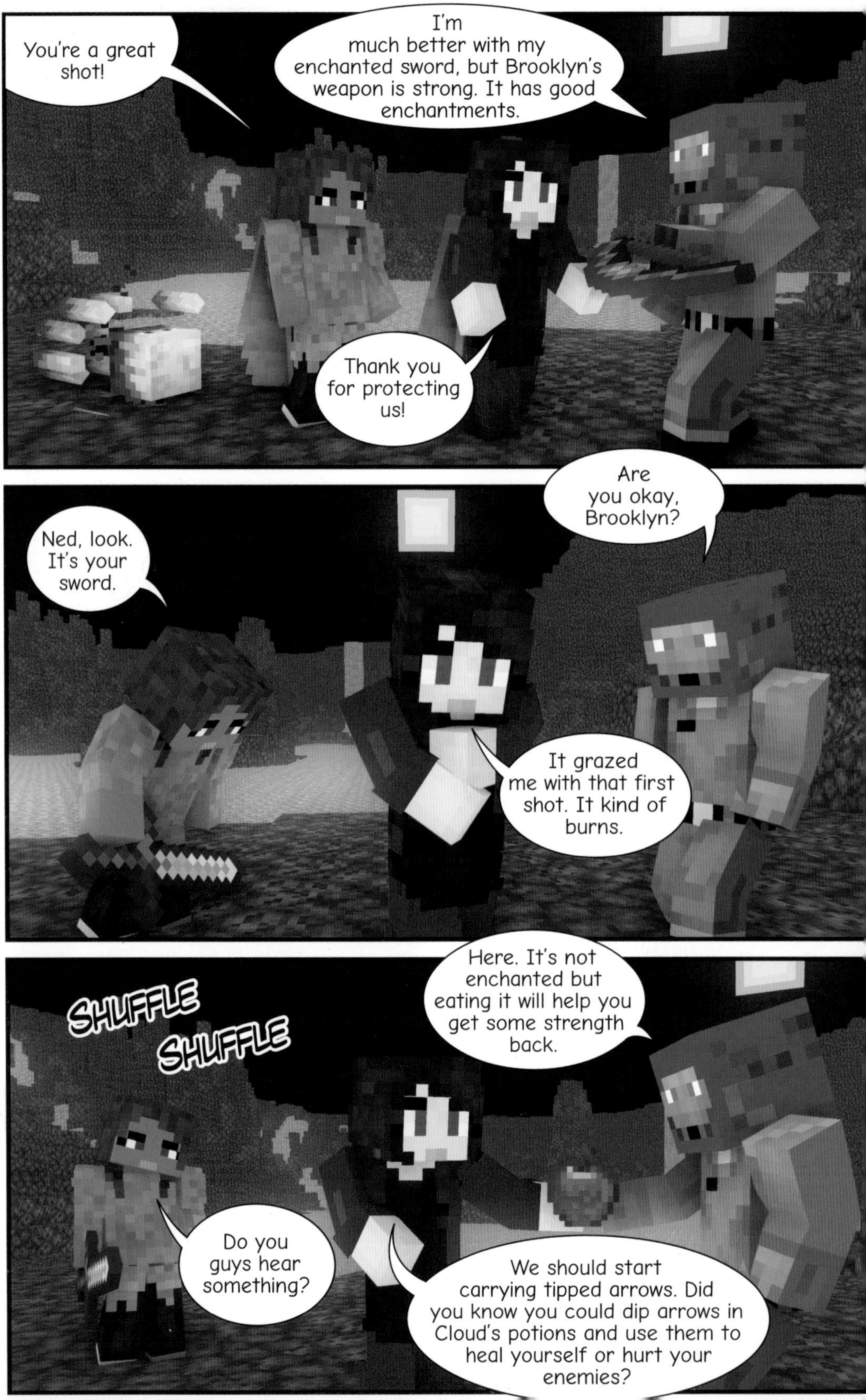

You're a great shot!
I'm much better with my enchanted sword, but Brooklyn's weapon is strong. It has good enchantments.
Thank you for protecting us!
Ned, look. It's your sword.
Are you okay, Brooklyn?
It grazed me with that first shot. It kind of burns.
SHUFFLE SHUFFLE
Here. It's not enchanted but eating it will help you get some strength back.
Do you guys hear something?
We should start carrying tipped arrows. Did you know you could dip arrows in Cloud's potions and use them to heal yourself or hurt your enemies?

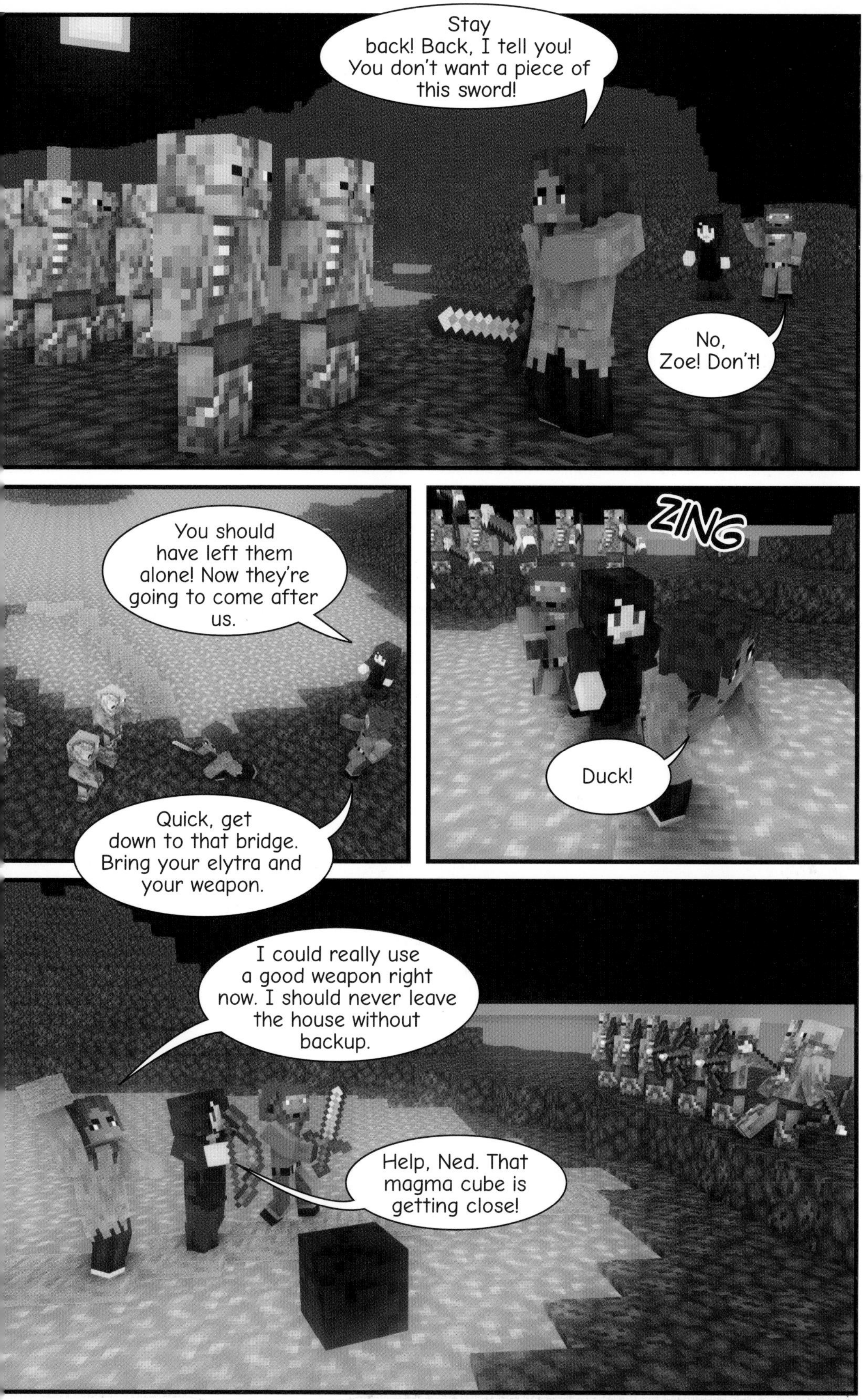
Stay back! Back, I tell you! You don't want a piece of this sword!
No, Zoe! Don't!
You should have left them alone! Now they're going to come after us.
Quick, get down to that bridge. Bring your elytra and your weapon.
ZING
Duck!
I could really use a good weapon right now. I should never leave the house without backup.
Help, Ned. That magma cube is getting close!

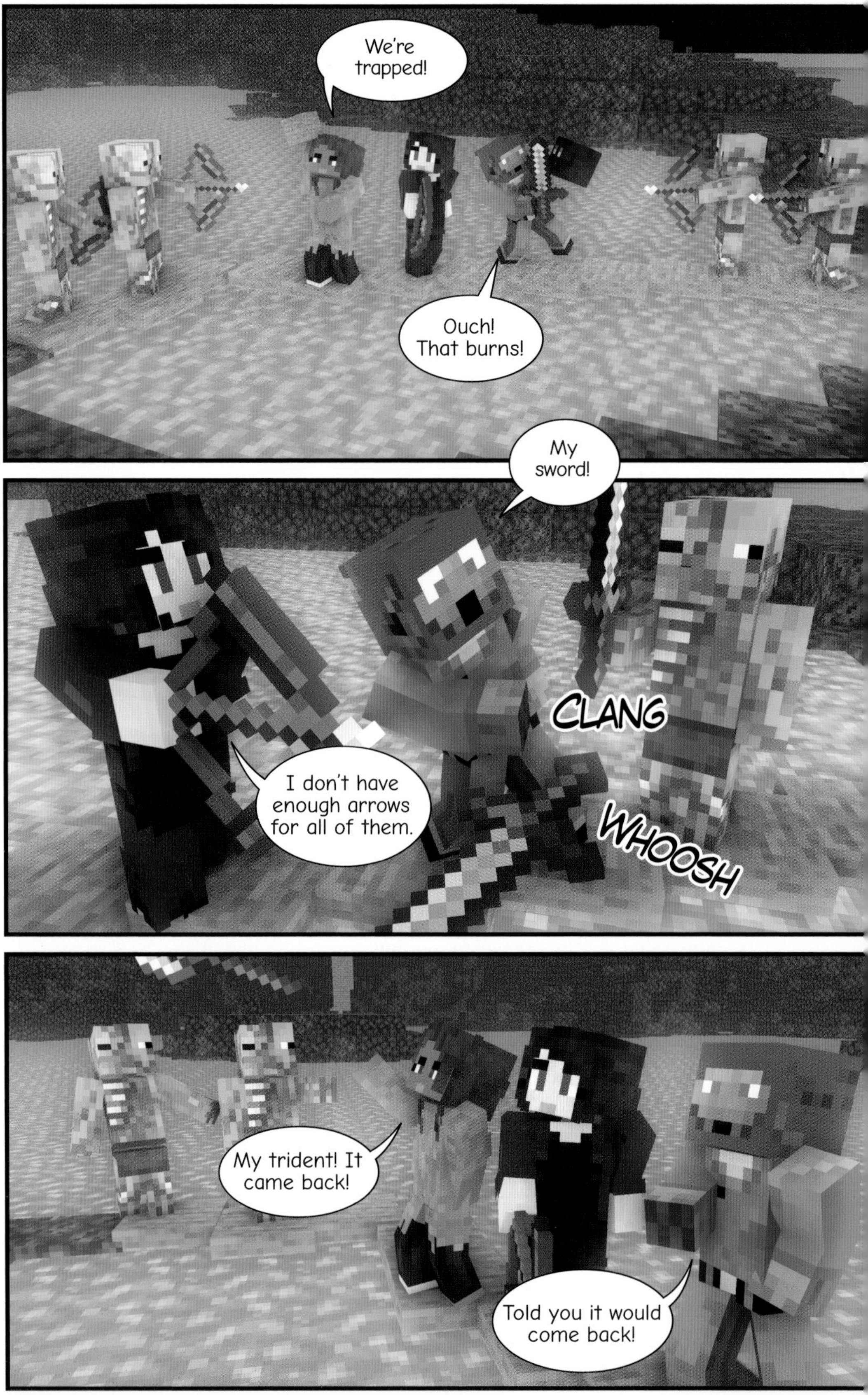

We're trapped!
Ouch! That burns!
My sword!
CLANG
I don't have enough arrows for all of them.
WHOOSH
My trident! It came back!
Told you it would come back!

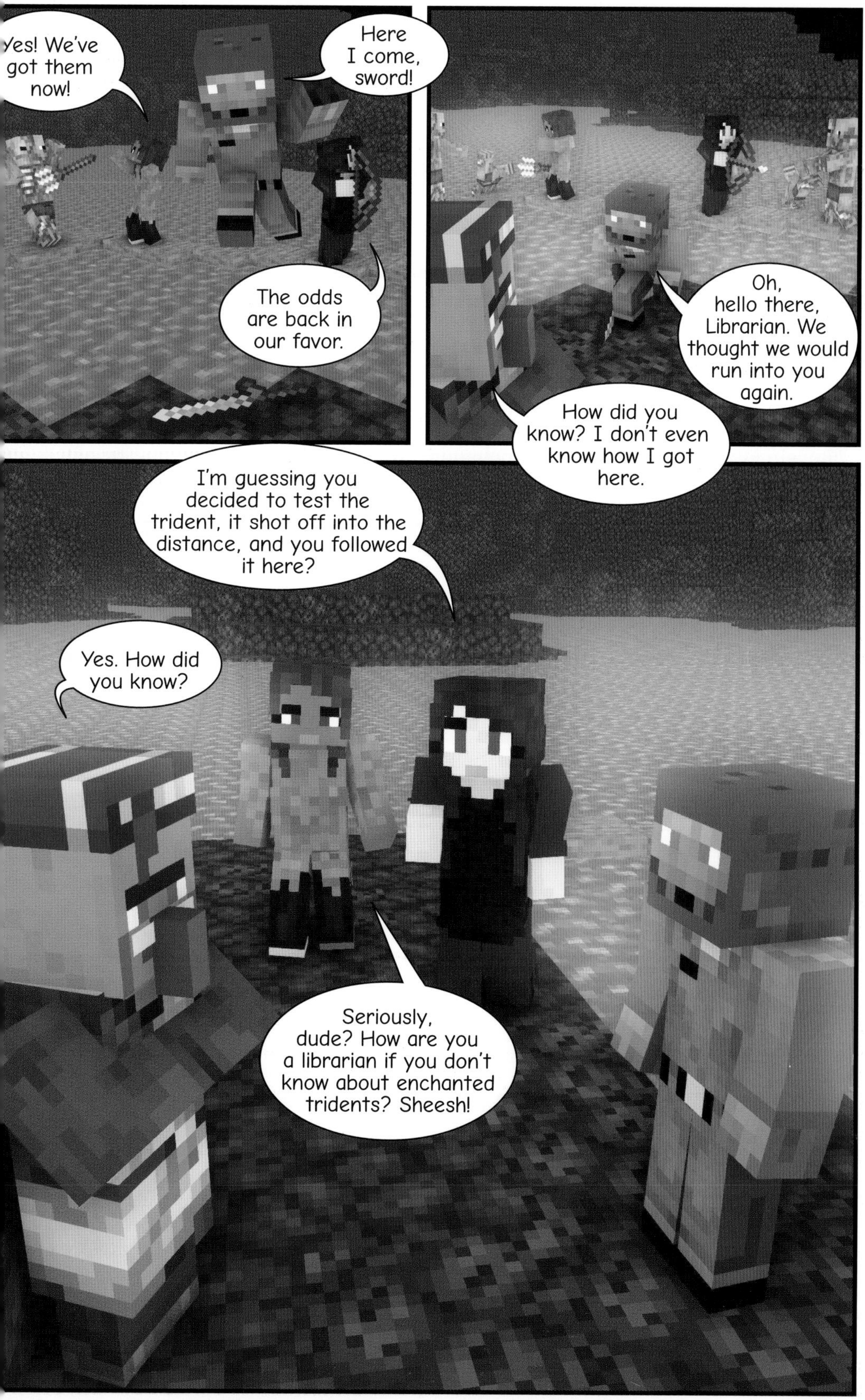

Yes! We've got them now!
Here I come, sword!
The odds are back in our favor.
Oh, hello there, Librarian. We thought we would run into you again.
How did you know? I don't even know how I got here.
I'm guessing you decided to test the trident, it shot off into the distance, and you followed it here?
Yes. How did you know?
Seriously, dude? How are you a librarian if you don't know about enchanted tridents? Sheesh!

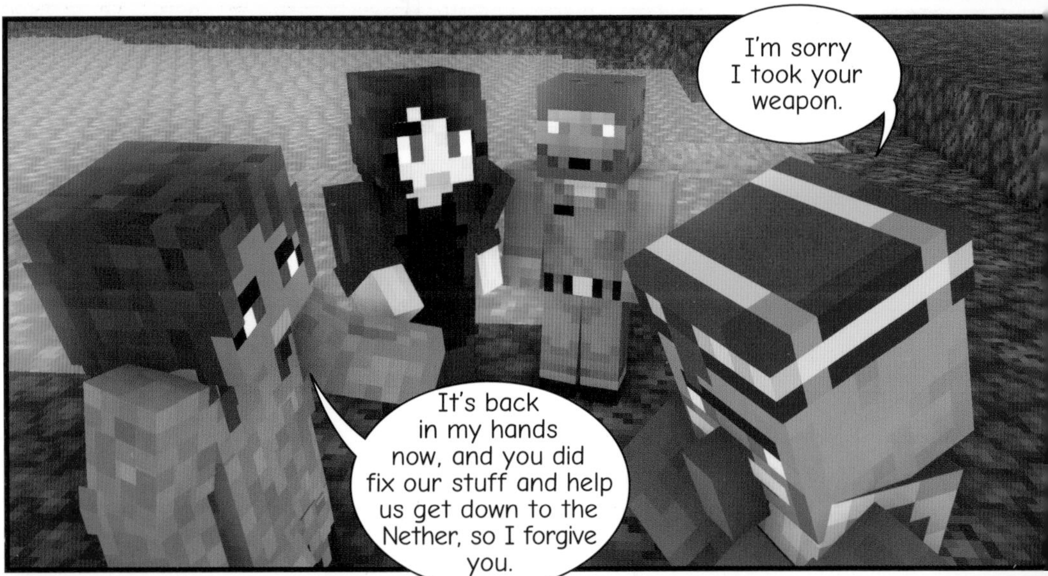
I'm sorry I took your weapon.
It's back in my hands now, and you did fix our stuff and help us get down to the Nether, so I forgive you.
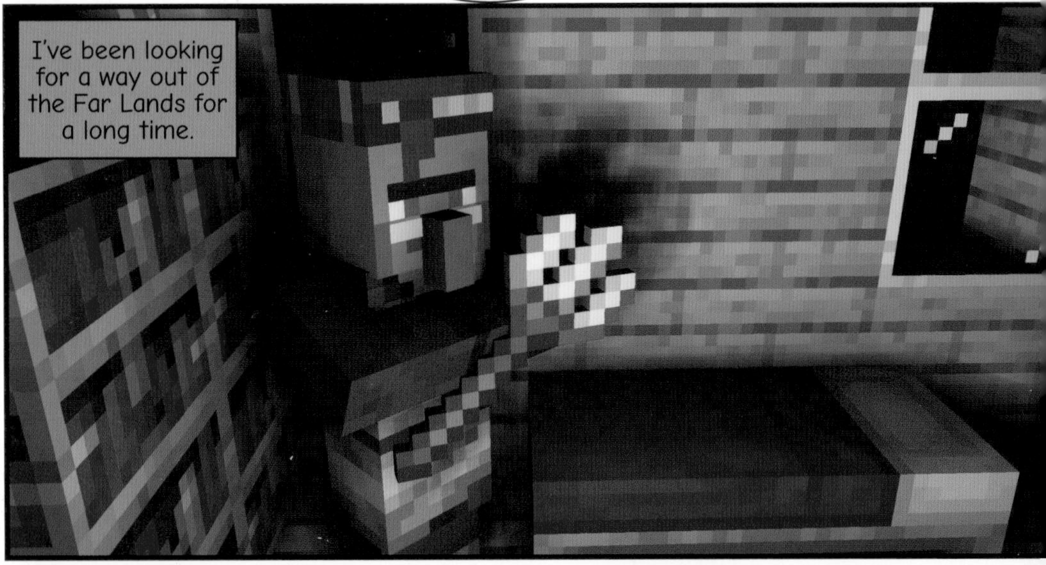
I've been looking for a way out of the Far Lands for a long time.
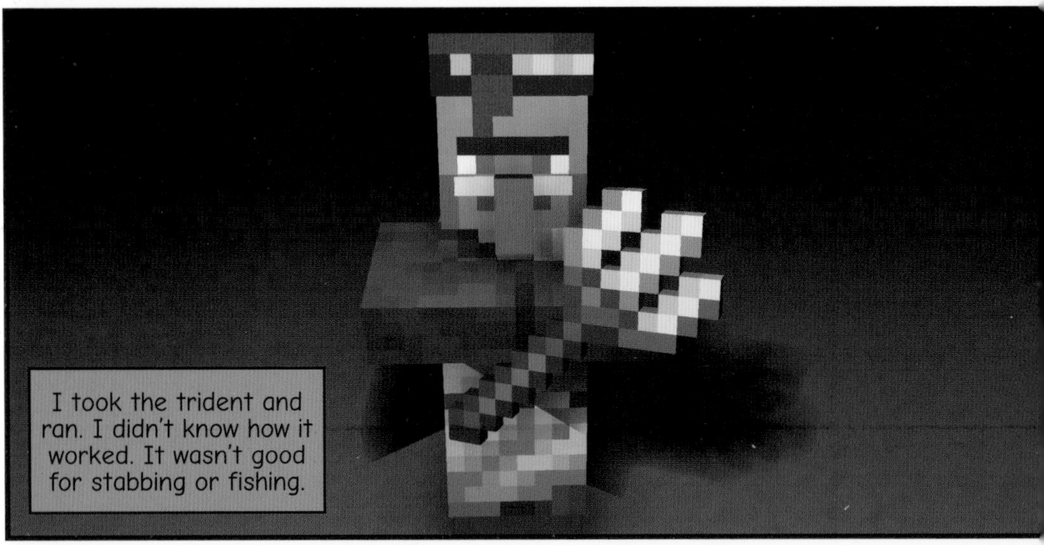
I took the trident and ran. I didn't know how it worked. It wasn't good for stabbing or fishing.

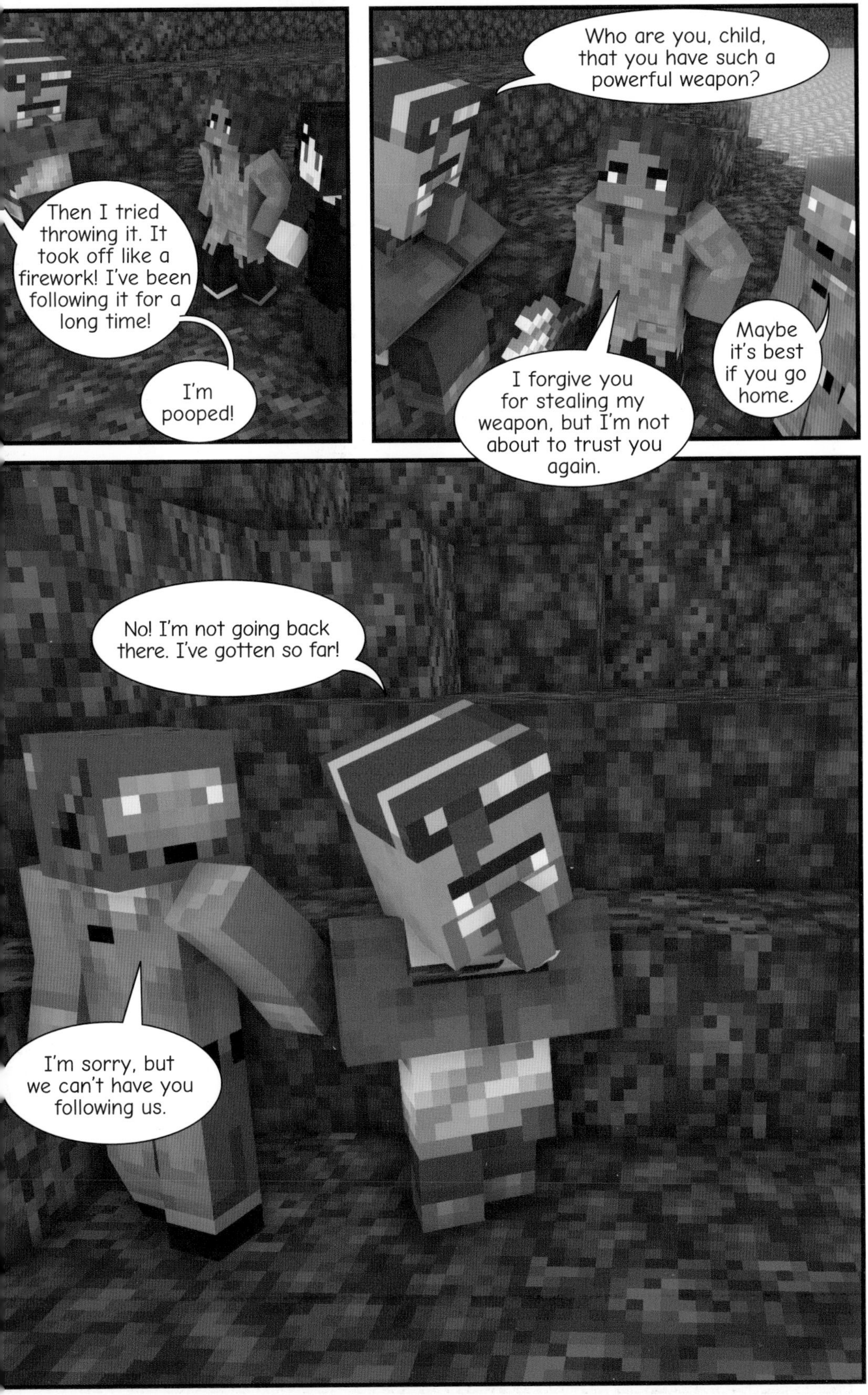
Then I tried throwing it. It took off like a firework! I've been following it for a long time!
I'm pooped!
Who are you, child, that you have such a powerful weapon?
I forgive you for stealing my weapon, but I'm not about to trust you again.
Maybe it's best if you go home.
No! I'm not going back there. I've gotten so far!
I'm sorry, but we can't have you following us.

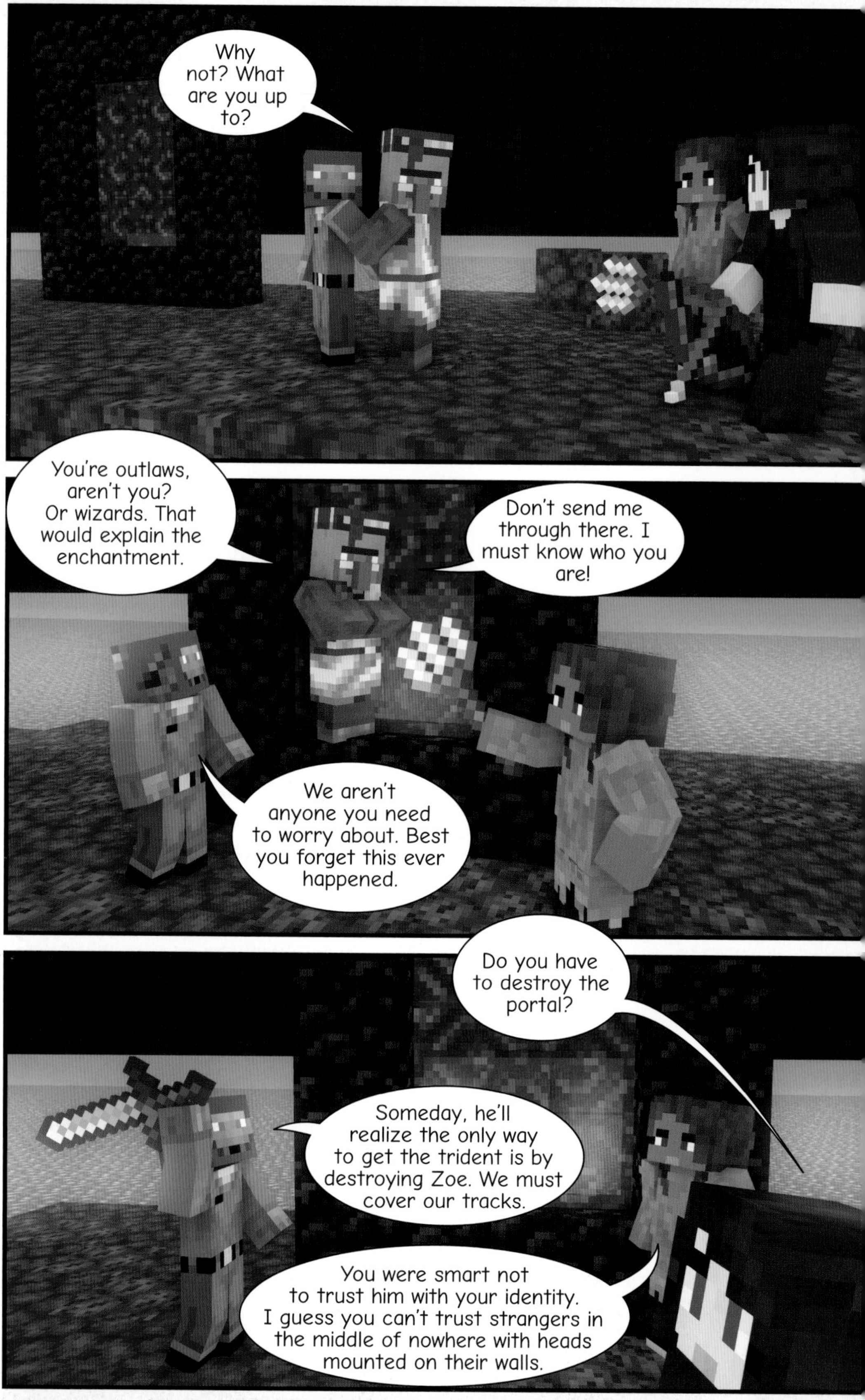
Why not? What are you up to?
You're outlaws, aren't you? Or wizards. That would explain the enchantment.
Don't send me through there. I must know who you are!
We aren't anyone you need to worry about. Best you forget this ever happened.
Do you have to destroy the portal?
Someday, he'll realize the only way to get the trident is by destroying Zoe. We must cover our tracks.
You were smart not to trust him with your identity. I guess you can't trust strangers in the middle of nowhere with heads mounted on their walls.

# CHAPTER 9

# THE ENDLESS MINE

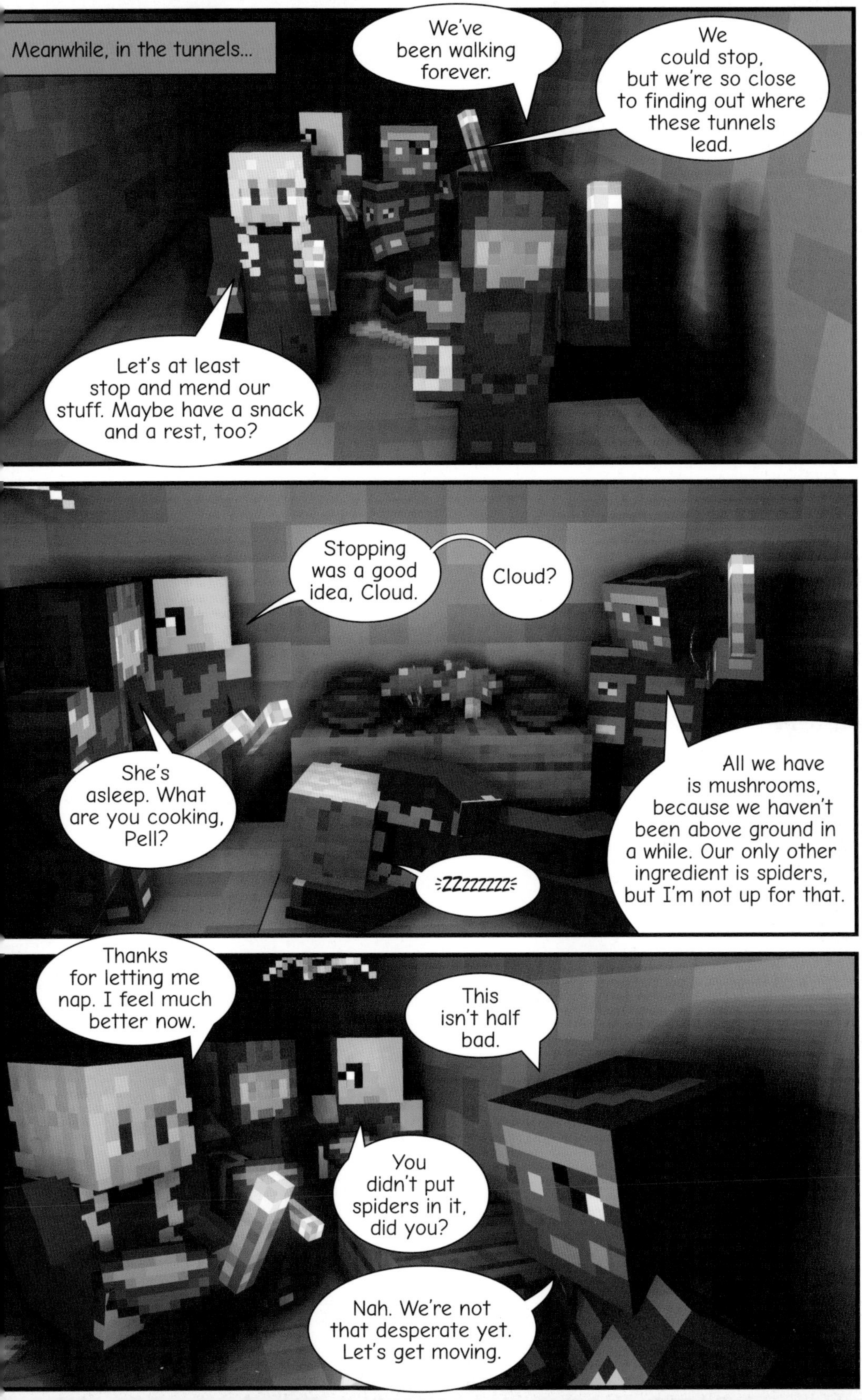
Meanwhile, in the tunnels...
We've been walking forever.
We could stop, but we're so close to finding out where these tunnels lead.
Let's at least stop and mend our stuff. Maybe have a snack and a rest, too?
Stopping was a good idea, Cloud.
Cloud?
She's asleep. What are you cooking, Pell?
ZZZZZZZZ
All we have is mushrooms, because we haven't been above ground in a while. Our only other ingredient is spiders, but I'm not up for that.
Thanks for letting me nap. I feel much better now.
This isn't half bad.
You didn't put spiders in it, did you?
Nah. We're not that desperate yet. Let's get moving.

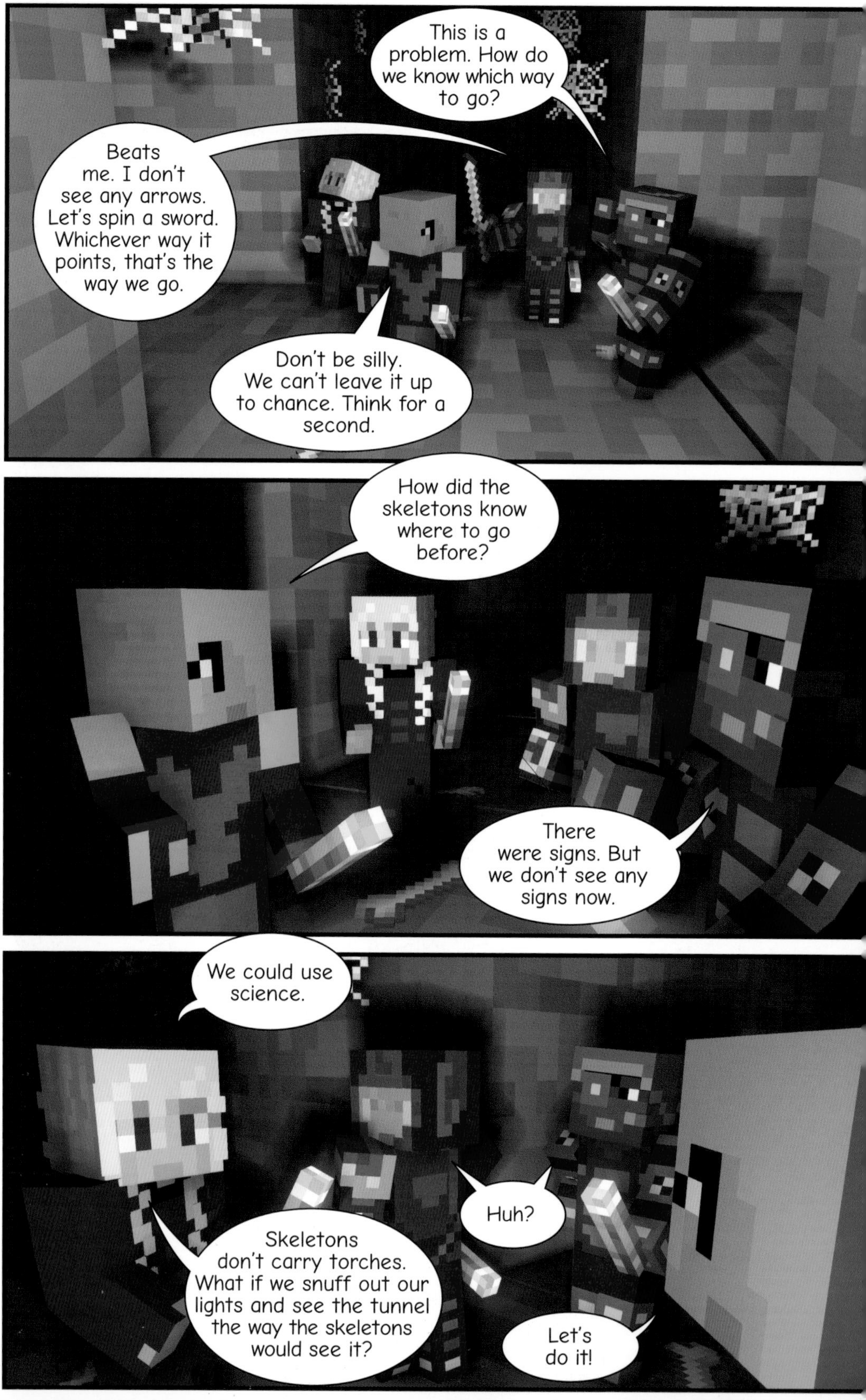
This is a problem. How do we know which way to go?
Beats me. I don't see any arrows. Let's spin a sword. Whichever way it points, that's the way we go.
Don't be silly. We can't leave it up to chance. Think for a second.
How did the skeletons know where to go before?
There were signs. But we don't see any signs now.
We could use science.
Huh?
Skeletons don't carry torches. What if we snuff out our lights and see the tunnel the way the skeletons would see it?
Let's do it!

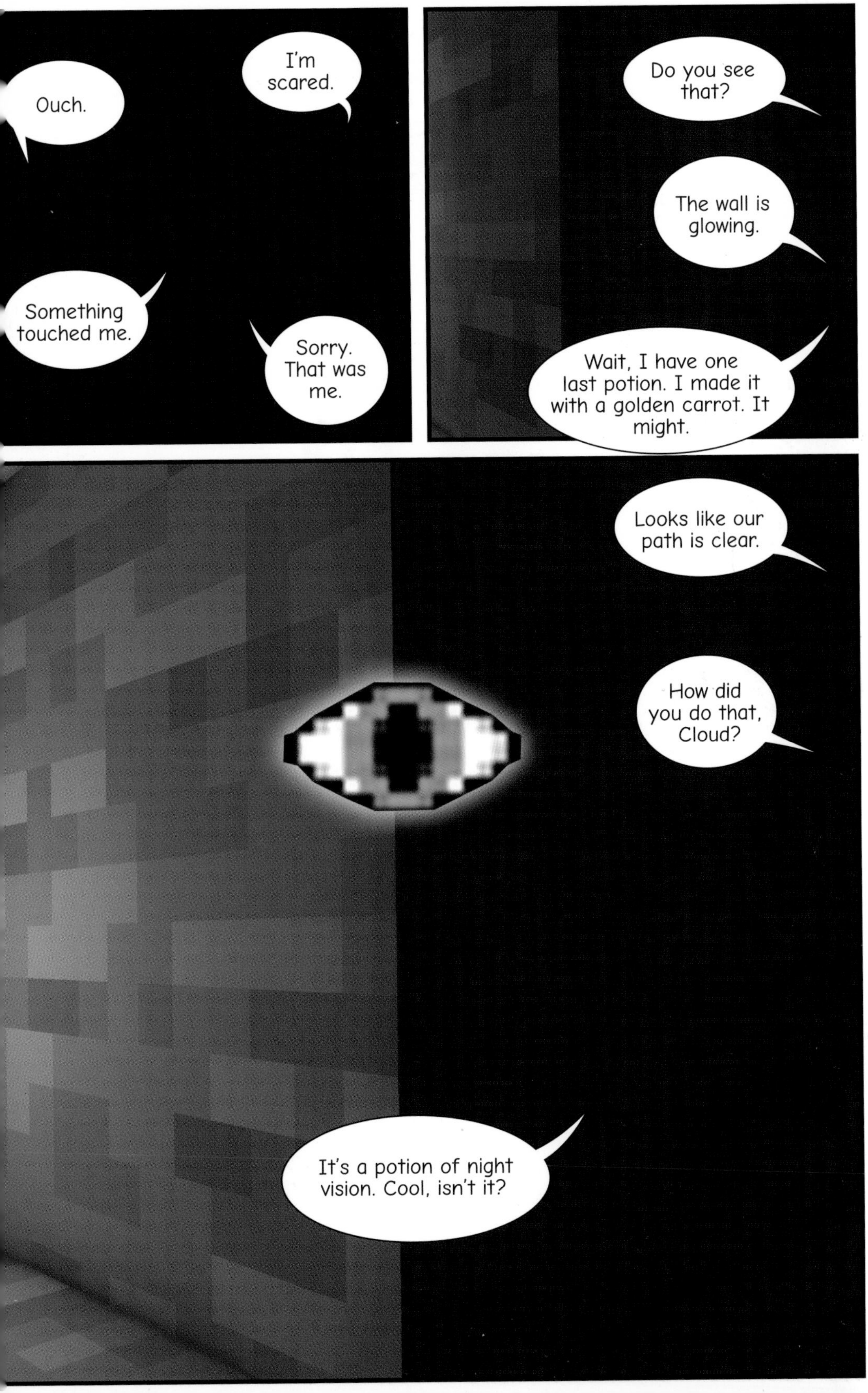
Ouch.
I'm scared.
Something touched me.
Sorry. That was me.
Do you see that?
The wall is glowing.
Wait, I have one last potion. I made it with a golden carrot. It might.
Looks like our path is clear.
How did you do that, Cloud?
It's a potion of night vision. Cool, isn't it?

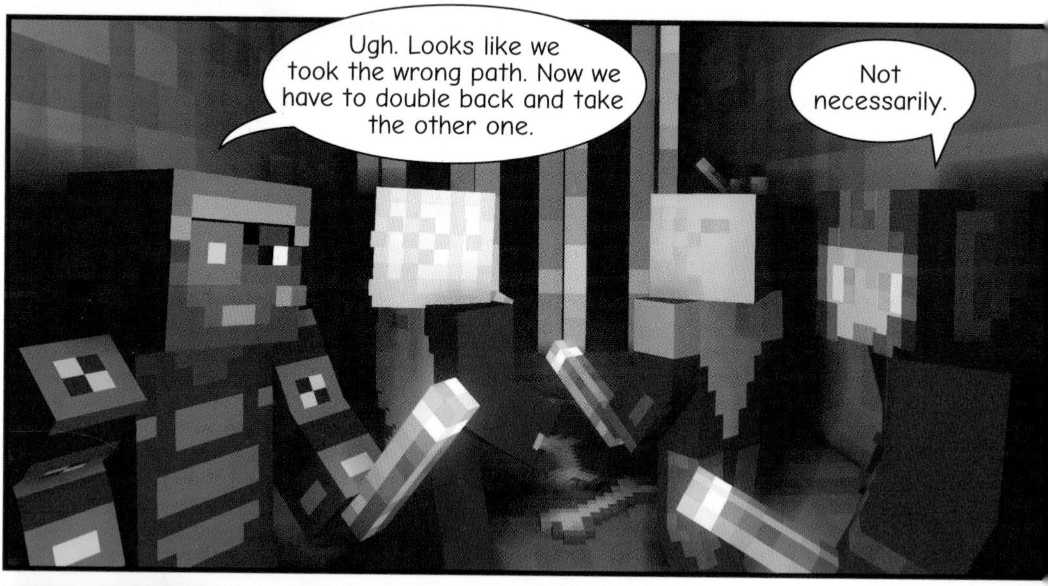
Ugh. Looks like we took the wrong path. Now we have to double back and take the other one.
Not necessarily.

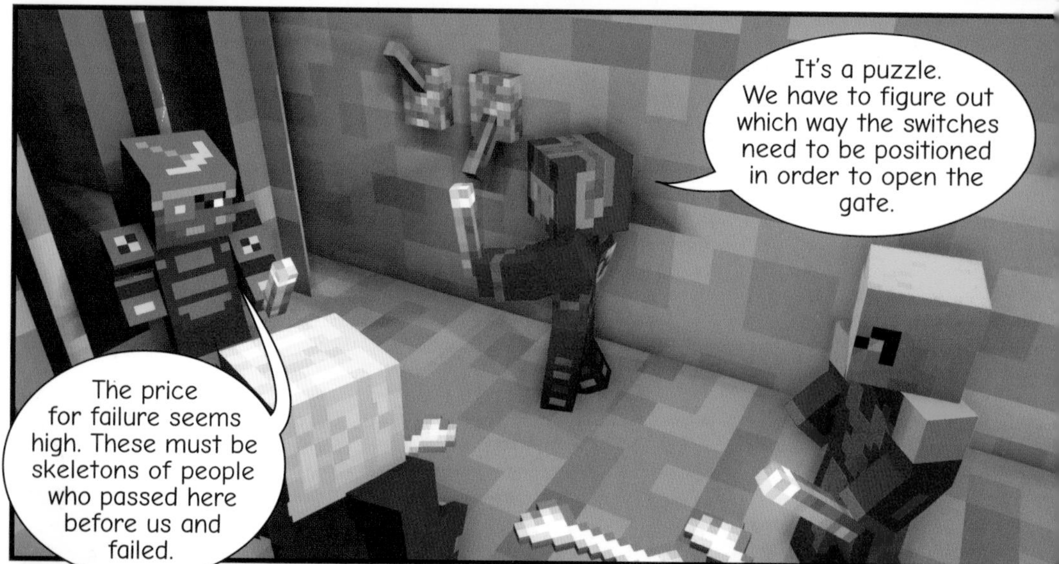
It's a puzzle. We have to figure out which way the switches need to be positioned in order to open the gate.
The price for failure seems high. These must be skeletons of people who passed here before us and failed.

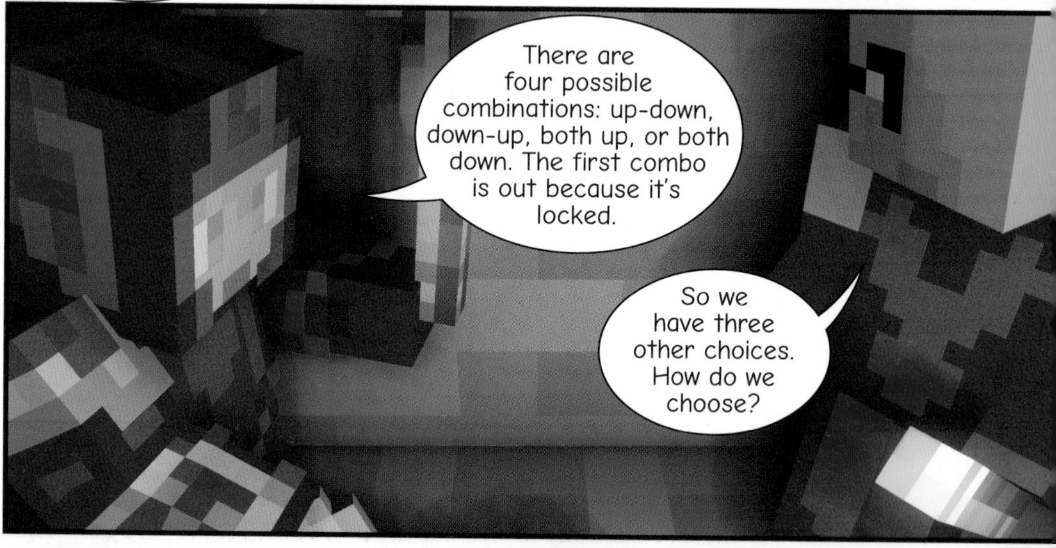
There are four possible combinations: up-down, down-up, both up, or both down. The first combo is out because it's locked.
So we have three other choices. How do we choose?

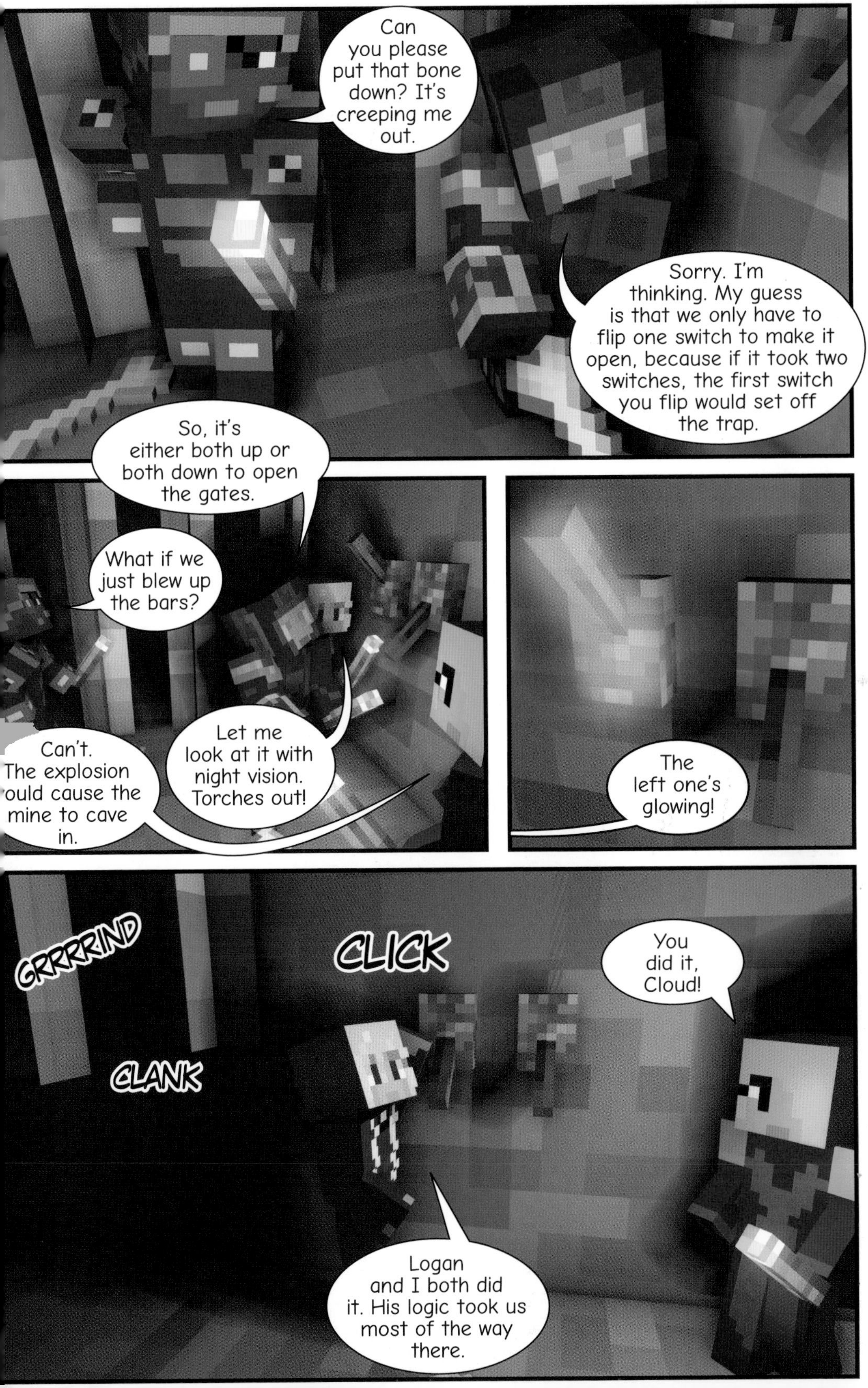
Can you please put that bone down? It's creeping me out.
Sorry. I'm thinking. My guess is that we only have to flip one switch to make it open, because if it took two switches, the first switch you flip would set off the trap.
So, it's either both up or both down to open the gates.
What if we just blew up the bars?
Can't. The explosion ould cause the mine to cave in.
Let me look at it with night vision. Torches out!
The left one's glowing!
GRRRRIND
CLICK
CLANK
You did it, Cloud!
Logan and I both did it. His logic took us most of the way there.

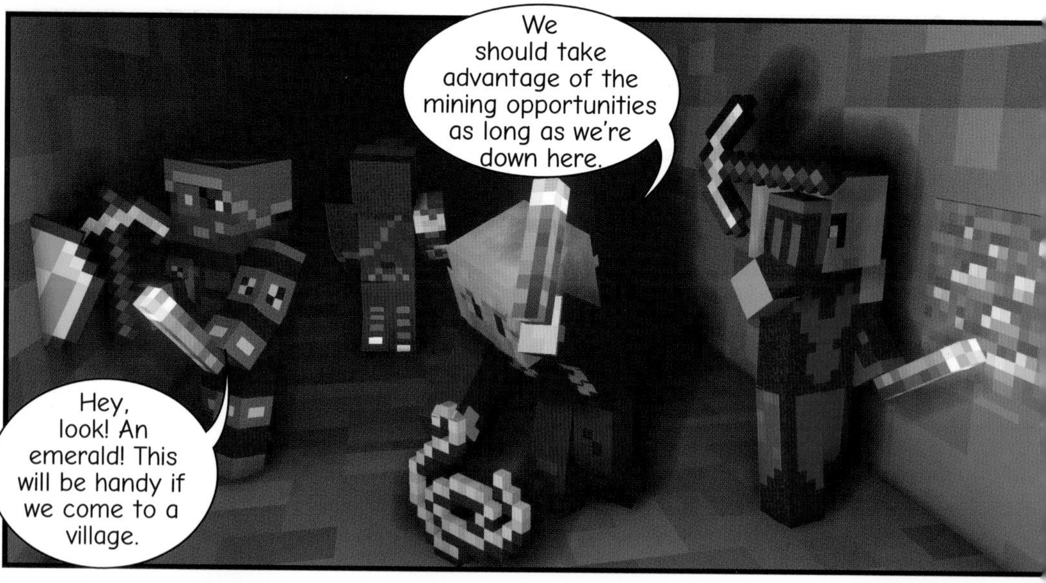
We should take advantage of the mining opportunities as long as we're down here.
Hey, look! An emerald! This will be handy if we come to a village.

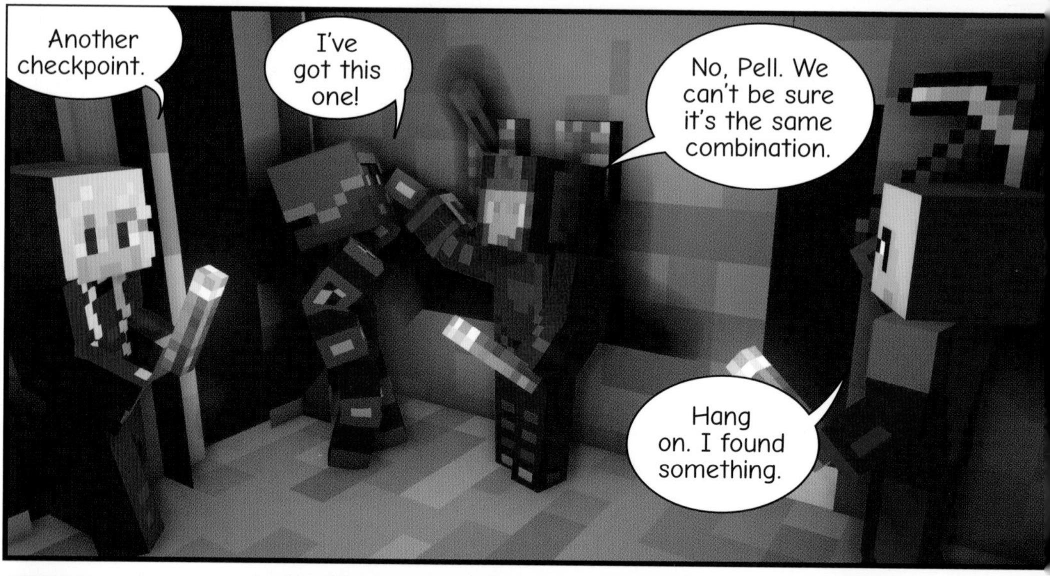
Another checkpoint.
I've got this one!
No, Pell. We can't be sure it's the same combination.
Hang on. I found something.

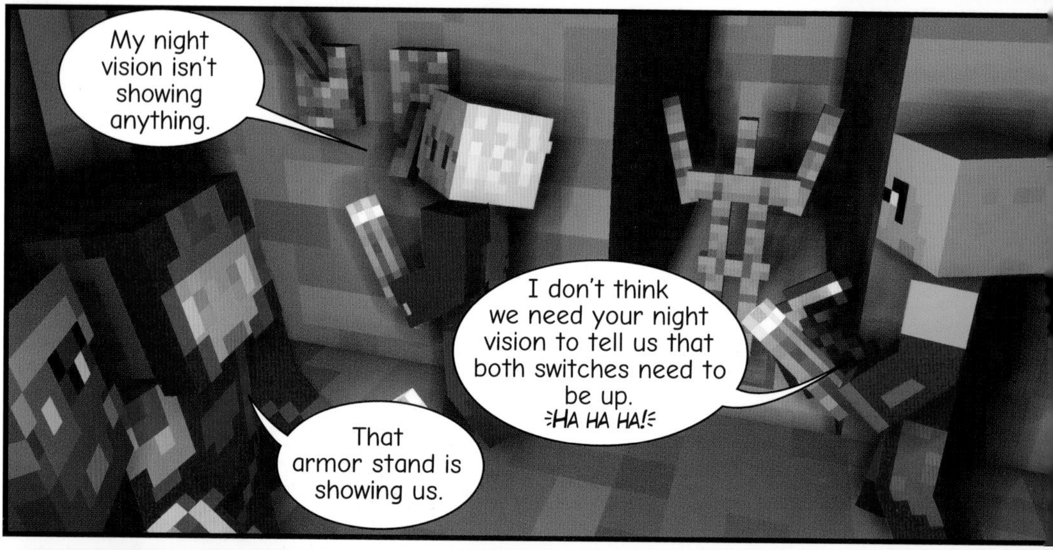
My night vision isn't showing anything.
I don't think we need your night vision to tell us that both switches need to be up.
HA HA HA!
That armor stand is showing us.

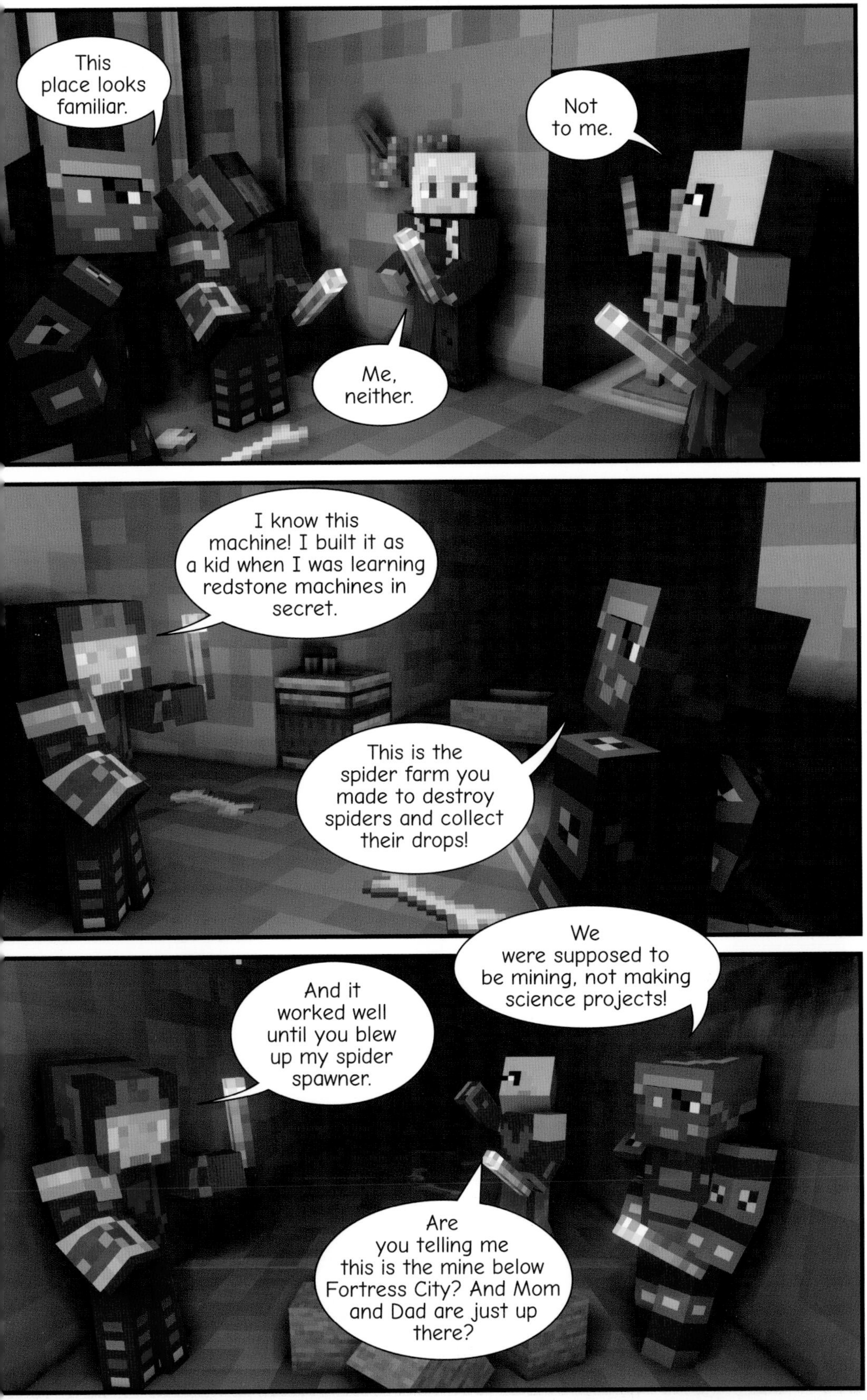
This place looks familiar.
Not to me.
Me, neither.
I know this machine! I built it as a kid when I was learning redstone machines in secret.
This is the spider farm you made to destroy spiders and collect their drops!
And it worked well until you blew up my spider spawner.
We were supposed to be mining, not making science projects!
Are you telling me this is the mine below Fortress City? And Mom and Dad are just up there?

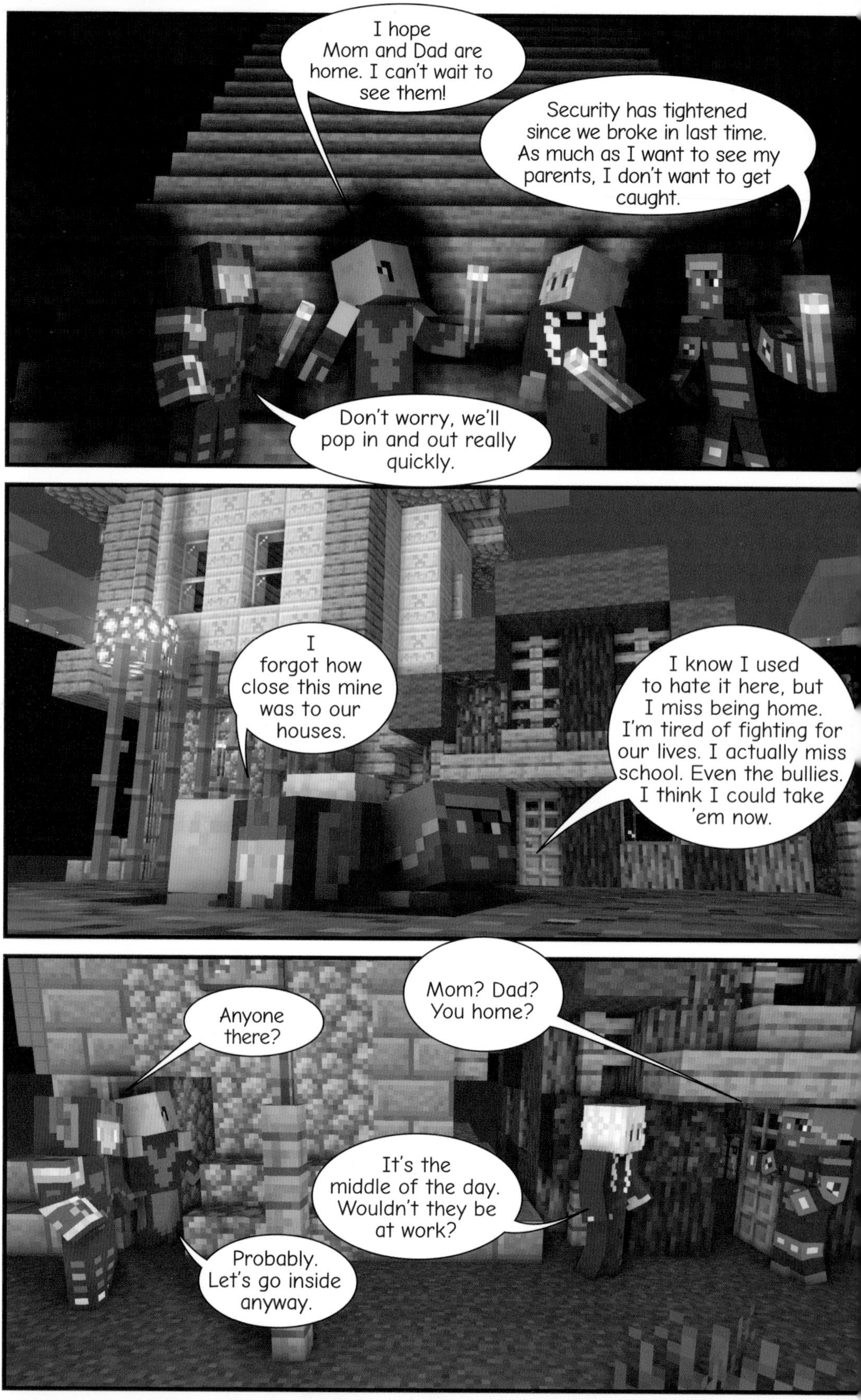
I hope Mom and Dad are home. I can't wait to see them!
Security has tightened since we broke in last time. As much as I want to see my parents, I don't want to get caught.
Don't worry, we'll pop in and out really quickly.
I forgot how close this mine was to our houses.
I know I used to hate it here, but I miss being home. I'm tired of fighting for our lives. I actually miss school. Even the bullies. I think I could take 'em now.
Anyone there?
Mom? Dad? You home?
It's the middle of the day. Wouldn't they be at work?
Probably. Let's go inside anyway.

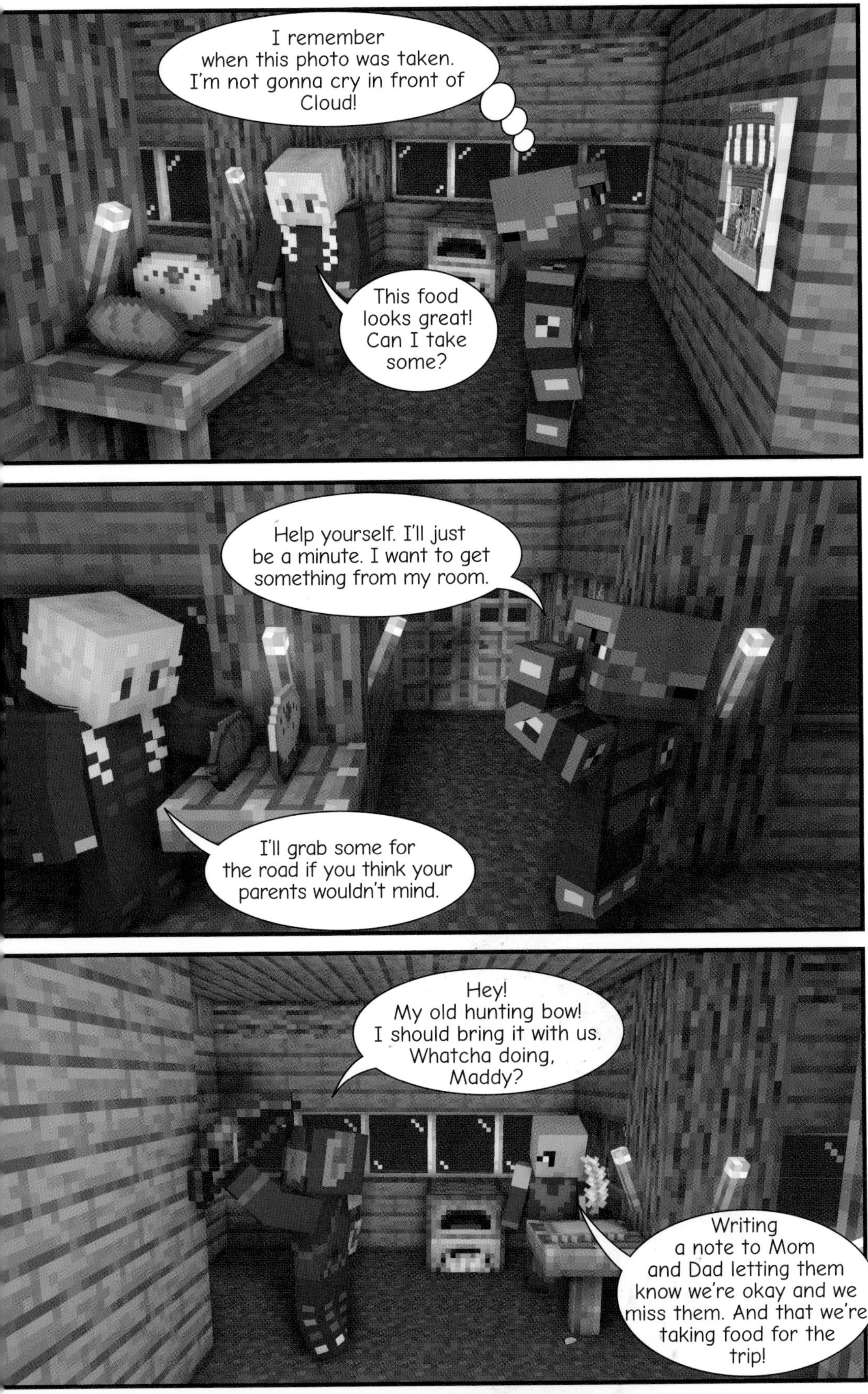
I remember when this photo was taken. I'm not gonna cry in front of Cloud!
This food looks great! Can I take some?
Help yourself. I'll just be a minute. I want to get something from my room.
I'll grab some for the road if you think your parents wouldn't mind.
Hey! My old hunting bow! I should bring it with us. Whatcha doing, Maddy?
Writing a note to Mom and Dad letting them know we're okay and we miss them. And that we're taking food for the trip!

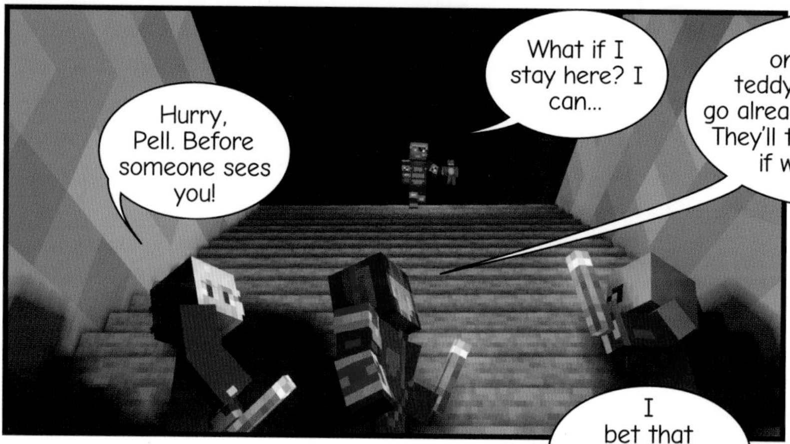

Hurry, Pell. Before someone sees you!
What if I stay here? I can...
Come on. Take your teddy bear and let's go already. We're outlaws. They'll throw us all in jail if we're caught.


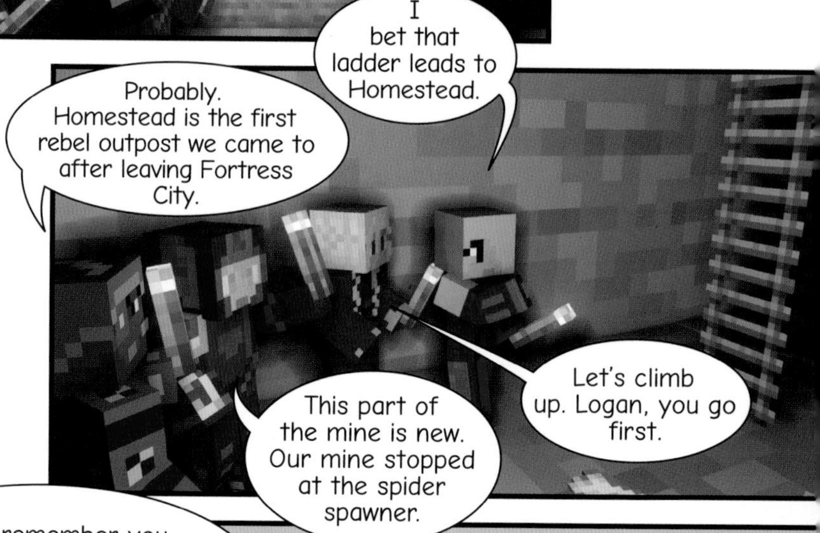

I bet that ladder leads to Homestead.
Probably. Homestead is the first rebel outpost we came to after leaving Fortress City.
This part of the mine is new. Our mine stopped at the spider spawner.
Let's climb up. Logan, you go first.


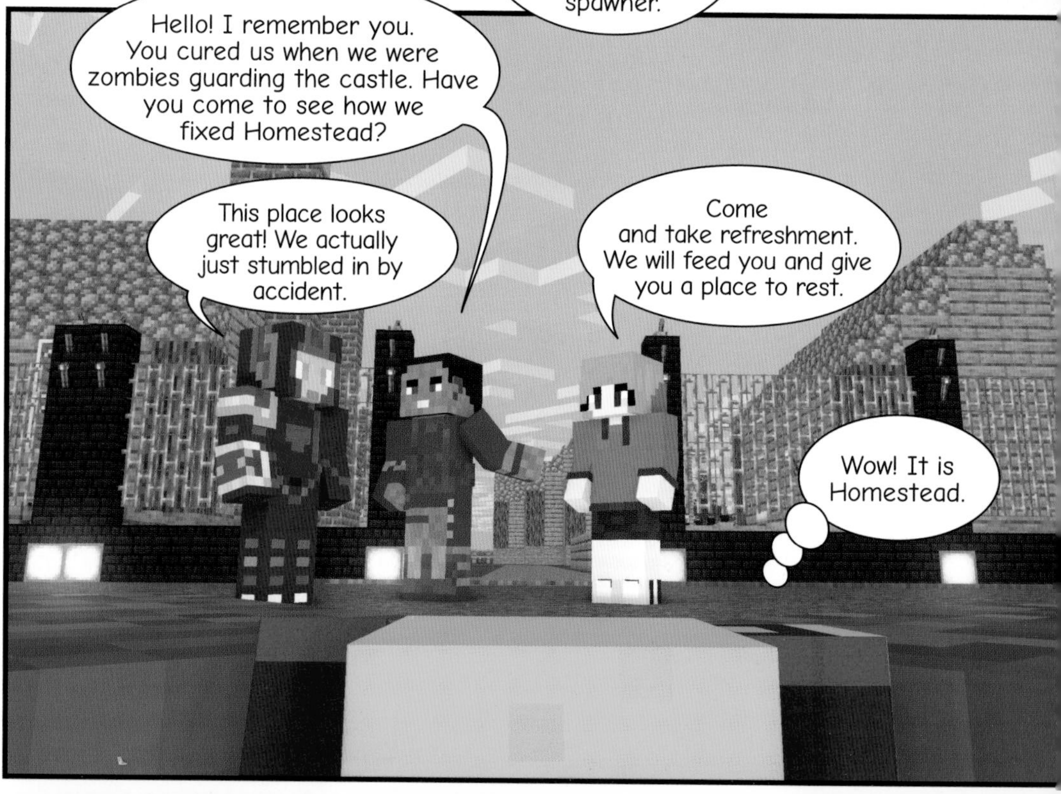

Hello! I remember you. You cured us when we were zombies guarding the castle. Have you come to see how we fixed Homestead?
This place looks great! We actually just stumbled in by accident.
Come and take refreshment. We will feed you and give you a place to rest.
Wow! It is Homestead.

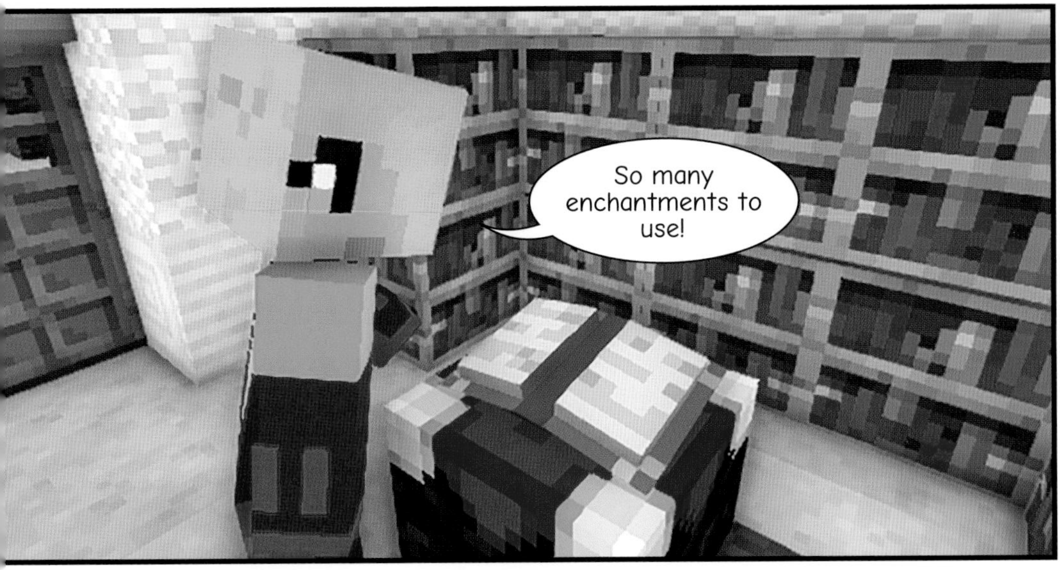
So many enchantments to use!

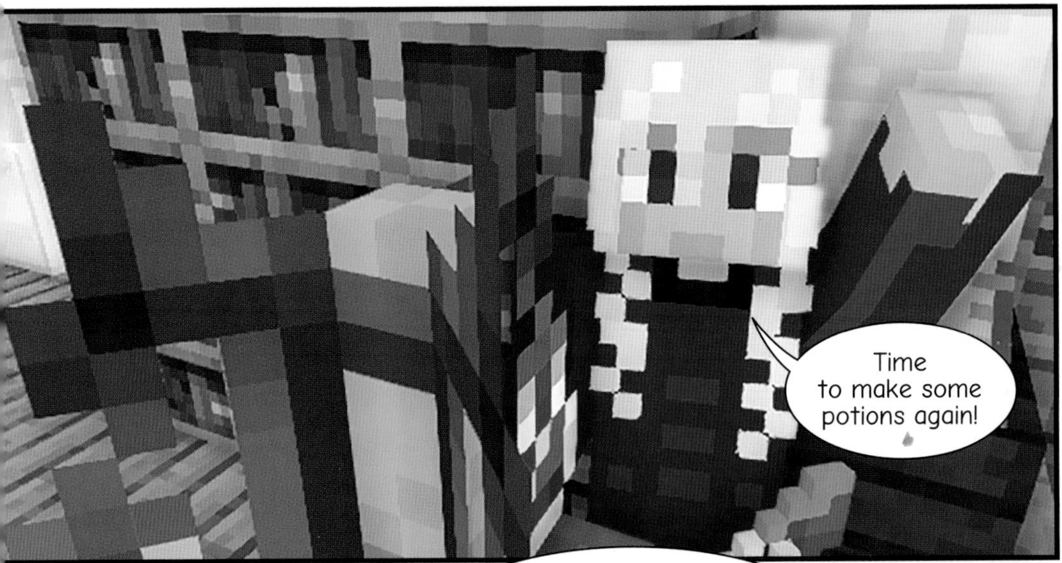
Time to make some potions again!

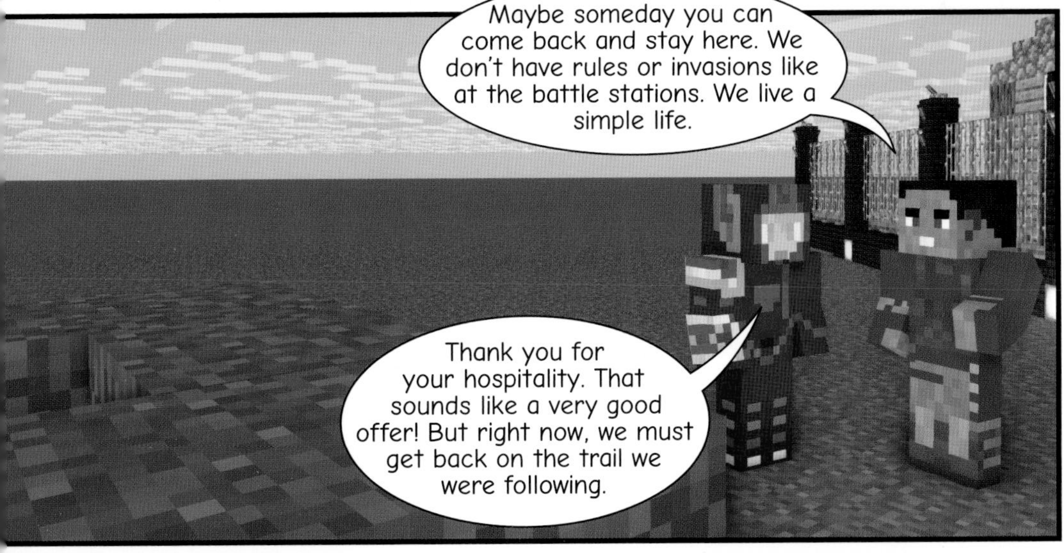
Maybe someday you can come back and stay here. We don't have rules or invasions like at the battle stations. We live a simple life.
Thank you for your hospitality. That sounds like a very good offer! But right now, we must get back on the trail we were following.

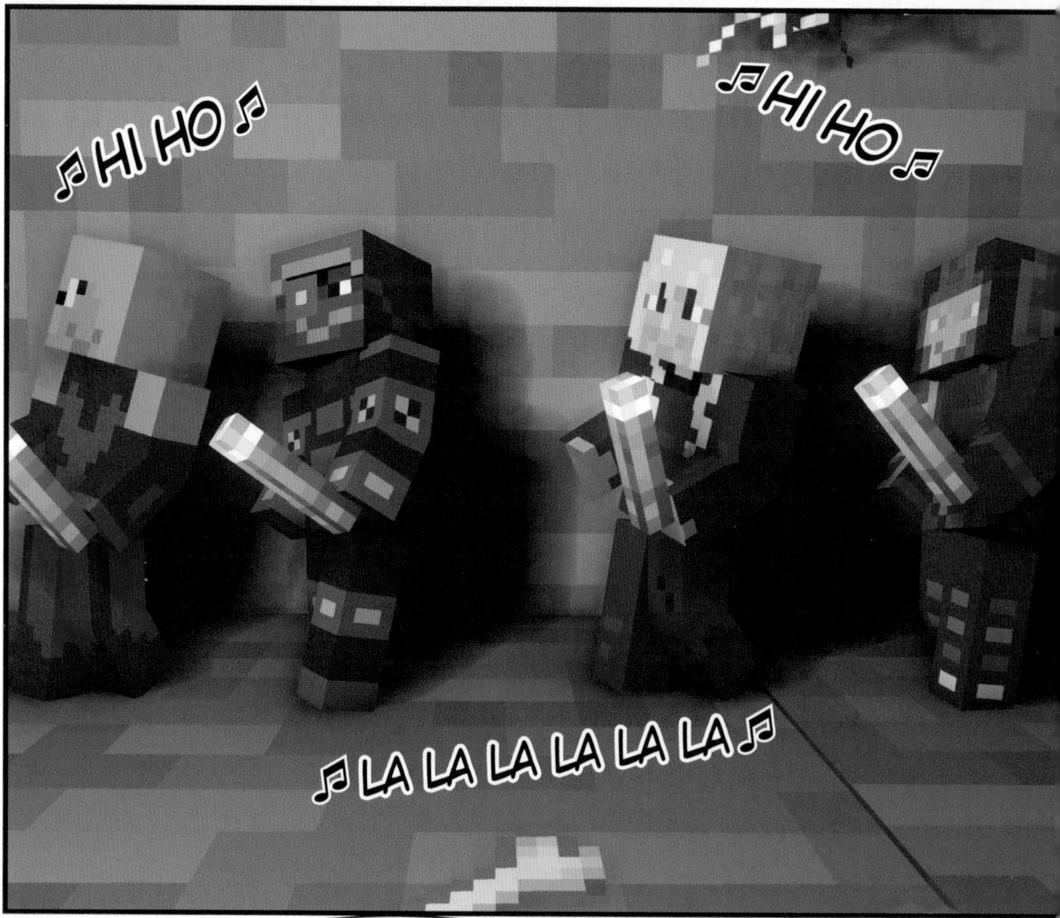
♫ HI HO ♫
♫ HI HO ♫
♫ LA LA LA LA LA LA ♫

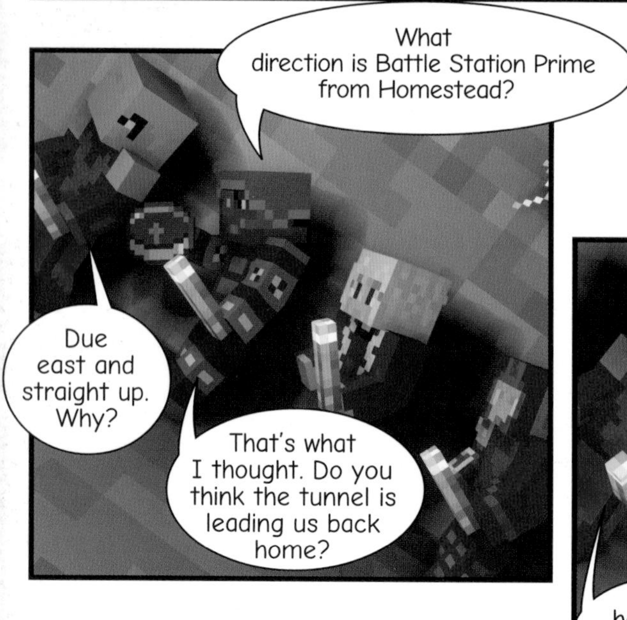
What direction is Battle Station Prime from Homestead?
Due east and straight up. Why?
That's what I thought. Do you think the tunnel is leading us back home?

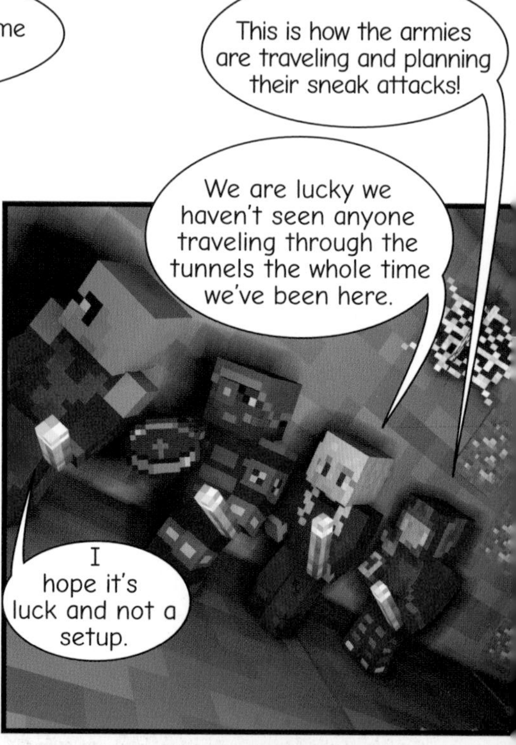
This is how the armies are traveling and planning their sneak attacks!
We are lucky we haven't seen anyone traveling through the tunnels the whole time we've been here.
I hope it's luck and not a setup.

# CHAPTER 10

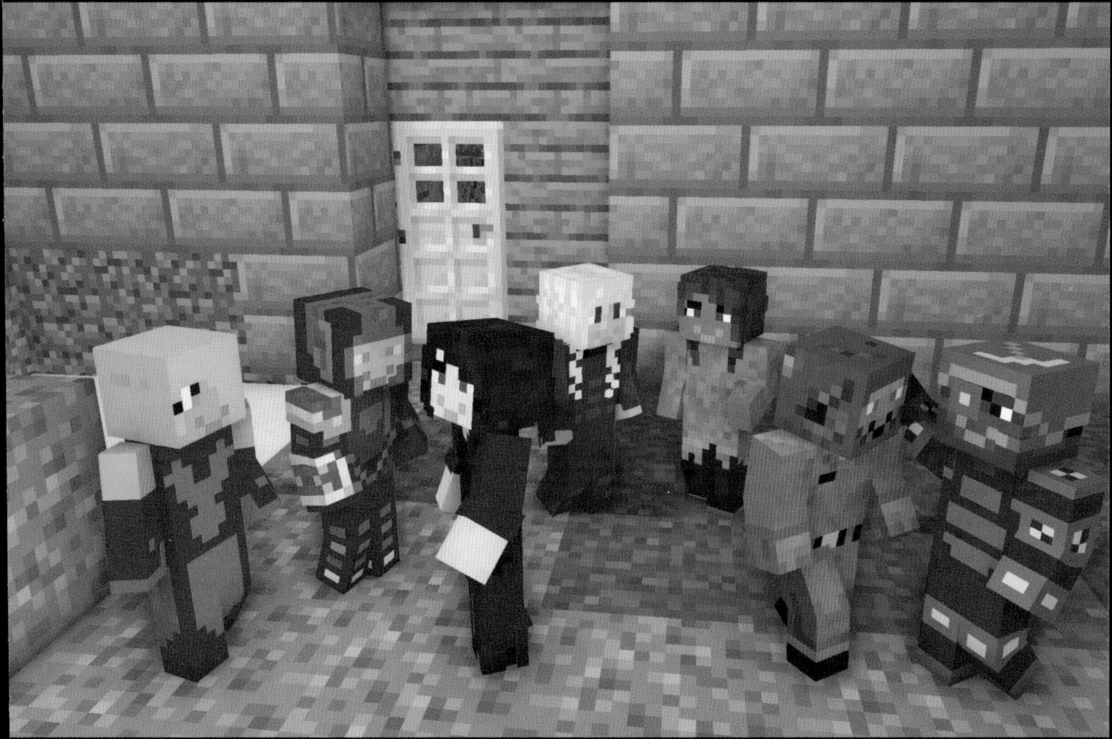

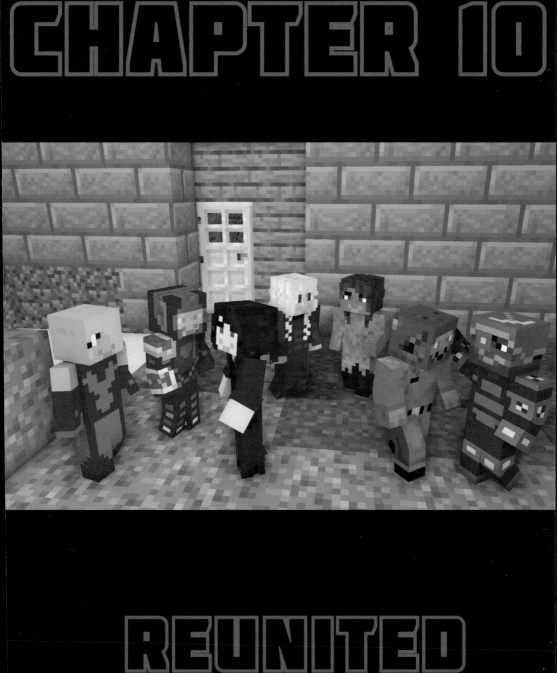

# REUNITED

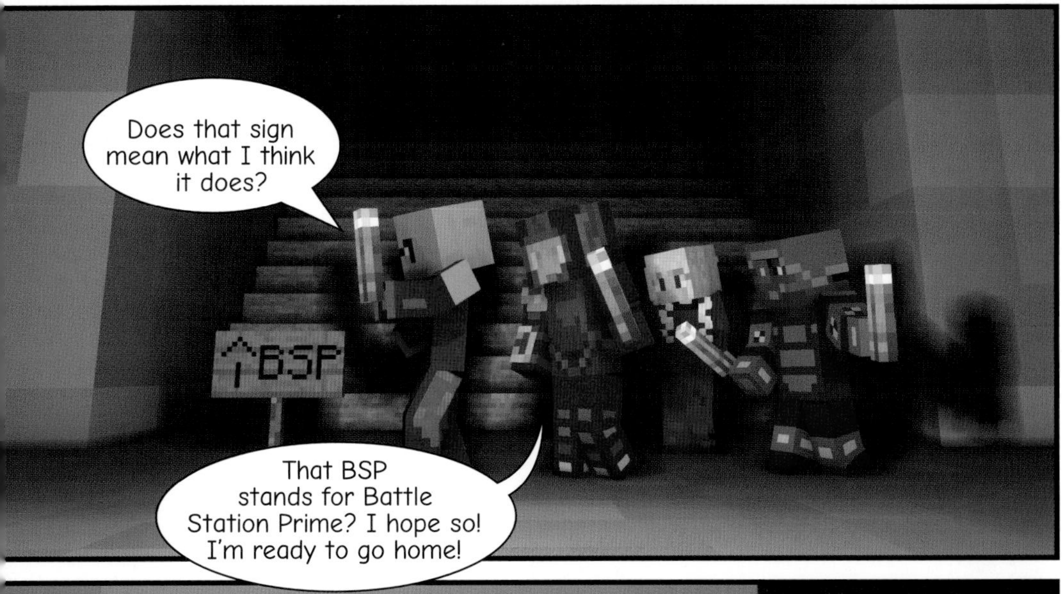
Does that sign mean what I think it does?
BSP
That BSP stands for Battle Station Prime? I hope so! I'm ready to go home!

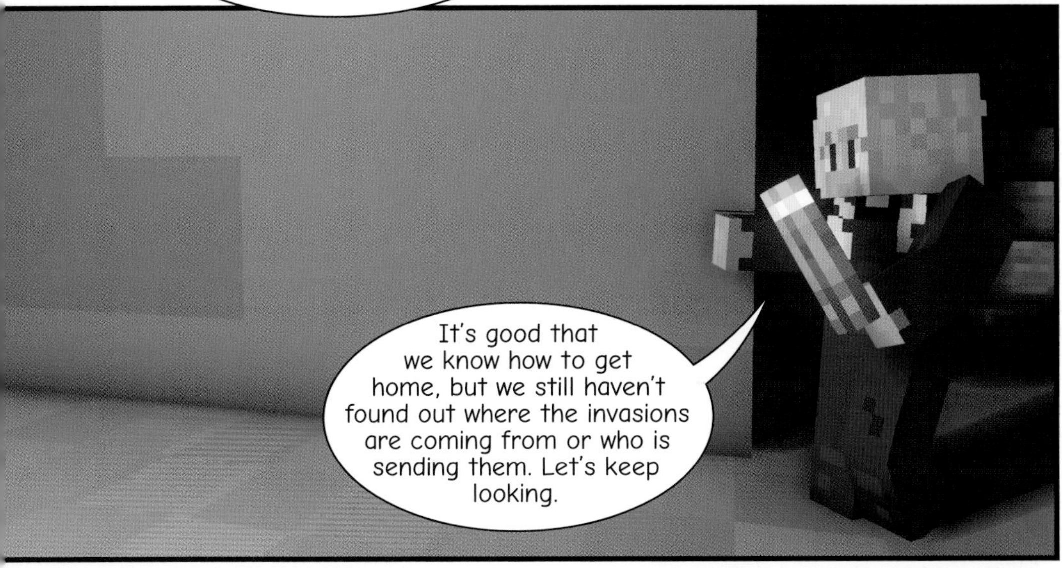
It's good that we know how to get home, but we still haven't found out where the invasions are coming from or who is sending them. Let's keep looking.

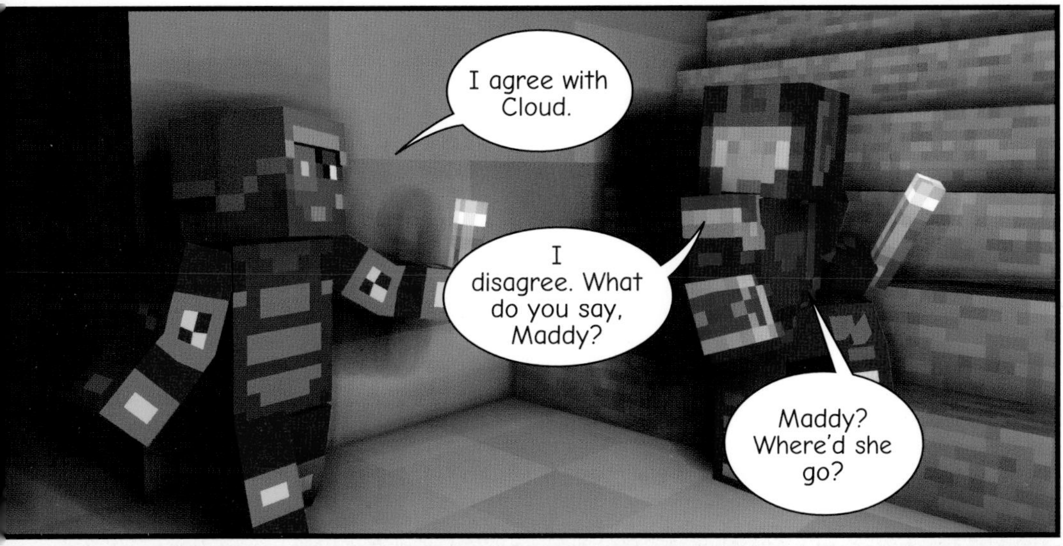
I agree with Cloud.
I disagree. What do you say, Maddy?
Maddy? Where'd she go?

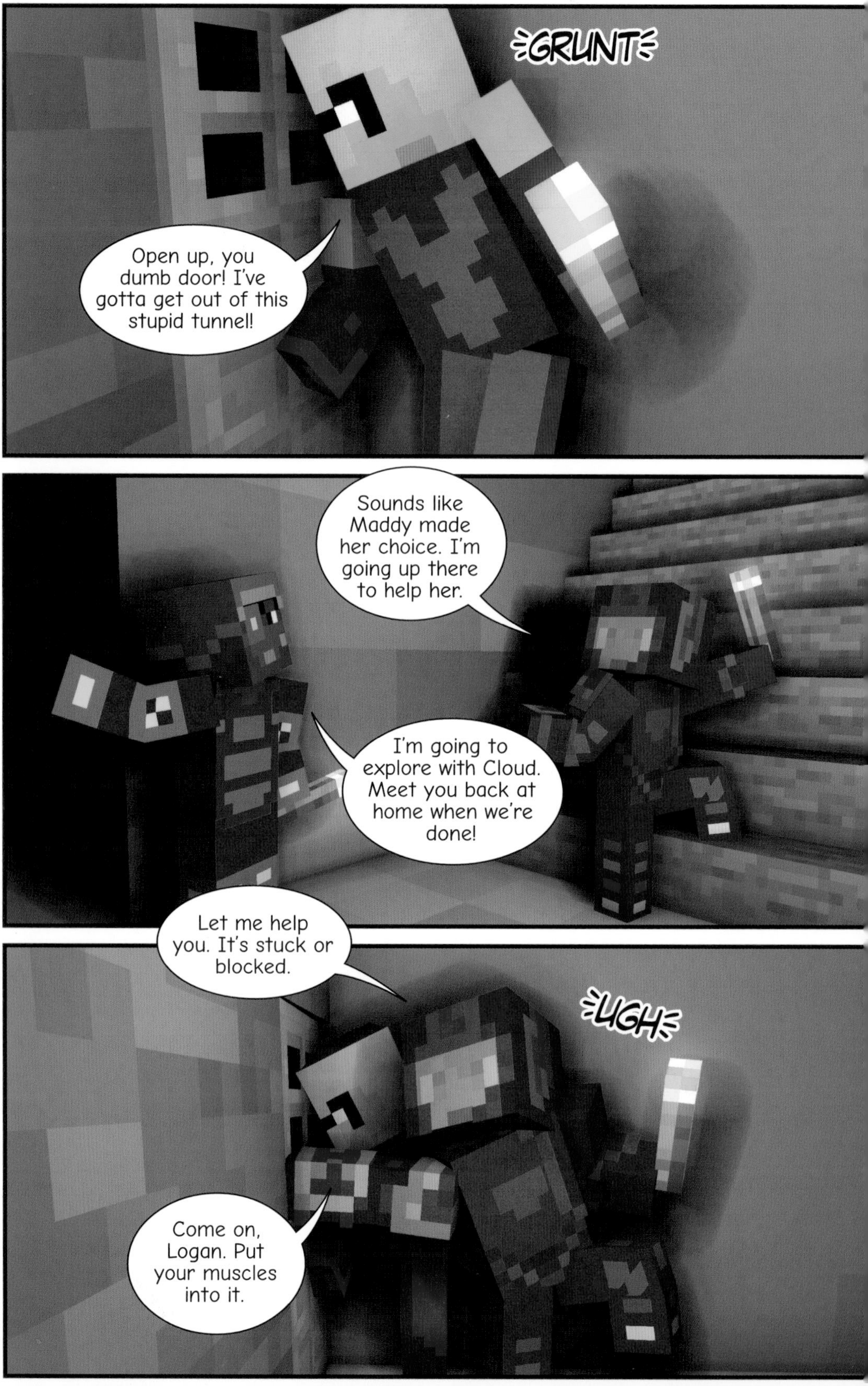
GRUNT
Open up, you dumb door! I've gotta get out of this stupid tunnel!
Sounds like Maddy made her choice. I'm going up there to help her.
I'm going to explore with Cloud. Meet you back at home when we're done!
Let me help you. It's stuck or blocked.
UGH
Come on, Logan. Put your muscles into it.

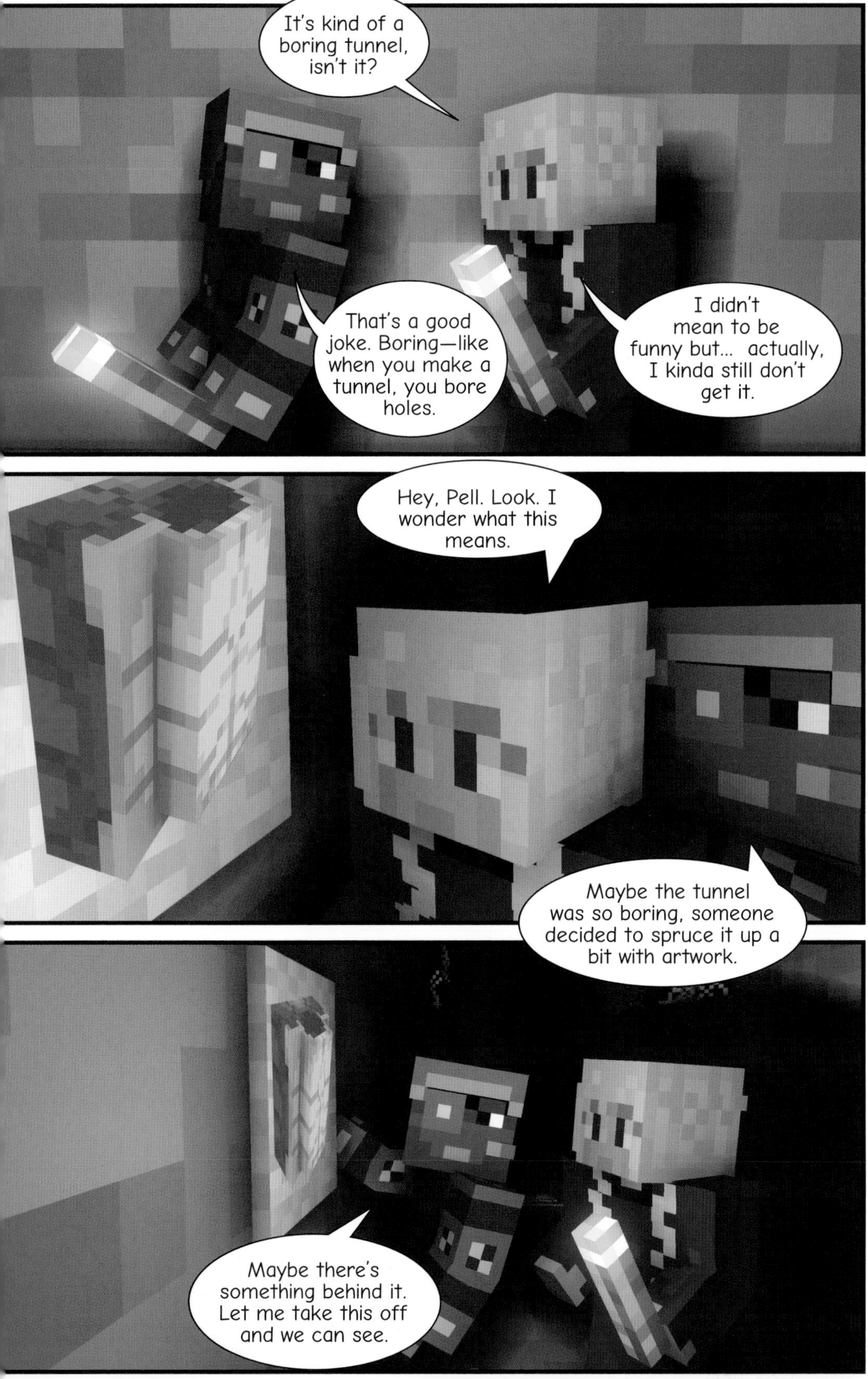
It's kind of a boring tunnel, isn't it?
That's a good joke. Boring—like when you make a tunnel, you bore holes.
I didn't mean to be funny but... actually, I kinda still don't get it.
Hey, Pell. Look. I wonder what this means.
Maybe the tunnel was so boring, someone decided to spruce it up a bit with artwork.
Maybe there's something behind it. Let me take this off and we can see.

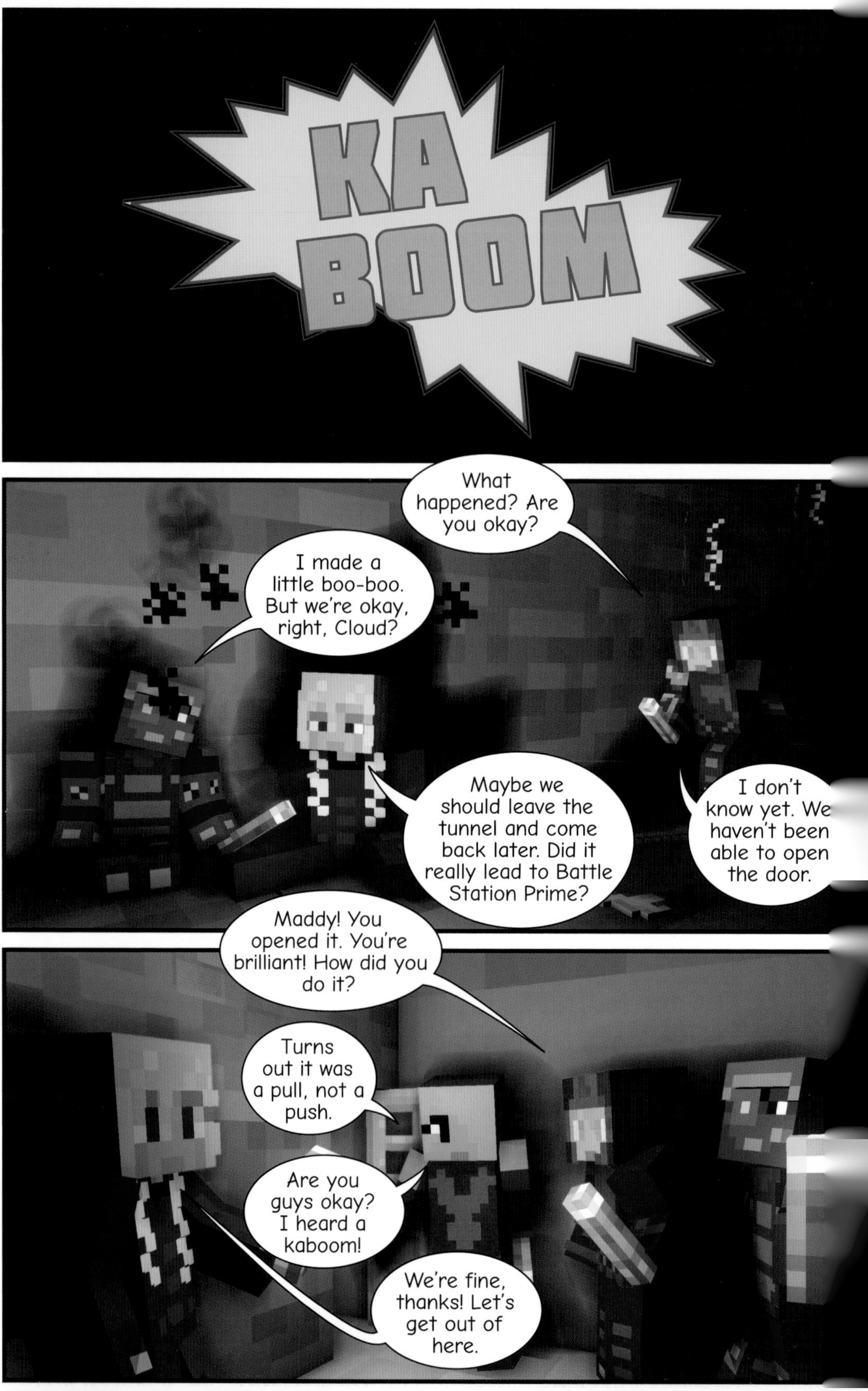
KA BOOM
What happened? Are you okay?
I made a little boo-boo. But we're okay, right, Cloud?
Maybe we should leave the tunnel and come back later. Did it really lead to Battle Station Prime?
I don't know yet. We haven't been able to open the door.
Maddy! You opened it. You're brilliant! How did you do it?
Turns out it was a pull, not a push.
Are you guys okay? I heard a kaboom!
We're fine, thanks! Let's get out of here.

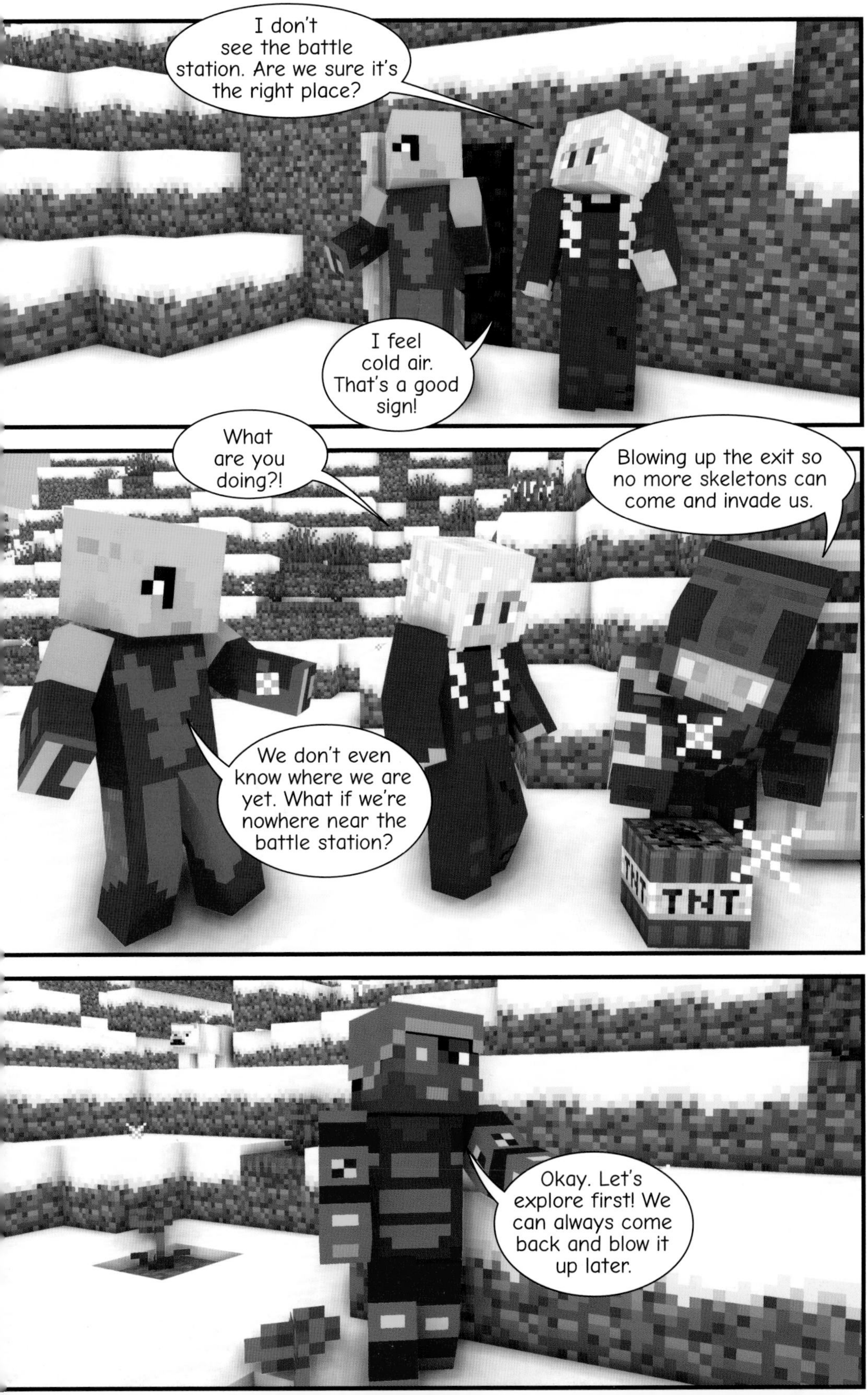
I don't see the battle station. Are we sure it's the right place?
I feel cold air. That's a good sign!
What are you doing?!
Blowing up the exit so no more skeletons can come and invade us.
We don't even know where we are yet. What if we're nowhere near the battle station?
TNT
Okay. Let's explore first! We can always come back and blow it up later.

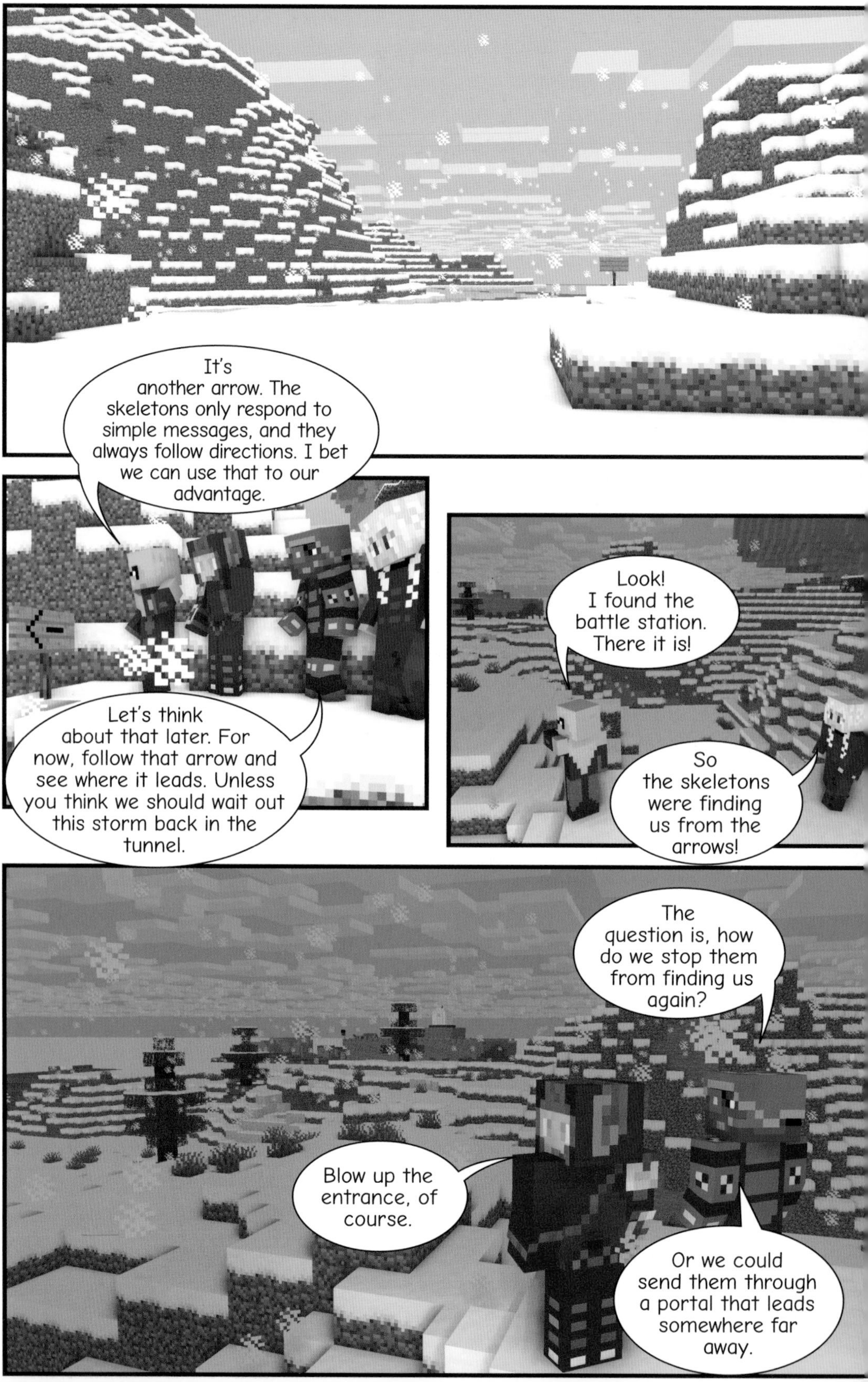
It's another arrow. The skeletons only respond to simple messages, and they always follow directions. I bet we can use that to our advantage.
Let's think about that later. For now, follow that arrow and see where it leads. Unless you think we should wait out this storm back in the tunnel.
Look! I found the battle station. There it is!
So the skeletons were finding us from the arrows!
The question is, how do we stop them from finding us again?
Blow up the entrance, of course.
Or we could send them through a portal that leads somewhere far away.

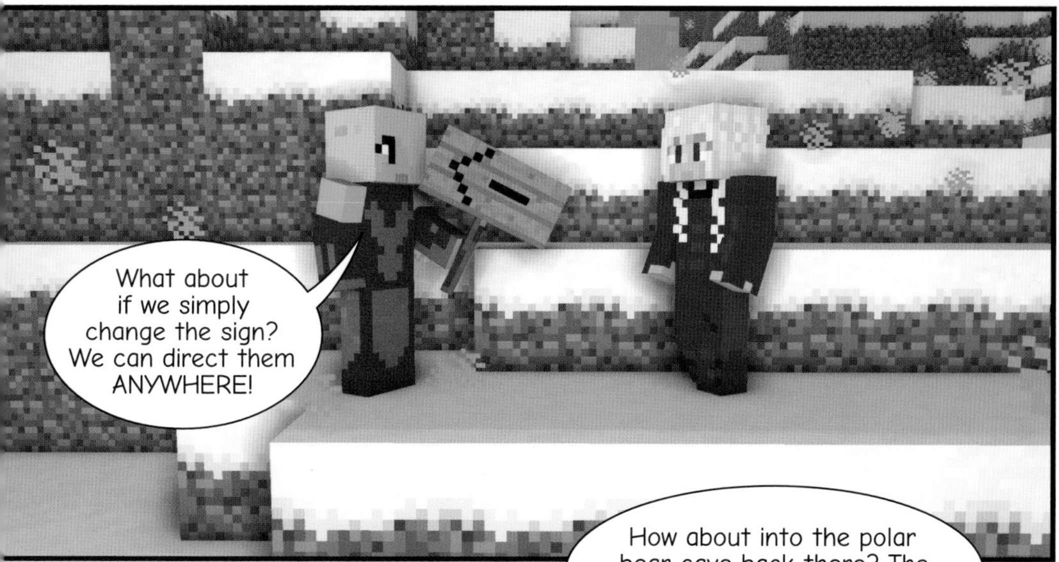
What about if we simply change the sign? We can direct them ANYWHERE!

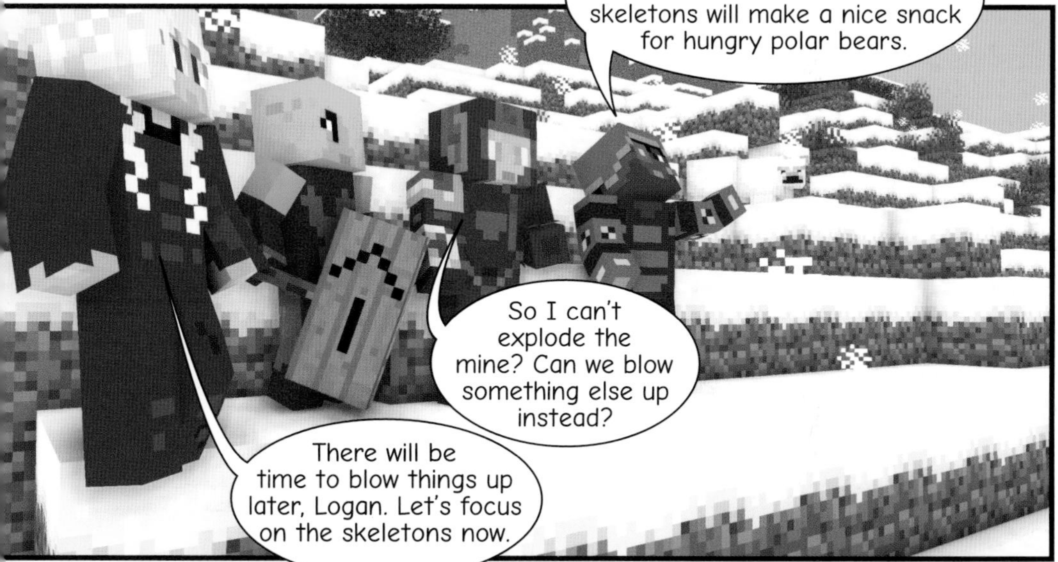
How about into the polar bear cave back there? The skeletons will make a nice snack for hungry polar bears.
So I can't explode the mine? Can we blow something else up instead?
There will be time to blow things up later, Logan. Let's focus on the skeletons now.

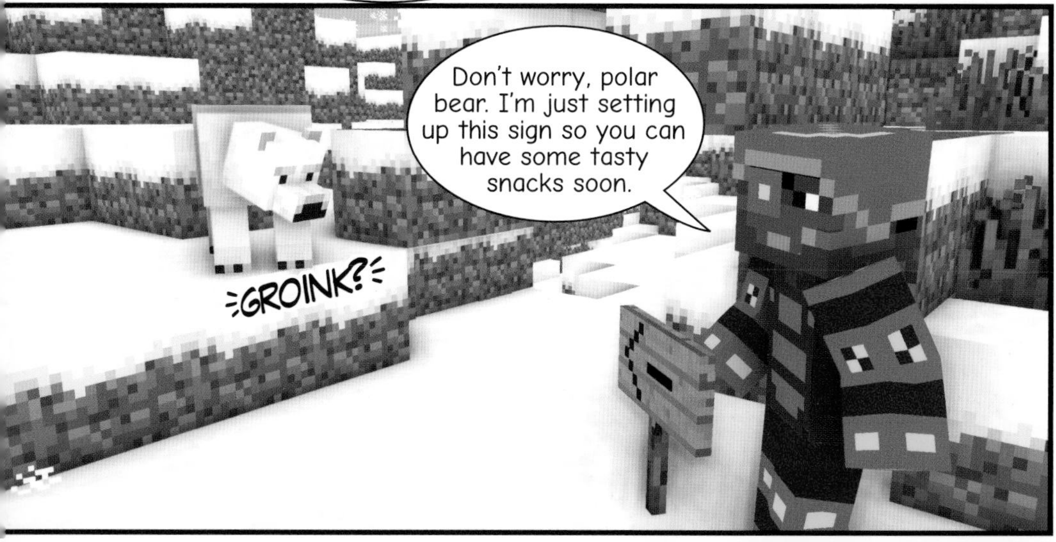
Don't worry, polar bear. I'm just setting up this sign so you can have some tasty snacks soon.
GROINK?

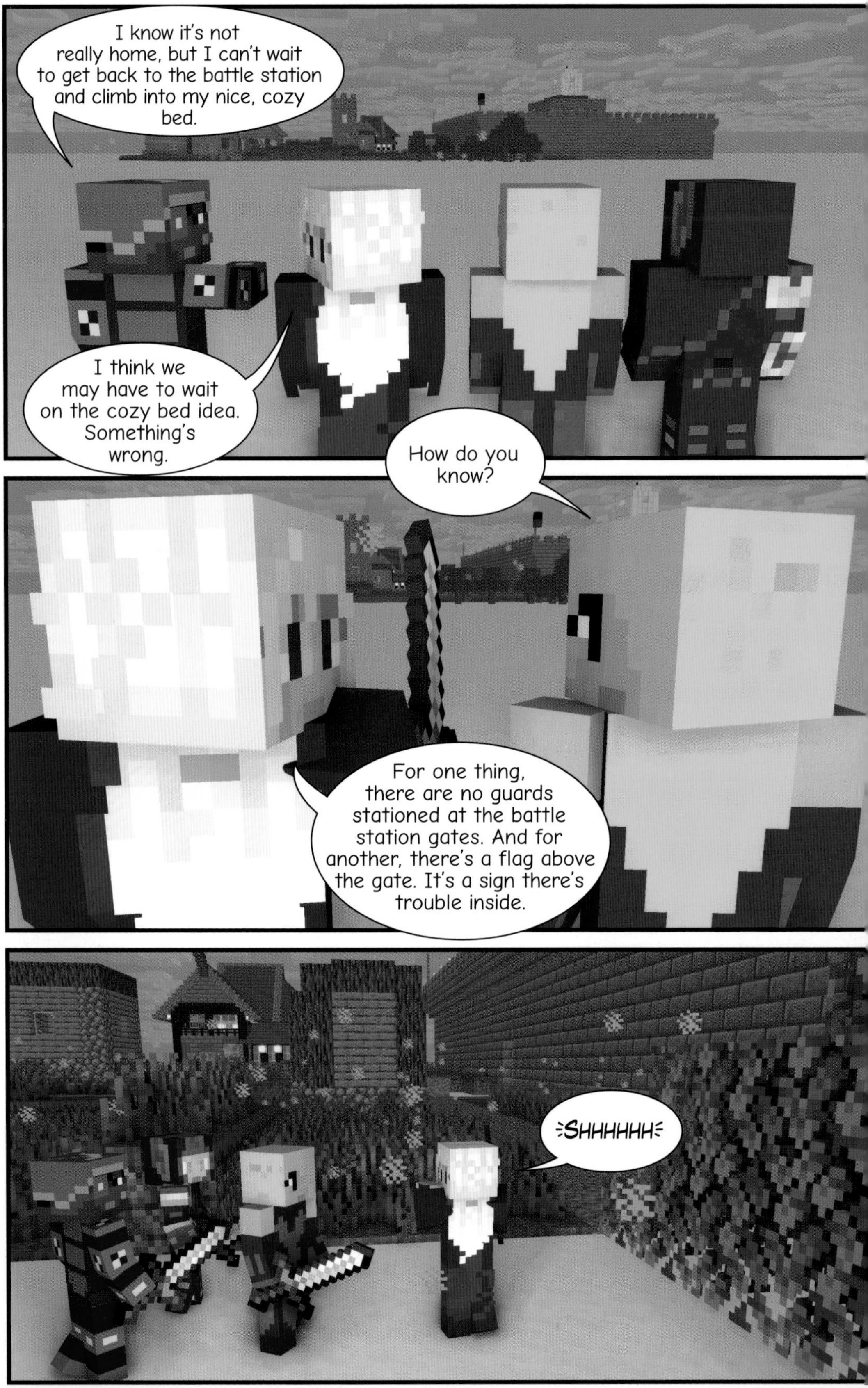
I know it's not really home, but I can't wait to get back to the battle station and climb into my nice, cozy bed.
I think we may have to wait on the cozy bed idea. Something's wrong.
How do you know?
For one thing, there are no guards stationed at the battle station gates. And for another, there's a flag above the gate. It's a sign there's trouble inside.
SHHHHHH

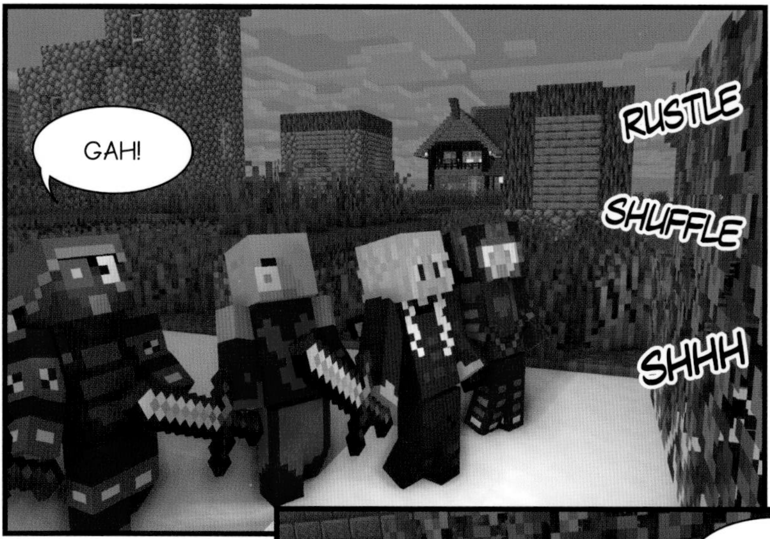
GAH!
RUSTLE
SHUFFLE
SHHH

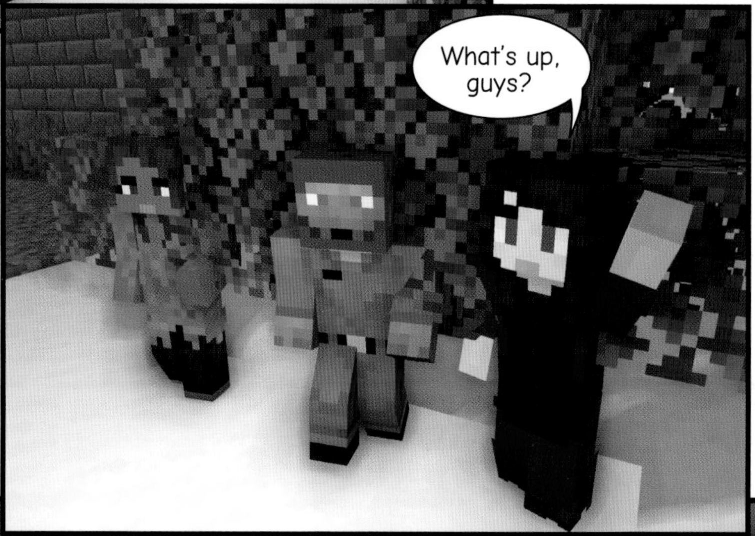
What's up, guys?

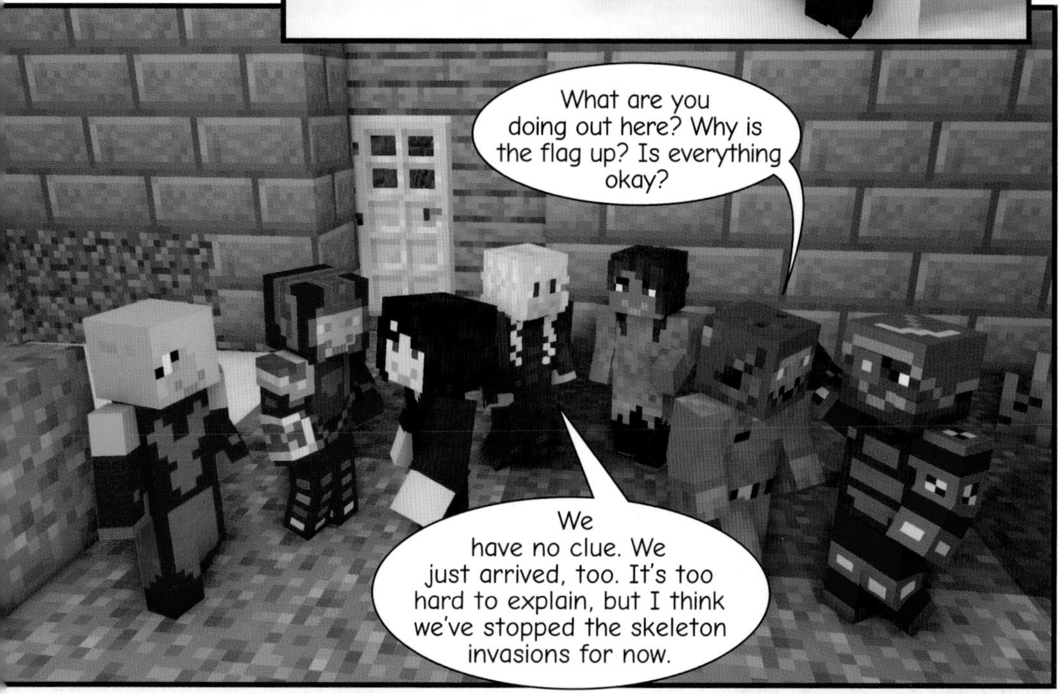
What are you doing out here? Why is the flag up? Is everything okay?
We have no clue. We just arrived, too. It's too hard to explain, but I think we've stopped the skeleton invasions for now.

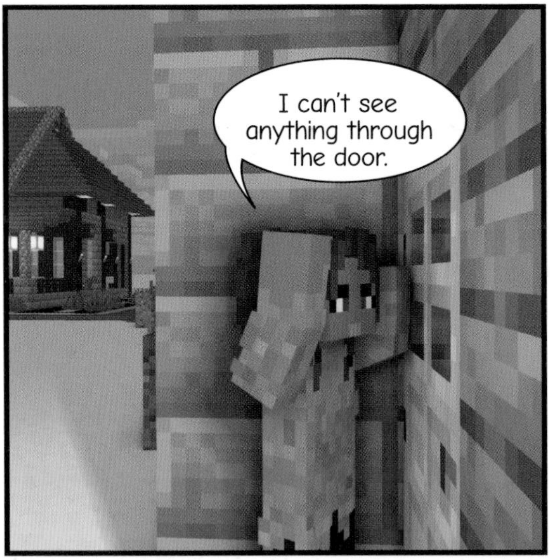
I can't see anything through the door.

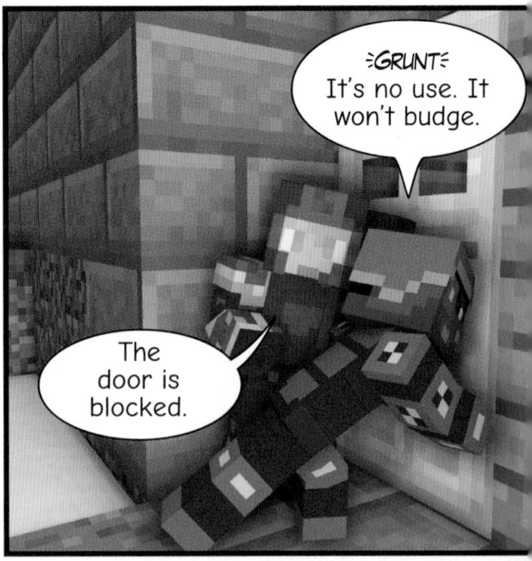
GRUNT
It's no use. It won't budge.
The door is blocked.

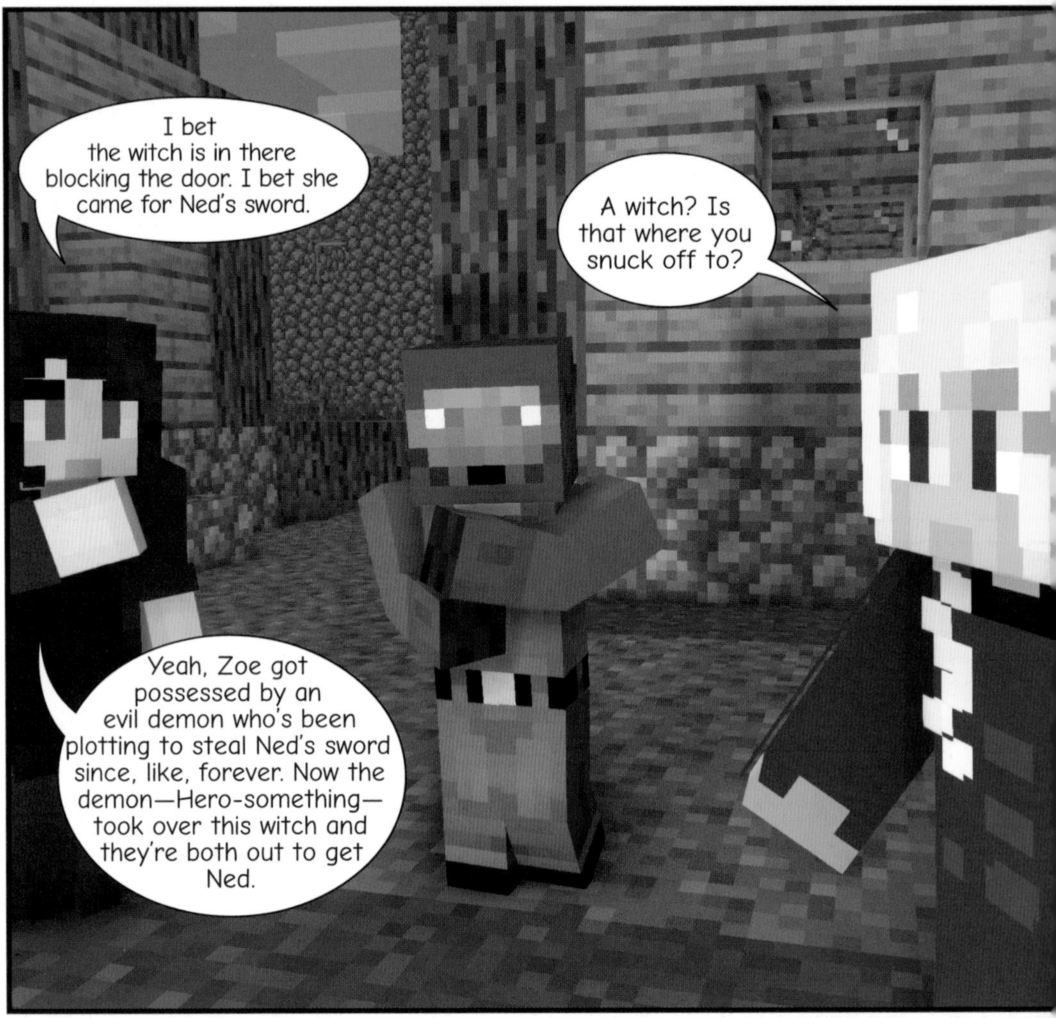
I bet the witch is in there blocking the door. I bet she came for Ned's sword.
A witch? Is that where you snuck off to?
Yeah, Zoe got possessed by an evil demon who's been plotting to steal Ned's sword since, like, forever. Now the demon—Hero-something—took over this witch and they're both out to get Ned.

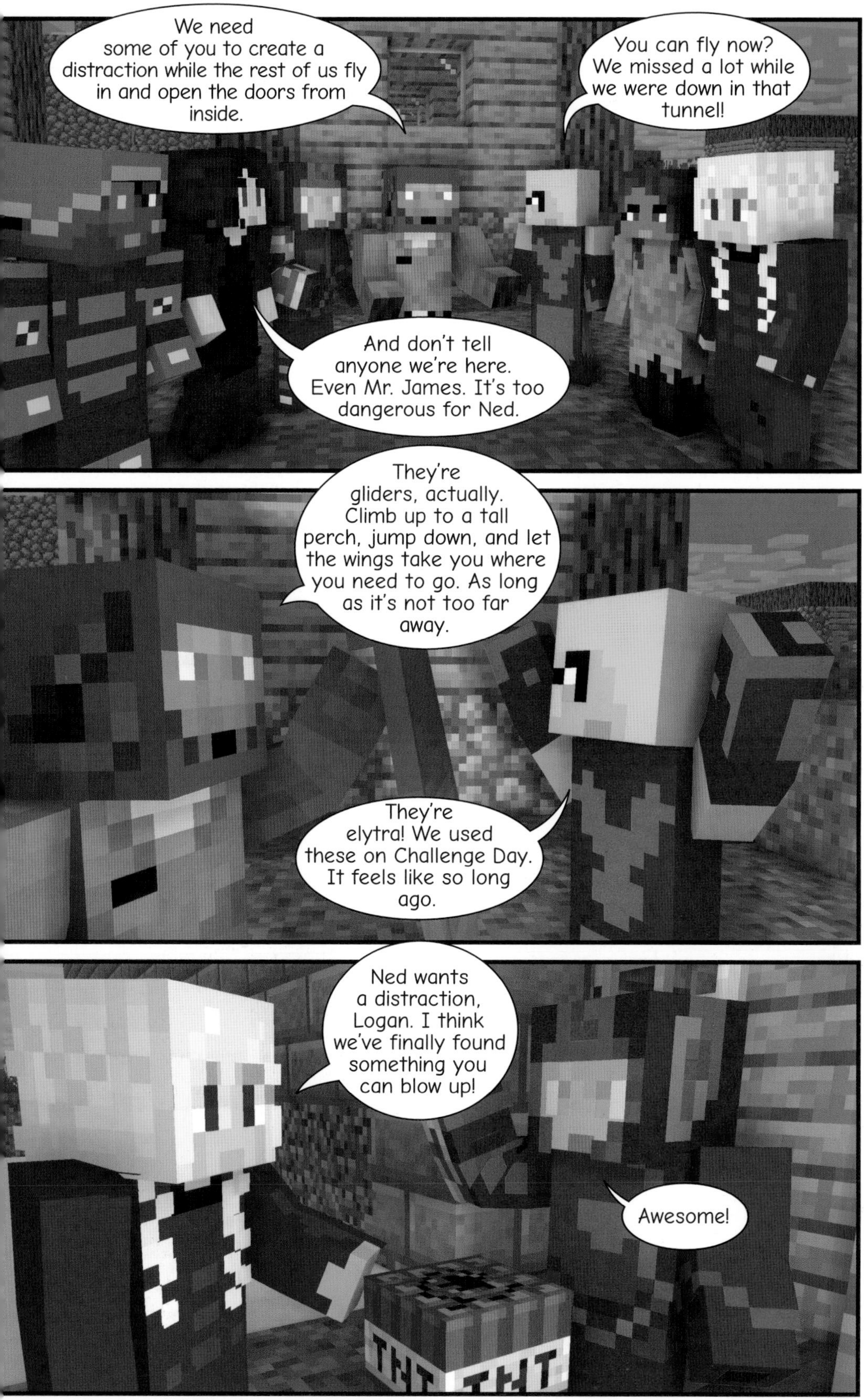
We need some of you to create a distraction while the rest of us fly in and open the doors from inside.
You can fly now? We missed a lot while we were down in that tunnel!
And don't tell anyone we're here. Even Mr. James. It's too dangerous for Ned.
They're gliders, actually. Climb up to a tall perch, jump down, and let the wings take you where you need to go. As long as it's not too far away.
They're elytra! We used these on Challenge Day. It feels like so long ago.
Ned wants a distraction, Logan. I think we've finally found something you can blow up!
Awesome!
TNT TNT

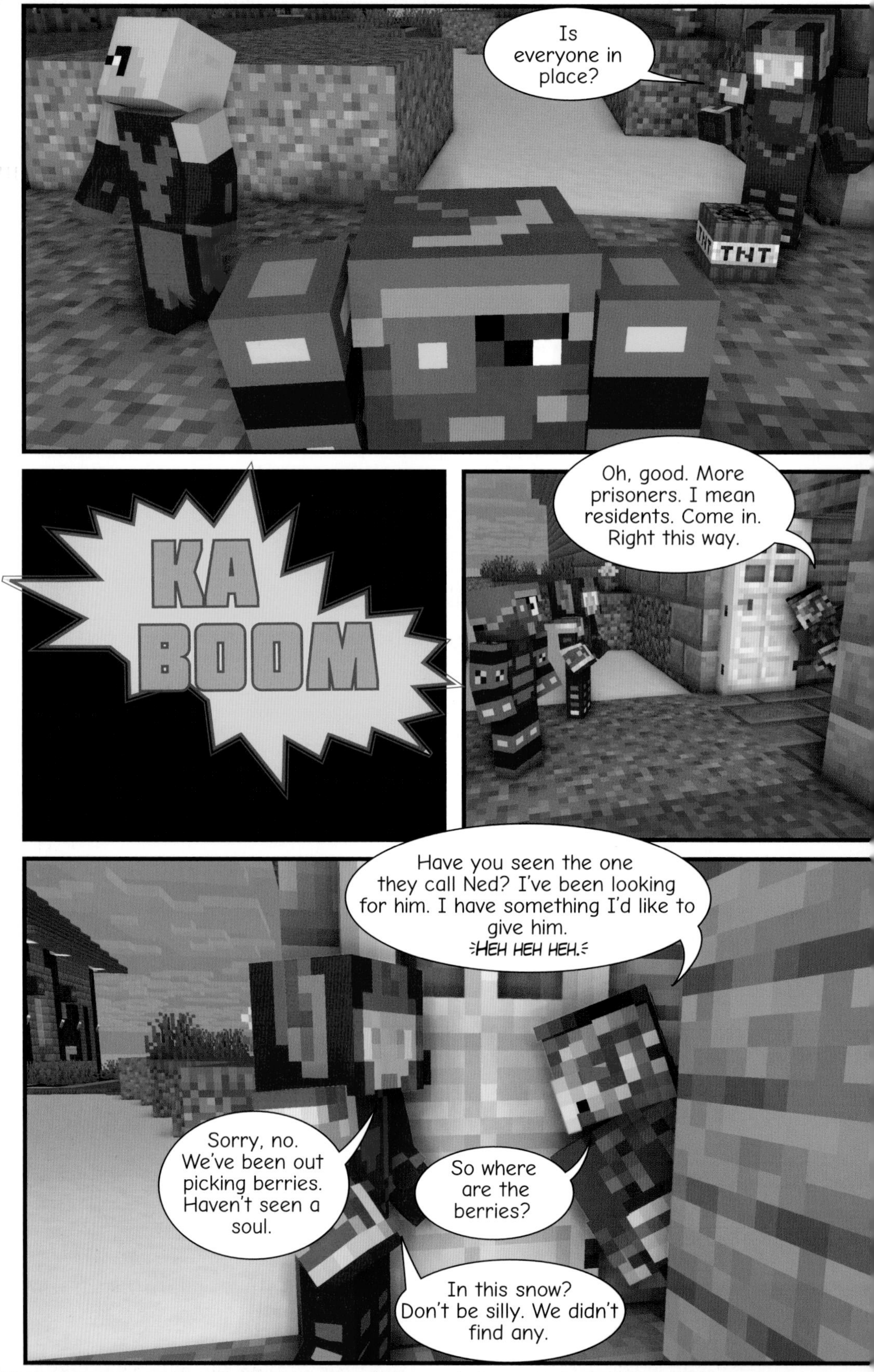
Is everyone in place?
KA BOOM
Oh, good. More prisoners. I mean residents. Come in. Right this way.
Have you seen the one they call Ned? I've been looking for him. I have something I'd like to give him.
HEH HEH HEH.
Sorry, no. We've been out picking berries. Haven't seen a soul.
So where are the berries?
In this snow? Don't be silly. We didn't find any.

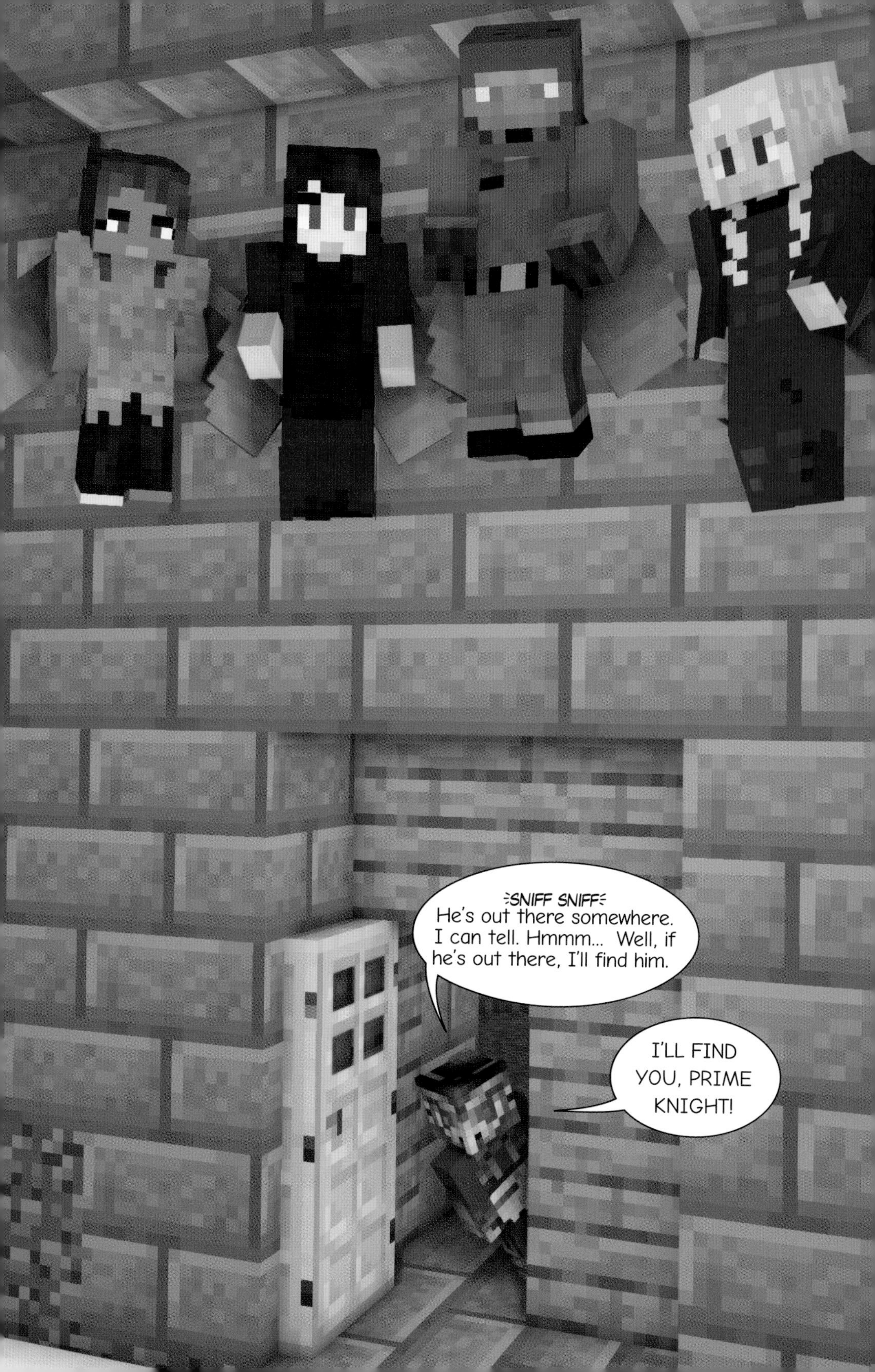
SNIFF SNIFF
He's out there somewhere. I can tell. Hmmm... Well, if he's out there, I'll find him.
I'LL FIND YOU, PRIME KNIGHT!

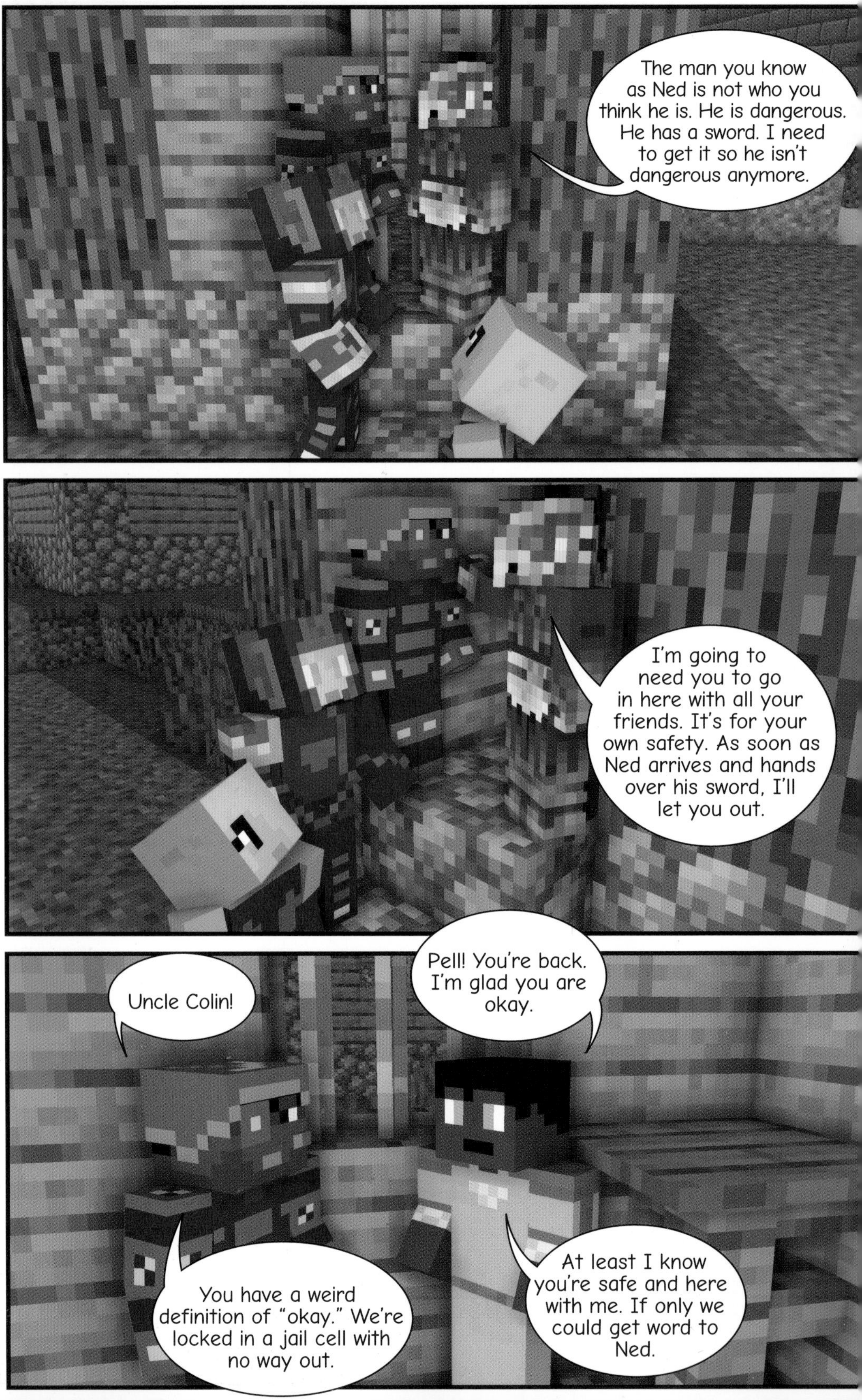
The man you know as Ned is not who you think he is. He is dangerous. He has a sword. I need to get it so he isn't dangerous anymore.
I'm going to need you to go in here with all your friends. It's for your own safety. As soon as Ned arrives and hands over his sword, I'll let you out.
Uncle Colin!
Pell! You're back. I'm glad you are okay.
You have a weird definition of "okay." We're locked in a jail cell with no way out.
At least I know you're safe and here with me. If only we could get word to Ned.

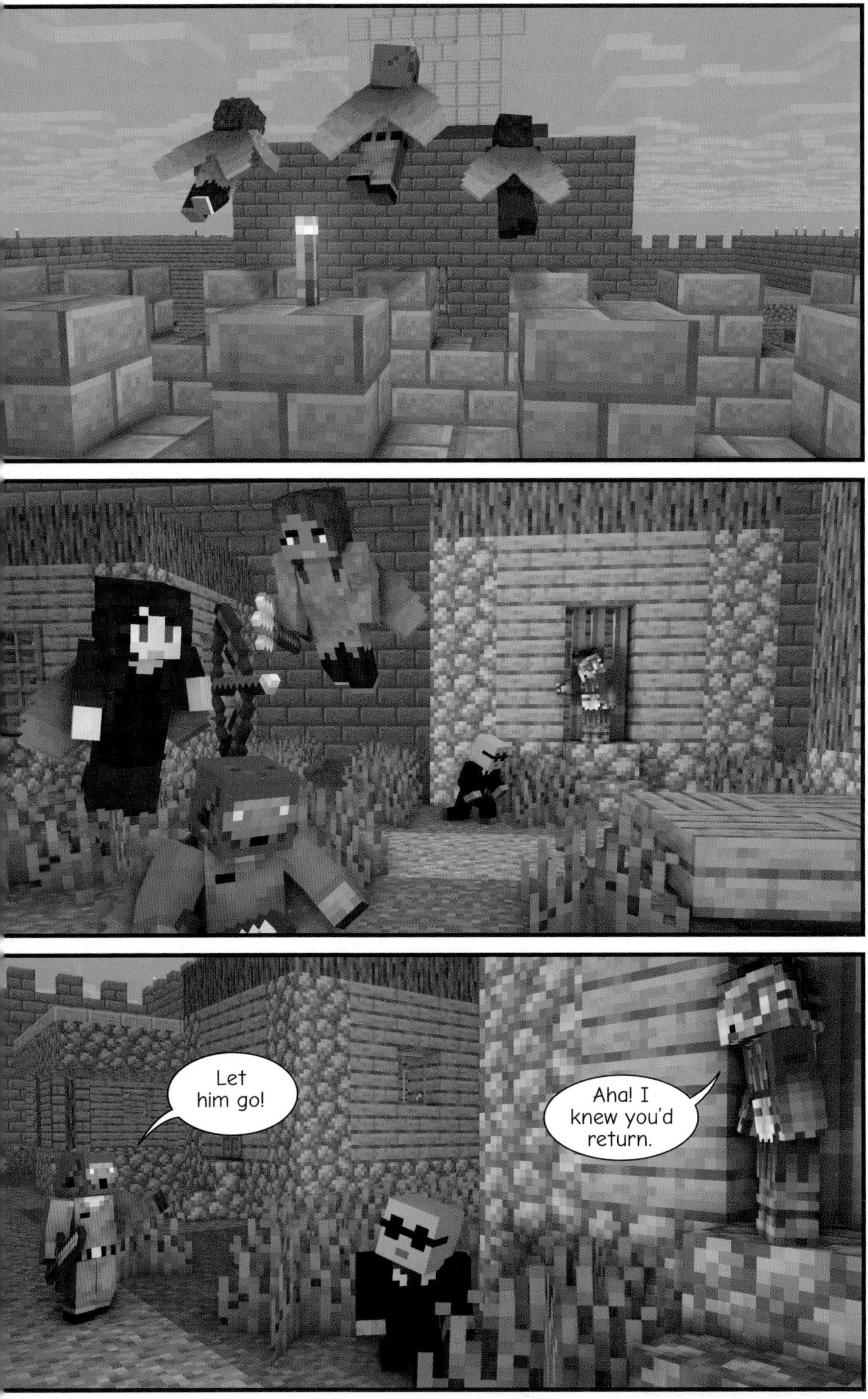
Let him go!
Aha! I knew you'd return.

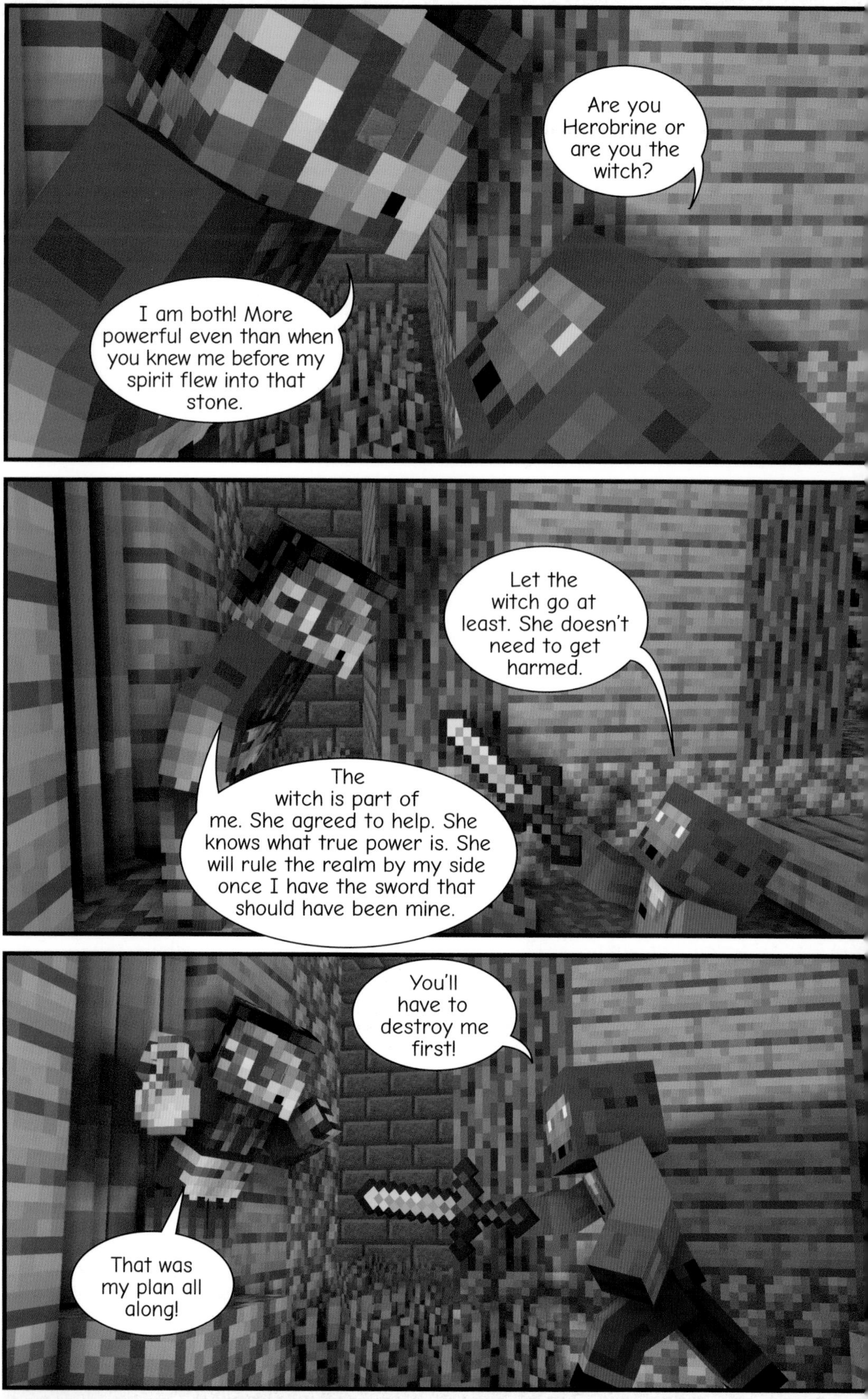
Are you Herobrine or are you the witch?
I am both! More powerful even than when you knew me before my spirit flew into that stone.
Let the witch go at least. She doesn't need to get harmed.
The witch is part of me. She agreed to help. She knows what true power is. She will rule the realm by my side once I have the sword that should have been mine.
You'll have to destroy me first!
That was my plan all along!

# CHAPTER 11

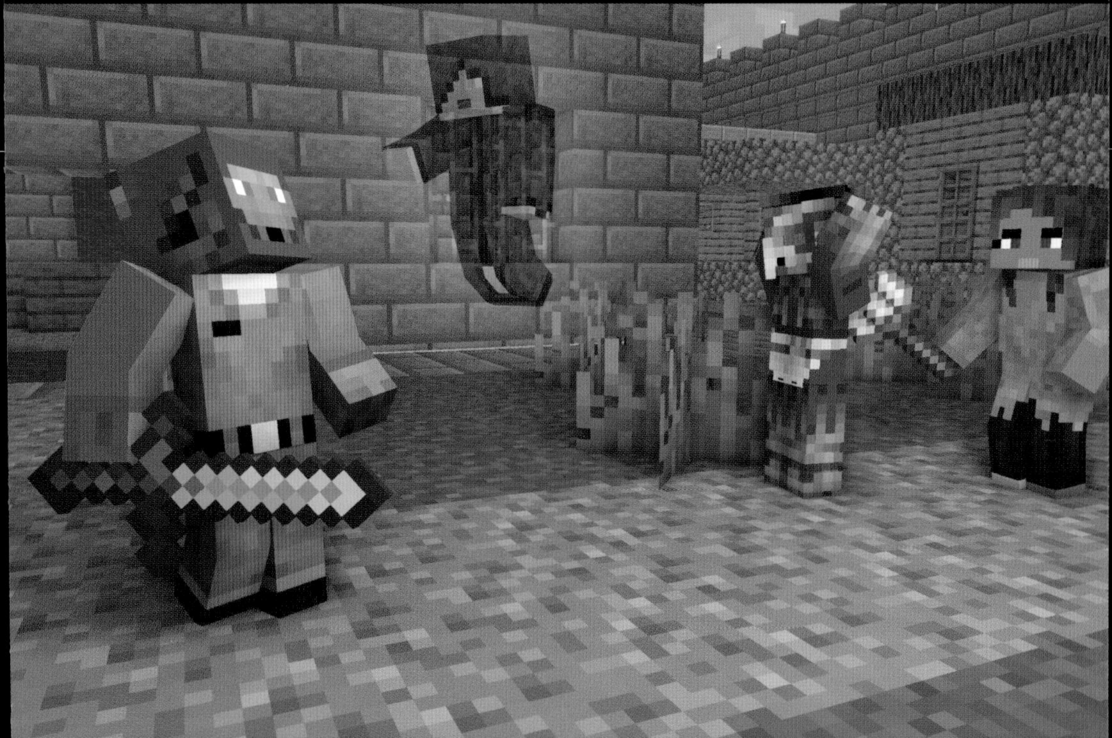

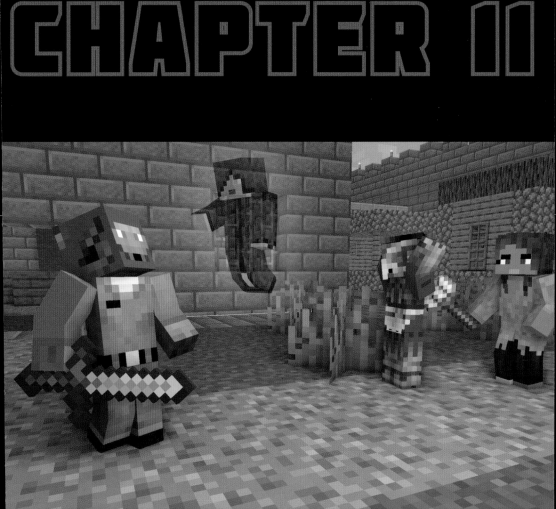

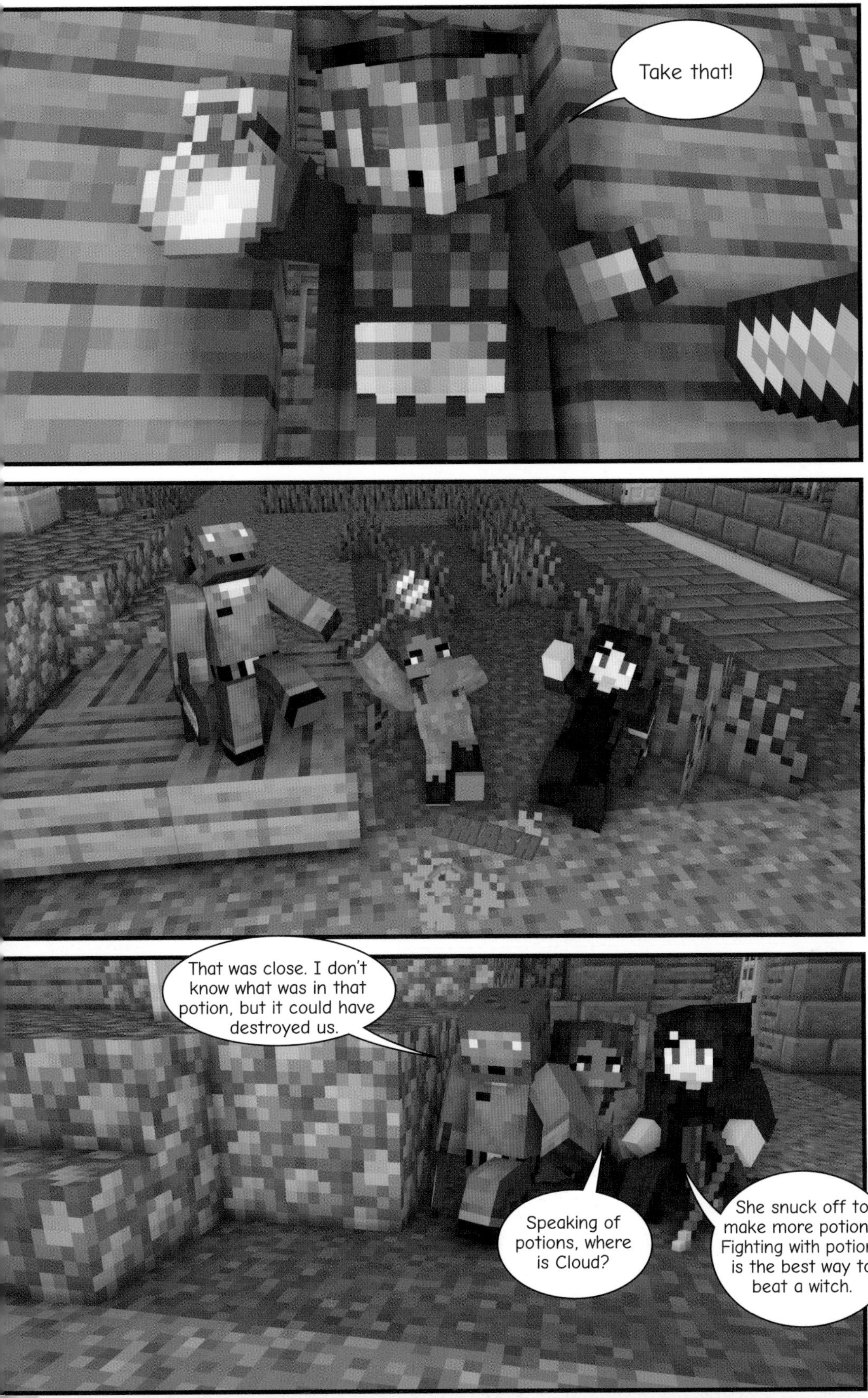
Take that!
That was close. I don't know what was in that potion, but it could have destroyed us.
Speaking of potions, where is Cloud?
She snuck off to make more potions. Fighting with potions is the best way to beat a witch.

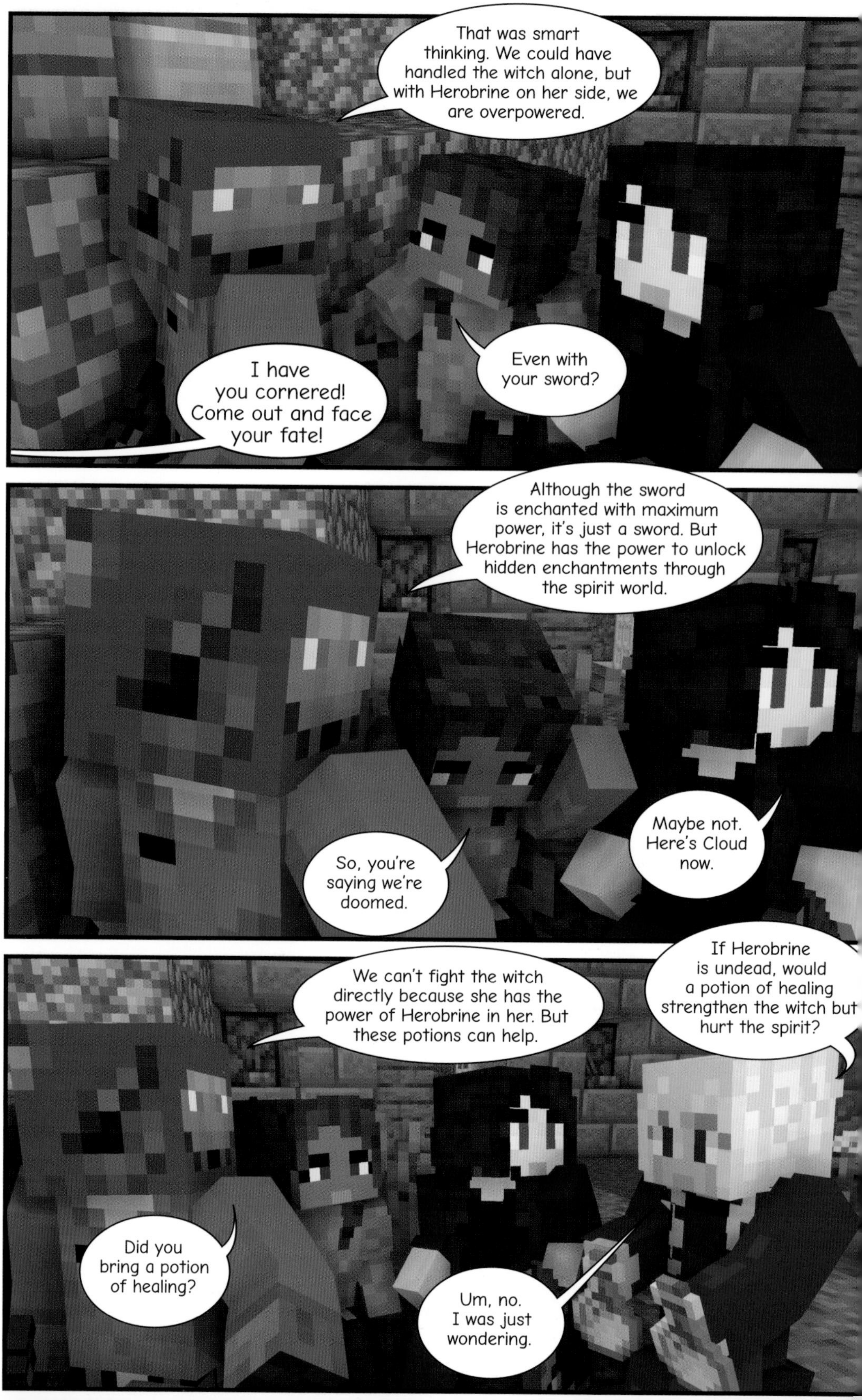
That was smart thinking. We could have handled the witch alone, but with Herobrine on her side, we are overpowered.
Even with your sword?
I have you cornered! Come out and face your fate!
Although the sword is enchanted with maximum power, it's just a sword. But Herobrine has the power to unlock hidden enchantments through the spirit world.
So, you're saying we're doomed.
Maybe not. Here's Cloud now.
We can't fight the witch directly because she has the power of Herobrine in her. But these potions can help.
If Herobrine is undead, would a potion of healing strengthen the witch but hurt the spirit?
Did you bring a potion of healing?
Um, no. I was just wondering.

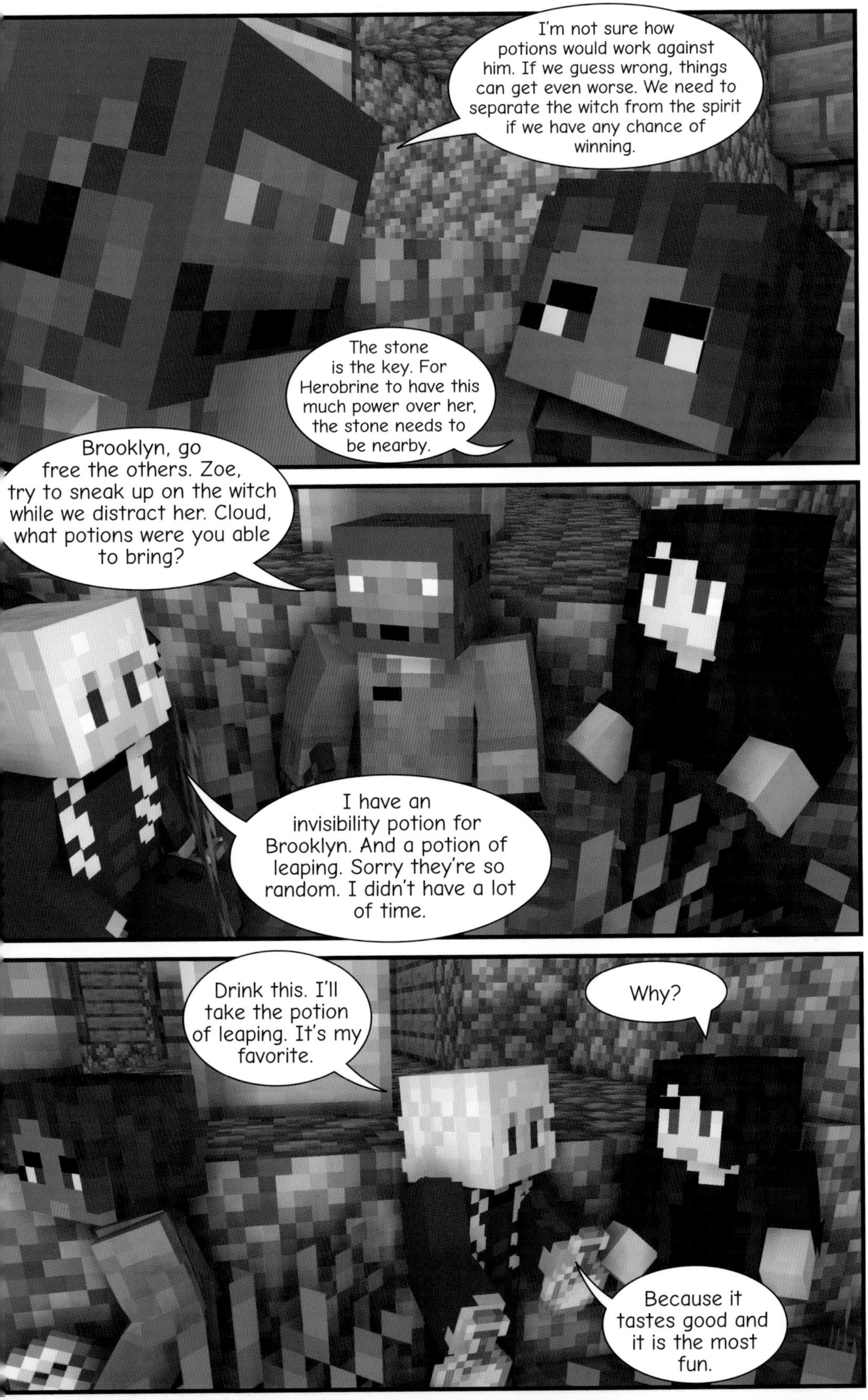
I'm not sure how potions would work against him. If we guess wrong, things can get even worse. We need to separate the witch from the spirit if we have any chance of winning.
The stone is the key. For Herobrine to have this much power over her, the stone needs to be nearby.
Brooklyn, go free the others. Zoe, try to sneak up on the witch while we distract her. Cloud, what potions were you able to bring?
I have an invisibility potion for Brooklyn. And a potion of leaping. Sorry they're so random. I didn't have a lot of time.
Drink this. I'll take the potion of leaping. It's my favorite.
Why?
Because it tastes good and it is the most fun.

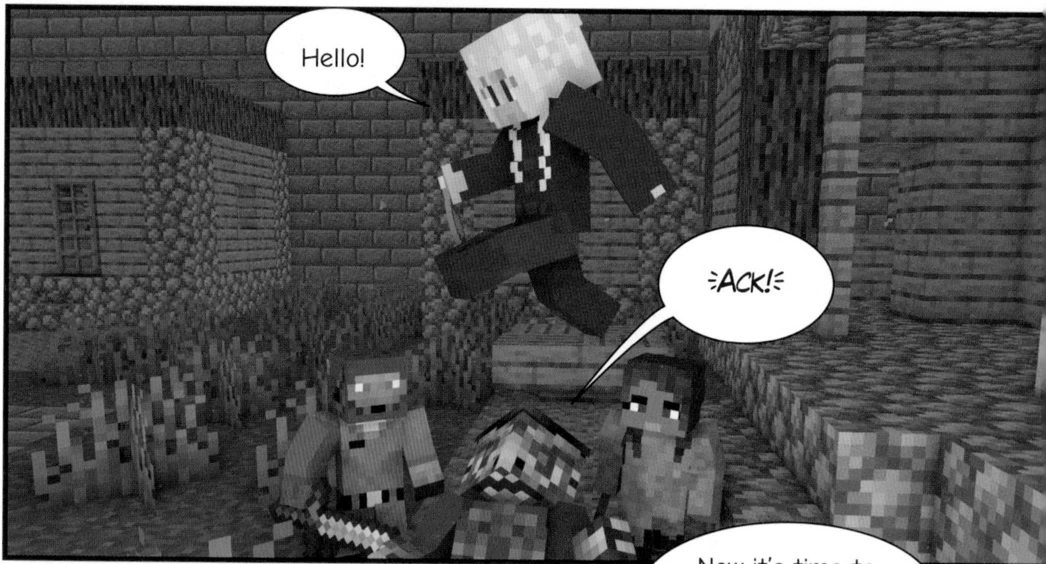
Hello!
ACK!

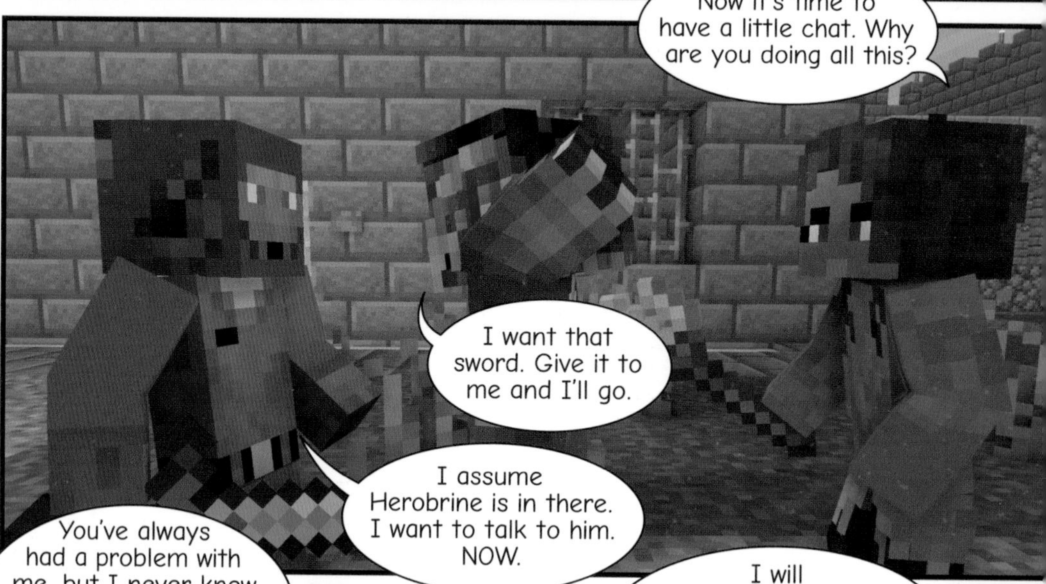
Now it's time to have a little chat. Why are you doing all this?
I want that sword. Give it to me and I'll go.
I assume Herobrine is in there. I want to talk to him. NOW.

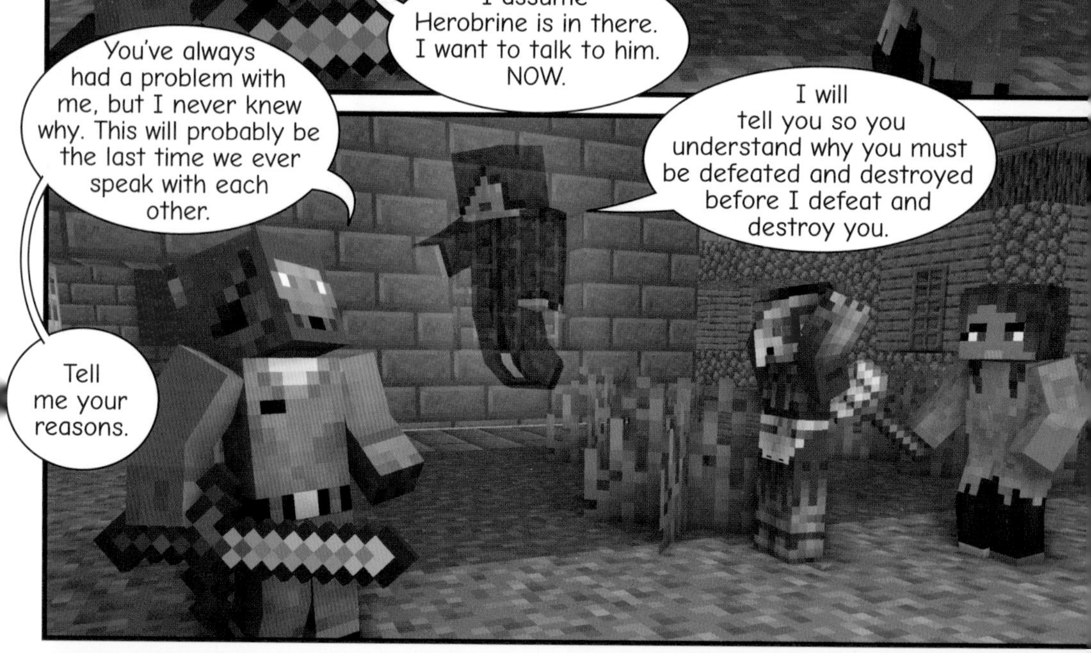
You've always had a problem with me, but I never knew why. This will probably be the last time we ever speak with each other.
I will tell you so you understand why you must be defeated and destroyed before I defeat and destroy you.
Tell me your reasons.

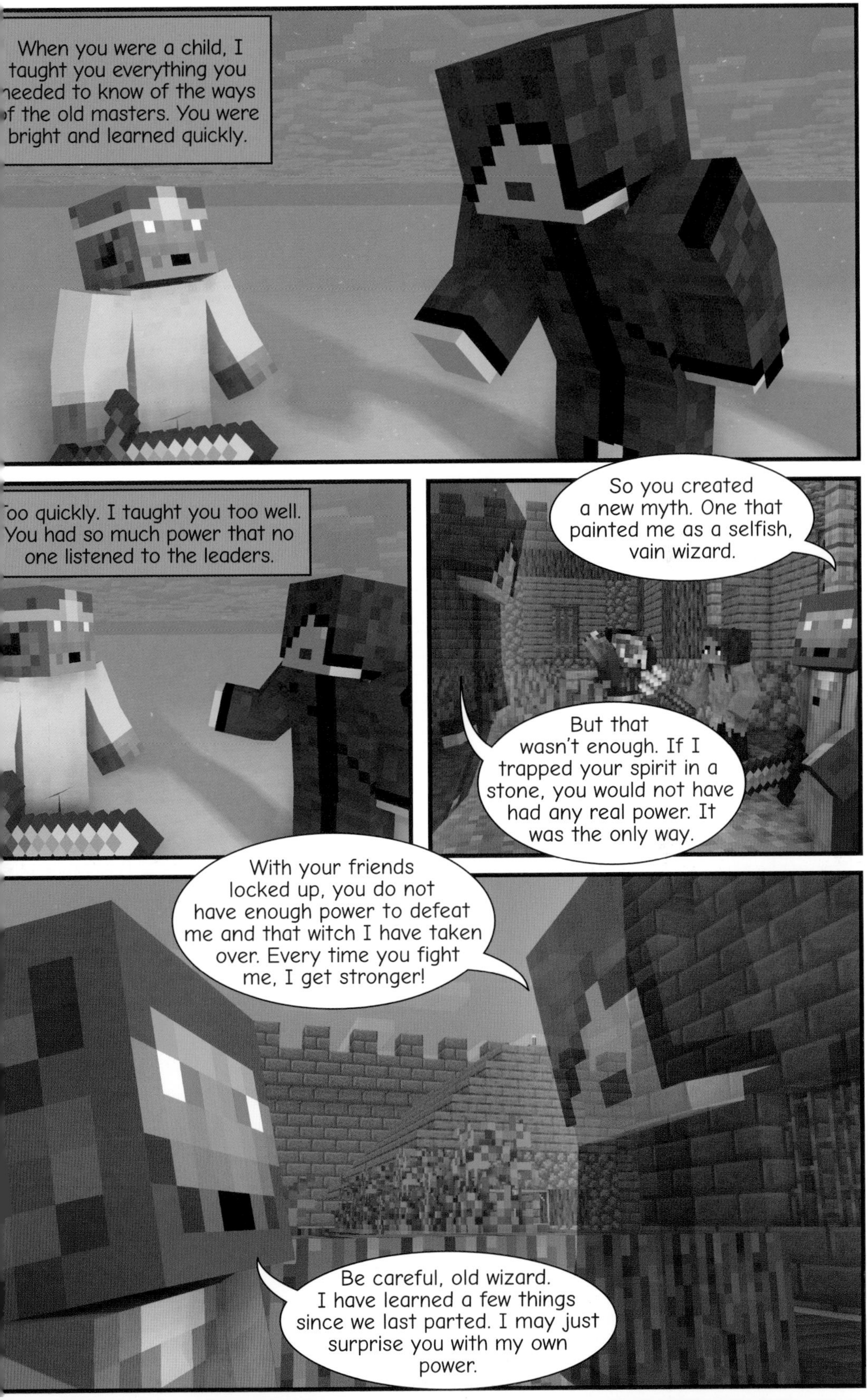
When you were a child, I taught you everything you needed to know of the ways of the old masters. You were bright and learned quickly.
Too quickly. I taught you too well. You had so much power that no one listened to the leaders.
So you created a new myth. One that painted me as a selfish, vain wizard.
But that wasn't enough. If I trapped your spirit in a stone, you would not have had any real power. It was the only way.
With your friends locked up, you do not have enough power to defeat me and that witch I have taken over. Every time you fight me, I get stronger!
Be careful, old wizard. I have learned a few things since we last parted. I may just surprise you with my own power.

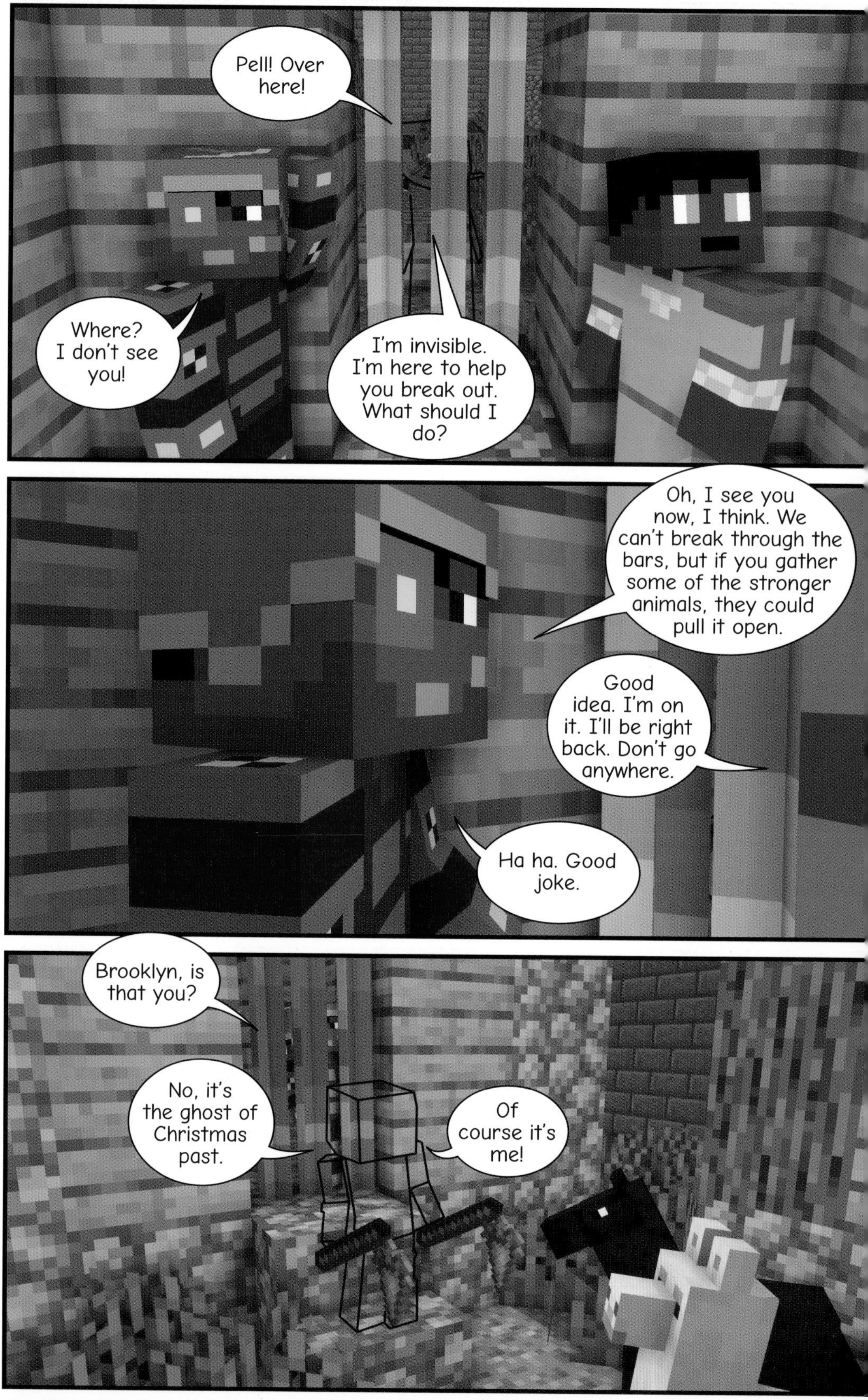
Pell! Over here!
Where? I don't see you!
I'm invisible. I'm here to help you break out. What should I do?
Oh, I see you now, I think. We can't break through the bars, but if you gather some of the stronger animals, they could pull it open.
Good idea. I'm on it. I'll be right back. Don't go anywhere.
Ha ha. Good joke.
Brooklyn, is that you?
No, it's the ghost of Christmas past.
Of course it's me!

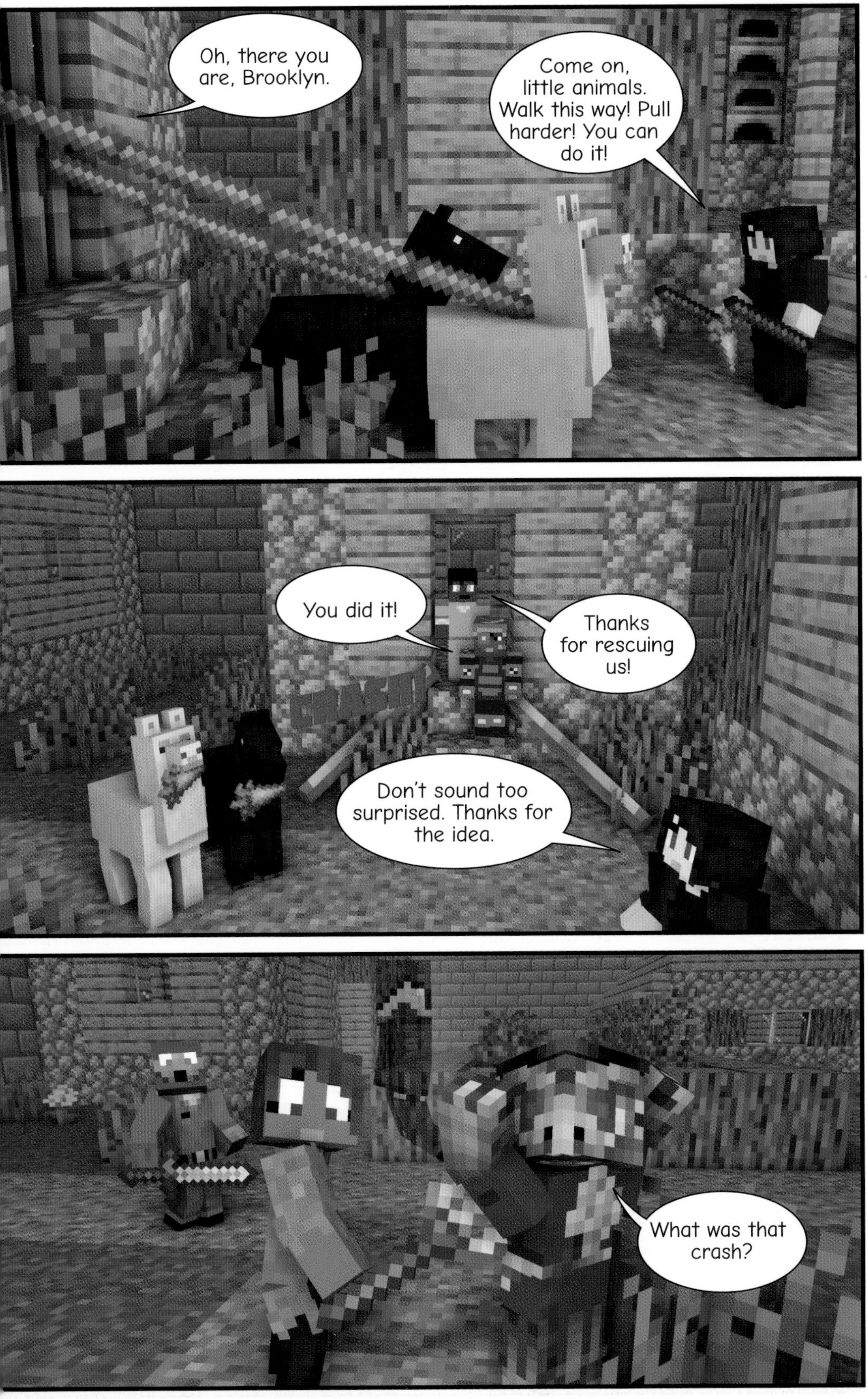
Oh, there you are, Brooklyn.
Come on, little animals. Walk this way! Pull harder! You can do it!
You did it!
Thanks for rescuing us!
CRASH!
Don't sound too surprised. Thanks for the idea.
What was that crash?

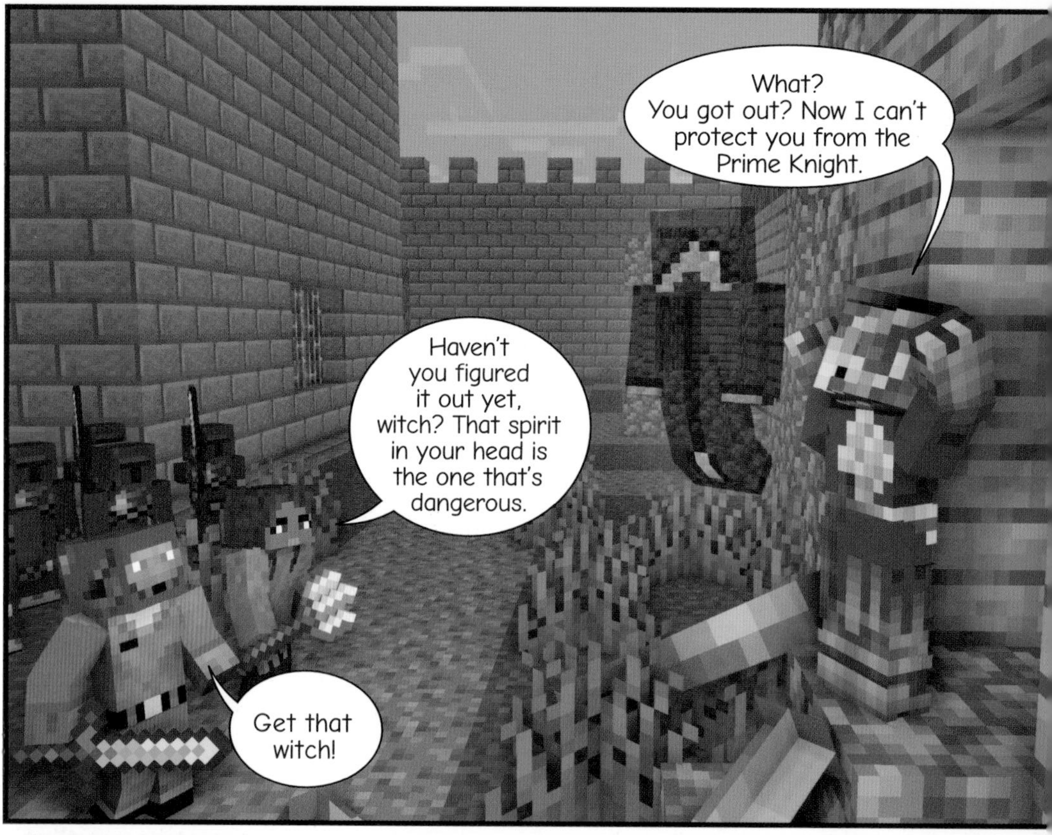
What? You got out? Now I can't protect you from the Prime Knight.
Haven't you figured it out yet, witch? That spirit in your head is the one that's dangerous.
Get that witch!

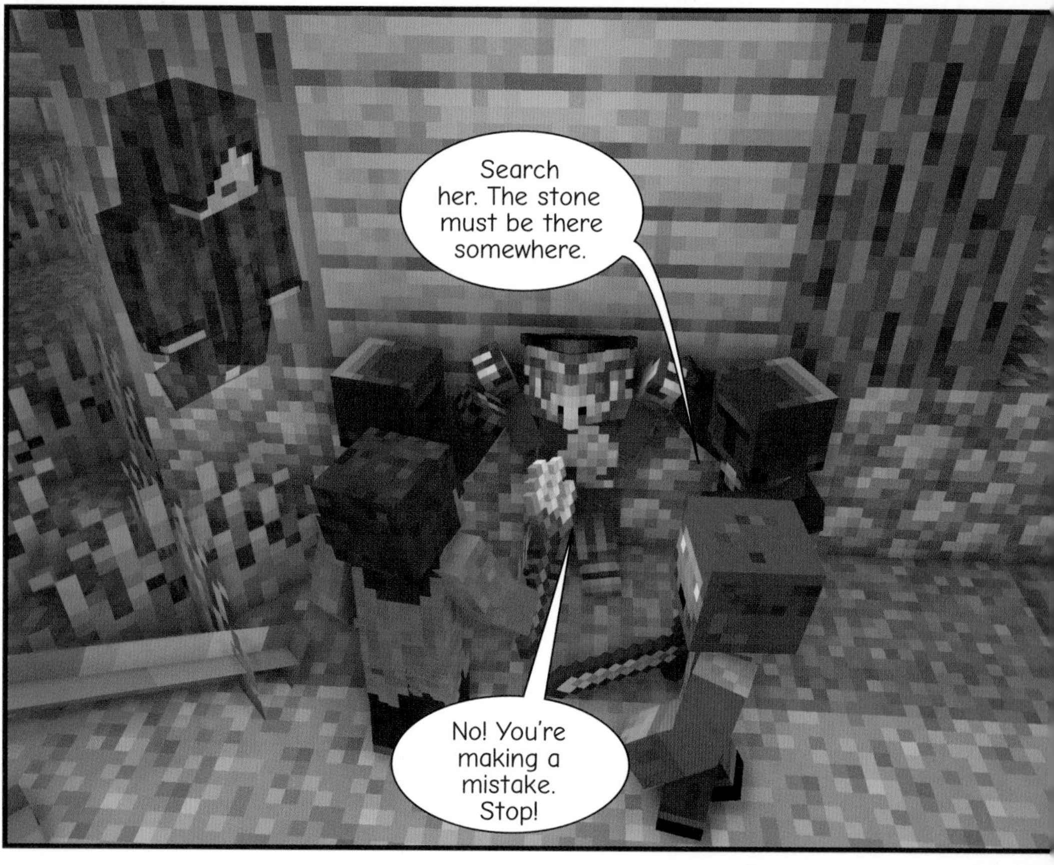
Search her. The stone must be there somewhere.
No! You're making a mistake. Stop!

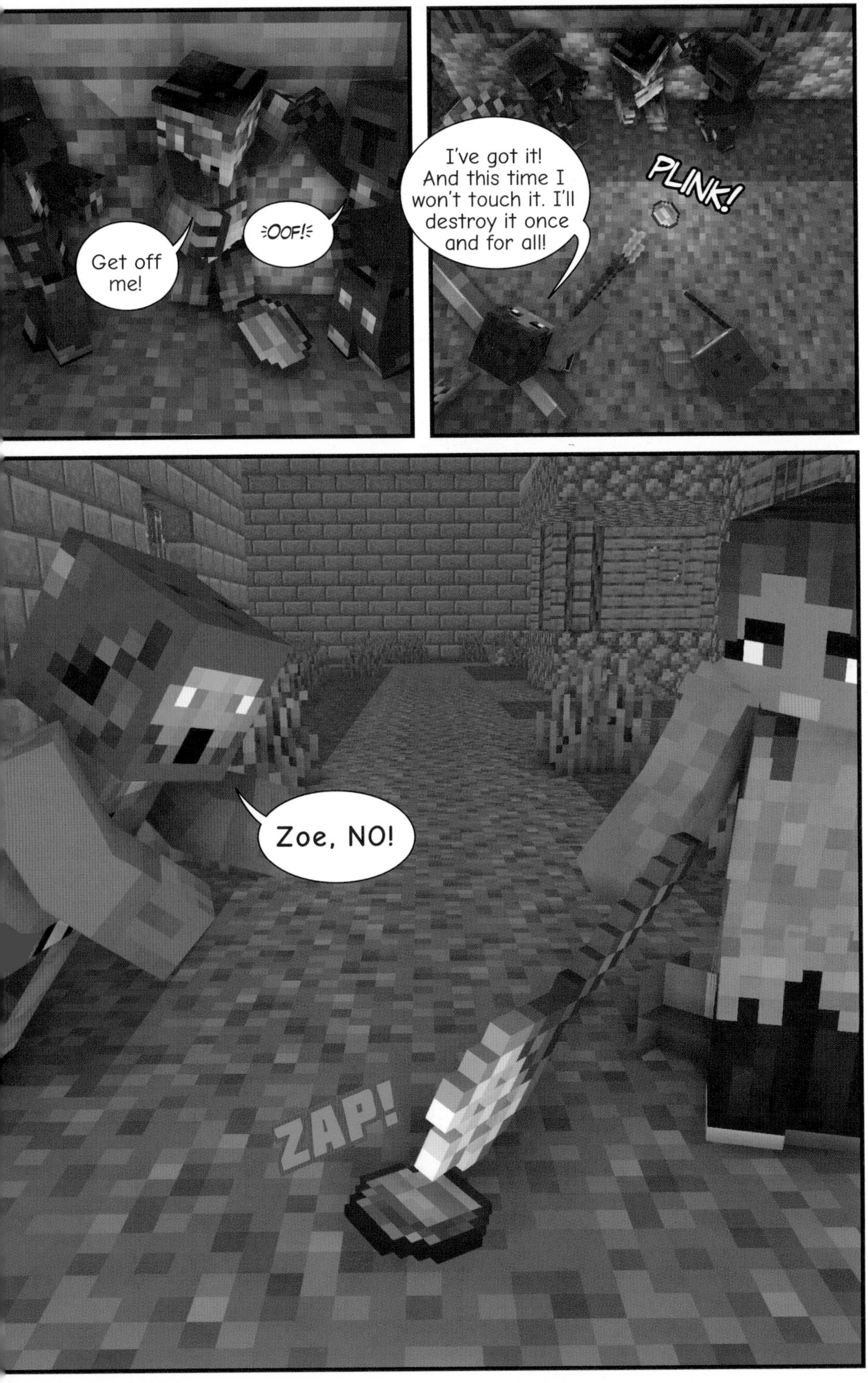

Get off me!
OOF!
I've got it! And this time I won't touch it. I'll destroy it once and for all!
PLINK!
Zoe, NO!
ZAP!

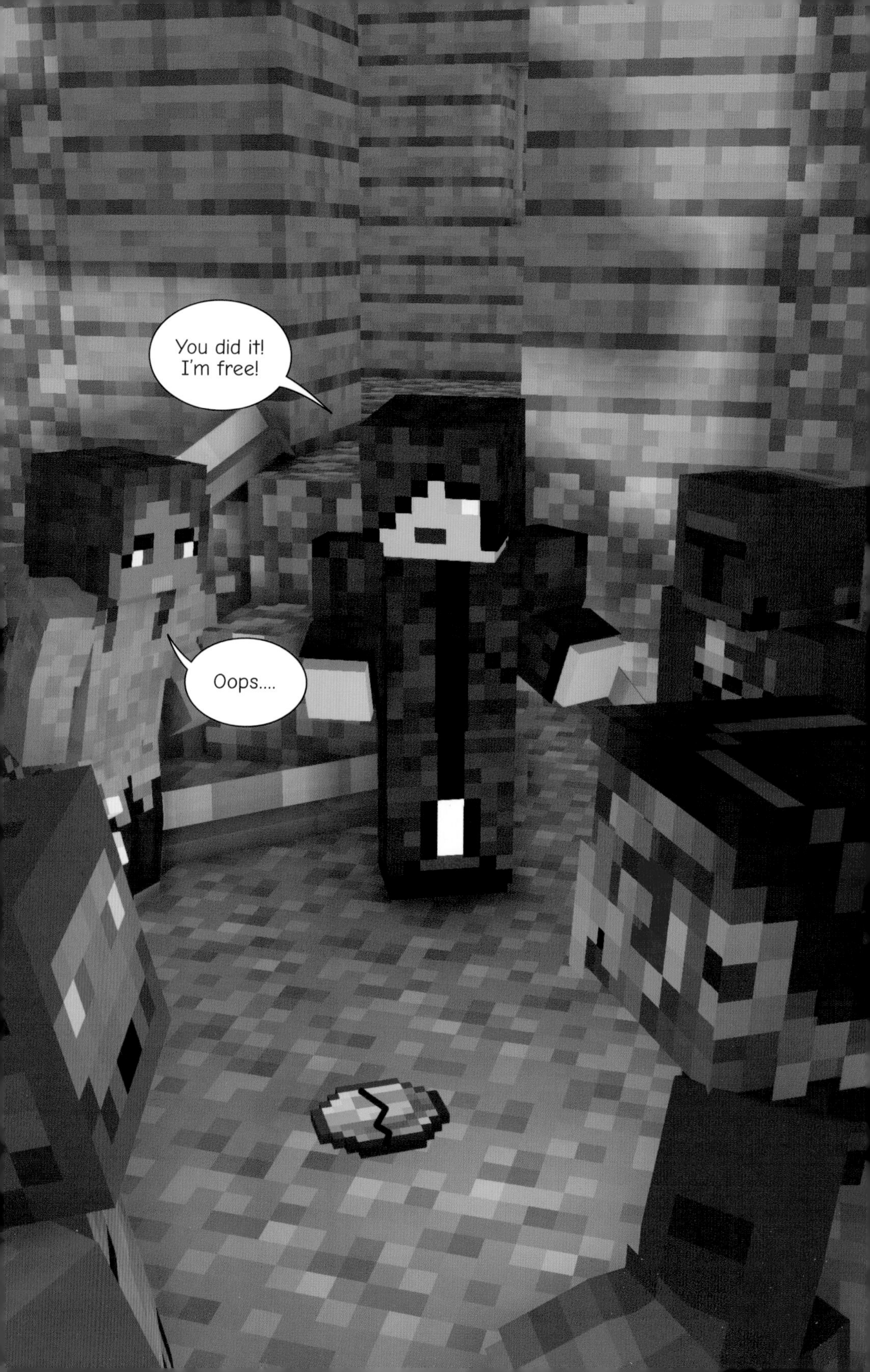
You did it! I'm free!
Oops....

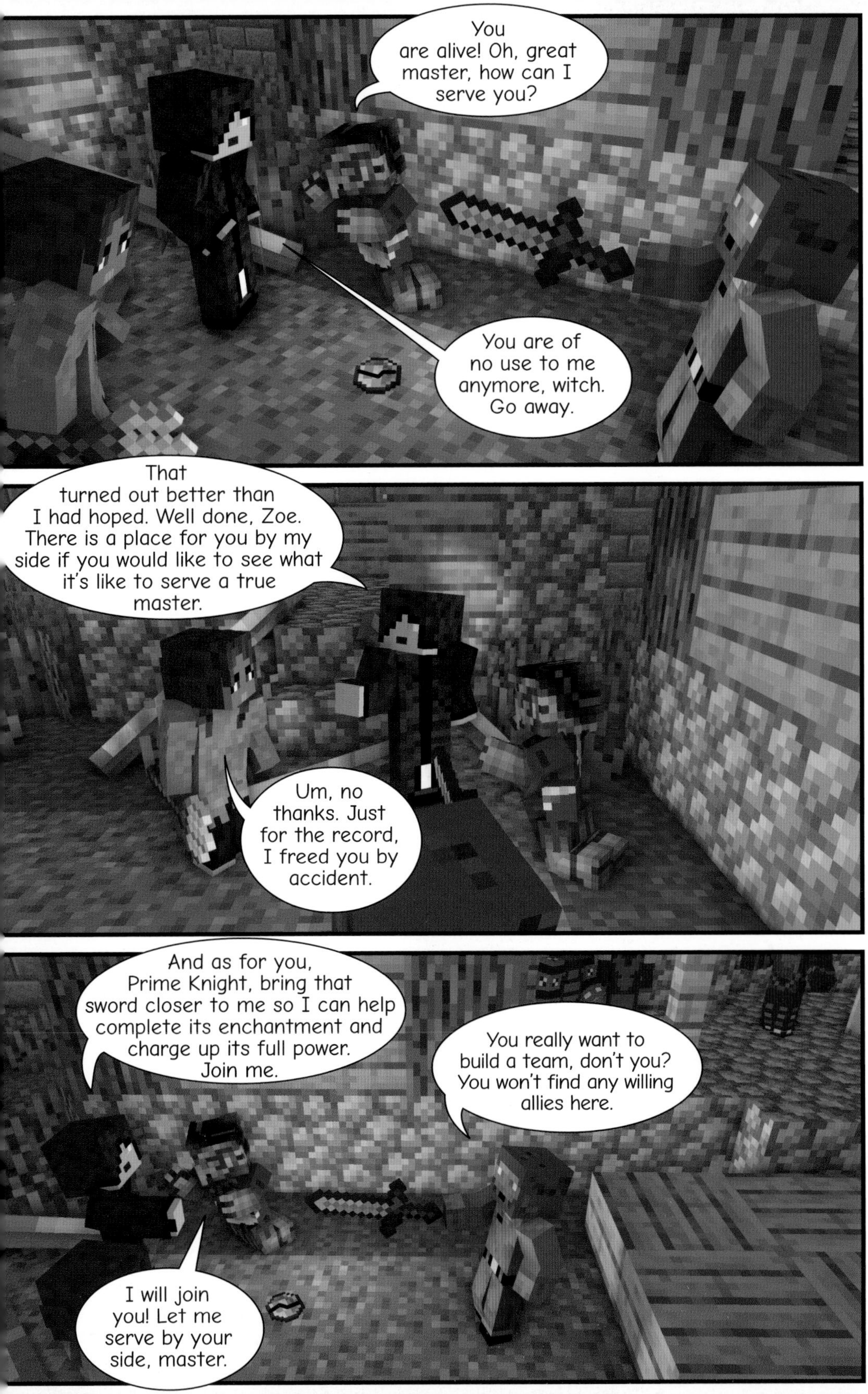
You are alive! Oh, great master, how can I serve you?
You are of no use to me anymore, witch. Go away.
That turned out better than I had hoped. Well done, Zoe. There is a place for you by my side if you would like to see what it's like to serve a true master.
Um, no thanks. Just for the record, I freed you by accident.
And as for you, Prime Knight, bring that sword closer to me so I can help complete its enchantment and charge up its full power. Join me.
You really want to build a team, don't you? You won't find any willing allies here.
I will join you! Let me serve by your side, master.

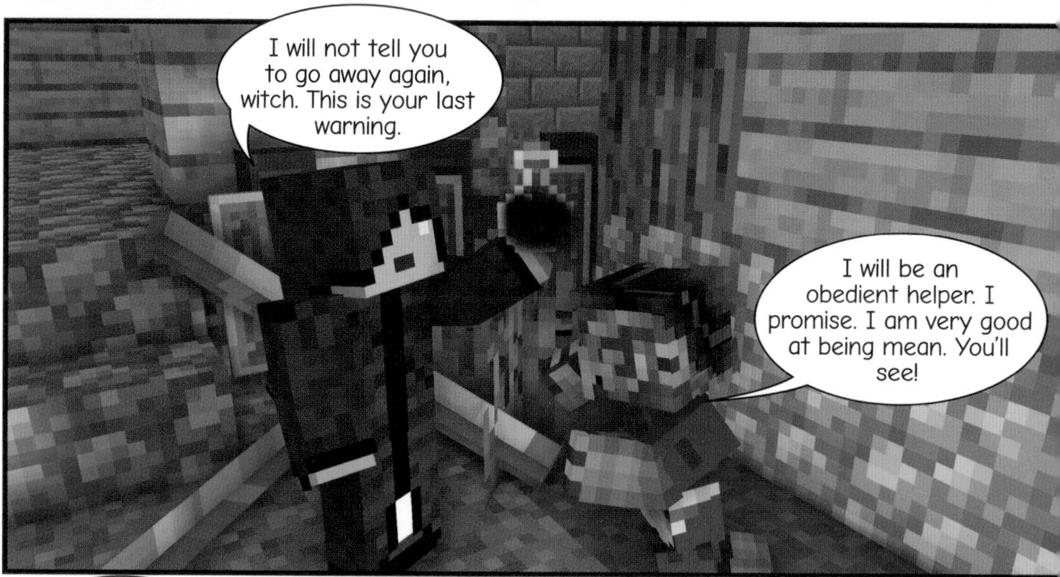
I will not tell you to go away again, witch. This is your last warning.
I will be an obedient helper. I promise. I am very good at being mean. You'll see!

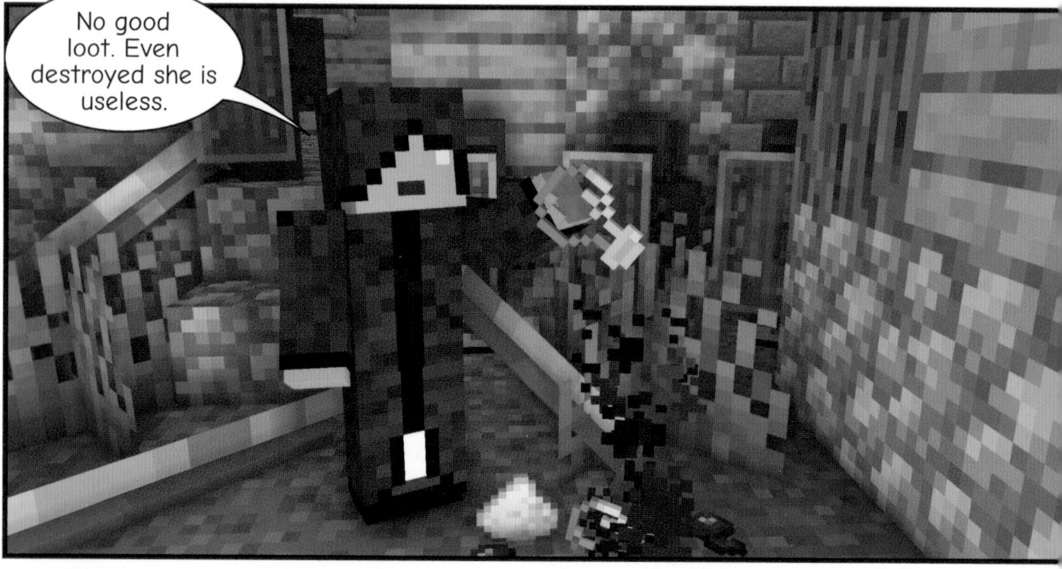
No good loot. Even destroyed she is useless.

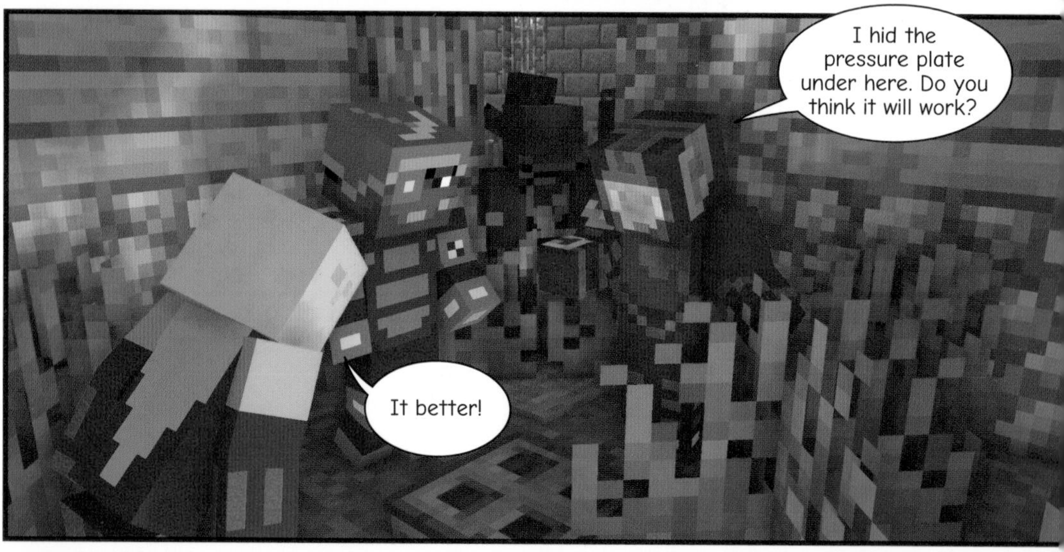
I hid the pressure plate under here. Do you think it will work?
It better!

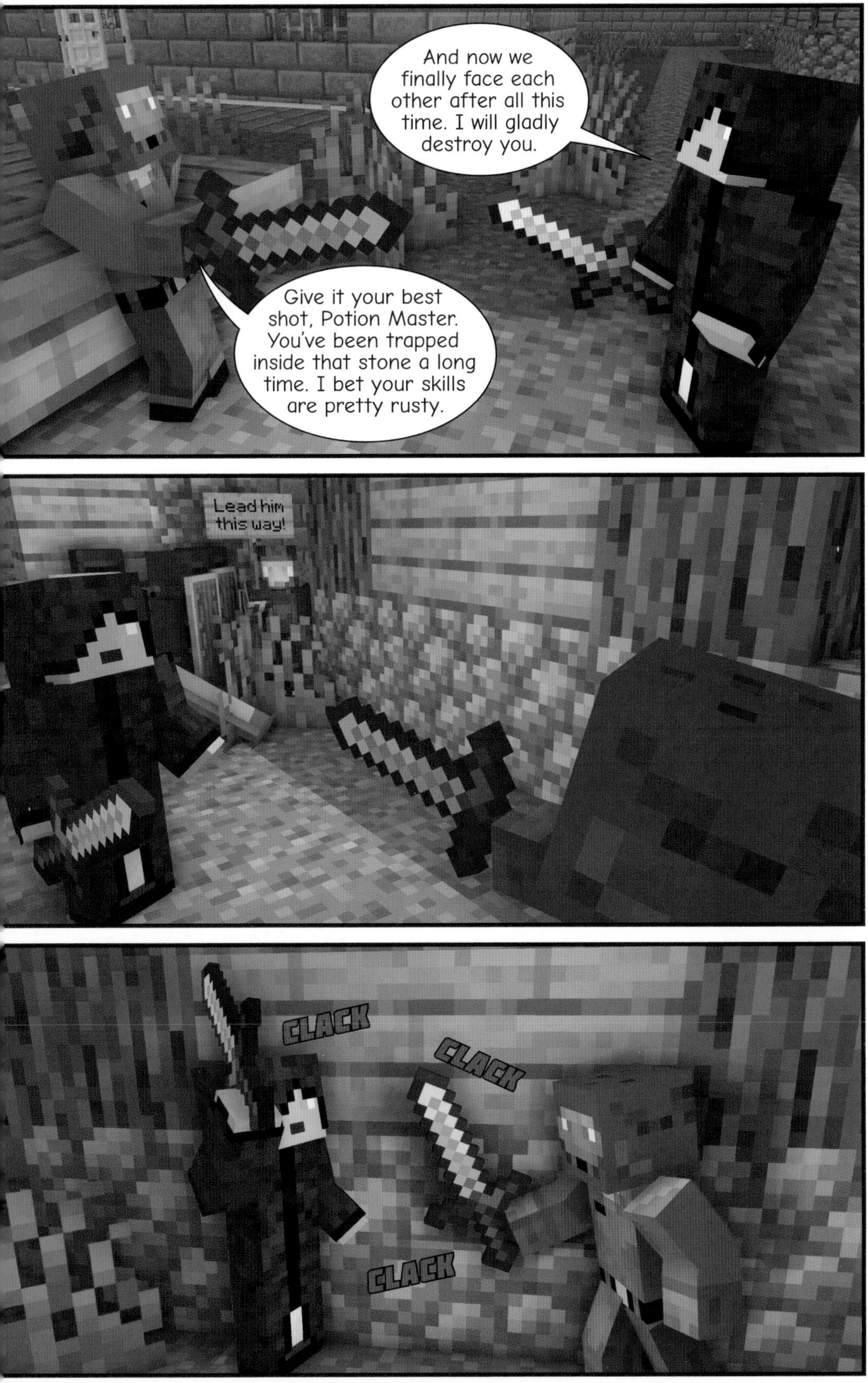
And now we finally face each other after all this time. I will gladly destroy you.
Give it your best shot, Potion Master. You've been trapped inside that stone a long time. I bet your skills are pretty rusty.
Lead him this way!
CLACK
CLACK
CLACK

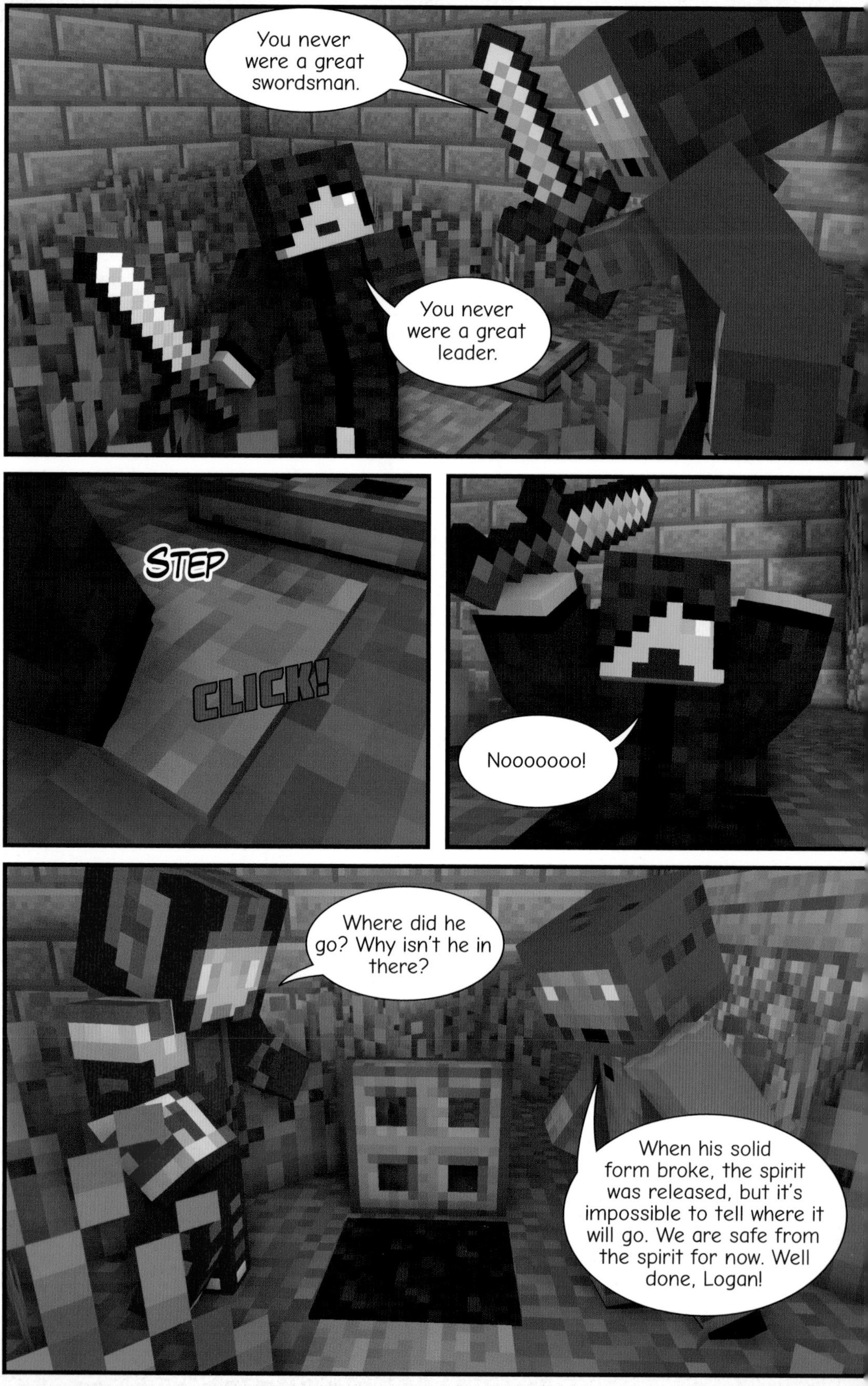
You never were a great swordsman.
You never were a great leader.
STEP
CLICK!
Noooooooo!
Where did he go? Why isn't he in there?
When his solid form broke, the spirit was released, but it's impossible to tell where it will go. We are safe from the spirit for now. Well done, Logan!

# CHAPTER 12

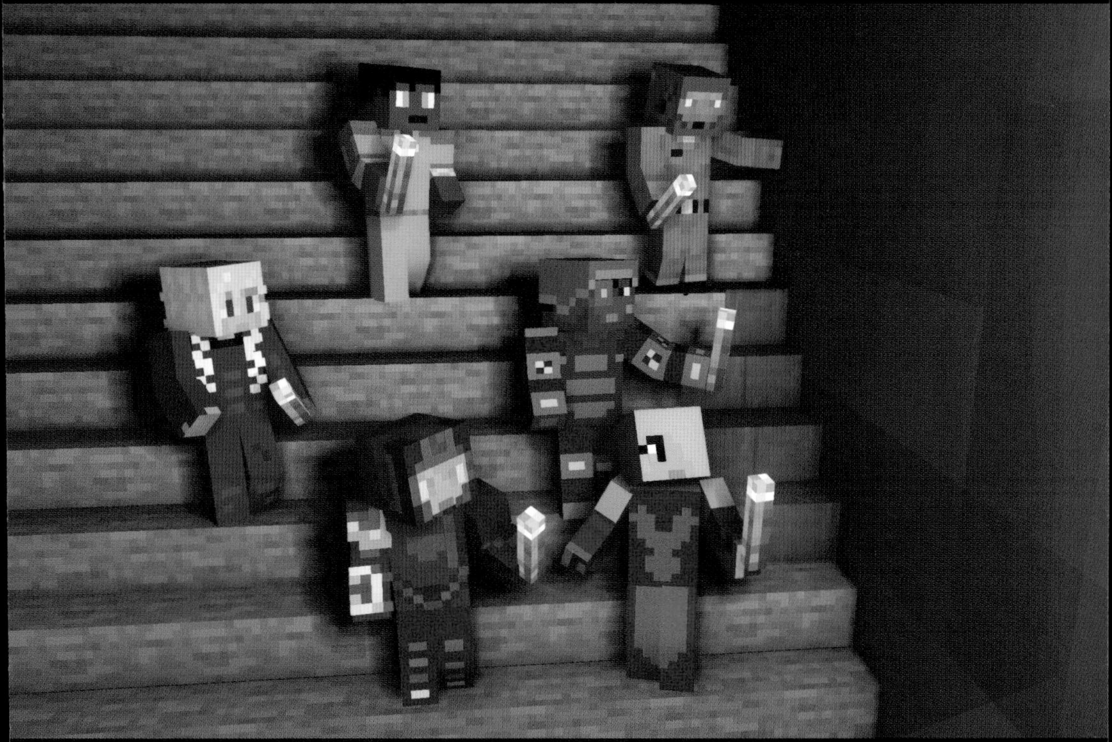

# KEEPING WATCH

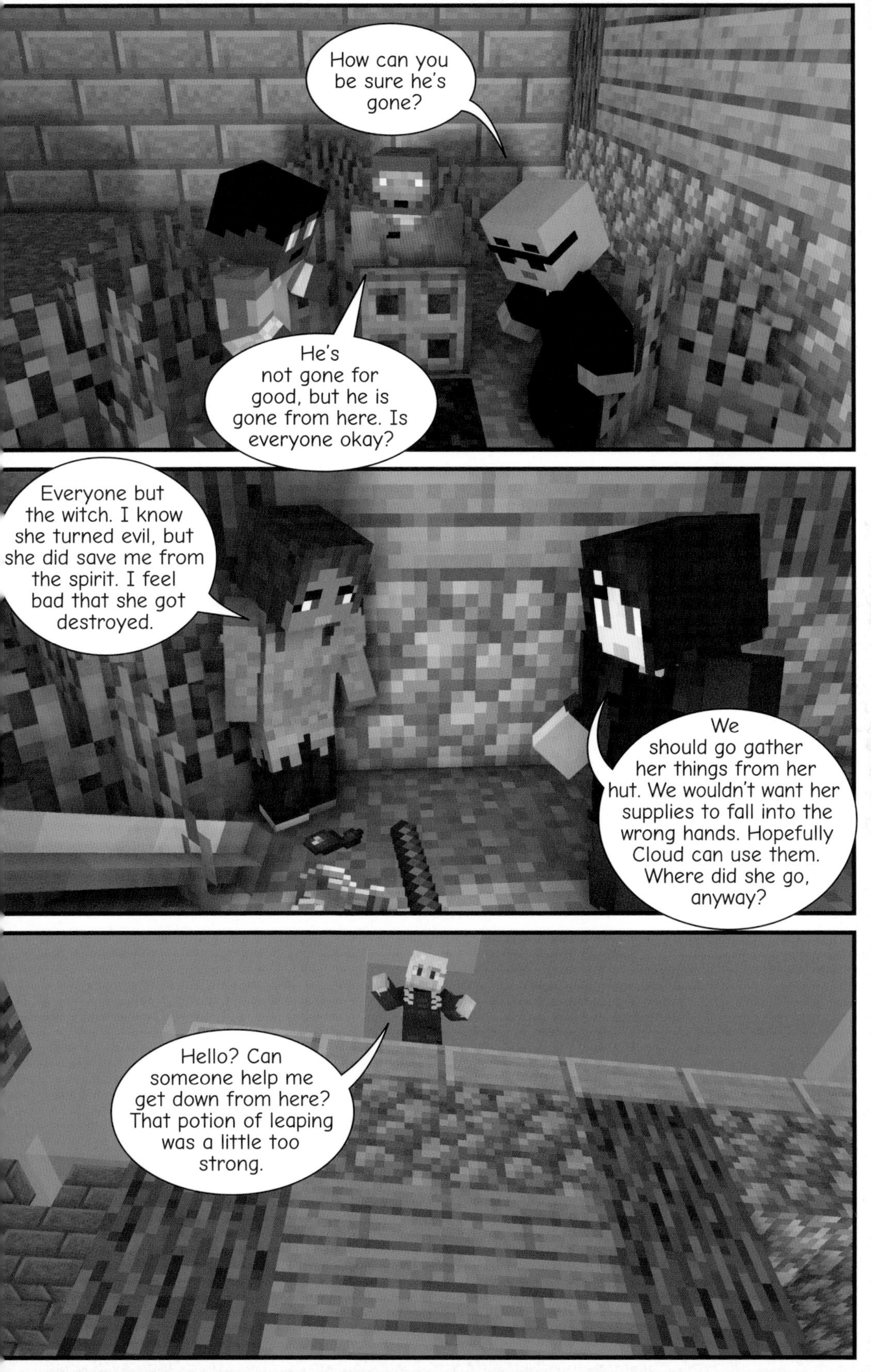
How can you be sure he's gone?
He's not gone for good, but he is gone from here. Is everyone okay?
Everyone but the witch. I know she turned evil, but she did save me from the spirit. I feel bad that she got destroyed.
We should go gather her things from her hut. We wouldn't want her supplies to fall into the wrong hands. Hopefully Cloud can use them. Where did she go, anyway?
Hello? Can someone help me get down from here? That potion of leaping was a little too strong.

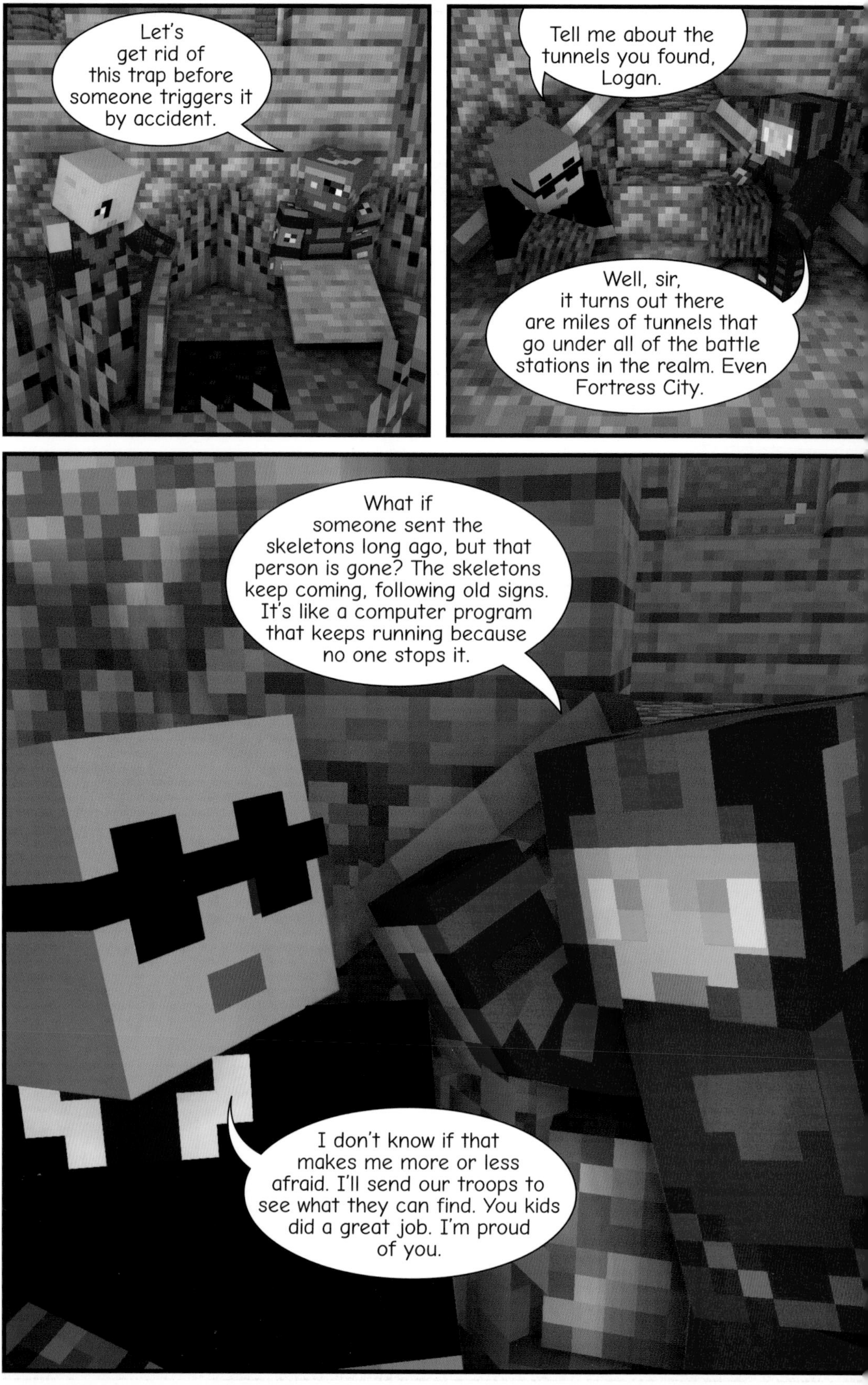
Let's get rid of this trap before someone triggers it by accident.
Tell me about the tunnels you found, Logan.
Well, sir, it turns out there are miles of tunnels that go under all of the battle stations in the realm. Even Fortress City.
What if someone sent the skeletons long ago, but that person is gone? The skeletons keep coming, following old signs. It's like a computer program that keeps running because no one stops it.
I don't know if that makes me more or less afraid. I'll send our troops to see what they can find. You kids did a great job. I'm proud of you.

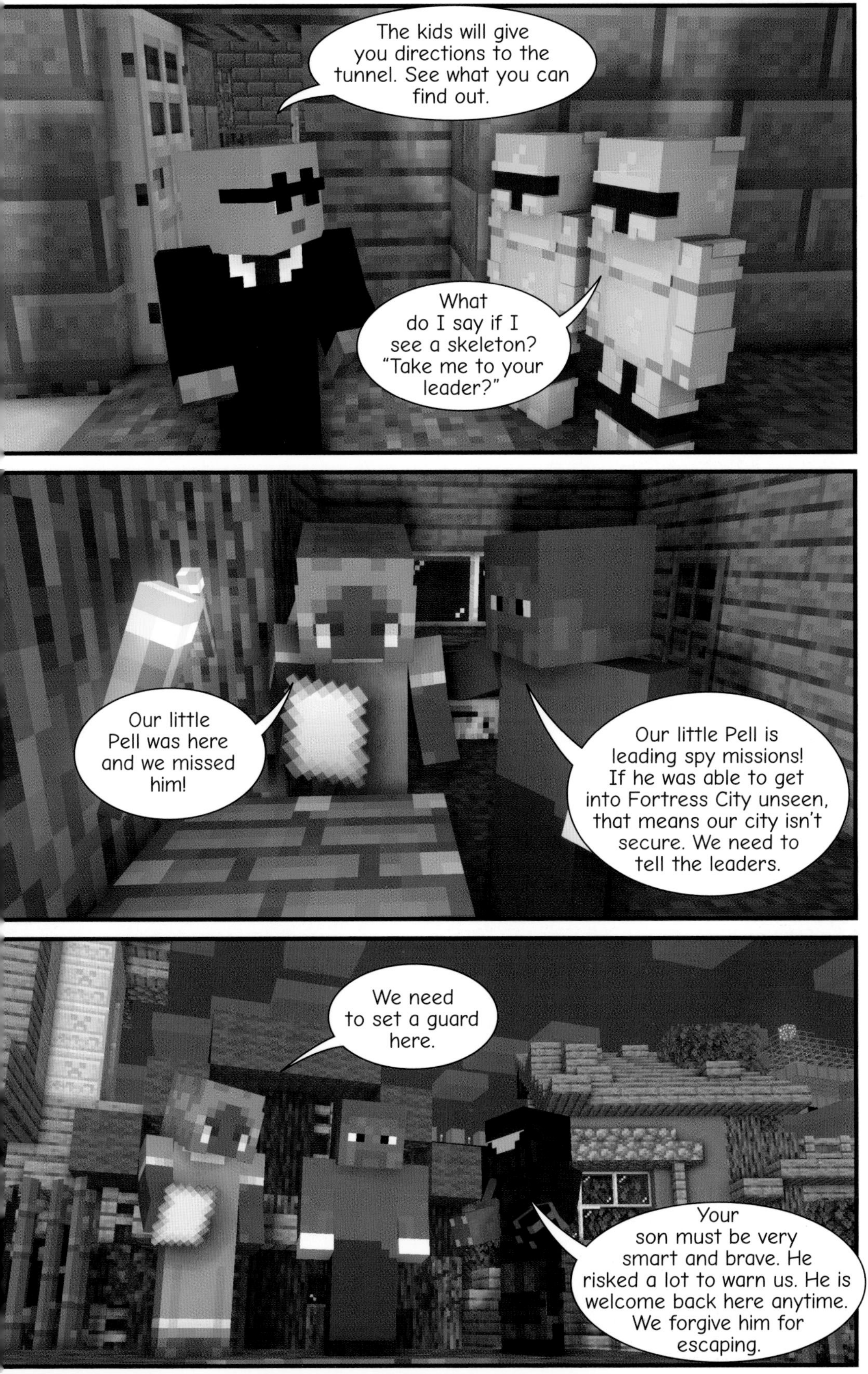
The kids will give you directions to the tunnel. See what you can find out.
What do I say if I see a skeleton? "Take me to your leader?"
Our little Pell was here and we missed him!
Our little Pell is leading spy missions! If he was able to get into Fortress City unseen, that means our city isn't secure. We need to tell the leaders.
We need to set a guard here.
Your son must be very smart and brave. He risked a lot to warn us. He is welcome back here anytime. We forgive him for escaping.

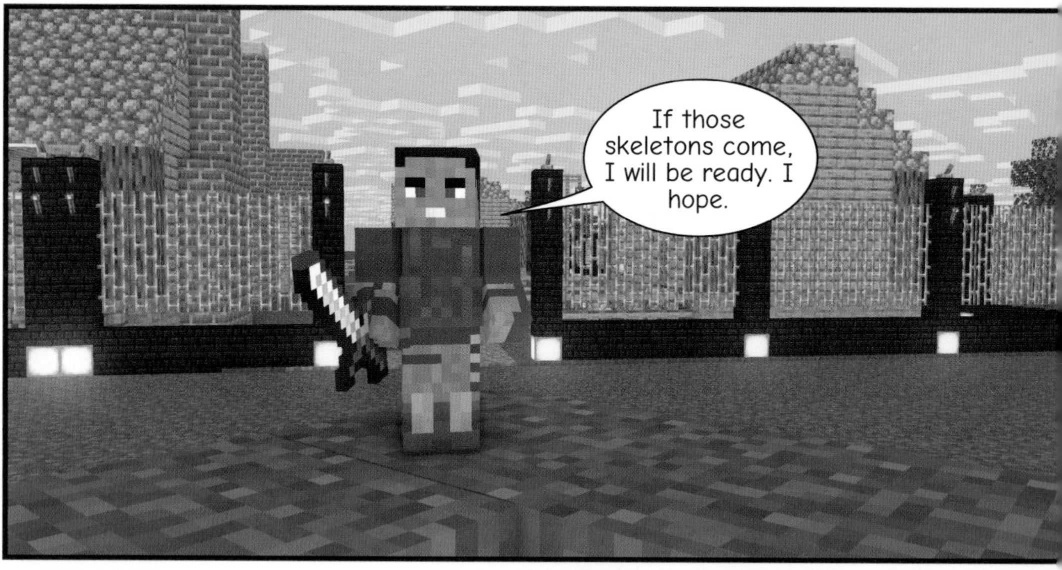
If those skeletons come, I will be ready. I hope.
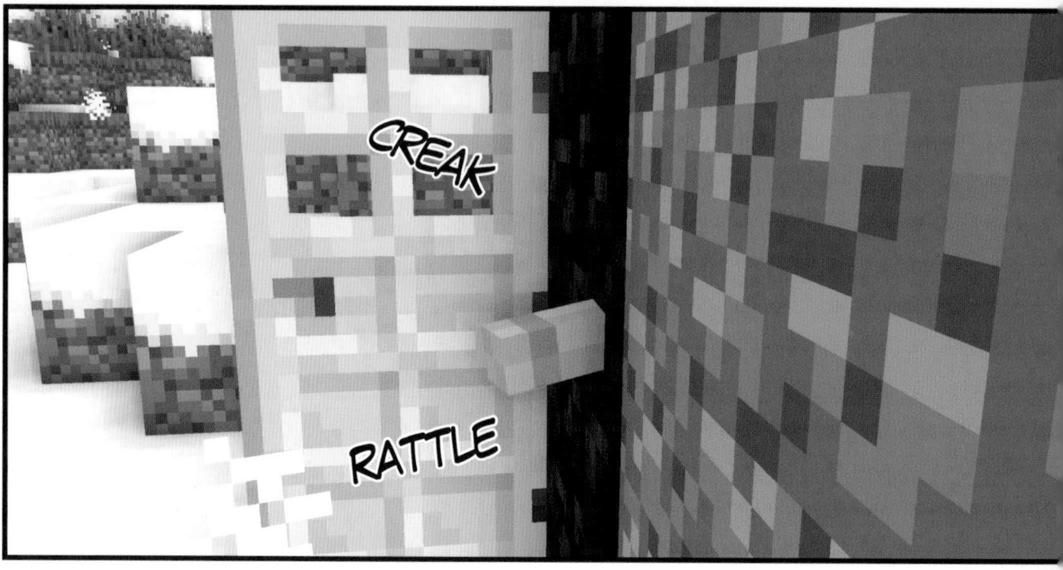
CREAK
RATTLE
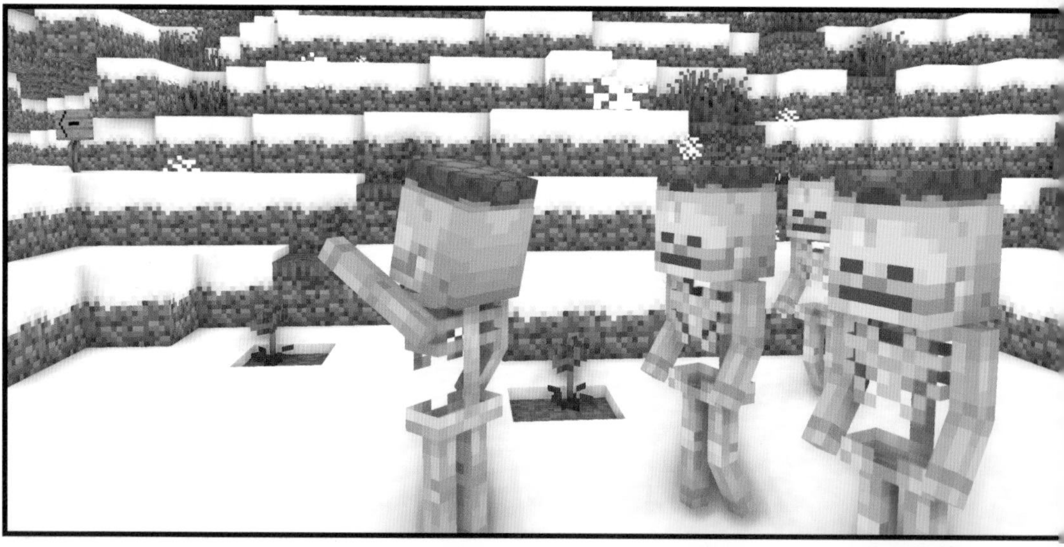

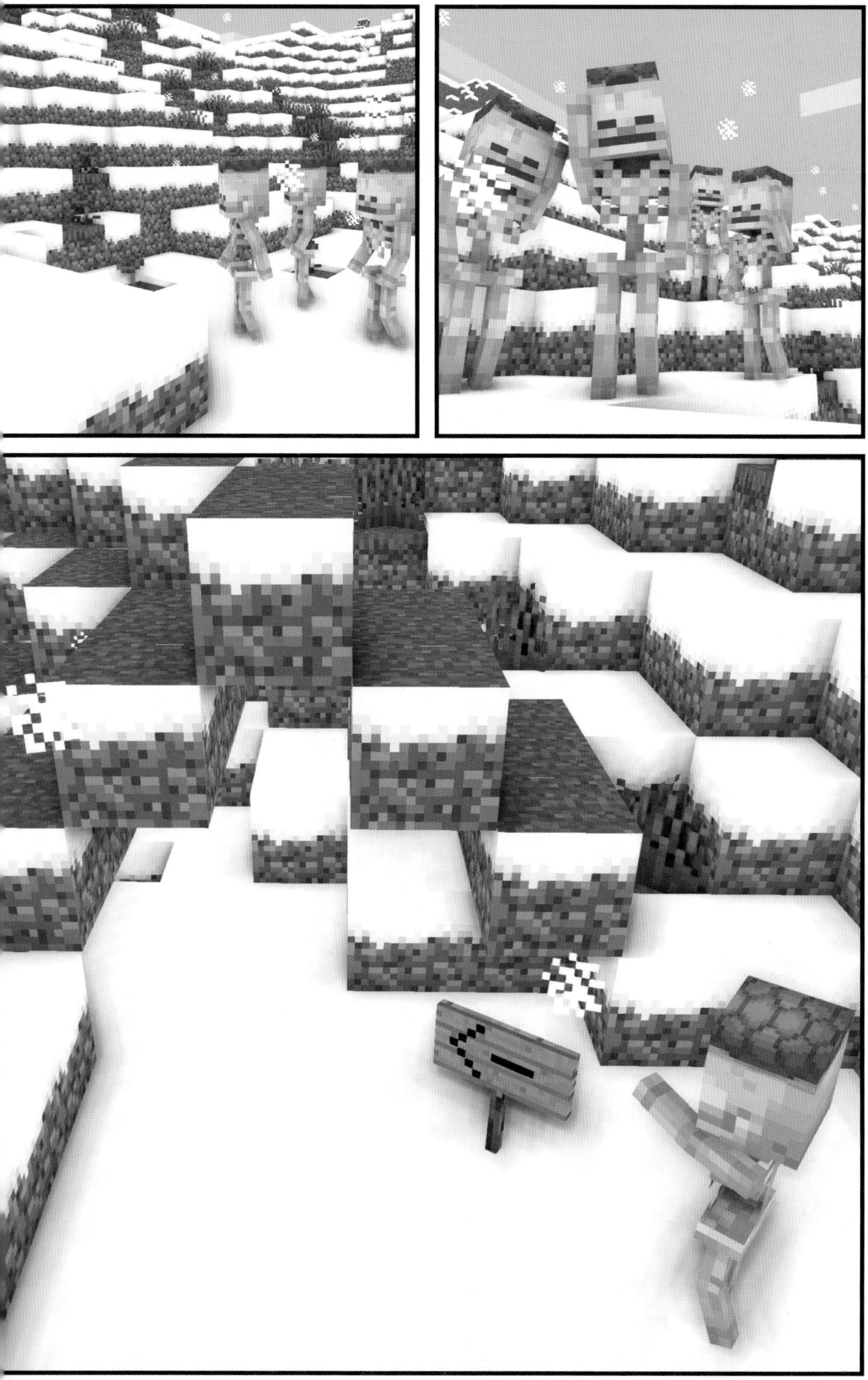

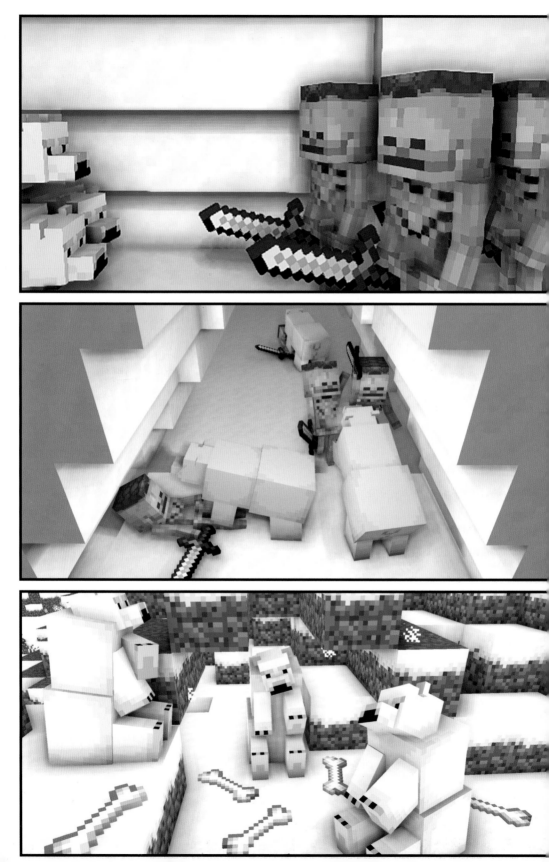

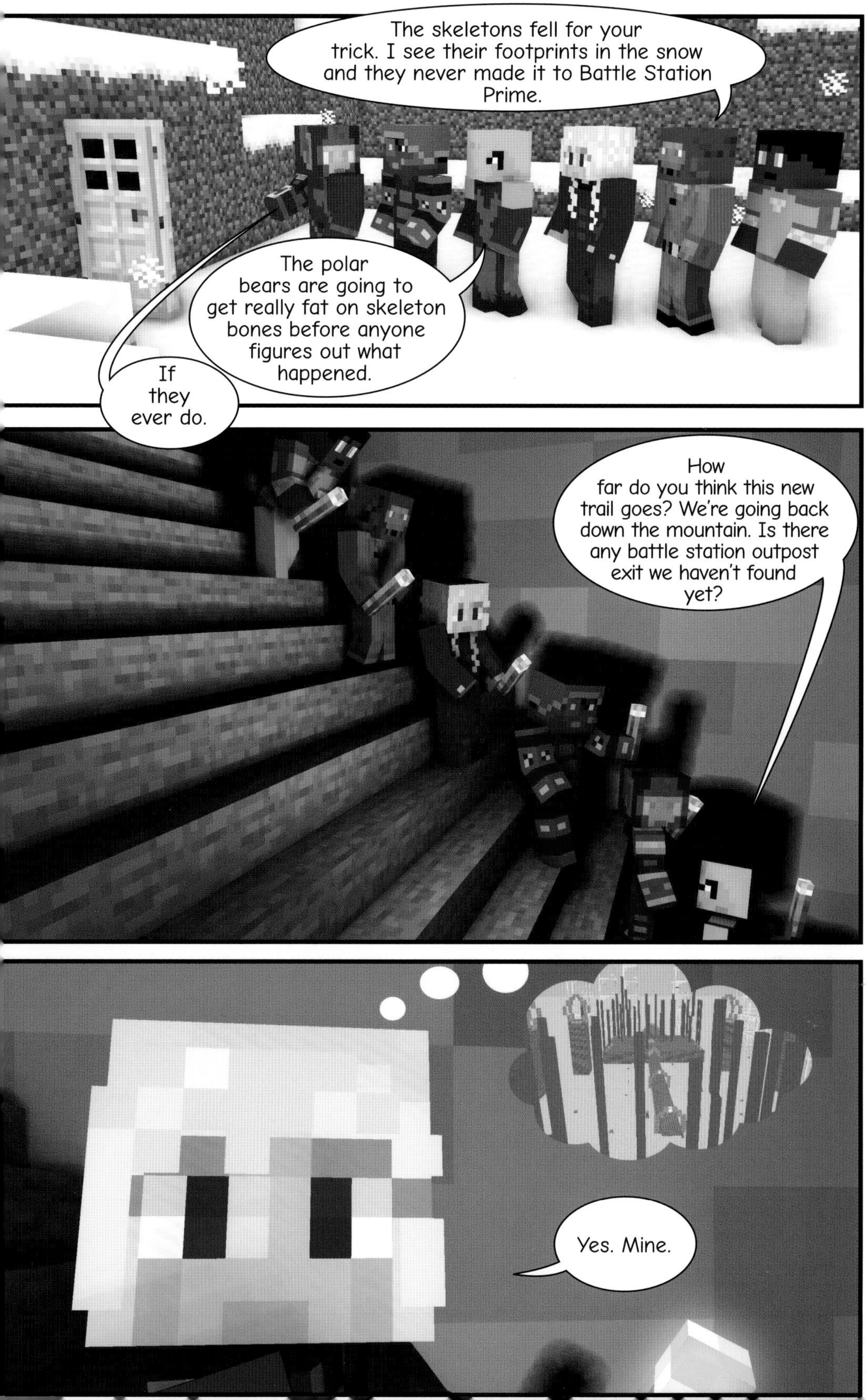
The skeletons fell for your trick. I see their footprints in the snow and they never made it to Battle Station Prime.
The polar bears are going to get really fat on skeleton bones before anyone figures out what happened.
If they ever do.
How far do you think this new trail goes? We're going back down the mountain. Is there any battle station outpost exit we haven't found yet?
Yes. Mine.

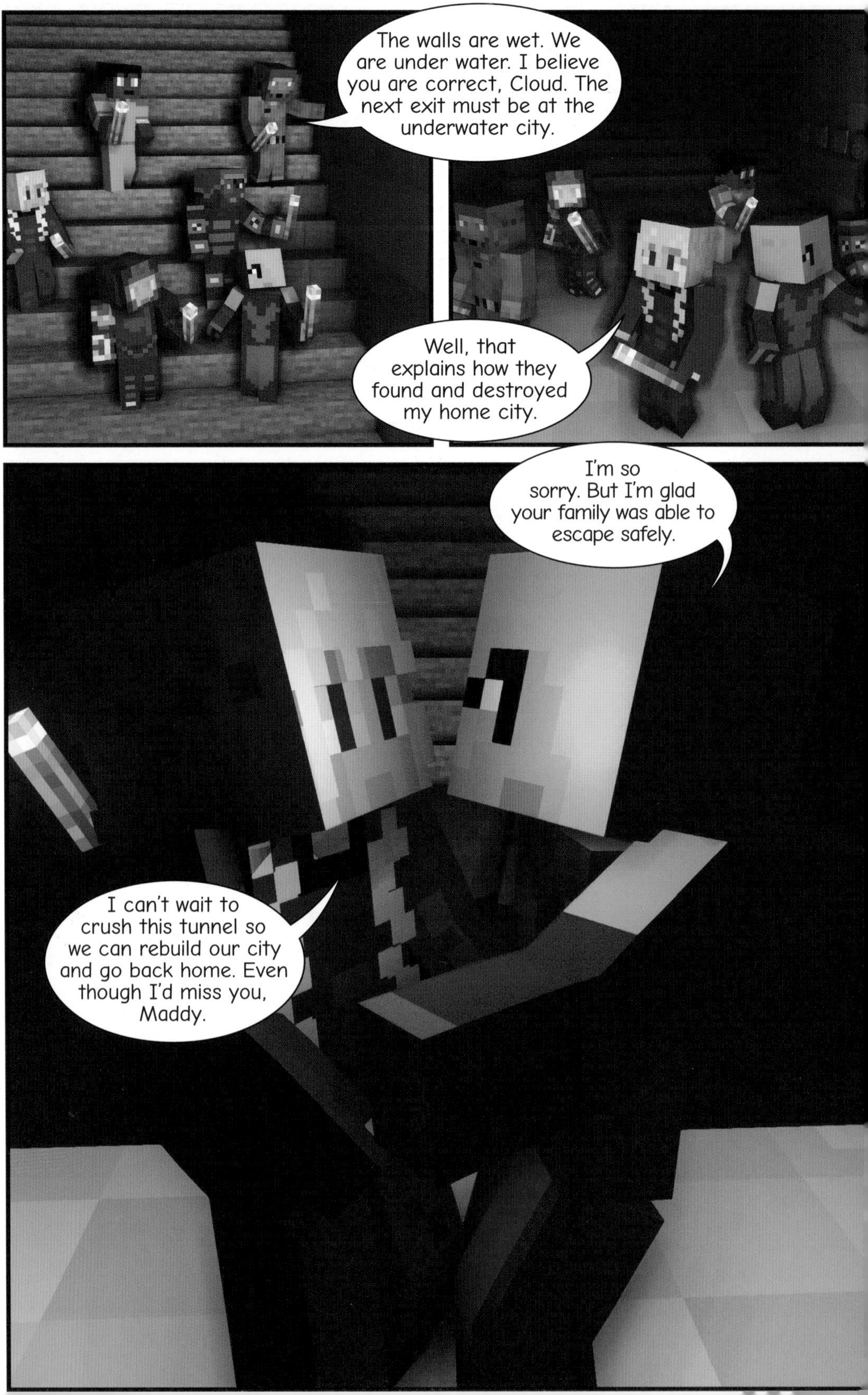
The walls are wet. We are under water. I believe you are correct, Cloud. The next exit must be at the underwater city.
Well, that explains how they found and destroyed my home city.
I'm so sorry. But I'm glad your family was able to escape safely.
I can't wait to crush this tunnel so we can rebuild our city and go back home. Even though I'd miss you, Maddy.

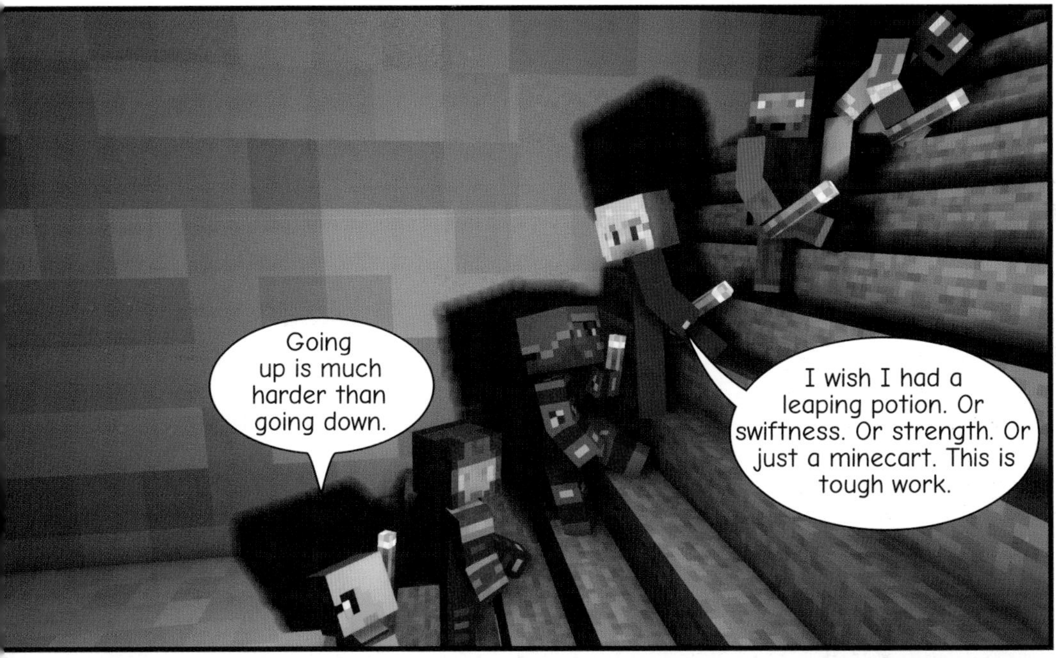
Going up is much harder than going down.
I wish I had a leaping potion. Or swiftness. Or strength. Or just a minecart. This is tough work.
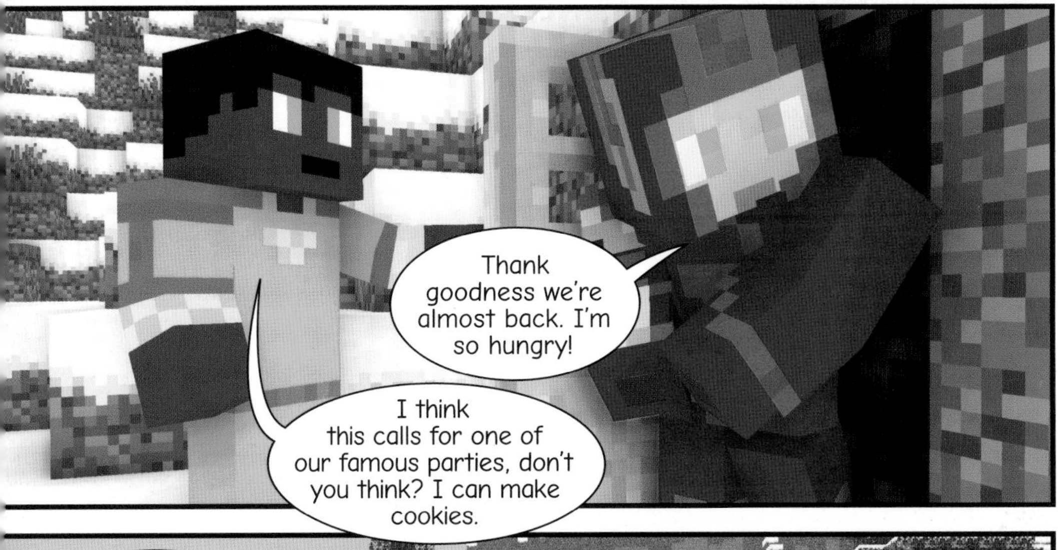
Thank goodness we're almost back. I'm so hungry!
I think this calls for one of our famous parties, don't you think? I can make cookies.
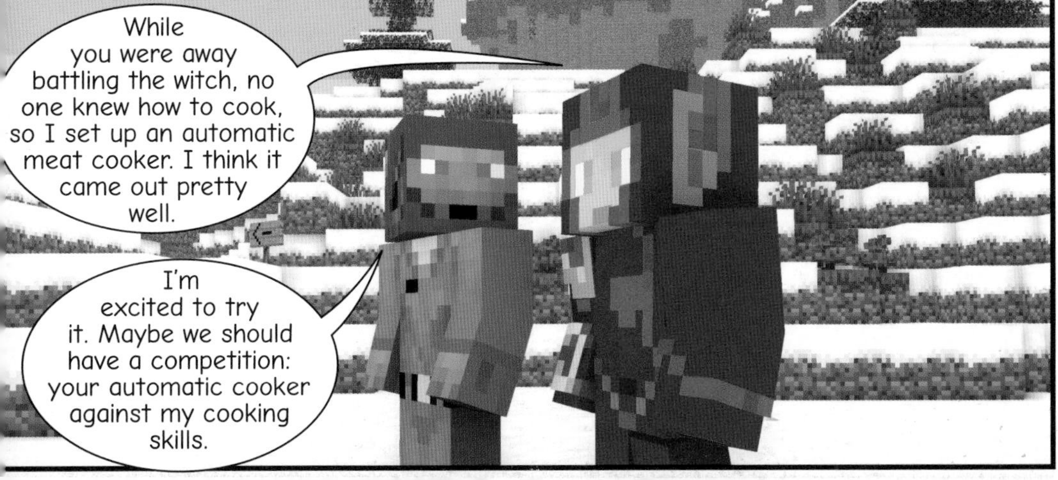
While you were away battling the witch, no one knew how to cook, so I set up an automatic meat cooker. I think it came out pretty well.
I'm excited to try it. Maybe we should have a competition: your automatic cooker against my cooking skills.

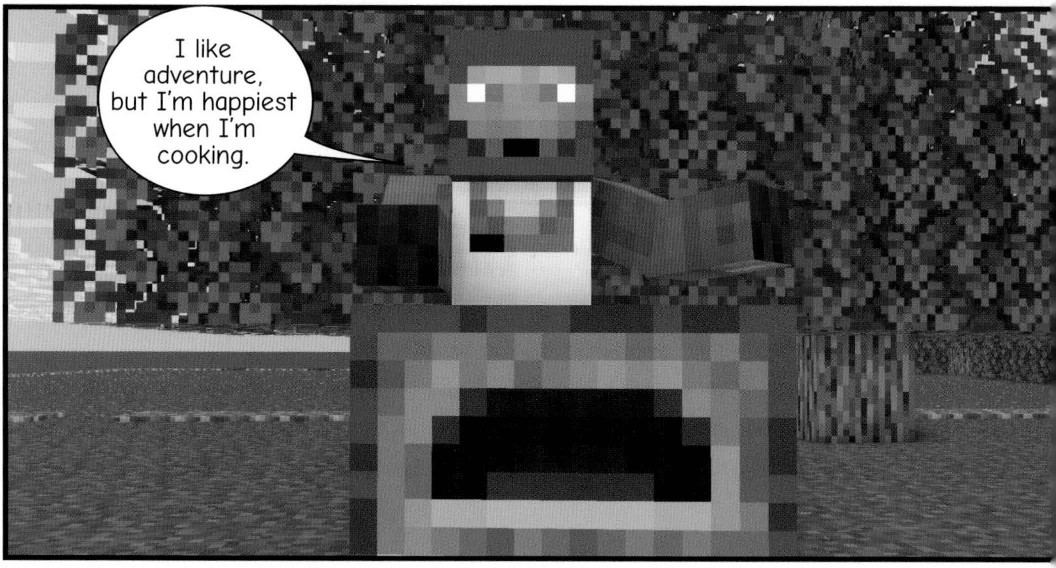
I like adventure, but I'm happiest when I'm cooking.

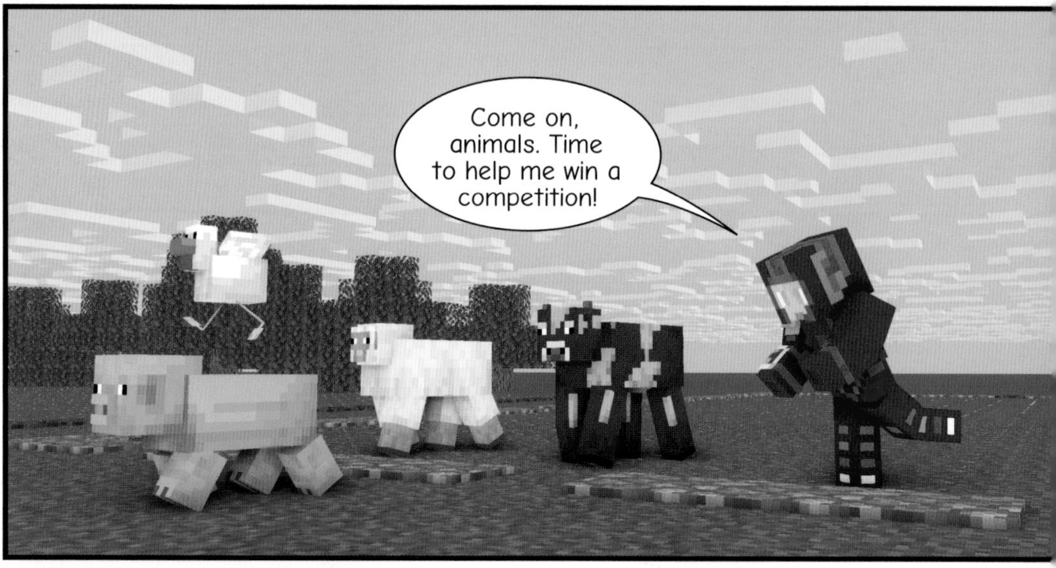
Come on, animals. Time to help me win a competition!

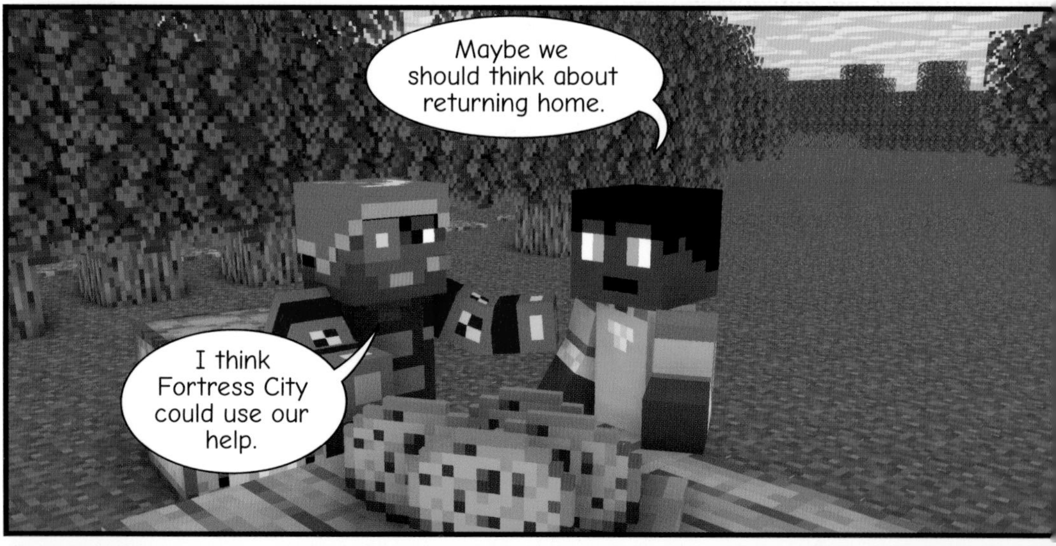
Maybe we should think about returning home.
I think Fortress City could use our help.

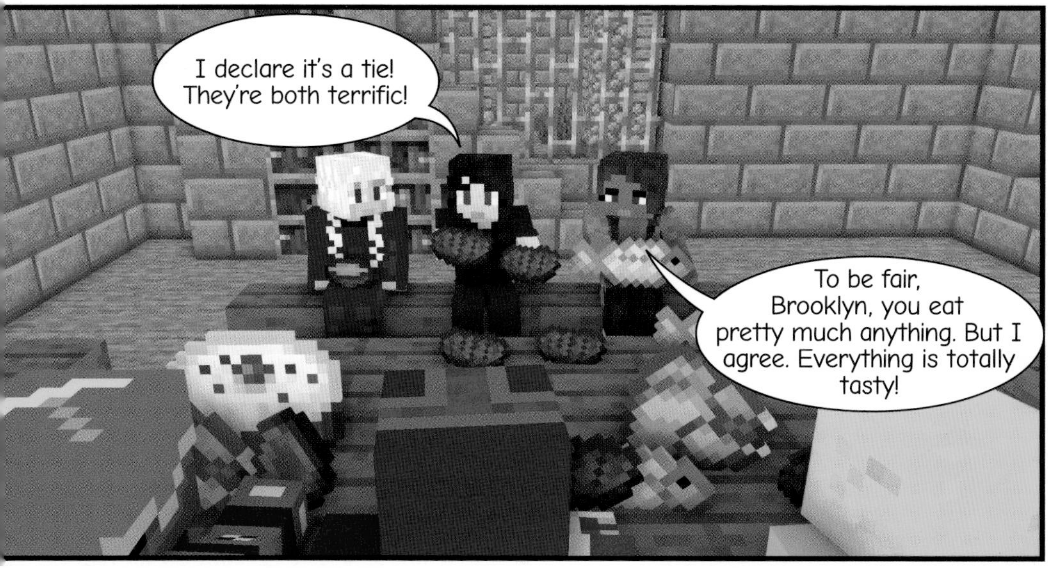
I declare it's a tie! They're both terrific!
To be fair, Brooklyn, you eat pretty much anything. But I agree. Everything is totally tasty!

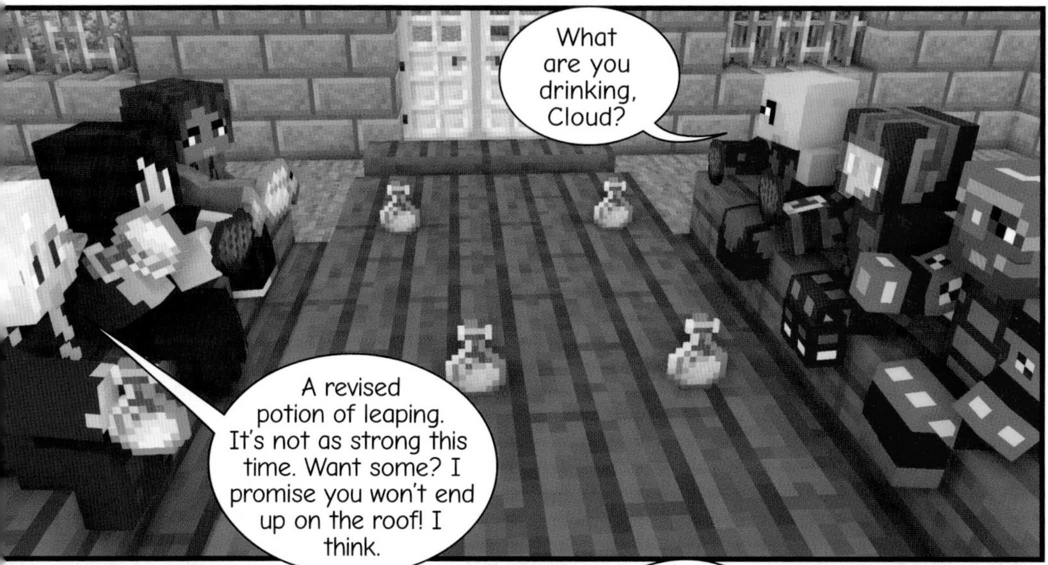
What are you drinking, Cloud?
A revised potion of leaping. It's not as strong this time. Want some? I promise you won't end up on the roof! I think.

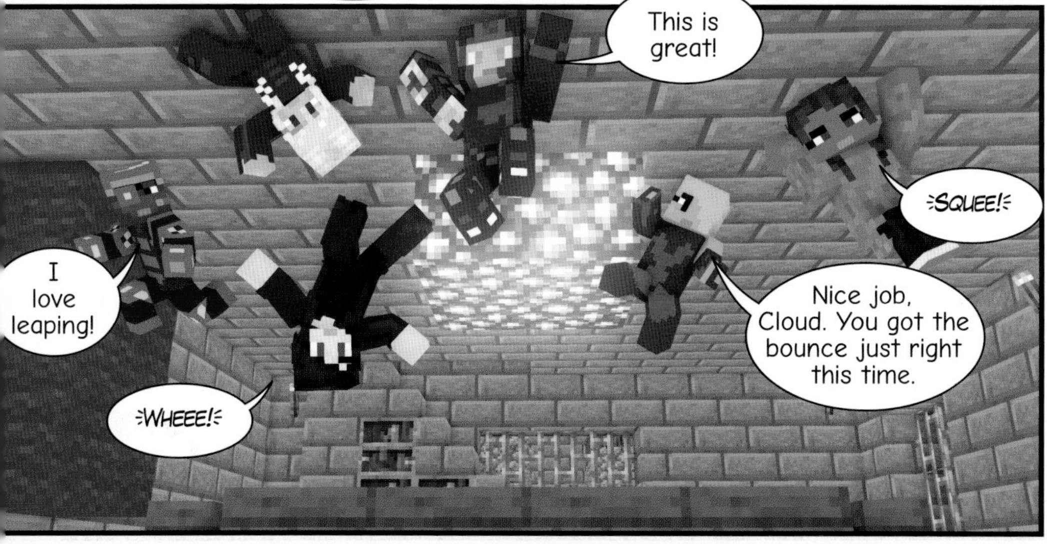
This is great!
SQUEE!
I love leaping!
Nice job, Cloud. You got the bounce just right this time.
WHEEE!

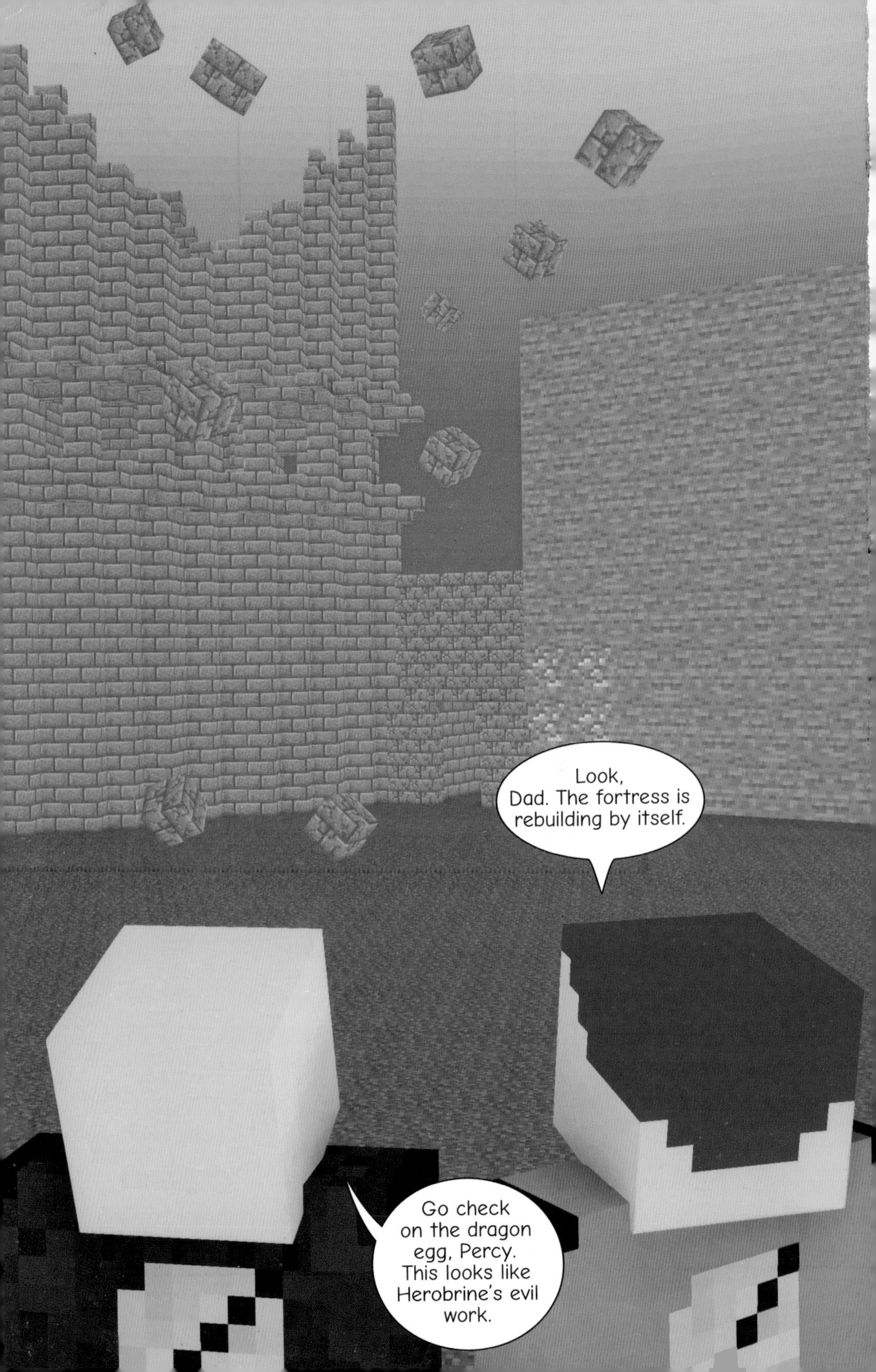
Look, Dad. The fortress is rebuilding by itself.
Go check on the dragon egg, Percy. This looks like Herobrine's evil work.

# ANATOMY
## OF STRENGTH
## TRAINING

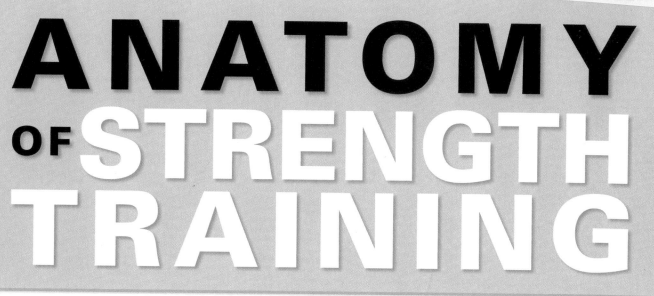

**General Disclaimer**

The contents of this book are intended to provide useful information to the general public. All materials, including texts, graphics, and images, are for informational purposes only and are not a substitute for medical diagnosis, advice, or treatment for specific medical conditions. All readers should seek expert medical care and consult their own physicians before commencing any exercise program or for any general or specific health issues. The author and publishers do not recommend or endorse specific treatments, procedures, advice, or other information found in this book and specifically disclaim all responsibility for any and all liability, loss, or risk, personal or otherwise, which is incurred as a consequence, directly or indirectly, of the use or application of any of the material in this publication.

Thunder Bay Press
An imprint of the Baker & Taylor Publishing Group
10350 Barnes Canyon Road, San Diego, CA 92121
www.thunderbaybooks.com

All notations of errors or omissions should be addressed to Thunder Bay Press, Editorial Department, at the above address. All other correspondence (author inquiries, permissions) concerning the content of this book should be addressed to Moseley Road, Inc., 123 Main Street, Irvington, NY 10533. www.moseleyroad.com.

ISBN-13: 978-1-60710-204-5
ISBN-10: 1-60710-204-8

Printed in Canada
2  3  4  5   14  13  12  11  10

# ANATOMY OF STRENGTH TRAINING

## The 5 Essential Exercises

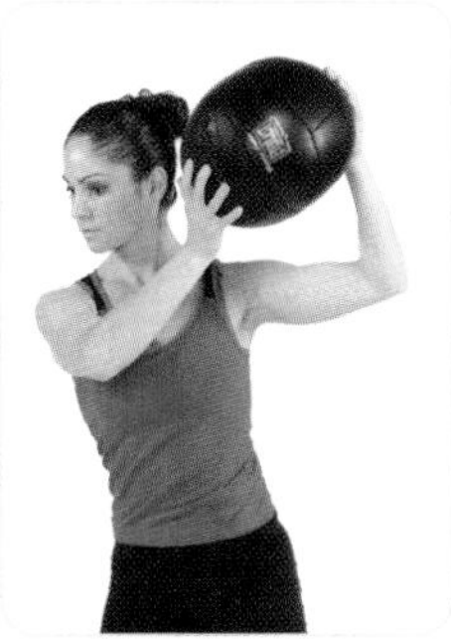
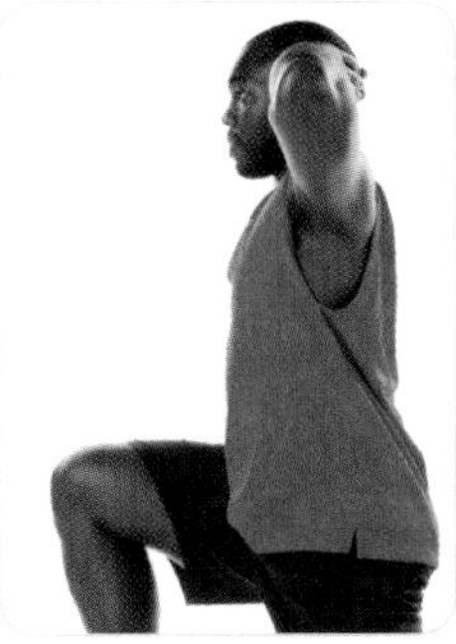
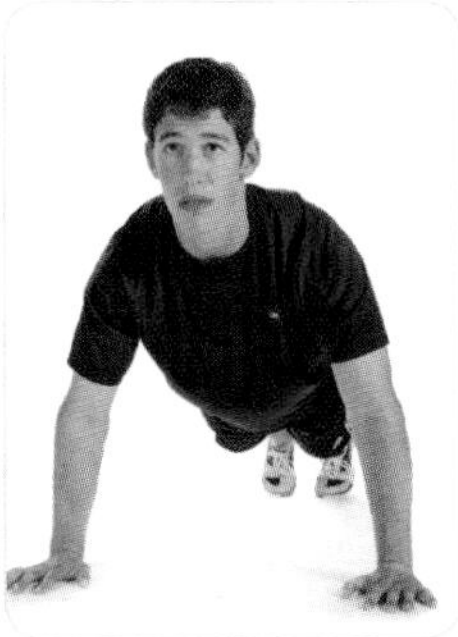
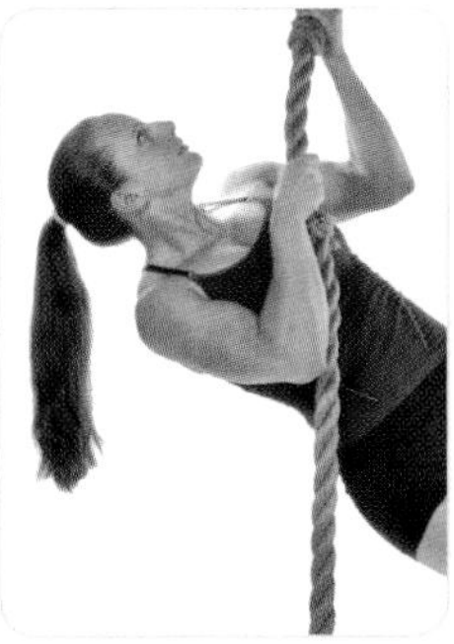
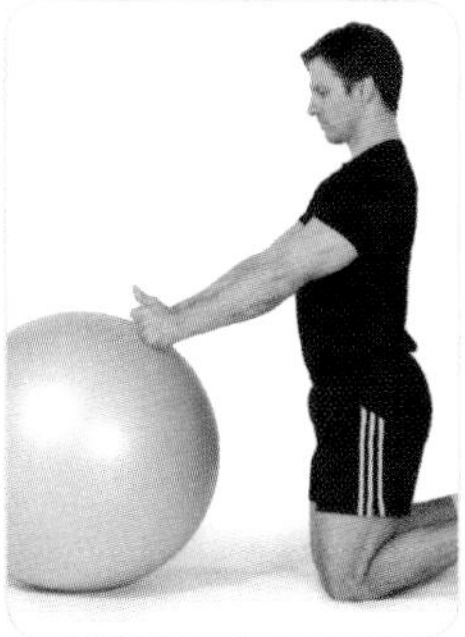

PAT MANOCCHIA

THUNDER BAY
P·R·E·S·S

San Diego, California

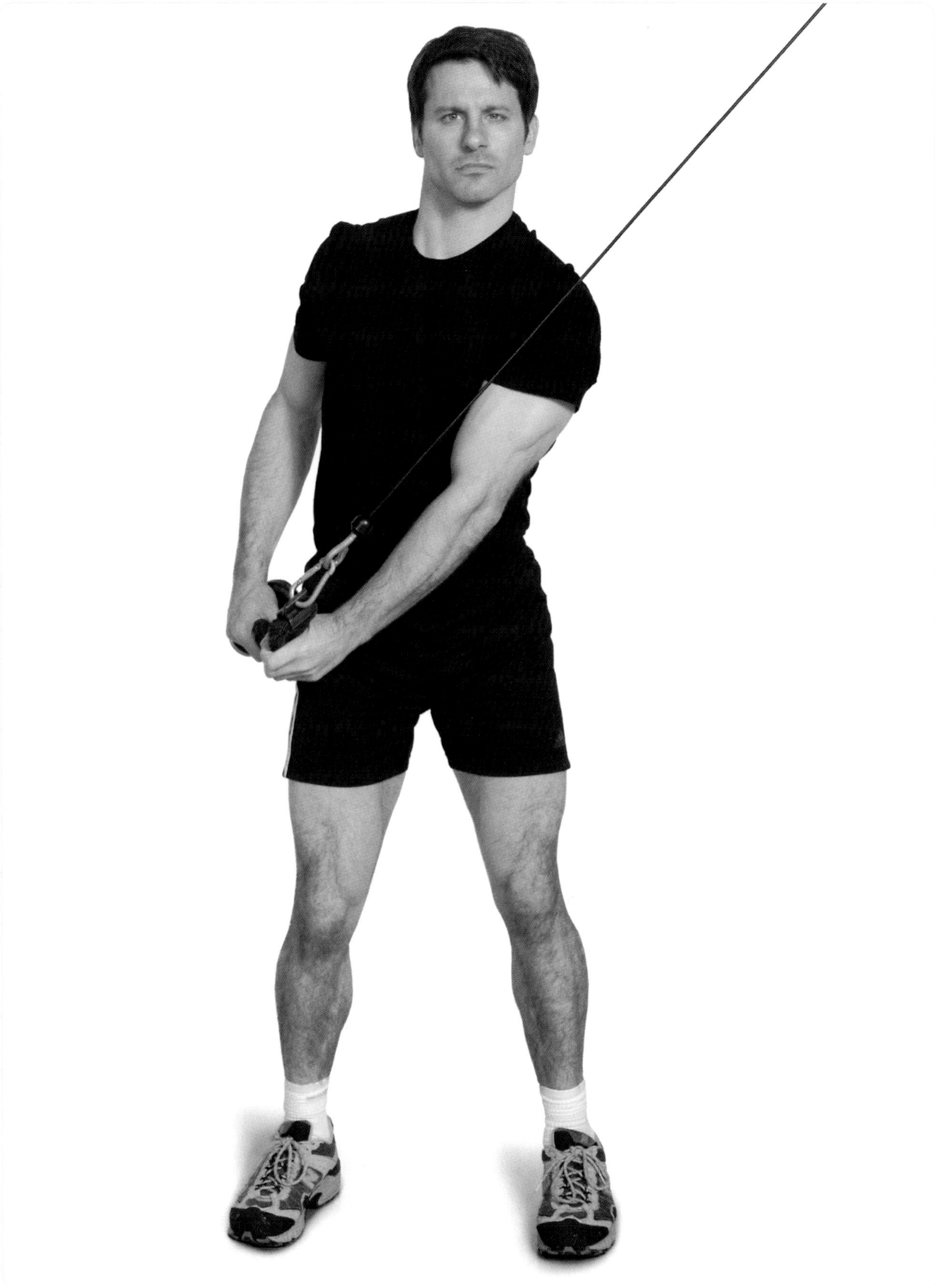

# CONTENTS

# THE 5 ESSENTIAL EXERCISES

The ultimate objective of any strength-training program is this: effectiveness. First and foremost, effective strength training or musculoskeletal conditioning must address all of the muscles, bones, joints, ligaments, and tendons of the body. This is because the body is a system, and that system (like any other system) is only as good as its weakest link.

Therefore, in order for any strength-training program to be truly effective, it must address the body as a system, and regardless of whether it is for a sixteen-year-old or a sixty-year-old, a linebacker or a librarian, in my opinion, the program must consist of 5 Essential Exercises.

The reason that this is the case is quite simply, that when broken down into components, the body does only five things: *flexion* (bending of a joint), *extension* (straightening of a joint), *adduction* (moving limb toward the body), *abduction* (moving limb away from the body), and *rotation* (turning or twisting). In this book, I've created categories of exercises that represent each movement, and in some cases combine two different ones depending on the joint being activated:

1. Deadlift

2. Lunge

3. Push-up

4. Chin-up

5. Ab Wheel

## 1. DEADLIFT

## 2. LUNGE

## 3. PUSH-UP

## 4. CHIN-UP

## 5. AB WHEEL

The categories provide a 5 Essential Exercise regimen that addresses each of the body's movements. Below are the five exercises, primary muscles, and movements addressed in each exercise category.

| EXERCISE | JOINTS | FUNCTION |
| --- | --- | --- |
| 1. Deadlift | Hip, Back, Knee | Extension |
| 2. Lunge | Hip, Knee | Extension, Adduction, Abduction |
| 3. Push-up | Shoulder, Elbow | Flexion, Adduction, Extension |
| 4. Chin-up | Shoulder, Elbow | Extension, Flexion |
| 5. Ab Wheel | Hip, Back, Knee | Flexion |

In this book, the rotational aspect of movement is basically addressed by either creating a rotational torque using unilateral resistance, or by using the same basic movement in a different plane.

I've included approximately ten to fifteen variations of each exercise, all of which make the specific category address slightly different aspects of the body's function. Any level of conditioning can be effectively built on these five movements with a very modest, very basic set of equipment.

This book includes visual and textual representations of each of the 5 Essential Exercises, as well as variations that you can make in order to adjust for skill level and intensity when using them. I've also included a basic matrix of conditioning programs depicting some different ways in which the exercises may be used. There are many, many ways to skin the proverbial cat, so consequently there is an almost unlimited amount of variety that can be created programmatically by mixing and matching elements from each of the five categories.

You must understand that the end result will also depend on how you use these essentials. The "how," or variables, that need to be manipulated for these exercises are *skill, time, intensity,* and *frequency*, or, more specifically, repetitions, sets, weights, sessions per week, increments of progression, and technique.

There are many excellent books on how to use these variables for a given desired effect, ranging from increased overall endurance and range of motion to absolute strength and the ability to generate power (force at high speeds), so I will not address anything in this book to that level of specificity. This book is designed to give anyone an understanding of the necessary elements of muscular conditioning and to guide you on how they should be used, with some basic programs as examples.

I also would like to be crystal clear from the beginning regarding the commitment required to be successful with a conditioning program: There are NO SHORTCUTS! I in no way want the reader to assume that this is a "seven-minute-a-day" deal. That is simply not ever the case. I am, and have always been, vehemently opposed to the idea of "shortening" or "condensing" the time required to become healthy and fit. It simply does not work like that. This book is ultimately about *process*, and the focus is specifically on how to maximize the quality of the process by organizing and simplifying it. I sincerely hope that the information here sheds some light on how to efficiently craft an exercise program for musculoskeletal conditioning, whether you are a rank beginner or an elite athlete.

# FULL-BODY ANATOMY

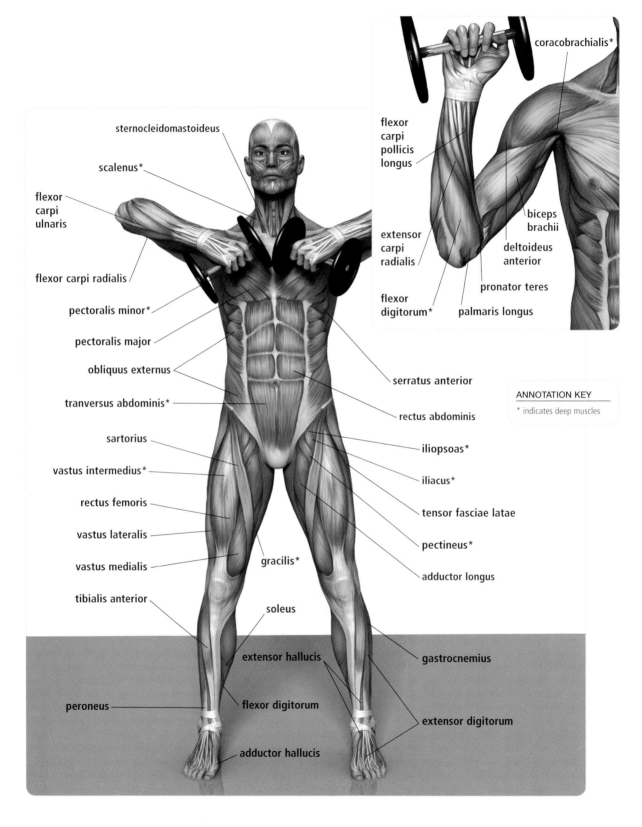

coracobrachialis*

flexor
carpi
pollicis
longus

extensor
carpi
radialis

flexor
digitorum*

biceps
brachii

deltoideus
anterior

pronator teres

palmaris longus

sternocleidomastoideus

scalenus*

flexor
carpi
ulnaris

flexor carpi radialis

pectoralis minor*

pectoralis major

obliquus externus

tranversus abdominis*

sartorius

vastus intermedius*

rectus femoris

vastus lateralis

vastus medialis

tibialis anterior

peroneus

serratus anterior

rectus abdominis

iliopsoas*

iliacus*

tensor fasciae latae

pectineus*

adductor longus

gracilis*

soleus

extensor hallucis

flexor digitorum

adductor hallucis

gastrocnemius

extensor digitorum

ANNOTATION KEY

* indicates deep muscles

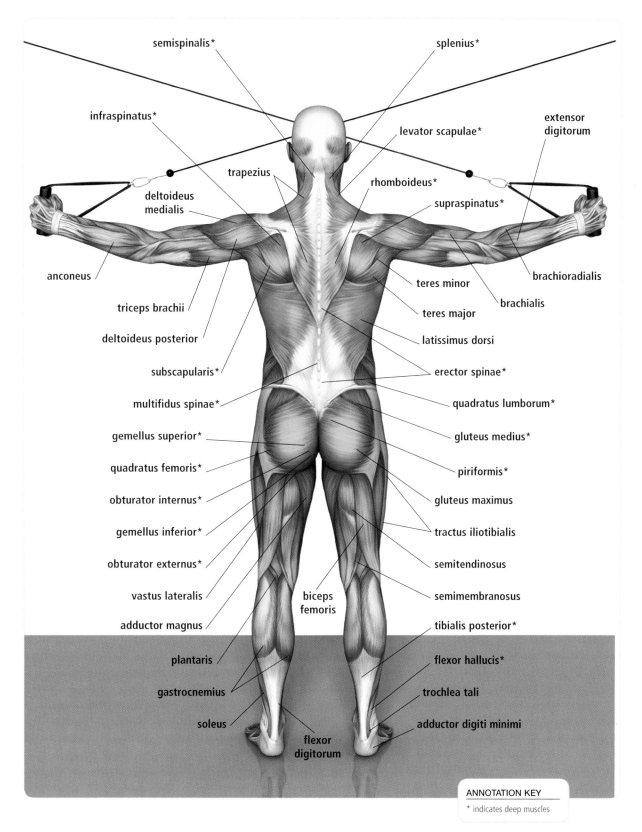

semispinalis*

splenius*

infraspinatus*

levator scapulae*

extensor digitorum

trapezius

deltoideus medialis

rhomboideus*

supraspinatus*

anconeus

brachioradialis

teres minor

triceps brachii

brachialis

teres major

deltoideus posterior

latissimus dorsi

subscapularis*

erector spinae*

multifidus spinae*

quadratus lumborum*

gemellus superior*

gluteus medius*

quadratus femoris*

piriformis*

obturator internus*

gluteus maximus

gemellus inferior*

tractus iliotibialis

obturator externus*

semitendinosus

vastus lateralis

semimembranosus

biceps femoris

adductor magnus

tibialis posterior*

plantaris

flexor hallucis*

gastrocnemius

trochlea tali

soleus

flexor digitorum

adductor digiti minimi

**ANNOTATION KEY**

* indicates deep muscles

II

# DEADLIFT

Of all the traditional movements that people perform while exercising, the deadlift is arguably the most important of them all. Why? Because it is the most applicable to everyday life: it is something we do every single day, young and old, rich and poor, weak and strong. From picking up our laundry bags to carrying our briefcases, this movement—and variations of it—*must* be a cornerstone of any exercise program.

The joints involved are the ankle, knee, hip, spine, and shoulder (and wrist isometrically). The primary muscles are the hamstrings; glutes; calf muscles; lower, middle, and upper back muscles; shoulder muscles; and forearm muscles. In this movement, all of these muscles function primarily as extensors.

Primary benefits are hip, leg, and lower-back strength, as well as improved spinal position (posture) and range of motion (flexibility).

# DEADLIFT

## FULL WITH BARBELL

1

**Starting Position:** With the barbell on the ground and your feet shoulder-width apart, stand so that your shins contact the bar. Grasp the bar with an alternating grip (with one palm facing toward you and the other away) or with palms facing inward (toward your body). Keep your spine neutral, positioned at a 45-degree angle to perpendicular. Drop and retract your hips so that your upper legs are parallel to the ground (or as close to parallel as your flexibility will allow). Position your shoulder joints directly over the bar. Make sure that your feet are flat and your weight is evenly distributed. Pull your chest, head, and rib cage up and your abdominal muscles up and in. Inhale at the bottom of the position.

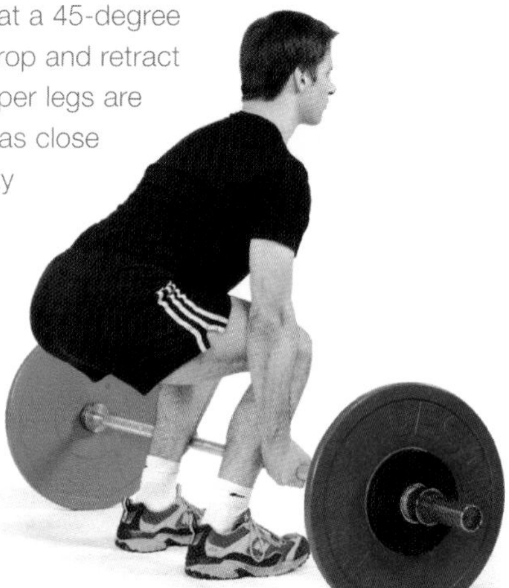

2

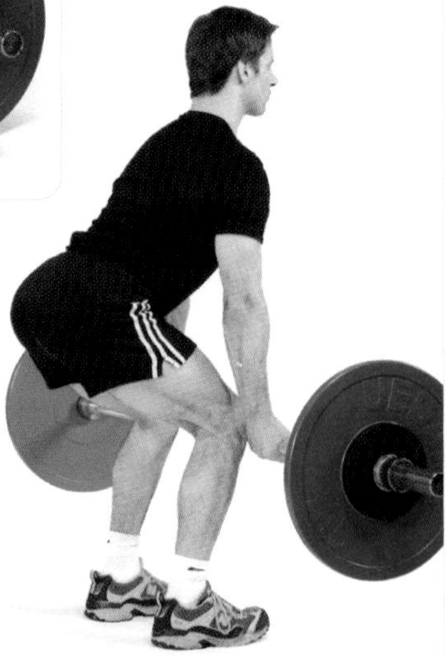

**Action:** Exhale, and drive your torso up and backward and your hips up and forward. Push your feet into the ground, extending your knees and pulling backward on the bar with your upper back and shoulders until you arrive at a vertical position.

3

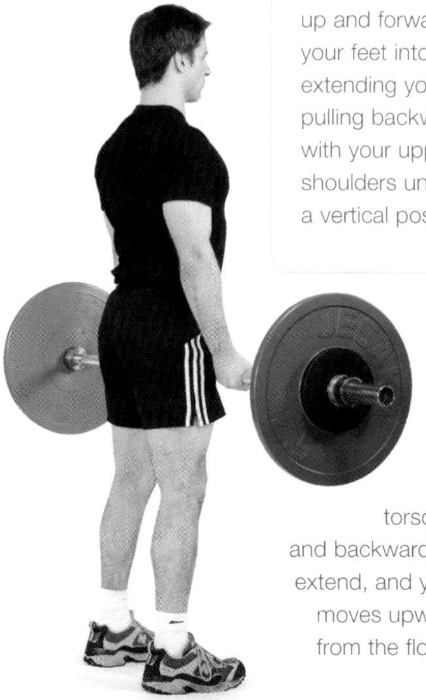

**Movement Path:** Your hips move upward and forward while your spine and torso move upward and backward, your knees extend, and your entire body moves upward and away from the floor.

### STABILIZE BY

- Keeping your rib cage high and your head up.
- Pushing your shoulders down and back, with your shoulder blades flat on your rib cage.
- Keeping your knees directly over your feet.

### LOOK FOR

- The angle of your spine to never drop below 45 degrees during the movement.
- A slight arch in your back throughout the movement.
- All of your joints to move at the same time and at the same rate.

### AVOID

- Straightening your knees prior to extending your back and hips.
- Rounding your back.
- Elevating your shoulders or lowering your head.
- Allowing your knees to migrate either inward or outward.

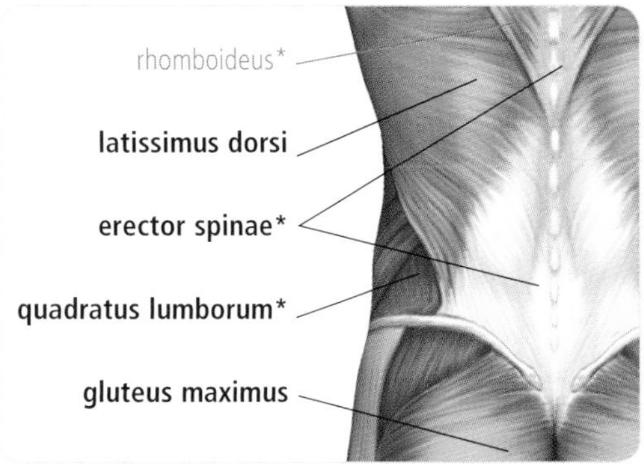
rhomboideus*
latissimus dorsi
erector spinae*
quadratus lumborum*
gluteus maximus

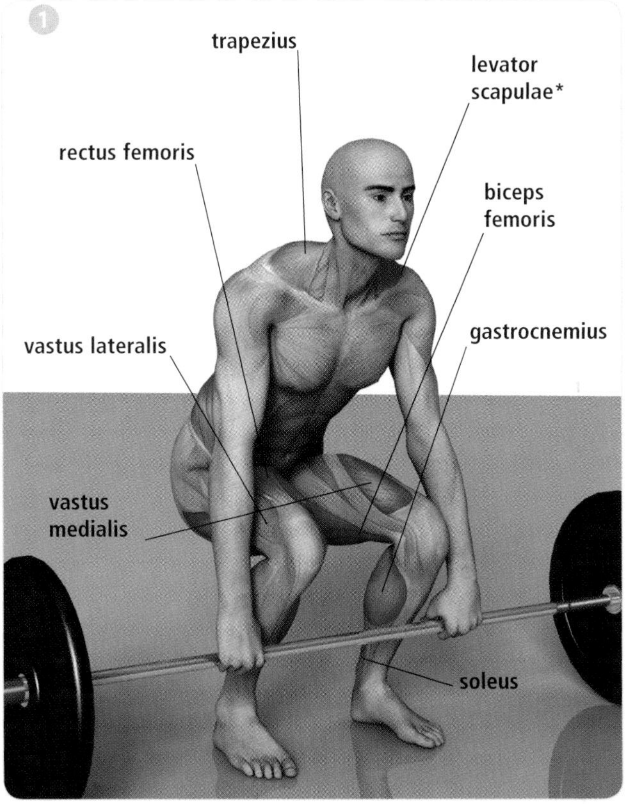
1
trapezius
levator scapulae*
rectus femoris
biceps femoris
vastus lateralis
gastrocnemius
vastus medialis
soleus

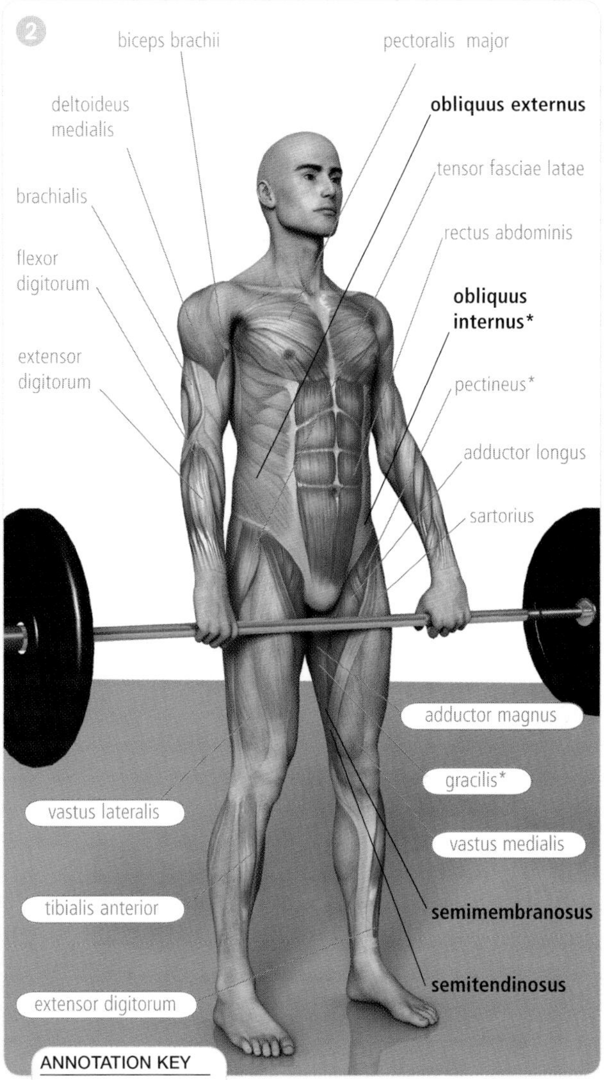
2
biceps brachii
pectoralis major
deltoideus medialis
obliquus externus
tensor fasciae latae
brachialis
rectus abdominis
flexor digitorum
obliquus internus*
extensor digitorum
pectineus*
adductor longus
sartorius
adductor magnus
gracilis*
vastus lateralis
vastus medialis
tibialis anterior
semimembranosus
semitendinosus
extensor digitorum

ANNOTATION KEY

**Black text indicates active muscles**

Gray text indicates stabilizing muscles

* indicates deep muscles

MODIFICATION

**Similar Difficulty:** Start with dumbbells on the ground adjacent to the outside of feet. Grasp dumbbells with palms facing inward. Follow same action and movement path.

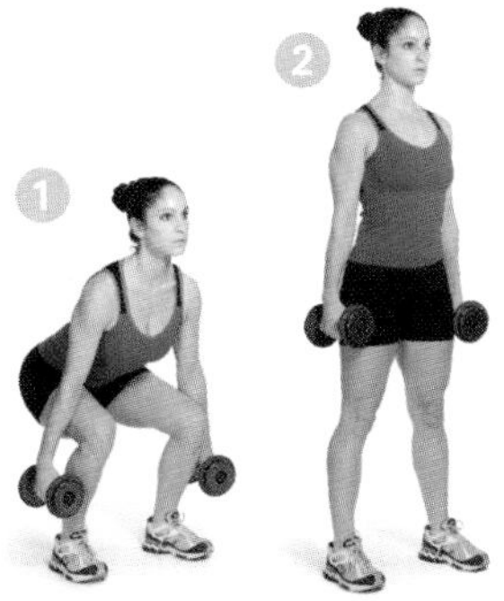
1
2

## BEST FOR

- biceps femoris
- erector spinae
- gluteus maximus
- latissimus dorsi
- levator scapulae
- obliquus externus
- quadratus lumborum
- rectus femoris
- rhomboideus
- semimembranosus
- semitendinosus
- soleus
- trapezius
- vastus lateralis
- vastus medialis

# STRAIGHT-LEG WITH BARBELL

## DEADLIFT

**Starting Position:** With a barbell on the ground and your feet shoulder-width apart, stand so that your shins contact the bar of the barbell. Grasp the bar with your palms facing outward (away from your body). Bend your knees slightly, keeping your spine in a neutral position and your hips elevated, so that your head, shoulders, and hips are in a straight line and parallel to the floor.

**Action:** Create tension from your hands through the back of your body, all the way to your heels. Drive your back up and your hips forward, drawing the bar in a straight line vertically adjacent to your shins, and continue until you are in a full standing position.

### LOOK FOR
- All movement to happen at the same time.
- Your spine to remain completely stable from hips to head.
- Your head to be up, with your eyes forward and looking upward.

### AVOID
- Allowing your spine to round (by flexing forward).
- Allowing your spine to change position in segments as it moves.
- Bending so that your hips are above your shoulders during the movement.
- Bending your elbows or shrugging your shoulders.
- Allowing your weight to rest in the front part of the foot or the bar to be forward of the toe line.

**Movement Path:** Your center of mass moves vertically upward as the line of your torso rotates in an arc.

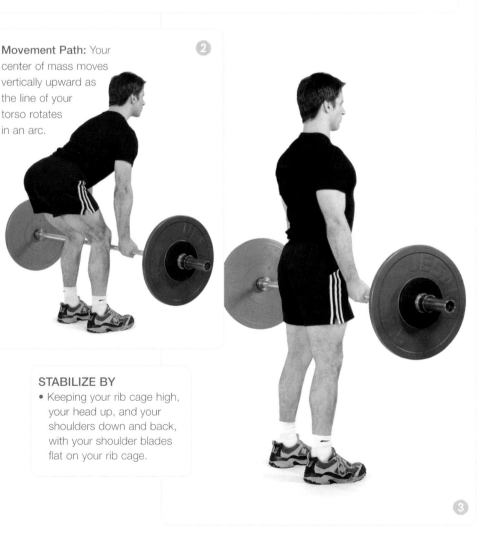

### STABILIZE BY
- Keeping your rib cage high, your head up, and your shoulders down and back, with your shoulder blades flat on your rib cage.

# STRAIGHT-LEG WITH BARBELL • DEADLIFT

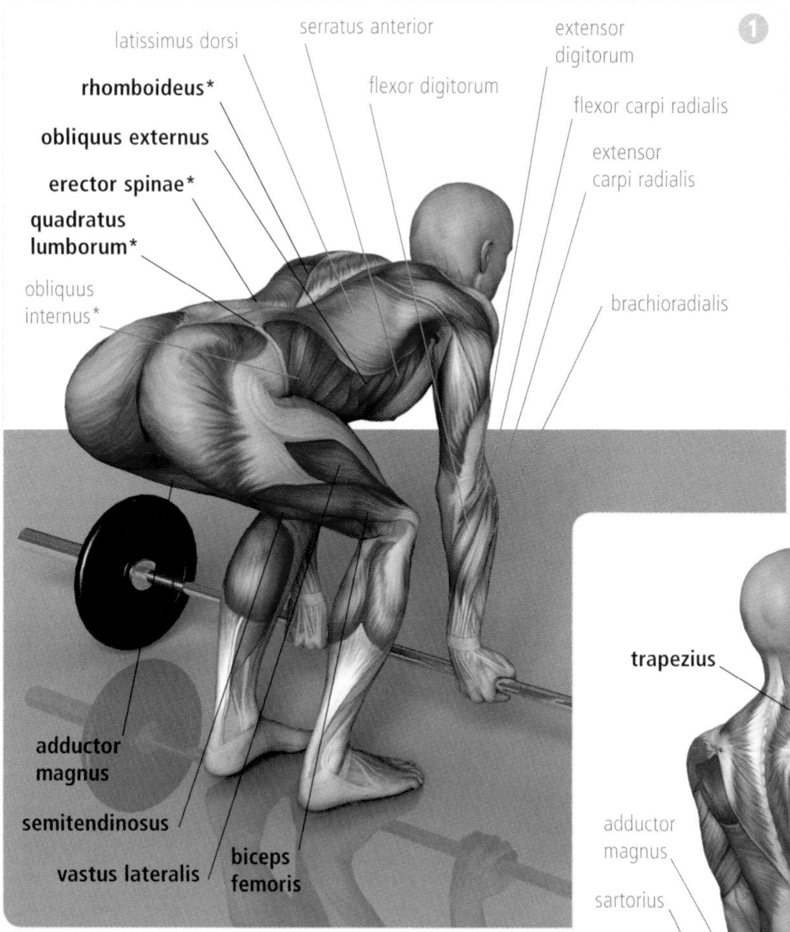

1
latissimus dorsi
serratus anterior
extensor digitorum
rhomboideus*
flexor digitorum
flexor carpi radialis
obliquus externus
extensor carpi radialis
erector spinae*
quadratus lumborum*
obliquus internus*
brachioradialis
adductor magnus
semitendinosus
vastus lateralis
biceps femoris


ANNOTATION KEY

**Black text indicates active muscles**

Gray text indicates stabilizing muscles

* indicates deep muscles

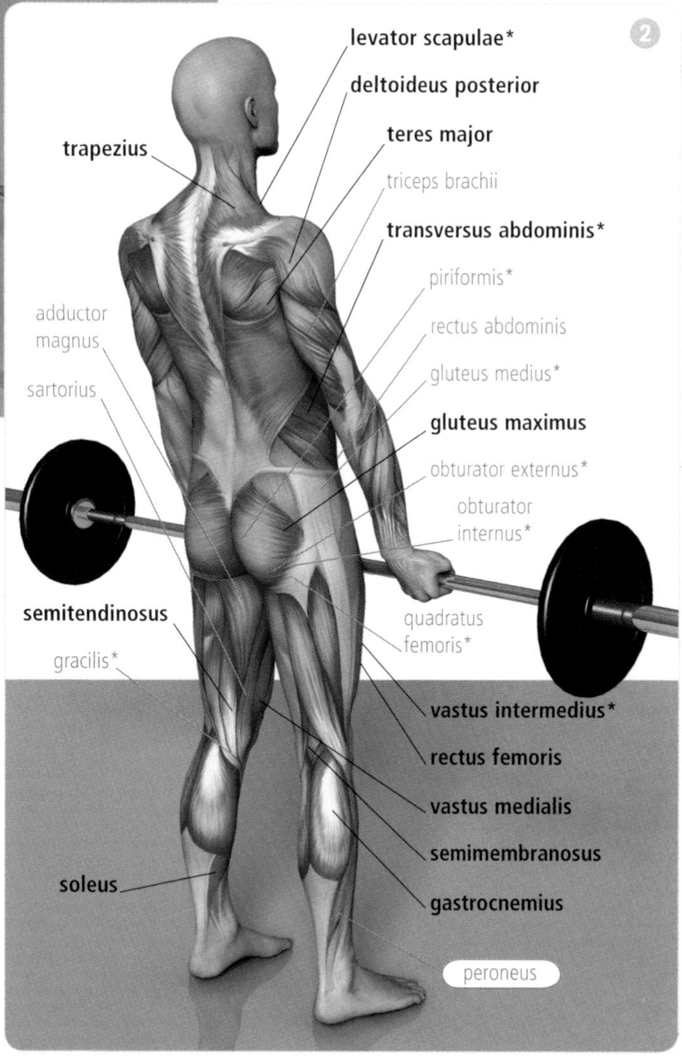

2
levator scapulae*
deltoideus posterior
trapezius
teres major
triceps brachii
transversus abdominis*
piriformis*
adductor magnus
rectus abdominis
gluteus medius*
sartorius
gluteus maximus
obturator externus*
obturator internus*
semitendinosus
quadratus femoris*
gracilis*
vastus intermedius*
rectus femoris
vastus medialis
semimembranosus
soleus
gastrocnemius
peroneus


## BEST FOR

- biceps femoris
- erector spinae
- gluteus maximus
- levator scapulae
- quadratus lumborum
- rhomboideus
- semimembranosus
- semitendinosus
- trapezius

# SUMO WITH KETTLEBELL

**DEADLIFT**

**Starting Position:** With the kettlebell on the ground and your feet slightly wider than shoulder-width apart, toes and knees pointed outward at 45-degree angles, grasp the bell with palms facing toward you. Your knees are bent so that they are directly over your toes. Keep your spine in a neutral position, positioned at a 45-degree angle to perpendicular. Your hips are dropped and retracted so that your upper legs are parallel to the ground (or as close to parallel as your flexibility will allow). Position your shoulder joints directly over the bell. Make sure that your feet are flat and your weight is evenly distributed. Pull your chest, head, and rib cage up and your abdominal muscles up and in. Inhale at the bottom of the position.

## STABILIZE BY
- Keeping your rib cage high and your head up.
- Pushing your shoulders down and back, with your shoulder blades flat on your rib cage.
- Keeping your knees directly over your feet.

**Action:** Exhale, and drive your torso up and backward and your hips up and forward. Push your feet into the ground, extending your knees so that they move in a scissorlike action inward, and pull backward on the kettlebell with your upper back and shoulders until you arrive at a vertical position.

## LOOK FOR
- The angle of your spine to never drop below 45 degrees during the movement.
- A slight arch in your back throughout the movement.
- All of your joints to move at the same time and at the same rate.

## AVOID
- Straightening your knees prior to extending your back and hips.
- Rounding your back.
- Elevating your shoulders or lowering your head.
- Allowing your knees to migrate either inward or outward.

**Movement Path:** Your hips move upward and forward, while your spine and torso move upward and backward, your knees extend and move inward, and your entire body moves upward and way from the floor.

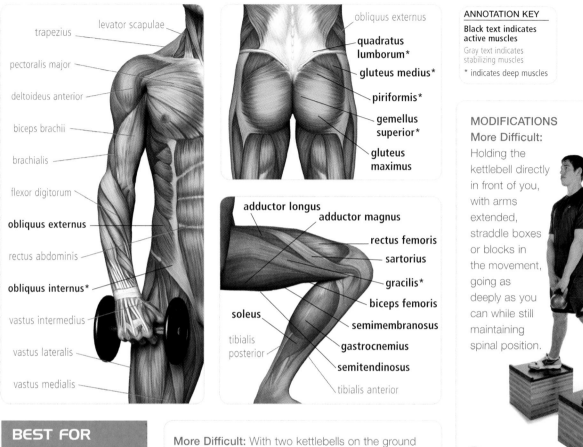

# SUMO WITH KETTLEBELL • DEADLIFT

levator scapulae
trapezius
pectoralis major
deltoideus anterior
biceps brachii
brachialis
flexor digitorum
obliquus externus
rectus abdominis
obliquus internus*
vastus intermedius
vastus lateralis
vastus medialis

obliquus externus
quadratus lumborum*
gluteus medius*
piriformis*
gemellus superior*
gluteus maximus

adductor longus
adductor magnus
rectus femoris
sartorius
gracilis*
biceps femoris
soleus
semimembranosus
tibialis posterior
gastrocnemius
semitendinosus
tibialis anterior

ANNOTATION KEY

**Black text indicates active muscles**

Gray text indicates stabilizing muscles

* indicates deep muscles

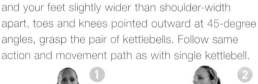

## BEST FOR

- quadratus lumborum
- rectus femoris
- soleus
- biceps femoris
- semitendinosus
- semimembranosus
- gastrocnemius
- adductor magnus
- adductor longus
- gracilis
- gluteus maximus
- rectus abdominis
- obliquus internus
- obliquus externus
- trapezius
- levator scapulae
- vastus lateralis
- vastus medialis
- vastus intermedius

**More Difficult:** With two kettlebells on the ground and your feet slightly wider than shoulder-width apart, toes and knees pointed outward at 45-degree angles, grasp the pair of kettlebells. Follow same action and movement path as with single kettlebell.

1

2

1

MODIFICATIONS

**More Difficult:** Holding the kettlebell directly in front of you, with arms extended, straddle boxes or blocks in the movement, going as deeply as you can while still maintaining spinal position.

2

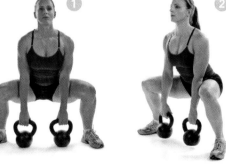

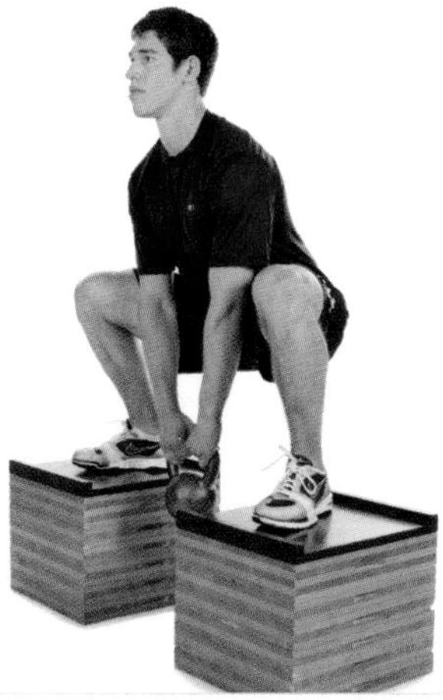

# FULL SINGLE-LEG WITH DUMBBELLS

## DEADLIFT

1

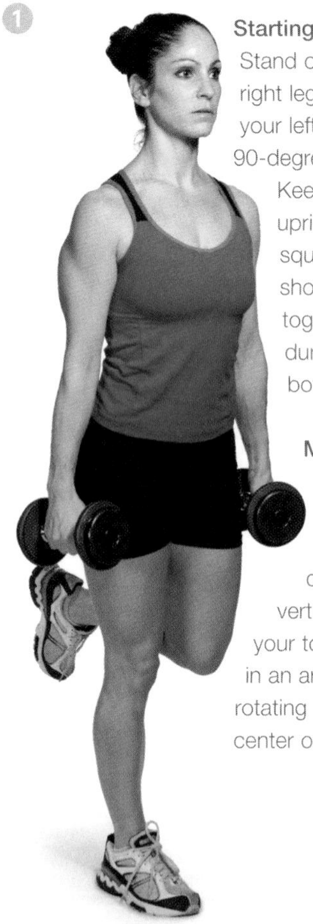

**Starting Position:** Stand on your right leg, and bend your left leg to a 90-degree angle. Keep your torso upright, and squeeze your shoulder blades together. Hold dumbbells in both hands.

**Movement Path:** Your center of mass descends vertically, and your torso moves in an arc, as though rotating around the center of a circle.

**STABILIZE BY**
- Maintaining a focus on balance—it is key! Look and focus on a spot in front of you as you bend over, balancing on one leg.
- Contracting your quadriceps on the eccentric movement and your hamstrings and gluteals on the concentric movement.

**Action:** Bend your right leg slightly as you bend over from your hips and reach the dumbbells toward the floor. Keep your chest up and your back slightly arched. Your left leg remains bent at 90 degrees throughout the exercise. Once you've touched the floor or gone as deep as you can, squeeze your gluteals and shoulder blades as you stand up again.

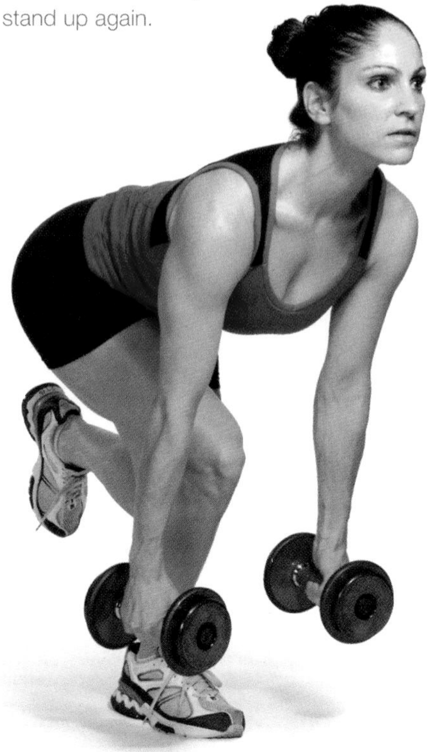

2

**LOOK FOR**
- Your spine to remain in a constant position throughout the movement.
- Your torso to flex forward from the hip joint.
- Your hamstrings to stretch; allow your pelvis to rotate forward from below the waist.

**AVOID**
- Improper form. Correct posture is extremely important: make sure that your chest is up and your back is slightly arched. If you can't bend over very far in this position, that's okay. It is better to have proper posture than greater range of motion.
- Rounding your back.
- Allowing your shoulder blades to slip forward.

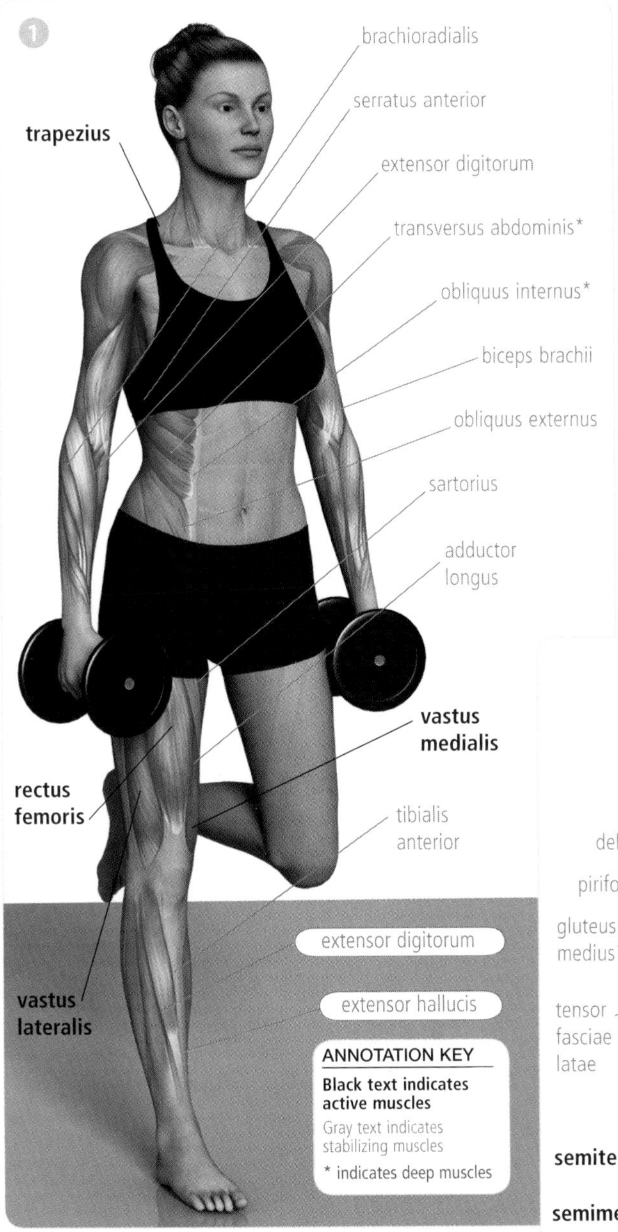
1
brachioradialis
serratus anterior
trapezius
extensor digitorum
transversus abdominis*
obliquus internus*
biceps brachii
obliquus externus
sartorius
adductor longus
vastus medialis
rectus femoris
tibialis anterior
extensor digitorum
extensor hallucis
vastus lateralis

ANNOTATION KEY
**Black text indicates active muscles**
Gray text indicates stabilizing muscles
* indicates deep muscles

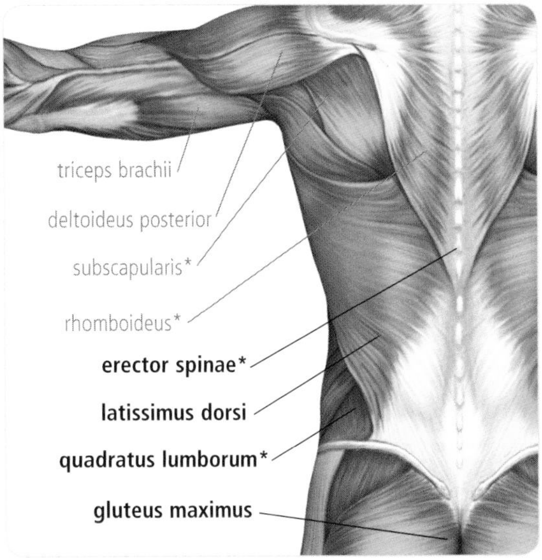
triceps brachii
deltoideus posterior
subscapularis*
rhomboideus*
erector spinae*
latissimus dorsi
quadratus lumborum*
gluteus maximus

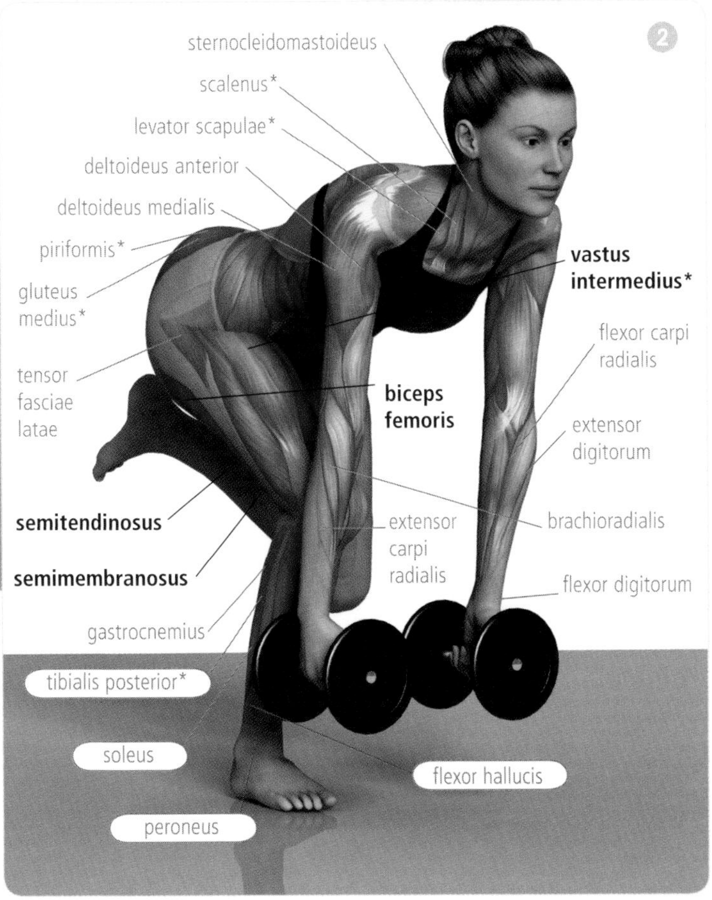
2
sternocleidomastoideus
scalenus*
levator scapulae*
deltoideus anterior
deltoideus medialis
piriformis*
gluteus medius*
tensor fasciae latae
vastus intermedius*
flexor carpi radialis
biceps femoris
extensor digitorum
semitendinosus
extensor carpi radialis
brachioradialis
semimembranosus
flexor digitorum
gastrocnemius
tibialis posterior*
soleus
flexor hallucis
peroneus

## BEST FOR

- biceps femoris
- erector spinae
- gluteus maximus
- latissimus dorsi
- quadratus lumborum
- rectus femoris
- semimembranosus
- semitendinosus
- vastus lateralis
- vastus medialis

# STRAIGHT-LEG WITH DUMBBELL



**Starting Position:** Holding the dumbbell directly in front of one leg, and your feet shoulder-width apart, place the opposite hand behind your head, elbow facing out to the side. Bend your knees slightly, keeping your spine in a neutral position and your hips elevated, so that your head, shoulders, and hips are in a straight line and parallel to the floor.

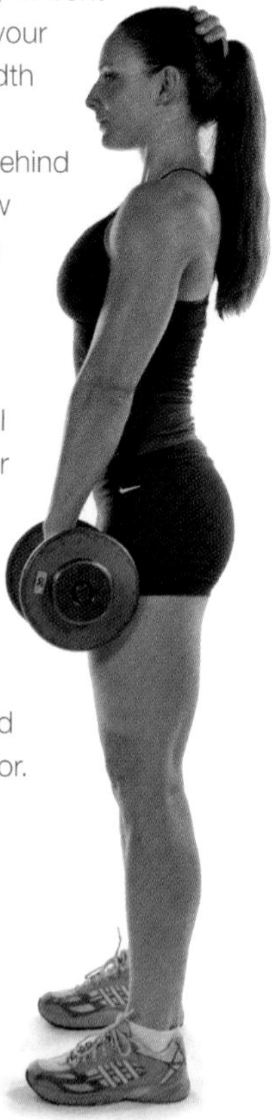

1

**Action:** Descend by retracting your hips and dropping your chest and rib cage forward. Create tension from your hands through the back of your body, all the way to your heels. Return by driving your back up and your hips forward, drawing the dumbbell in a straight line vertically adjacent to your shins, and continue until you are in a full standing position.

**Movement Path:** Push your feet into the ground as you drive your shoulders back and up and your hips forward simultaneously.

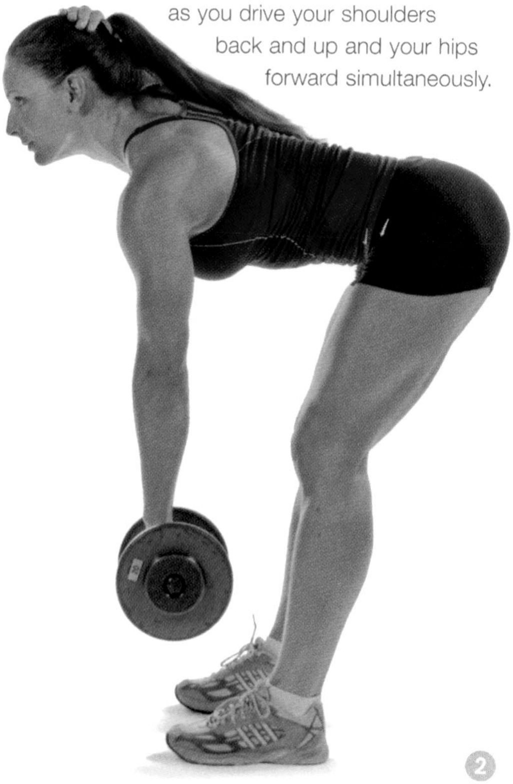

2

### LOOK FOR

- Keeping weight evenly distributed through hips, legs, and feet into the ground.
- All movement to happen at the same time.
- Your spine to remain completely stable from hips to head.
- Your head to be up, with your eyes forward and looking upward.

### AVOID

- Allowing your spine to round (by flexing forward) or change position in segments as it moves.
- A rotation of any part of the spine or upper body.
- Bending so that your hips are above your shoulders during the movement.
- Bending your elbows or shrugging your shoulders.
- Allowing your weight to rest in the front part of the foot or the dumbbell to be forward of the toe line.

### STABILIZE BY

- Keeping your rib cage high, your head up, and your shoulders down and back, with your shoulder blades flat on your rib cage.

## BEST FOR

- erector spinae
- rhomboideus
- quadratus lumborum
- vastus lateralis
- vastus medialis
- vastus intermedius
- rectus femoris
- soleus
- adductor magnus
- biceps femoris
- semitendinosus
- semimembranosus
- gastrocnemius

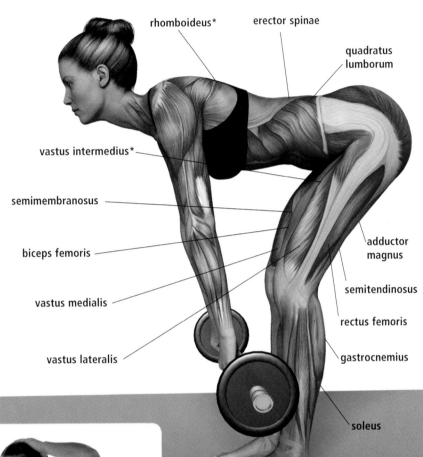

rhomboideus*

erector spinae

quadratus lumborum

vastus intermedius*

semimembranosus

biceps femoris

vastus medialis

vastus lateralis

adductor magnus

semitendinosus

rectus femoris

gastrocnemius

soleus

## MODIFICATION
**Similar Difficulty:**
Replace the dumbbell with a kettlebell and maintain the same action and movement path.

### ANNOTATION KEY

**Black text indicates active muscles**

Gray text indicates stabilizing muscles

\* indicates deep muscles

# SINGLE-LEG/STRAIGHT-LEG WITH KETTLEBELL

**DEADLIFT**

**Starting Position:** Stand on your right leg, and keep your left slightly behind your right heel, bearing little to no weight. Keep your torso upright, and squeeze your shoulder blades together. Hold the kettlebell in your left hand.

## STABILIZE BY
- Maintaining a focus on balance—it is key! Look and focus on a spot in front of you as you bend over, balancing on one leg.
- Contracting your quadriceps on the eccentric movement and your hamstrings and gluteals on the concentric movement.
- Keeping your low back solid and keeping opposite leg straight and gluteus contracted.

## LOOK FOR
- Spine to remain in a constant position throughout the movement.
- Torso to flex forward from the hip joint.
- Hamstrings to stretch and allow pelvis to rotate forward from below the belt.
- Opposite leg to work as a counterbalance.

## AVOID
- Improper form. Correct posture is extremely important: make sure that your chest is up and your back is slightly arched. If you can't bend over as far in this position, that is okay. It is better to have proper posture than greater range of motion.
- Rounding the back/spine.
- Allowing the shoulder blades to slip forward.
- Not keeping the opposite leg and spine in a straight line at all times.

**Action:** Bend your right leg very slightly as you bend over from your hip, and reach the kettlebell toward the floor. Make sure that you keep your chest up and your back slightly arched. Your left leg remains in line with your spine throughout the exercise. Once you've touched the floor or gone as deep as you can, squeeze your gluteal hamstrings and shoulder blades as you stand up on your right leg, while your left leg returns to starting position.

**Movement Path:** The movement path consists of starting in an erect position and going into a bent-over position, originating at the hip joint, and then returning to the erect position.

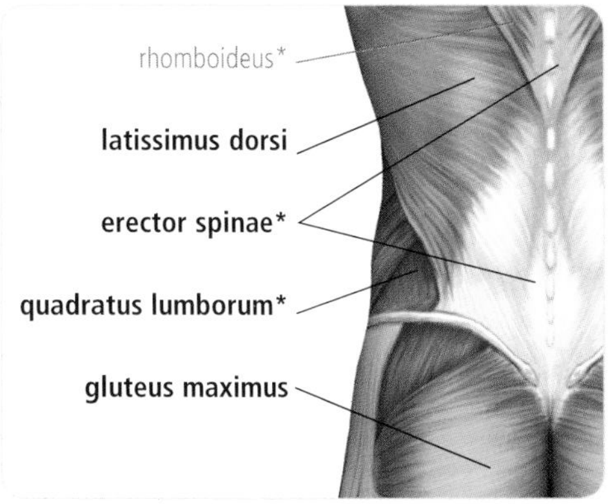
rhomboideus*
latissimus dorsi
erector spinae*
quadratus lumborum*
gluteus maximus

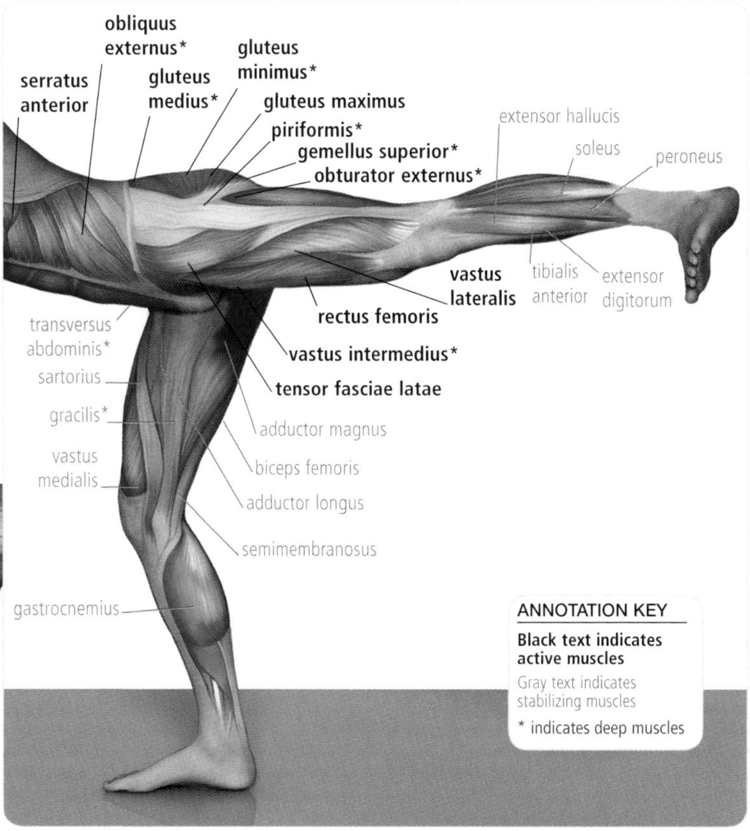
obliquus externus*
serratus anterior
gluteus medius*
gluteus minimus*
gluteus maximus
piriformis*
gemellus superior*
obturator externus*
extensor hallucis
soleus
peroneus
vastus lateralis
tibialis anterior
extensor digitorum
rectus femoris
transversus abdominis*
vastus intermedius*
sartorius
tensor fasciae latae
gracilis*
adductor magnus
vastus medialis
biceps femoris
adductor longus
semimembranosus
gastrocnemius
ANNOTATION KEY
Black text indicates active muscles
Gray text indicates stabilizing muscles
* indicates deep muscles

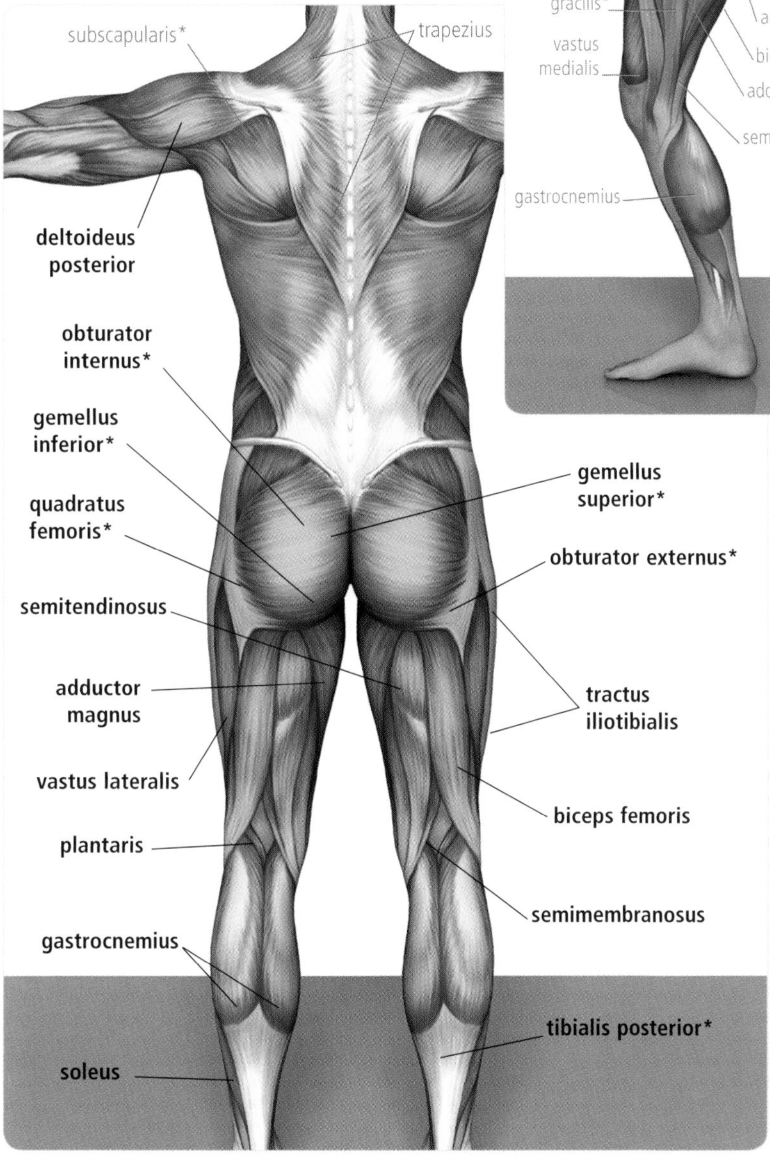
subscapularis*
trapezius
deltoideus posterior
obturator internus*
gemellus inferior*
gemellus superior*
quadratus femoris*
obturator externus*
semitendinosus
adductor magnus
tractus iliotibialis
vastus lateralis
biceps femoris
plantaris
semimembranosus
gastrocnemius
tibialis posterior*
soleus

## BEST FOR

- biceps femoris
- semitendinosus
- semimembranosus
- vastus lateralis
- vastus medialis
- vastus intermedius
- rectus femoris
- gluteus maximus
- erector spinae
- latissimus dorsi
- quadratus lumborum
- deltoideus posterior
- piriformis
- adductor longus
- adductor magnus
- gluteus medius
- gastrocnemius
- soleus
- tibialis posterior
- tibialis anterior
- peroneus
- flexor hallucis
- extensor hallucis
- transversus abdominis
- serratus anterior
- obliquus internus*
- subscapularis
- rhomboideus
- trapezius

# MEDICINE BALL RAISE



1

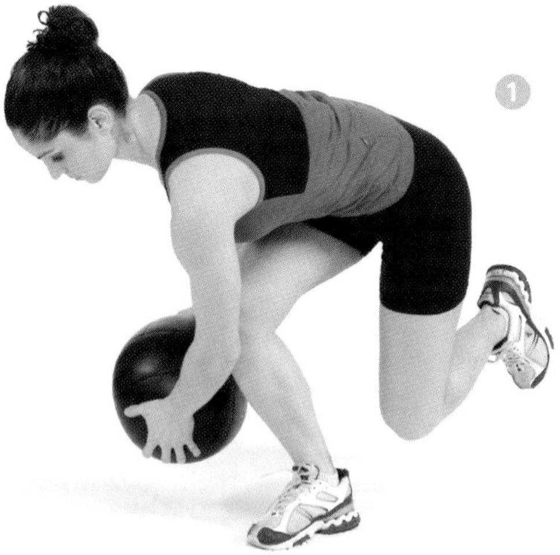

Starting Position: Stand on one foot, bending the raised knee, and grasp a medicine ball just below and to the outside of the knee on the standing leg.

**STABILIZE BY**
- Pulling your abdomen up and in.
- Distributing your weight evenly across your foot.
- Using all muscles and joints in a coordinated, relaxed manner.

2

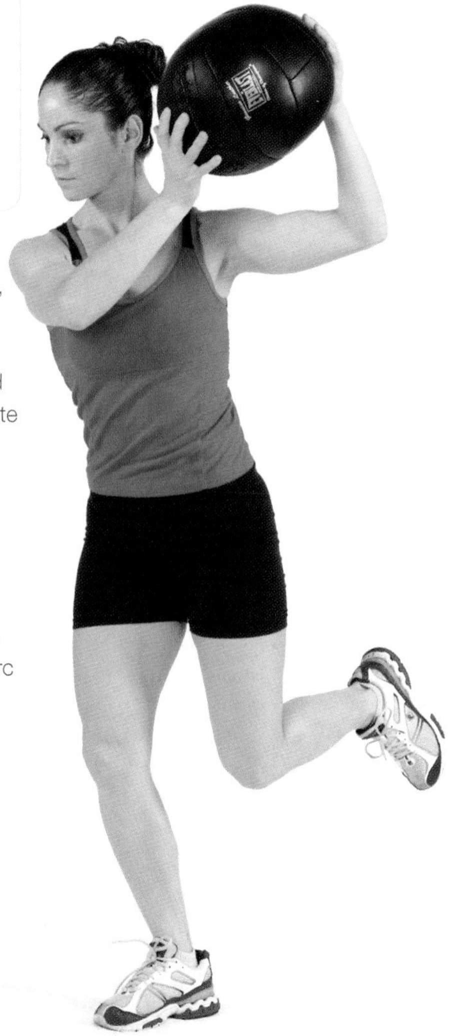

**Action:** Stand, extending your leg, while bringing the ball across your body to above and outside the opposite shoulder.

**Movement Path:** Your upper body rotates as your center of mass shifts upward. The ball moves in an arc across your body.

**LOOK FOR**
- Your knee and hip to extend and rise at the same time.
- The ball to remain equidistant from your torso throughout the movement.
- Your elbows to remain extended.

**AVOID**
- Excessive flexion of your torso and spine.
- Bringing the ball close to your body or lifting any part of your foot from the floor.

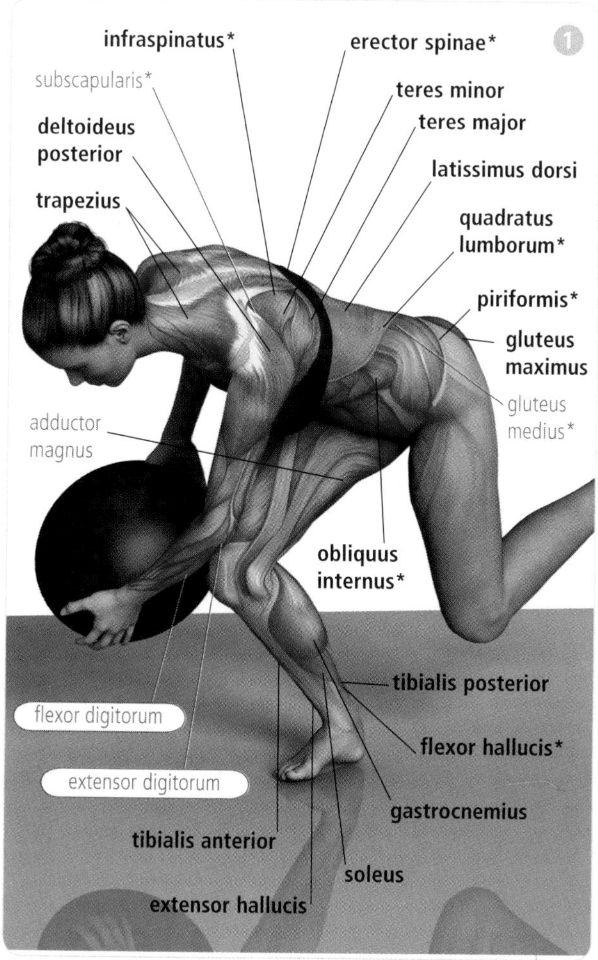
1
infraspinatus*
subscapularis*
erector spinae*
teres minor
teres major
deltoideus posterior
latissimus dorsi
trapezius
quadratus lumborum*
piriformis*
gluteus maximus
gluteus medius*
adductor magnus
obliquus internus*
tibialis posterior
flexor digitorum
flexor hallucis*
extensor digitorum
gastrocnemius
tibialis anterior
soleus
extensor hallucis

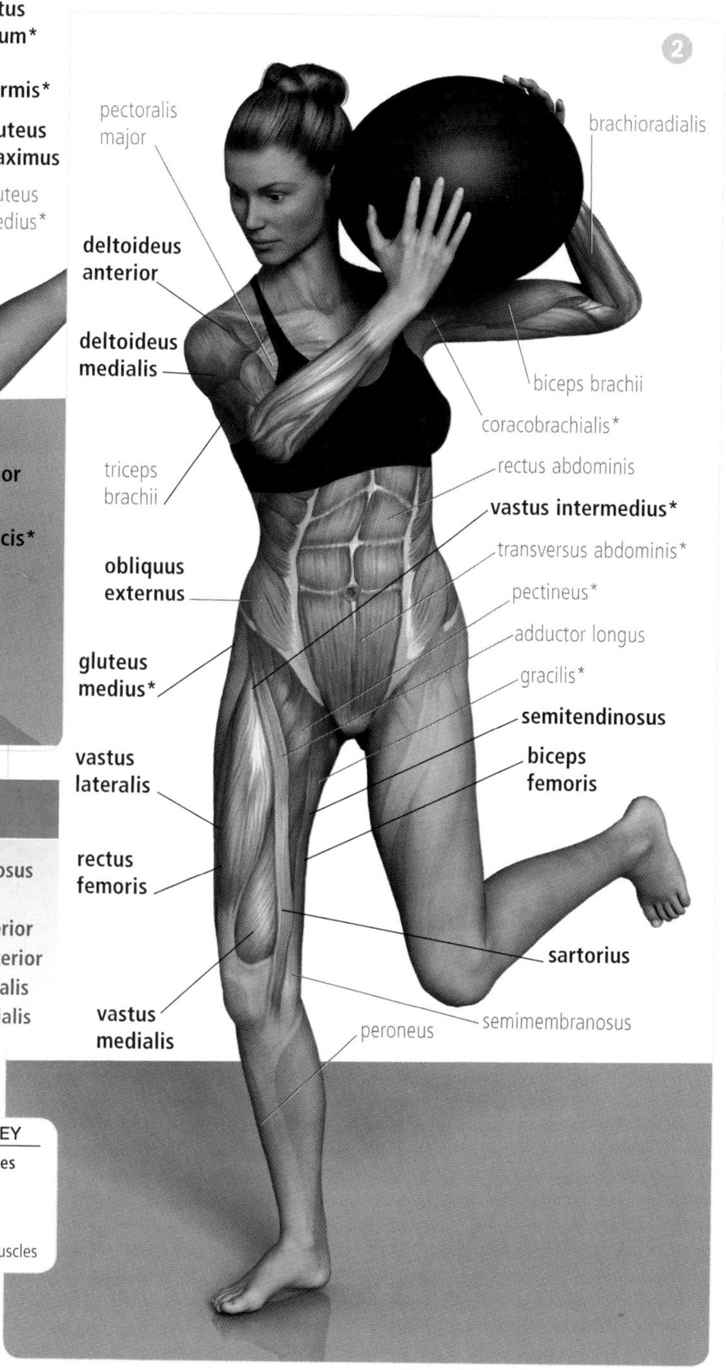
2
pectoralis major
brachioradialis
deltoideus anterior
deltoideus medialis
biceps brachii
coracobrachialis*
triceps brachii
rectus abdominis
vastus intermedius*
transversus abdominis*
obliquus externus
pectineus*
adductor longus
gluteus medius*
gracilis*
semitendinosus
biceps femoris
vastus lateralis
rectus femoris
sartorius
vastus medialis
peroneus
semimembranosus

## BEST FOR

- biceps femoris
- erector spinae
- extensor hallucis
- flexor hallucis
- gluteus maximus
- gluteus medius
- infraspinatus
- piriformis
- quadratus lumborum
- rectus femoris
- semimembranosus
- semitendinosus
- soleus
- tibialis anterior
- tibialis posterior
- vastus lateralis
- vastus medialis

ANNOTATION KEY

**Black text indicates active muscles**

Gray text indicates stabilizing muscles

* indicates deep muscles

# FULL CABLE WITH ROTATION

## DEADLIFT

**Starting Position:** Standing with feet slightly wider than shoulder-width apart, grasp the cable with both hands directly in front of you at your body's midline. See figure 1, page 31.

**Action:** Drop and retract your hips so that the tops of your legs are parallel to the ground (or as close to parallel as your flexibility will allow). Position your shoulder joints directly over your feet. Make sure that your feet are flat and your weight is evenly distributed. Pull your chest, head, and rib cage up and your abdominal muscles up and in. Inhale at the bottom of the position. Exhale, and drive your torso up and backward and your hips up and forward. Push your feet into the ground, extending your knees until you arrive at a vertical position.

**STABILIZE BY**
- Keeping your rib cage high and your head up.
- Pushing your shoulders down and back, with your shoulder blades flat on your rib cage.
- Keeping your knees directly over your feet.

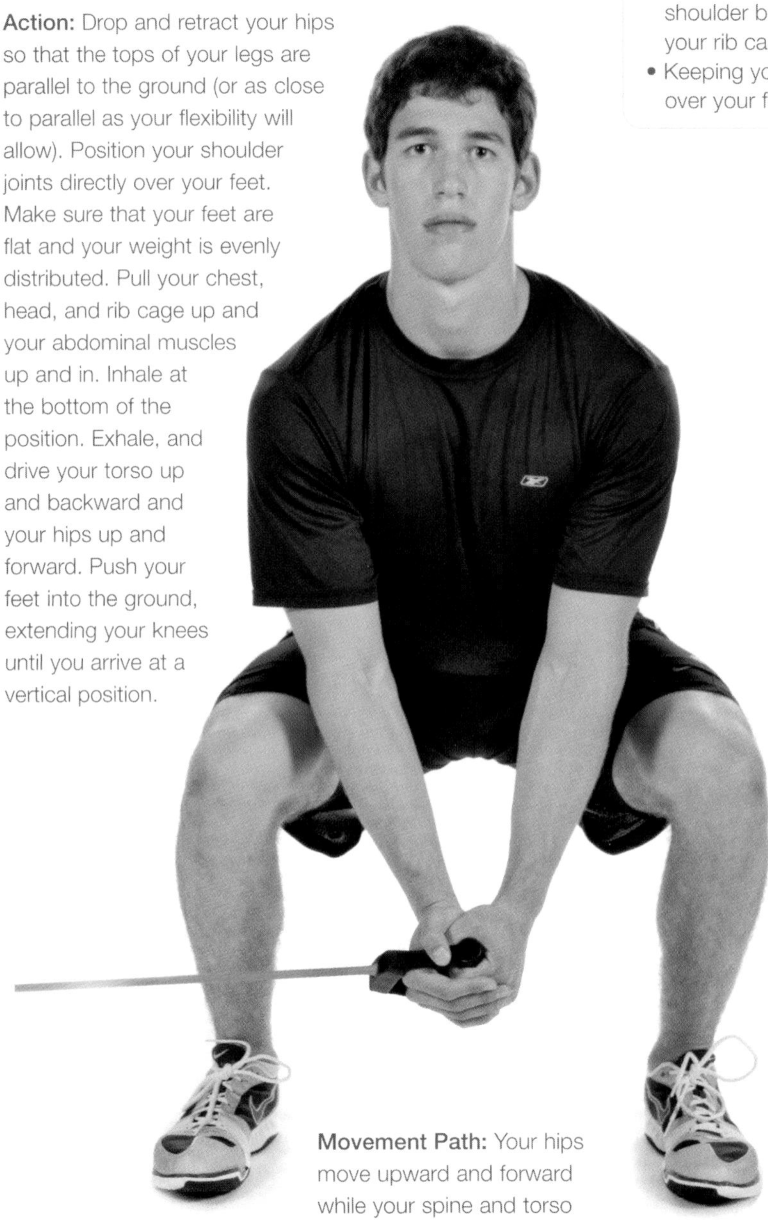

**LOOK FOR**
- The angle of your spine to never drop below 45 degrees during the movement.
- A slight arch in your back throughout the movement.
- All of your joints to move at the same time and at the same rate.

**AVOID**
- Straightening your knees prior to extending your back and hips.
- Rounding your back.
- Elevating your shoulders or lowering your head.
- Allowing your knees to migrate either inward or outward.

**Movement Path:** Your hips move upward and forward while your spine and torso move upward and backward, your knees extend, and your entire body moves upward and away from the floor.

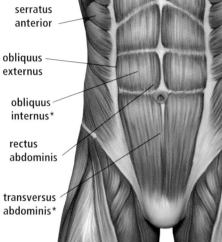

serratus anterior

obliquus externus

obliquus internus*

rectus abdominis

transversus abdominis*

## BEST FOR

- erector spinae
- rhomboideus
- latissimus dorsi
- teres major
- quadratus lumborum
- trapezius
- levator scapulae
- vastus lateralis
- vastus medialis
- vastus intermedius
- rectus femoris
- soleus
- biceps femoris
- semitendinosus
- semimembranosus
- gastrocnemius
- gluteus maximus
- rectus abdominis
- obliquus internus
- obliquus externus
- flexor digitorum
- deltoideus posterior
- adductor longus
- adductor magnus
- sartorius
- gracilis

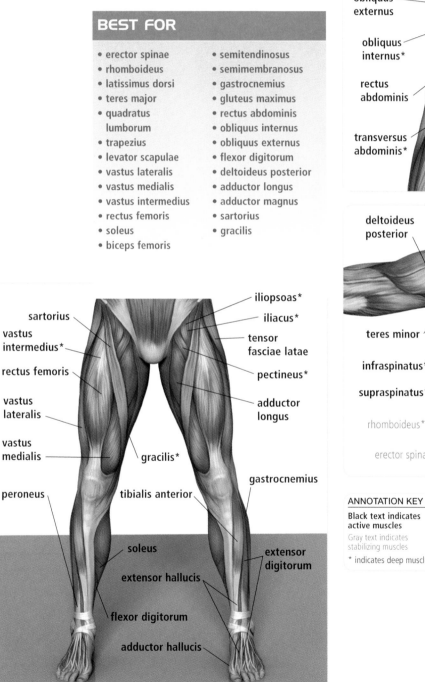

sartorius

vastus intermedius*

rectus femoris

vastus lateralis

vastus medialis

peroneus

soleus

extensor hallucis

flexor digitorum

adductor hallucis

tibialis anterior

gracilis*

iliopsoas*

iliacus*

tensor fasciae latae

pectineus*

adductor longus

gastrocnemius

extensor digitorum

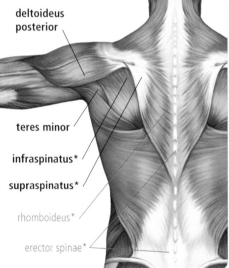

deltoideus posterior

teres minor

infraspinatus*

supraspinatus*

rhomboideus*

erector spinae*

**ANNOTATION KEY**

Black text indicates active muscles

Gray text indicates stabilizing muscles

* indicates deep muscles

# STRAIGHT-LEG CABLE

**DEADLIFT**

**Starting Position:** Grasp cable in one hand at your side so that the cable crosses the front of both legs. With your feet shoulder-width apart, place the opposite hand behind your head with elbow facing out to the side. Bend your knees slightly, keeping your spine in a neutral position and your hips elevated, so that your head, shoulders, and hips are in a straight line and parallel to the floor.

**Action:** Descend by retracting your hips and dropping your chest and rib cage forward. Create tension from your hand through the back of your body, all the way to your heels. Return by driving your back up and your hips forward, keeping your hand adjacent to your leg, your shoulder steady (continue until you are in a full standing position).

**Movement Path:** Push your feet into the ground as you drive your shoulders back and up and your hips forward simultaneously.

### LOOK FOR
- Keeping weight evenly distributed through hips, legs, and feet into the ground.
- All movement to happen at the same time.
- Your spine to remain stable from hips to head with no rotation.
- Your head to be up, with your eyes forward and looking upward.
- Knees and hips to remain parallel.

### AVOID
- Rotation of any part of the spine or upper body.
- Allowing your spine to round or change position in segments.
- Bending so that hips are above your shoulders.
- Bending your elbows or shrugging your shoulders.
- Allowing your weight to rest in the front part of the foot or the cable to be forward of the toe line.

### STABILIZE BY
- Keeping your rib cage high, your head up, and your shoulders down and back with your shoulder blades flat on your rib cage, hand with cable solid and stable.

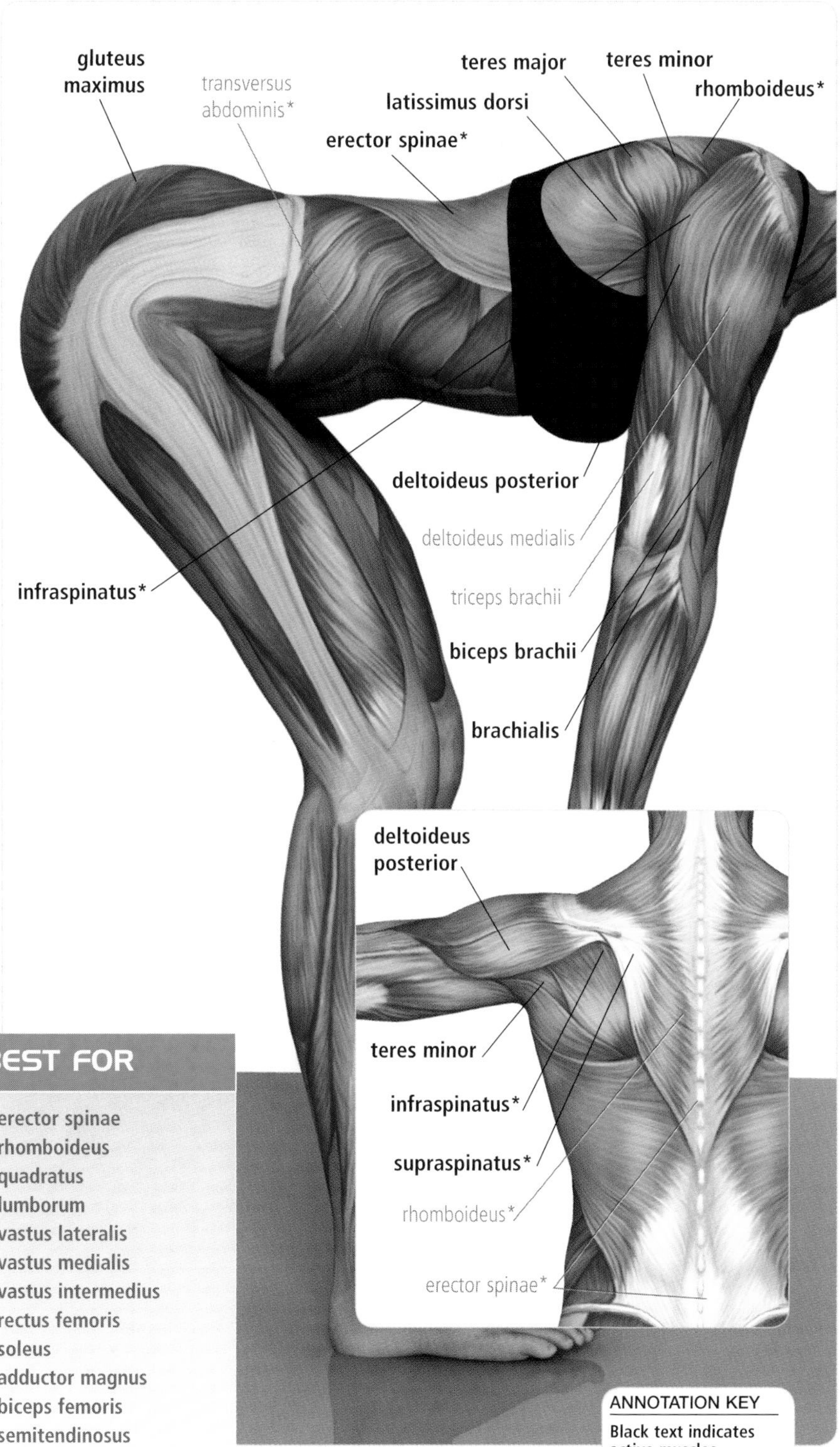
gluteus maximus
transversus abdominis*
teres major
teres minor
rhomboideus*
latissimus dorsi
erector spinae*
deltoideus posterior
deltoideus medialis
triceps brachii
infraspinatus*
biceps brachii
brachialis
deltoideus posterior
teres minor
infraspinatus*
supraspinatus*
rhomboideus*
erector spinae*

## BEST FOR

- erector spinae
- rhomboideus
- quadratus lumborum
- vastus lateralis
- vastus medialis
- vastus intermedius
- rectus femoris
- soleus
- adductor magnus
- biceps femoris
- semitendinosus
- semimembranosus
- gastrocnemius

ANNOTATION KEY

**Black text indicates active muscles**

Gray text indicates stabilizing muscles

* indicates deep muscles

MODIFICATION

More Difficult: Grasp the cable with both hands directly in front of you at the body's midline. Use the exact same action and movement path.

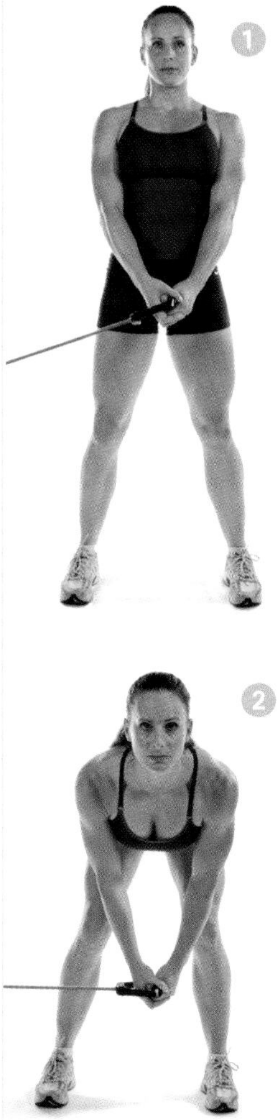
1
2

# BAG FLIP

**Starting Position:** With a punching bag on the ground and your feet shoulder-width apart, grasp the bag with your palms facing each another. Bend your knees so that your knees are over your toes. Keep your spine in a neutral position, positioned at a 45-degree angle to perpendicular. Your hips are dropped and retracted so that the tops of your legs are parallel to the ground (or as close to parallel as your flexibility will allow). Position your shoulder joints directly over the bag. Make sure that your feet are flat and your weight is evenly distributed. Pull your chest, head, and rib cage up and your abdominal muscles up and in. Inhale at the bottom of the position.

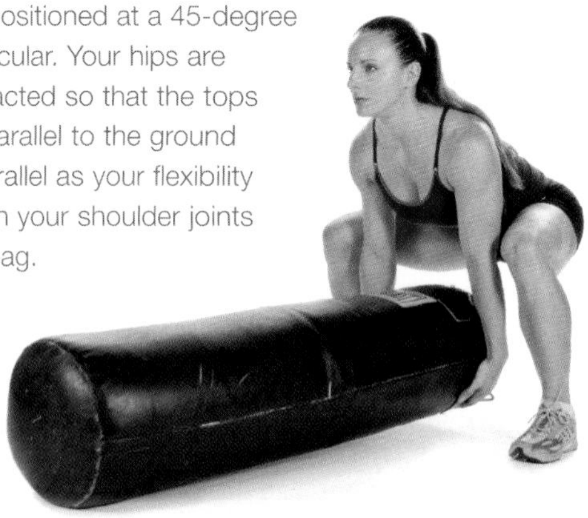

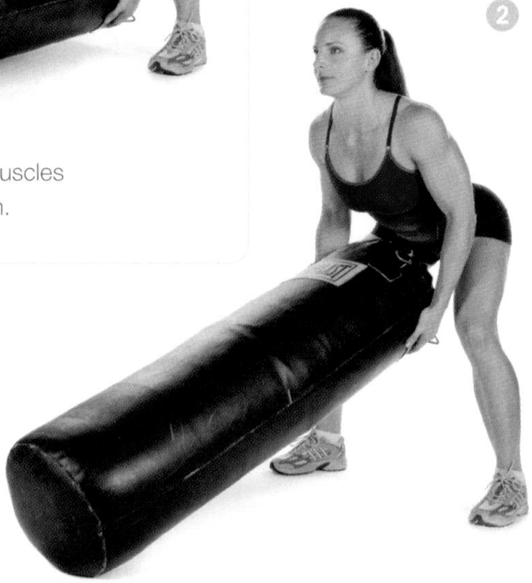

**Action:** Exhale, and drive your torso upward and your hips up and forward. Push your feet into the ground, extending your knees and pulling upward on the bag, forcefully and quickly, with your upper back, shoulders, and elbows. Elevate onto your toes, and follow through with your hands upward and forward away from your body, releasing the bag in one fluid movement.

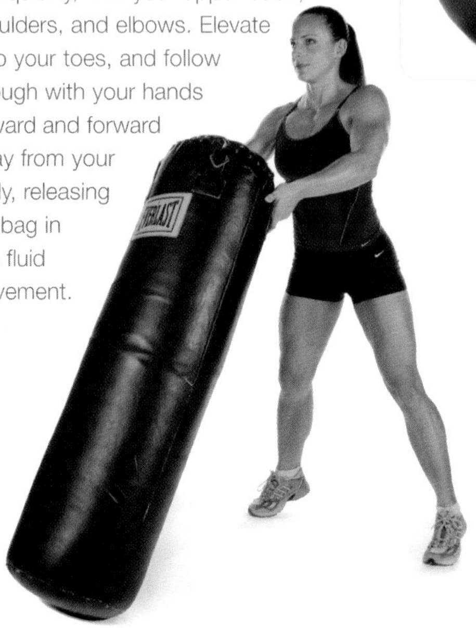

### LOOK FOR

- The angle of your spine to never drop below 45 degrees during the movement.
- A slight arch in your back throughout the movement.
- All of your joints to move at the same time and at the same rate.

### AVOID

- Straightening your knees prior to extending your back and hips.
- Rounding your back.
- Lowering your head.
- Allowing your knees to migrate either inward or outward.

### STABILIZE BY

- Keeping your rib cage high and your head up.
- Keeping your spine in a solid, neutral position.
- Keeping your knees directly over your feet.

## BEST FOR

- biceps femoris
- erector spinae
- gluteus maximus
- latissimus dorsi
- levator scapulae
- obliquus externus
- quadratus lumborum
- rectus femoris
- rhomboideus
- semimembranosus
- semitendinosus
- soleus
- trapezius
- vastus lateralis
- vastus medialis

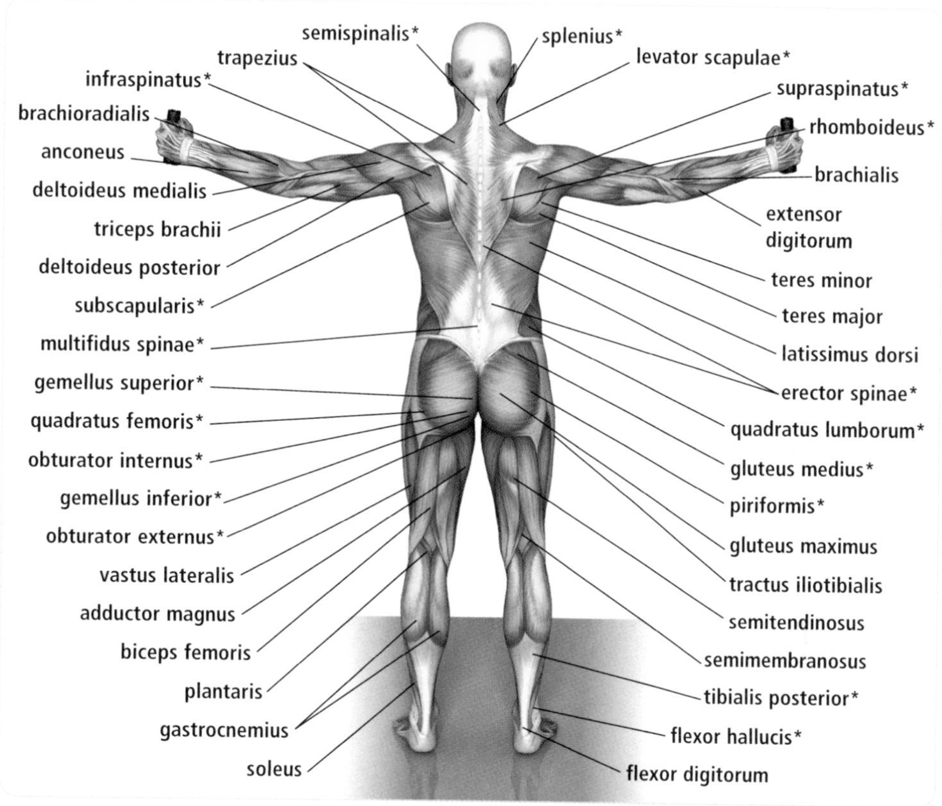
semispinalis*
splenius*
trapezius
levator scapulae*
infraspinatus*
supraspinatus*
brachioradialis
rhomboideus*
anconeus
brachialis
deltoideus medialis
extensor digitorum
triceps brachii
teres minor
deltoideus posterior
teres major
subscapularis*
latissimus dorsi
multifidus spinae*
erector spinae*
gemellus superior*
quadratus lumborum*
quadratus femoris*
gluteus medius*
obturator internus*
piriformis*
gemellus inferior*
gluteus maximus
obturator externus*
tractus iliotibialis
vastus lateralis
semitendinosus
adductor magnus
semimembranosus
biceps femoris
tibialis posterior*
plantaris
flexor hallucis*
gastrocnemius
flexor digitorum
soleus

ANNOTATION KEY

Black text indicates active muscles

Gray text indicates stabilizing muscles

* indicates deep muscles

**Movement Path:** Your hips move upward and forward while your spine and torso move upward and slightly backward, your knees extend, and your entire body moves upward and away from the floor.

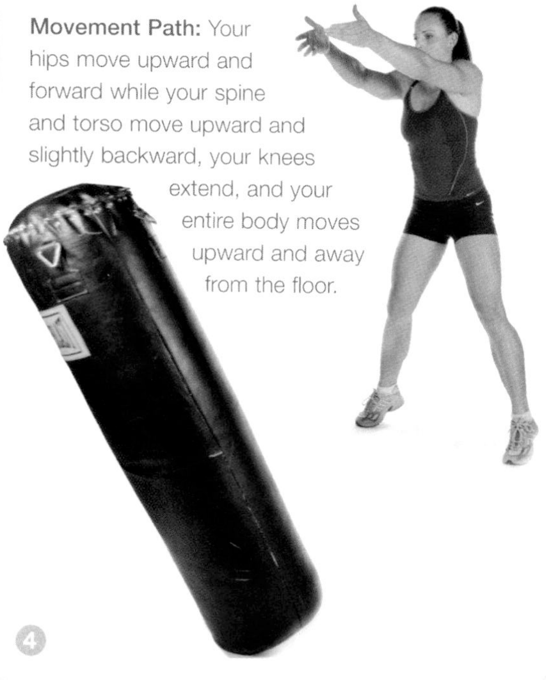
4

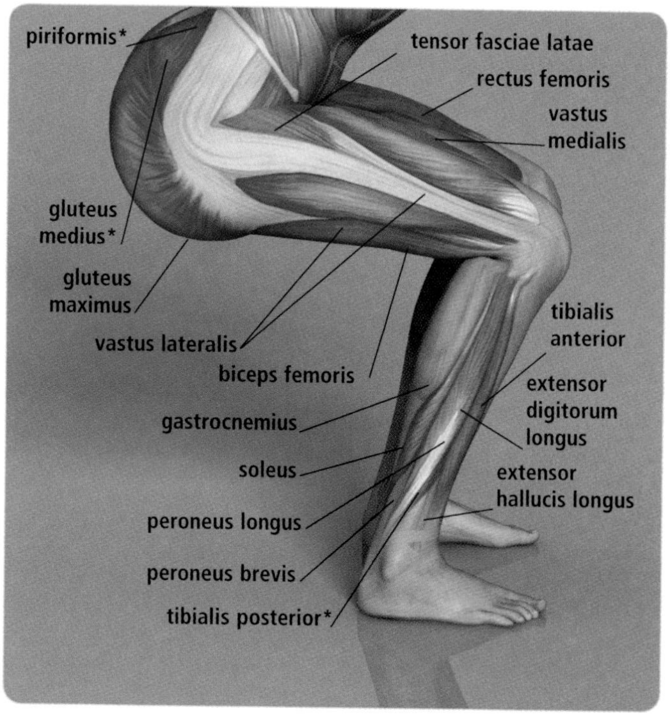
piriformis*
tensor fasciae latae
rectus femoris
vastus medialis
gluteus medius*
gluteus maximus
tibialis anterior
vastus lateralis
biceps femoris
extensor digitorum longus
gastrocnemius
soleus
extensor hallucis longus
peroneus longus
peroneus brevis
tibialis posterior*

# FULL WITH DUMBBELL

**Starting Position:** With the dumbbell on the ground and your feet slightly wider than shoulder-width apart, grasp the dumbbell with palm facing toward you. Place the other hand behind your head, elbows pointing outward. Your knees are positioned so that they are directly over your toes. Keep your spine in a neutral position.

**Action:** Bend as deeply as you can while still maintaining spinal position. Your hips are dropped and retracted so that your upper legs are parallel to the ground (or as close to parallel as your flexibility will allow). Position your shoulder joints directly over your feet. Make sure that your feet are flat and your weight is evenly distributed. Pull your chest, head, and rib cage up and your abdominal muscles up and in. Inhale at the bottom of the position. Exhale, and drive your torso up and backward and your hips up and forward. Push your feet into the ground, extending your knees and pulling upward on the dumbbell with your upper back and shoulders until you arrive at a vertical position.

STABILIZE BY
- Keeping your rib cage high and your head up.
- Pushing your shoulders down and back, with your shoulder blades flat on your rib cage.
- Keeping your knees directly over your feet.

LOOK FOR
- The angle of your spine to never drop below 45 degrees during the movement.
- A slight arch in your back throughout the movement.
- All of your joints to move at the same time and at the same rate.
- The dumbbell to drop in a straight vertical line.

AVOID
- Straightening your knees prior to extending your back and hips.
- Rounding your back.
- Elevating your shoulders or lowering your head.
- Allowing your knees to migrate either inward or outward.
- Any rotation of the torso, hips, or shoulders.

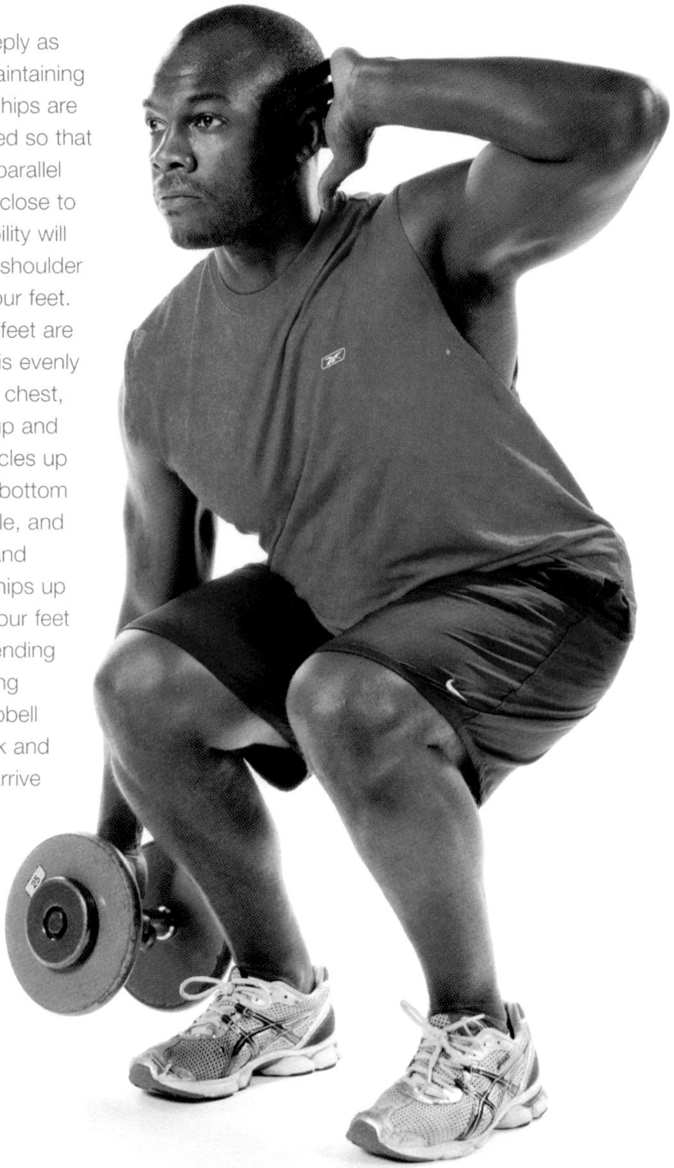

1

**Movement Path:** Your hips move upward and forward, while your spine and torso move upward and backward, your knees extend and move inward, and your entire body moves upward and away from the floor.

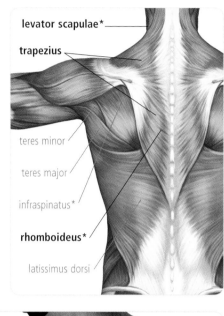

- levator scapulae*
- trapezius
- teres minor
- teres major
- infraspinatus*
- rhomboideus*
- latissimus dorsi

## BEST FOR

- erector spinae
- rhomboideus
- latissimus dorsi
- teres major
- quadratus lumborum
- levator scapulae
- trapezius
- vastus lateralis
- vastus medialis
- vastus intermedius
- rectus femoris
- soleus
- biceps femoris
- semitendinosus
- semimembranosus
- gastrocnemius
- adductor magnus
- adductor longus
- gracilis
- adductor brevis
- gluteus maximus
- rectus abdominis
- obliquus internus
- obliquus externus
- flexor digitorum
- deltoideus posterior
- obturator externus
- gluteus medius
- piriformis

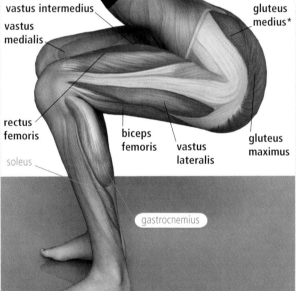

- vastus intermedius
- vastus medialis
- rectus femoris
- soleus
- gluteus medius*
- biceps femoris
- vastus lateralis
- gluteus maximus
- gastrocnemius

### ANNOTATION KEY

**Black text indicates active muscles**

Gray text indicates stabilizing muscles

* indicates deep muscles

# LUNGE

In order for the body to function properly, the legs, hips, and back must be strong, stable, and flexible. Lunges address all three of these body parts in one movement. Lower-back and disk-related injuries are rampant, as are knee injuries (such as to the anterior cruciate ligament and meniscus, patellofemoral pain, and iliotibial band syndrome). A vast majority of these injuries stem from one of the following three issues: strength imbalances, instability, and inflexibility. It is also common for injuries to result from a combination of two or all of them at once. A steady diet of lunges will, without question, improve strength, stability, and flexibility and lower the possibility of related injuries.

Joints involved are the ankle, knee, and hip. The muscles involved are those of the legs, glutes, lower back, and stomach.

Primary benefits are leg and hip strength, flexibility, and balance.

# STATIONARY

## LUNGE

LOOK FOR
- No translation forward from the hips (do not bend).
- Your spine to remain in the same position as it moves down and up.
- No lateral movement of your leg as you step, either landing or pushing.

AVOID
- Raising the heel of your stepping foot off the ground or rotating your hips or torso.

**Starting Position:** Stand with your feet close together and your hands on your hips.

**Action:** Keeping your head up, your spine in a neutral position, and your hands on your hips, take a step forward, bending your front knee to a 90-degree angle and dropping your front thigh until it is parallel to the ground. Your back knee drops straight down behind you, so that you are balancing on the toe of your foot to create a 90-degree angle in your knee joint and a straight line from your spine through your bottom knee. Return to the starting position by pushing on your front foot and elevating with your back leg until standing.

**Movement Path:** The general motion is forward and descending. Your spine stays in a vertical position and is translated forward and downward by the step and the descent.

STABILIZE BY
- Keeping your chest high, stomach up, and spine neutral.
- Evenly distributing your weight across your front foot, from front to back.
- Keeping your back foot on the toe and your weight in the back of the stepping leg.

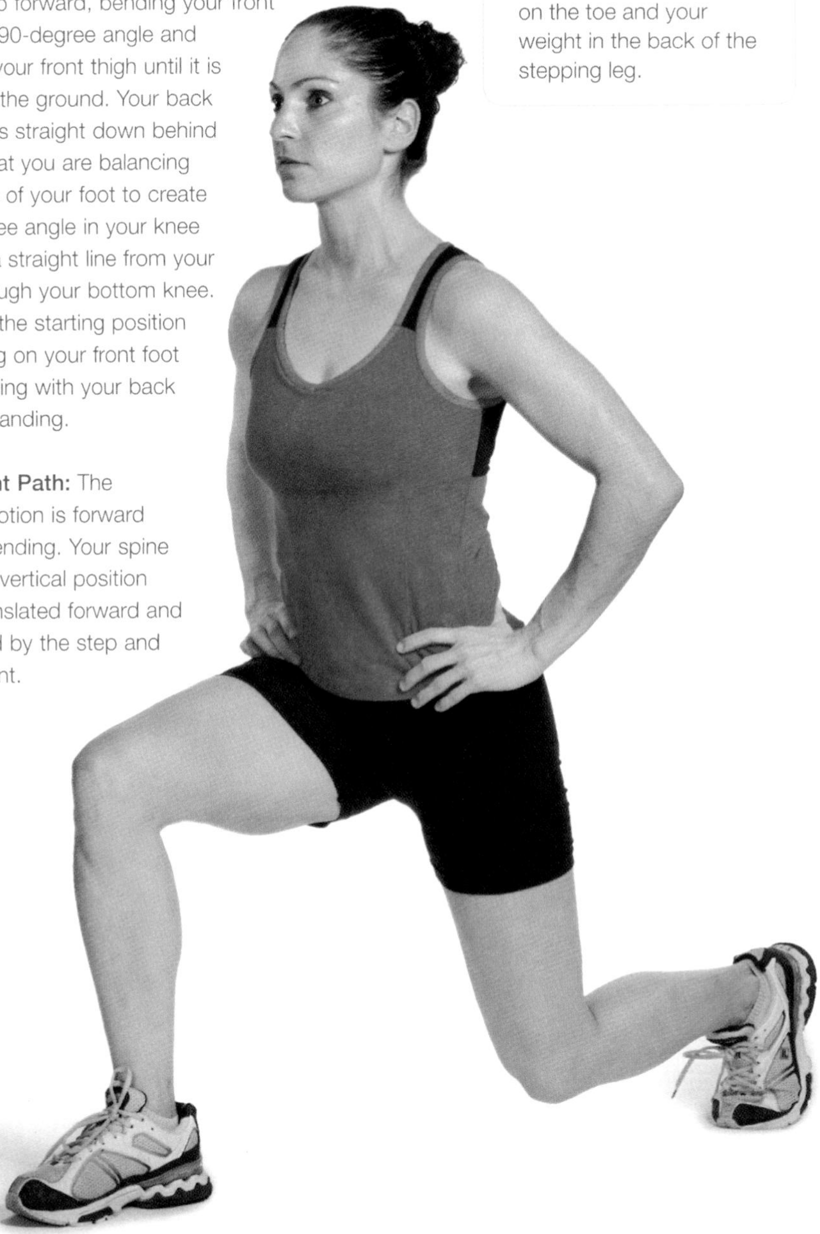

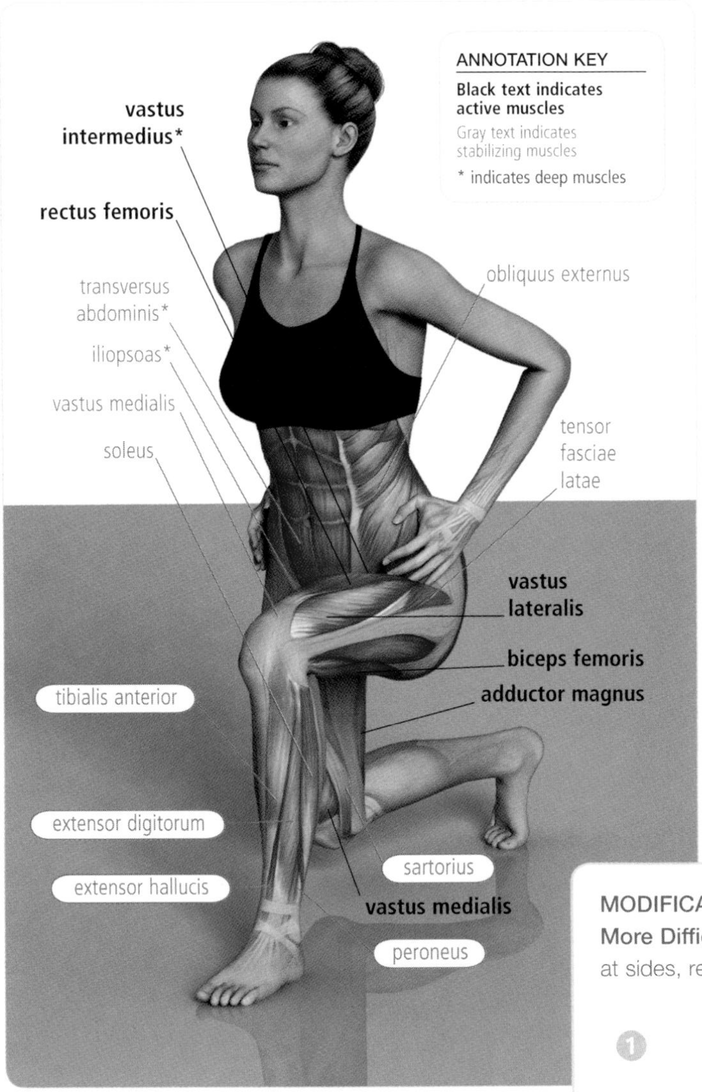
ANNOTATION KEY
Black text indicates active muscles
Gray text indicates stabilizing muscles
* indicates deep muscles
vastus intermedius*
rectus femoris
transversus abdominis*
iliopsoas*
vastus medialis
soleus
obliquus externus
tensor fasciae latae
vastus lateralis
biceps femoris
adductor magnus
tibialis anterior
extensor digitorum
extensor hallucis
sartorius
vastus medialis
peroneus

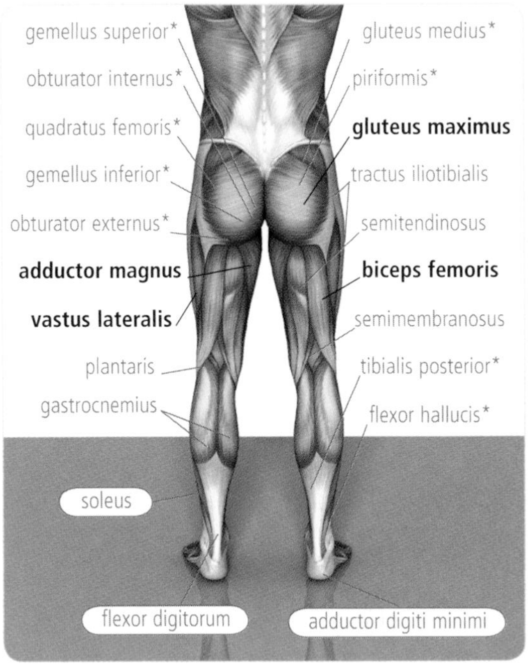
gemellus superior*
obturator internus*
quadratus femoris*
gemellus inferior*
obturator externus*
adductor magnus
vastus lateralis
plantaris
gastrocnemius
soleus
flexor digitorum
gluteus medius*
piriformis*
gluteus maximus
tractus iliotibialis
semitendinosus
biceps femoris
semimembranosus
tibialis posterior*
flexor hallucis*
adductor digiti minimi

## BEST FOR

- adductor magnus
- biceps femoris
- gluteus maximus
- rectus femoris
- vastus intermedius
- vastus lateralis
- vastus medialis

MODIFICATION

**More Difficult:** Holding a barbell overhead or dumbbells at sides, repeat the same action and movement path.

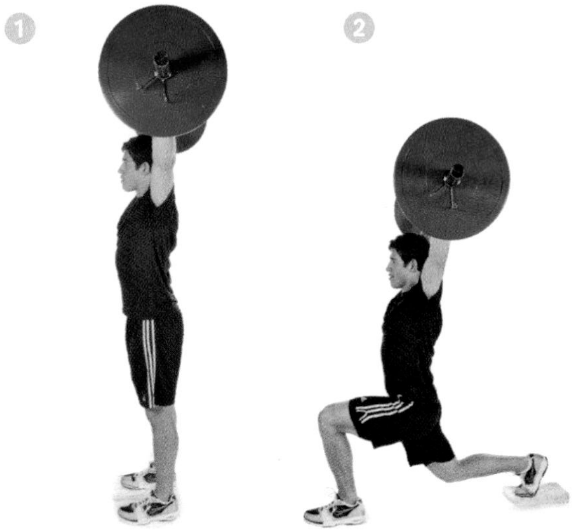
1
2

# WALKING WITH ROTATION

**① Starting Position:** Stand with your feet close together and your hands on your hips. With palms facing each other and arms extended at chest height, grasp a medicine ball on the sides.

**STABILIZE BY**
- Keeping your chest high, stomach up, and spine neutral.
- Evenly distributing your weight across your front foot, from front to back.
- Keeping your back foot on the toe and your weight in the back of the stepping leg.

**LOOK FOR**
- No translation forward from the hips or your spine.
- Your spine to remain in the same position as it moves down and up.
- No lateral movement of your leg as you step, either landing or pushing.

**AVOID**
- Raising the heel of your stepping foot off the ground or rotating your hips or torso.

**Action:** Keeping your head up, your spine in a neutral position, and both hands in front of you, step forward, bending your front knee to a 90-degree angle and dropping your front thigh until it is parallel to the ground. Your back knee drops straight down behind you, so that you are balancing on the toe of your foot, to create a 90-degree angle in your knee joint and a straight line from your spine through your bottom knee. During the stepping-out process, simultaneously move the ball across your body 45 degrees to the side of the forward leg, keeping arms extended and level.

**Movement Path:** A forward motion and a descending motion. Your spine stays in a vertical position and is translated forward and down by the step and the deceleration. Return to the starting position by pushing on your front foot and elevating with your back leg while bringing the ball back to starting position. Repeat with other leg.

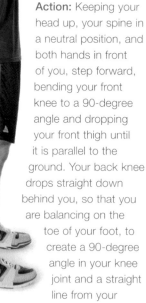

**②**

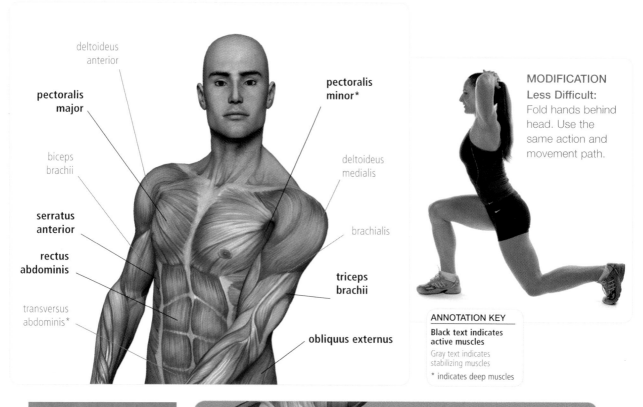

deltoideus anterior

pectoralis major

biceps brachii

serratus anterior

rectus abdominis

transversus abdominis*

pectoralis minor*

deltoideus medialis

brachialis

triceps brachii

obliquus externus

MODIFICATION
Less Difficult:
Fold hands behind head. Use the same action and movement path.

**ANNOTATION KEY**

**Black text indicates active muscles**

Gray text indicates stabilizing muscles

* indicates deep muscles

## BEST FOR

- gluteus maximus
- vastus lateralis
- vastus medialis
- vastus intermedius
- biceps femoris
- rectus femoris
- adductor magnus
- erector spinae
- soleus
- tibialis anterior

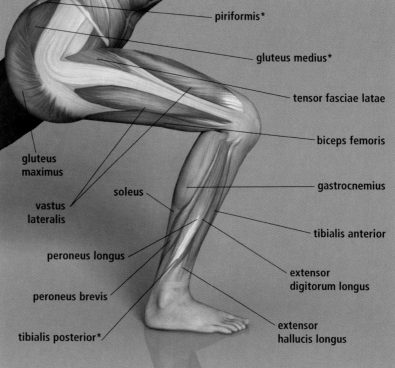

piriformis*

gluteus medius*

tensor fasciae latae

biceps femoris

gastrocnemius

tibialis anterior

extensor digitorum longus

extensor hallucis longus

gluteus maximus

vastus lateralis

soleus

peroneus longus

peroneus brevis

tibialis posterior*

# LATERAL

## LUNGE

**Starting Position:** Stand vertically with your feet directly below your hips and your hands on your hips.

### LOOK FOR
- A simultaneous movement of your arms and hips.
- Your chest to remain up and your shoulders to remain down.

### AVOID
- Any part of the stepping foot leaving contact with the ground or your knee extending forward beyond your toe.
- An excessive drop in torso angle beyond or below 45 degrees.

**Action:** Step directly out to the side at 180 degrees, retracting your hips and keeping your spine neutral. As your chest moves forward and your hips retract, extend your arms to ensure balance. Stop at the bottom of the movement when the upper thigh of your stepping leg is parallel to the ground. The opposite knee should be extended, your hips should be behind the stepping foot, and your knee should not exceed the toe line and should be directly over the foot. Your upper arms should be parallel to the ground. Pushing back off the stepping leg, return to the starting position.

**Movement Path:** As you move laterally to the side, your arms go forward and your hips go back. Your torso drops as your hips retract. Use one foot as both decelerator and accelerator. Use the standing or stationary foot as a balance lever.

### STABILIZE BY
- Keeping your hips retracted, your chest up, and using your arms as a counterbalance to the retraction of your hips.
- Keeping the opposite leg in contact with the floor, and maintaining tension on your quadriceps and hamstrings, so that your knee is locked and extended.

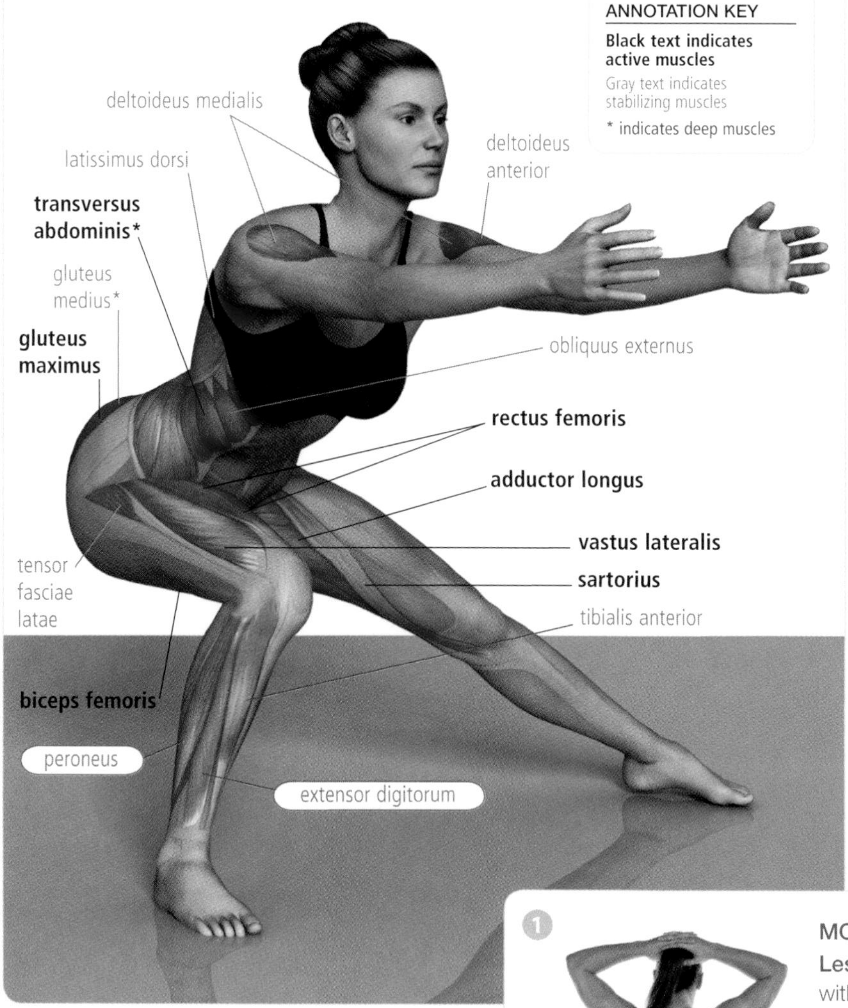
deltoideus medialis
latissimus dorsi
transversus abdominis*
gluteus medius*
gluteus maximus
deltoideus anterior
obliquus externus
rectus femoris
adductor longus
vastus lateralis
sartorius
tibialis anterior
tensor fasciae latae
biceps femoris
peroneus
extensor digitorum

ANNOTATION KEY

**Black text indicates active muscles**

Gray text indicates stabilizing muscles

* indicates deep muscles

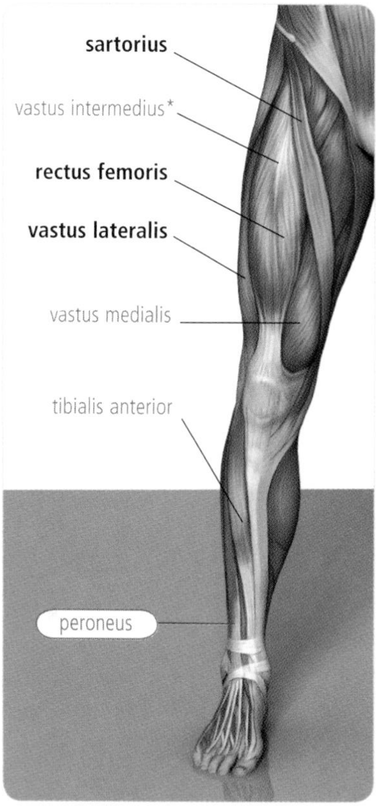
sartorius
vastus intermedius*
rectus femoris
vastus lateralis
vastus medialis
tibialis anterior
peroneus

## BEST FOR

- adductor longus
- adductor magnus
- biceps femoris
- gluteus maximus
- rectus femoris
- sartorius
- vastus lateralis

1

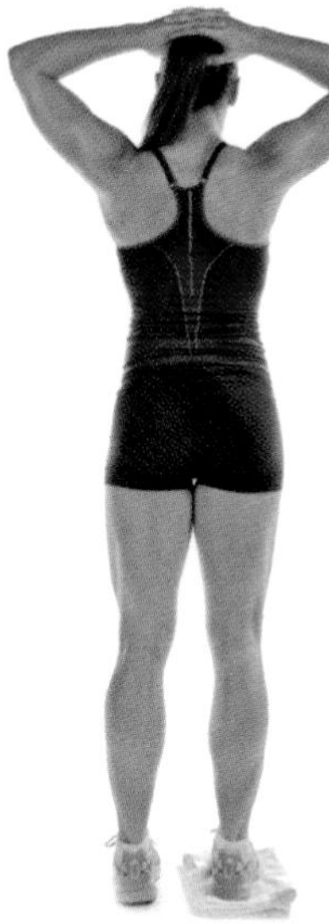

MODIFICATION

**Less Difficult:** Place hands behind head with elbows pointed wide and shoulders down. Follow same action and movement path. Repeat on other side.

2

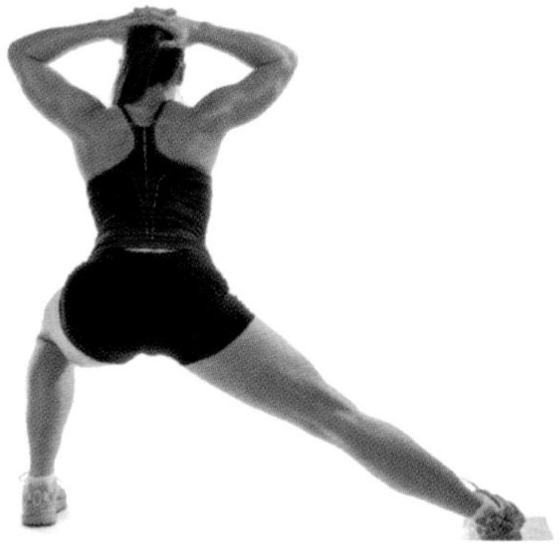

# 45-DEGREE TOWEL SLIDE

1

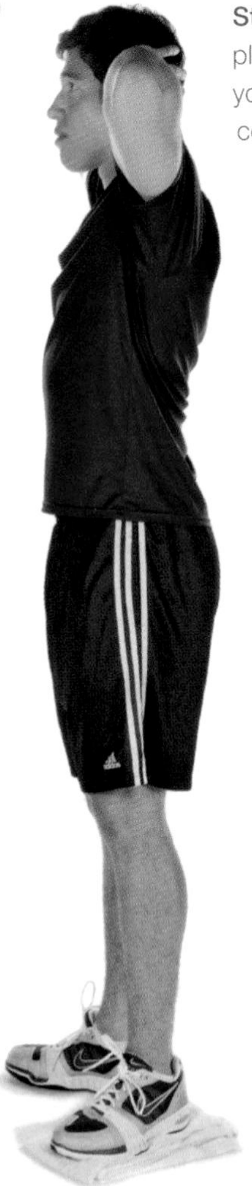

**Starting Position:** With your hands placed behind your head, start with your feet close together, one foot centered on a small towel.

**Action:** Looking straight ahead, keep your head neutral and spine long. Slide the foot with the towel directly out to the side at a 45-degree angle. As you begin the movement, your chest should move forward and your hips backward. Retract your hips on the stationary leg while keeping your spine neutral. This should allow the upper thigh to be parallel to the ground. Stop at the bottom of the movement when the towel-sliding leg is fully extended. Return to the starting position by pushing into the ground with the standing foot and sliding the foot with the towel underneath back toward the stationary front foot, moving the hips forward and spine upward to vertical.

**Movement Path:** The general motion of the hips and pelvis is lateral downward and backward at a 45-degree angle. Your spine flexes slightly forward and your arms extend, with weight focused on the nonmoving leg. The towel-sliding leg is moving with assistance from the towel. The towel foot bears little to no weight and is used primarily for balance. The stationary foot is the balance lever and prime mover.

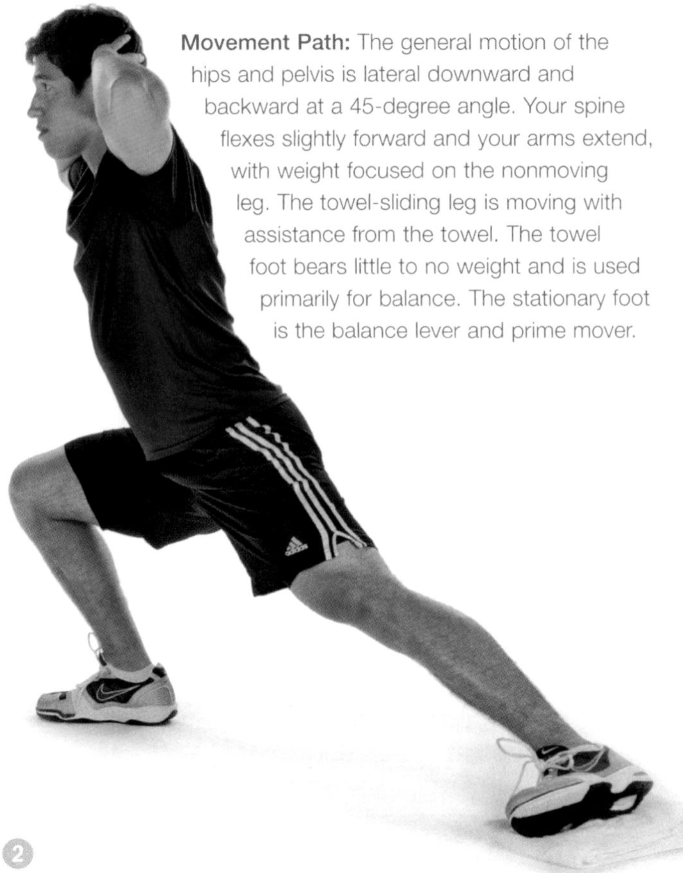

2

**LOOK FOR**

- A simultaneous movement of your legs and hips.
- Your chest to remain up and your shoulders to remain down.
- Your spine to remain in a neutral position as it translates forward and backward.
- The sliding leg to move backward and outward at a 45-degree angle to standing foot.

**AVOID**

- Back extension—shoulders should be slightly in front of the hips.
- Raising the heel of the front foot (non-towel-sliding foot) off the ground.

**STABILIZE BY**

- Keeping the torso solid and chest up.
- Keeping the hips and shoulders facing forward.

## BEST FOR

- biceps femoris
- vastus lateralis
- vastus medialis
- rectus femoris
- sartorius
- adductor magnus
- adductor longus
- erector spinae
- transversus abdominis
- trapezius
- rhomboideus
- gluteus medius
- gluteus minimus
- tibialis anterior
- erector spinae

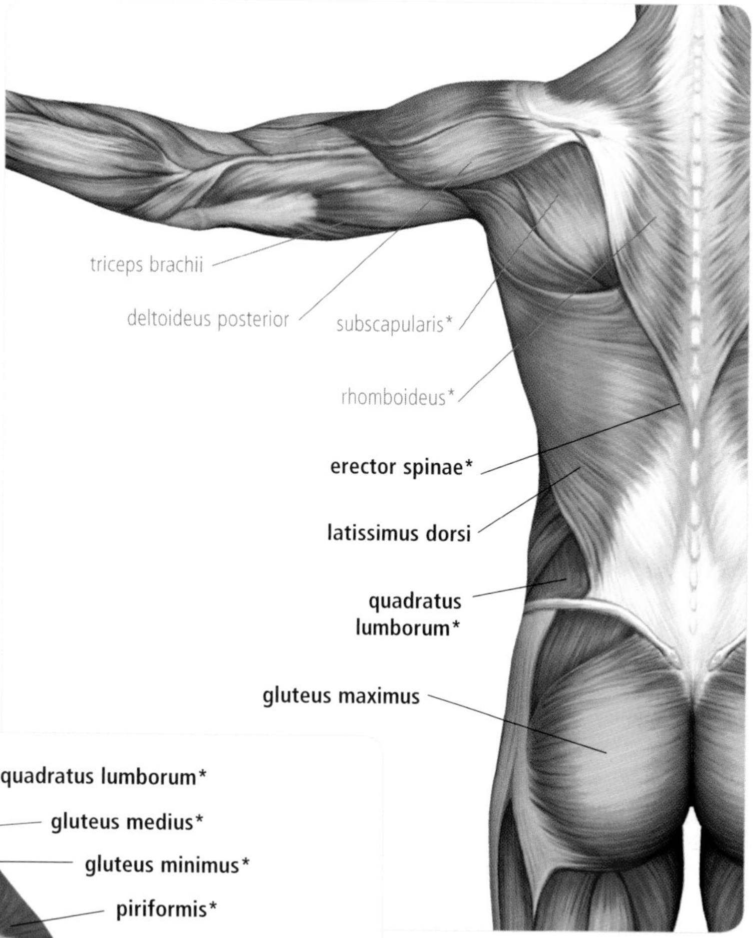
triceps brachii
deltoideus posterior
subscapularis*
rhomboideus*
erector spinae*
latissimus dorsi
quadratus lumborum*
gluteus maximus

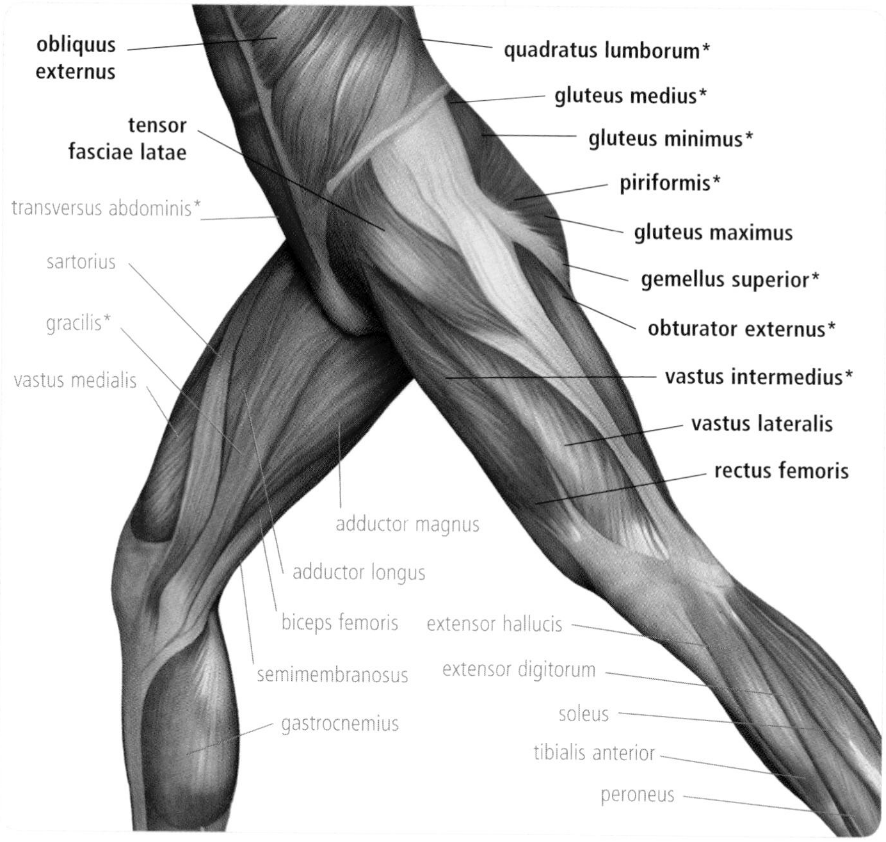
obliquus externus
tensor fasciae latae
transversus abdominis*
sartorius
gracilis*
vastus medialis
adductor magnus
adductor longus
biceps femoris
semimembranosus
gastrocnemius
quadratus lumborum*
gluteus medius*
gluteus minimus*
piriformis*
gluteus maximus
gemellus superior*
obturator externus*
vastus intermedius*
vastus lateralis
rectus femoris
extensor hallucis
extensor digitorum
soleus
tibialis anterior
peroneus

ANNOTATION KEY

**Black text indicates active muscles**

Gray text indicates stabilizing muscles

* indicates deep muscles

# BACKWARD TOWEL SLIDE



1

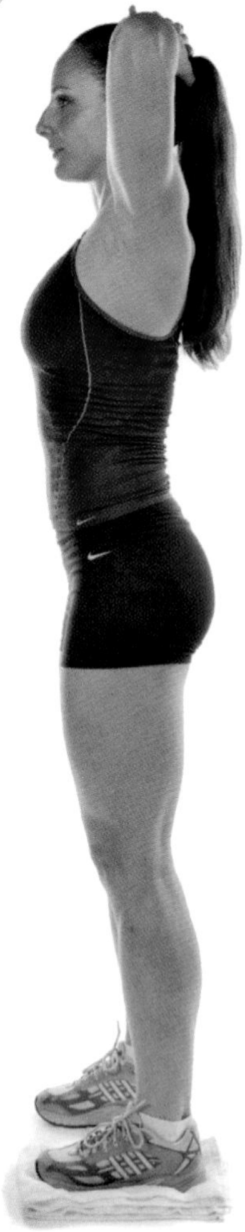

**Starting Position:** Stand with your hands placed behind your head and your feet close together, one foot centered on a small towel, bearing little to no weight.

STABILIZE BY
- Keeping the torso solid and chest up.
- Keeping the hips and shoulders facing forward.

**Action:** Looking straight ahead, keep your head neutral and spine long. Now, slide the foot with the towel underneath behind and across your body, so that you are balancing with the toe of your sliding foot. The standing leg bends and the hip drops until the front knee ends up in a 90-degree position, allowing your front thigh to be parallel to the ground. Return to the starting position by pushing the front foot into the floor, extending both the knee and hip, simultaneously sliding the foot with the towel underneath back toward the stationary front foot, and rise to a standing position.

**Movement Path:** The general motion of the hips and spine is backward and downward in a curvilinear fashion, or arc. Your spine stays in a vertical position with weight focused on the nonmoving leg. The rear leg is moving with assistance from the towel.

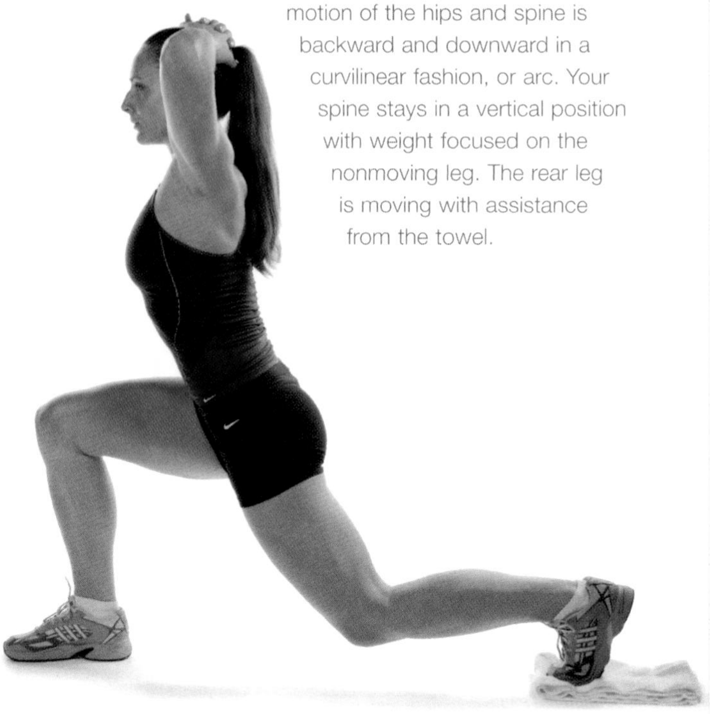

2

LOOK FOR
- Body to be in center of balance.
- Neutral spine position.
- Towel sliding at a 45-degree angle across and behind the standing foot.

AVOID
- Back extension—shoulders should be slightly in front of the hips.
- Raising the heel of the front foot (non-towel-sliding foot) off the ground.
- Back foot being dragged forward.
- Allowing the front knee to move forward and exceed the toe line.
- Allowing the front knee to migrate inward toward the midline.
- Keeping the back leg tense so that it remains straight.

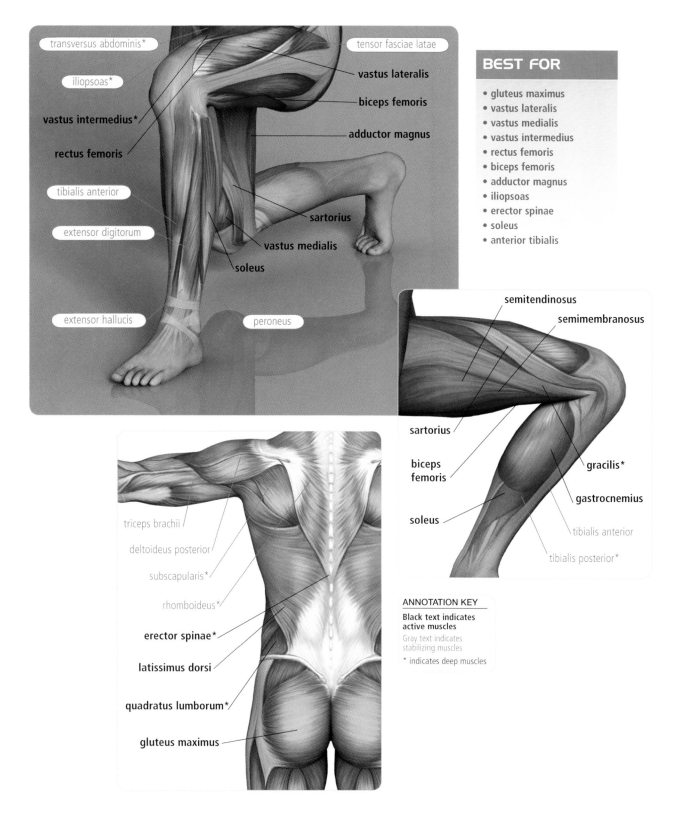

transversus abdominis*

iliopsoas*

vastus intermedius*

rectus femoris

tibialis anterior

extensor digitorum

extensor hallucis

tensor fasciae latae

vastus lateralis

biceps femoris

adductor magnus

sartorius

vastus medialis

soleus

peroneus

## BEST FOR

- gluteus maximus
- vastus lateralis
- vastus medialis
- vastus intermedius
- rectus femoris
- biceps femoris
- adductor magnus
- iliopsoas
- erector spinae
- soleus
- anterior tibialis

semitendinosus

semimembranosus

sartorius

biceps femoris

soleus

gracilis*

gastrocnemius

tibialis anterior

tibialis posterior*

triceps brachii

deltoideus posterior

subscapularis*

rhomboideus*

erector spinae*

latissimus dorsi

quadratus lumborum*

gluteus maximus

## ANNOTATION KEY

**Black text indicates active muscles**

Gray text indicates stabilizing muscles

* indicates deep muscles

# CROSS-BODY TOWEL SLIDE

1 **Starting Position:** With your hands placed behind your head, start with your feet close together, one foot centered on a small towel.

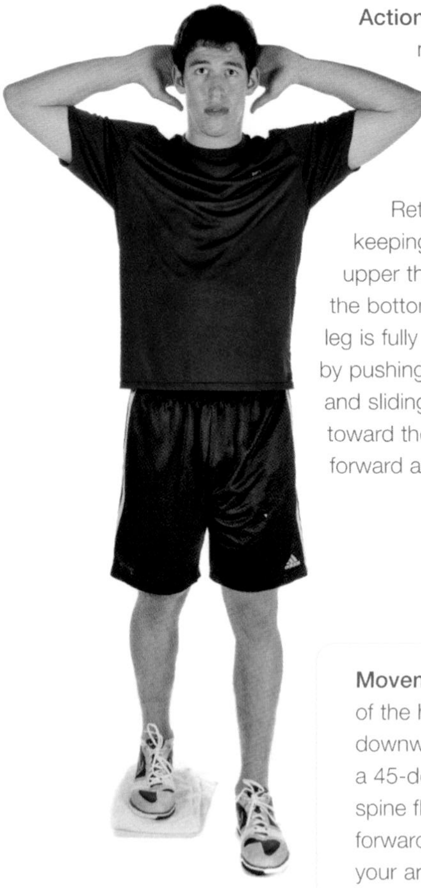

**Action:** Looking straight ahead, keep your head neutral and spine long. Now, slide the foot with the towel directly out to the side at a 45-degree angle. As you begin the movement, your chest should move forward and your hips backward. Retract your hips on the stationary leg while keeping your spine neutral. This should allow the upper thigh to be parallel to the ground. Stop at the bottom of the movement when the towel-sliding leg is fully extended. Return to the starting position by pushing into the ground with the standing foot and sliding the foot with the towel underneath back toward the stationary front foot, moving the hips forward and spine upward to vertical.

**Movement Path:** The general motion of the hips and pelvis is lateral downward and backward at a 45-degree angle. Your spine flexes slightly forward and your arms extend, with weight focused on the nonmoving leg. The towel-sliding leg is moving with assistance from the towel. The towel foot bears little to no weight and is used primarily for balance. The stationary foot is the balance lever and prime mover.

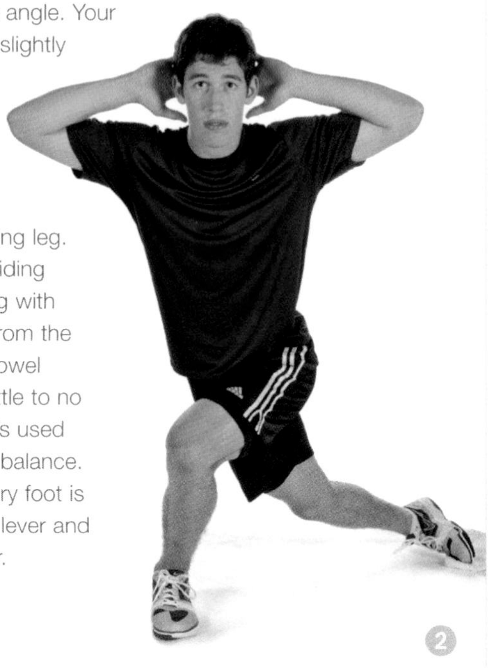

2

### LOOK FOR

- Body to be in center of balance.
- Neutral spine position.
- Towel to slide at a 45-degree angle across and behind standing foot.
- Shoulders to be slightly in front of the hips during back extension.

### AVOID

- Rotating the hips.
- Raising the heel of the front foot off the ground.
- Dragging the back foot forward.
- Allowing the front knee to move forward and exceed the toe line.
- Allowing the front knee to migrate inward toward the midline.
- Keeping the back leg tense so that it remains straight.

### STABILIZE BY

- Keeping the torso solid and chest up.
- Keeping the hips and shoulders facing forward.

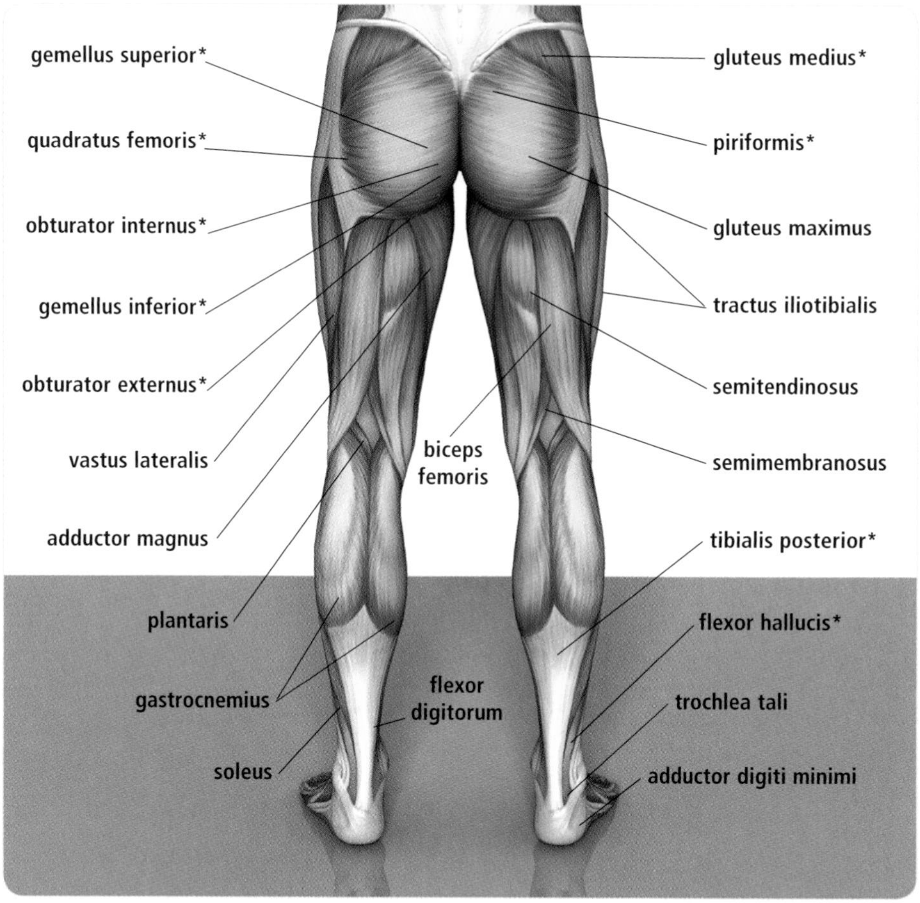
gemellus superior*
quadratus femoris*
obturator internus*
gemellus inferior*
obturator externus*
vastus lateralis
adductor magnus
plantaris
gastrocnemius
soleus
biceps femoris
flexor digitorum
gluteus medius*
piriformis*
gluteus maximus
tractus iliotibialis
semitendinosus
semimembranosus
tibialis posterior*
flexor hallucis*
trochlea tali
adductor digiti minimi

ANNOTATION KEY

Black text indicates active muscles

Gray text indicates stabilizing muscles

* indicates deep muscles

## BEST FOR

- gluteus maximus
- vastus lateralis
- vastus medialis
- vastus intermedius
- rectus femoris
- biceps femoris
- adductor magnus
- iliopsoas
- erector spinae
- soleus
- anterior tibialis

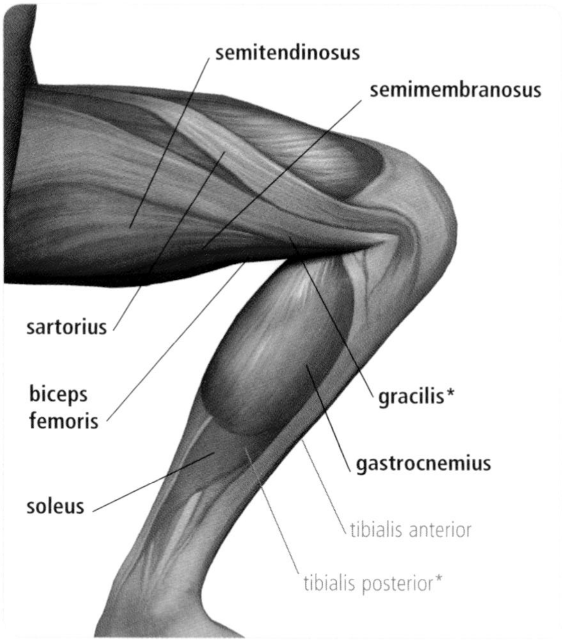
semitendinosus
semimembranosus
sartorius
biceps femoris
soleus
gracilis*
gastrocnemius
tibialis anterior
tibialis posterior*

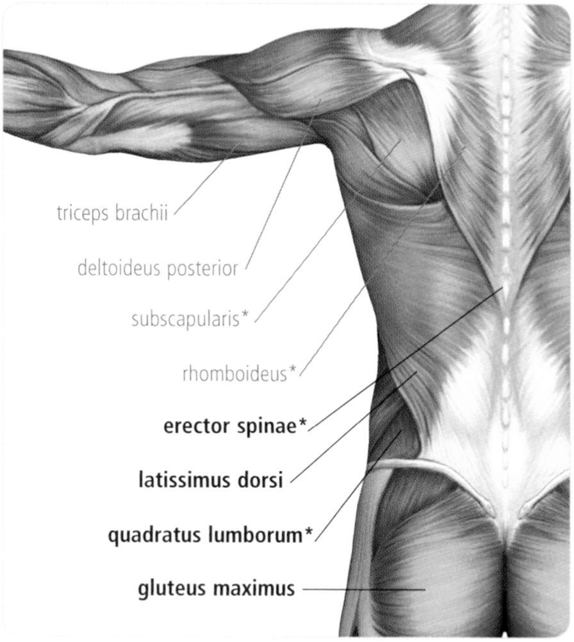
triceps brachii
deltoideus posterior
subscapularis*
rhomboideus*
erector spinae*
latissimus dorsi
quadratus lumborum*
gluteus maximus

# REVERSE BARBELL SLIDE



1

**Starting Position:** Hold a barbell directly above your head with hands wider than shoulder-width apart and your feet close together, one foot centered on a small towel, bearing little to no weight.

**Action:** Looking straight ahead, keep your head neutral and spine long. Slide the foot with the towel underneath directly behind you, so that you are balancing on the toe of your foot to create a 90-degree angle in your knee joint and a straight line from your spine through your bottom knee. The front knee should end up in a 90-degree position, allowing your front thigh to be parallel to the ground. Both the arms and bar remain directly above the head throughout the movement. Return to the starting position by pushing the front foot into the floor, extending both the knee and hip, simultaneously sliding the foot with the towel underneath back toward the stationary front foot as you rise to a standing position.

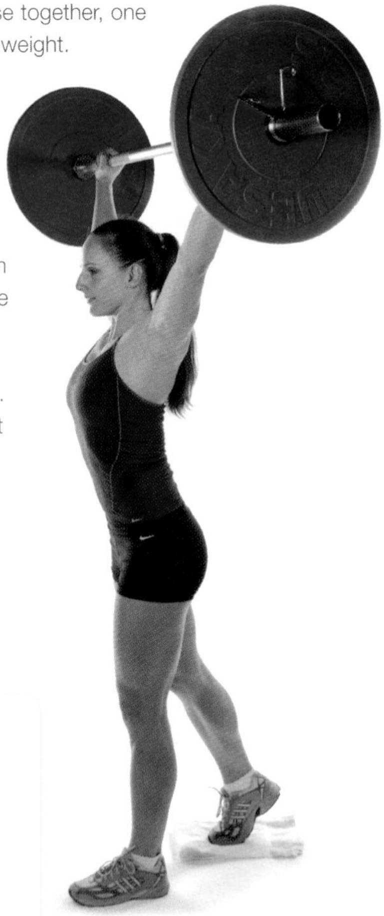

2

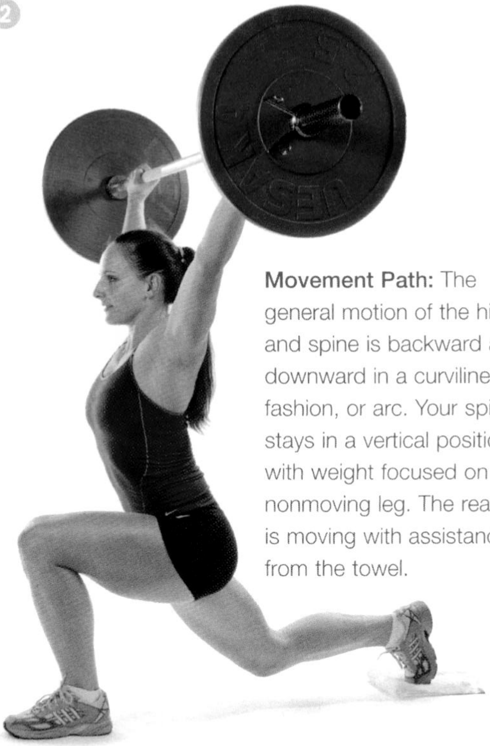

**Movement Path:** The general motion of the hips and spine is backward and downward in a curvilinear fashion, or arc. Your spine stays in a vertical position, with weight focused on the nonmoving leg. The rear leg is moving with assistance from the towel.

LOOK FOR
- Bar to remain directly above head, arms extended.
- Body to be in center of balance.
- Neutral spine position.
- Towel to slide straight back with deceleration.

AVOID
- Rotation of any kind.
- Back extension—shoulders should be directly above the hips.
- Raising the heel of the front foot (non-towel-sliding foot) off the ground.
- Back foot being dragged forward.
- Allowing the front knee to move forward and exceed the toe line.
- Allowing the front knee to migrate inward toward the midline.
- Keeping the back leg tense so that it remains straight.

STABILIZE BY
- Keeping the spine vertical and the rib cage pulled up and in.
- Keeping chest high and shoulders down.
- Extending your arms completely.

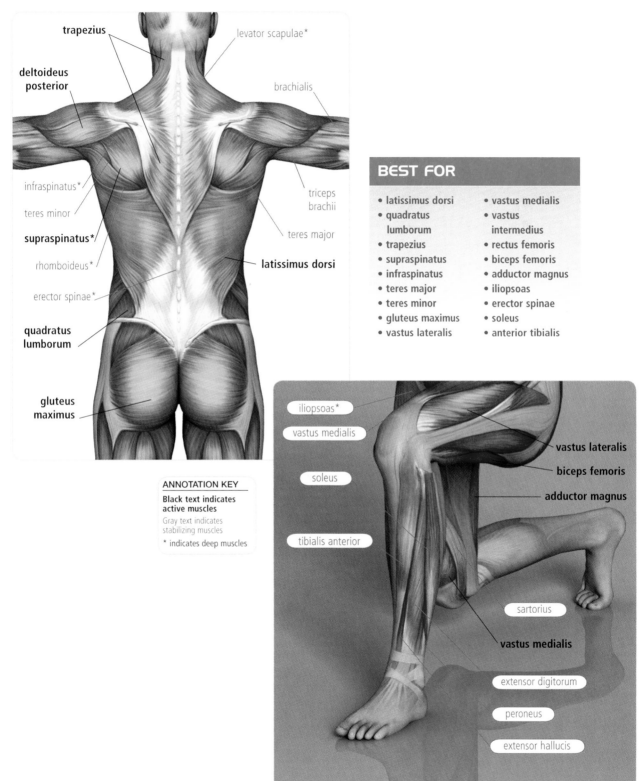

trapezius

levator scapulae*

deltoideus posterior

brachialis

infraspinatus*

triceps brachii

teres minor

supraspinatus*

teres major

rhomboideus*

latissimus dorsi

erector spinae*

quadratus lumborum

gluteus maximus

## BEST FOR

- latissimus dorsi
- quadratus lumborum
- trapezius
- supraspinatus
- infraspinatus
- teres major
- teres minor
- gluteus maximus
- vastus lateralis
- vastus medialis
- vastus intermedius
- rectus femoris
- biceps femoris
- adductor magnus
- iliopsoas
- erector spinae
- soleus
- anterior tibialis

## ANNOTATION KEY

**Black text indicates active muscles**

Gray text indicates stabilizing muscles

* indicates deep muscles

iliopsoas*

vastus medialis

vastus lateralis

biceps femoris

soleus

adductor magnus

tibialis anterior

sartorius

**vastus medialis**

extensor digitorum

peroneus

extensor hallucis

# REVERSE WITH OVERHEAD KETTLEBELL

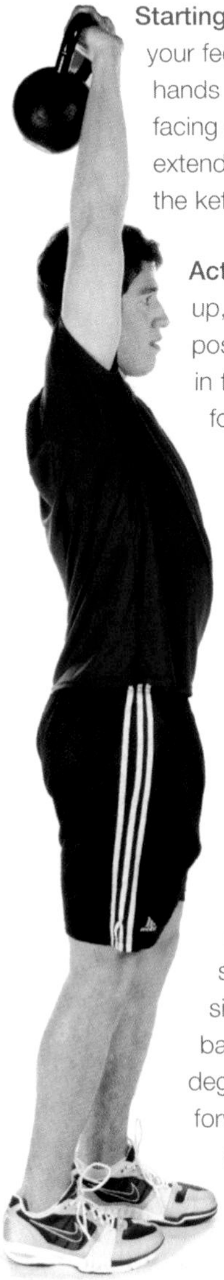

**Starting Position:** Stand with your feet close together and your hands on your hips. With palms facing each other and arms extended at chest height, grasp the kettlebell.

**Action:** Keeping your head up, your spine in a neutral position, and your hands in front of you, take a step forward, bending your front knee to a 90-degree angle and dropping your front thigh until it is parallel to the ground. Your back knee drops straight down behind you, so that you are balancing on the toe of your foot, to create a 90-degree angle in your knee joint and a straight line from your spine through your bottom knee. During the stepping-out process, simultaneously move the ball across your body 45 degrees to the side of the forward leg, keeping arms extended and level.

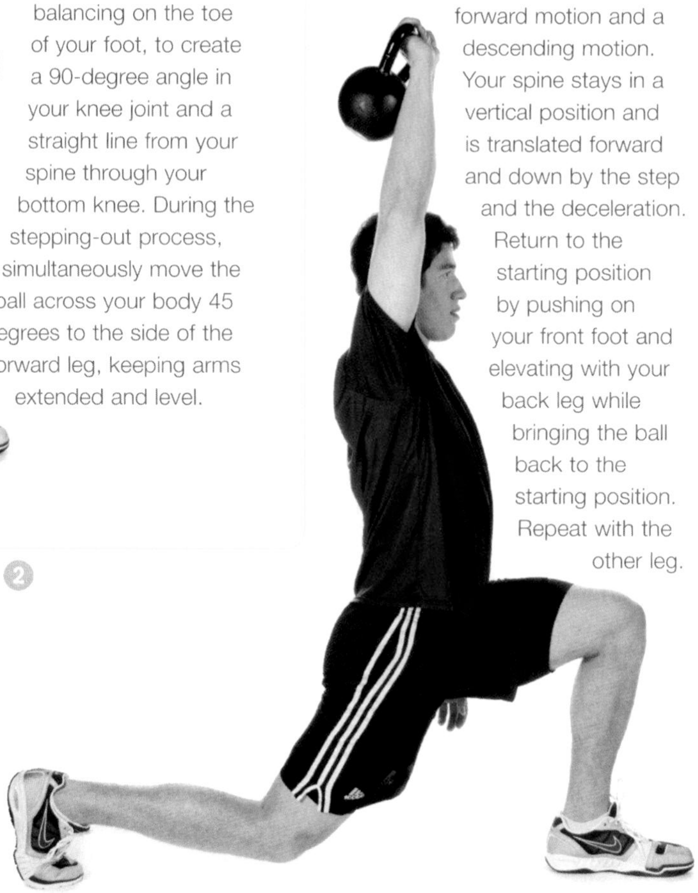

**Movement Path:** A forward motion and a descending motion. Your spine stays in a vertical position and is translated forward and down by the step and the deceleration. Return to the starting position by pushing on your front foot and elevating with your back leg while bringing the ball back to the starting position. Repeat with the other leg.

STABILIZE BY
- Keeping your chest high, stomach up, and spine neutral.
- Evenly distributing your weight across your front foot, from front to back.
- Keeping your back foot on the toe line and your weight in the back of the stepping leg.

LOOK FOR
- Body to be in center of balance.
- Neutral spine position.

AVOID
- Back extension—shoulders should be slightly in front of the hips.
- Raising the heel of the front foot off the ground.
- Back foot being dragged forward.
- Allowing the front knee to move forward and exceed the toe line.
- Allowing the front knee to migrate inward toward the midline.
- Keeping the back leg tense so it remains straight.

# REVERSE WITH OVERHEAD KETTLEBELL • LUNGE

MODIFICATIONS

**Less Difficult:** Fold hands behind head. Use same action and movement path.

**More Difficult:** Rest a barbell across your shoulders. Maintain the same activation pattern and movement sequence, keeping the bar's weight balanced on your torso. Keep your shoulders down, with your hands wider than shoulder-width apart, your torso vertical, and your chest and chin up.

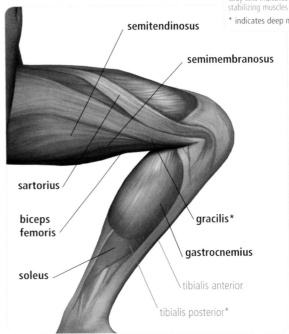

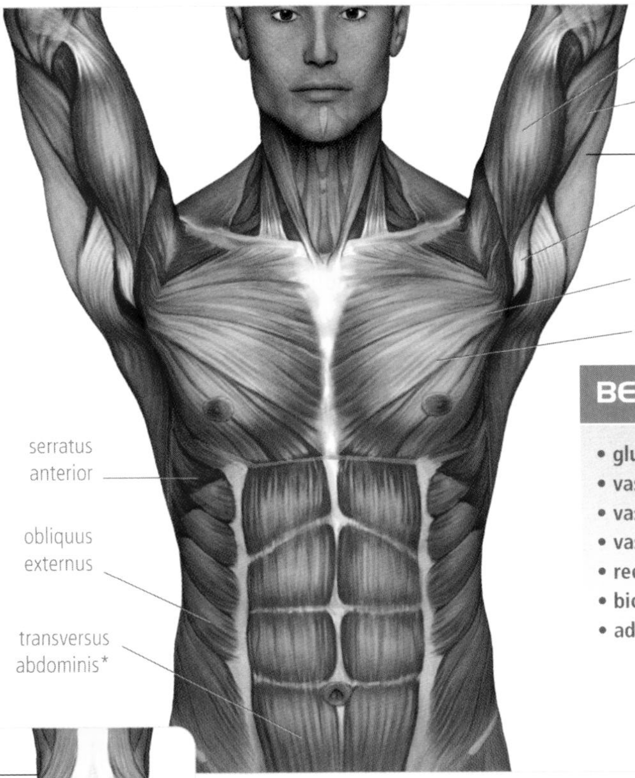

biceps brachii
brachialis
triceps brachii
coracobrachialis*
pectoralis minor*
pectoralis major
serratus anterior
obliquus externus
transversus abdominis*


## BEST FOR

- gluteus maximus
- vastus lateralis
- vastus medialis
- vastus intermedius
- rectus femoris
- biceps femoris
- adductor magnus

ANNOTATION KEY

**Black text indicates active muscles**

Gray text indicates stabilizing muscles

* indicates deep muscles

levator scapulae*
trapezius
triceps brachii
deltoideus posterior
infraspinatus*
teres major
rhomboideus*
erector spinae*
quadratus lumborum*
gluteus maximus

semitendinosus
semimembranosus
sartorius
biceps femoris
soleus
gracilis*
gastrocnemius
tibialis anterior
tibialis posterior*

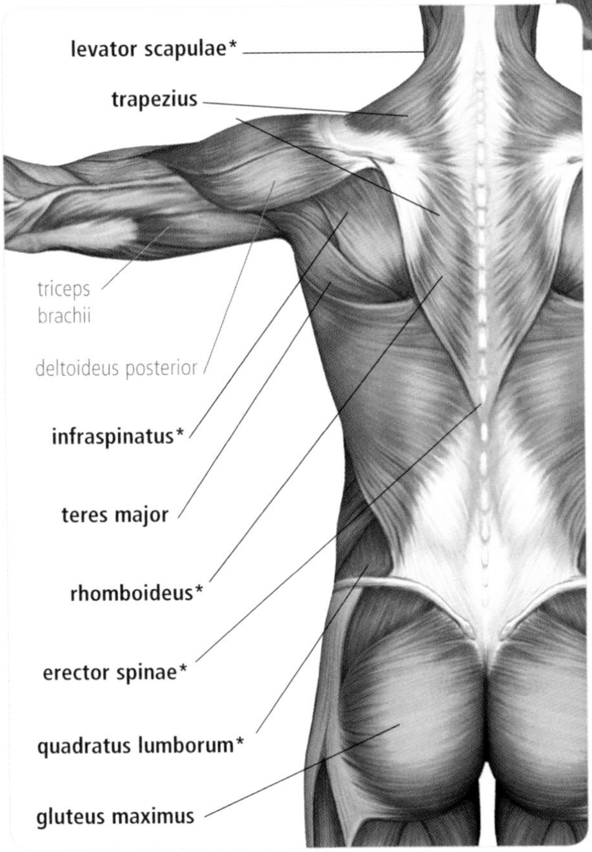

# UP TO BOX

**Starting Position:** Stand vertically with your feet directly below your hips and your hands either on your hips or clasped behind your head, elbows pointing outward.

**Action:** Step forward, placing one foot on a step in front of you, dropping the front thigh and hip so that both the raised knee and hip are close to a 90-degree angle. Make sure that your body is vertical, your chest is up, and your front knee is directly over your foot. Your raised knee should not exceed the toe line, and your foot should be flat on the surface of the step. The back knee and hip drop directly downward, the spine remains erect. Keeping your back leg bent, push through your top leg, extending your knee and hips simultaneously to drive your body upward and backward. Do not allow your back leg to push off the floor.

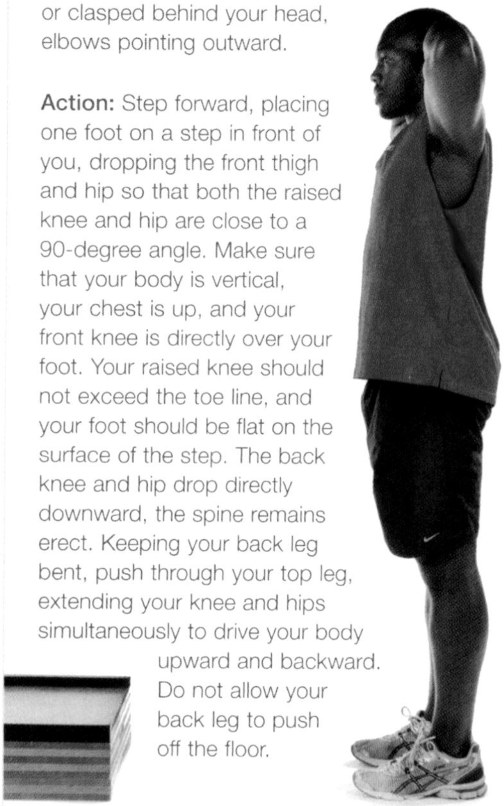

1

### STABILIZE BY

- Keeping your upper back muscles and shoulders down and back.
- Not allowing your momentum to bring your torso forward.
- Keeping your hip, shoulder, and ankle in a line from the bottom weight.

### LOOK FOR

- A slight forward translation and directly upward movement of your spine.

### AVOID

- Straightening your back knee.
- Allowing your front knee to slip forward beyond the toe line or any part of your front foot to lift off the step.
- Moving your knee either laterally or medially; keep it directly over the stepping foot.

**Movement Path:** A forward and slightly downward movement. Your head should begin above the moving foot and end directly between both feet. Allow your arms to simply stabilize the weight, keeping shoulders back. Ascend in the same fashion.

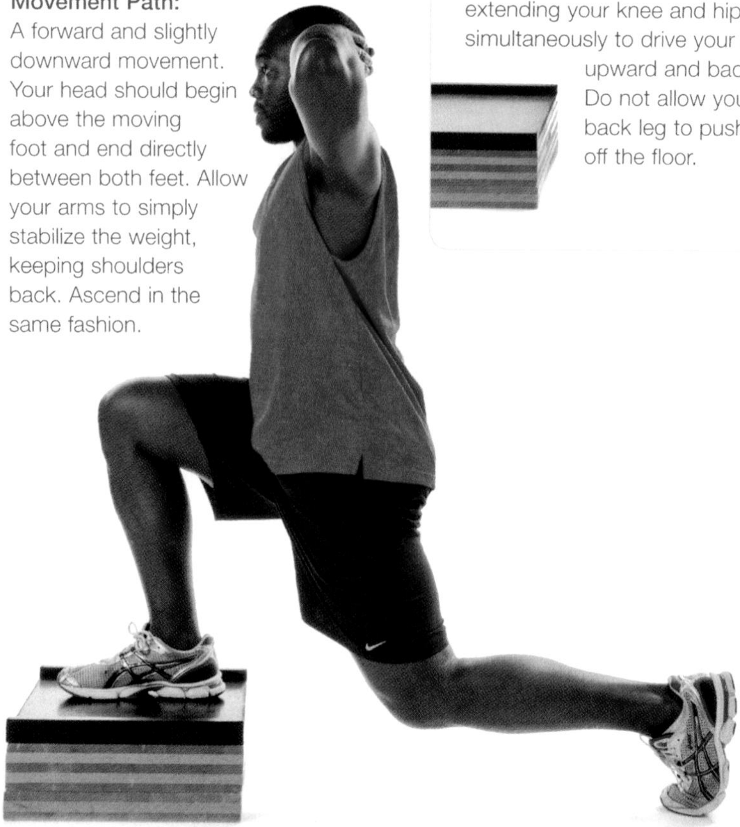

2

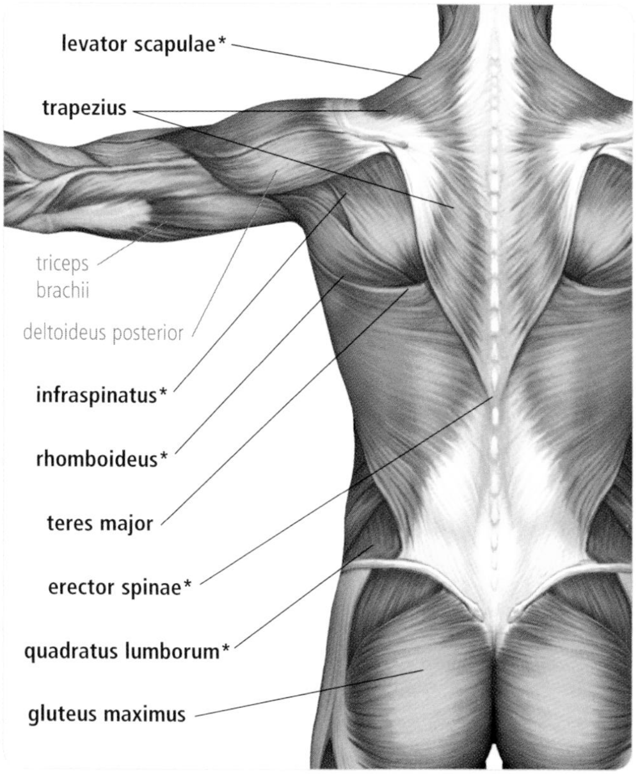
levator scapulae*
trapezius
triceps brachii
deltoideus posterior
infraspinatus*
rhomboideus*
teres major
erector spinae*
quadratus lumborum*
gluteus maximus

MODIFICATION

**More Difficult:** Holding a barbell directly above your head, shoulders down, elbows extending, repeat the same action and movement path.

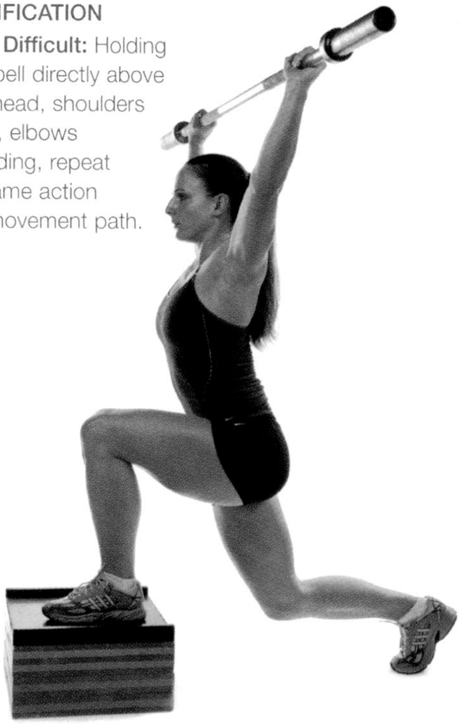

## BEST FOR

- rectus femoris
- sartorius
- biceps femoris
- semitendinosus
- semimembranosus
- soleus
- tibialis posterior
- tibialis anterior
- adductor magnus

ANNOTATION KEY

**Black text indicates active muscles**

Gray text indicates stabilizing muscles

* indicates deep muscles

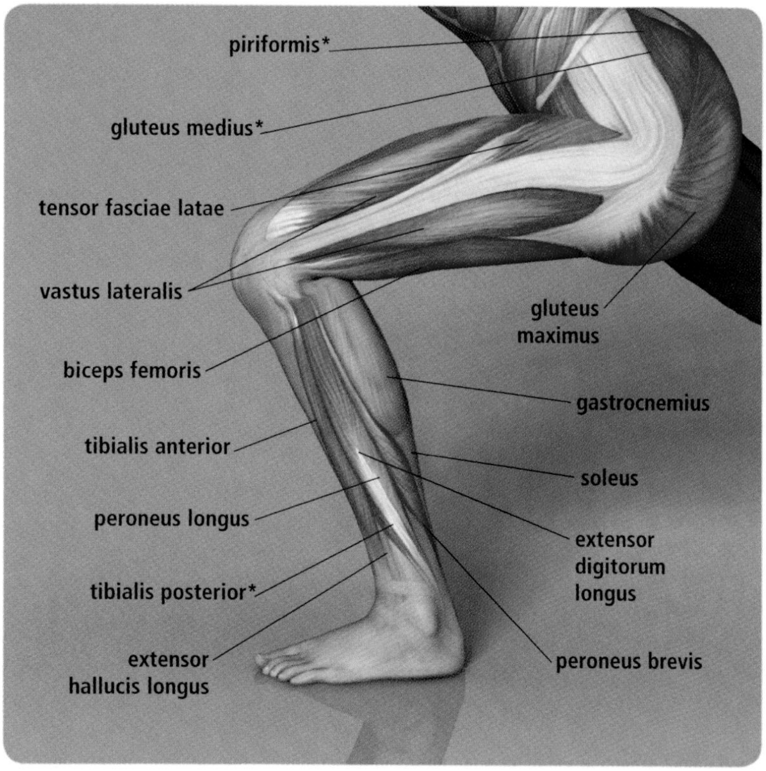
piriformis*
gluteus medius*
tensor fasciae latae
vastus lateralis
biceps femoris
tibialis anterior
peroneus longus
tibialis posterior*
extensor hallucis longus
gluteus maximus
gastrocnemius
soleus
extensor digitorum longus
peroneus brevis

# OFF BOX

## LUNGE

**Starting Position:** Begin by standing in a vertical position on a block, feet together, hands clasped behind head, chest erect, and head high.

**①**

**Action:** Step directly forward off the block, bending your knee and allowing your torso to ride forward. The torso remains erect as the front foot contacts the ground. Drop the torso and hips directly down by bending both the front and back knee until the front thigh is parallel to the ground and the back knee comes almost to the ground.

**②**

### LOOK FOR
- Your head to remain directly above your hip.
- Your knee and hips to move simultaneously.

### AVOID
- Extending your knee beyond your toe line.
- Any rotation in your hips or torso.
- Any deviation of the standing knee from above the weight-bearing foot.

### STABILIZE BY
- Keeping your spinal muscles active, your shoulders retracted and depressed, the opposite leg involved, and your opposite foot relaxed.

**Movement Path:** While descending directly down, allow your hips to translate forward and downward, while keeping your spine, chest, and head high.

## BEST FOR

- vastus lateralis
- vastus medialis
- vastus intermedius
- rectus femoris
- sartorius
- semitendinosus
- semimembranosus
- gluteus maximus
- erector spinae
- quadratus lumborum
- deltoideus posterior
- transversus abdominis
- rhomboideus
- adductor magnus
- tensor fasciae latae
- gluteus medius

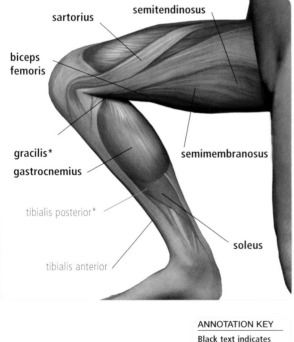

sartorius

semitendinosus

biceps femoris

gracilis*

gastrocnemius

semimembranosus

tibialis posterior*

soleus

tibialis anterior

### ANNOTATION KEY

**Black text indicates active muscles**

Gray text indicates stabilizing muscles

\* indicates deep muscles

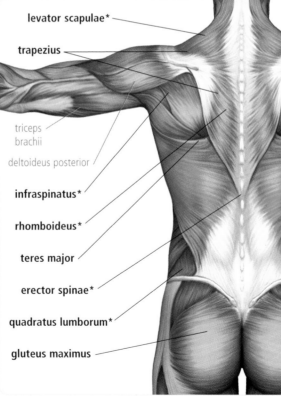

levator scapulae*

trapezius

triceps brachii

deltoideus posterior

infraspinatus*

rhomboideus*

teres major

erector spinae*

quadratus lumborum*

gluteus maximus

# PUSH-UP

The classic. The mighty mighty push-up has been around as an exercise for thousands of years—and for very good reason. It has the reputation of being a very simple exercise, and if done correctly, it can contribute to almost every part of the body in meaningful and beneficial ways.

The push-up can be used as a diagnostic tool during a fitness evaluation to measure not only chest and arm endurance but also shoulder stability, abdominal and lower-back strength, hip stability, and leg endurance.

Joints involved are the shoulder, elbow, and wrist. The primary muscles are the chest, shoulder, and triceps.

The primary benefits of this exercise are shoulder, back, and hip stability; upper-body strength and endurance; and abdominal endurance.

# PUSH-UP

**Starting Position:** Lie flat on the ground, facedown. Place your hands slightly outside of your shoulders and your fingertips parallel to your collarbone. Make sure that your elbows are at 45-degree angles to your torso. Place both feet on your tiptoes.

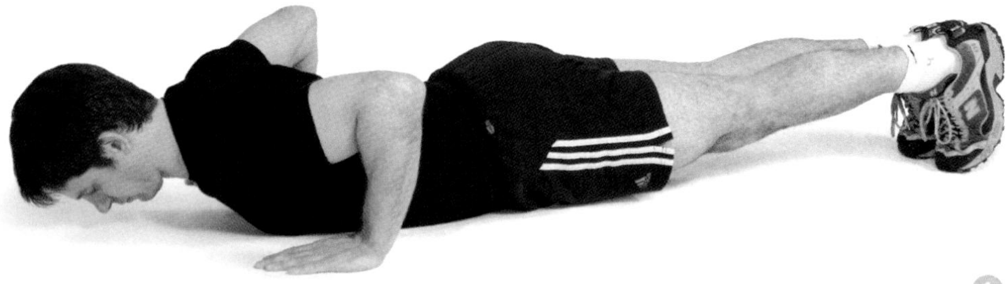

1

**Action:** Raise your legs and hips off the ground. Your lower back should arch slightly. Extend your arms, pushing into the ground. To return, lower your body in a single plane by bending your arms.

**Movement Path:** The plane of your body rotates upward in an arc. Use your feet as a lever.

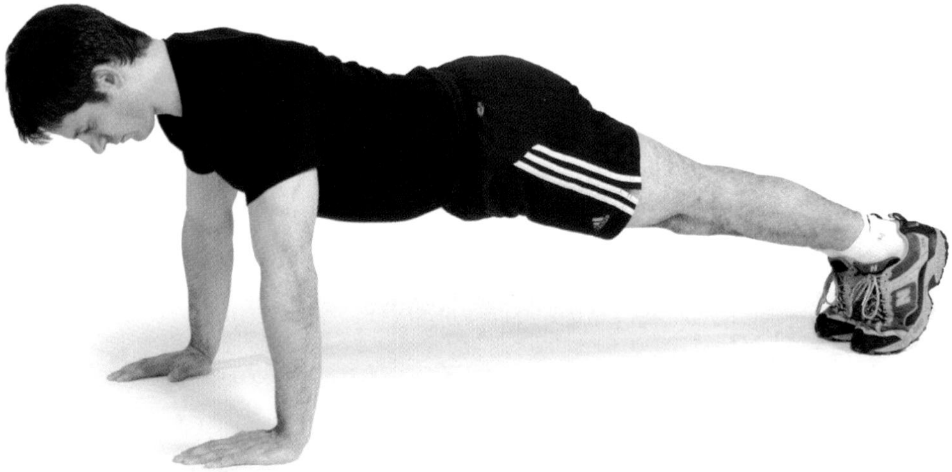

2

**LOOK FOR**
- A single plane of movement, i.e., a straight line from head to ankle.

**AVOID**
- Segmental elevation, i.e., your shoulders rising before your hips, or vice versa.
- Elevating your shoulders toward your ears.
- Moving your head forward.

**STABILIZE BY**
- Keeping your knees locked.
- Fixing your ankles in a stable position.
- Keeping your hips, abdominal muscles, and lower back rigid.

## BEST FOR

- deltoideus anterior
- coracobrachialis
- pectoralis major
- pectoralis minor
- triceps brachii

ANNOTATION KEY

**Black text indicates active muscles**

Gray text indicates stabilizing muscles

\* indicates deep muscles

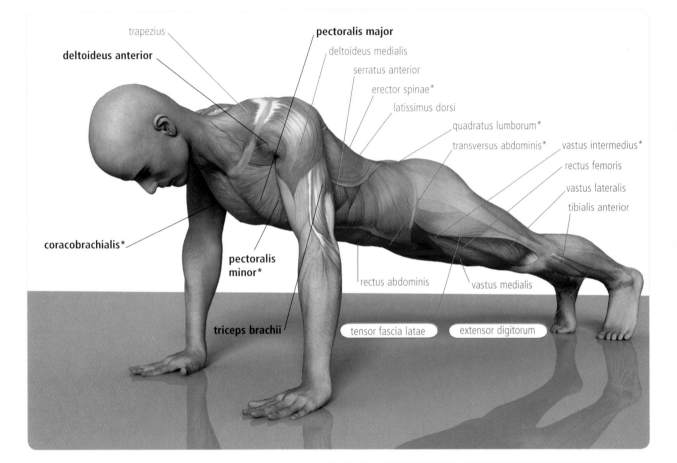

trapezius

**pectoralis major**

**deltoideus anterior**

deltoideus medialis

serratus anterior

erector spinae\*

latissimus dorsi

quadratus lumborum\*

transversus abdominis\*

vastus intermedius\*

rectus femoris

vastus lateralis

tibialis anterior

**coracobrachialis\***

**pectoralis minor\***

rectus abdominis

vastus medialis

**triceps brachii**

tensor fascia latae

extensor digitorum

## MODIFICATIONS

**Less Difficult:** Shorten the lever by bending your knees to the floor. Maintain the same action and movement path.

**More Difficult:** Raise the angle of elevation to 45 degrees by placing your hands on a physio ball.

**More Difficult:** Place your feet on a Swiss ball.

**More Difficult:** Raise one leg and maintain the same activation pattern and movement sequence.

# PUSH-UP & ROLL-OUT



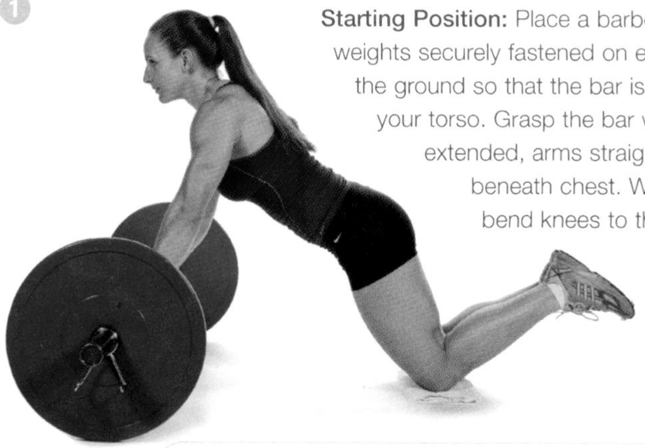

**Starting Position:** Place a barbell with weights securely fastened on each end on the ground so that the bar is horizontal to your torso. Grasp the bar with elbows extended, arms straight, and bar beneath chest. With body rigid, bend knees to the floor.

**Action:** Keeping your elbows at 45-degree angles to your torso, use your knees as a fulcrum, and let your body drop until your chest touches the bar. Extend elbows, and push up and away until arms are fully extended. Pause. Then, putting pressure on the heel of the hand, push on the bar, rolling it forward with arms remaining extended. Pause briefly, and then pull back on the bar, returning it to the starting position.

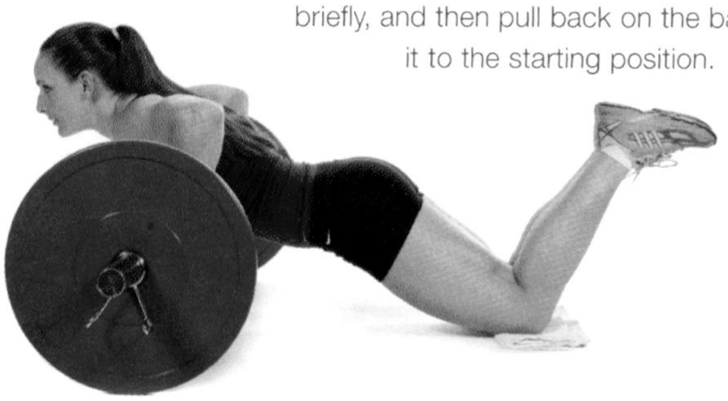

**Movement Path:** First, lower your body in a single plane by bending your arms. Your hips and shoulders should move simultaneously upward. Use your feet as a lever. Then, elevate your arms and allow your torso to drop.

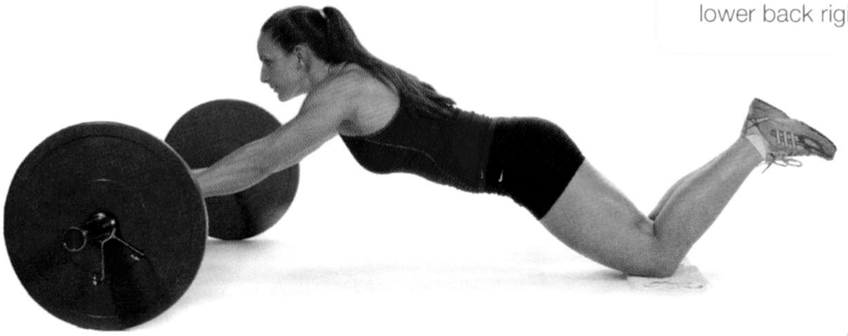

LOOK FOR
- Spine to remain motionless throughout both movements of the arms and shoulders.
- Spine to remain solid.
- Shoulders to remain down.
- Bar to not move during push-up phase.

AVOID
- A segmental elevation, i.e., your shoulders rising before your hips, or vice versa.
- Elevating your shoulders toward your ears.
- Moving your head forward.
- Rolling the bar forward or backward unevenly.

STABILIZE BY
- Keeping your knees locked.
- Fixing your ankles in a stable position.
- Keeping your hips, abdominal muscles, and lower back rigid.

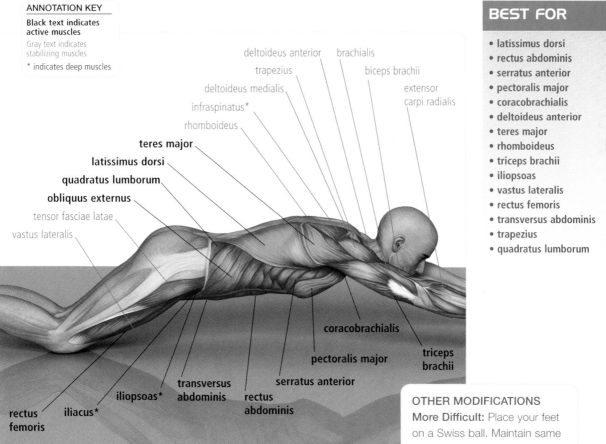

**ANNOTATION KEY**

**Black text indicates active muscles**

Gray text indicates stabilizing muscles

\* indicates deep muscles

deltoideus anterior
brachialis
trapezius
biceps brachii
deltoideus medialis
extensor carpi radialis
infraspinatus\*
rhomboideus
**teres major**
**latissimus dorsi**
**quadratus lumborum**
**obliquus externus**
tensor fasciae latae
vastus lateralis
**coracobrachialis**
**pectoralis major**
**triceps brachii**
**transversus abdominis**
**serratus anterior**
**iliopsoas\***
**rectus abdominis**
**rectus femoris**
**iliacus\***

**BEST FOR**

- latissimus dorsi
- rectus abdominis
- serratus anterior
- pectoralis major
- coracobrachialis
- deltoideus anterior
- teres major
- rhomboideus
- triceps brachii
- iliopsoas
- vastus lateralis
- rectus femoris
- transversus abdominis
- trapezius
- quadratus lumborum

### OTHER MODIFICATIONS

**More Difficult:** Place your feet on a Swiss ball. Maintain same action and movement path.

**More Difficult:** Raise one leg and maintain same action and movement path.

### MODIFICATIONS

**More Difficult:** Extend your legs so that your body is rigid. Maintain same action and movement path.

# ON PHYSIO BALL & BLOCKS

## PUSH-UP

1

**Starting Position:** With your hands wider than shoulder-width apart and your fingertips parallel to collarbone, place hands on blocks (or bench) and place feet on physio ball with ankles fixed at 90-degree angles, toes down, so that body is horizontal.

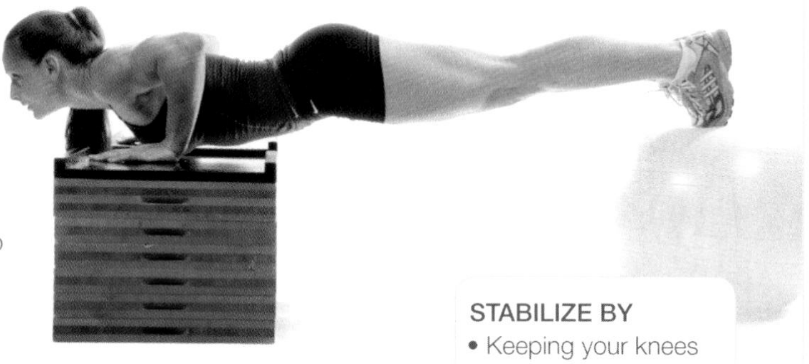

**STABILIZE BY**
- Keeping your knees locked.
- Fixing your ankles in a stable position.
- Keeping your hips, abdominal muscles, and lower back rigid.

2

**Action:** Lower your entire body by allowing the elbows to bend until your torso has dropped into a position where your chest is at the level of your hands. Return by extending the elbows and pushing into the blocks, elevating entire body simultaneously.

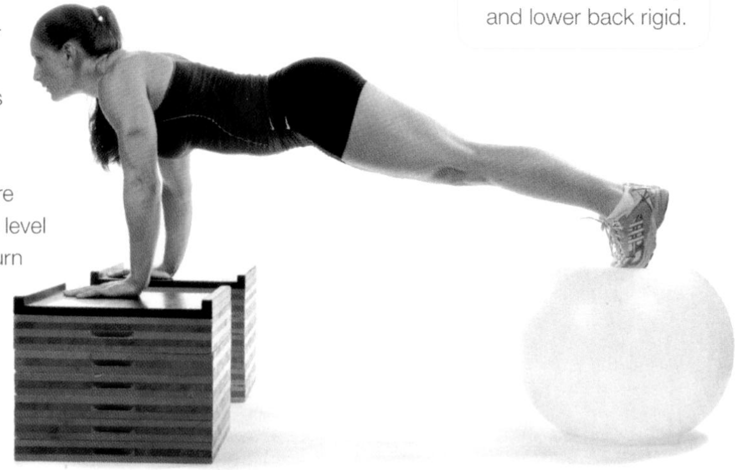

3 **Movement Path:** The plane of your body rotates upward in an arc. Use your feet as a lever.

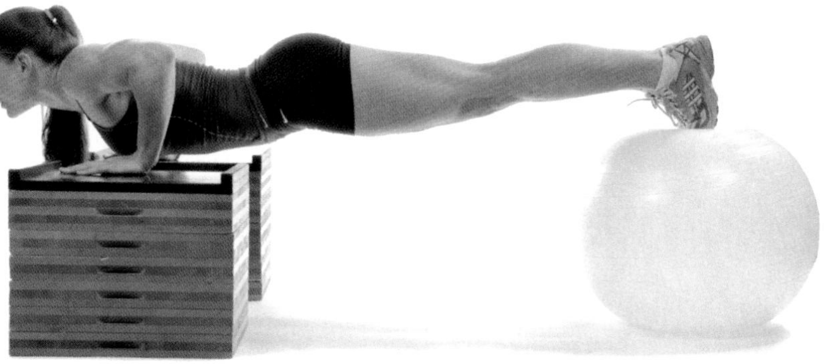

**LOOK FOR**
- A single plane of movement, i.e., a straight line from head to ankle.

**AVOID**
- A segmental elevation, i.e., your shoulders rising before your hips, or vice versa.
- Elevating your shoulders toward your ears.
- Moving your head forward.
- Allowing the ankles to change position.
- Allowing the ball or body to migrate laterally.

MODIFICATION

**More Difficult:** Keeping toes of one foot on physio ball, elevate other leg. Follow same action and movement path.

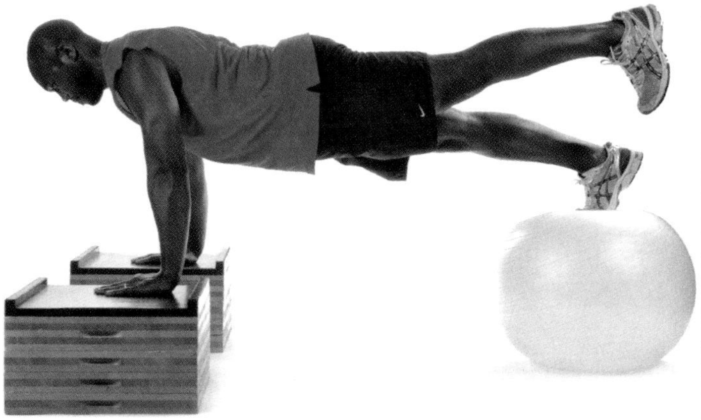

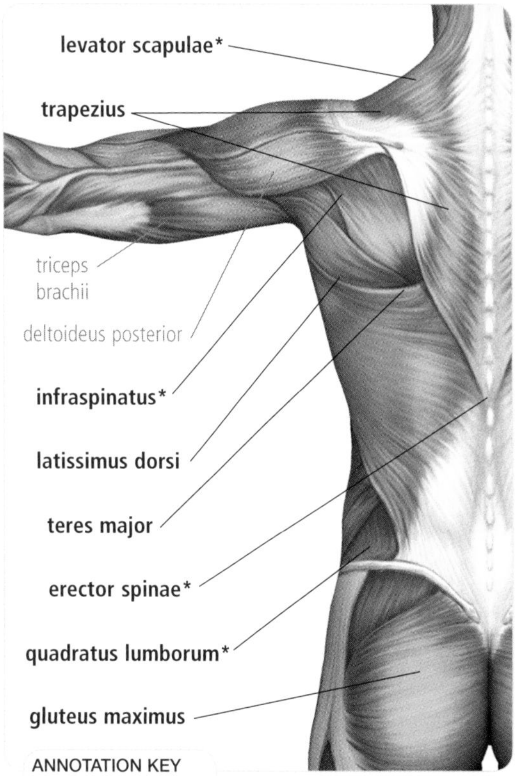

levator scapulae*
trapezius
triceps brachii
deltoideus posterior
infraspinatus*
latissimus dorsi
teres major
erector spinae*
quadratus lumborum*
gluteus maximus


ANNOTATION KEY

**Black text indicates active muscles**

Gray text indicates stabilizing muscles

* indicates deep muscles

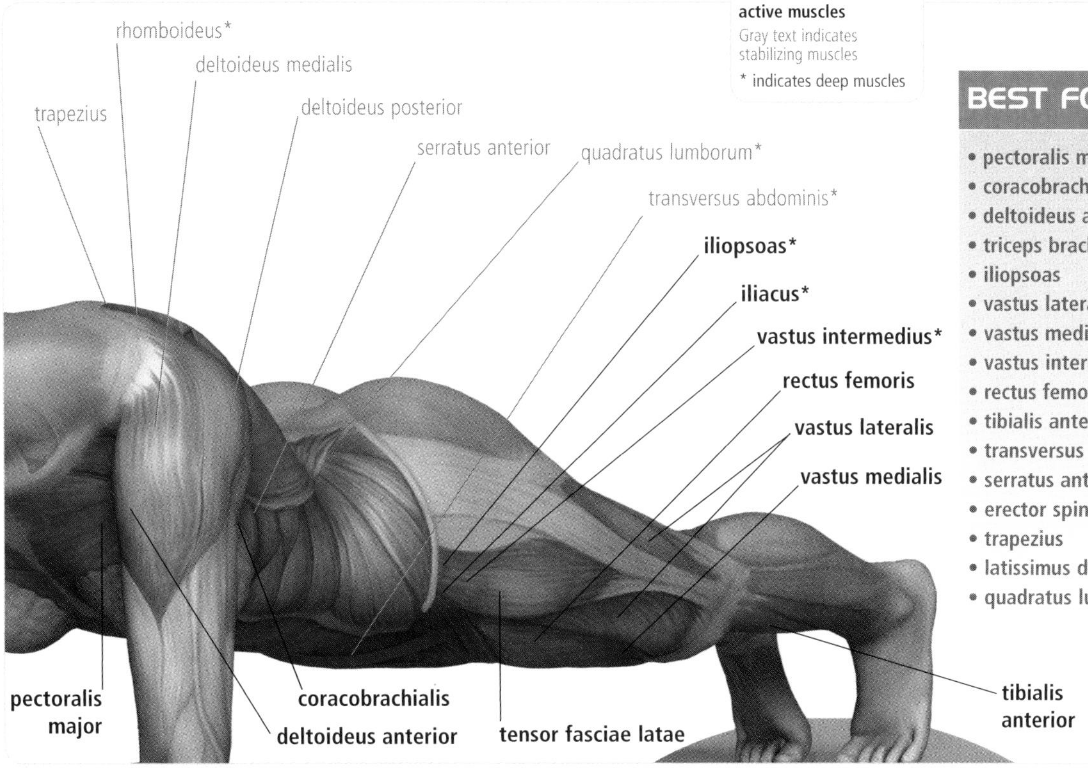

rhomboideus*
deltoideus medialis
trapezius
deltoideus posterior
serratus anterior
quadratus lumborum*
transversus abdominis*
iliopsoas*
iliacus*
vastus intermedius*
rectus femoris
vastus lateralis
vastus medialis
pectoralis major
coracobrachialis
deltoideus anterior
tensor fasciae latae
tibialis anterior


## BEST FOR

- pectoralis major
- coracobrachialis
- deltoideus anterior
- triceps brachii
- iliopsoas
- vastus lateralis
- vastus medialis
- vastus intermedius
- rectus femoris
- tibialis anterior
- transversus abdominis
- serratus anterior
- erector spinae
- trapezius
- latissimus dorsi
- quadratus lumborum

# ON DUMBBELLS WITH ROTATION



1

**Starting Position:** Lie flat on the floor with your hands slightly wider than shoulder width, grasping the dumbbells so that the dumbbell handles are parallel to your spine. Point your elbows directly at the ceiling. Your feet should be slightly wider than shoulder width and your spine should be neutral.

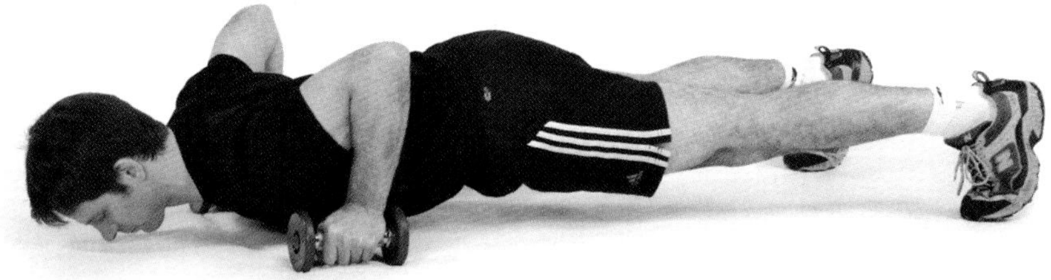

2

**Action:** Push up toward the ceiling; once your arms are fully extended, rotate your hips and feet, lifting one arm in an arc toward the ceiling so that your arms are aligned in a straight line and your feet are split apart, with your weight on the edges of your shoes. Your torso, hips, and legs are rigid.

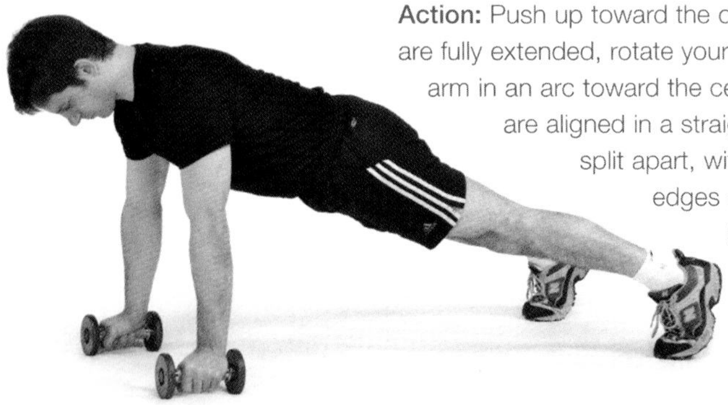

3

**Movement Path:** Your entire body moves up and away from the floor, and then rotates around your spine 180 degrees.

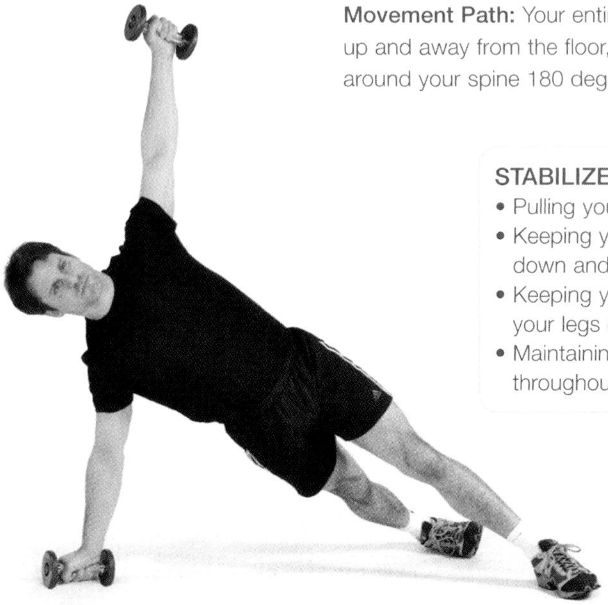

### STABILIZE BY

- Pulling your abdomen up and in.
- Keeping your shoulder blades down and flat.
- Keeping your knees straight and your legs contracted.
- Maintaining a neutral spinal position throughout the movement.

### LOOK FOR

- Your shoulders to remain depressed.
- Your neck to remain long.
- Your hips to remain elevated.
- Your shoulders, hips, and feet to remain in the same plane from the floor.

### AVOID

- Bending your knees or dropping your hips.
- Excessive rotation in shoulder and hip.

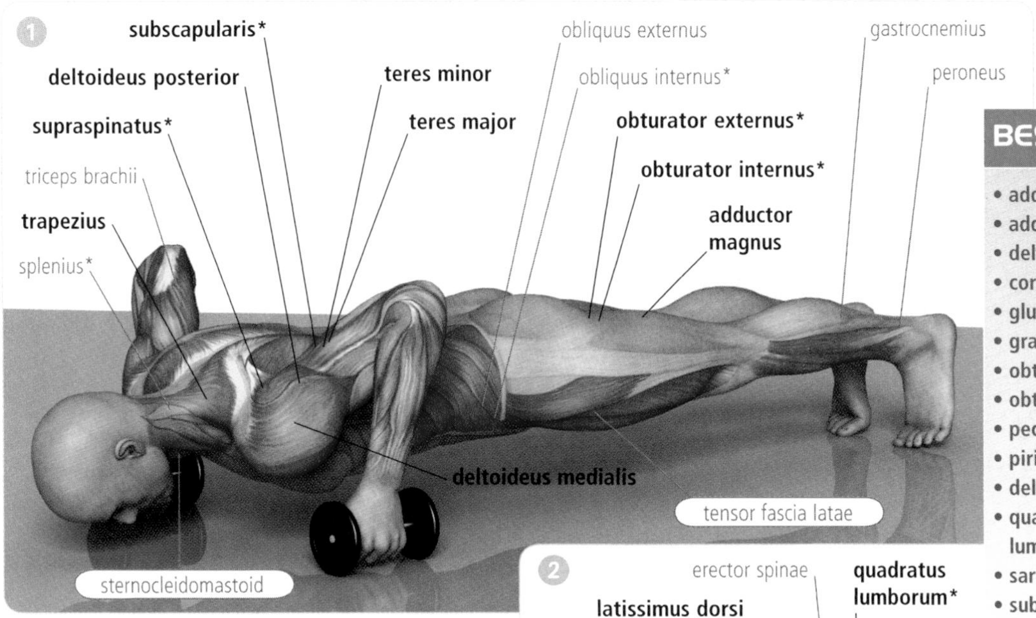
1
subscapularis*
deltoideus posterior
supraspinatus*
triceps brachii
trapezius
splenius*
teres minor
teres major
obliquus externus
obliquus internus*
obturator externus*
obturator internus*
adductor magnus
gastrocnemius
peroneus
deltoideus medialis
tensor fascia latae
sternocleidomastoid

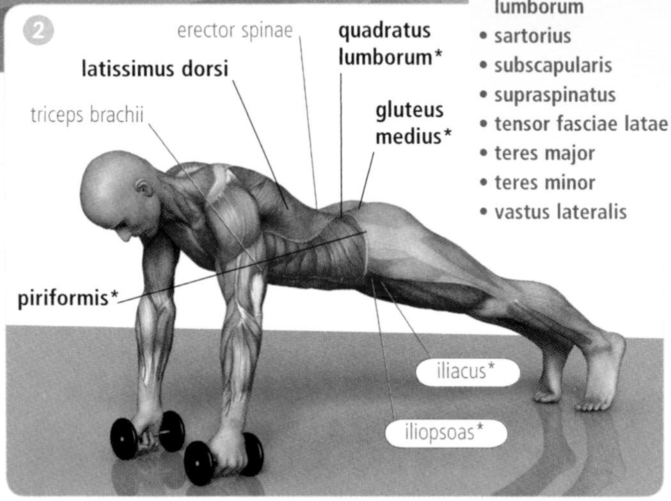
2
erector spinae
quadratus lumborum*
latissimus dorsi
triceps brachii
gluteus medius*
piriformis*
iliacus*
iliopsoas*

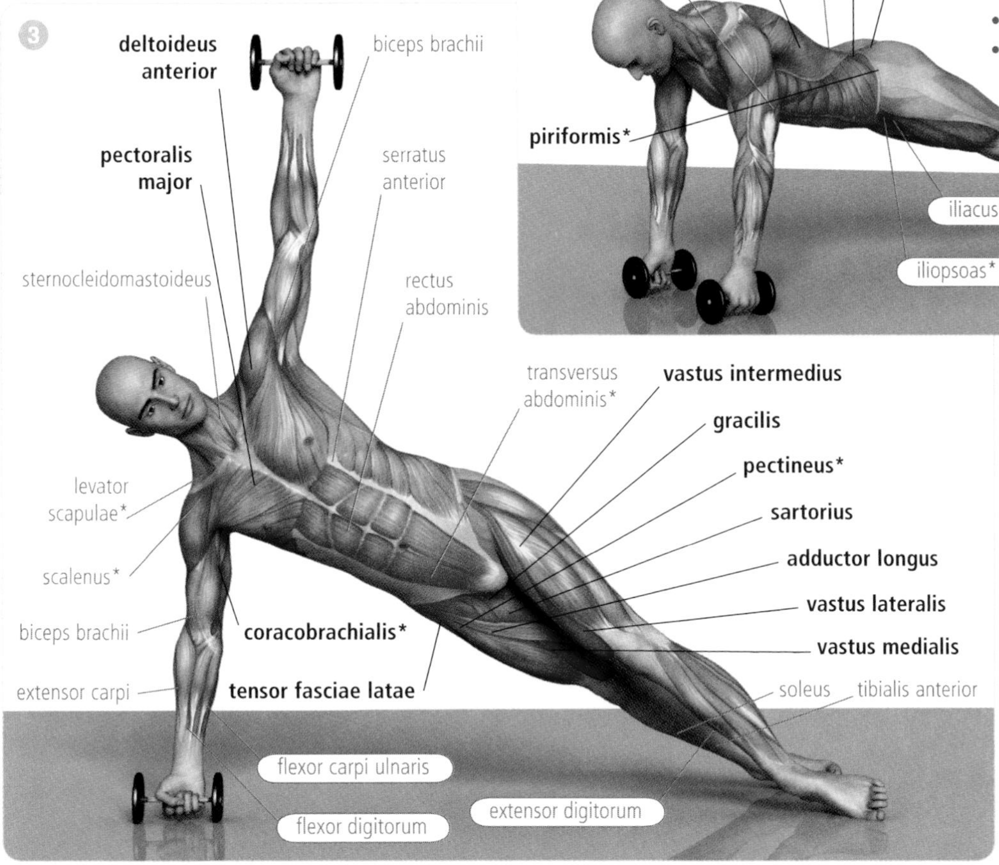
3
deltoideus anterior
biceps brachii
pectoralis major
serratus anterior
sternocleidomastoideus
rectus abdominis
transversus abdominis*
vastus intermedius
gracilis
pectineus*
sartorius
adductor longus
vastus lateralis
vastus medialis
levator scapulae*
scalenus*
biceps brachii
coracobrachialis*
extensor carpi
tensor fasciae latae
soleus
tibialis anterior
flexor carpi ulnaris
flexor digitorum
extensor digitorum

## BEST FOR

- adductor longus
- adductor magnus
- deltoideus anterior
- coracobrachialis
- gluteus medius
- gracilis
- obturator externus
- obturator internus
- pectoralis major
- piriformis
- deltoideus posterior
- quadratus lumborum
- sartorius
- subscapularis
- supraspinatus
- tensor fasciae latae
- teres major
- teres minor
- vastus lateralis

ANNOTATION KEY

**Black text indicates active muscles**

Gray text indicates stabilizing muscles

* indicates deep muscles

# TOWEL FLY



1

**Starting Position:** With your arms fully extended, start from the top of the push-up position, with your hands wider than shoulder width and placed on a towel so that the towel is taut between your hands and directly under your chest.

**Action:** Move your hands together while keeping your torso rigid and your arms extended. Return by spreading your hands to the starting position.

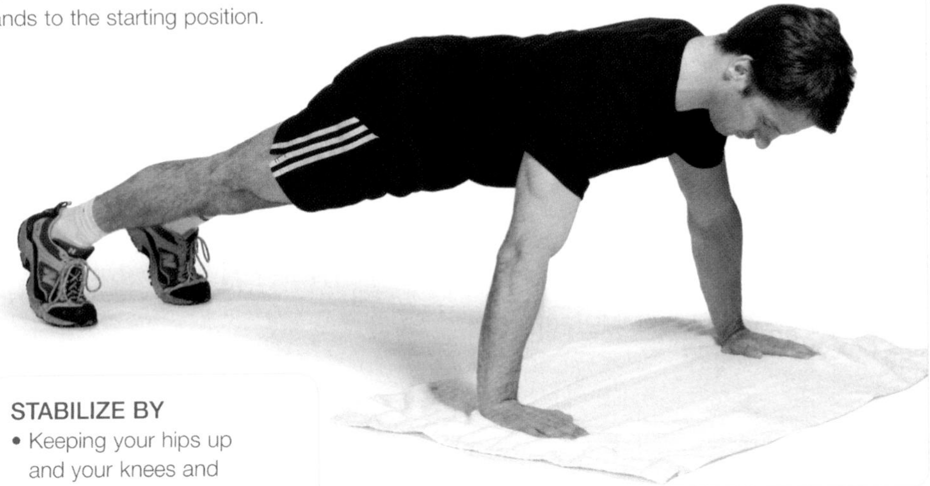

LOOK FOR
- Your arms to remain directly below your chest and perpendicular to your torso.

AVOID
- Dropping your head forward or bending or extending your elbows.
- Any change in your spinal position.
- Elevating or widening your shoulder blades.

STABILIZE BY
- Keeping your hips up and your knees and ankles locked.
- Keeping your shoulders retracted and depressed throughout the movement.

2

**Movement Path:** As your hands slide together, your torso (spine), hips, and legs elevate, using your toes as a lever.

Your hand movements should be smooth and simultaneous.

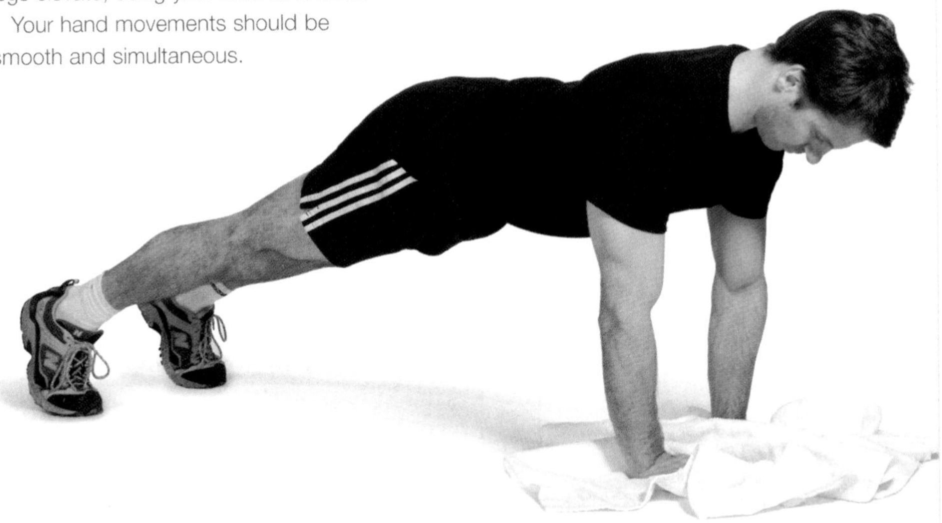

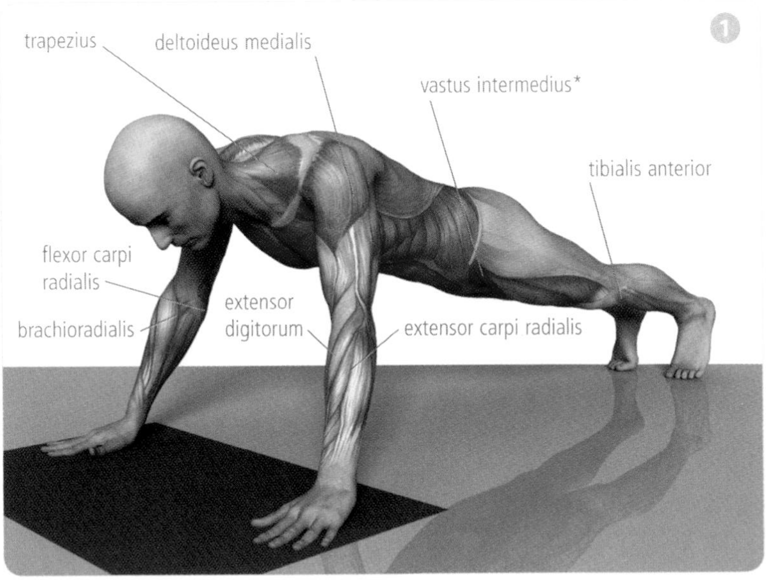
1
trapezius
deltoideus medialis
vastus intermedius*
tibialis anterior
flexor carpi radialis
brachioradialis
extensor digitorum
extensor carpi radialis

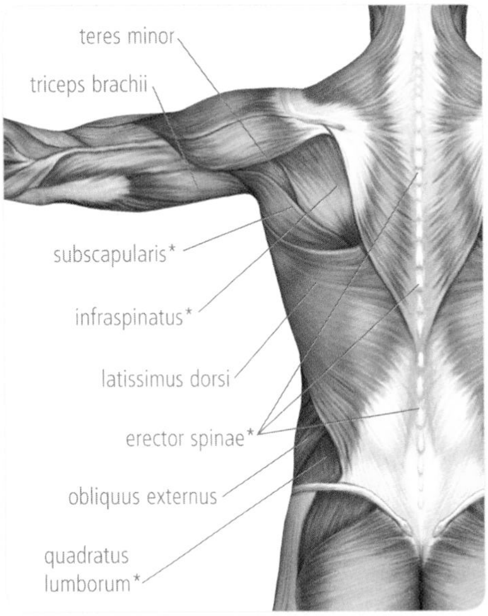
teres minor
triceps brachii
subscapularis*
infraspinatus*
latissimus dorsi
erector spinae*
obliquus externus
quadratus lumborum*

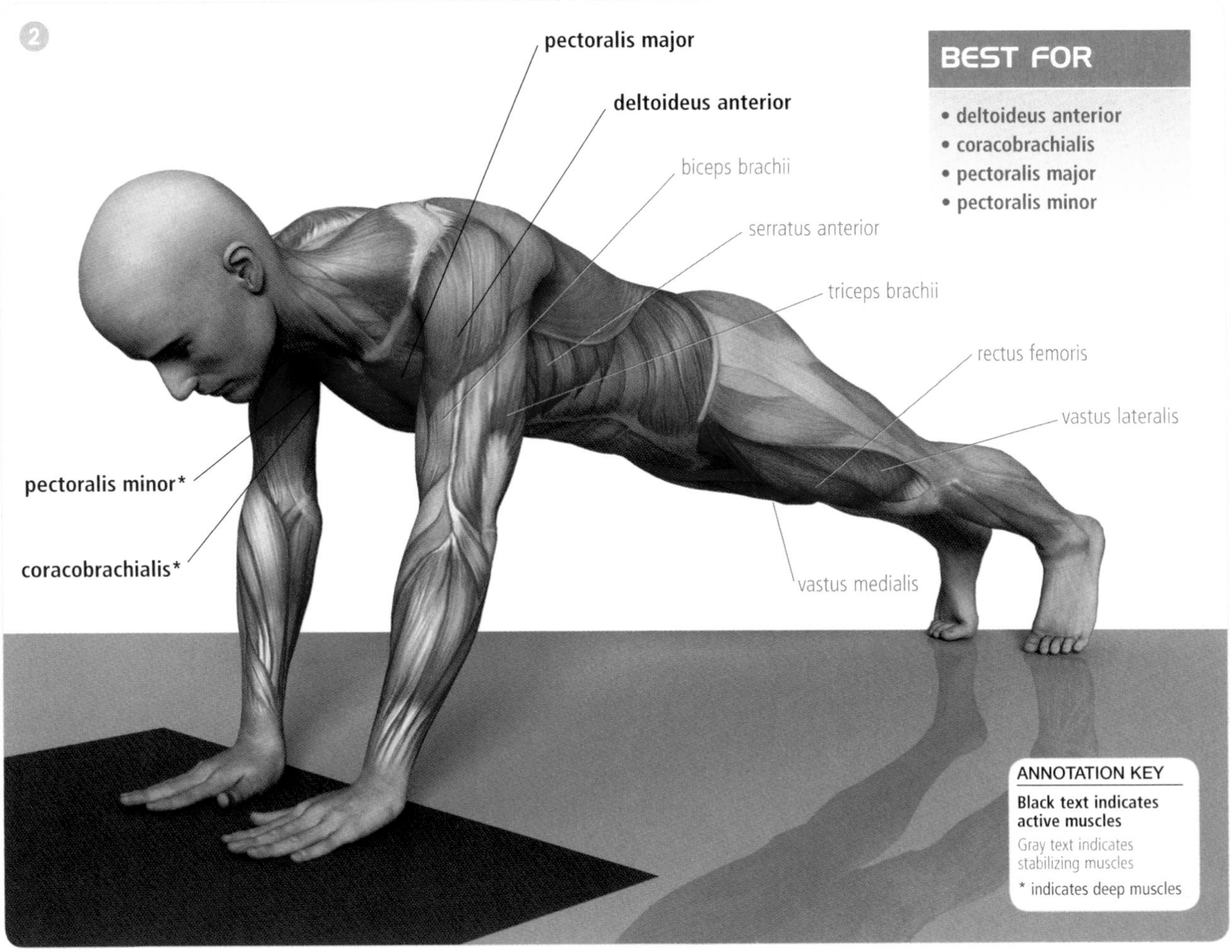
2
**pectoralis major**
**deltoideus anterior**
biceps brachii
serratus anterior
triceps brachii
rectus femoris
vastus lateralis
**pectoralis minor***
**coracobrachialis***
vastus medialis

## BEST FOR

- **deltoideus anterior**
- **coracobrachialis**
- **pectoralis major**
- **pectoralis minor**

ANNOTATION KEY

**Black text indicates active muscles**

Gray text indicates stabilizing muscles

* indicates deep muscles

# PIKE & PRESS



LOOK FOR
- A single plane of movement, i.e., a straight line from head to ankle.

AVOID
- A segmental elevation, i.e., your shoulders rising before your hips, or vice versa.
- Elevating your shoulders toward your ears.
- Moving your head forward.
- Allowing the ankles to change position.
- Allowing the ball or body to migrate laterally.

1

**Starting Position:** Place hands on blocks (or a bench), and place feet with ankles fixed at 90-degree angles on a physio ball, toes down, so that your body is horizontal. Your hands should be wider than shoulder width, and your fingertips parallel to your collarbone. Place your feet on the ball with the top of your feet (shoelaces) contacting the ball, your toes pointed.

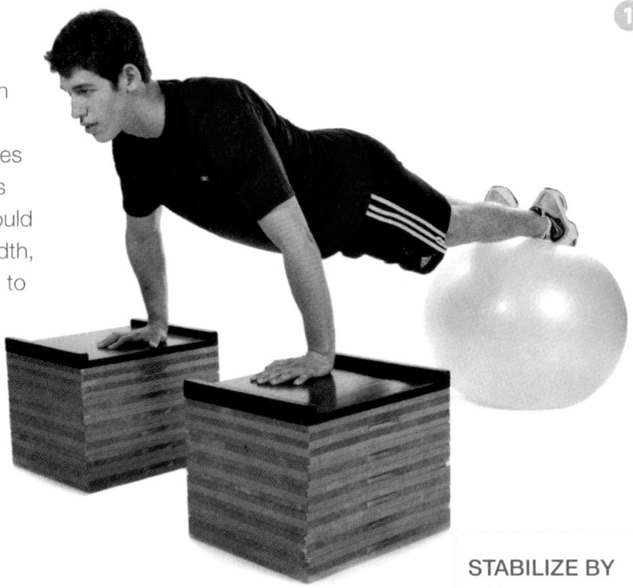

STABILIZE BY
- Keeping your knees locked.
- Fixing your ankles in a stable position.
- Keeping your hips, abdominal muscles, and lower back rigid.

**Action:** Lower your entire body by allowing the elbows to bend until your torso has dropped into a position where the chest is at the level of your hands. Return by extending the elbows and pushing into the blocks, elevating entire body simultaneously.

From top position, pull ball forward by flexing your feet and drawing the toes and hips upward so that the torso is bent at the hips. Toes are on top of the ball and both feet are at 90-degree angles. Your upper body and head are facing downward. Keeping your torso in that position, bend your elbows and drop your spine (headfirst) between hands. Return by pushing your hands into blocks until your elbows are fully extended. Then, drop your hips and extend your toes until your body returns to horizontal.

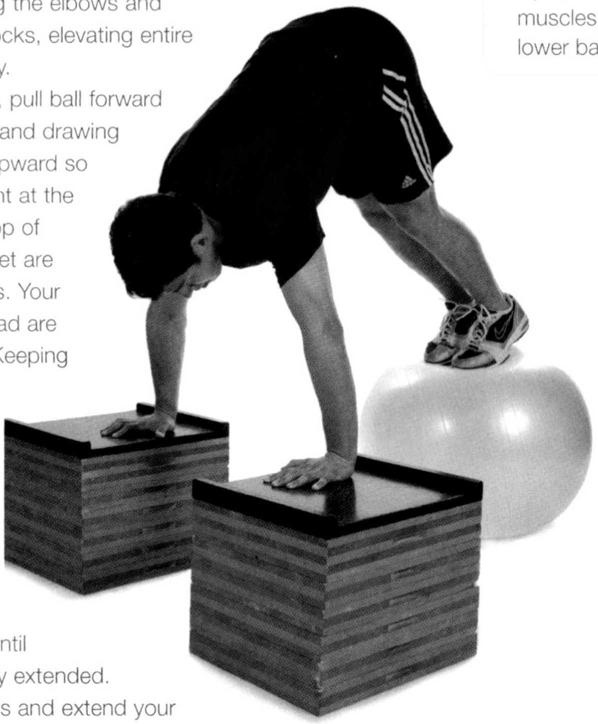

2

**Movement Path:** The plane of your body rotates upward in an arc. Use your feet as a lever.

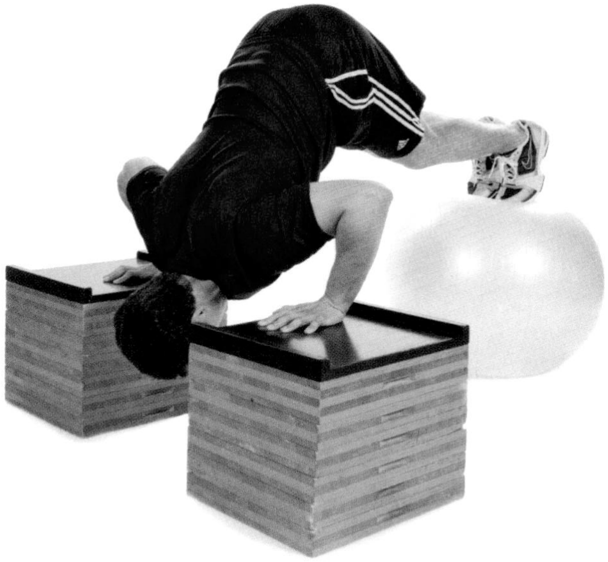

3

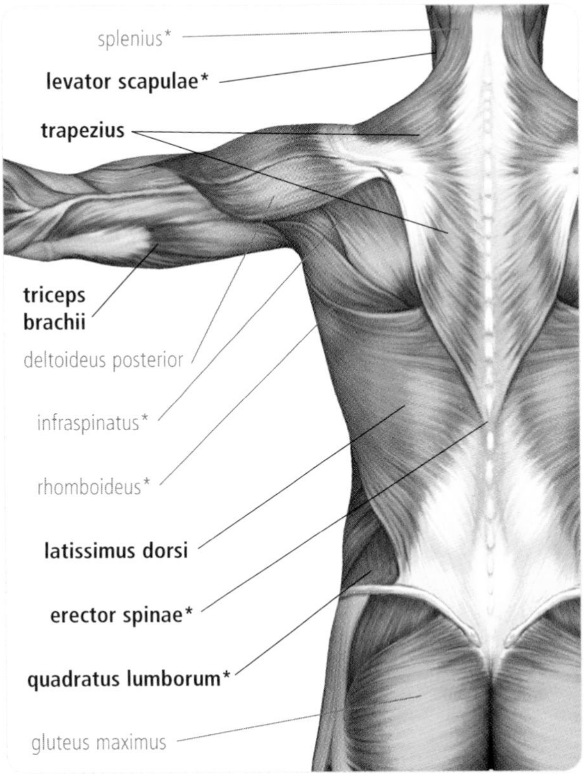
splenius*
levator scapulae*
trapezius
triceps brachii
deltoideus posterior
infraspinatus*
rhomboideus*
latissimus dorsi
erector spinae*
quadratus lumborum*
gluteus maximus

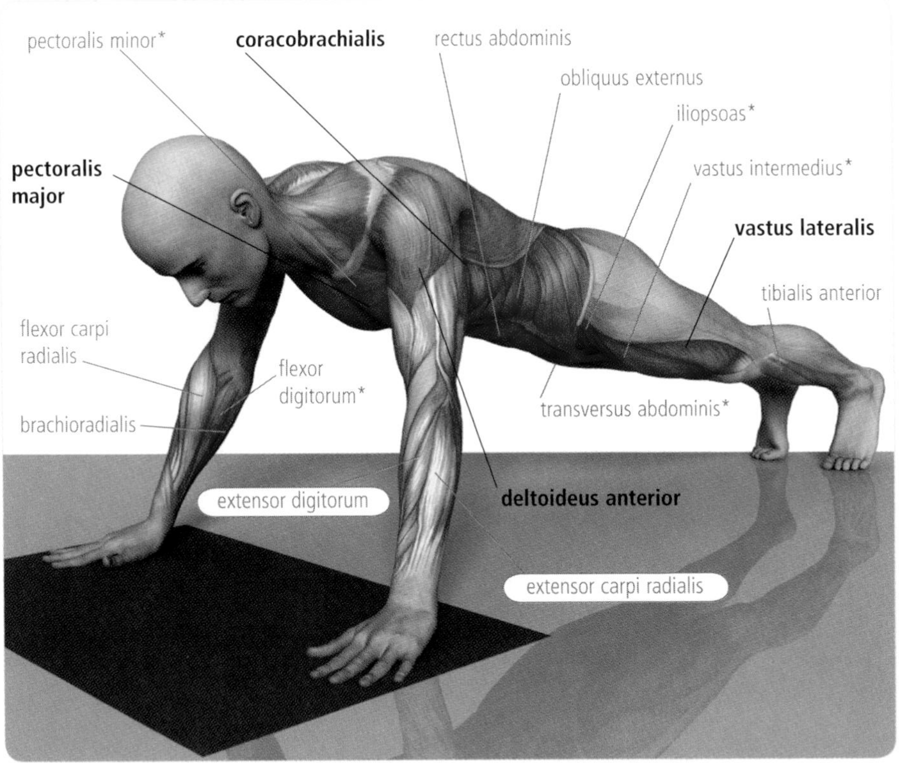
pectoralis minor*
coracobrachialis
rectus abdominis
obliquus externus
iliopsoas*
vastus intermedius*
vastus lateralis
tibialis anterior
pectoralis major
flexor carpi radialis
flexor digitorum*
brachioradialis
transversus abdominis*
extensor digitorum
deltoideus anterior
extensor carpi radialis

## BEST FOR

- pectoralis major
- pectoralis minor
- coracobrachialis
- deltoideus anterior
- triceps brachii
- iliopsoas
- vastus lateralis
- vastus intermedius
- rectus femoris
- tibialis anterior
- transversus abdominis
- serratus anterior
- erector spinae
- trapezius
- latissimus dorsi
- quadratus lumborum

ANNOTATION KEY

**Black text indicates active muscles**

Gray text indicates stabilizing muscles

* indicates deep muscles

# LOWER-BODY ROTATION

**1** **Starting Position:** With hand position same as in a push-up, rotate the lower body with either feet split and bottom foot forward, or one foot on top of the other.

## LOOK FOR
- Fingertips to remain parallel.
- Hips to remain in position throughout movement.
- Feet to remain rigid and contact the ground only with the edges.

## AVOID
- Elevating shoulders toward the ears.
- Allowing ankles to drop and contact the ground.

**2** **Action:** Raise your legs and hips off the ground. Your lower back should arch slightly. Extend your arms, pushing into the ground. To return, lower your body in a single plane by bending your arms. Repeat on opposite side.

**Movement Path:** The plane of your body rotates upward in an arc. Use your feet as a lever.

## STABILIZE BY
- Keeping your knees locked.
- Fixing your ankles in a stable position.
- Keeping your hips, abdominal muscles, and lower back rigid.

ANNOTATION KEY
**Black text indicates active muscles**
Gray text indicates stabilizing muscles
* indicates deep muscles

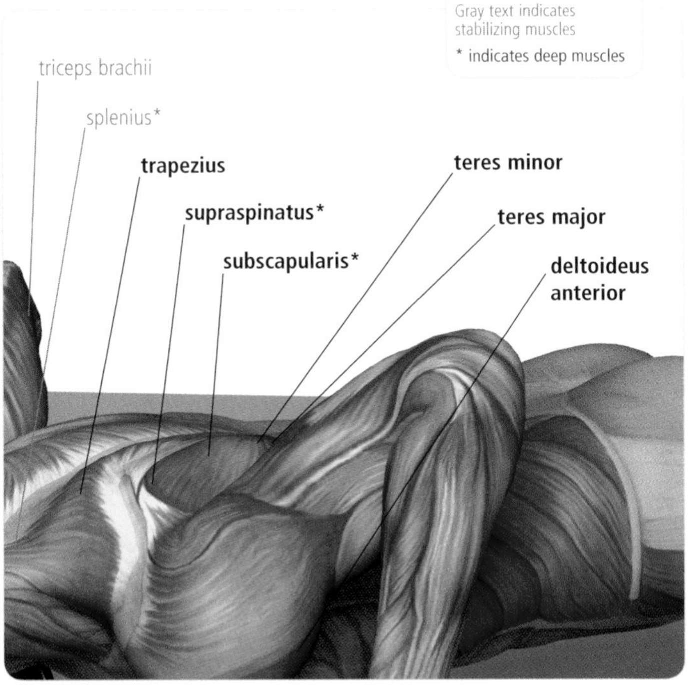
triceps brachii
splenius*
trapezius
supraspinatus*
subscapularis*
teres minor
teres major
deltoideus anterior

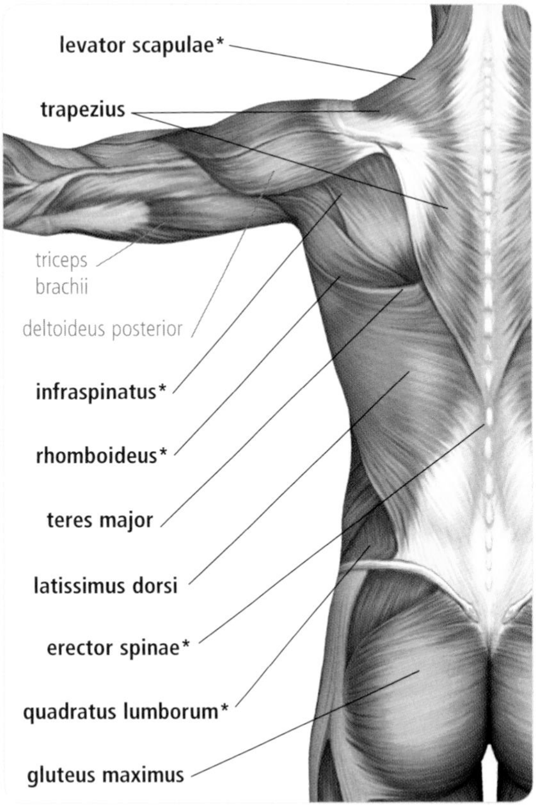
levator scapulae*
trapezius
triceps brachii
deltoideus posterior
infraspinatus*
rhomboideus*
teres major
latissimus dorsi
erector spinae*
quadratus lumborum*
gluteus maximus

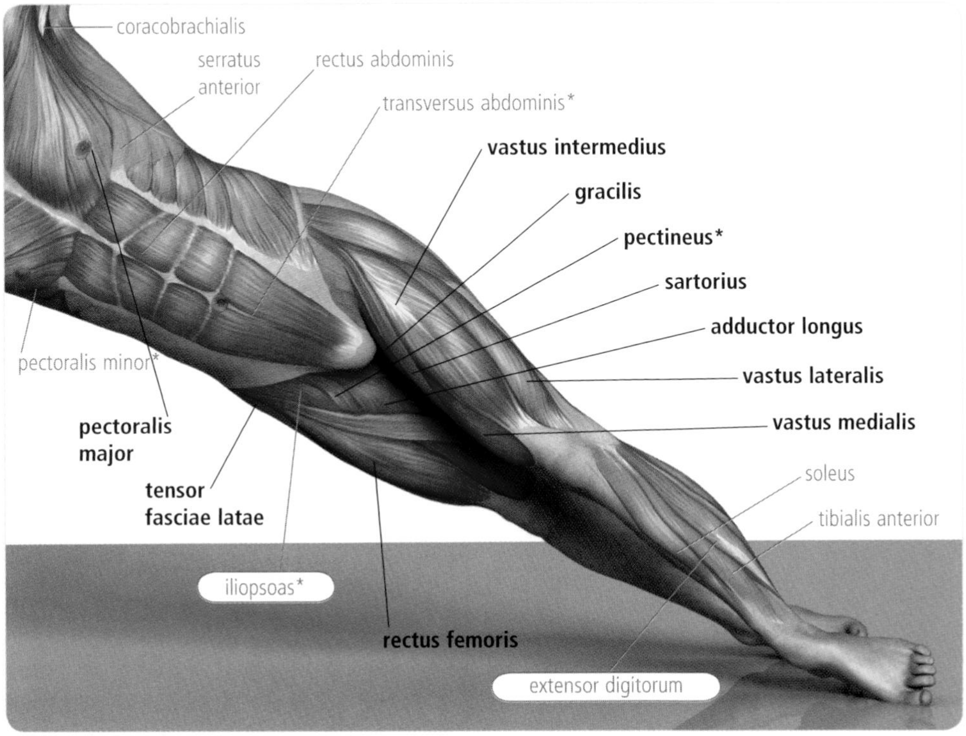
coracobrachialis
serratus anterior
rectus abdominis
transversus abdominis*
vastus intermedius
gracilis
pectineus*
sartorius
adductor longus
vastus lateralis
vastus medialis
pectoralis minor*
pectoralis major
tensor fasciae latae
soleus
tibialis anterior
iliopsoas*
rectus femoris
extensor digitorum

## BEST FOR

- pectoralis major
- pectoralis minor
- coracobrachialis
- deltoideus anterior
- triceps brachii
- iliopsoas
- vastus lateralis
- vastus medialis
- vastus intermedius
- rectus femoris
- tibialis anterior
- transversus abdominis
- serratus anterior
- erector spinae
- trapezius
- latissimus dorsi
- quadratus lumborum

# CLAP PUSH-UP

**1** **Starting Position:** Lie flat on the ground, facedown. Place your hands slightly outside of your shoulders and your fingertips parallel to your collarbone. Make sure that your elbows are at 45-degree angles to your torso. Place both feet on tiptoes.

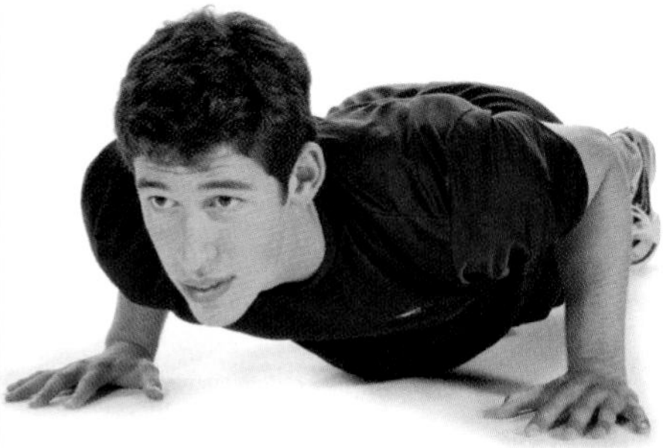

**2**

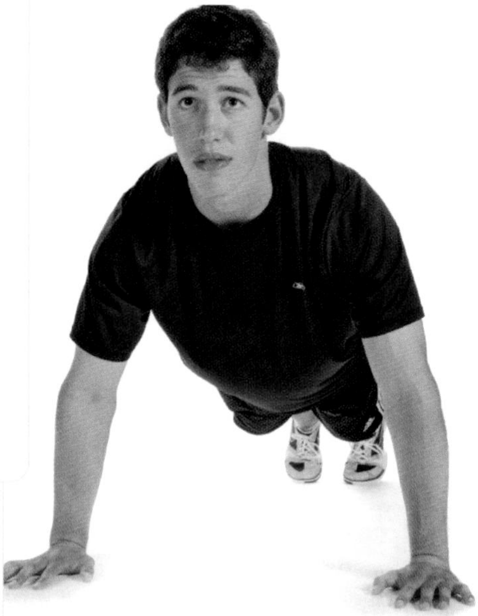

**LOOK FOR**
- Body to remain rigid.
- Hands to return to original position.
- Continuous movement.

**AVOID**
- Stopping at the bottom of the movement.
- Allowing hand position to vary substantially.

**3** **Action:** Keeping your body rigid, forcefully and quickly push your hands into the ground so that enough momentum is generated for the hands to come off the ground. Just as your body reaches its highest point, remove your hands and clap them directly underneath your chest. Immediately return them to their original position, and allow your body to return toward the start position, decelerating as it descends to a position just above the floor. Quickly repeat.

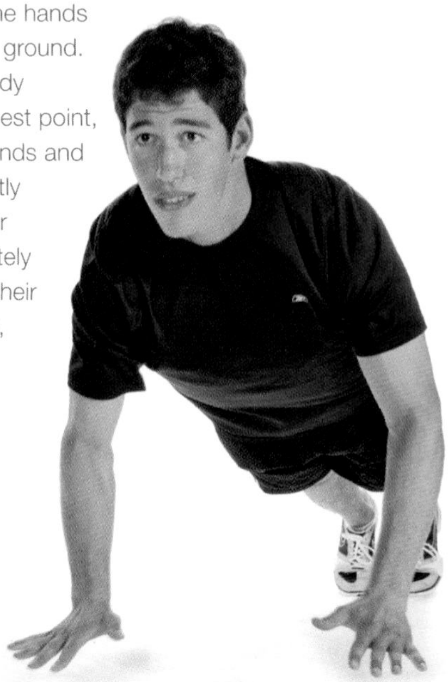

**STABILIZE BY**
- Keeping your knees locked.
- Fixing your ankles in a stable position.
- Keeping your hips, abdominal muscles, and lower back rigid.

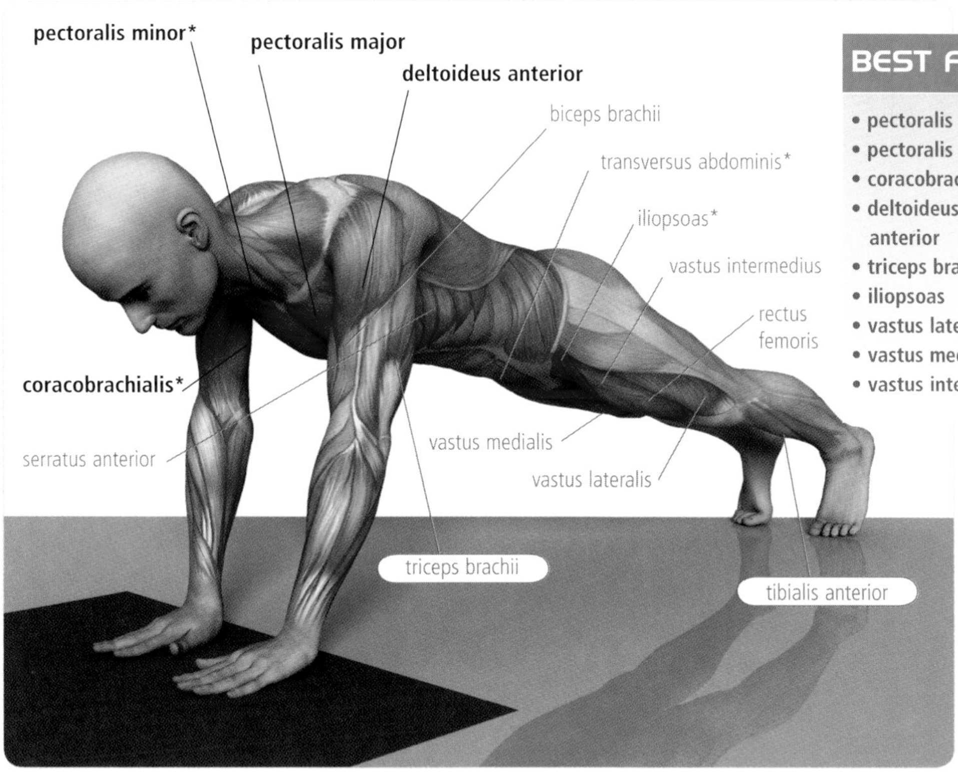
pectoralis minor*
pectoralis major
deltoideus anterior
biceps brachii
transversus abdominis*
iliopsoas*
vastus intermedius
rectus femoris
coracobrachialis*
serratus anterior
vastus medialis
vastus lateralis
triceps brachii
tibialis anterior

## BEST FOR

- pectoralis major
- pectoralis minor
- coracobrachialis
- deltoideus anterior
- triceps brachii
- iliopsoas
- vastus lateralis
- vastus medialis
- vastus intermedius
- rectus femoris
- tibialis anterior
- transversus abdominis
- serratus anterior
- erector spinae
- trapezius
- latissimus dorsi
- quadratus lumborum

ANNOTATION KEY

**Black text indicates active muscles**

Gray text indicates stabilizing muscles

* indicates deep muscles

4

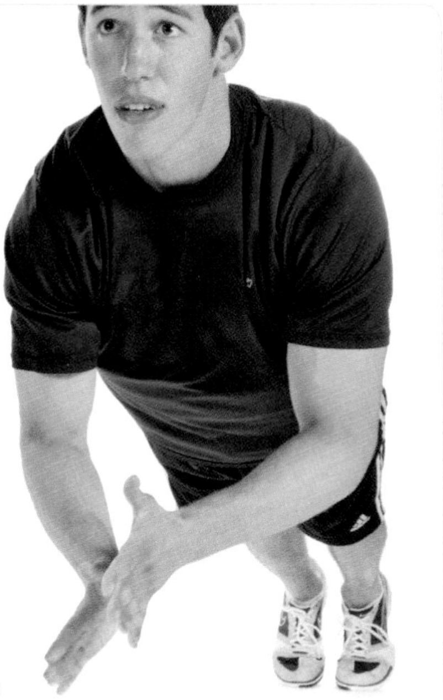

**Movement Path:** The plane of your body rotates upward in an arc. Use your feet as a lever.

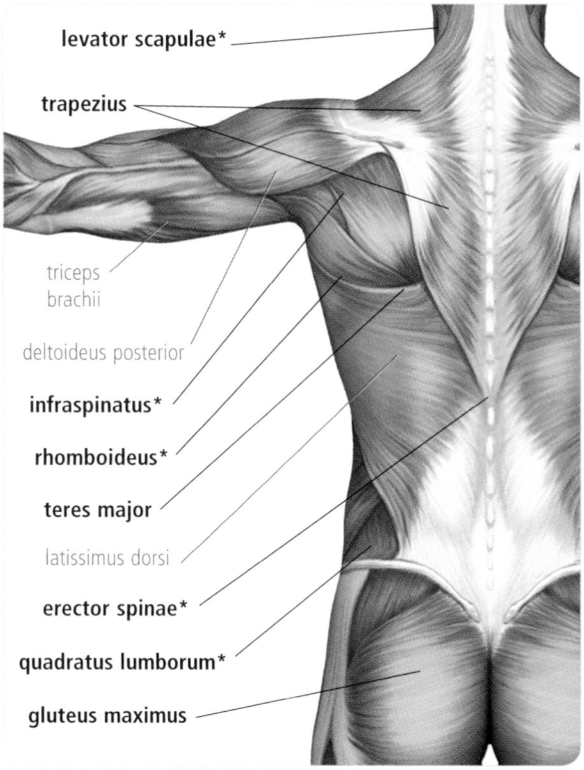
levator scapulae*
trapezius
triceps brachii
deltoideus posterior
infraspinatus*
rhomboideus*
teres major
latissimus dorsi
erector spinae*
quadratus lumborum*
gluteus maximus

# ON KETTLEBELLS

## PUSH-UP

**Starting Position:** Grasp handles of kettlebells set on ground at slightly wider than shoulder width and parallel to your collarbone. Make sure that your elbows are at 45-degree angles to your torso. Place both feet on tiptoes.

**Action:** Raise your legs and hips off the ground. Your lower back should arch slightly. Extend your arms, pushing into the ground. To return, lower your body in a single plane by bending your arms.

### LOOK FOR
- A single plane of movement, i.e., a straight line from head to ankle.

### AVOID
- A segmental elevation, i.e., your shoulders rising before your hips, or vice versa.
- Elevating your shoulders toward your ears.
- Moving your head forward.

### STABILIZE BY
- Keeping your knees locked.
- Fixing your ankles in a stable position.
- Keeping your hips, abdominal muscles, and lower back rigid.

**Movement Path:** The plane of your body rotates upward in an arc. Use your feet as a lever.

MODIFICATION

**More Difficult:** Place one hand on a medicine ball, the other on the floor. Follow same action and movement path.

1

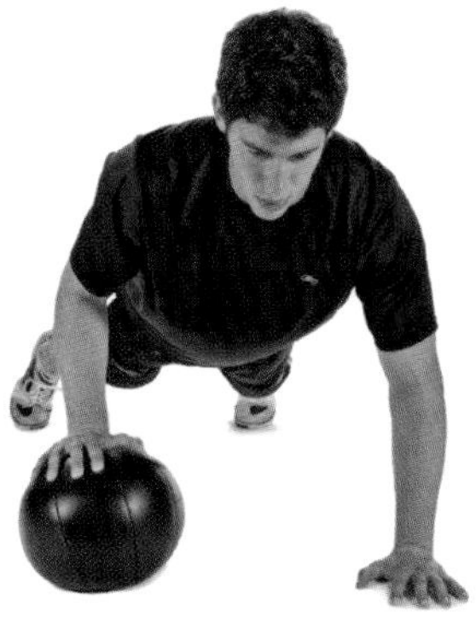

2

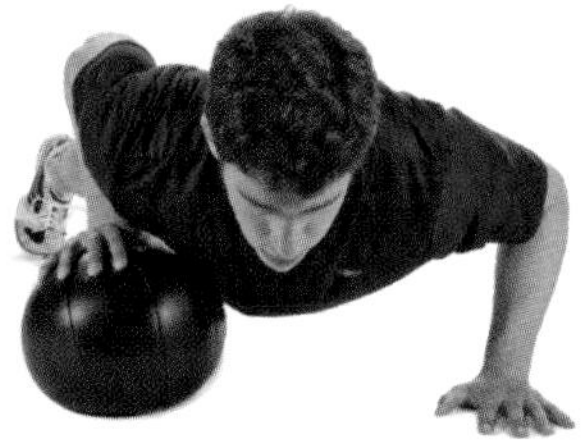

## BEST FOR

- pectoralis major
- pectoralis minor
- coracobrachialis
- deltoideus anterior
- triceps brachii
- iliopsoas
- vastus lateralis
- vastus medialis
- vastus intermedius
- rectus femoris
- tibialis anterior
- transversus abdominis
- serratus anterior
- erector spinae
- trapezius
- latissimus dorsi
- quadratus lumborum

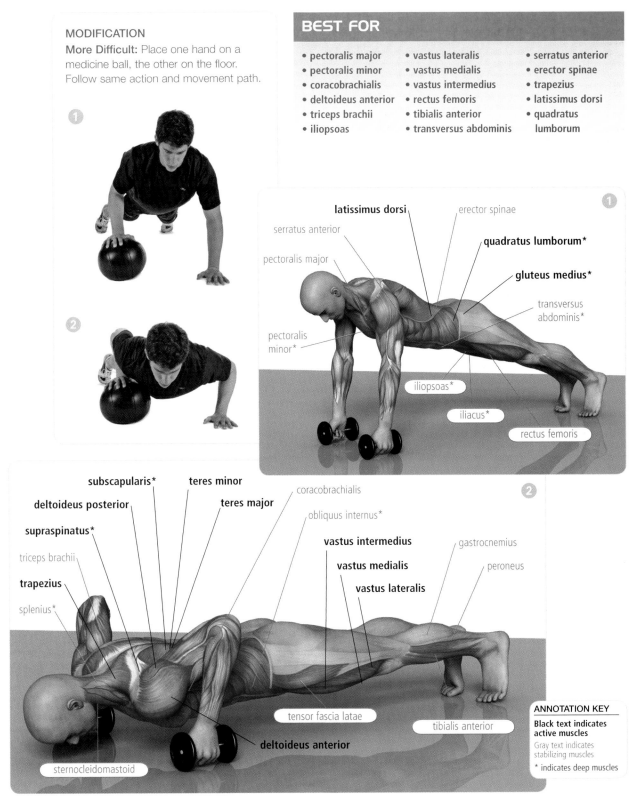

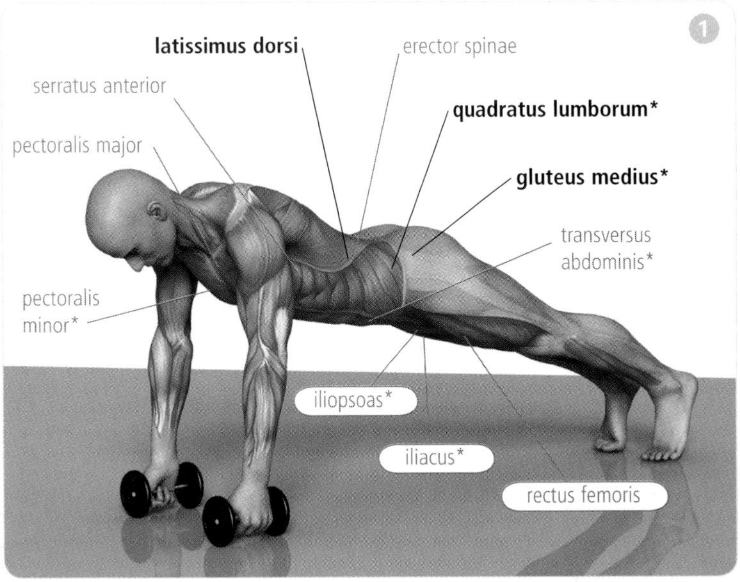
1
latissimus dorsi
erector spinae
serratus anterior
quadratus lumborum*
pectoralis major
gluteus medius*
transversus abdominis*
pectoralis minor*
iliopsoas*
iliacus*
rectus femoris

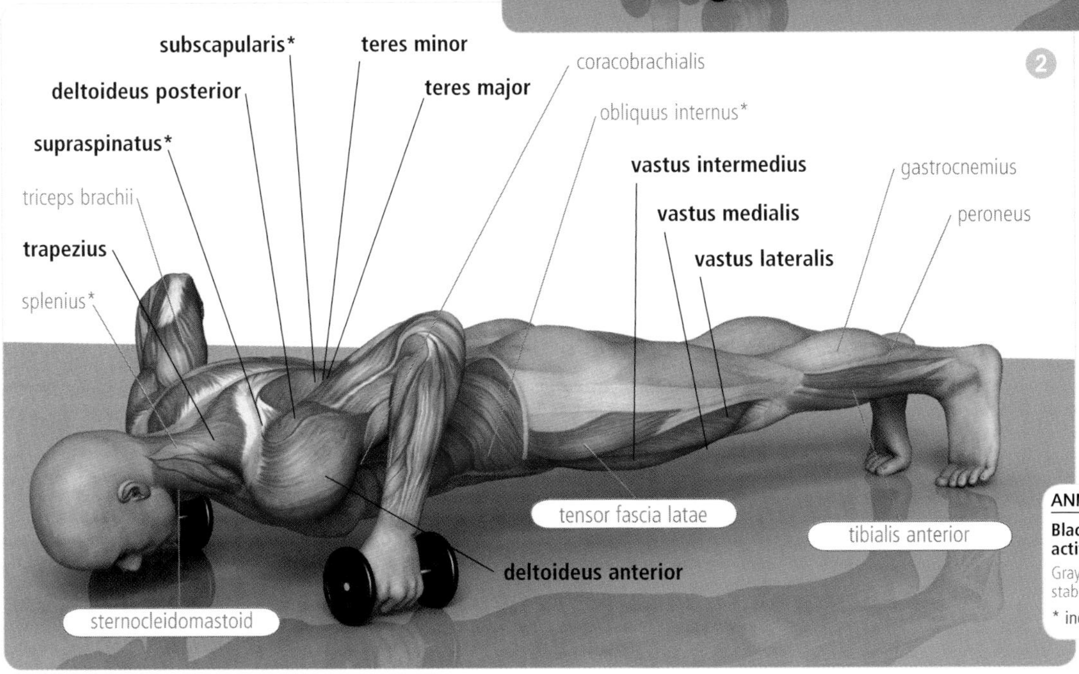
2
subscapularis*
teres minor
deltoideus posterior
teres major
coracobrachialis
obliquus internus*
supraspinatus*
vastus intermedius
gastrocnemius
triceps brachii
vastus medialis
peroneus
trapezius
vastus lateralis
splenius*
tensor fascia latae
tibialis anterior
deltoideus anterior
sternocleidomastoid

ANNOTATION KEY

**Black text indicates active muscles**

Gray text indicates stabilizing muscles

* indicates deep muscles

# HAND WALKOVER

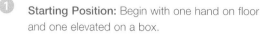

**① Starting Position:** Begin with one hand on floor and one elevated on a box.

## STABILIZE BY
- Keeping torso rigid.
- Keeping legs straight and feet firm but relaxed.

**Action:** Perform a push-up with hands narrow. Once you've returned to starting position, place both hands on block. Move the other hand off the box slightly farther than shoulder width. Keeping feet in position, repeat push-up. From starting position, return bottom hand to box, and repeat.

## LOOK FOR
- Shoulders to remain horizontal.
- Rib cage and chest to remain up.
- Elbow of elevated hand to be slightly bent, while other is completely straight at top position.

## AVOID
- Dropping one shoulder.
- Any sagging or extending of the hips.
- Bending knees.

②

③

78

4

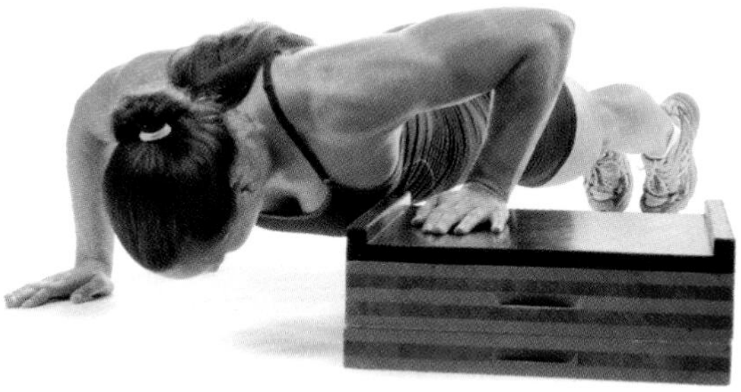

**Movement Path:** The spine moves in a horizontal plane in an arc with the feet as a fulcrum, torso descending directly toward the floor and returning.

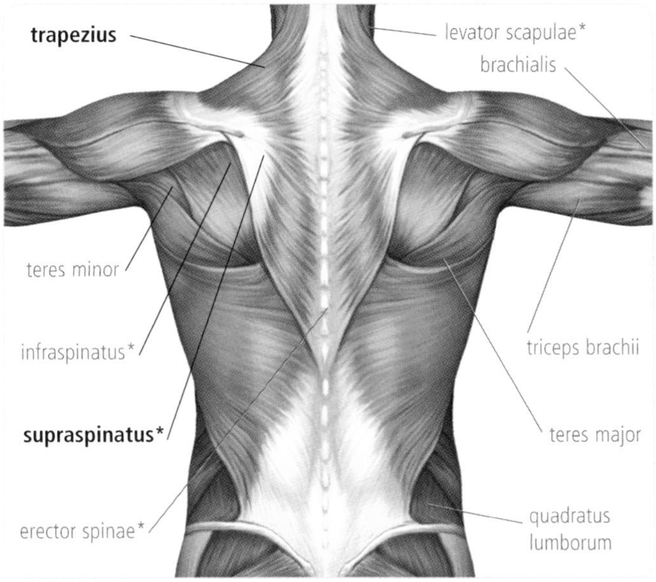
trapezius
levator scapulae*
brachialis
teres minor
infraspinatus*
supraspinatus*
erector spinae*
triceps brachii
teres major
quadratus lumborum

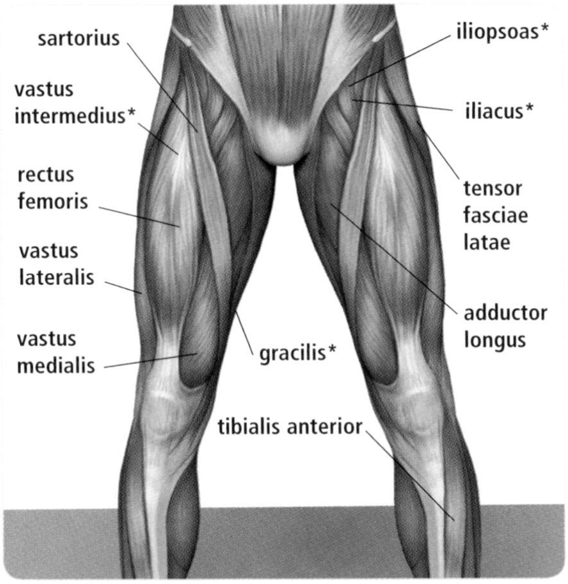
sartorius
vastus intermedius*
rectus femoris
vastus lateralis
vastus medialis
gracilis*
tibialis anterior
iliopsoas*
iliacus*
tensor fasciae latae
adductor longus

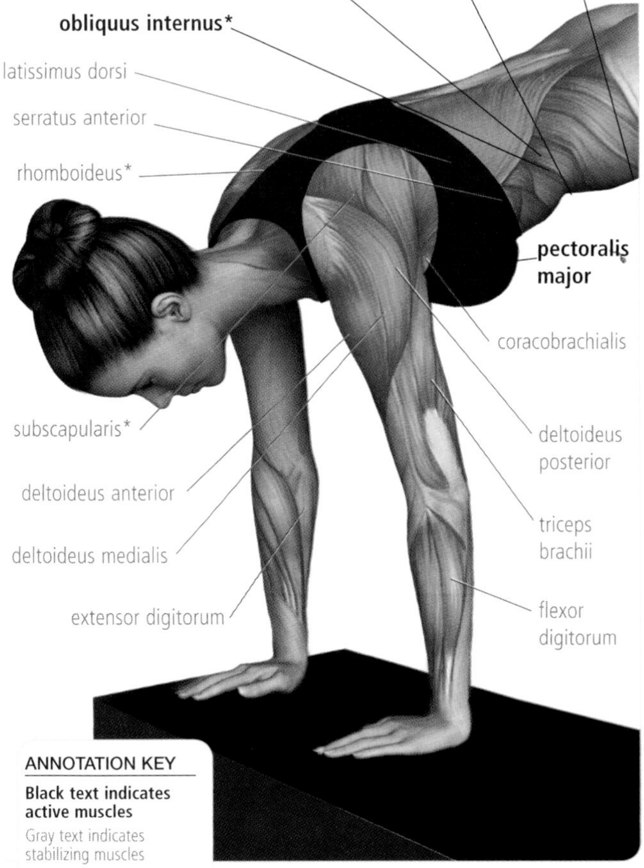
rectus abdominis
transversus abdominis*
obliquus externus
obliquus internus*
latissimus dorsi
serratus anterior
rhomboideus*
pectoralis major
coracobrachialis
subscapularis*
deltoideus anterior
deltoideus medialis
extensor digitorum
deltoideus posterior
triceps brachii
flexor digitorum

ANNOTATION KEY

**Black text indicates active muscles**

Gray text indicates stabilizing muscles

* indicates deep muscles

## BEST FOR

- pectoralis major
- pectoralis minor
- coracobrachialis
- deltoideus anterior
- triceps brachii
- iliopsoas
- vastus lateralis
- vastus medialis
- vastus intermedius
- rectus femoris
- tibialis anterior
- transversus abdominis
- serratus anterior
- erector spinae
- trapezius
- latissimus dorsi
- quadratus lumborum

# HANDS ON RINGS



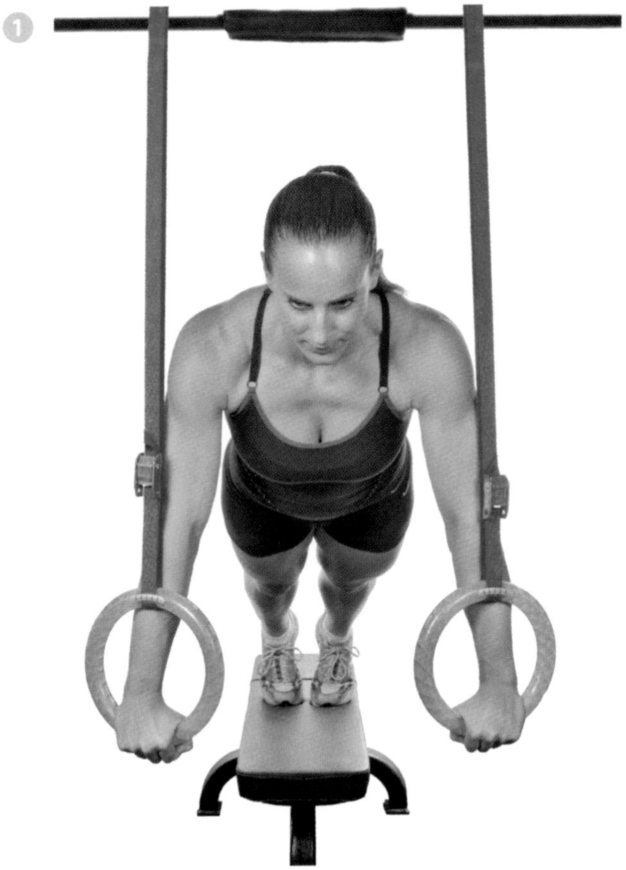

**Starting Position:** With your body rigid, grasp the rings slightly wider than shoulder-width apart with a palms-down grip, so that the rings are parallel and directly above your chest.

**Action:** Allow the entire body to descend chest-first in a controlled manner by allowing your elbows to bend and using your toes as a fulcrum. While descending, move your hands apart laterally, until your chest is directly between your hands at ring level, and your elbows are bent to 90 degrees. Return by extending your arms, pushing toward the floor until your elbows are straightened.

LOOK FOR
- A single plane of movement, i.e., a straight line from head to ankle.

AVOID
- Segmental elevation, i.e., your shoulders rising before your hips, or vice versa.
- Elevating your shoulders toward your ears.
- Moving your head forward.

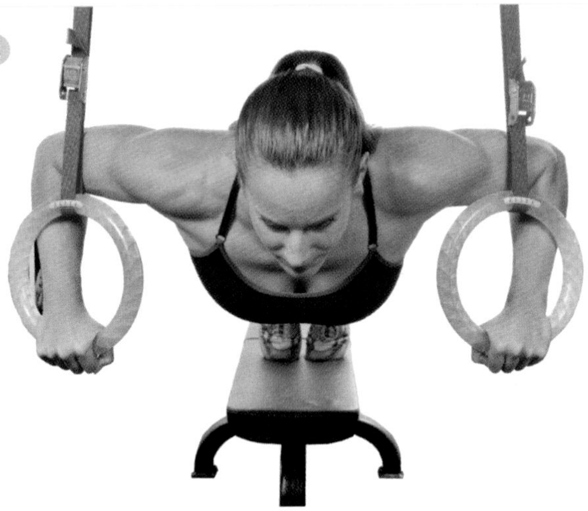

**Movement Path:** Your torso moves directly downward, and your hands move outward on the descent and inward on the ascent.

STABILIZE BY
- Keeping your knees locked.
- Fixing your ankles in a stable position.
- Keeping your hips, abdominal muscles, and lower back rigid.

## BEST FOR

- pectoralis major
- pectoralis minor
- coracobrachialis
- deltoideus anterior
- triceps brachii
- iliopsoas
- vastus lateralis
- vastus medialis
- vastus intermedius
- rectus femoris
- tibialis anterior
- transversus abdominis
- serratus anterior
- erector spinae
- trapezius
- latissimus dorsi
- quadratus lumborum

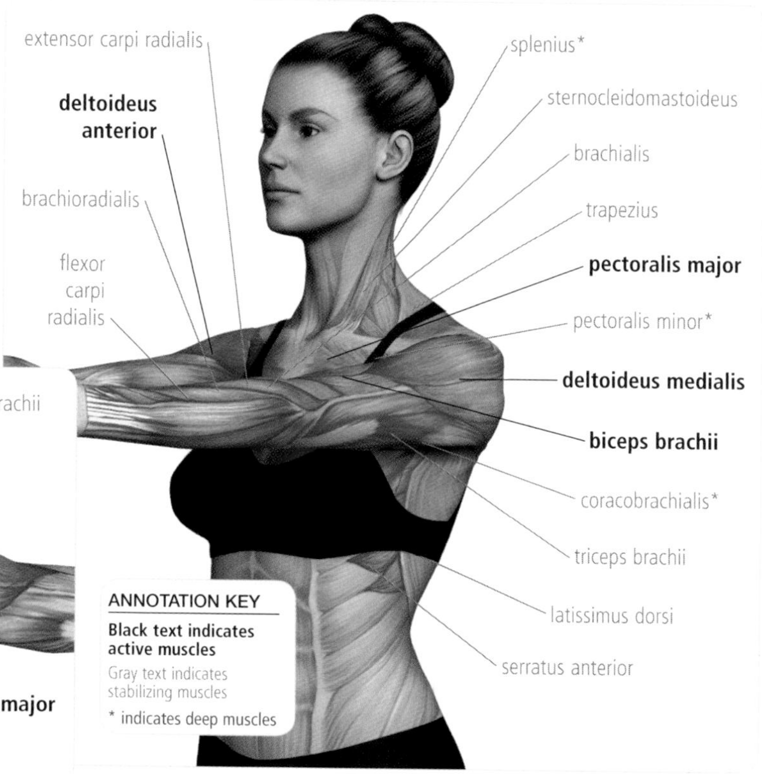
extensor carpi radialis
deltoideus anterior
brachioradialis
flexor carpi radialis
splenius*
sternocleidomastoideus
brachialis
trapezius
pectoralis major
pectoralis minor*
deltoideus medialis
biceps brachii
coracobrachialis*
triceps brachii
latissimus dorsi
serratus anterior
ANNOTATION KEY
Black text indicates active muscles
Gray text indicates stabilizing muscles
* indicates deep muscles

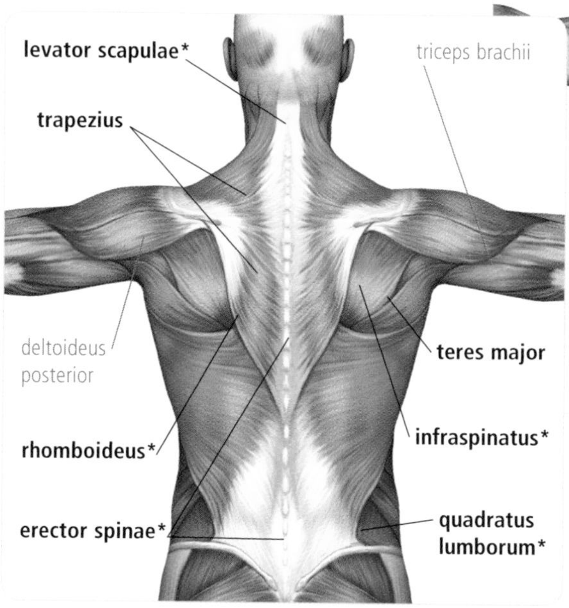
levator scapulae*
trapezius
triceps brachii
deltoideus posterior
teres major
rhomboideus*
infraspinatus*
erector spinae*
quadratus lumborum*

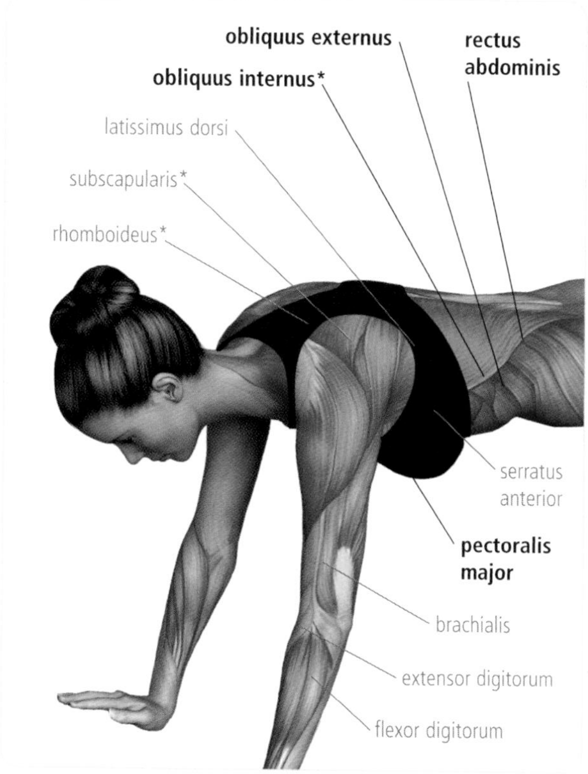
obliquus externus
rectus abdominis
obliquus internus*
latissimus dorsi
subscapularis*
rhomboideus*
serratus anterior
pectoralis major
brachialis
extensor digitorum
flexor digitorum

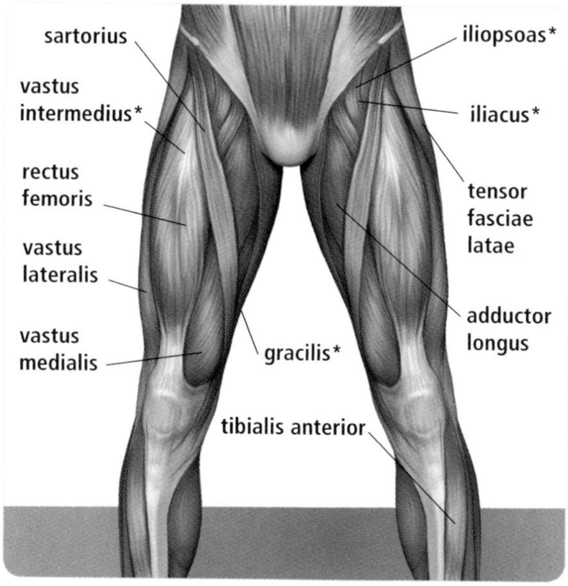
sartorius
iliopsoas*
vastus intermedius*
iliacus*
rectus femoris
tensor fasciae latae
vastus lateralis
adductor longus
vastus medialis
gracilis*
tibialis anterior

# SINGLE-ARM FORWARD SLIDE

**① Starting Position:** On a smooth, flat surface (preferably wood), assume a push-up position with legs straight and each hand placed on a small individual towel. Hands are directly beneath shoulders.

## LOOK FOR
- Smooth transitions.
- All parts to move at once.

## AVOID
- Touching the ground with the torso.
- Bending knees.
- Allowing body to rotate.

**② Action:** Bend one elbow and simultaneously slide the other hand upward, keeping that elbow straight to cause your torso to descend. Return by pushing into the floor with the bent arm and pulling downward with the overhead, straightened one, until your torso returns to its original position. Alternate arms.

**③ Movement Path:** Your spine moves directly downward. One arm moves upward.

## STABILIZE BY
- Keeping tension on both hands.
- Keeping legs straight and hips even.

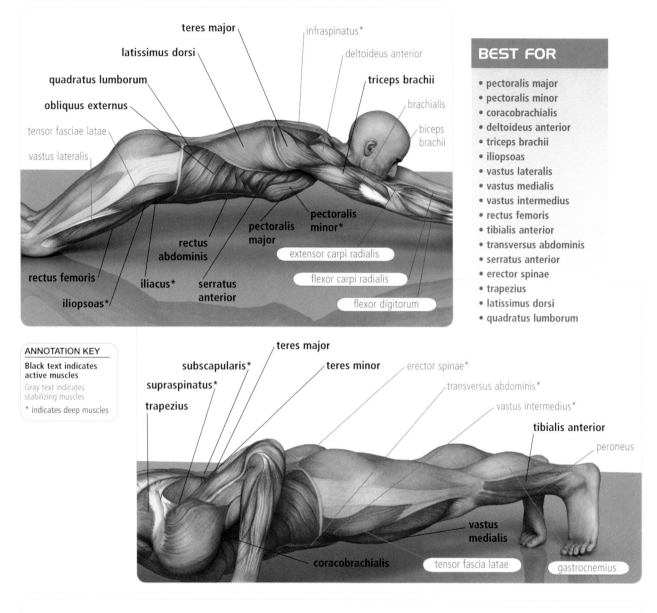

# SINGLE-ARM FORWARD SLIDE • PUSH-UP

teres major
latissimus dorsi
quadratus lumborum
obliquus externus
tensor fasciae latae
vastus lateralis
infraspinatus*
deltoideus anterior
triceps brachii
brachialis
biceps brachii
pectoralis minor*
pectoralis major
rectus abdominis
extensor carpi radialis
flexor carpi radialis
flexor digitorum
rectus femoris
iliacus*
serratus anterior
iliopsoas*


## BEST FOR

- pectoralis major
- pectoralis minor
- coracobrachialis
- deltoideus anterior
- triceps brachii
- iliopsoas
- vastus lateralis
- vastus medialis
- vastus intermedius
- rectus femoris
- tibialis anterior
- transversus abdominis
- serratus anterior
- erector spinae
- trapezius
- latissimus dorsi
- quadratus lumborum

ANNOTATION KEY

**Black text indicates active muscles**

Gray text indicates stabilizing muscles

* indicates deep muscles

teres major
subscapularis*
teres minor
erector spinae*
supraspinatus*
transversus abdominis*
trapezius
vastus intermedius*
tibialis anterior
peroneus
vastus medialis
coracobrachialis
tensor fascia latae
gastrocnemius


MODIFICATION

**Less Difficult:** Assume a push-up position with your knees bent. Follow the same action and movement path.

1 2 3

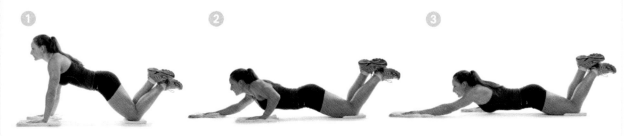

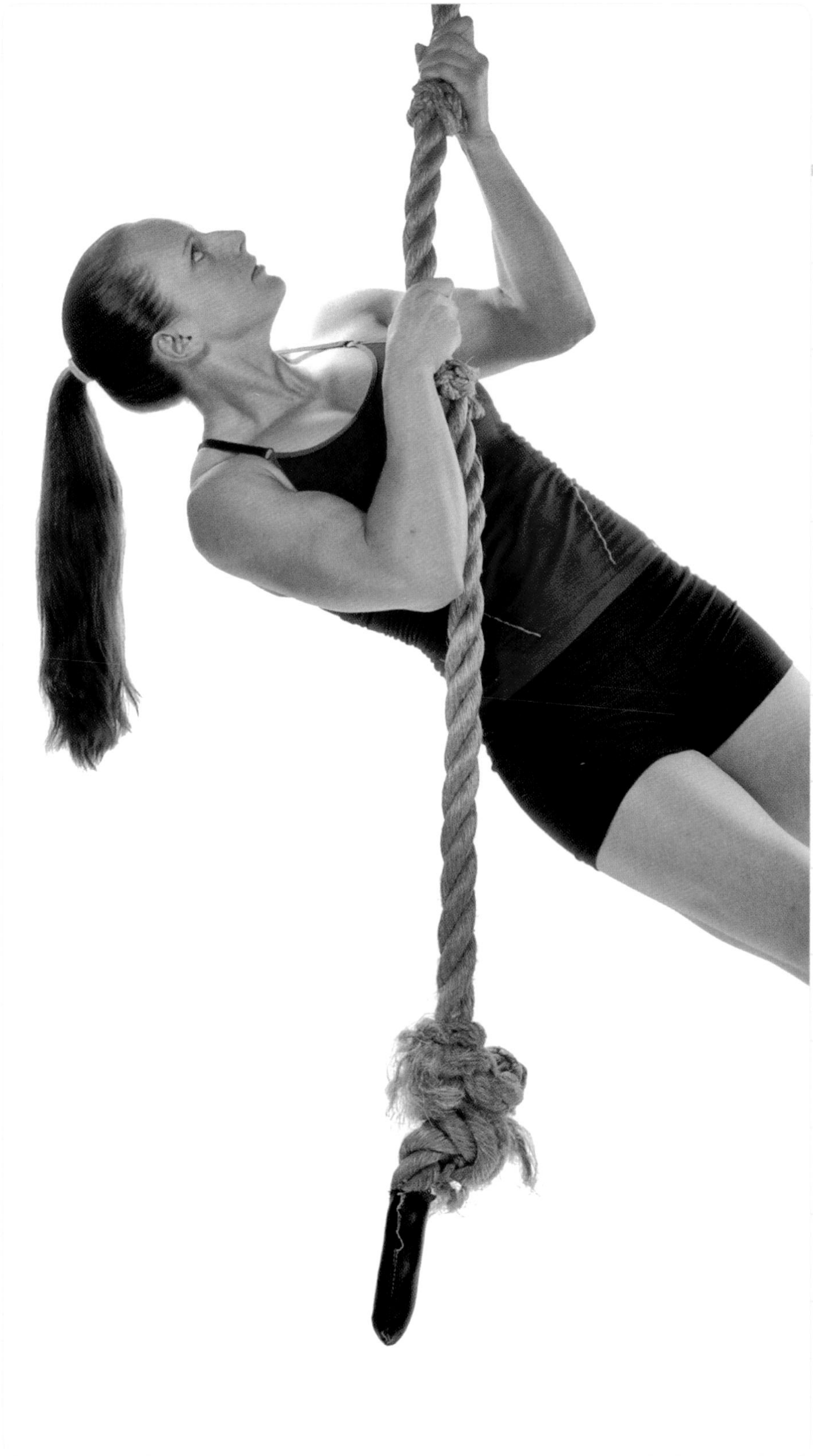

# CHIN-UP

Like its other half (the push-up), the chin-up has also been around as an exercise for thousands of years. These two are the yin and yang of the upper body's function: push and pull. The chin-up is perhaps the most intimidating of all exercises because there is only you and the bar, and either you can pull yourself up to it or you cannot. Gravity is relentless, and no matter how strong you are, when you begin to fail (and you will), there is no way to cheat it: when you're done, you're done. As an upper-body conditioning exercise, it is rivaled by only its partner the push-up (and perhaps the dip) as an absolute necessity for anyone at any level.

The joints involved are the shoulder, elbow, and wrist. The muscles used are the back, shoulders, and biceps.

The primary benefits derived from chin-ups are upper-body pulling strength and endurance, shoulder stability, grip strength, and posture.

# BASIC

## CHIN-UP

**Starting Position:** Gripping the bar with your palms in (facing your body), hang with your knees bent only very slightly. Keep your head in a neutral alignment. Your hands should be shoulder-width apart.

**Action:** Pull your body up vertically until your upper chest is aligned with the bar; this is the end of the concentric phase. Lower your body back down to the starting position with your elbows fully extended (the end of the eccentric phase).

**LOOK FOR**
- Your arms to return to a full extension.
- You shoulder blades to draw together and downward at the beginning of the movement.

**AVOID**
- Swinging, jerking, chin "pecking," or hyperextension of elbows.

**Movement Path:** Your body moves vertically up. Your upper body tilts back slightly to allow your chin to smoothly pass the bar line.

**STABILIZE BY**
- Retracting your scapula.
- Keeping your core tight to prevent swinging.

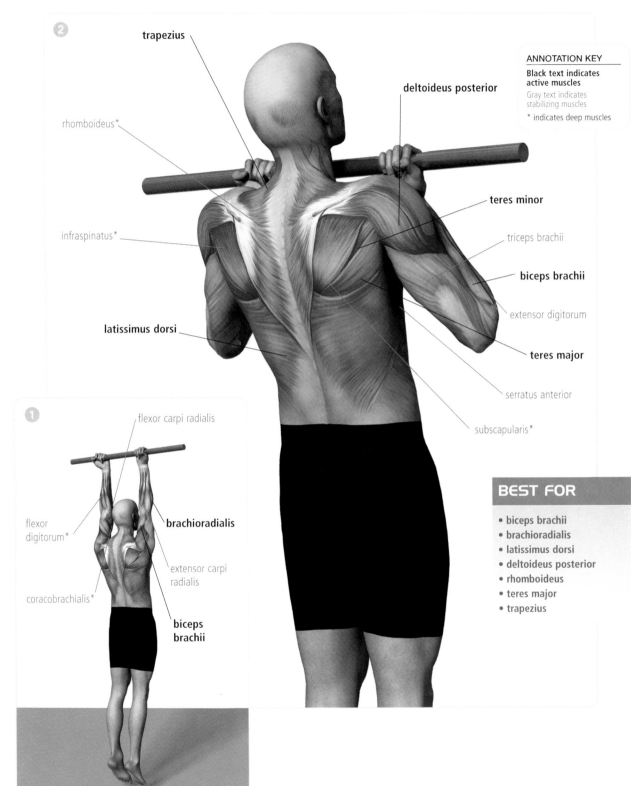

2
trapezius
deltoideus posterior
rhomboideus*
teres minor
infraspinatus*
triceps brachii
biceps brachii
extensor digitorum
latissimus dorsi
teres major
serratus anterior
subscapularis*

ANNOTATION KEY
**Black text indicates active muscles**
Gray text indicates stabilizing muscles
* indicates deep muscles

1
flexor carpi radialis
flexor digitorum*
brachioradialis
extensor carpi radialis
coracobrachialis*
biceps brachii

## BEST FOR

- biceps brachii
- brachioradialis
- latissimus dorsi
- deltoideus posterior
- rhomboideus
- teres major
- trapezius

# PULL-UP GRIP

## CHIN-UP

**Starting Position:** Gripping the bar with your palms out (facing away from your body), hang with your knees bent and your ankles crossed. Keep your head in a neutral alignment. Your hands should be shoulder-width apart.

**Action:** Pull your body up vertically until your upper chest is aligned with the bar; this is the end of the concentric phase. Lower your body back down to the starting position with your elbows fully extended (the end of the eccentric phase).

**Movement Path:** Your body moves vertically up. Your upper body tilts back slightly to allow your chin to smoothly pass the bar line.

### LOOK FOR
- Your arms to return to a full extension.
- Your shoulder blades to draw together and downward at the beginning of the movement.

### AVOID
- Swinging, jerking, chin "pecking," or hyperextension of elbows.

### STABILIZE BY
- Retracting your scapula
- Keeping your core tight to prevent swinging

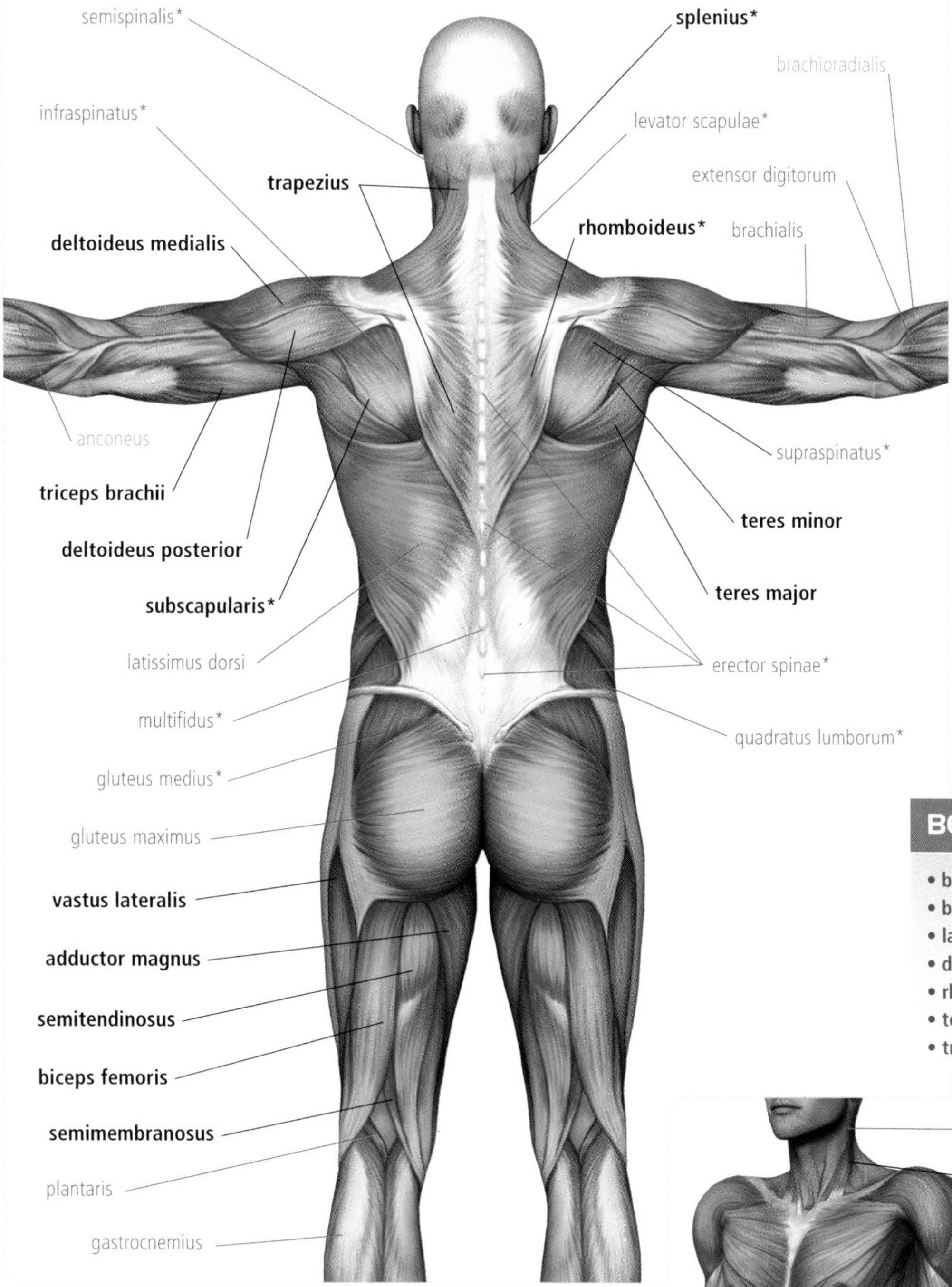
semispinalis*
splenius*
brachioradialis
infraspinatus*
levator scapulae*
extensor digitorum
trapezius
deltoideus medialis
rhomboideus*
brachialis
anconeus
supraspinatus*
triceps brachii
teres minor
deltoideus posterior
teres major
subscapularis*
latissimus dorsi
erector spinae*
multifidus*
quadratus lumborum*
gluteus medius*
gluteus maximus
vastus lateralis
adductor magnus
semitendinosus
biceps femoris
semimembranosus
plantaris
gastrocnemius

ANNOTATION KEY

**Black text indicates active muscles**

Gray text indicates stabilizing muscles

* indicates deep muscles

## BEST FOR

- **biceps brachii**
- **brachioradialis**
- **latissimus dorsi**
- **deltoideus posterior**
- **rhomboideus**
- **teres major**
- **trapezius**

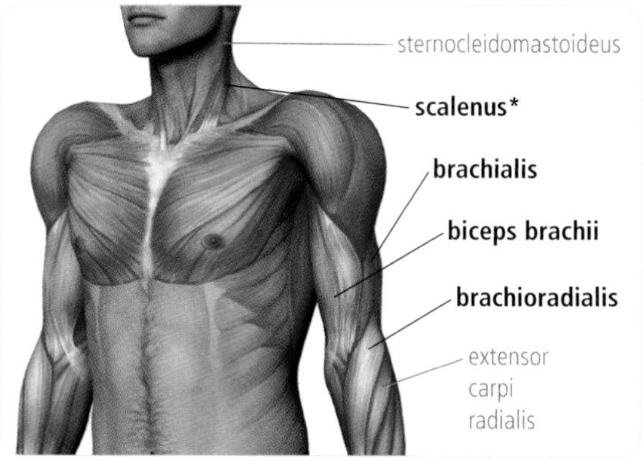
sternocleidomastoideus
scalenus*
brachialis
biceps brachii
brachioradialis
extensor carpi radialis

# 45-DEGREE BODY ROW



**Starting Position:** Hang from a bar with your body in a flat plane. The line of your body should be at a 45-degree angle to the floor. Grasp the bar with both arms in supine or prone grips. Your elbows should be at 90-degree angles.

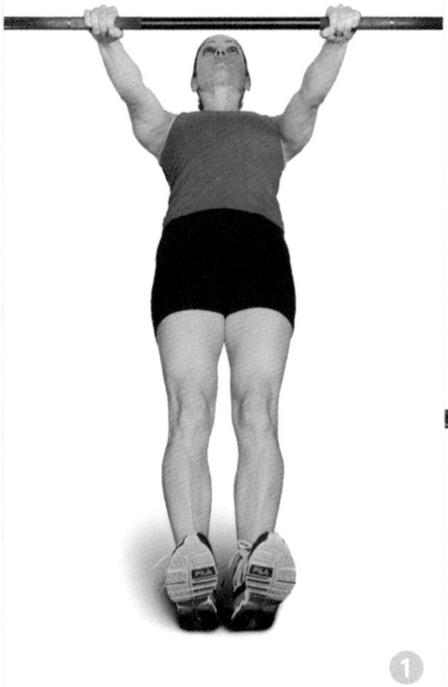

**STABILIZE BY**

- Fixing your shoulders in one position.
- Locking your knees.
- Keeping your ankles in a fixed position.
- Keeping your hips, abdominal muscles, and lower back rigid.

**LOOK FOR**

- A single plane of movement, maintaining a straight line from your head to your ankles.

**AVOID**

- A segmental elevation, such as your shoulders rising before your hips, or vice versa.
- Elevating your shoulders toward your ears.
- Moving your head forward.

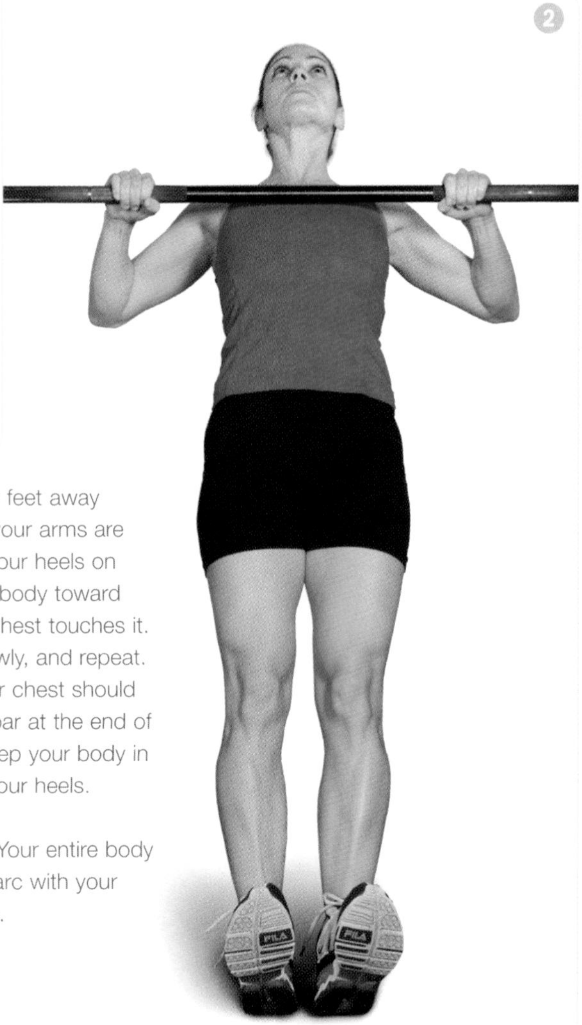

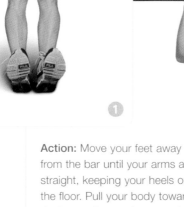

**Action:** Move your feet away from the bar until your arms are straight, keeping your heels on the floor. Pull your body toward the bar until your chest touches it. Lower yourself slowly, and repeat. The bottom of your chest should always touch the bar at the end of the movement. Keep your body in a straight line on your heels.

**Movement Path:** Your entire body moves in a single arc with your feet as the fulcrum.

## BEST FOR

- biceps brachii
- brachialis
- brachioradialis
- infraspinatus
- latissimus dorsi
- rhomboideus
- teres major
- teres minor
- trapezius

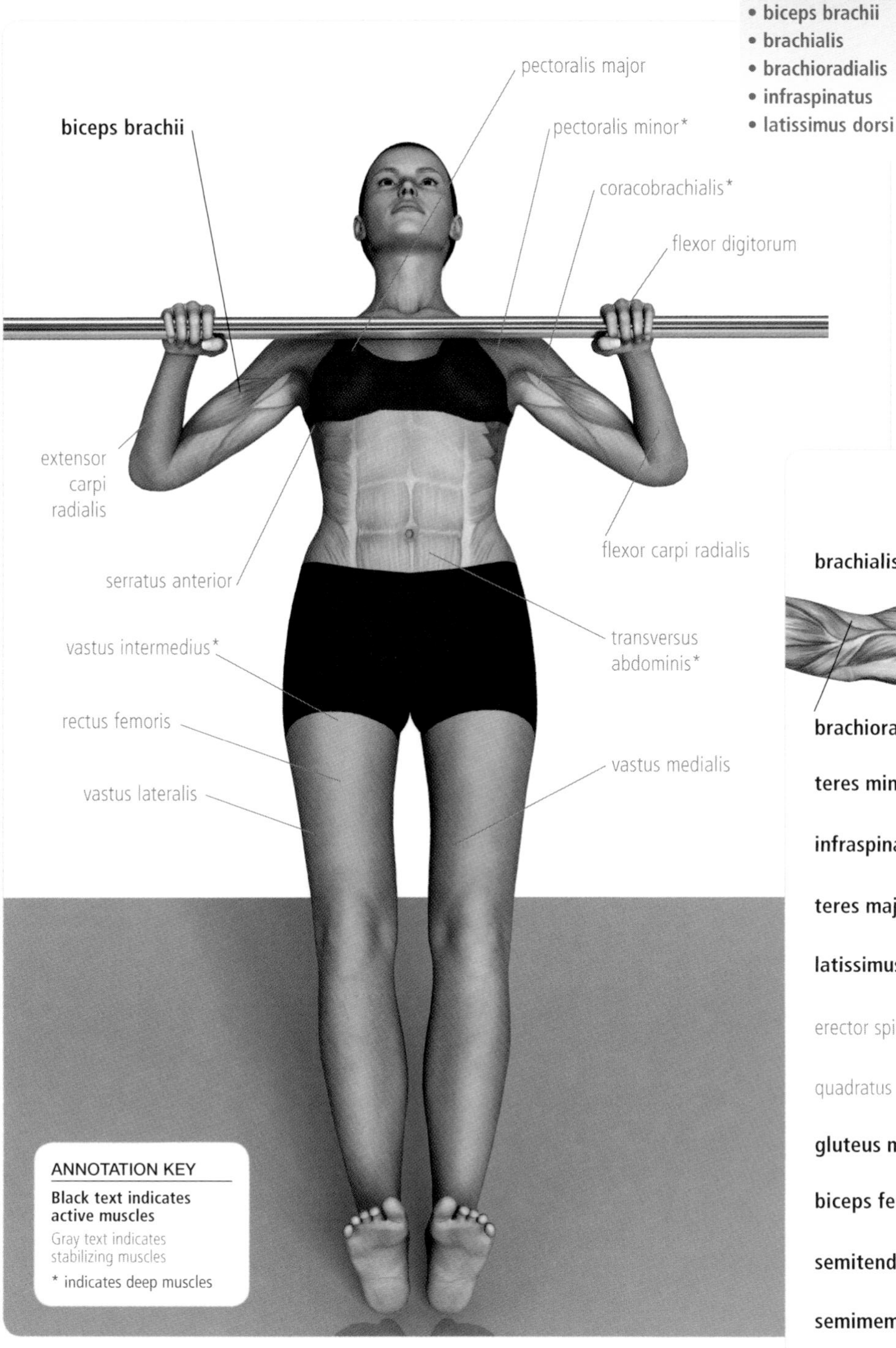
pectoralis major
biceps brachii
pectoralis minor*
coracobrachialis*
flexor digitorum
extensor carpi radialis
flexor carpi radialis
serratus anterior
transversus abdominis*
vastus intermedius*
rectus femoris
vastus medialis
vastus lateralis
ANNOTATION KEY
Black text indicates active muscles
Gray text indicates stabilizing muscles
* indicates deep muscles

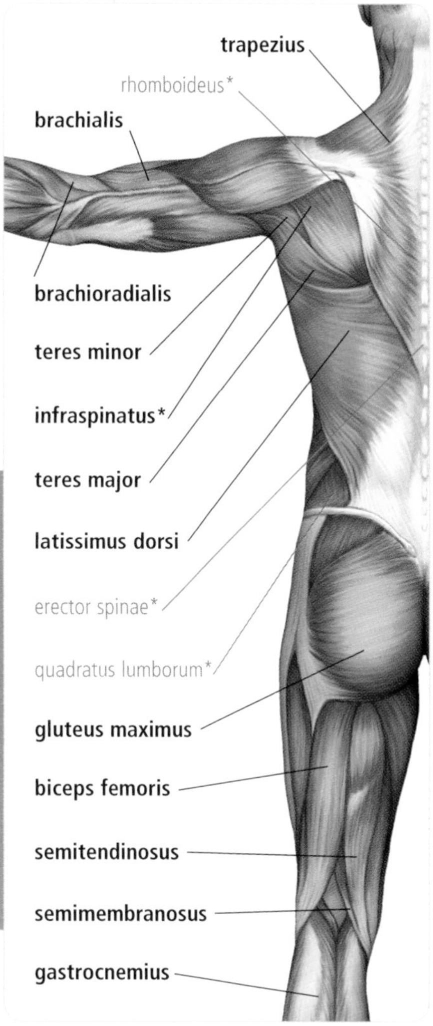
trapezius
rhomboideus*
brachialis
brachioradialis
teres minor
infraspinatus*
teres major
latissimus dorsi
erector spinae*
quadratus lumborum*
gluteus maximus
biceps femoris
semitendinosus
semimembranosus
gastrocnemius

# HORIZONTAL BODY ROW

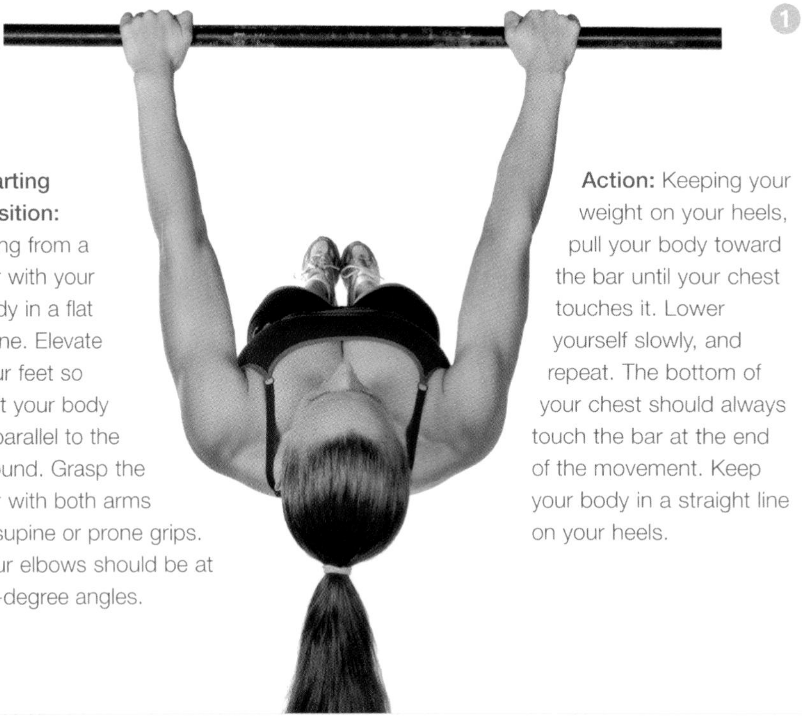

**Starting Position:** Hang from a bar with your body in a flat plane. Elevate your feet so that your body is parallel to the ground. Grasp the bar with both arms in supine or prone grips. Your elbows should be at 90-degree angles.

**Action:** Keeping your weight on your heels, pull your body toward the bar until your chest touches it. Lower yourself slowly, and repeat. The bottom of your chest should always touch the bar at the end of the movement. Keep your body in a straight line on your heels.

LOOK FOR

- A single plane of movement, maintaining a straight line from your head to your ankles.

AVOID

- A segmental elevation, such as your shoulders rising before your hips, or vice versa.
- Elevating your shoulders toward your ears.
- Moving your head forward.

STABILIZE BY

- Fixing your shoulders in one position.
- Locking your knees.
- Keeping your ankles in a fixed position.
- Keeping your hips, abdominal muscles, and lower back rigid.

**Movement Path:** Your entire body moves in a single arc with your feet as the fulcrum.

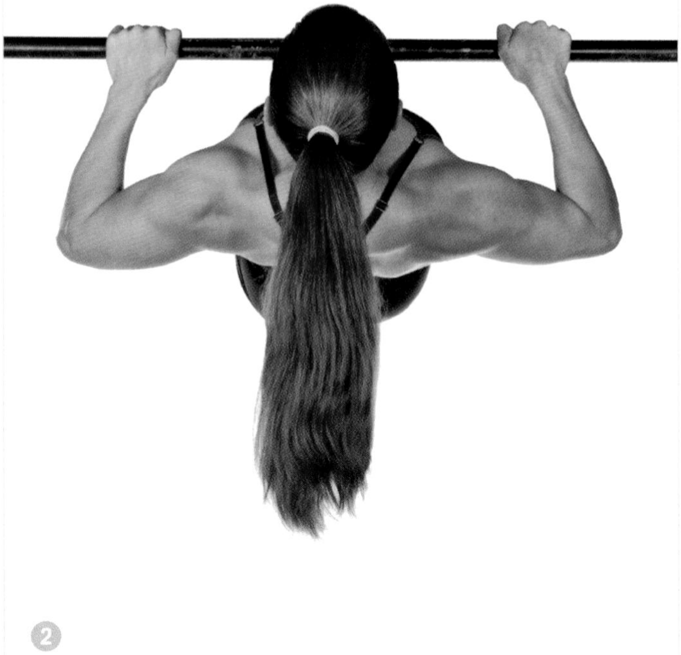

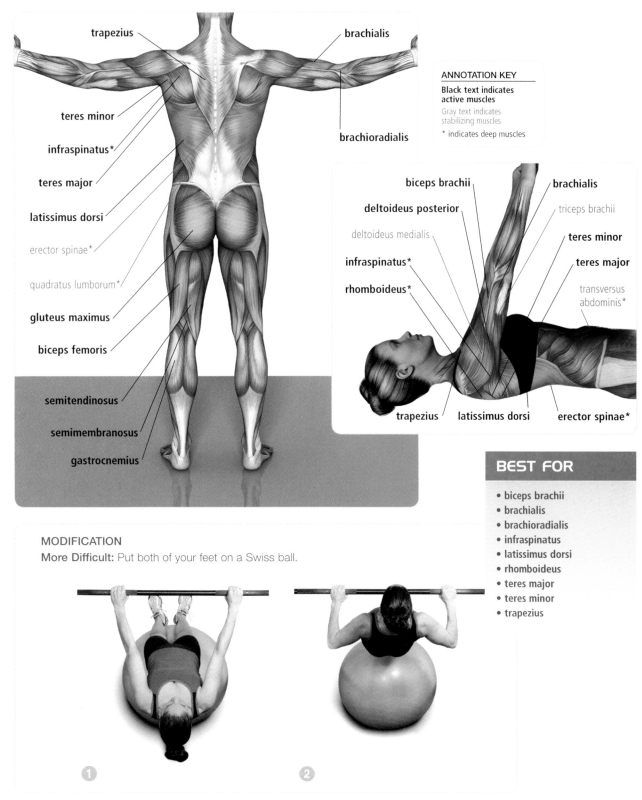

trapezius

brachialis

teres minor

infraspinatus*

teres major

latissimus dorsi

erector spinae*

quadratus lumborum*

gluteus maximus

biceps femoris

semitendinosus

semimembranosus

gastrocnemius

brachioradialis

**ANNOTATION KEY**

**Black text indicates active muscles**

Gray text indicates stabilizing muscles

* indicates deep muscles

biceps brachii

deltoideus posterior

deltoideus medialis

infraspinatus*

rhomboideus*

brachialis

triceps brachii

teres minor

teres major

transversus abdominis*

trapezius

latissimus dorsi

erector spinae*

**BEST FOR**

- biceps brachii
- brachialis
- brachioradialis
- infraspinatus
- latissimus dorsi
- rhomboideus
- teres major
- teres minor
- trapezius

**MODIFICATION**
**More Difficult:** Put both of your feet on a Swiss ball.

①

②

# LATERAL ROPE PULL



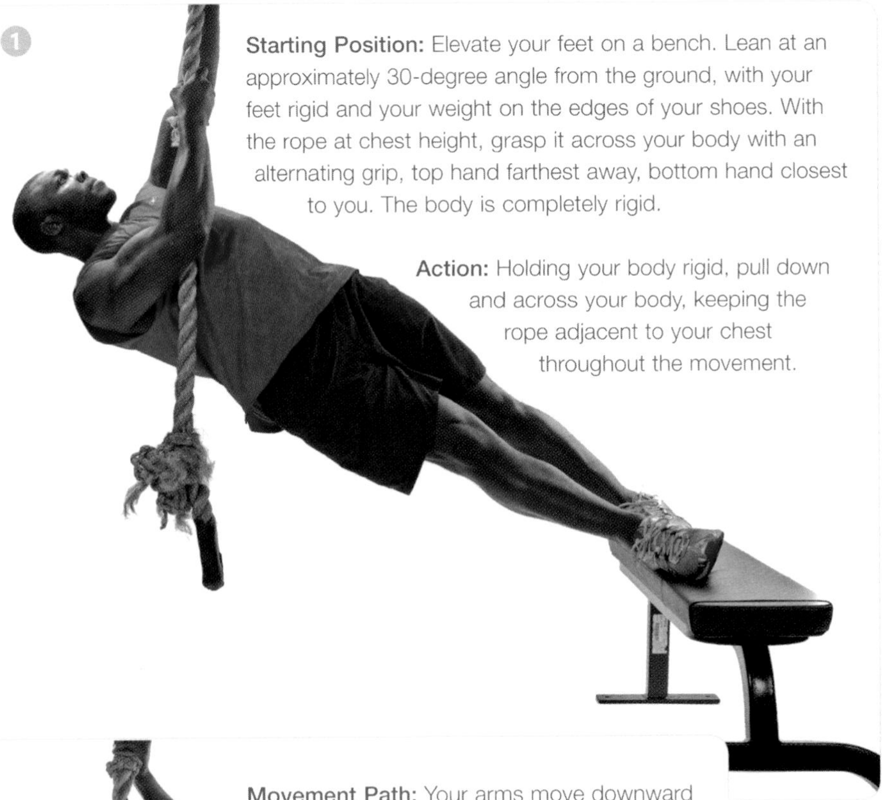

**Starting Position:** Elevate your feet on a bench. Lean at an approximately 30-degree angle from the ground, with your feet rigid and your weight on the edges of your shoes. With the rope at chest height, grasp it across your body with an alternating grip, top hand farthest away, bottom hand closest to you. The body is completely rigid.

**Action:** Holding your body rigid, pull down and across your body, keeping the rope adjacent to your chest throughout the movement.

LOOK FOR
- Your feet to work as a fulcrum.
- The rope to remain adjacent to chest.

AVOID
- Dropping your hips.
- Allowing the body to rotate.

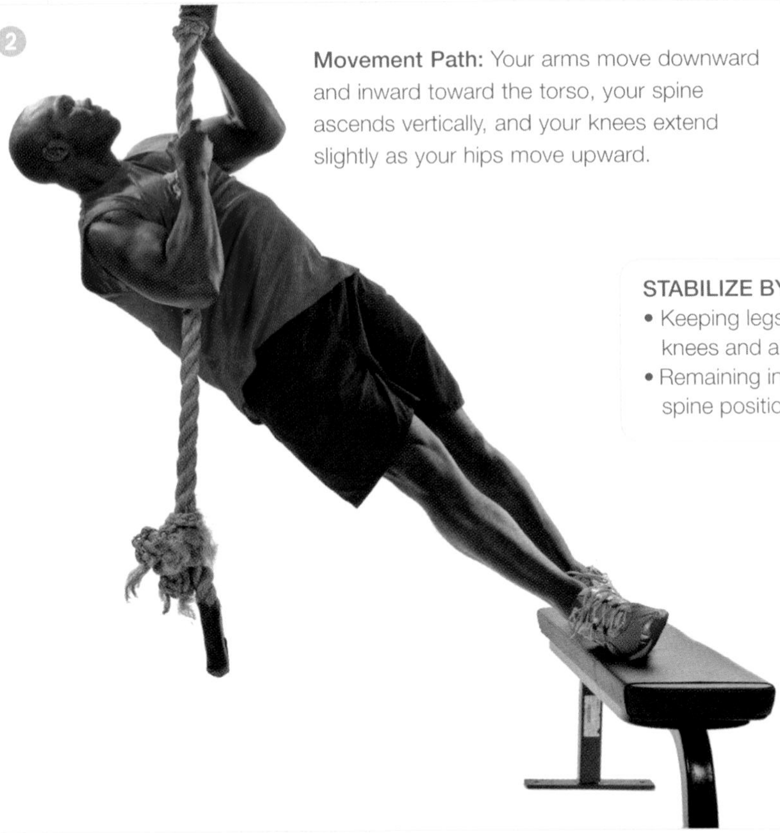

**Movement Path:** Your arms move downward and inward toward the torso, your spine ascends vertically, and your knees extend slightly as your hips move upward.

STABILIZE BY
- Keeping legs straight and knees and ankles solid.
- Remaining in a neutral spine position.

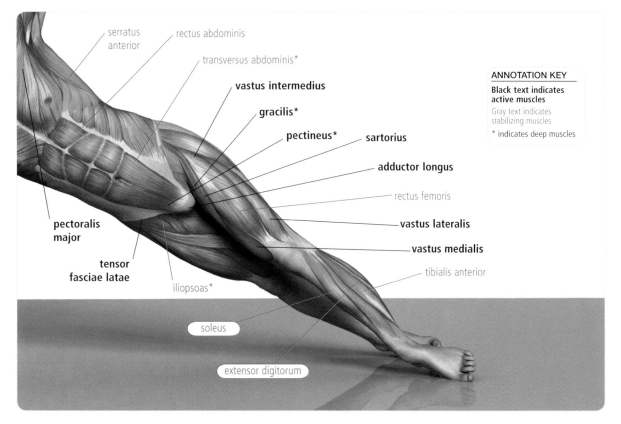

serratus anterior

rectus abdominis

transversus abdominis*

**vastus intermedius**

**gracilis***

**pectineus***

**sartorius**

**adductor longus**

rectus femoris

**vastus lateralis**

**vastus medialis**

pectoralis major

tensor fasciae latae

iliopsoas*

tibialis anterior

soleus

extensor digitorum

**ANNOTATION KEY**

**Black text indicates active muscles**

Gray text indicates stabilizing muscles

* indicates deep muscles

## BEST FOR

- serratus anterior
- rectus abdominis
- deltoideus posterior
- teres minor
- triceps brachii
- pectoralis major
- latissimus dorsi
- transversus abdominis
- gluteus medius
- iliopsoas
- gluteus maximus
- pectineus
- vastus lateralis
- vastus medialis
- vastus intermedius
- rectus femoris
- tensor fasciae latae
- adductor longus
- gracilis
- quadratus lumborum
- erector spinae

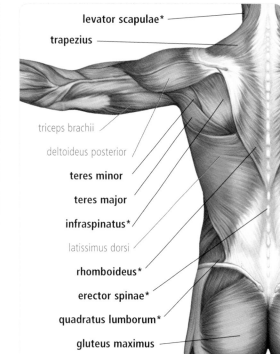

levator scapulae*

trapezius

triceps brachii

deltoideus posterior

**teres minor**

**teres major**

**infraspinatus***

latissimus dorsi

**rhomboideus***

**erector spinae***

**quadratus lumborum***

**gluteus maximus**

# PULL-UP NEUTRAL GRIP



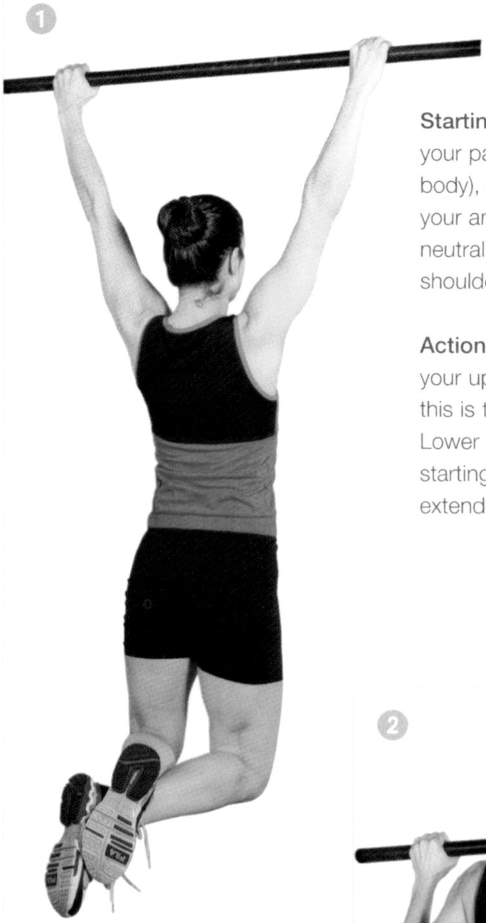

**Starting Position:** Gripping the bar with your palms out (facing away from your body), hang with your knees bent and your ankles crossed. Keep your head in a neutral alignment. Your hands should be shoulder-width apart.

**Action:** Pull your body up vertically until your upper chest is aligned with the bar; this is the end of the concentric phase. Lower your body back down to the starting position with your elbows fully extended (the end of the eccentric phase).

LOOK FOR
- Your arms to return to a full extension.
- Your shoulder blades to draw together and downward at the beginning of the movement.

AVOID
- Swinging, jerking, chin "pecking," or hyperextension of elbows.

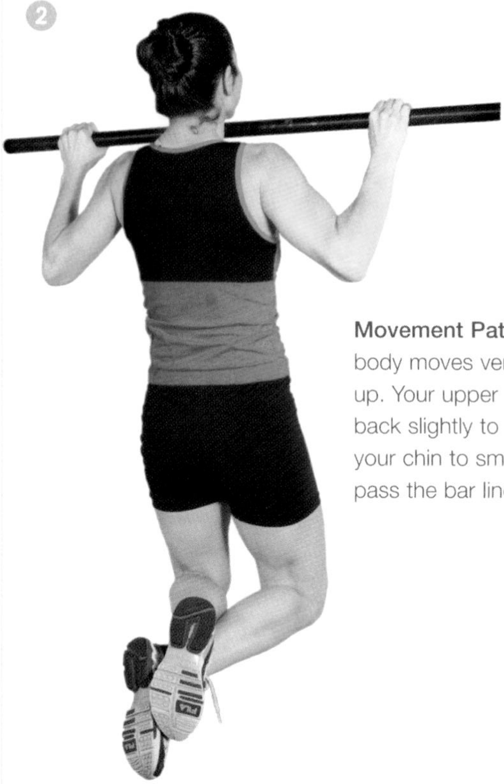

**Movement Path:** Your body moves vertically up. Your upper body tilts back slightly to allow your chin to smoothly pass the bar line.

STABILIZE BY
- Retracting your scapula.
- Keeping your core tight to prevent swinging.

## BEST FOR

- biceps brachii
- brachioradialis
- latissimus dorsi
- deltoideus posterior
- rhomboideus
- teres major
- trapezius

ANNOTATION KEY

**Black text indicates active muscles**

Gray text indicates stabilizing muscles

* indicates deep muscles

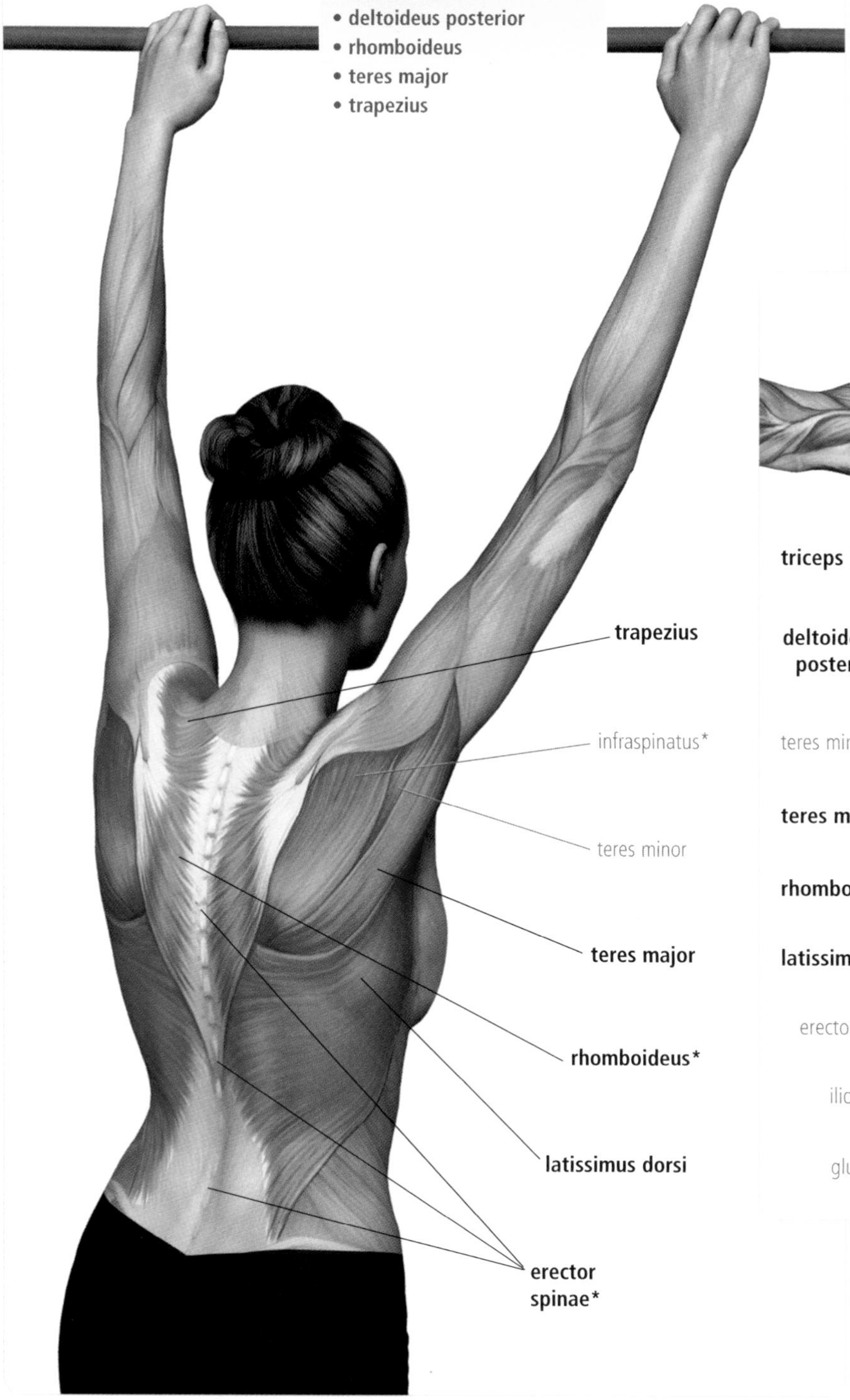
trapezius
infraspinatus*
teres minor
teres major
rhomboideus*
latissimus dorsi
erector spinae*

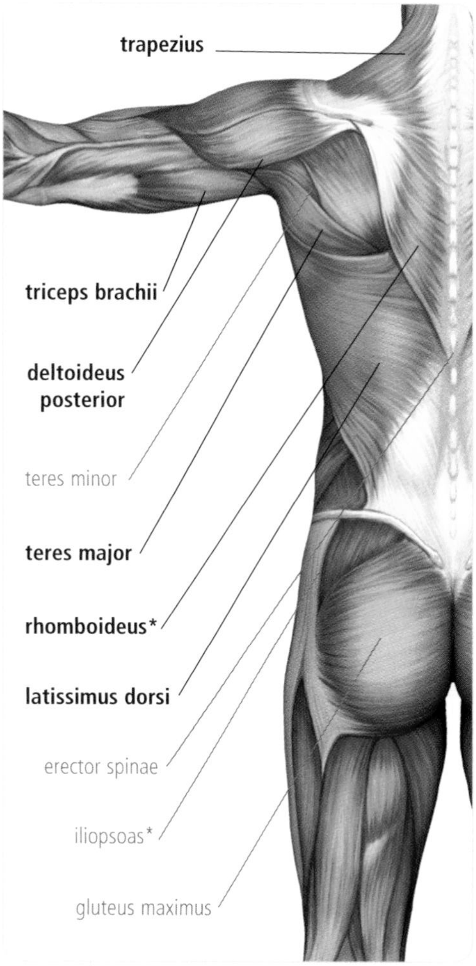
trapezius
triceps brachii
deltoideus posterior
teres minor
teres major
rhomboideus*
latissimus dorsi
erector spinae
iliopsoas*
gluteus maximus

# STAND-PULL

## CHIN-UP

1

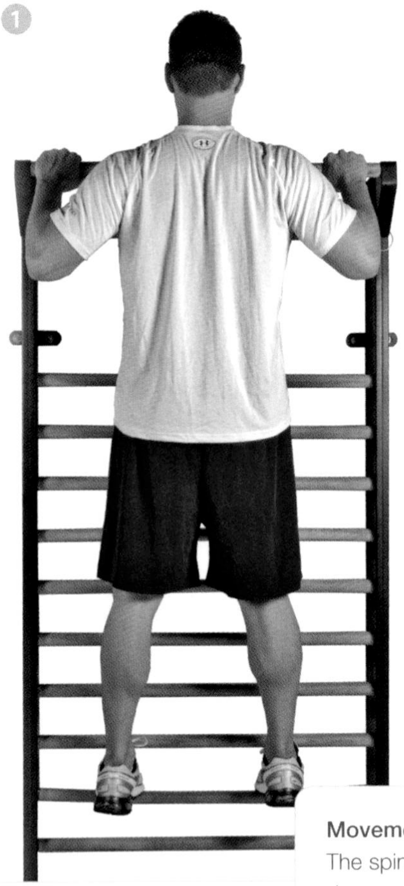

**Starting Position:** In standing position, grasp a bar at collarbone height with your palms slightly wider than shoulder-width apart and facing away from you. The tops of your shoes should be directly beneath your hands, distributing your weight so that if you were to let go of the bar, you would fall backward.

**Action:** Drop your hips down and backward, bending the knees, extending the arms, and keeping the spine in a vertical and neutral position until the arms are fully extended. Return by simultaneously pulling downward with the elbows and the arms and extending the knees and hips again, keeping the spine vertical and neutral.

**Movement Path:** The spine travels downward and backward, the arms extend upward and forward, the hips retract and drop, and the upper legs move up toward the torso. The lower legs remain stationary.

2

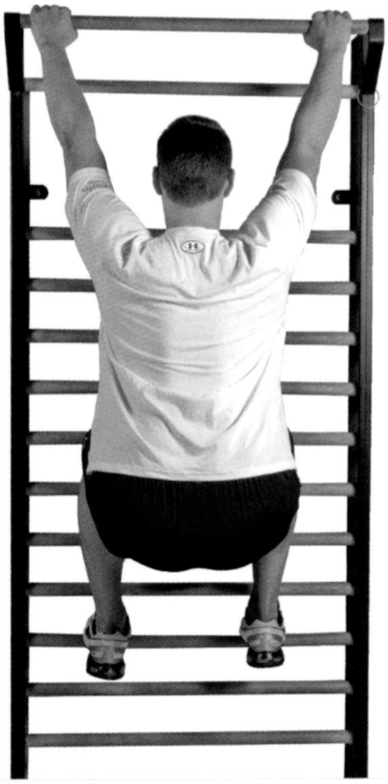

LOOK FOR
- Simultaneous movement of all parts.
- Your head and spine to remain vertical throughout the movement.
- Your chest to be pulled up and to the bar.
- The elbows to remain adjacent to the torso at top position.

AVOID
- Allowing the torso to drop forward.
- Pulling the elbows backward on the pull-up phase.

STABILIZE BY
- Keeping the feet flat and weight evenly distributed.
- Keeping the spine solid, and the rib cage and head up.

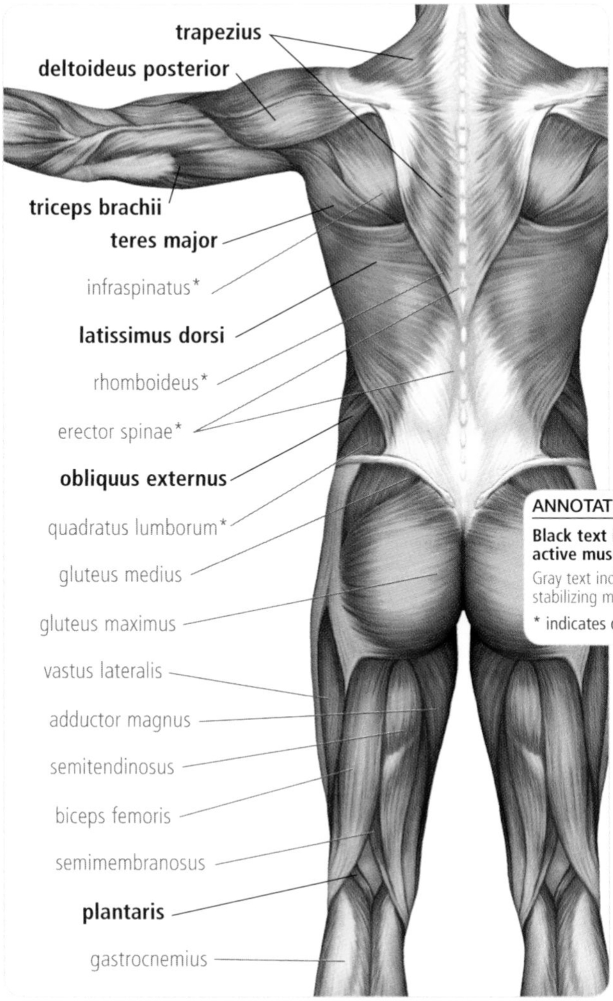
trapezius
deltoideus posterior
triceps brachii
teres major
infraspinatus*
latissimus dorsi
rhomboideus*
erector spinae*
obliquus externus
quadratus lumborum*
gluteus medius
gluteus maximus
vastus lateralis
adductor magnus
semitendinosus
biceps femoris
semimembranosus
plantaris
gastrocnemius

ANNOTATION KEY
**Black text indicates active muscles**
Gray text indicates stabilizing muscles
* indicates deep muscles

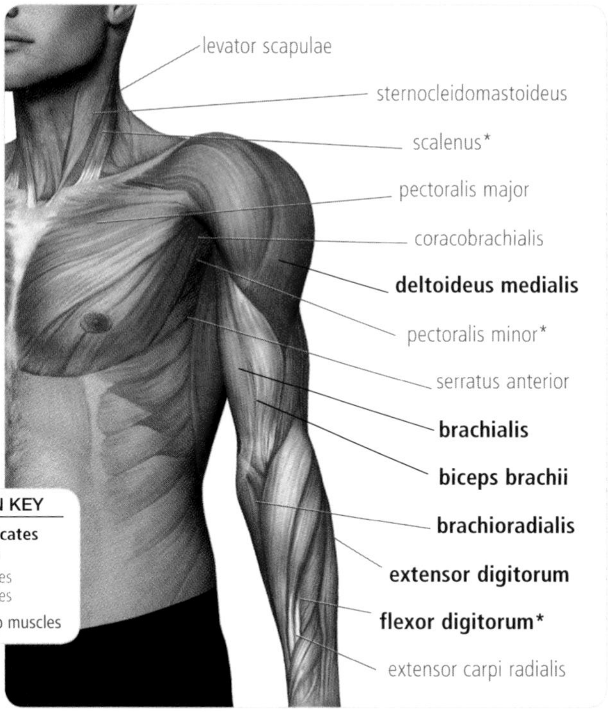
levator scapulae
sternocleidomastoideus
scalenus*
pectoralis major
coracobrachialis
deltoideus medialis
pectoralis minor*
serratus anterior
brachialis
biceps brachii
brachioradialis
extensor digitorum
flexor digitorum*
extensor carpi radialis

## BEST FOR

- latissimus dorsi
- rhomboideus
- trapezius
- erector spinae
- infraspinatus
- teres major
- deltoideus posterior
- deltoideus medialis
- brachialis
- biceps brachii
- brachioradialis
- gluteus maximus
- biceps femoris
- semitendinosus
- semimembranosus
- gastrocnemius
- pectoralis major
- pectoralis minor
- coracobrachialis
- extensor carpi radialis
- extensor digitorum
- flexor digitorum
- infraspinatus
- levator scapulae
- triceps brachii
- serratus anterior
- vastus lateralis
- quadratus lumborum

MODIFICATION

**Similar Difficulty:** Grasping a rope at chest height, stand with a slight lean backward. Sit down and backward with the hips, and keep tension on the rope as the arms extend forward and the knees bend. Return by pulling upward and extending both knees and hips.

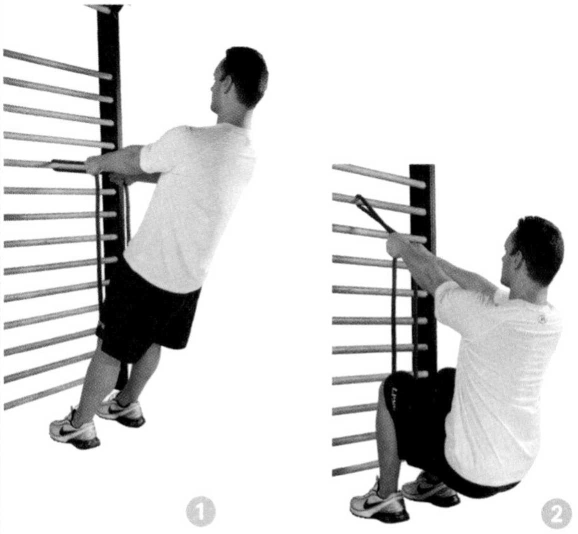
1
2

# STEP CHIN

## STABILIZE BY
- Keeping the chest high and shoulders down.
- Keeping the hips and shoulders parallel.

**Starting Position:** Begin with your head higher than the bar and your palms down, wider than shoulder width. Place one foot on a step with only the ball of the foot bearing weight, and the other leg straight and slightly behind the weight-bearing foot.

## LOOK FOR
- Non-weight-bearing leg to remain in the same plane as the spine.
- All joints to move at the same time.

## AVOID
- Allowing the shoulder to elevate.
- Rotation in the hips.
- Allowing the spine to deviate from vertical.

**Action:** Begin by dropping and reaching downward with the free foot. Allow the arms to extend completely and the weight-bearing leg to bend at both the hip and the knee. During this movement, the non-weight-bearing foot should never touch the ground. Return by pulling the elbows down and pushing through the weight-bearing foot.

**Movement Path:** The spine travels downward and backward, the arms extend upward and forward, the hips retract and drop, and the upper legs move up toward the torso. The lower legs remain stationary.

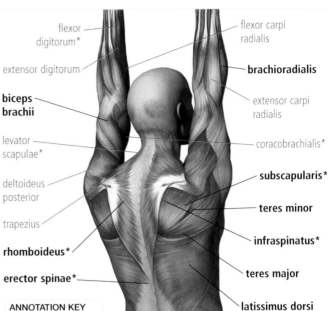

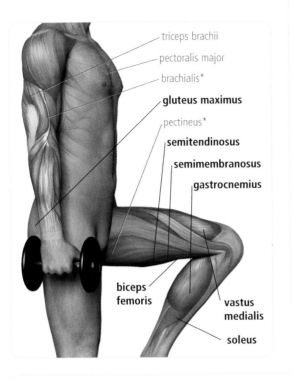

triceps brachii

pectoralis major

brachialis*

**gluteus maximus**

pectineus*

**semitendinosus**

**semimembranosus**

**gastrocnemius**

**biceps femoris**

**vastus medialis**

**soleus**

flexor digitorum*

extensor digitorum

**biceps brachii**

levator scapulae*

deltoideus posterior

trapezius

**rhomboideus***

**erector spinae***

flexor carpi radialis

**brachioradialis**

extensor carpi radialis

coracobrachialis*

**subscapularis***

**teres minor**

**infraspinatus***

**teres major**

**latissimus dorsi**

### ANNOTATION KEY

**Black text indicates active muscles**

Gray text indicates stabilizing muscles

\* indicates deep muscles

### MODIFICATION

**Similar Difficulty:** Stand with your feet directly under the bar and slightly wider than hip width. Grasp the bar at neck height with one hand slightly narrower than shoulder width. Grasp a dumbbell with the other hand, the arm extended and relaxed adjacent to the hip.

Drop the hips downward and backward in a controlled manner, allowing the arm grasping the bar to extend fully while bending the knees and hips. Return by simultaneously pulling and standing, keeping the spine vertical and the dumbbell arm straight and adjacent to the side.

### BEST FOR

- latissimus dorsi
- rhomboideus
- erector spinae
- infraspinatus
- trapezius
- teres major
- teres minor
- deltoideus posterior
- biceps brachii
- brachioradialis
- gluteus maximus
- biceps femoris
- semitendinosus
- semimembranosus
- gastrocnemius
- vastus medialis
- soleus
- pectoralis major
- coracobrachialis
- extensor carpi radialis
- flexor carpi radialis
- extensor digitorum
- flexor digitorum
- infraspinatus
- subscapularis
- levator scapulae
- triceps brachii
- erector spinae

# VERTICAL ROPE WITH ALTERNATE GRIP

1

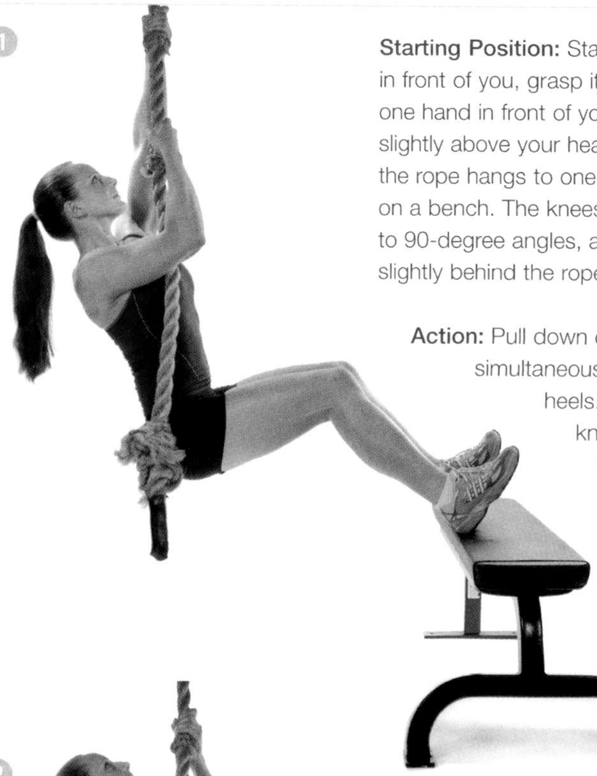

**Starting Position:** Standing with a rope directly in front of you, grasp it with an alternating grip, one hand in front of your chin, and the other slightly above your head. Step forward so that the rope hangs to one hip, and place your heels on a bench. The knees and hips should be bent to 90-degree angles, and the chest should be slightly behind the rope, with the arms extended.

**Action:** Pull down on the rope while simultaneously pushing down on your heels. Be sure to keep the knees bent and torso upright throughout the movement.

2

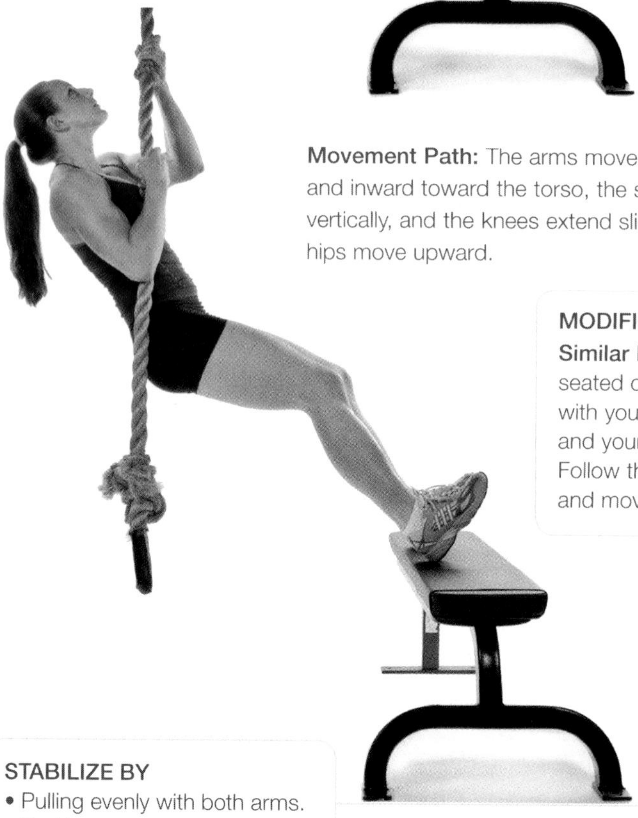

**Movement Path:** The arms move downward and inward toward the torso, the spine ascends vertically, and the knees extend slightly as the hips move upward.

**LOOK FOR**

- Hips to remain adjacent to rope.
- Spinal position to remain consistent.

**AVOID**

- Extending the knees excessively.
- Allowing the torso to rotate.

**MODIFICATIONS**

**Similar Difficulty:** Start seated on the ground with your feet on floor and your knees bent. Follow the same action and movement path.

**STABILIZE BY**

- Pulling evenly with both arms.
- Pushing evenly with both feet.
- Keeping chest and head up.

# VERTICAL ROPE WITH ALTERNATE GRIP • CHIN-UP

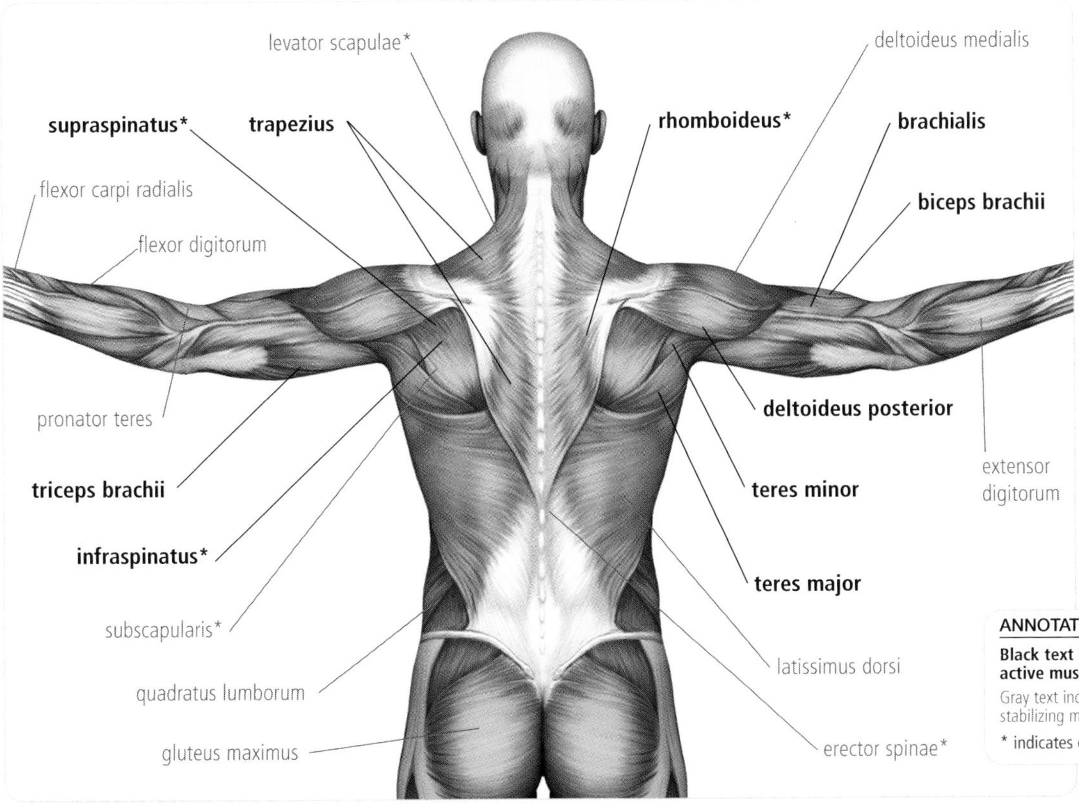

levator scapulae*
deltoideus medialis
supraspinatus*
trapezius
rhomboideus*
brachialis
flexor carpi radialis
biceps brachii
flexor digitorum
pronator teres
deltoideus posterior
triceps brachii
teres minor
extensor digitorum
infraspinatus*
teres major
subscapularis*
latissimus dorsi
quadratus lumborum
gluteus maximus
erector spinae*
ANNOTATION KEY
Black text indicates active muscles
Gray text indicates stabilizing muscles
* indicates deep muscles


## BEST FOR

- biceps brachii
- latissimus dorsi
- deltoideus posterior
- deltoideus medialis
- rhomboideus
- teres major
- teres minor
- trapezius
- biceps femoris
- gastrocnemius
- flexor carpi radialis
- flexor digitorum
- extensor hallucis longus
- extensor digitorum longus
- triceps brachii
- brachialis
- pronator teres
- peroneus longus
- peroneus brevis
- levator scapulae
- subscapularis
- infraspinatus
- quadratus lumborum
- gluteus maximus
- extensor digitorum
- erector spinae
- tensor fasciae latae
- rectus femoris
- vastus medialis
- tibialis anterior
- tibialis posterior
- vastus lateralis
- piriformis
- gluteus medius

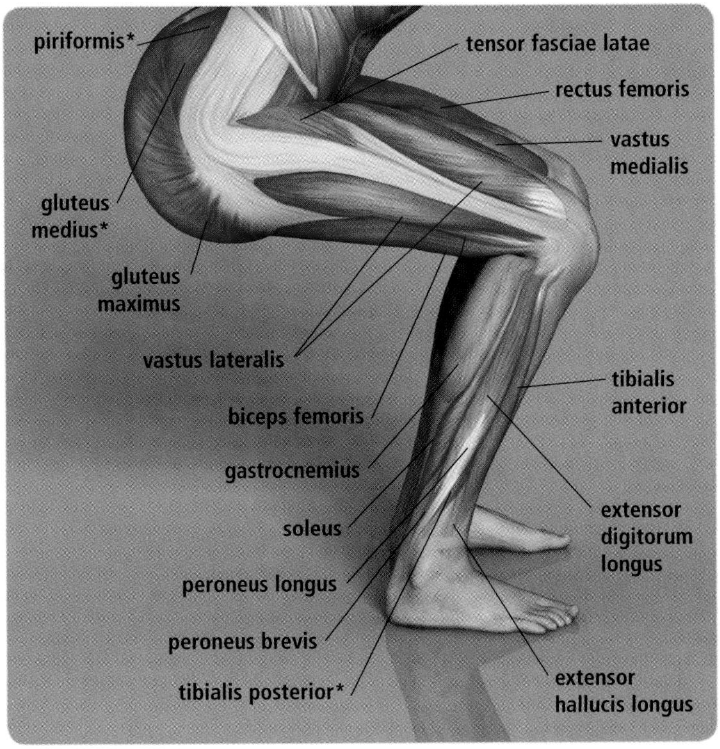

piriformis*
tensor fasciae latae
rectus femoris
vastus medialis
gluteus medius*
gluteus maximus
vastus lateralis
tibialis anterior
biceps femoris
gastrocnemius
soleus
extensor digitorum longus
peroneus longus
peroneus brevis
tibialis posterior*
extensor hallucis longus

# DROP & PULL

**LOOK FOR**
- All body parts to move at once.
- The feet to be involved in the movement.

**AVOID**
- Allowing hips to sag.
- Segmental movement of knees, hips, and spine.

**STABILIZE BY**
- Keeping the legs, hips, and spine rigid.
- Keeping your weight on the edge of your shoe as the body rotates.

1

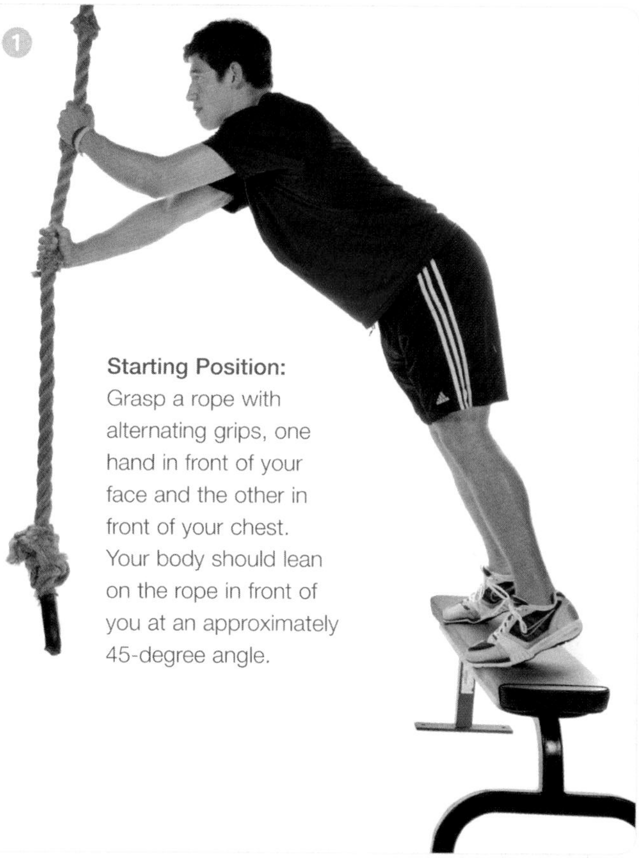

**Starting Position:** Grasp a rope with alternating grips, one hand in front of your face and the other in front of your chest. Your body should lean on the rope in front of you at an approximately 45-degree angle.

2

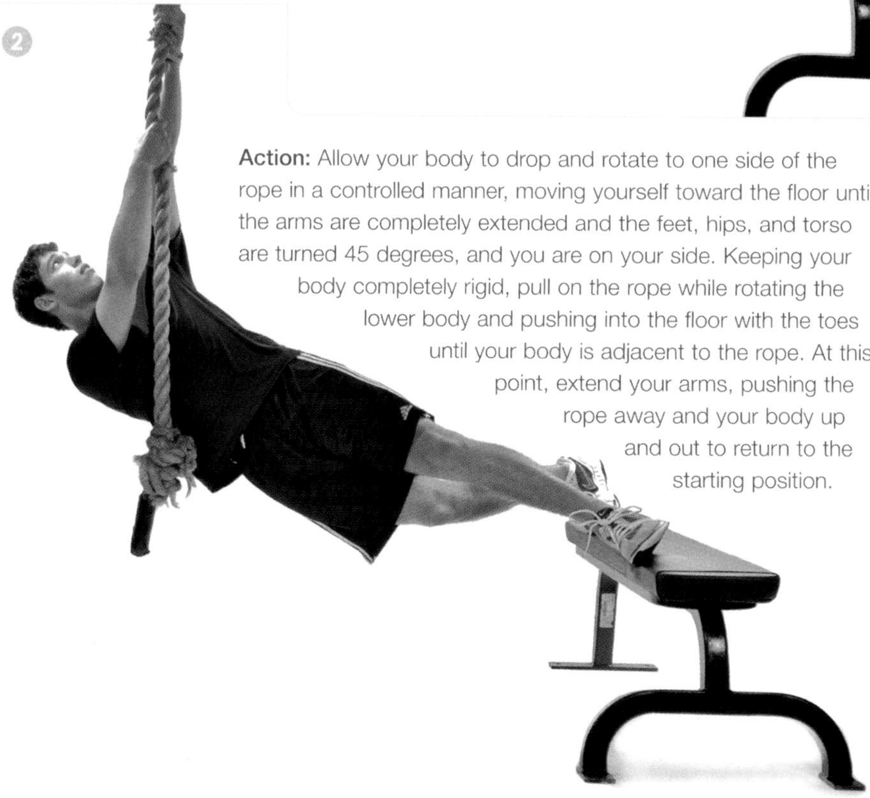

**Action:** Allow your body to drop and rotate to one side of the rope in a controlled manner, moving yourself toward the floor until the arms are completely extended and the feet, hips, and torso are turned 45 degrees, and you are on your side. Keeping your body completely rigid, pull on the rope while rotating the lower body and pushing into the floor with the toes until your body is adjacent to the rope. At this point, extend your arms, pushing the rope away and your body up and out to return to the starting position.

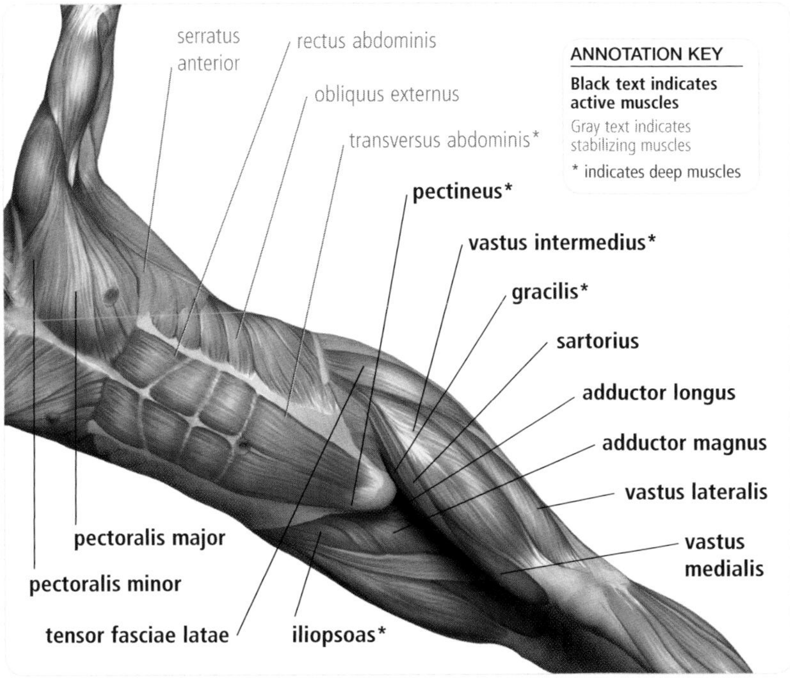
serratus anterior
rectus abdominis
obliquus externus
transversus abdominis*
pectineus*
vastus intermedius*
gracilis*
sartorius
adductor longus
adductor magnus
vastus lateralis
vastus medialis
pectoralis major
pectoralis minor
tensor fasciae latae
iliopsoas*

ANNOTATION KEY

**Black text indicates active muscles**

Gray text indicates stabilizing muscles

* indicates deep muscles

## BEST FOR

- serratus anterior
- obliquus externus
- rectus abdominis
- deltoideus posterior
- teres major
- teres minor
- infraspinatus
- subscapularis
- triceps brachii
- pectoralis major
- pectoralis minor
- latissimus dorsi
- transversus abdominis
- gluteus medius
- iliopsoas
- gluteus maximus
- pectineus
- vastus lateralis
- vastus medialis
- vastus intermedius
- biceps femoris
- semitendinosus
- tensor fasciae latae
- adductor longus
- adductor magnus
- gracilis
- quadratus lumborum
- erector spinae

**Movement Path:** The torso moves downward and rotates. The arms move toward the torso, and then across and away.

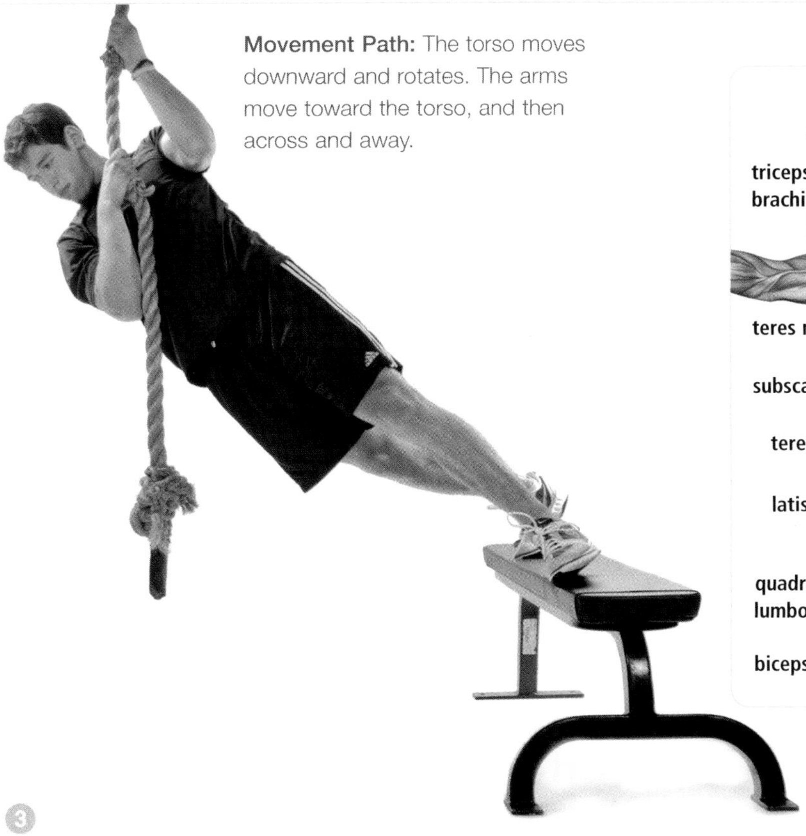
3

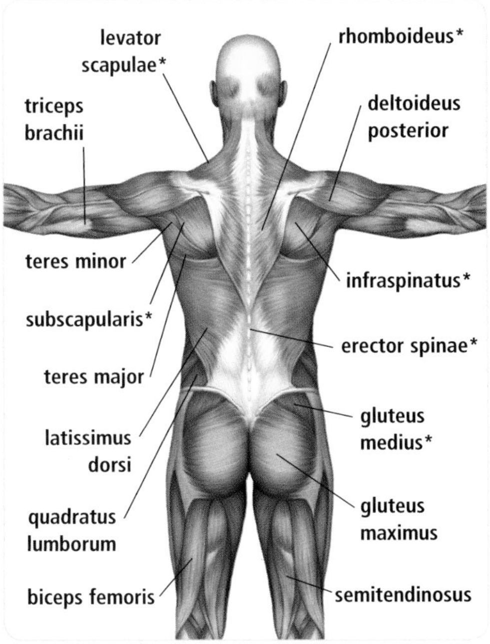
levator scapulae*
rhomboideus*
triceps brachii
deltoideus posterior
teres minor
infraspinatus*
subscapularis*
erector spinae*
teres major
gluteus medius*
latissimus dorsi
gluteus maximus
quadratus lumborum
biceps femoris
semitendinosus

# ROPE CHINS



1

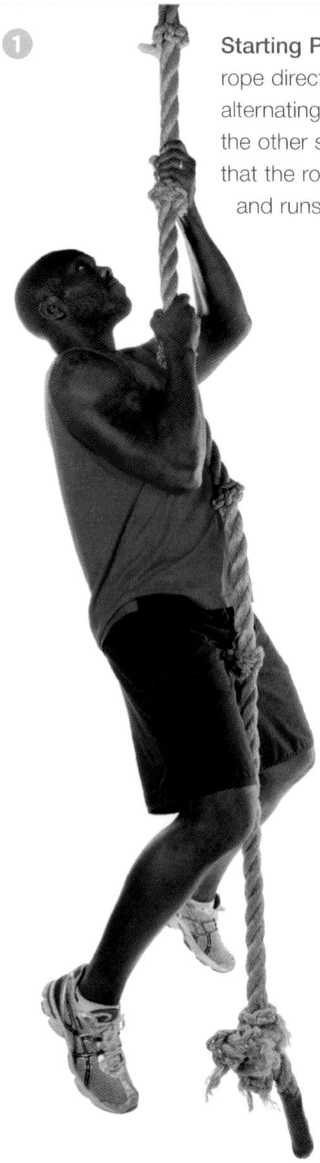

**Starting Position:** Standing on your tiptoes with a rope directly in front of you, grasp the rope with an alternating grip, one arm completely extended, and the other slightly above your head. Step forward so that the rope hangs directly adjacent to your chest and runs down the middle of your body.

2

**Action:** Bend your knees slightly and remove your body weight from the floor so that you are hanging onto the rope with only your hands. Pull down on the rope until your chin rises above your bottom hand. Be sure to keep the knees bent and the torso upright throughout the movement. Let yourself down slowly and repeat.

**Movement Path:** The arms move downward and inward toward the torso, the spine ascends vertically, and the knees remain slightly bent.

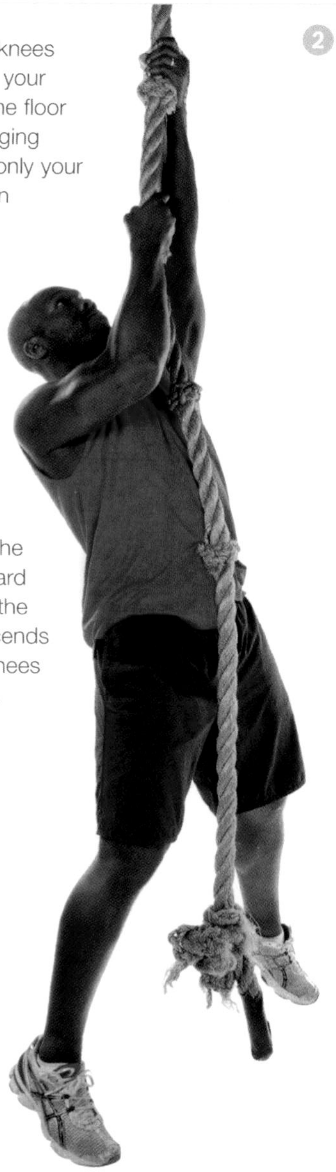

LOOK FOR

- Hips and chest to remain adjacent to rope.
- Spinal position to remain consistent.

AVOID

- Allowing the torso to rotate.

STABILIZE BY

- Pulling evenly with both arms.
- Keeping chest and head up.

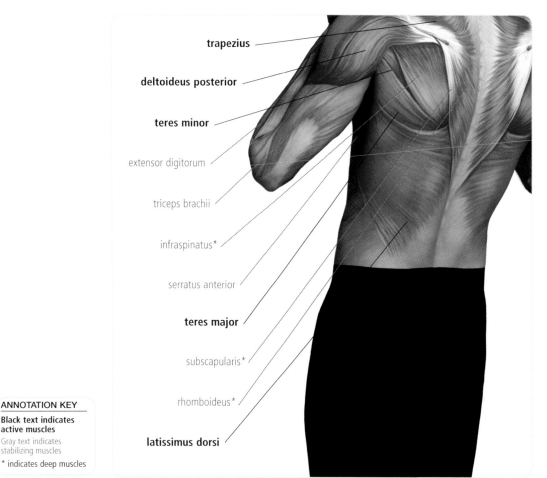

trapezius

deltoideus posterior

teres minor

extensor digitorum

triceps brachii

infraspinatus*

serratus anterior

teres major

subscapularis*

rhomboideus*

latissimus dorsi

**ANNOTATION KEY**

**Black text indicates active muscles**

Gray text indicates stabilizing muscles

* indicates deep muscles

pectoralis minor*

biceps brachii

brachialis

latissimus dorsi

brachioradialis

palmaris longus

pronator teres

flexor digitorum

flexor carpi radialis

## BEST FOR

- biceps brachii
- brachioradialis
- latissimus dorsi
- deltoideus posterior
- rhomboideus
- infraspinatus
- teres major
- teres minor
- trapezius
- pronator teres
- flexor carpi radialis
- flexor digitorum
- pectoralis minor
- deltoideus
- triceps brachii
- brachialis
- palmaris longus

# AB WHEEL

I chose this type of abdominal exercise for a very specific reason: the abdominals are the muscles that get the most attention paid to them with the least results. I have seen thousands of people perform endless ab crunches with very little to show for it—other than sore necks and backs.

The ab wheel—and variations I've chosen—generally involve a lot of muscles and, as far as bang for the buck, are without question the most effective movements I've seen. They produce results.

The joints involved are the hips, shoulders, and knees. The primary muscles used are the abdominals, obliques, and hip flexors. The muscles of the back and chest are all involved.

The primary benefits of this exercise are stomach and hip strength and flexibility, lower-back flexibility, and spinal and shoulder stability.

# AB WHEEL



**LOOK FOR**
- All joints to move at the same time.
- Your head and spine to remain aligned.

**AVOID**
- Rounding or arching your spine.
- Allowing your joints to move sequentially.
- Moving quickly in either direction.

**Starting Position:** On your knees, bend your torso forward at a 45-degree angle, with your spine in a neutral position. Extend your arms forward at a 45- to 90-degree angle to your torso, with your elbows straight and your hands grasping the wheel.

1

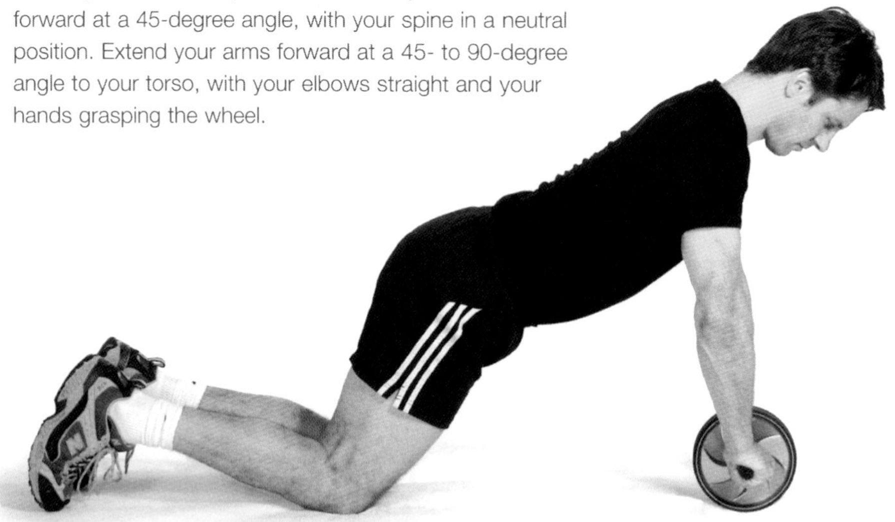

**Action:** Inhale, and extend your arms forward, allowing your torso to drop until your chest is almost parallel to the floor, rolling the wheel in a straight line away from you. Your hips move forward, following your torso, but your knees remain stationary. Exhale, and draw your arms and hips back simultaneously; your torso elevates and returns to the starting position.

2

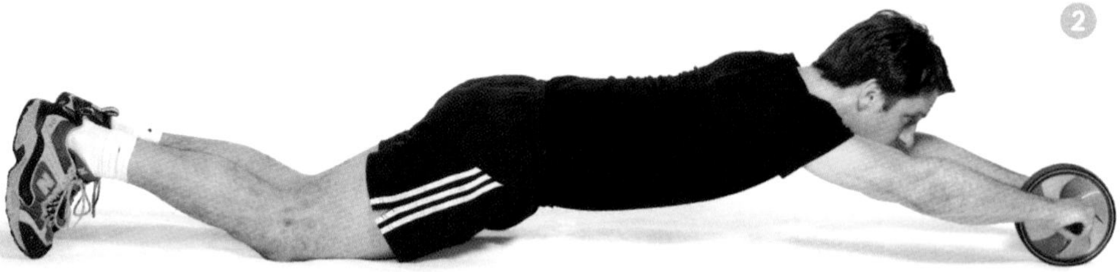

**Movement Path:** Your center of mass is translated forward and downward as your arms and hips extend into a linear position, with your knees as the fulcrum.

**STABILIZE BY**
- Pulling your abdomen up and in.
- Keeping your shoulders down and back throughout the movement.
- Keeping your arms extended and your wrists solid.
- Maintaining a neutral spinal position throughout the movement.

## BEST FOR

- iliacus
- iliopsoas
- latissimus dorsi
- obliquus externus
- obliquus internus
- pectoralis major
- rectus abdominis
- rectus femoris
- serratus anterior
- teres major
- teres minor
- triceps brachii
- deltoideus
- rhomboideus
- tensor fasciae latae
- infraspinatus
- triceps brachii
- brachialis
- biceps brachii
- extensor carpi radialis
- flexor carpi radialis
- flexor digitorum
- extensor digitorum
- quadratus lumborum

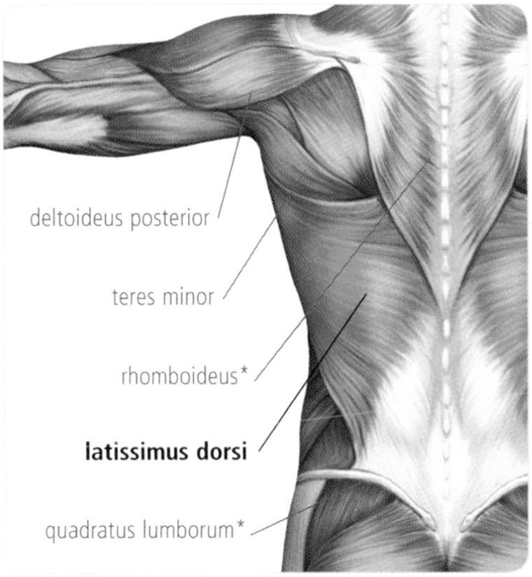
deltoideus posterior
teres minor
rhomboideus*
latissimus dorsi
quadratus lumborum*

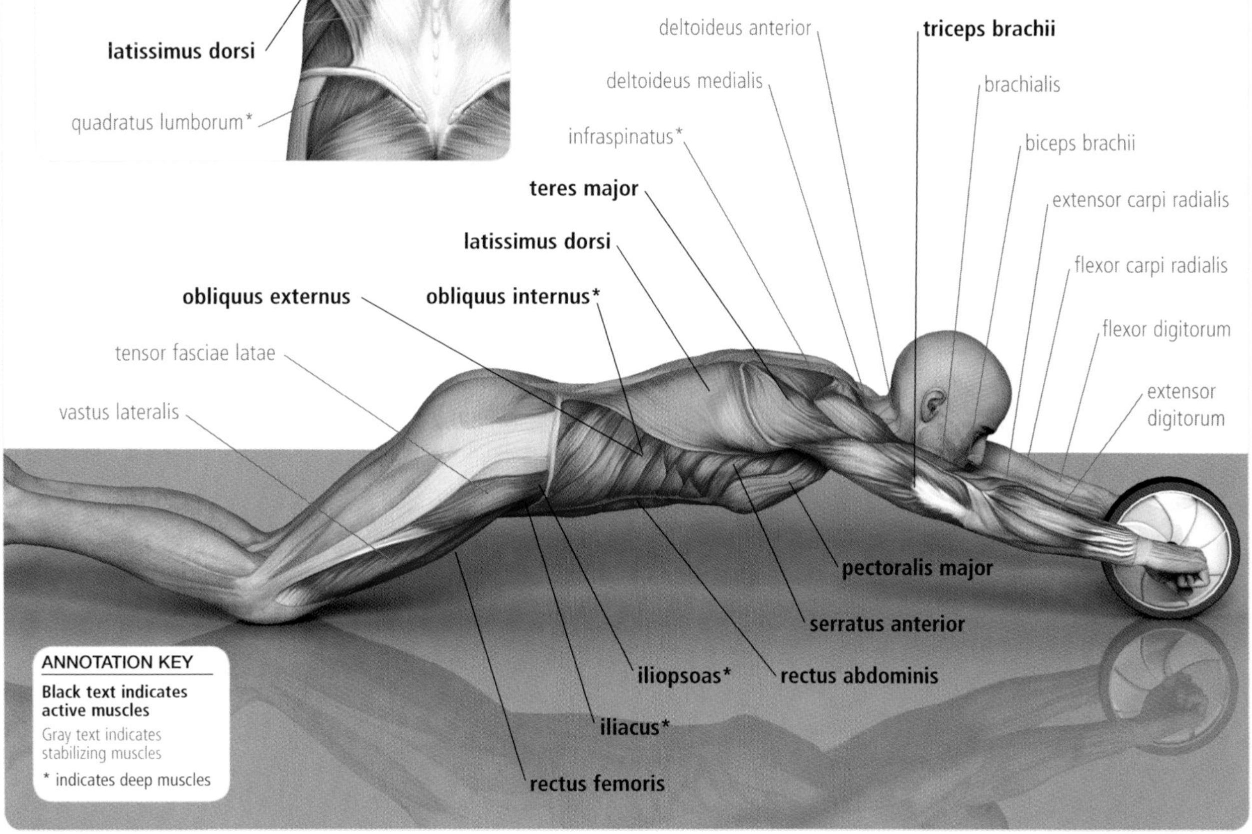
deltoideus anterior
triceps brachii
deltoideus medialis
brachialis
infraspinatus*
biceps brachii
teres major
extensor carpi radialis
latissimus dorsi
flexor carpi radialis
obliquus externus
obliquus internus*
flexor digitorum
tensor fasciae latae
extensor digitorum
vastus lateralis
pectoralis major
serratus anterior
iliopsoas*
rectus abdominis
iliacus*
rectus femoris

ANNOTATION KEY
**Black text indicates active muscles**
Gray text indicates stabilizing muscles
* indicates deep muscles

MODIFICATION
**Similar Difficulty:**
Replace the wheel with a physio ball; your hands begin higher up.

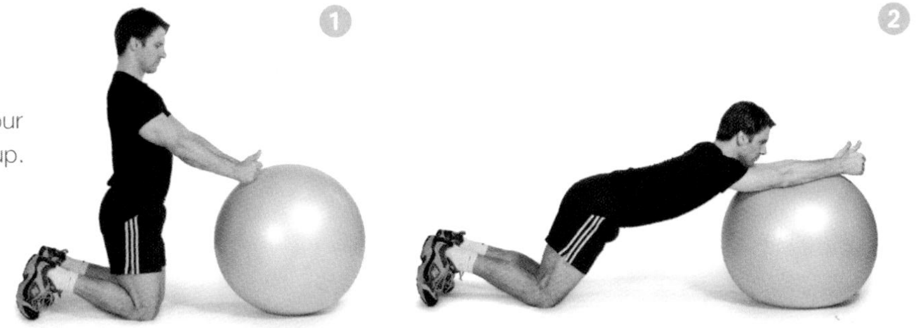
1
2

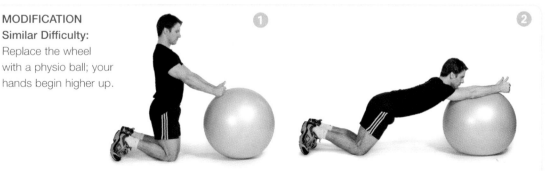

# PLOW ON PHYSIO BALL



**Starting Position:** Place your hands on the ground, with your legs extended so that the tops of your shoes are on top of a physio ball in a push-up position. Keep your spine neutral.

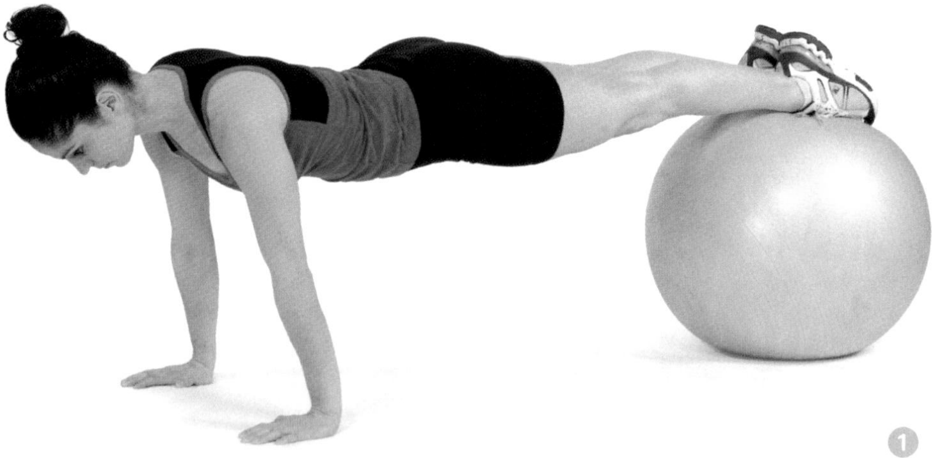

1

**Action:** Pull your knees up toward your chest while flexing your feet, balancing your toes on the ball, driving your hips toward the ceiling, and retracting your abdomen.

**Movement Path:** Your torso flexes in a straight line and a single plane. Your feet move up toward your midline in a horizontal plane.

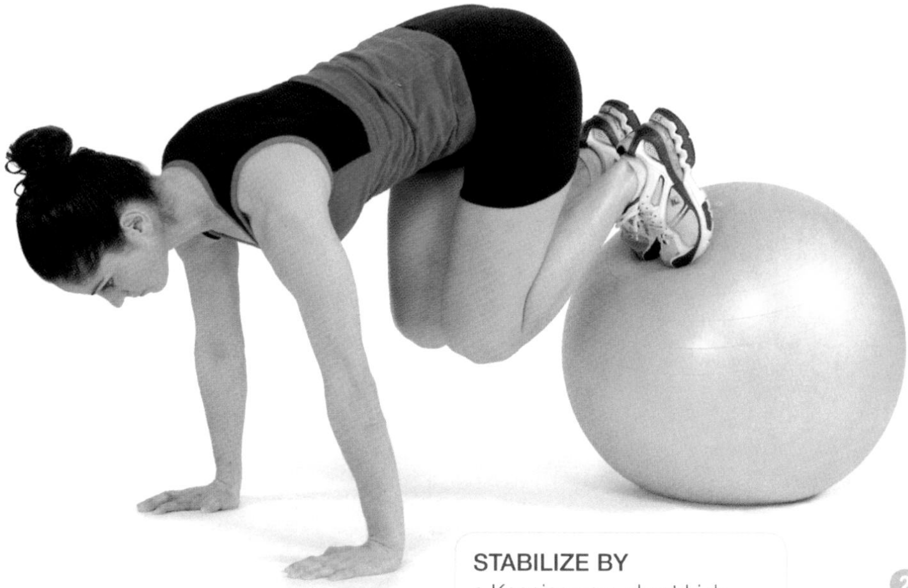

2

LOOK FOR

- A simultaneous movement while your hips raise, so that your spine is at a 45-degree angle from your hip to your shoulder from the ground.

AVOID

- Dropping your knees toward the floor.
- Bending your elbows.
- Allowing your shoulders to either elevate toward your ears or round forward.

STABILIZE BY

- Keeping your chest high and contracted.
- Elongating your neck and extending your elbows throughout the movement.

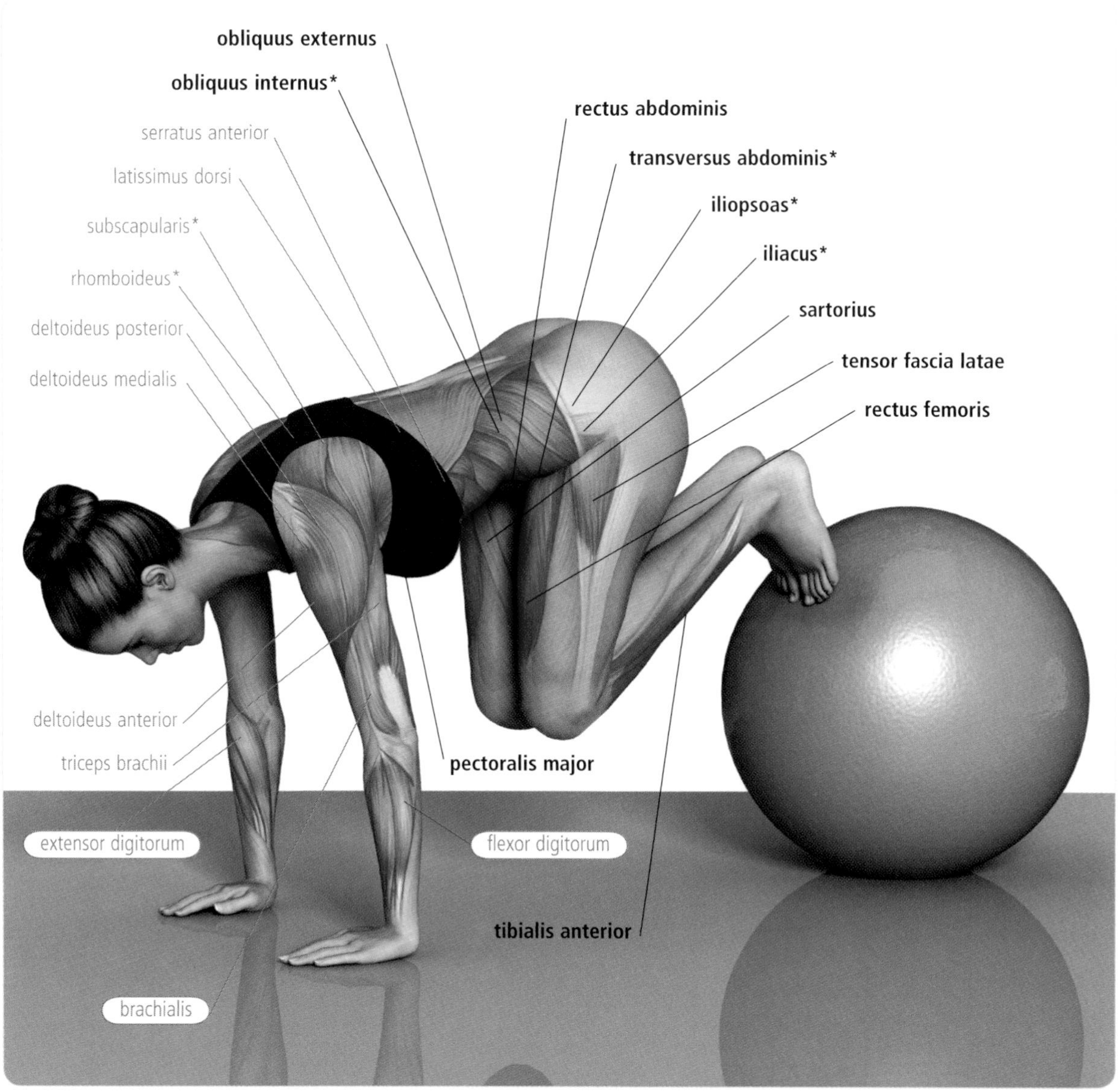

obliquus externus
obliquus internus*
serratus anterior
latissimus dorsi
subscapularis*
rhomboideus*
deltoideus posterior
deltoideus medialis
rectus abdominis
transversus abdominis*
iliopsoas*
iliacus*
sartorius
tensor fascia latae
rectus femoris
deltoideus anterior
triceps brachii
pectoralis major
extensor digitorum
flexor digitorum
tibialis anterior
brachialis


ANNOTATION KEY

**Black text indicates active muscles**

Gray text indicates stabilizing muscles

* indicates deep muscles

## BEST FOR

- iliacus
- iliopsoas
- obliquus externus
- obliquus internus
- rectus abdominis
- sartorius
- tibialis anterior
- transversus abdominis
- tensor fasciae latae
- rectus femoris
- serratus anterior
- brachialis
- extensor digitorum
- triceps brachii
- deltoideus posterior
- rhomboideus
- subscapularis
- latissimus dorsi
- pectoralis major

# PLOW WITH ROTATION



1 **Starting Position:** Assume the top of a push-up position with your hands slightly wider than shoulder width, with your feet on a towel or a small physio ball.

**Action:** Keeping your shoulder girdle solid, draw both knees upward while simultaneously rotating the hips and lower body until the ankle is rotated 90 degrees and both feet are on edge and pointing to one side. Extend the knees and hips, and rotate back to the starting position. Repeat on other side.

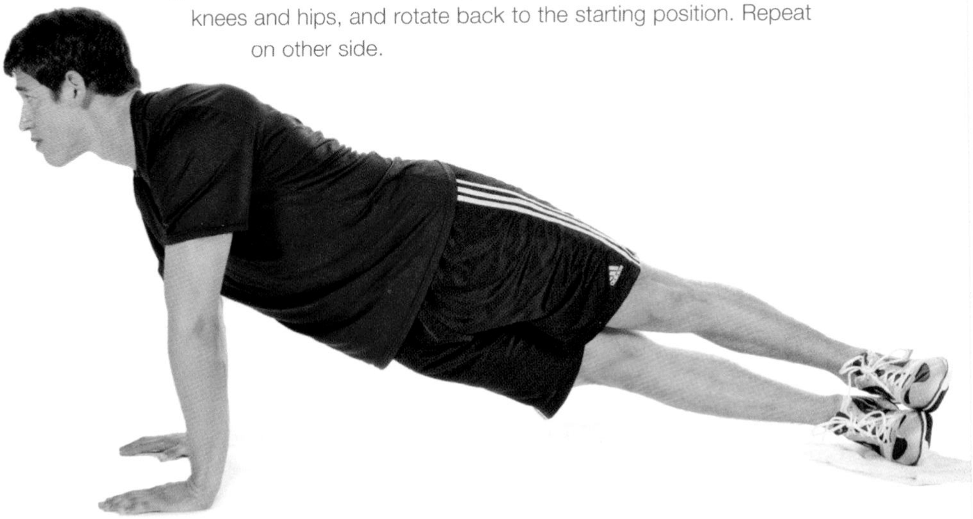

**LOOK FOR**
- A smooth and even movement.
- The hips to remain at the same height throughout the movement.
- Your feet to be solid and bearing weight on the edge of the shoe.
- The knees to remain parallel.

**AVOID**
- Allowing your back to either arch or sag.
- Moving your shoulders.
- Separating either your knees or feet.

**Movement Path:** The torso remains stationary, while the hips and knees flex and rotate.

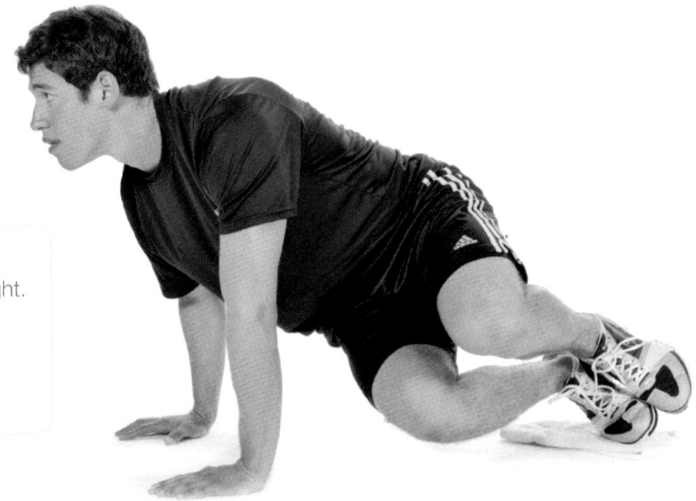

2

**STABILIZE BY**
- Keeping elbows straight.
- Keeping spine high.
- Allowing weight to be evenly distributed on support.

## BEST FOR

- rectus abdominis
- obliquus internus
- obliquus externus
- transversus abdominis
- rectus femoris
- sartorius
- iliopsoas
- iliacus
- triceps brachii
- deltoideus anterior
- rhomboideus
- infraspinatus
- teres major
- latissimus dorsi
- quadratus lumborum
- serratus anterior
- coracobrachialis
- erector spinae
- gluteus maximus

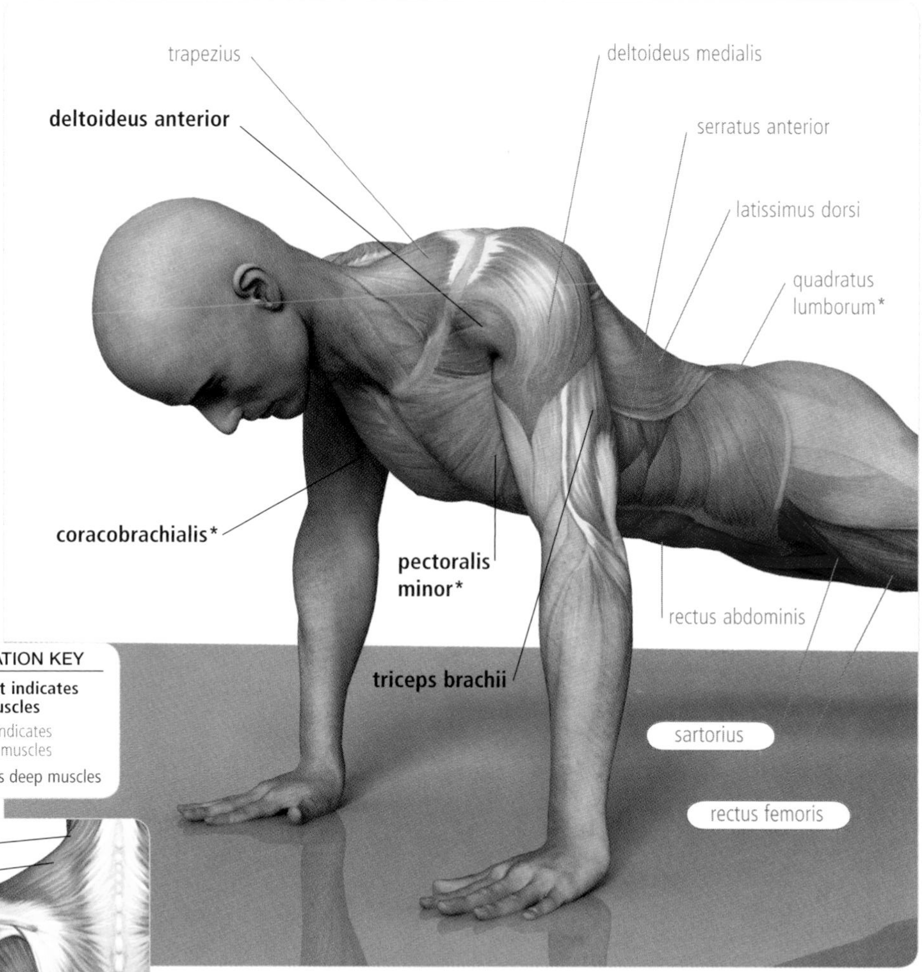

trapezius
deltoideus medialis
deltoideus anterior
serratus anterior
latissimus dorsi
quadratus lumborum*
coracobrachialis*
pectoralis minor*
rectus abdominis
triceps brachii
sartorius
rectus femoris


ANNOTATION KEY

**Black text indicates active muscles**

Gray text indicates stabilizing muscles

* indicates deep muscles

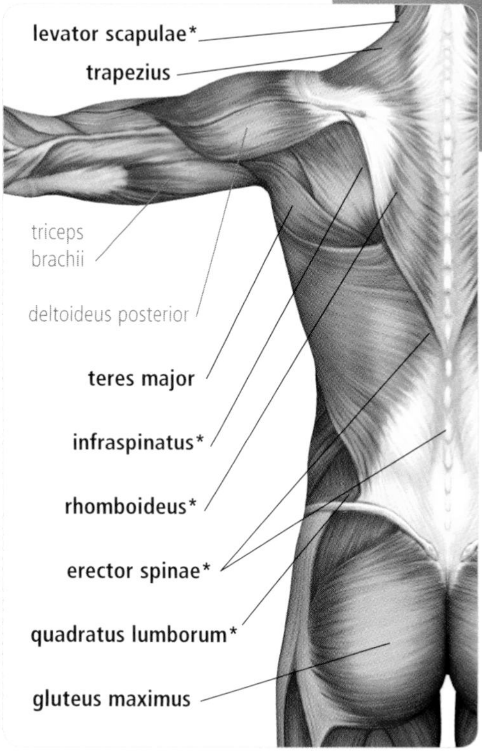

levator scapulae*
trapezius
triceps brachii
deltoideus posterior
teres major
infraspinatus*
rhomboideus*
erector spinae*
quadratus lumborum*
gluteus maximus


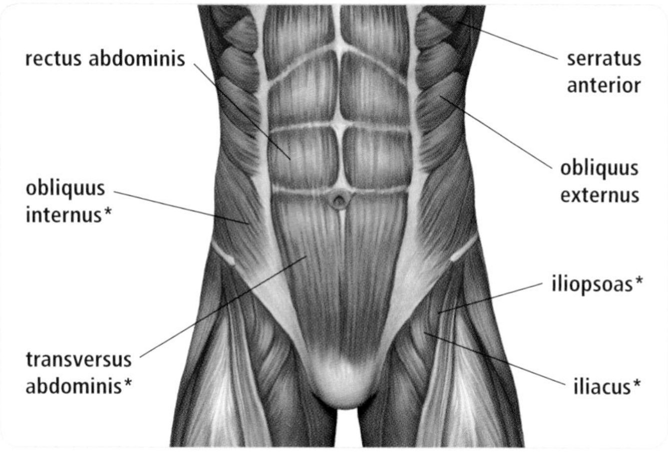

rectus abdominis
serratus anterior
obliquus externus
obliquus internus*
iliopsoas*
transversus abdominis*
iliacus*

# STRAIGHT-LEG HANGING RAISE

AB WHEEL

**Starting Position:** Grab a bar with your palms facing forward and preferably with your back against a wall. The feet should not be contacting the ground.

**Action:** Pulling on the bar so that the shoulders are down and away from your ears, keep the legs straight (knees and ankles taut). Kick forward, bringing both legs up to horizontal, keeping your lower back flat, and exhaling. Slowly allow your legs to drop in a controlled manner until they are directly beneath you.

## LOOK FOR
- Legs to move in a controlled manner.
- A 90-degree angle in torso/hip.
- Shoulders to remain down.

## AVOID
- Swinging and creating momentum.
- Allowing hips to roll upward and forward.
- Arching the back.

**Movement Path:** The torso remains motionless and the lower body flexes and moves upward and forward in a curvilinear fashion to 90 degrees at the hips.

## STABILIZE BY
- Keeping stomach tight, your chest up, and your legs completely rigid.

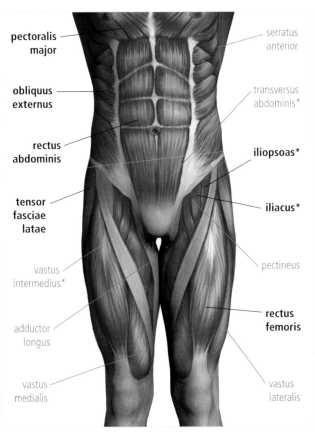

pectoralis major

serratus anterior

obliquus externus

transversus abdominis*

rectus abdominis

iliopsoas*

tensor fasciae latae

iliacus*

vastus intermedius*

pectineus

adductor longus

rectus femoris

vastus medialis

vastus lateralis

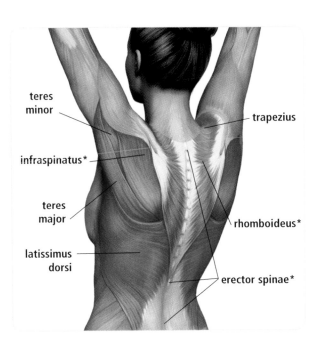

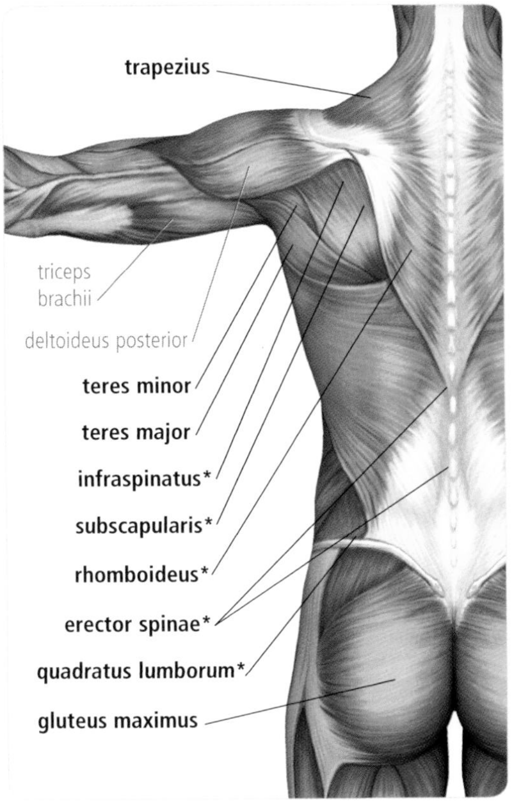

teres minor

trapezius

infraspinatus*

teres major

rhomboideus*

latissimus dorsi

erector spinae*

trapezius

triceps brachii

deltoideus posterior

teres minor

teres major

infraspinatus*

subscapularis*

rhomboideus*

erector spinae*

quadratus lumborum*

gluteus maximus

## BEST FOR

- rectus abdominis
- obliquus externus
- iliopsoas
- iliacus
- rectus femoris
- tensor fasciae latae
- pectoralis major
- latissimus dorsi
- teres major
- teres minor
- triceps brachii
- trapezius

- rhomboideus
- subscapularis
- infraspinatus
- transversus abdominis
- vastus lateralis
- vastus medialis
- vastus intermedius
- rectus femoris
- erector spinae
- quadratus lumborum

### ANNOTATION KEY

**Black text indicates active muscles**

Gray text indicates stabilizing muscles

* indicates deep muscles

# BENT-KNEE HANGING RAISE WITH MEDICINE BALL

**STABILIZE BY**
- Keeping your upper arms parallel and your shoulders down.
- Gripping the stirrups firmly.
- Keeping your legs parallel.

**LOOK FOR**
- Your knees to bend as your upper legs are raised (your lower legs remain vertical).
- Your legs to move upward together.

**AVOID**
- Swinging.
- Extending your arms upward to more than 5 degrees above horizontal.
- Moving your hips backward.

**Starting Position:** Clasping a medicine ball between your knees, hang with your upper arms in stirrups, with your elbows bent at 90-degree angles, pointing forward just above shoulder height. Grasp the stirrups with your hands and make sure your torso, legs, and hips are straight.

**Action:** Pull your upper arms and elbows downward and your upper legs and knees upward toward your elbows, flexing at the hips. Tuck your hips forward and bring your chest forward slightly. Return to the starting position in a slow and controlled manner. Exhale as you rise and inhale as you return to the starting position.

**Movement Path:** Your torso rounds slightly as your hips flex upward and your upper arms are pulled downward. Your center of mass makes no appreciable movement.

# BENT-KNEE HANGING RAISE WITH MEDICINE BALL • AB WHEEL

## BEST FOR

- iliacus
- iliopsoas
- pectineus
- rectus abdominis
- rectus femoris
- tensor fasciae latae
- pectoralis major
- pectoralis minor
- obliquus externus
- vastus intermedius
- adductor longus
- vastus medialis
- serratus anterior
- coracobrachialis
- triceps brachii
- teres minor
- teres major
- rhomboideus
- infraspinatus
- latissimus dorsi
- trapezius

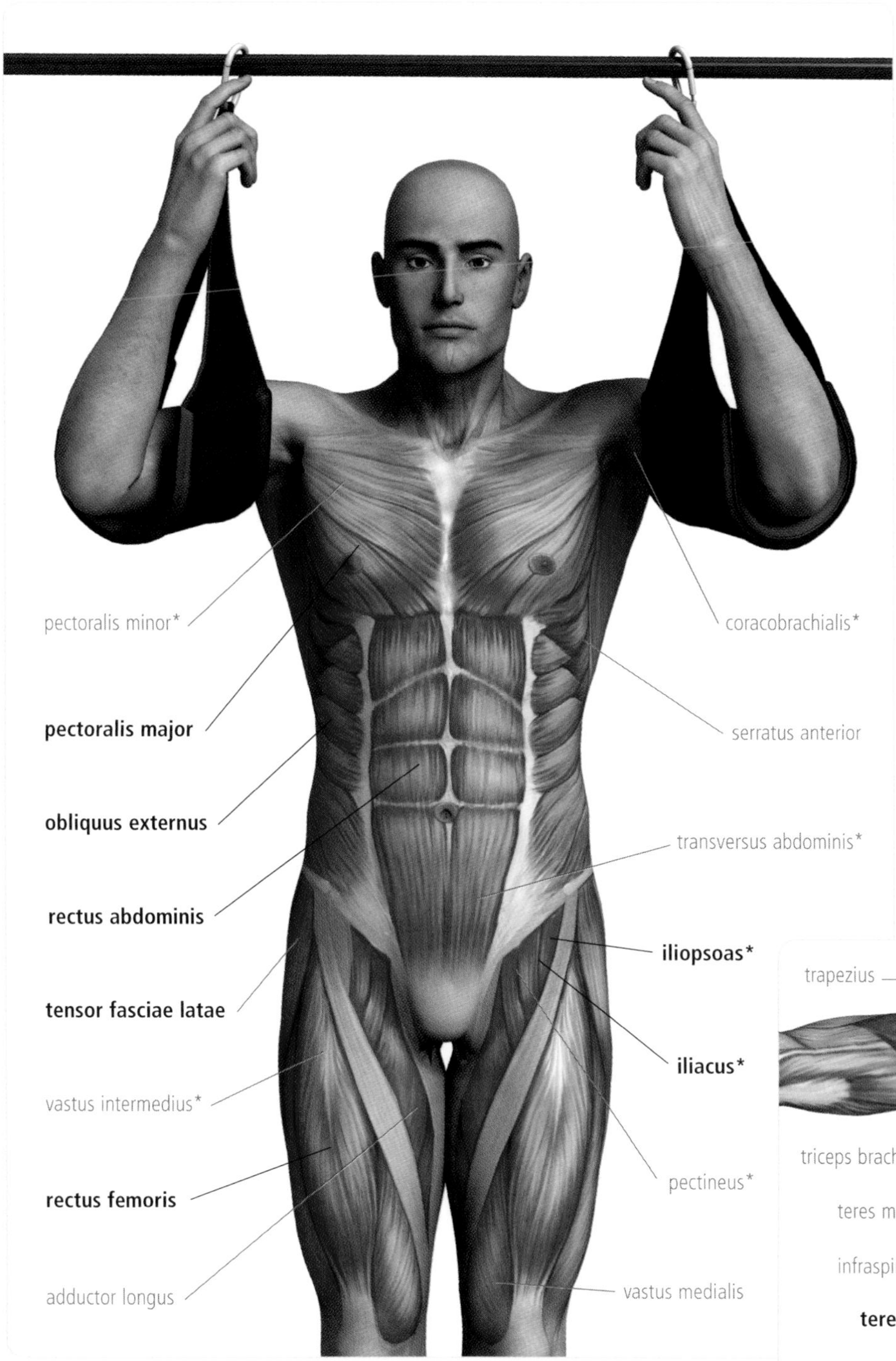
pectoralis minor*
pectoralis major
obliquus externus
rectus abdominis
tensor fasciae latae
vastus intermedius*
rectus femoris
adductor longus
coracobrachialis*
serratus anterior
transversus abdominis*
iliopsoas*
iliacus*
pectineus*
vastus medialis

ANNOTATION KEY

**Black text indicates active muscles**

Gray text indicates stabilizing muscles

* indicates deep muscles

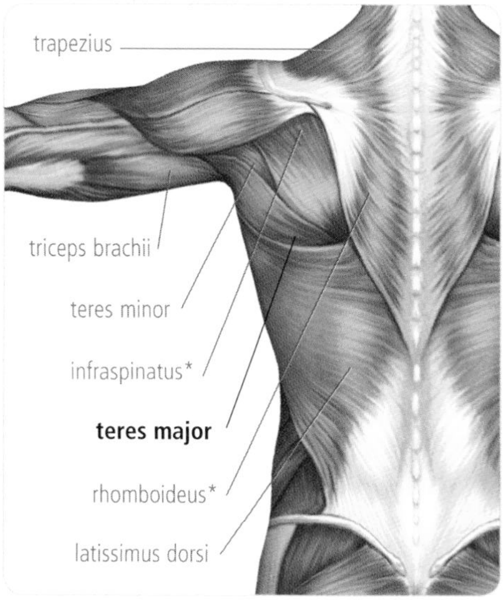
trapezius
triceps brachii
teres minor
infraspinatus*
teres major
rhomboideus*
latissimus dorsi

# HANGING RAISE WITH ROTATION



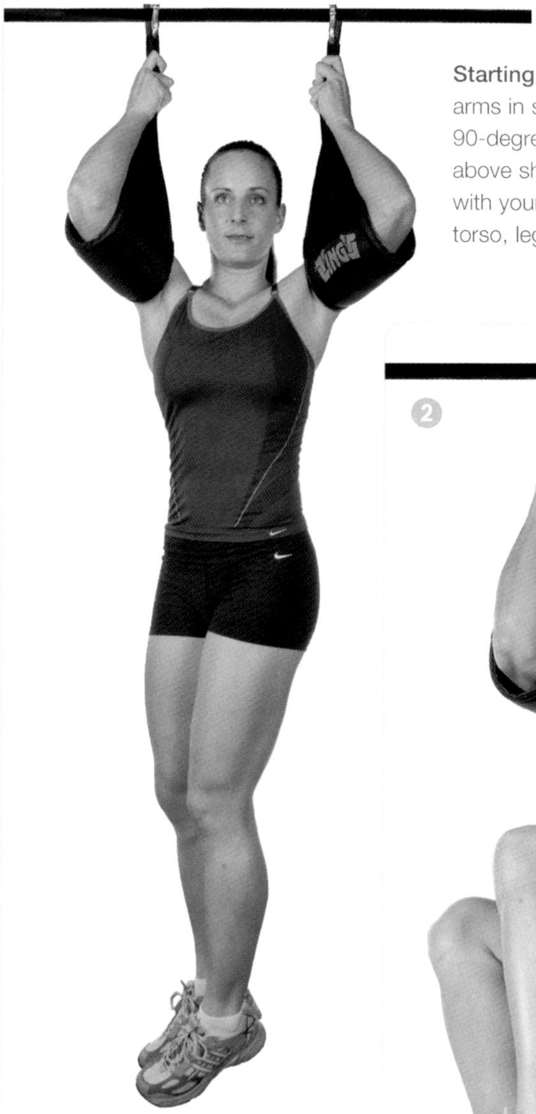

1

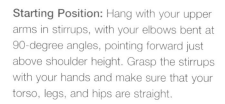

**Starting Position:** Hang with your upper arms in stirrups, with your elbows bent at 90-degree angles, pointing forward just above shoulder height. Grasp the stirrups with your hands and make sure that your torso, legs, and hips are straight.

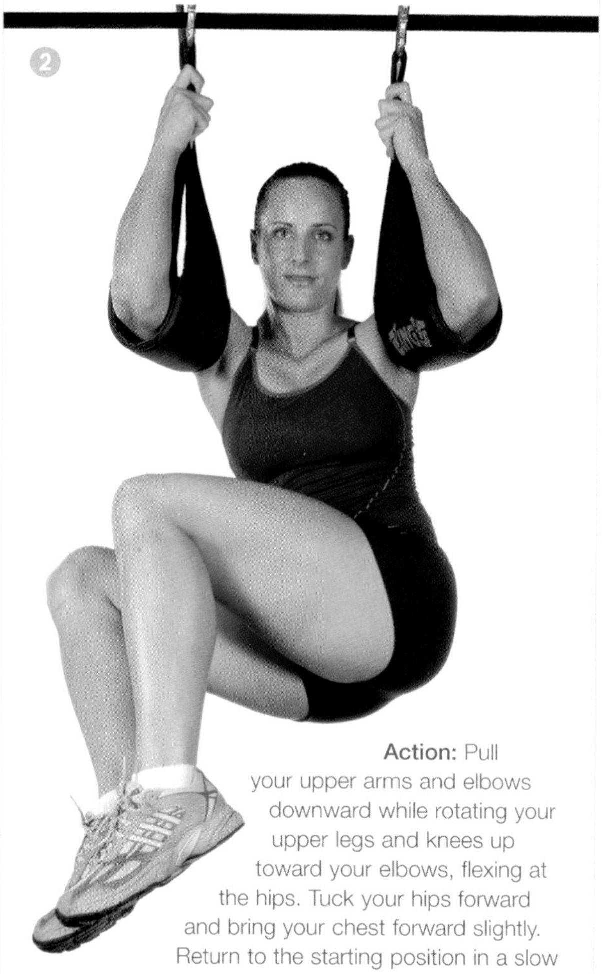

2

**Action:** Pull your upper arms and elbows downward while rotating your upper legs and knees up toward your elbows, flexing at the hips. Tuck your hips forward and bring your chest forward slightly. Return to the starting position in a slow and controlled manner. Exhale as you rise, and inhale as you return to the starting position.

LOOK FOR
- Your knees to bend as your upper legs are raised (your lower legs remain vertical).
- Your legs to move upward together.
- Your legs to remain parallel.

AVOID
- Swinging.
- Extending your arms upward to more than 5 degrees above horizontal.
- Moving your hips backward.

STABILIZE BY
- Keeping your upper arms parallel and your shoulders down.
- Gripping the stirrups firmly.
- Keeping your legs parallel.

## BEST FOR

- iliacus
- iliopsoas
- rectus abdominis
- rectus femoris
- tensor fasciae latae
- pectoralis major
- pectineus
- vastus intermedius
- adductor longus
- vastus lateralis
- vastus medialis
- coracobrachialis
- serratus anterior
- trapezius
- triceps brachii
- teres major
- infraspinatus
- rhomboideus
- subscapularis
- transversus abdominis
- trapezius
- deltoideus
- quadratus lumborum
- gluteus medius
- obliquus externus
- obliquus internus

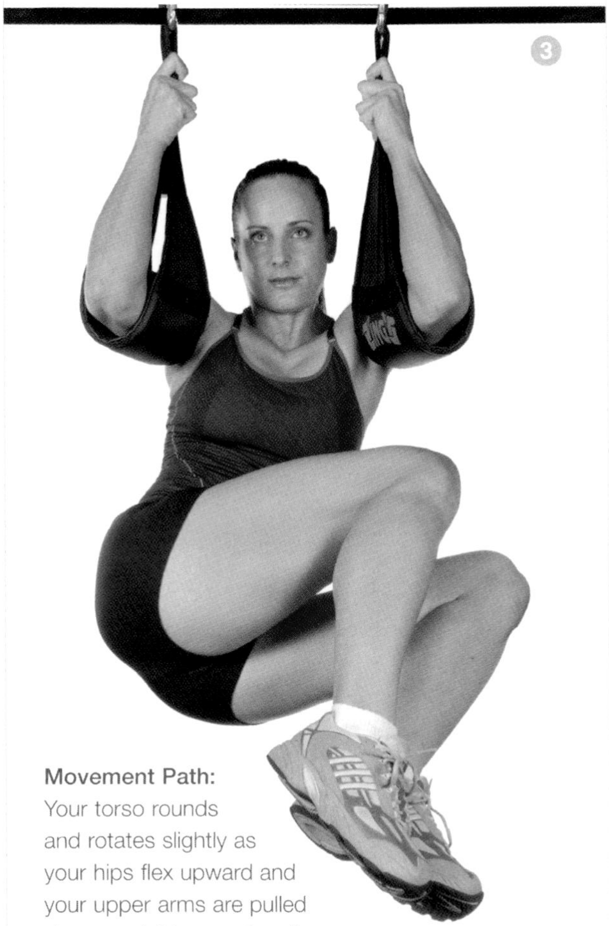
3

**Movement Path:** Your torso rounds and rotates slightly as your hips flex upward and your upper arms are pulled downward. Your center of mass makes no appreciable movement.

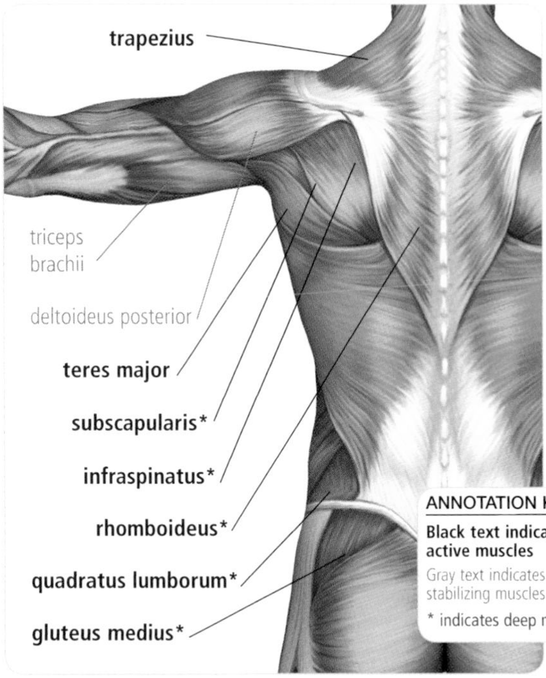
trapezius
triceps brachii
deltoideus posterior
teres major
subscapularis*
infraspinatus*
rhomboideus*
quadratus lumborum*
gluteus medius*

ANNOTATION KEY
**Black text indicates active muscles**
Gray text indicates stabilizing muscles
* indicates deep muscles

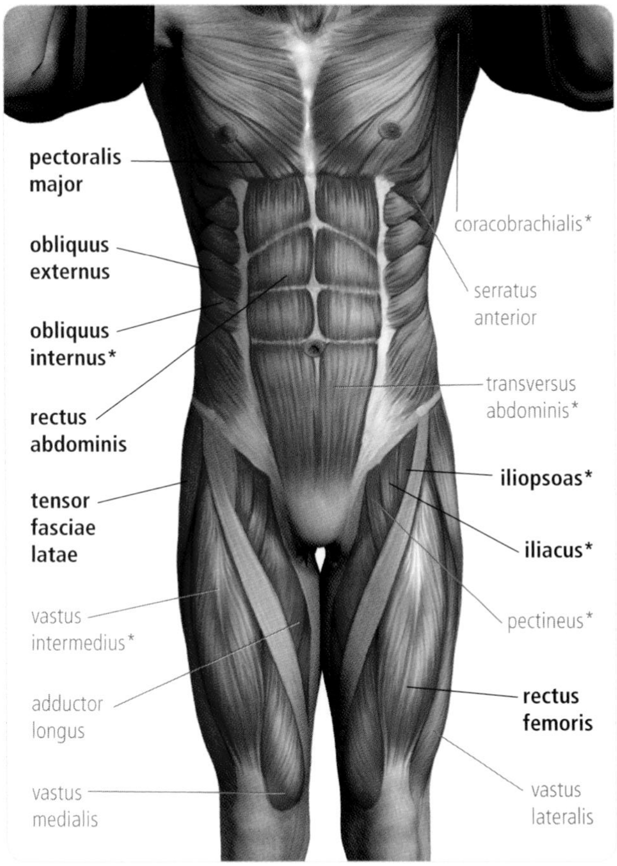
pectoralis major
obliquus externus
obliquus internus*
rectus abdominis
tensor fasciae latae
vastus intermedius*
adductor longus
vastus medialis
coracobrachialis*
serratus anterior
transversus abdominis*
iliopsoas*
iliacus*
pectineus*
rectus femoris
vastus lateralis

# V-UPS WITH PHYSIO BALL

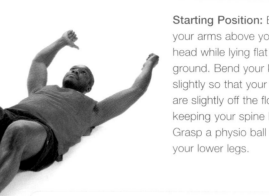

1

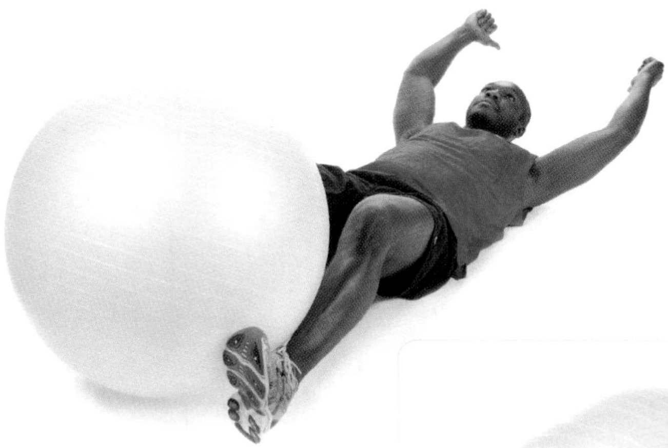

**Starting Position:** Extend your arms above your head while lying flat on the ground. Bend your knees slightly so that your feet are slightly off the floor, keeping your spine long. Grasp a physio ball with your lower legs.

2

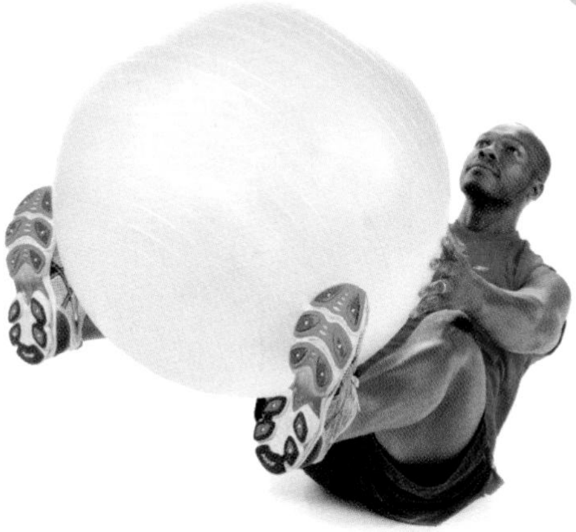

**Action:** Push your lower back into the ground, keeping your spine long. Contract your abdominal muscles and lift your upper back off the ground and forward, exhaling as you come up. Simultaneously reach upward with both arms and legs by folding the torso. Transfer the ball from your feet to your hands, and slowly return to the starting position. Repeat, and return the ball to your feet.

**Movement Path:** Your torso curves from your mid-lower back to the top of your head, in a straight line up toward the knees.

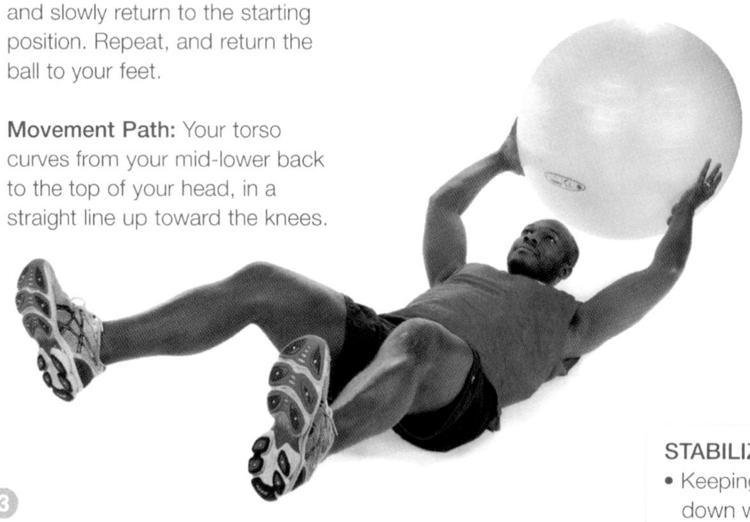

3

**LOOK FOR**
- A slight pause at the top of the movement.
- A smooth movement throughout the entire length of your spine.
- Your abdominal muscles to contract and pull in.
- Your hips to remain stable.
- The knees to remain in the same position.

**AVOID**
- Bending the knees excessively.
- Using momentum for any part of the movement.
- Arching your back or elevating your feet.

**STABILIZE BY**
- Keeping your shoulders down with your elbows widely spread.
- Keeping your hips even and your feet flat.

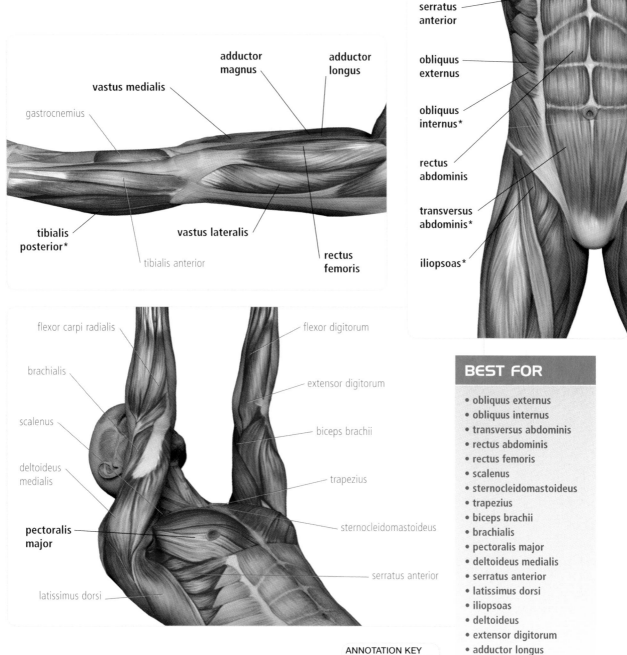

**serratus anterior**

**obliquus externus**

**obliquus internus***

**rectus abdominis**

**transversus abdominis***

**iliopsoas***

**adductor magnus**

**adductor longus**

**vastus medialis**

gastrocnemius

tibialis posterior*

tibialis anterior

**vastus lateralis**

**rectus femoris**

flexor carpi radialis

flexor digitorum

brachialis

extensor digitorum

scalenus

biceps brachii

deltoideus medialis

trapezius

pectoralis major

sternocleidomastoideus

serratus anterior

latissimus dorsi

## BEST FOR

- obliquus externus
- obliquus internus
- transversus abdominis
- rectus abdominis
- rectus femoris
- scalenus
- sternocleidomastoideus
- trapezius
- biceps brachii
- brachialis
- pectoralis major
- deltoideus medialis
- serratus anterior
- latissimus dorsi
- iliopsoas
- deltoideus
- extensor digitorum
- adductor longus
- adductor magnus
- vastus medialis
- vastus lateralis
- tibialis posterior
- gastrocnemius
- tibialis anterior
- flexor digitorum

### ANNOTATION KEY

**Black text indicates active muscles**

Gray text indicates stabilizing muscles

* indicates deep muscles

# HAND WALK-OUT



**Starting Position:** From a standing position, bend forward from the waist, and place your hands on the ground in front of you, slightly wider than your feet. Keep your knees as straight as possible.

1

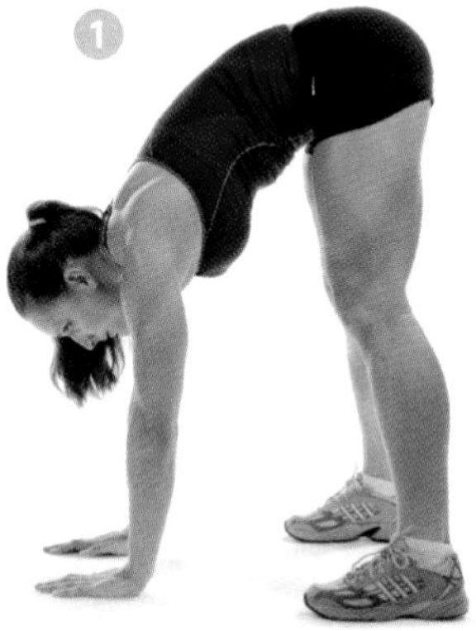

2

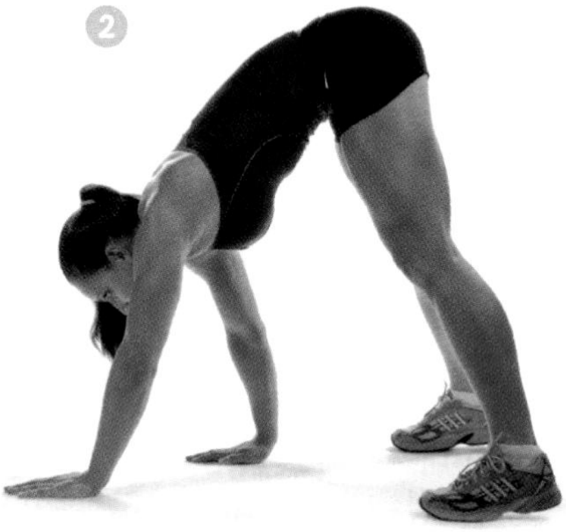

**Action:** Shift your weight to your hands and slowly "walk" them forward while keeping the knees straight, the hips up, and the spine straight. Continue dropping out until you've reached horizontal or push-up position. Return by walking your hands back toward the starting position and pushing your hips upward, folding the torso at the hips.

3

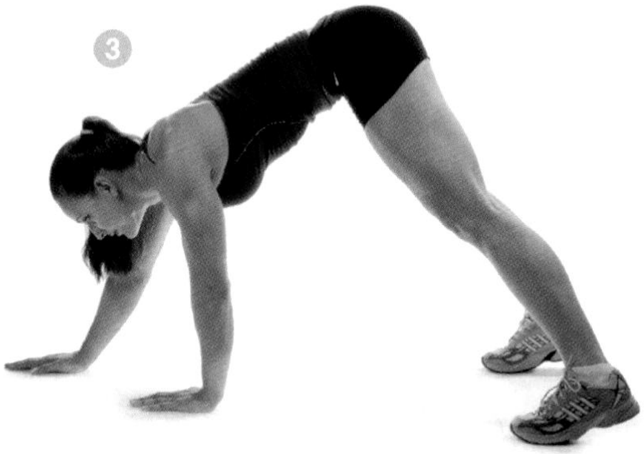

**Movement Path:** The shoulders move forward as the hips and legs move downward.

4

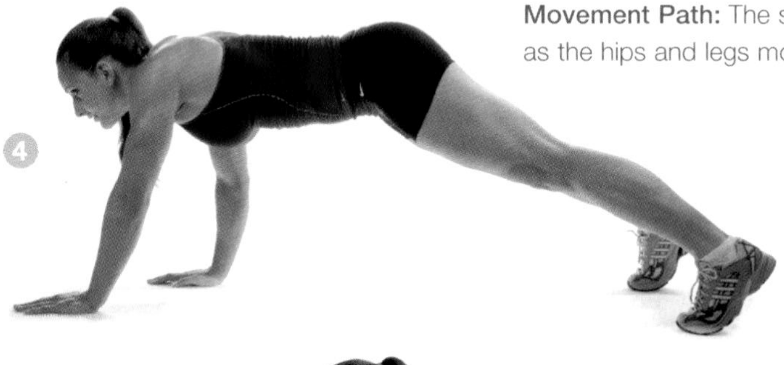

5

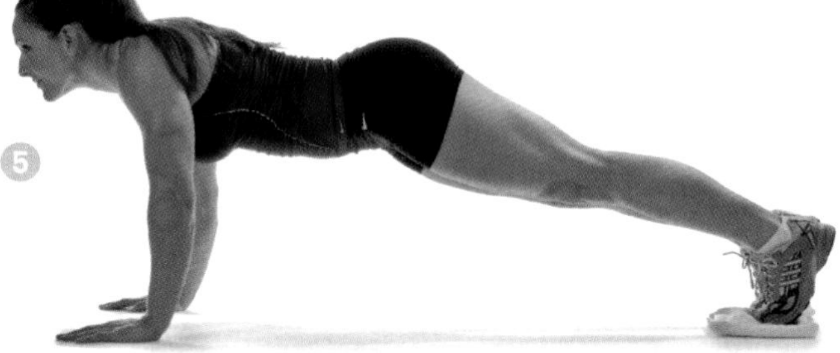

STABILIZE BY
- Pulling your abdomen up and in.
- Keeping the spine and legs straight.

LOOK FOR
- Spine and legs to remain straight.
- Slow, steady movement.

AVOID
- Bending the knees or spine.
- Allowing the elbows to bend.

deltoideus anterior

trapezius

triceps brachii

latissimus dorsi

serratus anterior

iliopsoas*

vastus intermedius*

rectus femoris

tibialis anterior

flexor carpi radialis

vastus medialis

vastus lateralis

extensor digitorum

extensor carpi radialis

**ANNOTATION KEY**

**Black text indicates active muscles**

Gray text indicates stabilizing muscles

* indicates deep muscles

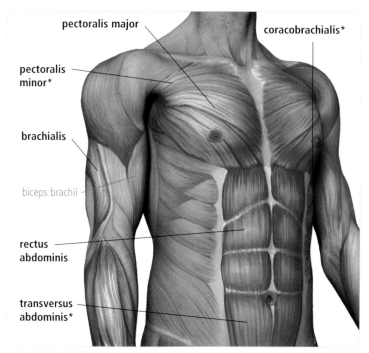

pectoralis major

coracobrachialis*

pectoralis minor*

brachialis

biceps brachii

rectus abdominis

transversus abdominis*

## BEST FOR

- pectoralis major
- pectoralis minor
- coracobrachialis
- deltoideus anterior
- triceps brachii
- iliopsoas
- vastus lateralis
- vastus medialis
- vastus intermedius
- rectus femoris
- transversus abdominis
- serratus anterior
- erector spinae
- trapezius
- latissimus dorsi
- quadratus lumborum
- brachialis
- tibialis anterior
- flexor carpi radialis
- extensor digitorum
- extensor carpi radialis
- biceps brachii

# FRONT PLANK



**Starting Position:** Lie facedown on the ground and fold your hands directly beneath your chin, with your elbows by your sides and both feet on your tiptoes.

**Action:** Raise the length of your torso to a horizontal position, with a slight arch in your lower back. Your shoulder blades should be flat and your spine long. Hold for 10 to 30 seconds.

**Movement Path:** None.

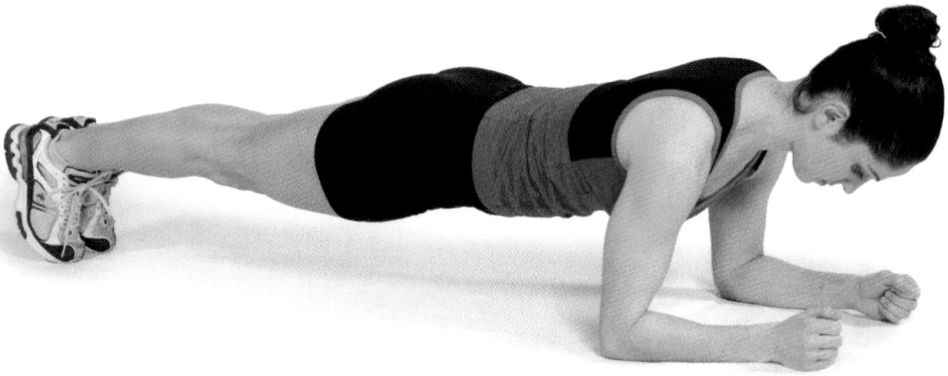

### LOOK FOR

- A neutral spinal position.
- Locked knees, with your ankles at 90-degree angles and your elbows directly under your shoulder joints.

### AVOID

- Rounding your spine, dropping your hips, and elevating your shoulders toward your ears.

### STABILIZE BY

- Keeping your spine neutral.
- Keeping your shoulders down and your head up.
- Maintaining the contraction of your gluteals and legs.
- Keeping your legs straight and your ankles bent at 90-degree angles, with your toes pointing directly into the ground.

### MODIFICATION

**Easier:** Raise your feet and rest your weight on your knees to shorten the lever.

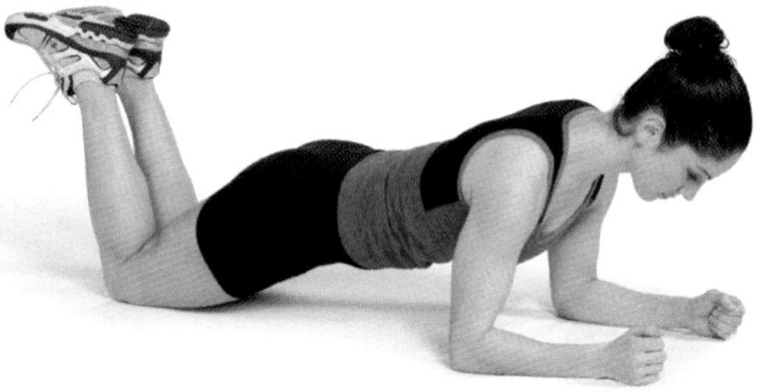

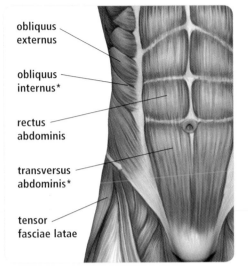

- obliquus externus
- obliquus internus*
- rectus abdominis
- transversus abdominis*
- tensor fasciae latae

## BEST FOR

- erector spinae
- iliacus
- iliopsoas
- obliquus internus
- obliquus externus
- rectus abdominis
- transversus abdominis
- rectus femoris
- serratus anterior
- splenius
- tibialis anterior
- vastus intermedius
- deltoideus
- pectoralis major
- rhomboideus
- latissimus dorsi
- quadratus lumborum
- tibialis anterior
- sartorius
- tensor fasciae latae

### ANNOTATION KEY

**Black text indicates active muscles**

Gray text indicates stabilizing muscles

* indicates deep muscles

latissimus dorsi

rhomboideus*

erector spinae*

serratus anterior

quadratus lumborum*

splenius*

iliopsoas*

iliacus*

vastus intermedius*

pectoralis major

deltoideus anterior

sartorius

rectus femoris

tibialis anterior

# PLANK TO PIKE

**Starting Position:** Place your hands on the ground, and place your feet on a physio ball with the ankles fixed at 90-degree angles, toes down, so that the body is horizontal. Your hands are wider than shoulder width, and your fingertips are parallel to your collarbone. Your feet are placed on the ball with the top of the foot (shoelaces) contacting the ball, and the toes are pointed.

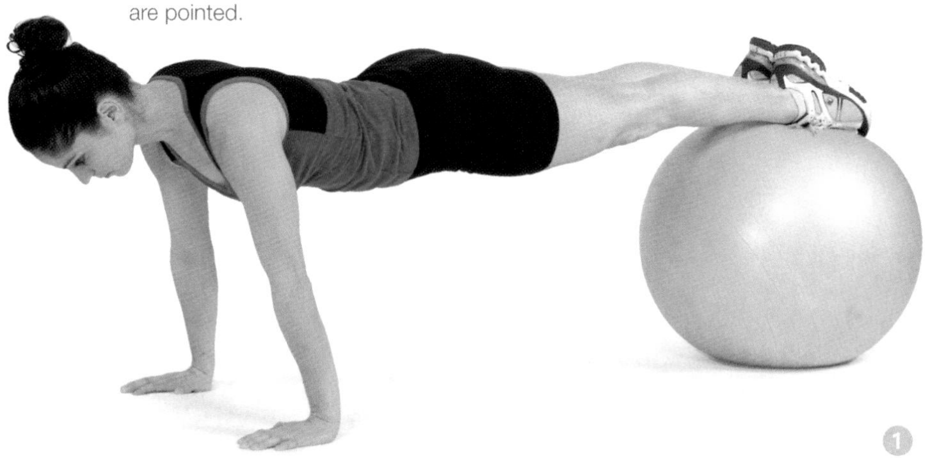

1

**LOOK FOR**

- A single plane of movement, i.e., a straight line from head to ankle.

**AVOID**

- A segmental elevation, i.e., your shoulders rising before your hips, or vice versa.
- Elevating your shoulders toward your ears.
- Moving your head forward.
- Allowing the ankles to change position.
- Allowing the ball or body to migrate laterally.

**Action:** Lower your entire body by allowing the elbows to bend until your torso has dropped into a position where the chest is at the level of your hands. Return by extending the elbows and pushing into the ground, elevating the entire body simultaneously. From the top position, pull the ball forward by flexing your feet and drawing the toes and hips upward so that the torso is bent at the hips. Your toes are on top of the ball and both feet are at 90-degree angles. The upper body and head face downward. Return by dropping your hips and extending your toes until your body returns to horizontal.

**Movement Path:** The plane of your body rotates upward in an arc. Use your feet as a lever.

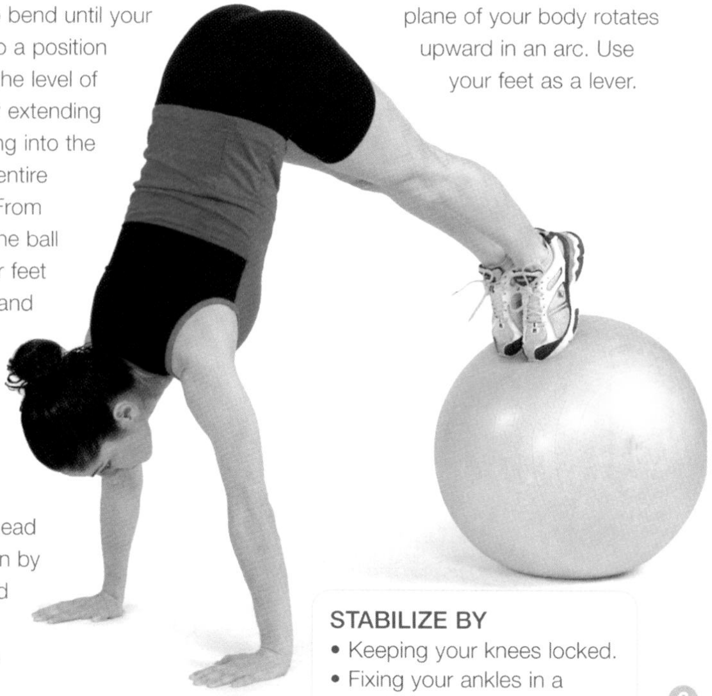

2

**STABILIZE BY**

- Keeping your knees locked.
- Fixing your ankles in a stable position.
- Keeping your hips, abdominal muscles, and lower back rigid.

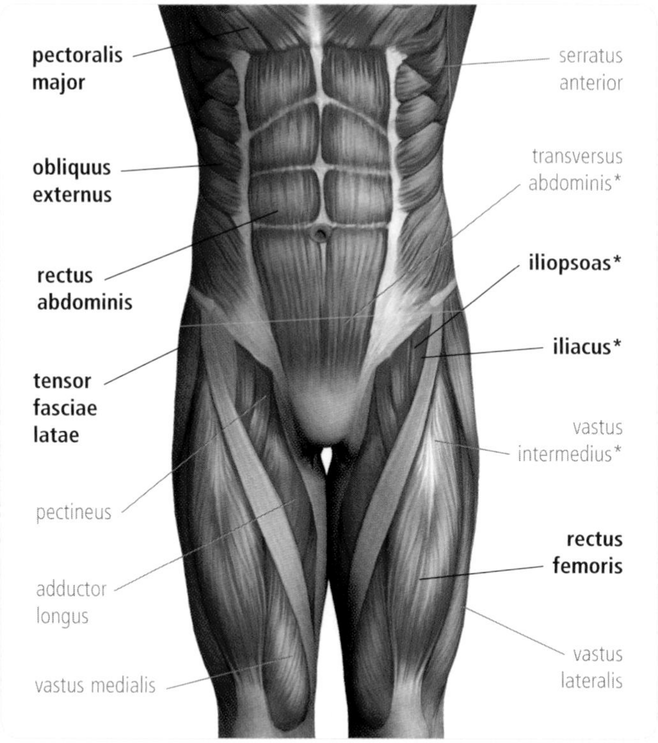
pectoralis major
obliquus externus
rectus abdominis
tensor fasciae latae
pectineus
adductor longus
vastus medialis
serratus anterior
transversus abdominis*
iliopsoas*
iliacus*
vastus intermedius*
rectus femoris
vastus lateralis

## BEST FOR

- pectoralis major
- pectoralis minor
- coracobrachialis
- deltoideus anterior
- triceps brachii
- iliopsoas
- iliacus
- vastus lateralis
- vastus medialis
- vastus intermedius
- rectus femoris
- transversus abdominis
- serratus anterior
- erector spinae
- trapezius
- latissimus dorsi
- quadratus lumborum
- adductor longus
- obliquus externus
- pectineus

ANNOTATION KEY

**Black text indicates active muscles**

Gray text indicates stabilizing muscles

* indicates deep muscles

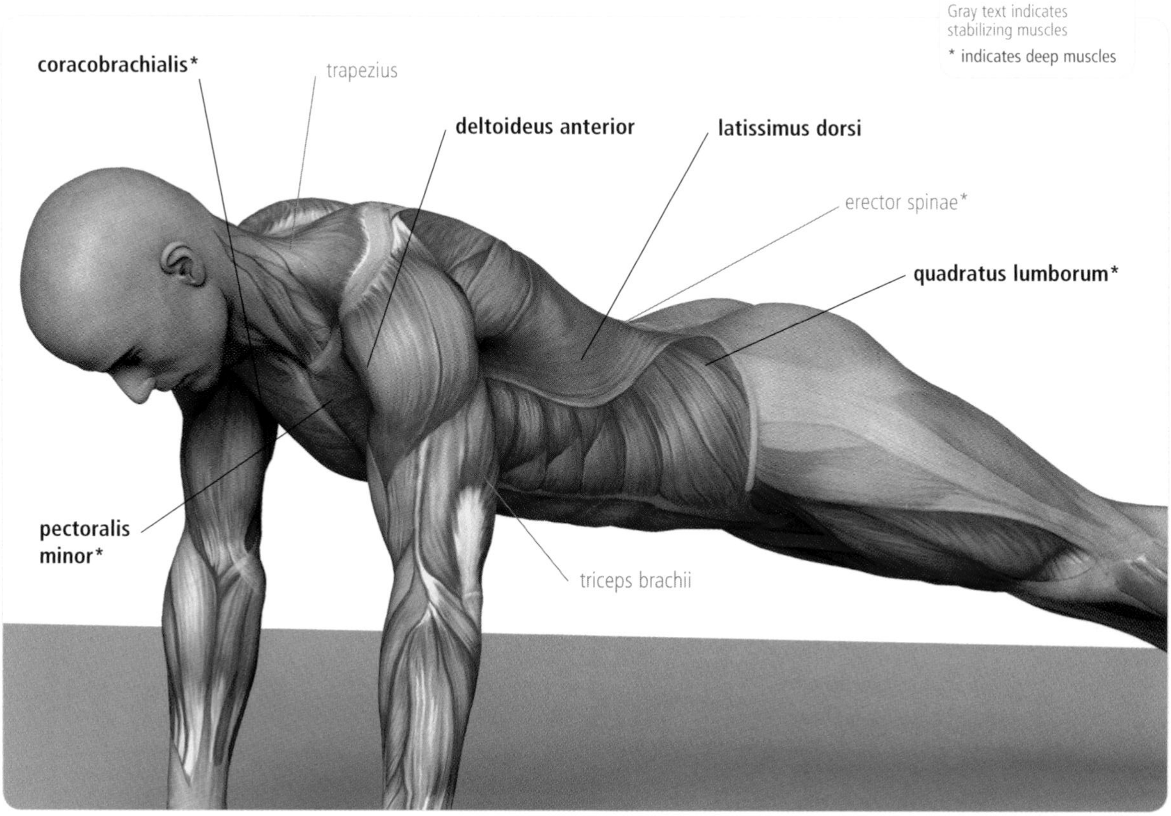
coracobrachialis*
trapezius
deltoideus anterior
latissimus dorsi
erector spinae*
quadratus lumborum*
pectoralis minor*
triceps brachii

# LAYOUT ON RINGS



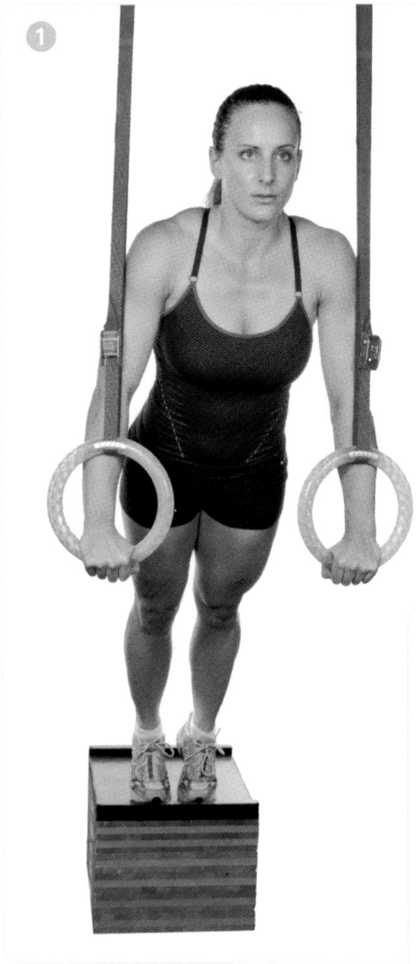

**Starting Position:** With your body rigid and at a 45-degree angle to the floor, grasp the rings directly under your shoulders with a palms-down grip, so that the rings are parallel and directly beneath the chest. The legs, hips, and spine form a straight line.

**Action:** Allowing the entire body to descend in a controlled manner with the arms straight, push the hands forward and outward, using the toes as a fulcrum. While descending, keep the hands parallel, allowing the body to descend until the arms are in a horizontal position. Return by pulling the arms back toward the floor until the body returns to the starting position.

LOOK FOR
- Arms to remain straight and parallel.
- A single plane of movement, i.e., a straight line from head to ankle.

AVOID
- Segmental elevation, i.e., your shoulders rising before your hips, or vice versa.
- Elevating your shoulders toward your ears.
- Moving your head forward.

STABILIZE BY
- Keeping shoulders down.
- Keeping your knees locked.
- Fixing your ankles in a stable position.
- Keeping your hips, abdominal muscles, and lower back rigid.

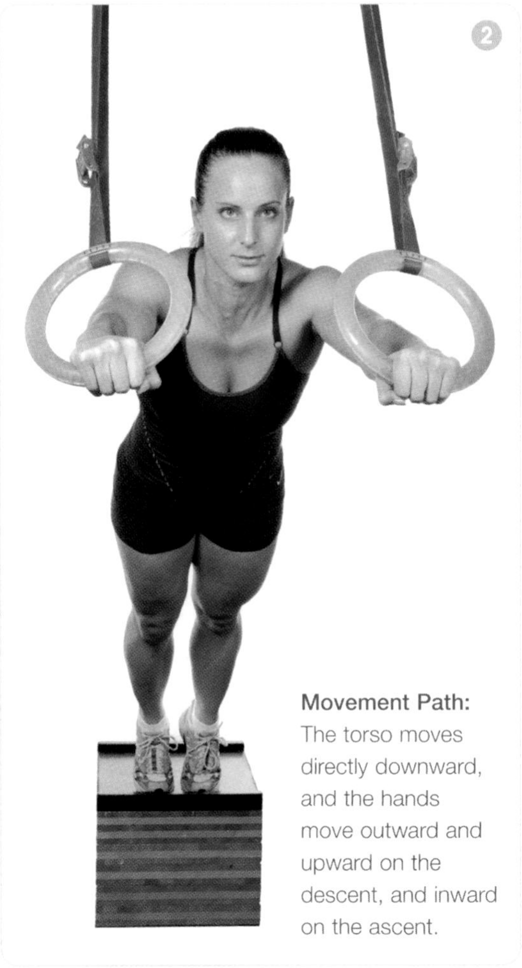

**Movement Path:** The torso moves directly downward, and the hands move outward and upward on the descent, and inward on the ascent.

## BEST FOR

- latissimus dorsi
- pectoralis major
- pectoralis minor
- coracobrachialis
- deltoideus
- rectus abdominis
- serratus anterior
- triceps brachii
- extensor digitorum
- iliopsoas
- iliacus
- pectineus
- vastus lateralis
- vastus medialis
- vastus intermedius
- rectus femoris
- tibialis anterior
- transversus abdominis
- serratus anterior
- erector spinae
- trapezius
- quadratus lumborum
- tensor fasciae latae
- erector spinae
- rhomboideus
- infraspinatus
- teres major
- teres minor
- brachialis
- obliquus internus
- obliquus externus

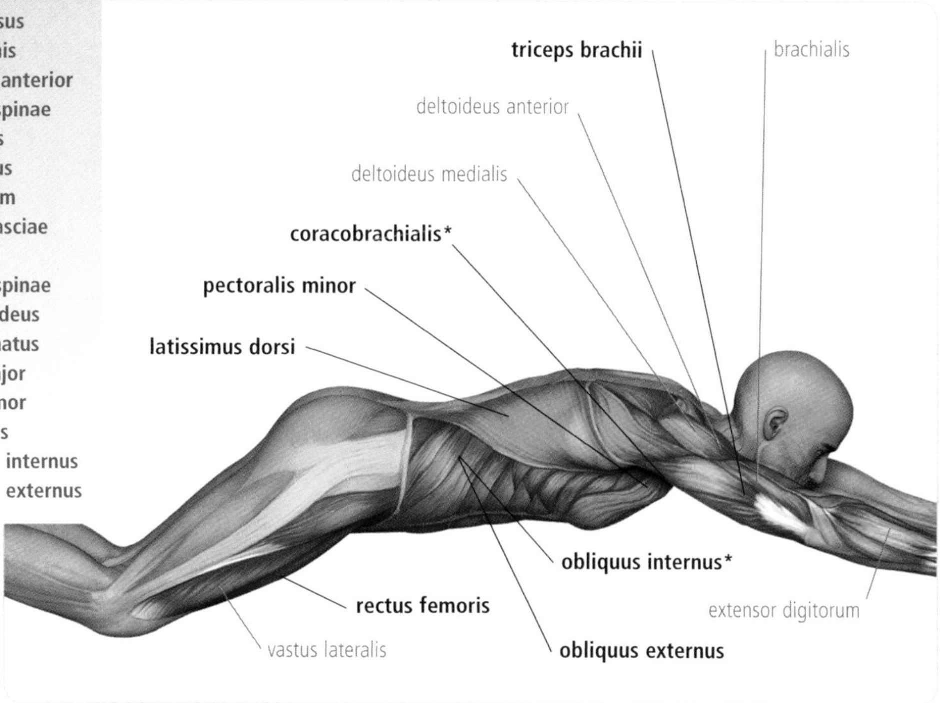

triceps brachii
brachialis
deltoideus anterior
deltoideus medialis
coracobrachialis*
pectoralis minor
latissimus dorsi
obliquus internus*
rectus femoris
extensor digitorum
vastus lateralis
obliquus externus


ANNOTATION KEY

**Black text indicates active muscles**

Gray text indicates stabilizing muscles

* indicates deep muscles

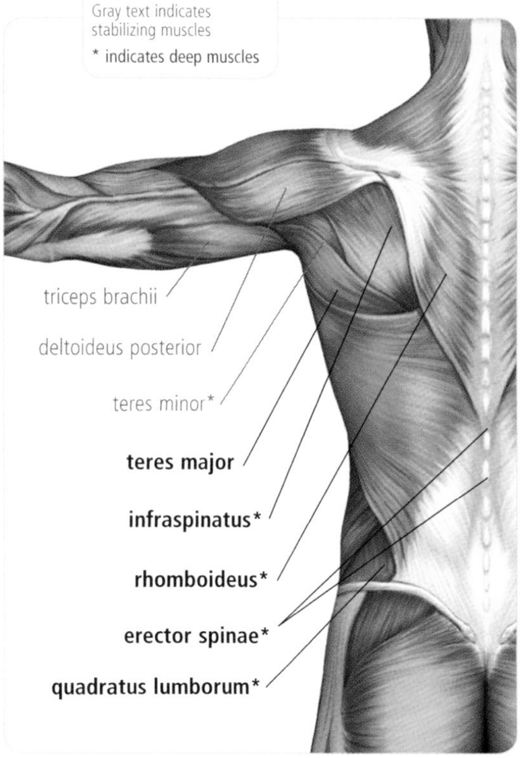

triceps brachii
deltoideus posterior
teres minor*
teres major
infraspinatus*
rhomboideus*
erector spinae*
quadratus lumborum*


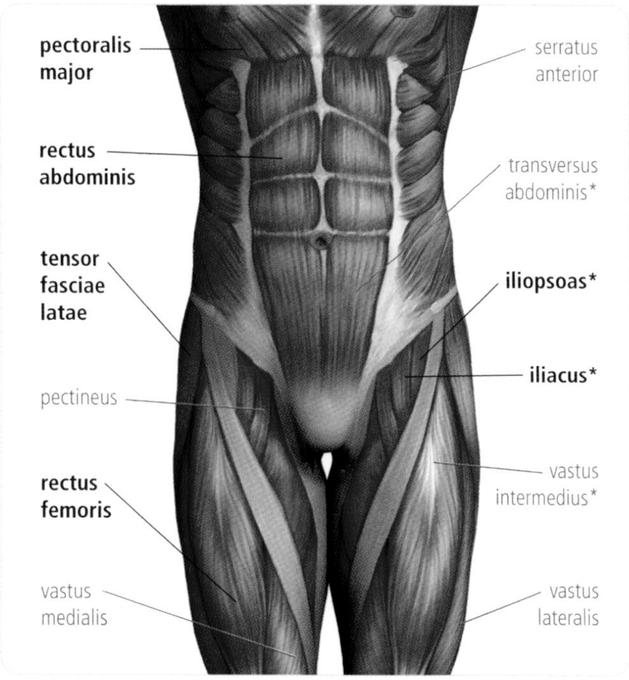

pectoralis major
serratus anterior
rectus abdominis
transversus abdominis*
tensor fasciae latae
iliopsoas*
iliacus*
pectineus
vastus intermedius*
rectus femoris
vastus medialis
vastus lateralis

# PROGRAMS

The following pages contain twelve sample exercise programs: four beginner, four intermediate, and four advanced. Each program consists of two pages. Included are:

- Specific exercise groupings, or "workouts"
- A visual representation of each exercise to be performed, with its page reference
- The weeks in which the workouts are to be performed
- A Program box, detailing both the number of times per week and the workouts to be performed
- A Prescription box, giving weekly volume and rest periods for a given workout. Please note that the weight/progression category must be tailored to each individual, according to size and fitness level; therefore all weights for the first week of any program are designated "TBD" (to be determined).
- An Exercise Sequence box, showing the order of exercises for a given workout
- A Notes section, which gives basic information on how the program should be used
- Space for user notes

Below are the Legend and Programs Glossary boxes, defining the elements and nomenclature used in the programs section. Opposite is a master list that includes all twelve programs. On page 135, there is a sample of how a workout may be logged.

Please remember that these workouts only address musculoskeletal conditioning. Warm-up, cardiovascular components, and flexibility are not addressed here. Before beginning any exercise program, you should always consult your physician.

## LEGEND

**Numbers** = Days per week

**Letters** = Specific workouts

**Roman numerals** = Programs or prescription

**Level** = Subjective categorization of both exercises and workouts based on technical difficulty and complexity

## PROGRAMS GLOSSARY

**BW:** Body weight

**Exercise:** Specific movement from a given category

**5 Essentials:** Category or type of exercise

**Programs:** Group of workouts

**Sequence:** Order in which the five ingredients are reinforced in a given workout

**TBD:** To be determined

**Workout:** Group of exercises

| | BEGINNER | | | | | INTERMEDIATE | | | | | ADVANCED | | | | |
|---|---|---|---|---|---|---|---|---|---|---|---|---|---|---|---|
| | Program I (6 weeks) | | | | | Program II (8 weeks) | | | | | Program III (8 weeks) | | | | |
| Weeks | Days | | | | | Days | | | | | Days | | | | |
| | 1 | 2 | | | | 1 | 2 | | | | 1 | 2 | | | |
| 1 | A | B | | | | A | B | | | | A | E | | | |
| 2 | A | B | | | | C | D | | | | B | D | | | |
| 3 | A | B | | | | A | B | | | | F | A | | | |
| 4 | B | A | | | | C | D | | | | C | D | | | |
| 5 | B | A | | | | B | A | | | | B | E | | | |
| 6 | B | A | | | | D | C | | | | F | C | | | |
| 7 | | | | | | B | A | | | | D | F | | | |
| 8 | | | | | | D | C | | | | E | A | | | |
| | Program IV (6 weeks) | | | | | Program V (6 weeks) | | | | | Program VI (4 weeks) | | | | |
| Weeks | Days | | | | | Days | | | | | Days | | | | |
| | 1 | 2 | 3 | | | 1 | 2 | 3 | | | 1 | 2 | 3 | | |
| 1 | C | A | D | | A | A | B | C | | | D | E | F | | |
| 2 | C | A | D | | D | D | E | F | | | D | E | F | | |
| 3 | C | A | D | | A | A | B | C | | | D | E | F | | |
| 4 | D | C | A | | D | D | E | F | | | D | E | F | | |
| 5 | D | C | A | | A | A | B | C | | | | | | | |
| 6 | D | C | A | | D | D | E | F | | | | | | | |
| | Program VII (4 weeks) | | | | | Program VIII (4 weeks) | | | | | Program IX (4 weeks) | | | | |
| Weeks | Days | | | | | Days | | | | | Days | | | | |
| | 1 | 2 | 3 | 4 | | 1 | 2 | 3 | 4 | | 1 | 2 | 3 | 4 | |
| 1 | G | H | G | H | | I | J | K | L | | M | N | O | D | |
| 2 | G | H | G | H | | I | J | K | L | | M | N | O | D | |
| 3 | H | G | H | G | | I | J | K | L | | M | N | O | D | |
| 4 | H | G | H | G | | I | J | K | L | | M | N | O | D | |
| | Program X (4 weeks) | | | | | Program XI (4 weeks) | | | | | Program XII (4 weeks) | | | | |
| Weeks | Days | | | | | Days | | | | | Days | | | | |
| | 1 | 2 | 3 | 4 | 5 | 1 | 2 | 3 | 4 | 5 | 1 | 2 | 3 | 4 | 5 |
| 1 | Q | S | R | U | T | I | J | K | P | Z | V | W | X | Y | Z |
| 2 | Q | S | R | U | T | I | J | Z | K | P | V | W | X | Y | Z |
| 3 | Q | S | R | U | T | I | J | K | P | Z | V | W | X | Y | Z |
| 4 | Q | S | R | U | T | I | J | Z | P | K | V | W | X | Y | Z |

# PROGRAM I

BEGINNER

WORKOUTS

| A weeks 1–3 | B weeks 1–3 | B weeks 4–6 | A weeks 4–6 |
|---|---|---|---|
| 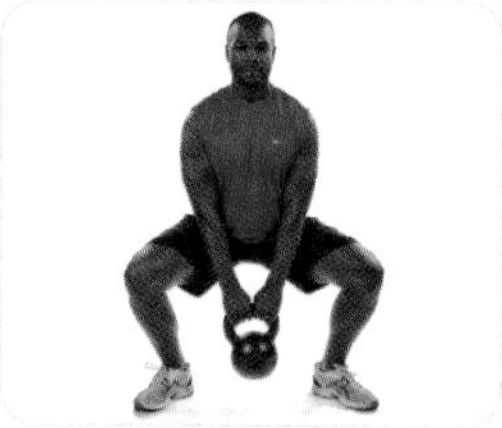<br>Sumo with Kettlebell<br>page 18 | 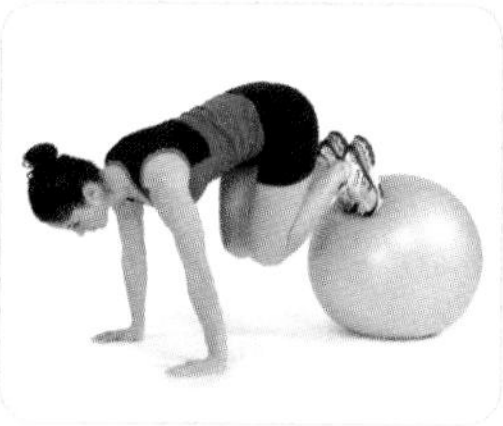<br>Plow on Physio Ball<br>page 112 | 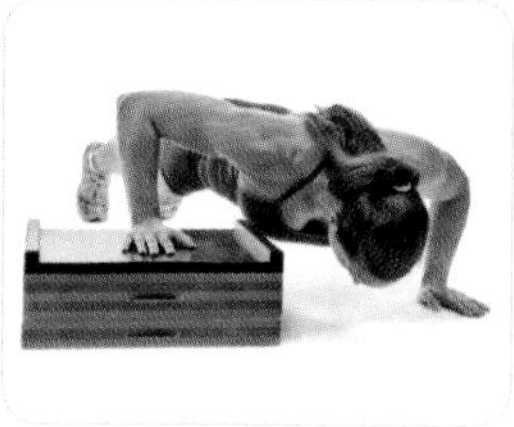<br>Hand Walkover<br>page 78 | 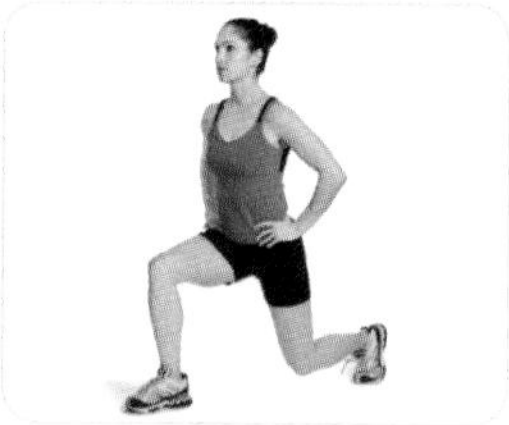<br>Stationary Lunge<br>page 38 |
| 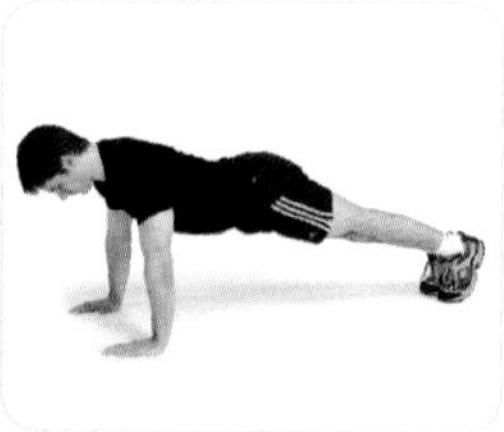<br>Basic Push-up<br>page 60 | 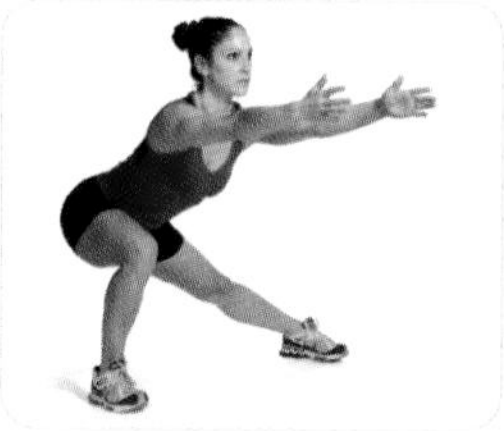<br>Lateral Lunge<br>page 42 | 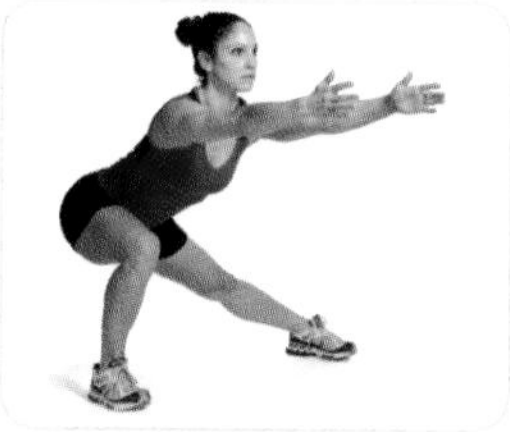<br>Lateral Lunge<br>page 42 | 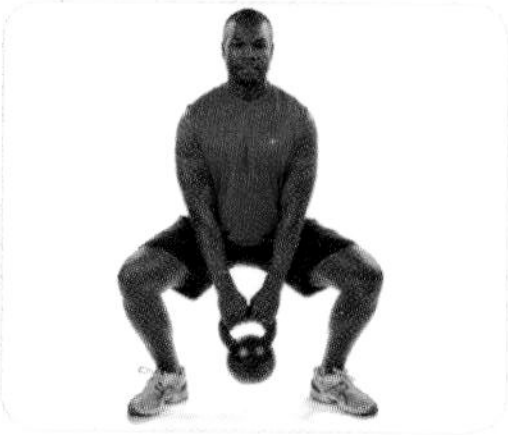<br>Sumo with Kettlebell<br>page 18 |
| 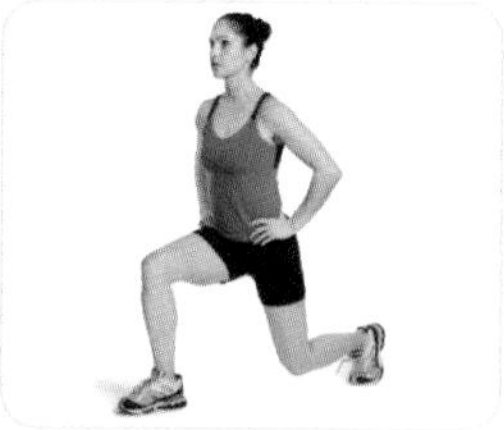<br>Stationary Lunge<br>page 38 | 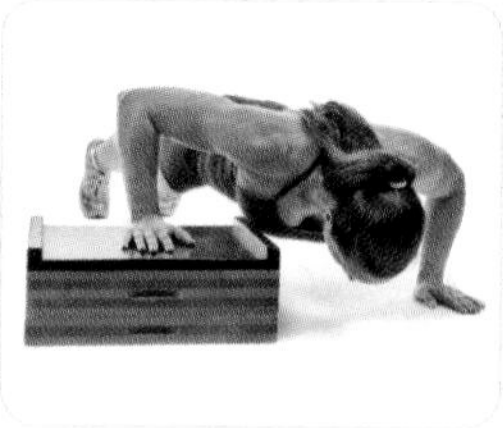<br>Hand Walkover<br>page 78 | 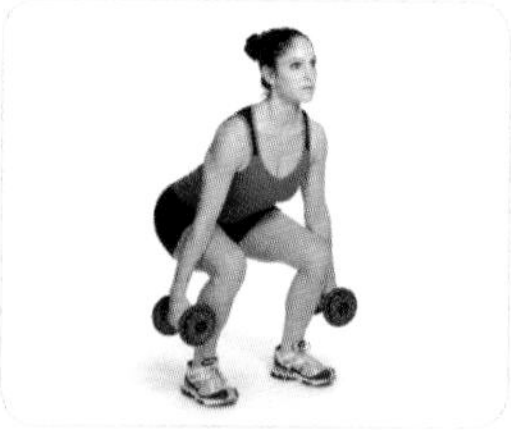<br>Full with Dumbbells<br>page 15 | 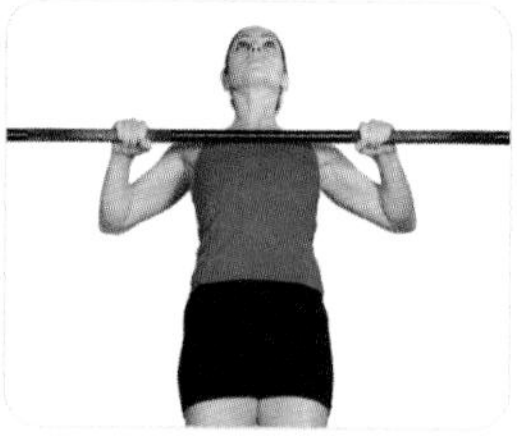<br>45-Degree Body Row<br>page 90 |
| 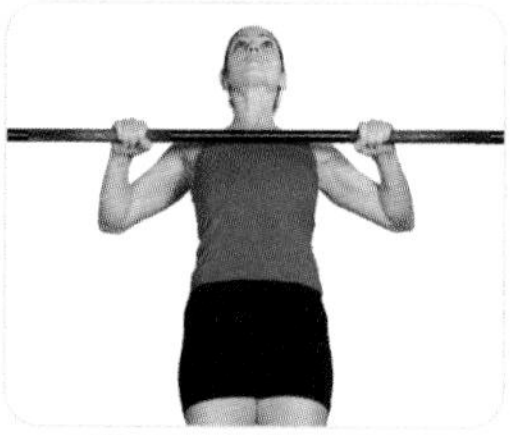<br>45-Degree Body Row<br>page 90 | 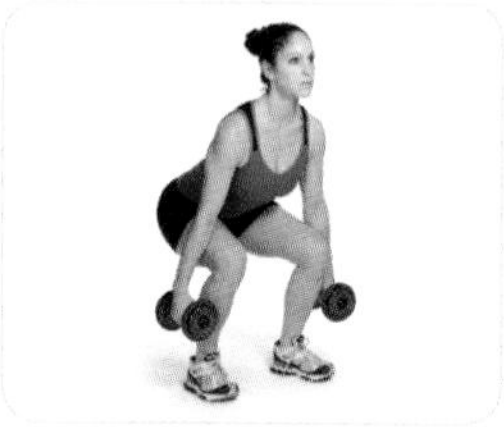<br>Full with Dumbbells<br>page 15 | 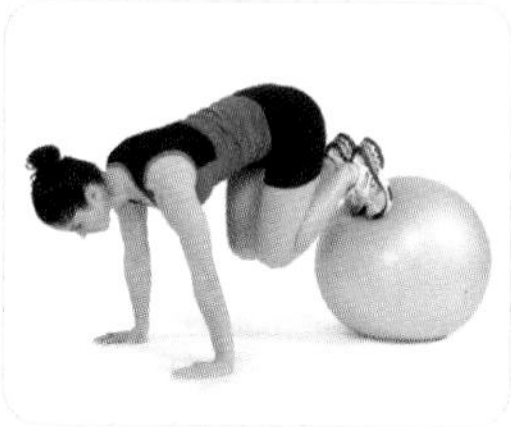<br>Plow on Physio Ball<br>page 112 | 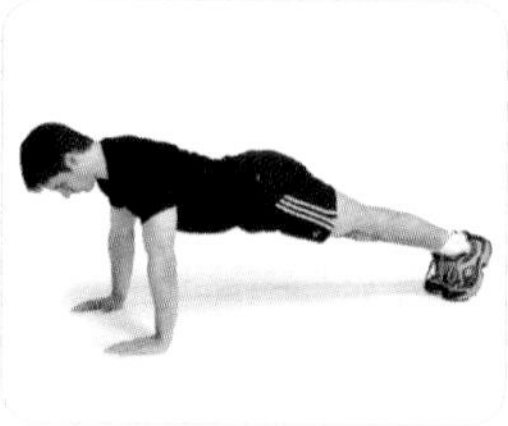<br>Basic Push-up<br>page 60 |
| 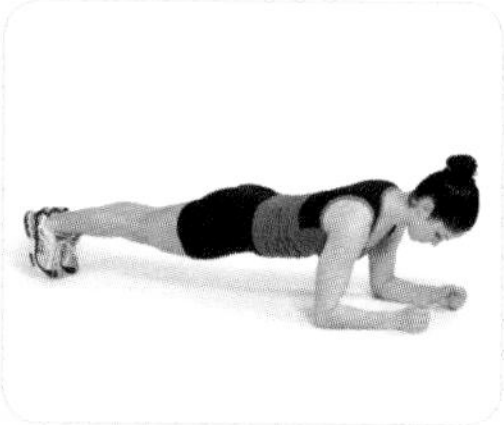<br>Front Plank<br>page 126 | 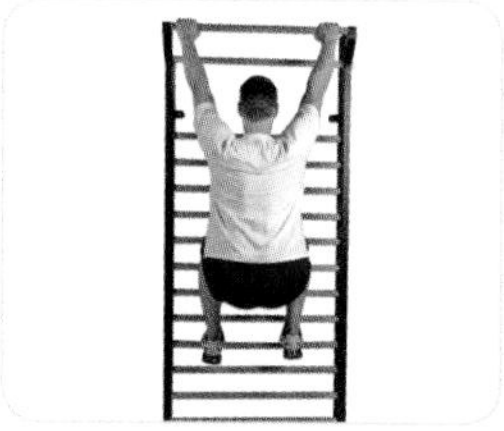<br>Stand-Pull<br>page 98 | 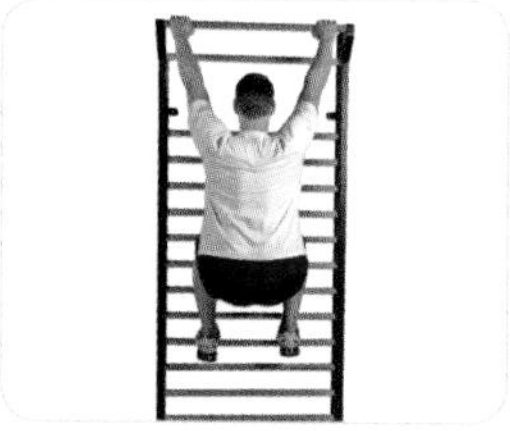<br>Stand-Pull<br>page 98 | 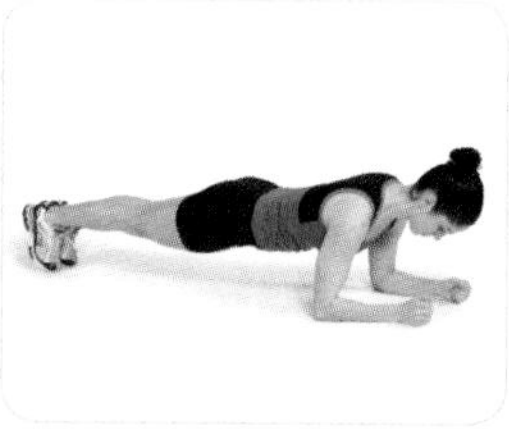<br>Front Plank<br>page 126 |

# PROGRAM 1 · BEGINNER

## SAMPLE PROGRAM LOG

| A | Sets | Reps | Weight | Rest | Sets | Reps | Weight | Rest | Sets | Reps | Weight | Rest | Sets | Reps | Weight | Rest |
|---|---|---|---|---|---|---|---|---|---|---|---|---|---|---|---|---|
| | | Week 1 | | | | Week 2 | | | | Week 3 | | | | Week 4 | | |
| Sumo | | | | | | | | | | | | | | | | |
| Stationary | | | | | | | | | | | | | | | | |
| Basic | | | | | | | | | | | | | | | | |
| 45-Degree Body Row | | | | | | | | | | | | | | | | |
| Front Plank | | | | | | | | | | | | | | | | |

## PROGRAM: 1 DURATION: 6 WEEKS

Days per week: 3
Total weeks: 6
Type: Intermediate
Endurance

| Weeks \ Days | 1 | 2 |
|---|---|---|
| 1 | A | B |
| 2 | A | B |
| 3 | A | B |
| 4 | B | A |
| 5 | B | A |
| 6 | B | A |

## PRESCRIPTION

| Week | Sets | Repetitions | Weight/Progression | Rest Set/Exercise |
|---|---|---|---|---|
| 1 | 3 | 8 | TBD | :75 / :90 |
| 2 | 3 | 10 | Same as week 1 | :60 / :75 |
| 3 | 3 | 12 | Same as week 1 | :45 / :60 |
| 4 | 3 | 10 | Increase 10% BW (2–5 reps) | :60 / :90 |
| 5 | 3 | 8 | Increase 10% BW (2–5 reps) | :75 / :90 |
| 6 | 3 | 6 | Increase 10% BW (2–5 reps) | :75 / :90 |

## EXERCISE SEQUENCE

| Order \ Workout | A | B | B | A |
|---|---|---|---|---|
| 1 | Deadlift | Ab Wheel | Push-up | Lunge |
| 2 | Push-up | Lunge | Lunge | Deadlift |
| 3 | Lunge | Push-up | Deadlift | Chin-up |
| 4 | Chin-up | Deadlift | Ab Wheel | Push-up |
| 5 | Ab Wheel | Chin-up | Chin-up | Ab Wheel |

Notes: In weeks 1–3 the exercise order remains consistent. In weeks 4–6 both the exercise sequence and workout schedule (workout B is done first) change.

# PROGRAM II



## WORKOUTS

| A<br>weeks 1, 3, 5, 7 | B<br>weeks 1, 3, 5, 7 | C<br>weeks 2, 4, 6, 8 | D<br>weeks 2, 4, 6, 8 |
|---|---|---|---|
| 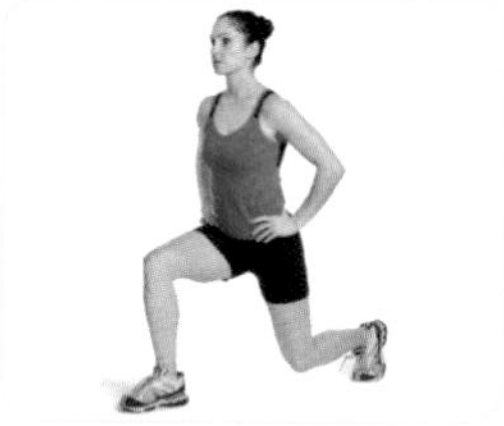<br>Stationary Lunge<br>page 38 | 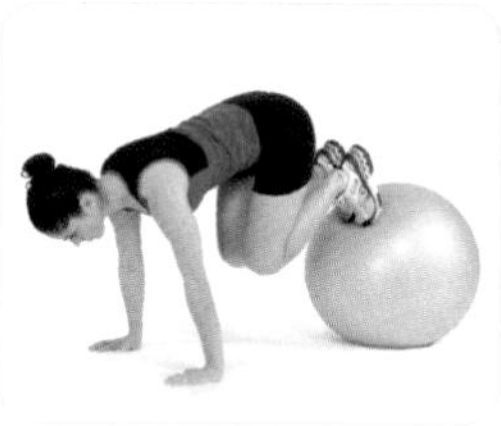<br>Plow on Physio Ball<br>page 112 | 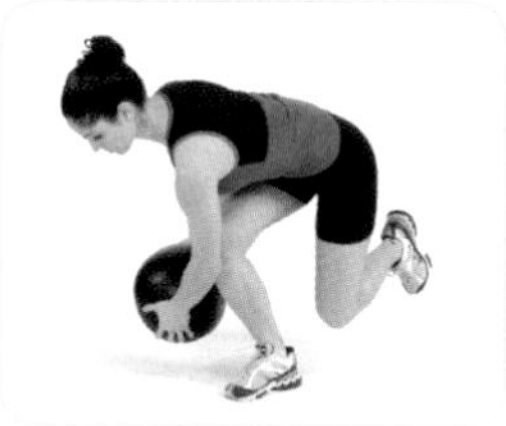<br>Medicine Ball Raise<br>page 26 | 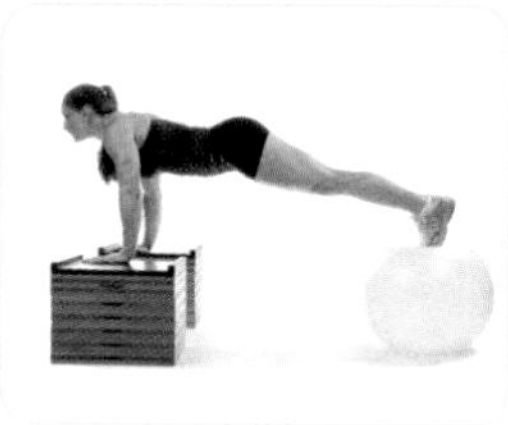<br>On Physio Ball & Blocks<br>page 64 |
| 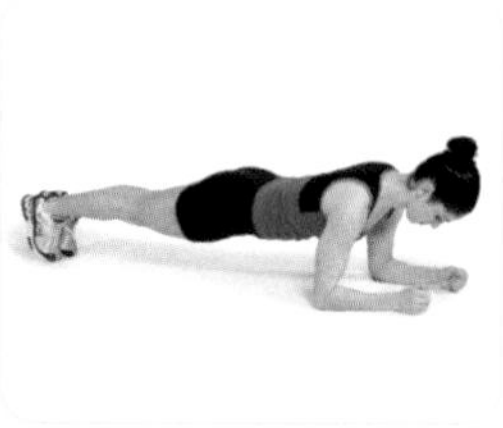<br>Front Plank<br>page 126 | 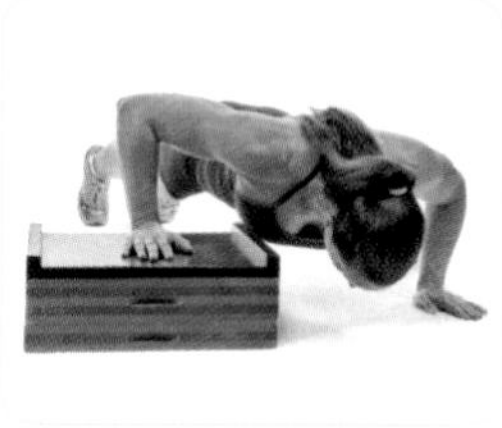<br>Hand Walkover<br>page 78 | 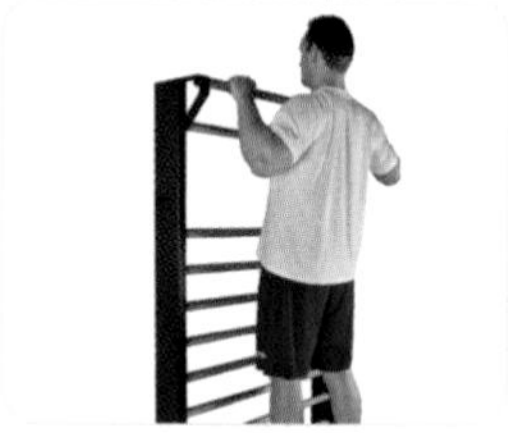<br>Step Chin<br>page 100 | 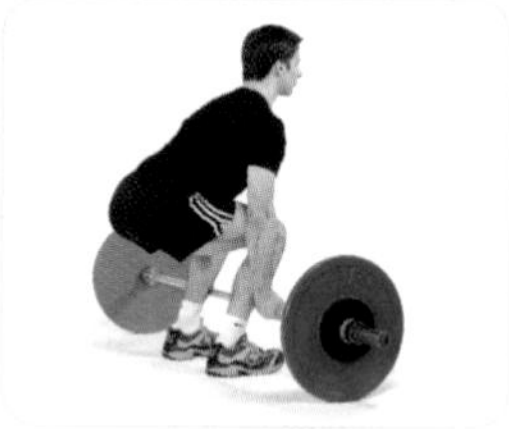<br>Full with Barbell<br>page 14 |
| 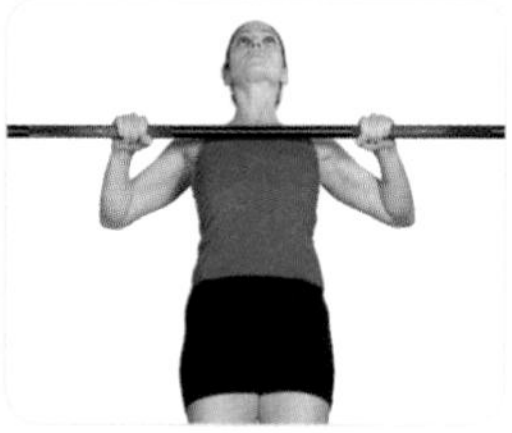<br>45-Degree Body Row<br>page 90 | 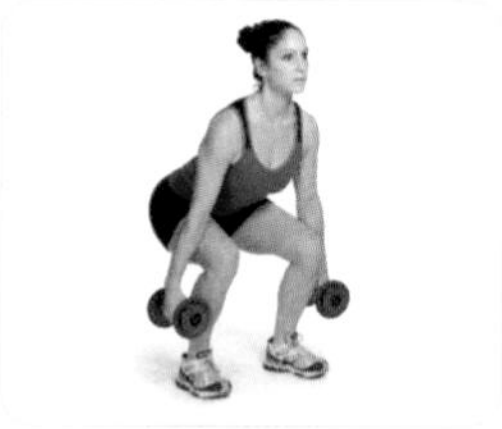<br>Full with Dumbbells<br>page 15 | 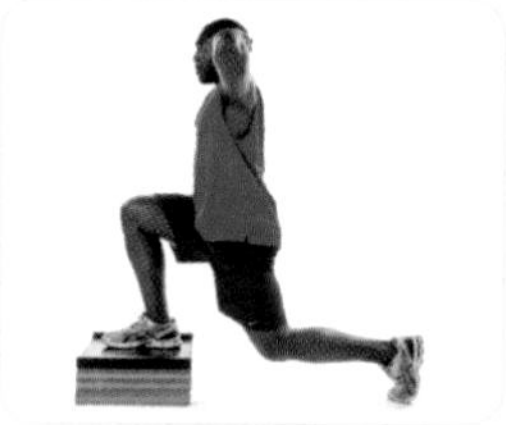<br>Up to Box<br>page 54 | 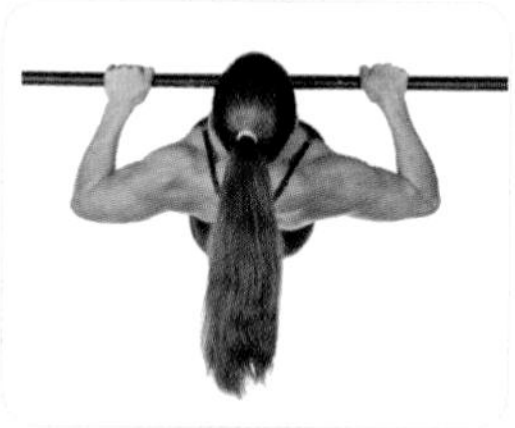<br>Horizontal Body Row<br>page 92 |
| 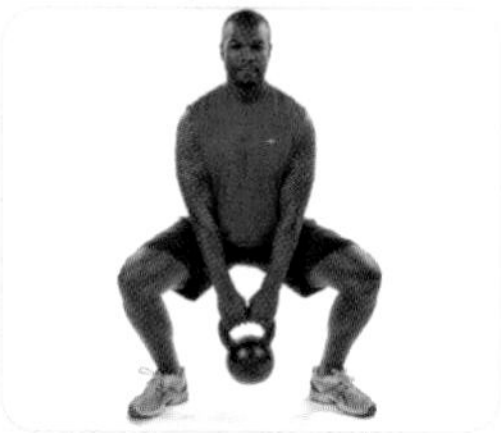<br>Sumo with Kettlebell<br>page 18 | 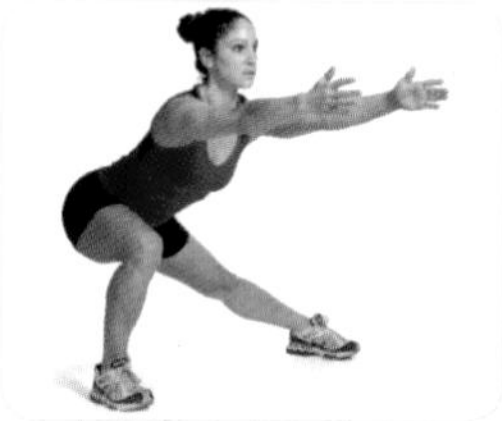<br>Lateral Lunge<br>page 42 | 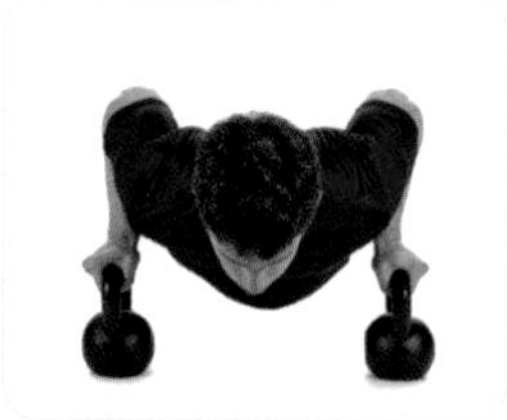<br>Push-up on Kettlebells<br>page 76 | 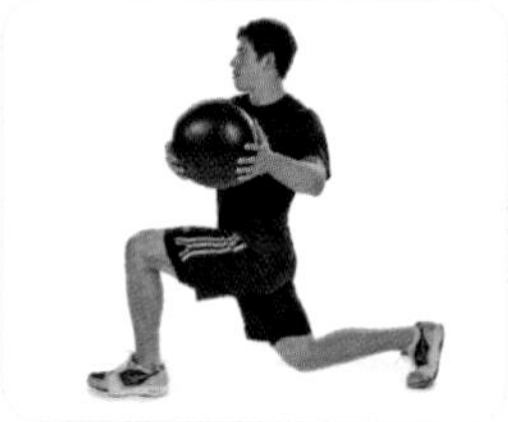<br>Walking with Rotation<br>page 40 |
| 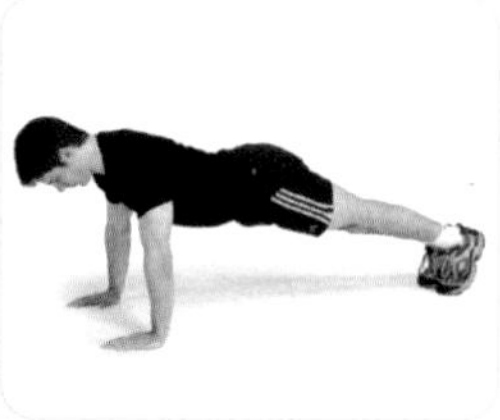<br>Basic Push-up<br>page 60 | 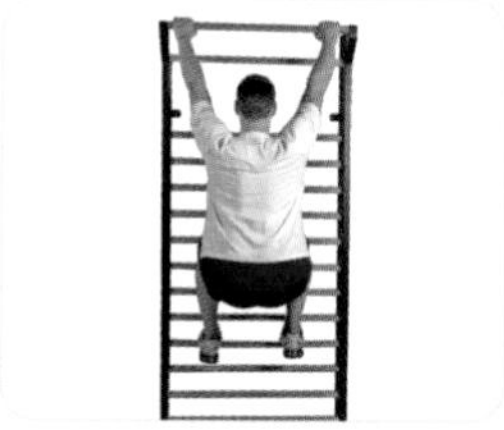<br>Stand-Pull<br>page 98 | 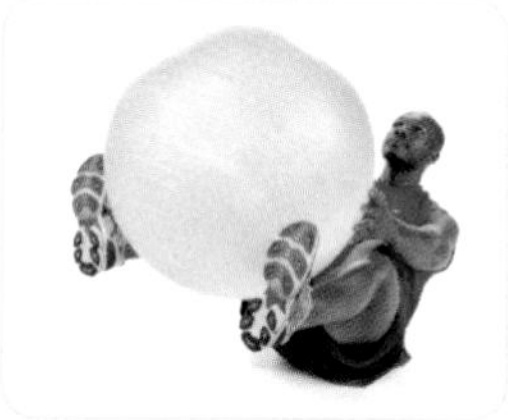<br>V-ups with Physio Ball<br>page 122 | 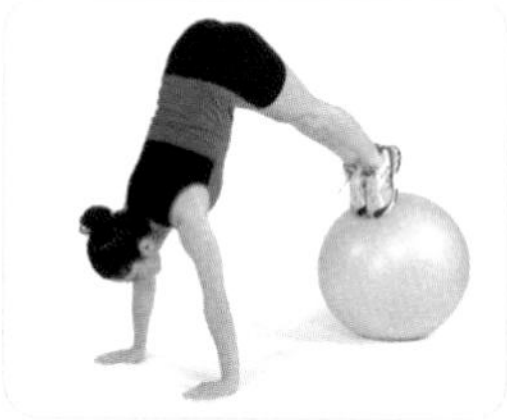<br>Plank to Pike<br>page 128 |

# PROGRAM II • INTERMEDIATE

## USER NOTES

## PROGRAM: II DURATION: 8 WEEKS

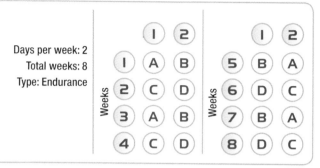

Days per week: 2
Total weeks: 8
Type: Endurance

| Weeks | | |
|---|---|---|
| | ① | ② |
| ① | A | B |
| ② | C | D |
| ③ | A | B |
| ④ | C | D |

| Weeks | | |
|---|---|---|
| | ① | ② |
| ⑤ | B | A |
| ⑥ | D | C |
| ⑦ | B | A |
| ⑧ | D | C |

## PRESCRIPTION

| Week | Sets | Repetitions | Weight/Progression | Rest Set/Exercise |
|---|---|---|---|---|
| ① | ③ | ⑧ | TBD | :75 / :90 |
| ② | ③ | ⑩ | Same | :75 / :75 |
| ③ | ③ | ⑫ | Same | :75 / :75 |
| ④ | ③ | ⑮ | Same | :90 / :75 |
| ⑤ | ④ | ⑥ | Increase weight 10% | :75 / :90 |
| ⑥ | ④ | ⑧ | Same | :75 / :90 |
| ⑦ | ④ | ⑩ | Same | :75 / :90 |
| ⑧ | ④ | ⑫ | Same | :90 / :90 |

## EXERCISE SEQUENCE

| | Workout | | | |
|---|---|---|---|---|
| Order | A | B | C | D |
| ① | Lunge | Ab Wheel | Deadlift | Push-up |
| ② | Ab Wheel | Push-up | Chin-up | Deadlift |
| ③ | Chin-up | Deadlift | Lunge | Chin-up |
| ④ | Deadlift | Lunge | Push-up | Lunge |
| ⑤ | Push-up | Chin-up | Ab Wheel | Ab Wheel |

**Notes:** There must be at least one day between workouts; two or three is optimal (e.g., Monday/Thursday or Tuesday/Friday).

# PROGRAM III

ADVANCED

WORKOUTS

| A<br>weeks 1, 3, 8 | B<br>weeks 2, 5 | C<br>weeks 4, 6 | D<br>weeks 2, 4, 7 |
| --- | --- | --- | --- |
| 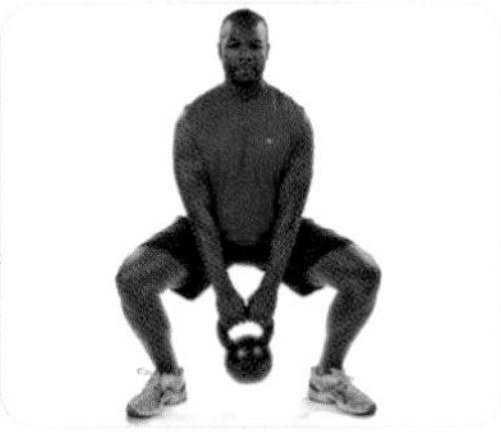<br>Sumo with Kettlebell<br>page 18 | 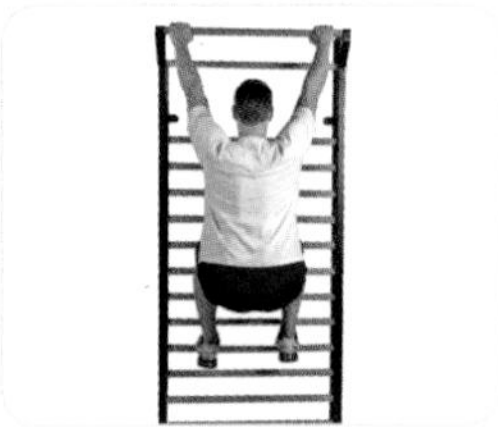<br>Stand-Pull<br>page 98 | 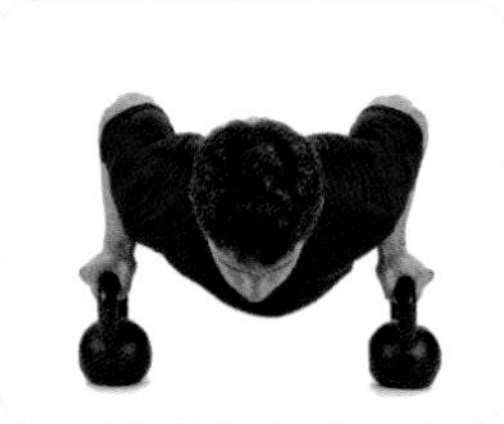<br>Push-up on Kettlebells<br>page 76 | 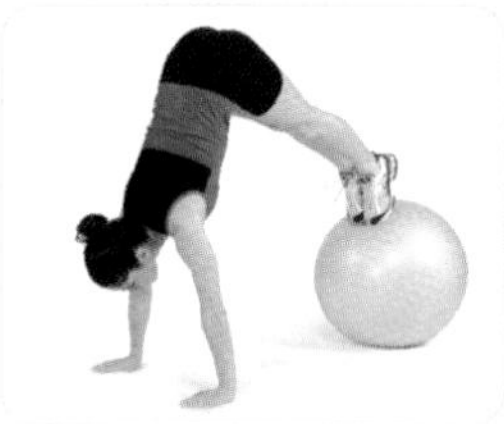<br>Plank to Pike<br>page 128 |
| 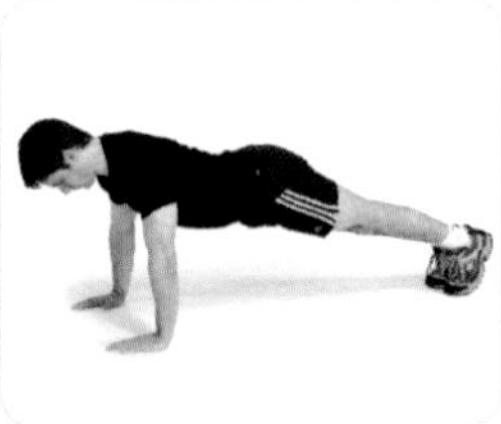<br>Basic Push-up<br>page 60 | 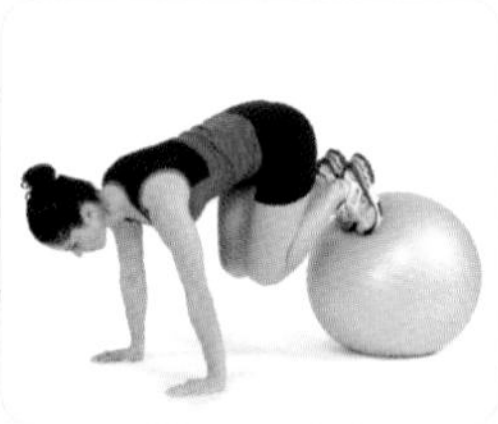<br>Plow on Physio Ball<br>page 112 | 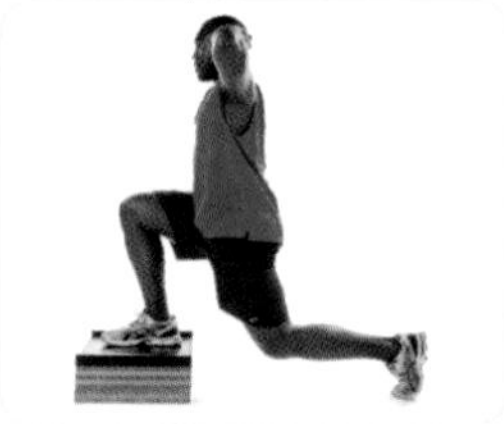<br>Up to Box<br>page 54 | 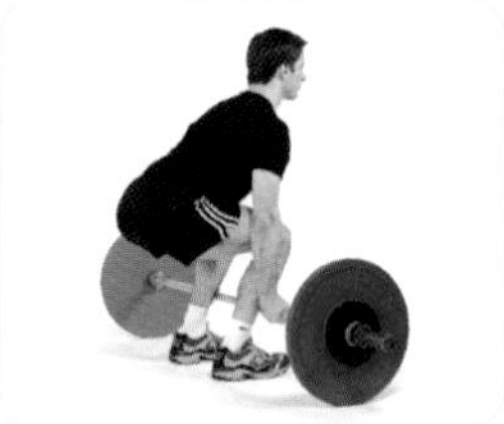<br>Full with Barbell<br>page 14 |
| 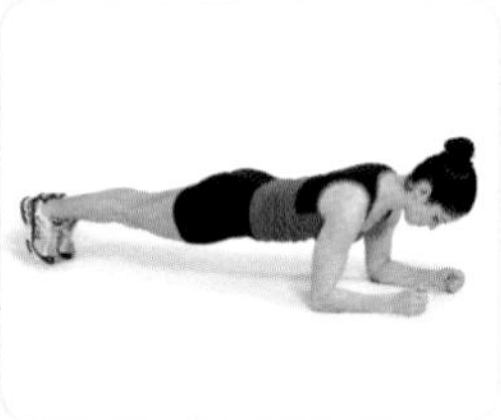<br>Front Plank<br>page 126 | 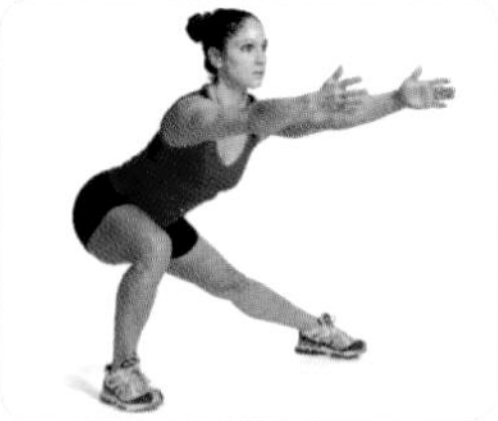<br>Lateral Lunge<br>page 42 | 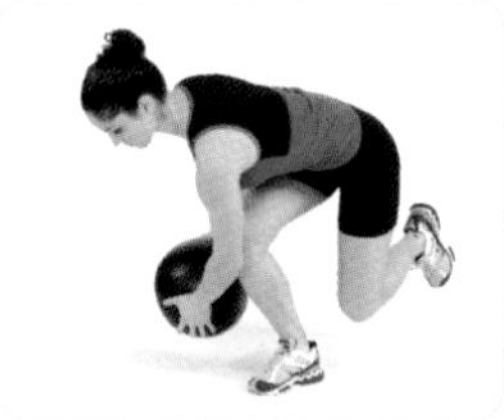<br>Medicine Ball Raise<br>page 26 | 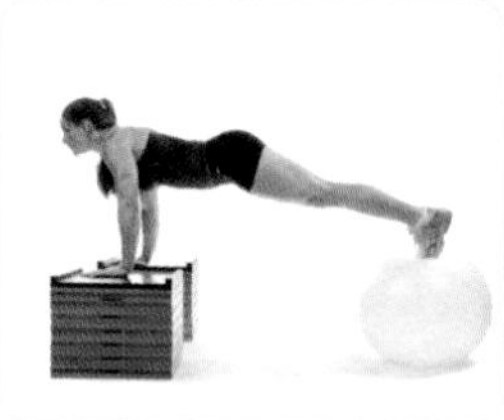<br>On Physio Ball & Blocks<br>page 64 |
| 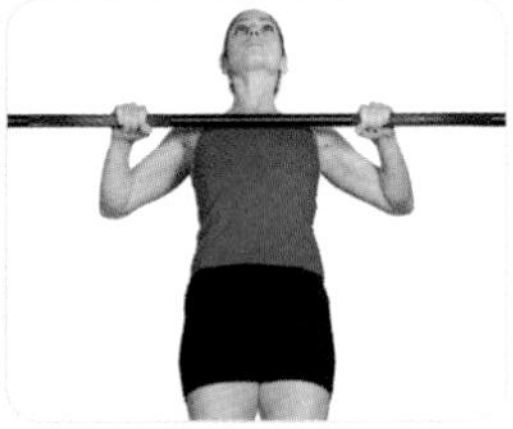<br>45-Degree Body Row<br>page 90 | 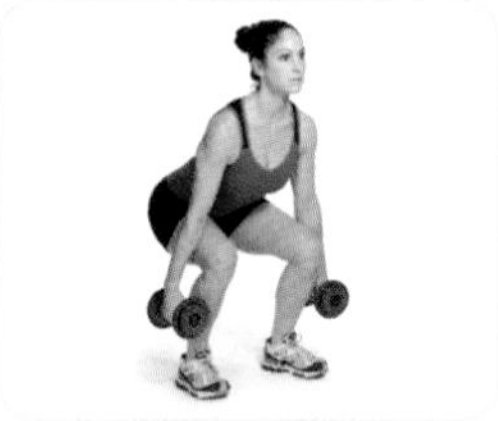<br>Full with Dumbbells<br>page 15 | 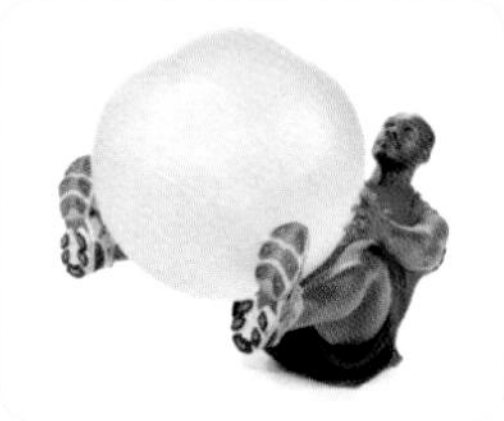<br>V-ups with Physio Ball<br>page 122 | 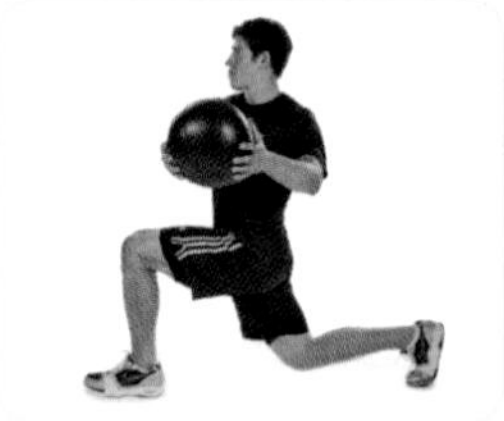<br>Walking with Rotation<br>page 40 |
| 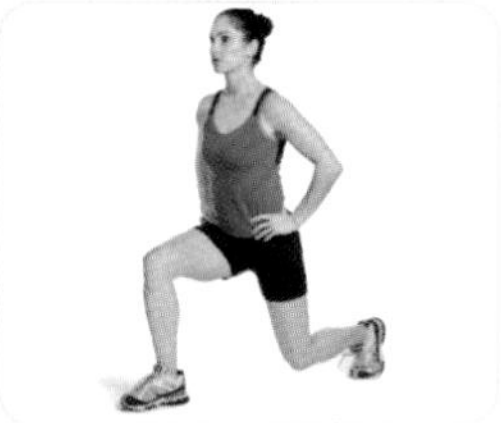<br>Stationary Lunge<br>page 38 | 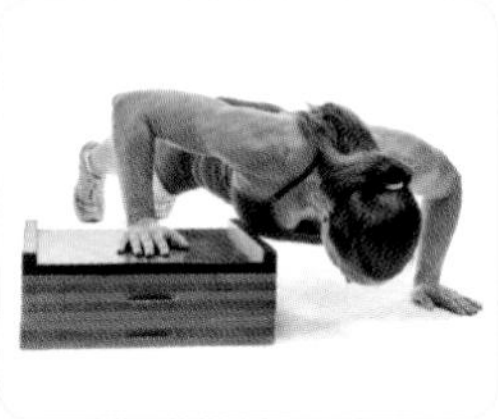<br>Hand Walkover<br>page 78 | 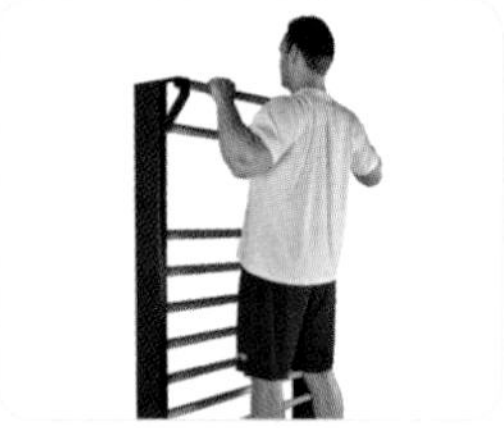<br>Step Chin<br>page 100 | 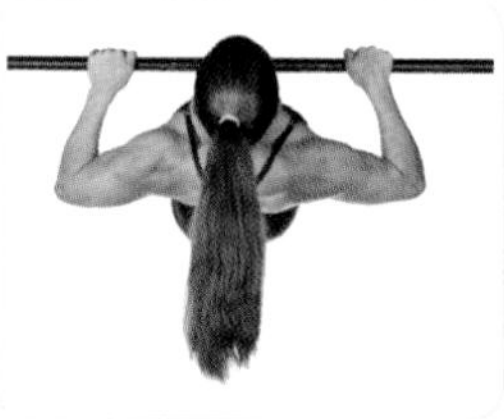<br>Horizontal Body Row<br>page 92 |

| E weeks 1, 5, 8 | F weeks 3, 6, 7 |
| --- | --- |

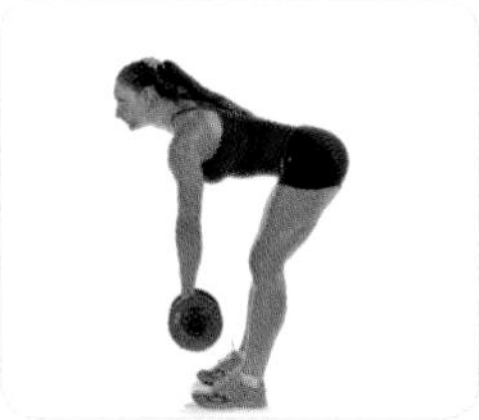
Straight-Leg with Dumbbell
page 22

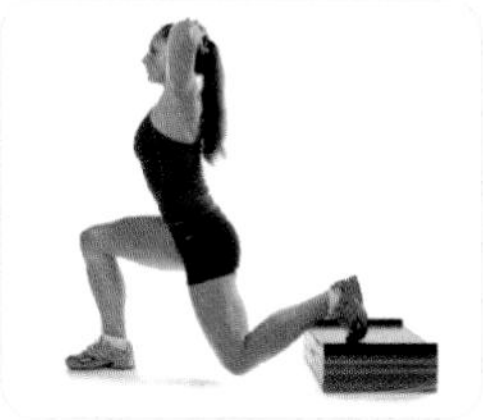
Off Box
page 56

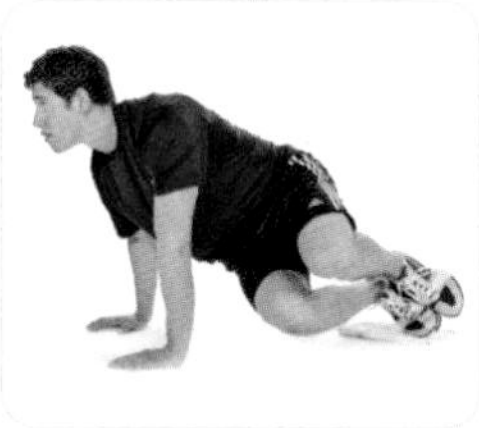
Plow with Rotation
page 114

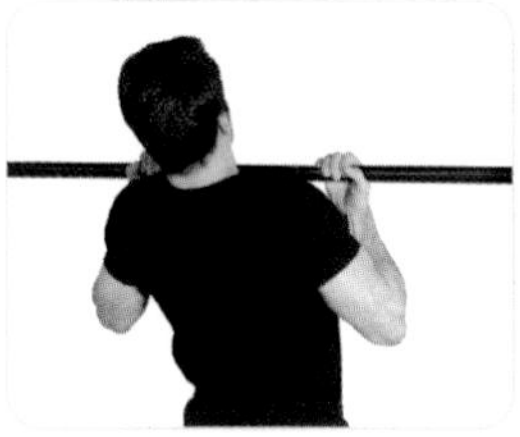
Basic Chin-up
page 86

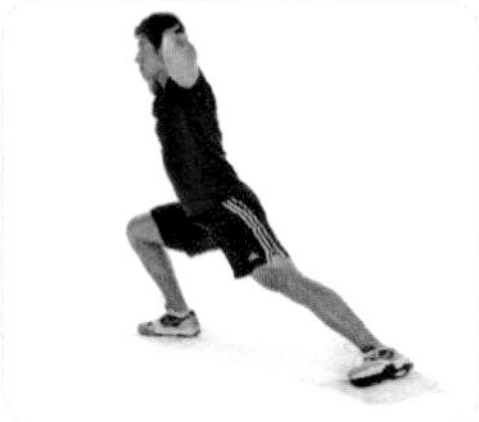
45-Degree Towel Slide
page 44

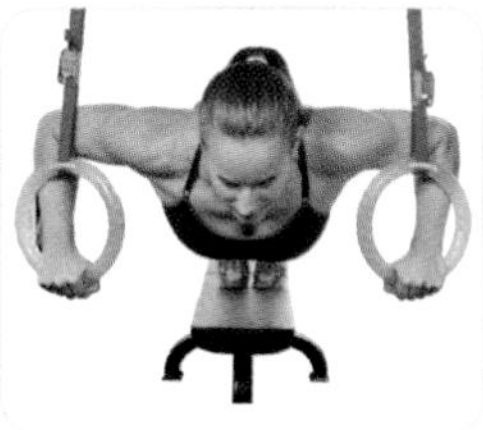
Hands on Rings
page 80

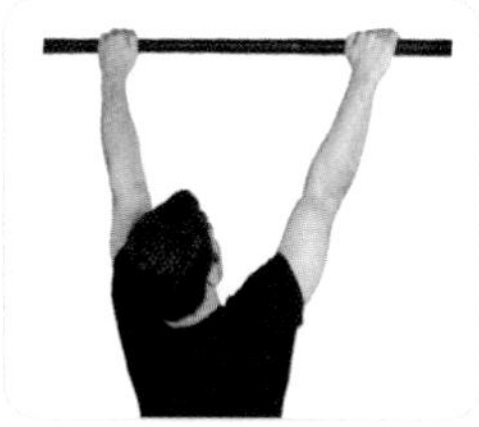
Pull-up Grip
page 88

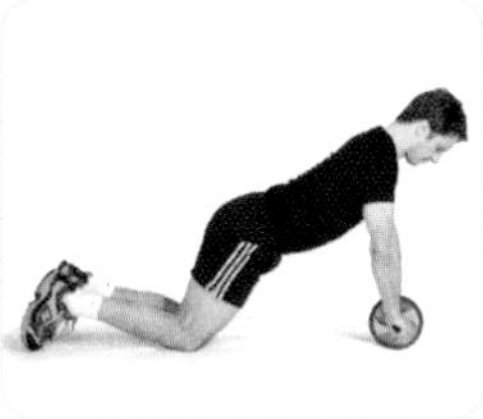
Ab Wheel
page 110

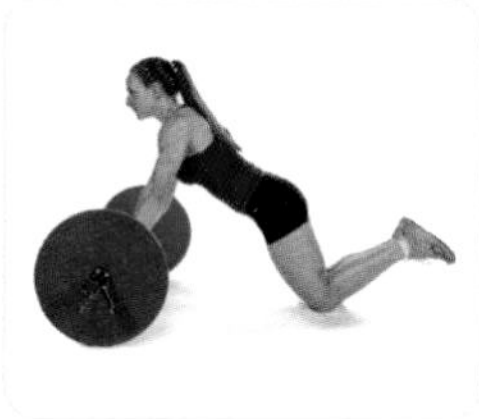
Push-up & Roll-out
page 62

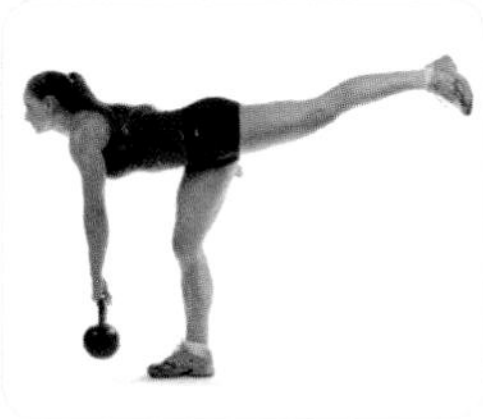
Single-Leg/Straight-Leg with
Kettlebells page 24

## PROGRAM: III DURATION: 8 WEEKS

Days per week: 2
Total weeks: 8
Type: Advanced
Cardiovascular
Endurance

| Weeks | 1 | 2 | Weeks | 1 | 2 |
| --- | --- | --- | --- | --- | --- |
| 1 | A | E | 5 | B | E |
| 2 | B | D | 6 | F | C |
| 3 | F | A | 7 | D | F |
| 4 | C | D | 8 | E | A |

## PRESCRIPTION

| Week | Sets | Repetitions | Weight/Progression | Rest Set/Exercise |
| --- | --- | --- | --- | --- |
| 1 | 5 | 6 | TBD | :60 / 0 |
| 2 | 5 | 6 | Same | :45 / 0 |
| 3 | 5 | 8 | Same | :60 / 0 |
| 4 | 5 | 8 | Same | :45 / 0 |
| 5 | 5 | 10 | Same | :60 / 0 |
| 6 | 5 | 10 | Same | :45 / 0 |
| 7 | 5 | 12 | Same | :60 / 0 |
| 8 | 5 | 12 | same | :45 / 0 |

## EXERCISE SEQUENCE

Workout

| Order | A | B | C | D | E | F |
| --- | --- | --- | --- | --- | --- | --- |
| 1 | Deadlift | Chin-up | Push-up | Ab Wheel | Deadlift | Lunge |
| 2 | Push-up | Ab Wheel | Lunge | Deadlift | Ab Wheel | Chin-up |
| 3 | Ab Wheel | Lunge | Deadlift | Push-up | Lunge | Push-up |
| 4 | Chin-up | Deadlift | Ab Wheel | Lunge | Chin-up | Ab Wheel |
| 5 | Lunge | Push-up | Chin-up | Chin-up | Push-up | Deadlift |

**Notes:** Exercises in this program are to be done in "circuit" fashion. There is no rest between exercises. All five movements are to be done consecutively, with rest to be taken between rounds or groups.

# PROGRAM IV

**BEGINNER**

## WORKOUTS

| A | B | C |
|---|---|---|
| weeks 1–6 | weeks 1–6 | weeks 1–6 |

Up to Box
page 54

Full with Barbell
page 14

Front Plank
page 126

Step Chin
page 100

Towel Fly
page 68

Stationary Lunge
page 38

Medicine Ball Raise
page 26

Walking Lunge with Rotation
page 40

Basic Push-up
page 60

Push-up on Kettlebells
page 76

Horizontal Body Row
page 92

Sumo with Kettlebell
page 18

V-ups with Physio Ball
page 122

Plank to Pike
page 128

45-Degree Body Row
page 90

## USER NOTES

## PROGRAM: IV  DURATION: 6 WEEKS

Days per week: 3
Total weeks: 6
Type: Strength/Endurance

| Weeks \ Days | 1 | 2 | 3 |
|---|---|---|---|
| 1 | C | A | B |
| 2 | C | A | B |
| 3 | C | A | B |
| 4 | B | C | A |
| 5 | B | C | A |
| 6 | B | C | A |

## PRESCRIPTION

| Week | Sets | Repetitions | Weight/Progression | Rest Set/Exercise |
|---|---|---|---|---|
| 1 | 3 | 10 | TBD | :120 / :120 |
| 2 | 3 | 8 | Increase 10% BW 2–5 reps | :90 / :120 |
| 3 | 3 | 6 | Increase 10% BW 2–5 reps | :120 / :120 |
| 4 | 3 | 8 | Same as week 3 | :90 / :120 |
| 5 | 3 | 10 | Same as week 3 | :90 / :90 |
| 6 | 3 | 12 | Same as week 3 | :75 / :90 |

## EXERCISE SEQUENCE

| Order \ Workout | A | B | C |
|---|---|---|---|
| 1 | Lunge | Deadlift | Ab Wheel |
| 2 | Chin-up | Push-up | Lunge |
| 3 | Deadlift | Lunge | Push-up |
| 4 | Push-up | Chin-up | Deadlift |
| 5 | Ab Wheel | Ab Wheel | Chin-up |

**Notes:** There must be at least one day between workouts. This program is optimally suited for Monday/Wednesday/Friday training.

# PROGRAM V

INTERMEDIATE

## WORKOUTS

| A weeks 1, 3, 5 | B weeks 1, 3, 5 | C weeks 1, 3, 5 | D weeks 2, 4, 6 |

Sumo with Kettlebell
page 18

Lateral Lunge
page 42

Push-up on Kettlebells
page 76

Full with Barbell
page 14

Stationary Lunge
page 38

Hand Walkover
page 78

V-ups with Physio Ball
page 122

Walking with Rotation
page 40

Basic Push-up
page 60

Full with Dumbbells
page 15

Up to Box
page 54

On Physio Ball & Blocks
page 64

45-Degree Body Row
page 90

Plow on Physio Ball
page 112

Step Chin
page 100

Horizontal Body Row
page 92

Front Plank
page 126

Stand-Pull
page 98

Medicine Ball Raise
page 26

Plank to Pike
page 128

## E
weeks 2, 4, 6

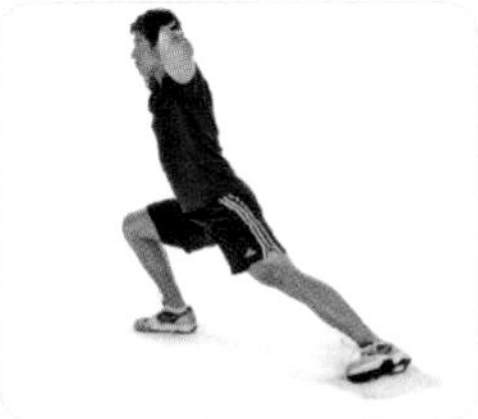
45-Degree Towel Slide
page 44

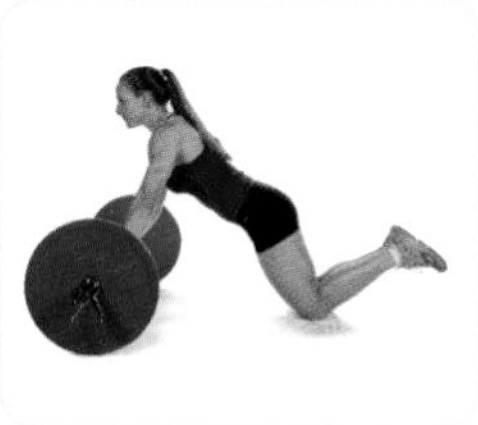
Push-up & Roll-out
page 62

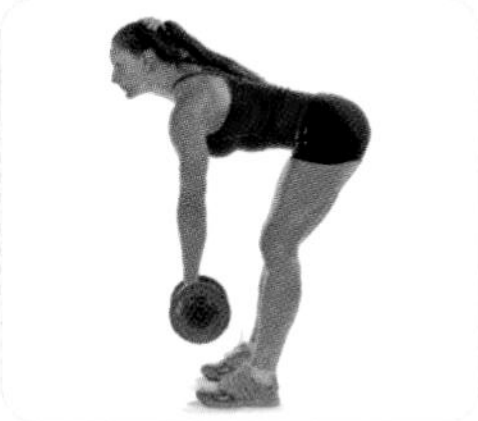
Straight-Leg with Dumbbell
page 22

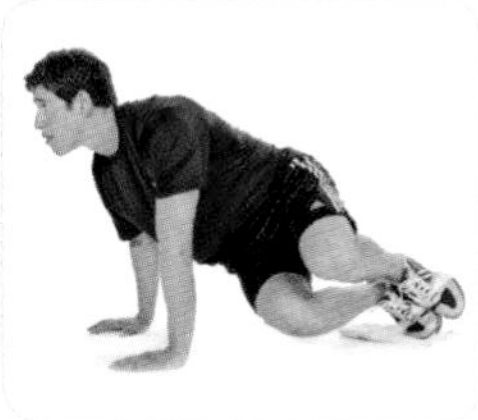
Plow with Rotation
page 114

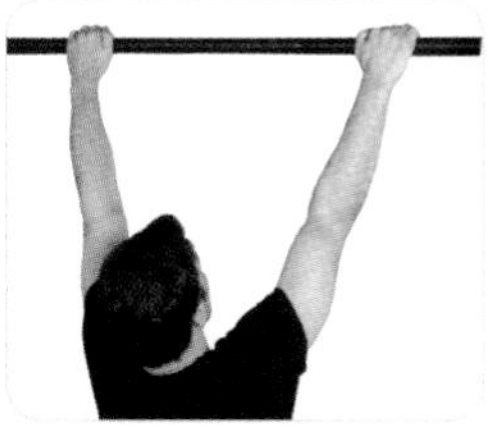
Pull-up Grip
page 88

## F
weeks 2, 4, 6

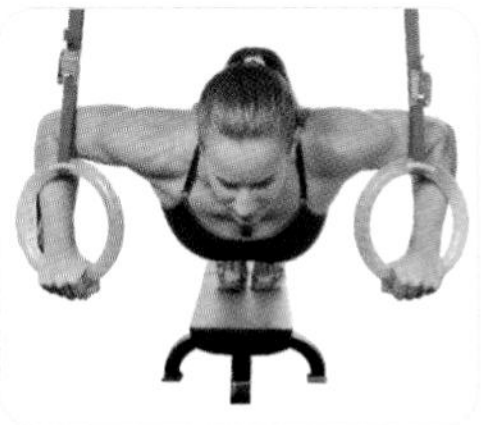
Hands on Rings
page 80

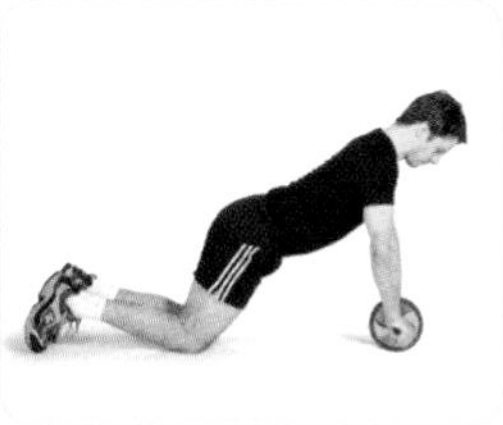
Ab Wheel
page 110

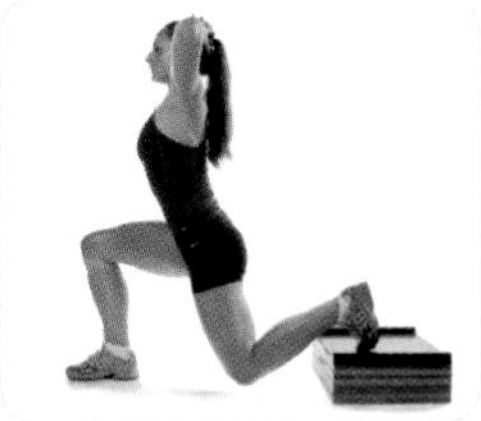
Off Box
page 56

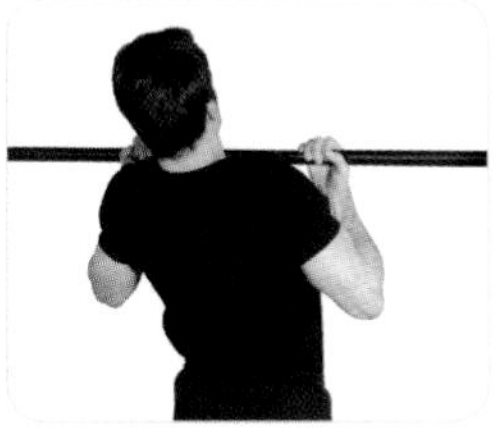
Basic Chin-up
page 86

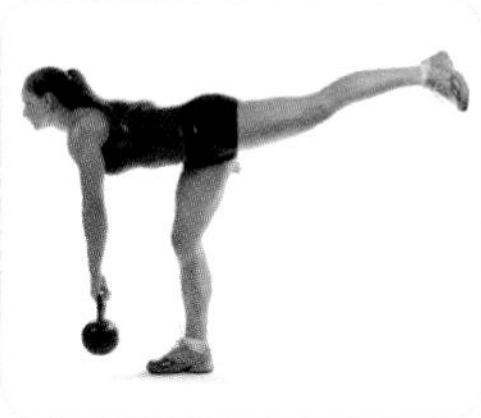
Single-Leg/Straight-Leg with Kettlebells page 24

## PROGRAM: V DURATION: 6 WEEKS

Days per week: 3
Total weeks: 6
Type: Intermediate Endurance

| Weeks | Day 1 | Day 2 | Day 3 |
|---|---|---|---|
| 1 | A | B | C |
| 2 | D | E | F |
| 3 | A | B | C |
| 4 | D | E | F |
| 5 | A | B | C |
| 6 | D | E | F |

## PRESCRIPTION

| Week | Sets | Repetitions | Weight/Progression | Rest Set/Exercise |
|---|---|---|---|---|
| 1 | 3 | 10 | TBD | :75 / :90 |
| 2 | 3 | 10 | TBD | :60 / :75 |
| 3 | 4 | 8 | Same as week 1 | :60 / :75 |
| 4 | 4 | 8 | Same as week 2 | :60 / :75 |
| 5 | 4 | 10 | Same as week 3 | :60 / :60 |
| 6 | 4 | 10 | Same as week 4 | :60 / :60 |

## EXERCISE SEQUENCE

| Order | Workout A | Workout B | Workout C | Workout D | Workout E | Workout F |
|---|---|---|---|---|---|---|
| 1 | Deadlift | Lunge | Push-up | Deadlift | Lunge | Push-up |
| 2 | Lunge | Push-up | Ab Wheel | Lunge | Push-up | Ab Wheel |
| 3 | Push-up | Deadlift | Lunge | Push-up | Deadlift | Lunge |
| 4 | Chin-up | Ab Wheel | Chin-up | Chin-up | Ab Wheel | Chin-up |
| 5 | Ab Wheel | Chin-up | Deadlift | Ab Wheel | Chin-up | Deadlift |

**Notes:** Due to the volume and intensity of work, a two-day rest between workouts is acceptable, with variability from week to week depending on the body's ability to recover.

# PROGRAM VI

ADVANCED

WORKOUTS

| D<br>weeks 1–4 | E<br>weeks 1–4 | F<br>weeks 1–4 |
|---|---|---|
| 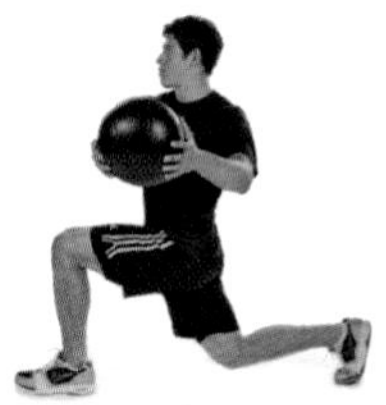<br>Walking with Rotation<br>page 40 | 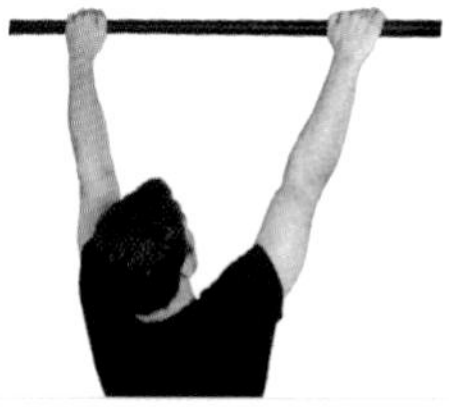<br>Pull-up Grip<br>page 88 | 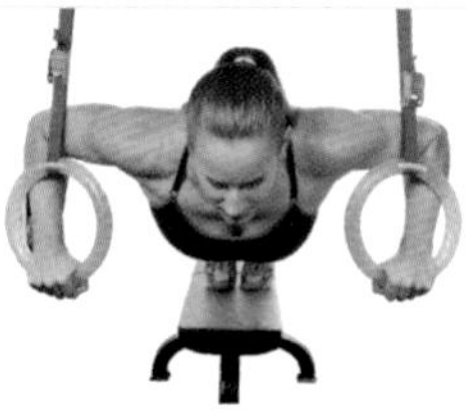<br>Hands on Rings<br>page 80 |
| 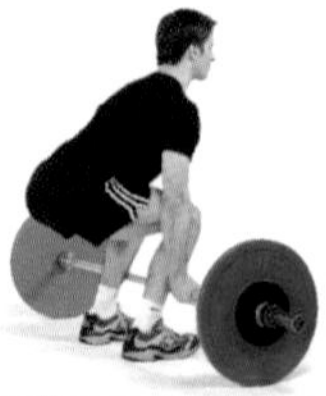<br>Full with Barbell<br>page 14 | 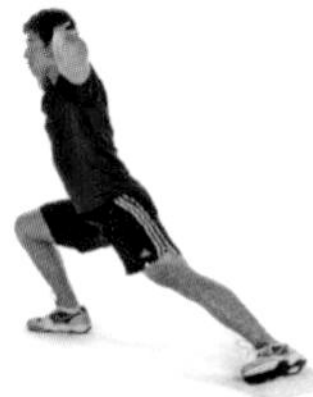<br>45-Degree Towel Slide<br>page 44 | 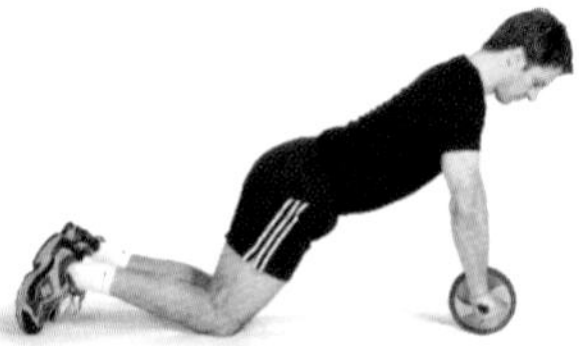<br>Ab Wheel<br>page 110 |
| 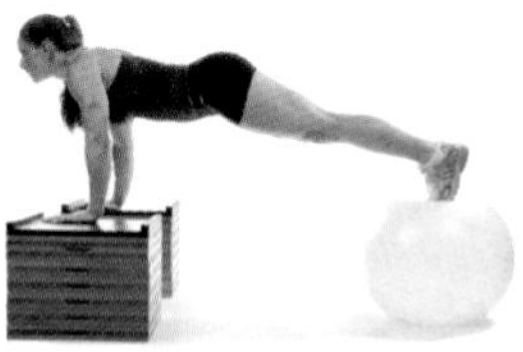<br>On Physio Ball & Blocks<br>page 64 | 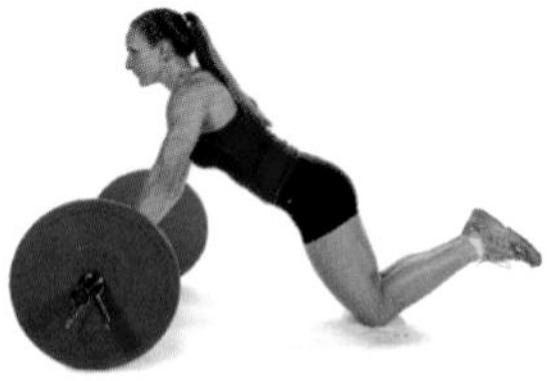<br>Push-up & Roll-out<br>page 62 | 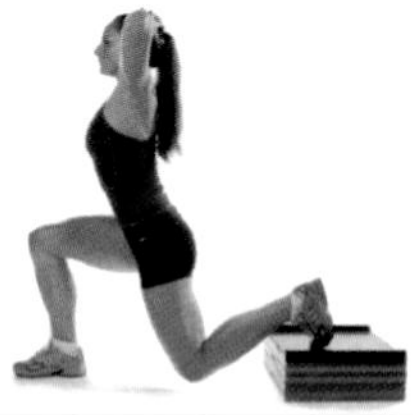<br>Off Box<br>page 56 |
| 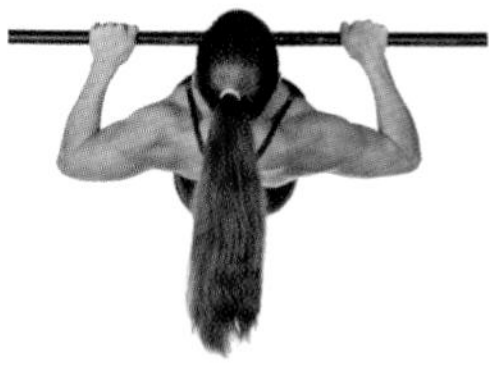<br>Horizontal Body Row<br>page 92 | 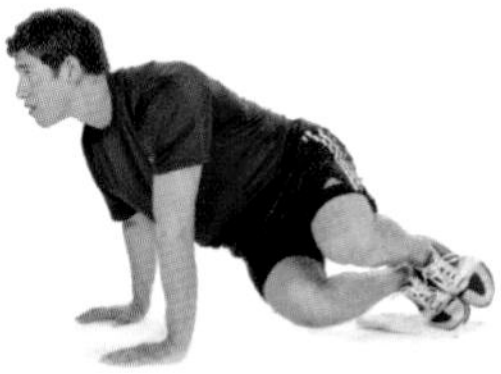<br>Plow with Rotation<br>page 114 | 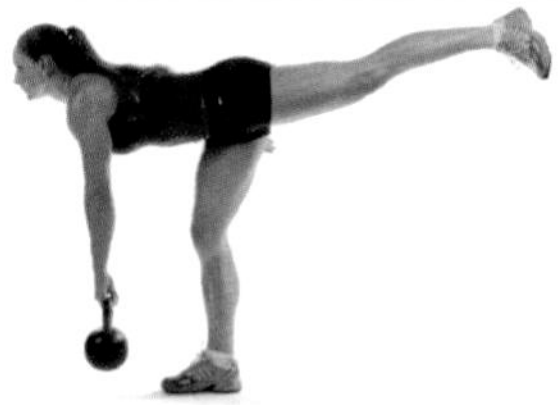<br>Single-Leg/Straight-Leg with Kettlebells<br>page 24 |
| 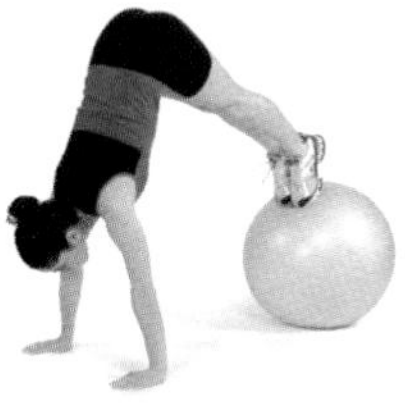<br>Plank to Pike<br>page 128 | 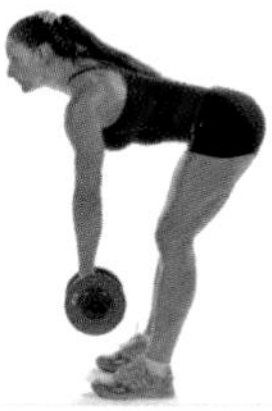<br>Straight-Leg with Dumbbell<br>page 22 | 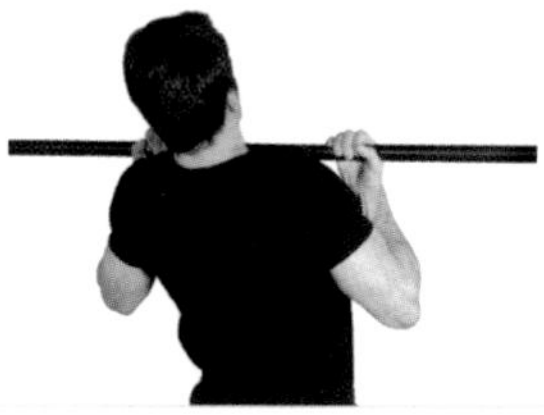<br>Basic Chin-up<br>page 86 |

## USER NOTES

## PROGRAM: VI  DURATION: 4 WEEKS

Days per week: 3
Total weeks: 4
Type: Advanced Strength

|  | Days | | |
|---|---|---|---|
| Weeks | 1 | 2 | 3 |
| 1 | D | E | F |
| 2 | D | E | F |
| 3 | D | E | F |
| 4 | D | E | F |

## PRESCRIPTION

| Week | Sets | Repetitions | Weight/Progression | Rest Set/Exercise |
|---|---|---|---|---|
| 1 | 5 | 10 | TBD | :90 / :120 |
| 2 | 5 | 8 | Up weight by 15% BW 5 reps | :90 / :120 |
| 3 | 5 | 6 | Up weight 10–15% BW 5–10 reps | :120 / :120 |
| 4 | 5 | 10 | Same as week 1 | :90 / :90 |

## EXERCISE SEQUENCE

| | Workout | | |
|---|---|---|---|
| Order | D | E | F |
| 1 | Lunge | Chin-up | Push-up |
| 2 | Deadlift | Lunge | Ab Wheel |
| 3 | Push-up | Push-up | Lunge |
| 4 | Chin-up | Ab Wheel | Deadlift |
| 5 | Ab Wheel | Deadlift | Chin-up |

**Notes:** Due to the volume and intensity of these workouts, a two-day rest between workouts is acceptable, with variability from week to week depending on the body's ability to recover.

# PROGRAM VII

BEGINNER

## WORKOUTS

| G weeks 1–2 | H weeks 1–2 | H weeks 3–4 | G weeks 3–4 |
|---|---|---|---|
| 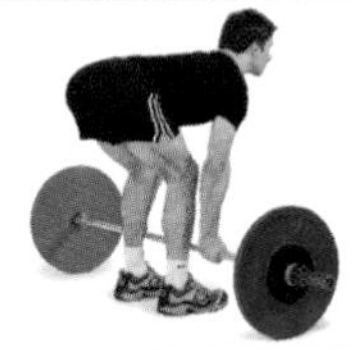 Straight-Leg with Barbell page 16 | 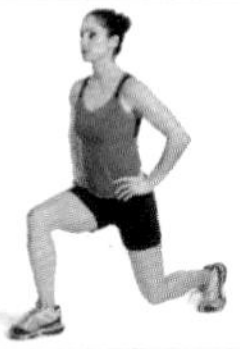 Stationary Lunge page 38 | 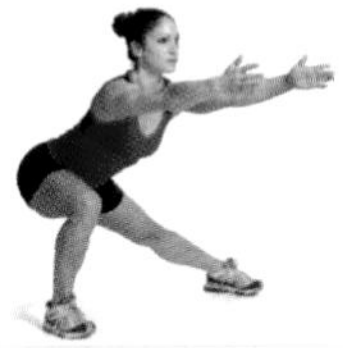 Lateral Lunge page 42 | 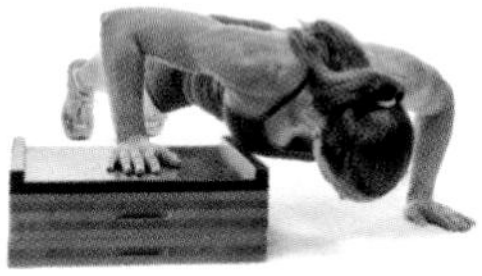 Hand Walkover page 78 |
| 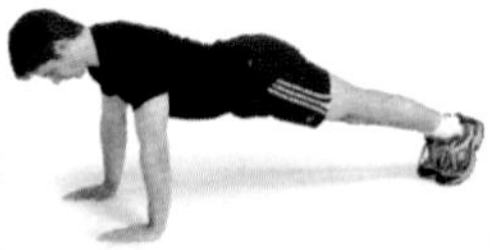 Basic Push-up page 60 | 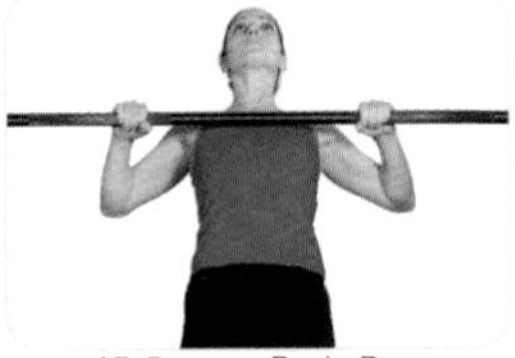 45-Degree Body Row page 90 | 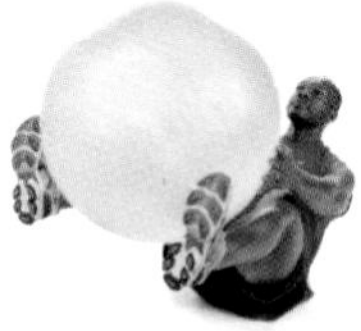 V-ups with Physio Ball page 122 | 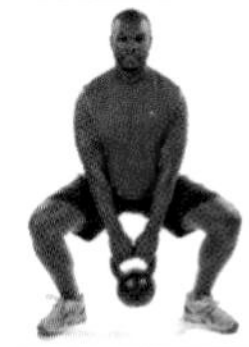 Sumo with Kettlebell page 18 |
| 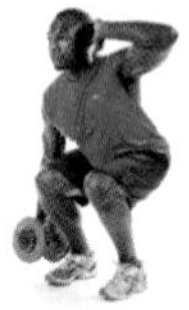 Full with Dumbbell page 34 | 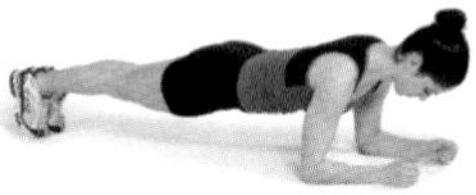 Front Plank page 126 | 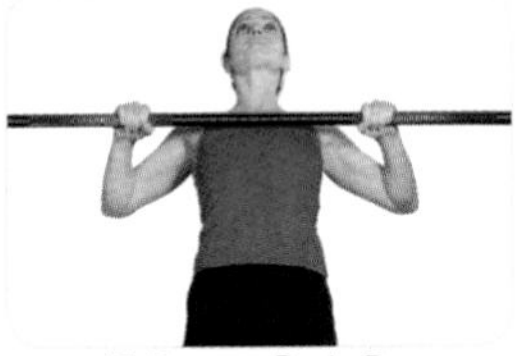 45-Degree Body Row page 90 | 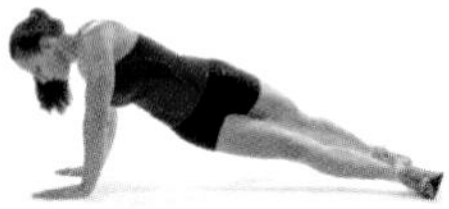 Lower Body Rotation page 72 |
| 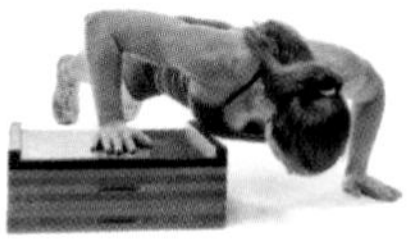 Hand Walkover page 78 | 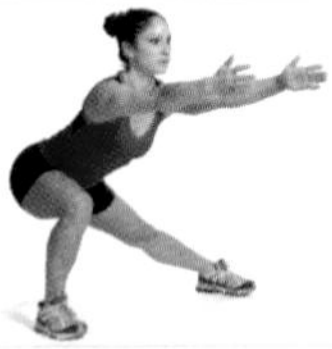 Lateral Lunge page 42 | 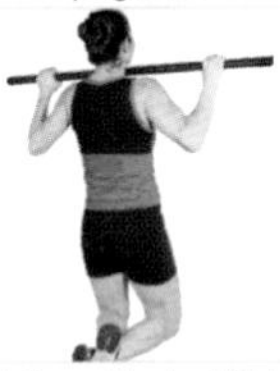 Pull-up Neutral Grip page 96 | 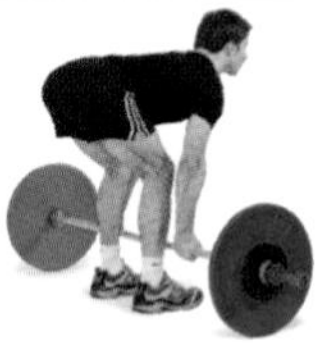 Straight-Leg with Barbell page 16 |
| 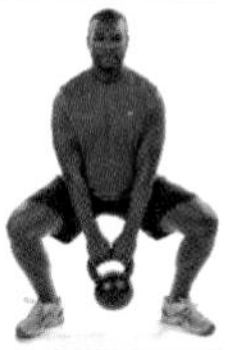 Sumo with Kettlebell page 18 | 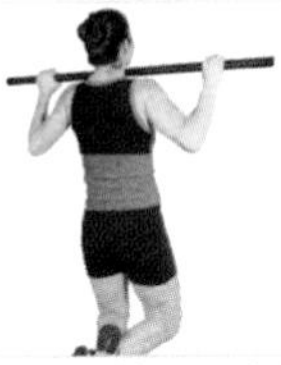 Pull-up Neutral Grip page 96 | 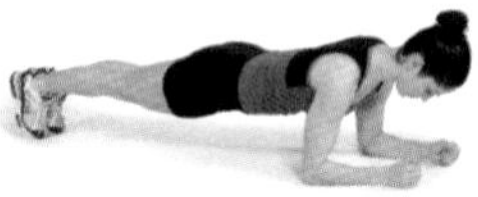 Front Plank page 126 | 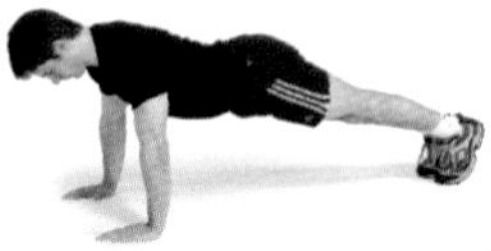 Basic Push-up page 60 |
| 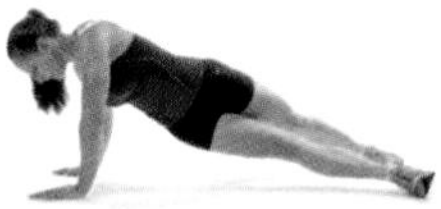 Lower Body Rotation page 72 | 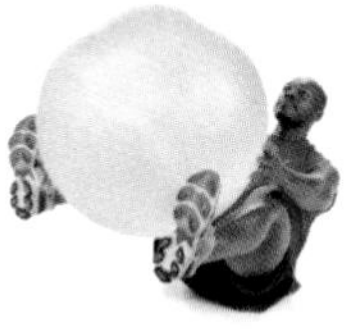 V-ups with Physio Ball page 122 | 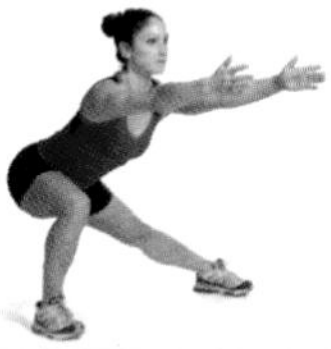 Lateral Lunge page 42 | 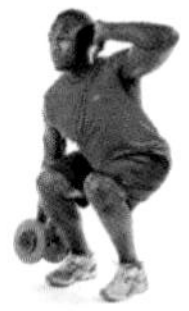 Full with Dumbbell page 34 |

## USER NOTES

## PROGRAM: VII  DURATION: 4 WEEKS

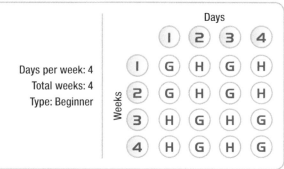

Days per week: 4
Total weeks: 4
Type: Beginner

| Weeks \ Days | 1 | 2 | 3 | 4 |
|---|---|---|---|---|
| 1 | G | H | G | H |
| 2 | G | H | G | H |
| 3 | H | G | H | G |
| 4 | H | G | H | G |

## PRESCRIPTION

| Week | Sets | Repetitions | Weight/Progression | Rest Set/Exercise |
|---|---|---|---|---|
| 1 | 2 | 10 | TBD | None / :60 |
| 2 | 2 | 12 | Weights remain the same throughout the program. | None / :60 |
| 3 | 2 | 15 | | None / :60 |
| 4 | 2 | 20 | | None / :75 |

## EXERCISE SEQUENCE

| Order \ Workout | G | H | H | G |
|---|---|---|---|---|
| 1 | Deadlift | Lunge | Lunge | Push-up |
| 2 | Push-up | Chin-up | Ab Wheel | Deadlift |
| 3 | Deadlift | Ab Wheel | Chin-up | Push-up |
| 4 | Push-up | Lunge | Chin-up | Deadlift |
| 5 | Deadlift | Chin-up | Ab Wheel | Push-up |
| 6 | Push-up | Ab Wheel | Lunge | Deadlift |

**Notes:** Exercises are to be performed in pairs, or "supersets." Complete three sets of the first two exercises, then three sets of the third and fourth exercises, and then finally move on to the fifth and sixth exercises.

# PROGRAM VIII



## WORKOUTS

### I
weeks 1–4

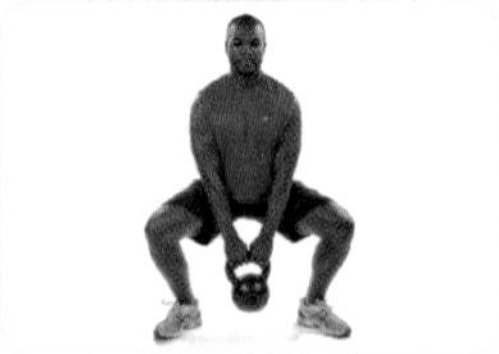
Sumo with Kettlebell
page 18

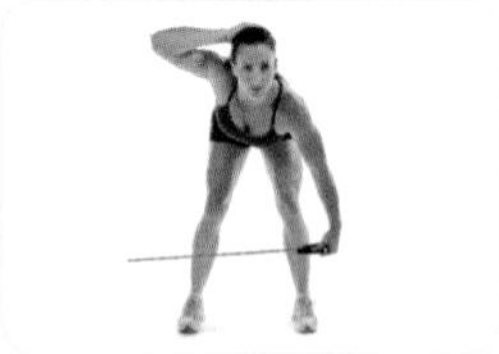
Straight-Leg Cable
page 30

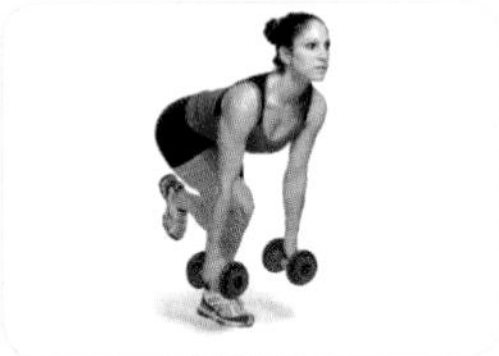
Full Single-Leg with Dumbbells
page 20

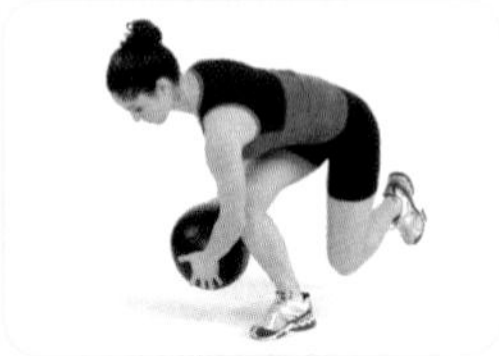
Medicine Ball Raise
page 26

### J
weeks 1–4

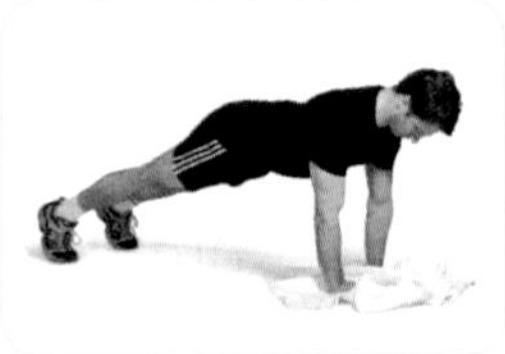
Towel Fly
page 68

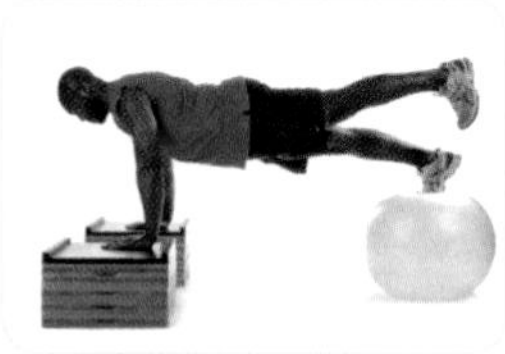
On Physio Ball & Blocks
page 65

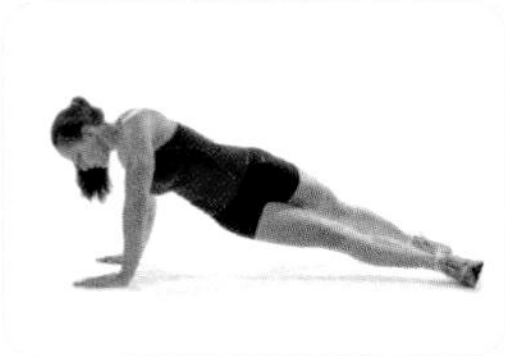
Lower Body Rotation
page 72

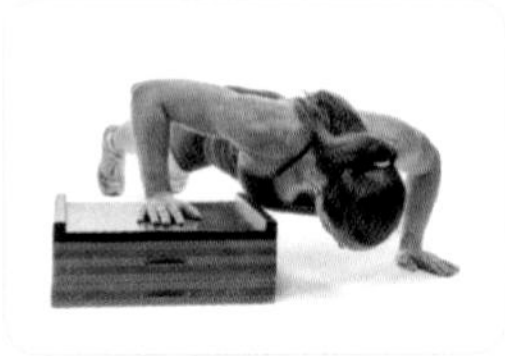
Hand Walkover
page 78

### K
weeks 1–4

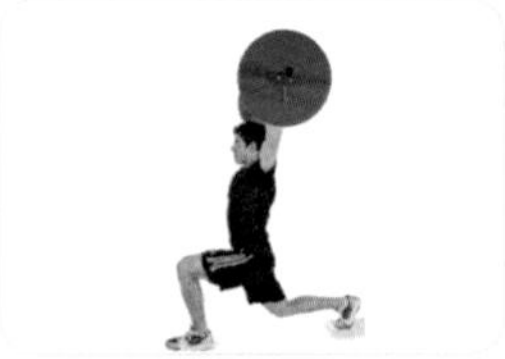
Stationary with Barbell
page 39

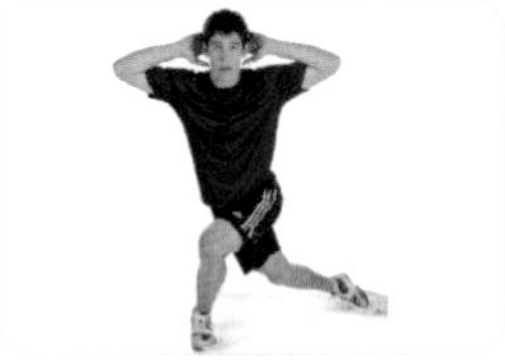
Cross-Body Towel Slide
page 48

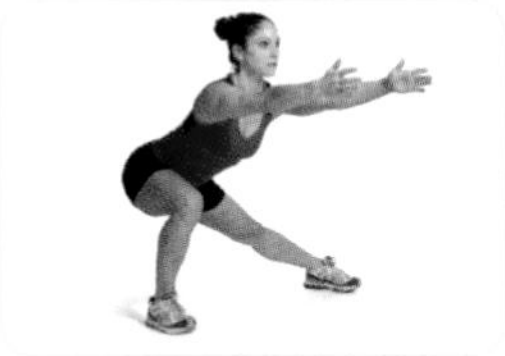
Lateral Lunge
page 42

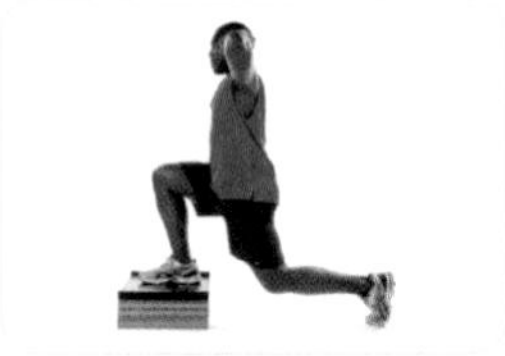
Up to Box
page 54

### L
weeks 1–4

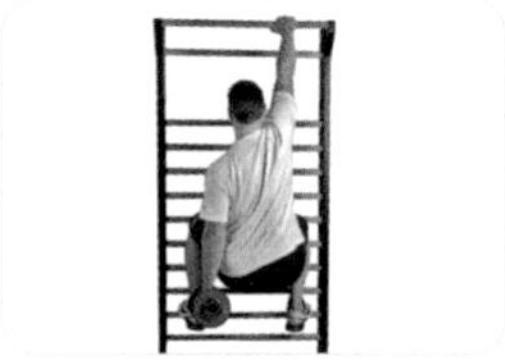
Step Chin with Dumbbell
page 101

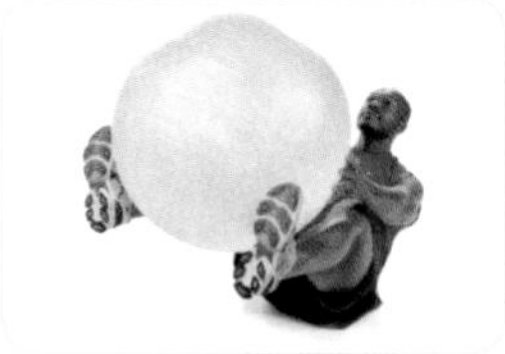
V-ups with Physio Ball
page 122

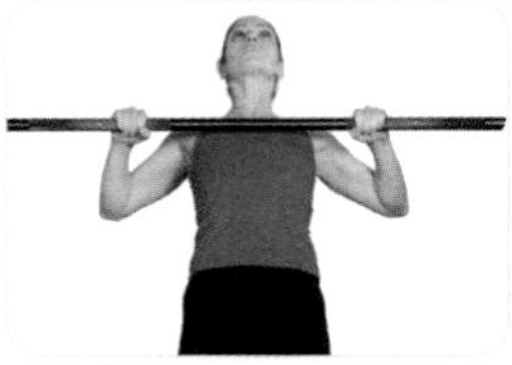
45-Degree Body Row
page 90

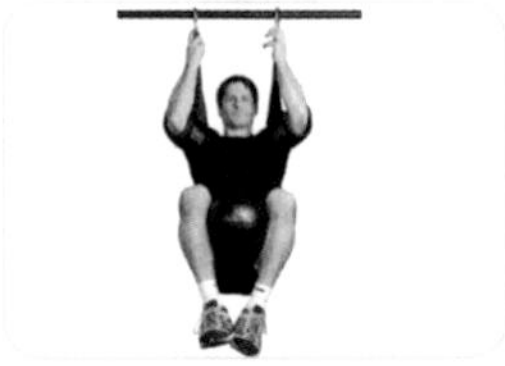
Bent-Knee Hanging Raise with
Medicine Ball page 118

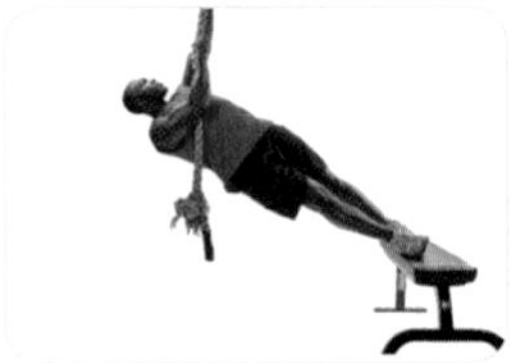
Lateral Rope
page 94

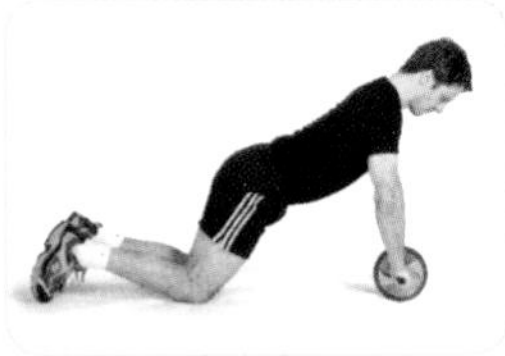
Ab Wheel
page 110

# PROGRAM VIII • INTERMEDIATE

## USER NOTES

## PROGRAM: VIII  DURATION: 4 WEEKS

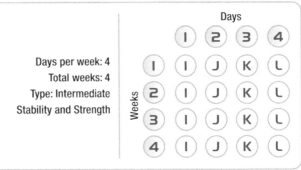

Days per week: 4
Total weeks: 4
Type: Intermediate
Stability and Strength

| Weeks | Day 1 | Day 2 | Day 3 | Day 4 |
|-------|-------|-------|-------|-------|
| 1 | I | J | K | L |
| 2 | I | J | K | L |
| 3 | I | J | K | L |
| 4 | I | J | K | L |

## PRESCRIPTION

| Week | Sets | Repetitions | Weight/Progression | Rest Set/Exercise |
|------|------|-------------|--------------------|--------------------|
| 1 | 3 | 10 | 80–85% max | :90 / :90 |
| 2 | 3 | 8 | Increase weight 5%/BW 3 reps | :90 / :90 |
| 3 | 3 | 6 | Increase weight 5%/BW 3 reps | :90 / :90 |
| 4 | 3 | 10 | Original weight | :90 / :90 |

## EXERCISE SEQUENCE

| Order | Workout I | J | K | L |
|-------|-----------|---|---|---|
| 1 | Deadlift | Push-up | Lunge | Chin-ups / Ab Wheel |
| 2 | Deadlift | Push-up | Lunge | Chin-ups / Ab Wheel |
| 3 | Deadlift | Push-up | Lunge | Chin-ups / Ab Wheel |
| 4 | Deadlift | Push-up | Lunge | Chin-ups / Ab Wheel |
| 5 | | | | Chin-ups / Ab Wheel |
| 6 | | | | Chin-ups / Ab Wheel |

**Notes:** This program is two days on, one off, two on, followed by a two-day rest. For body-weight exercises, reps should increase in weeks 2 and 3 until close to failure.

# PROGRAM IX

ADVANCED

## WORKOUTS

### M
weeks 1–4

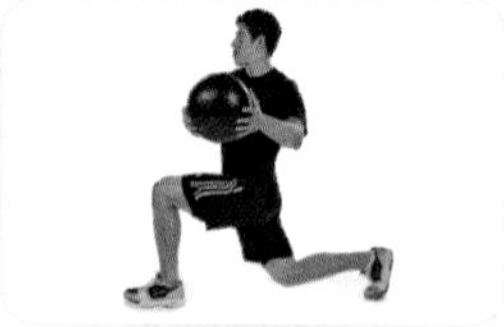
Walking with Rotation
page 40

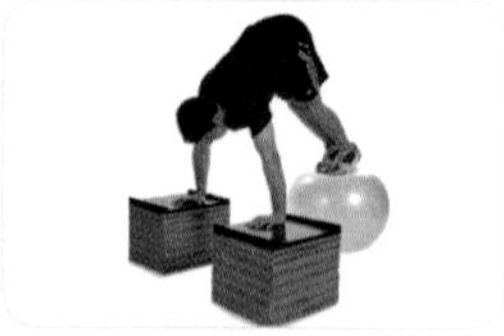
Pike & Press
page 70

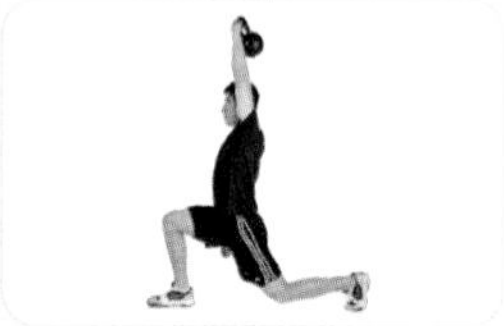
Reverse with Overhead Kettlebell
page 52

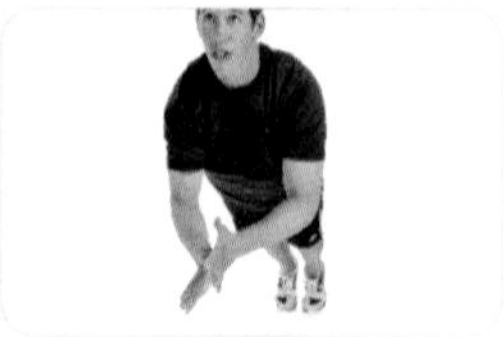
Clap
page 74

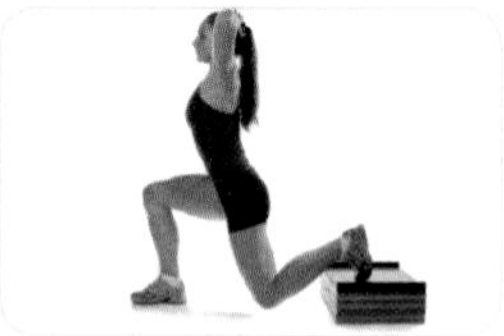
Off Box
page 56

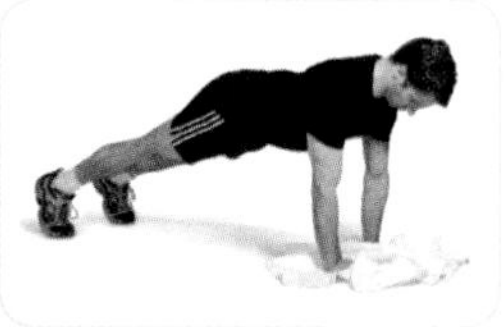
Towel Fly
page 68

### N
weeks 1–4

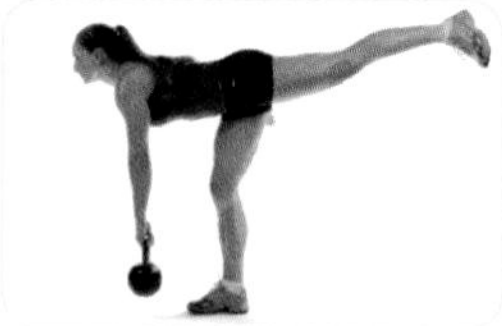
Single-Leg/Straight-Leg with Kettlebell
page 24

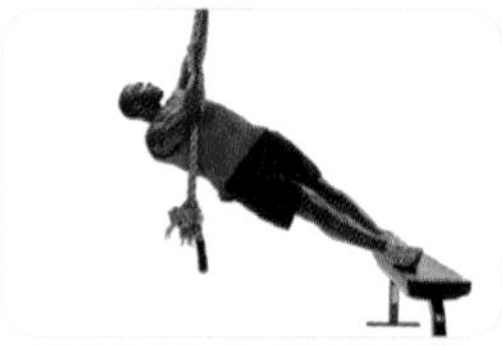
Lateral Rope
page 94

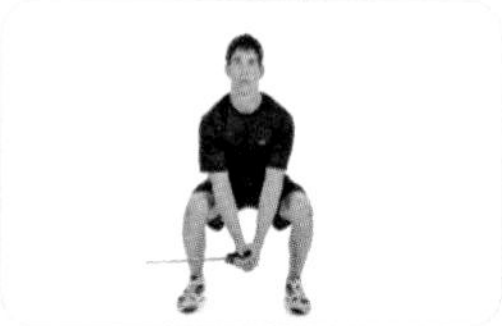
Full Cable with Rotation
page 28

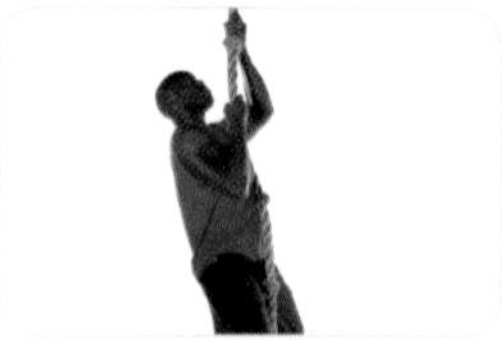
Rope Chins
page 107

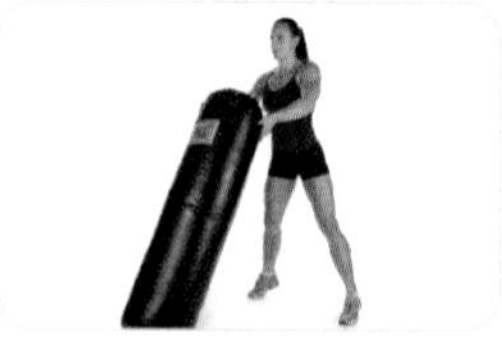
Bag Flip
page 32

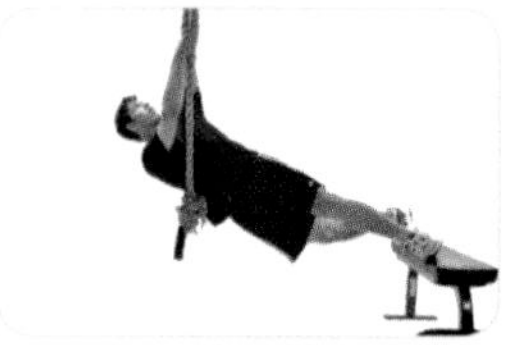
Drop & Pull
page 104

### O
weeks 1–4

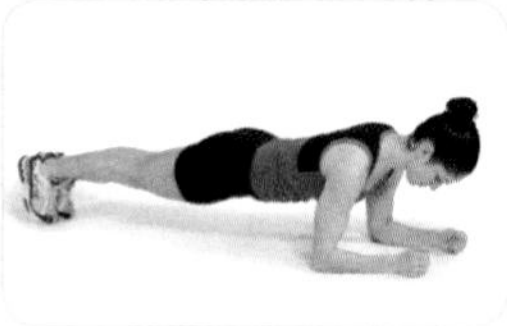
Front Plank
page 126

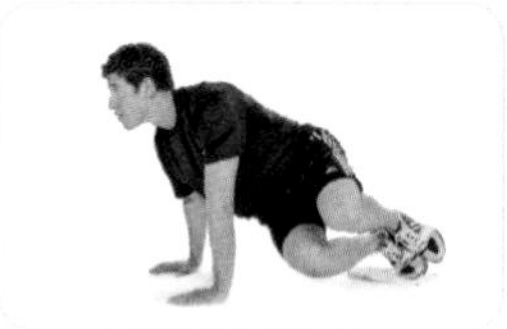
Plow with Rotation
page 114

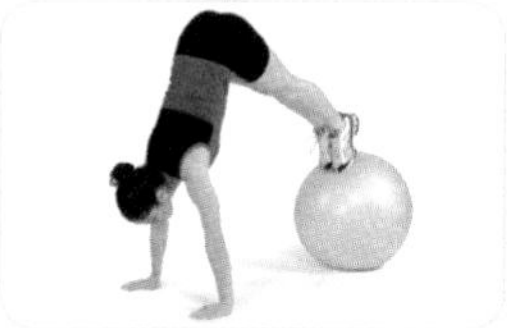
Pike to Plank
page 128

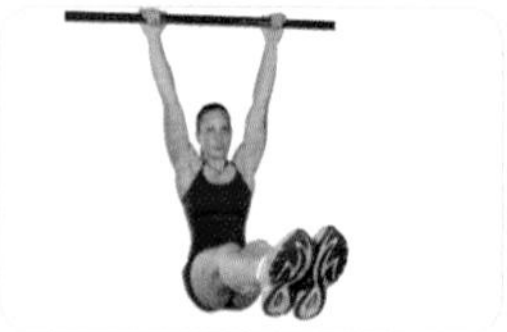
Straight-Leg Hanging Raise
page 116

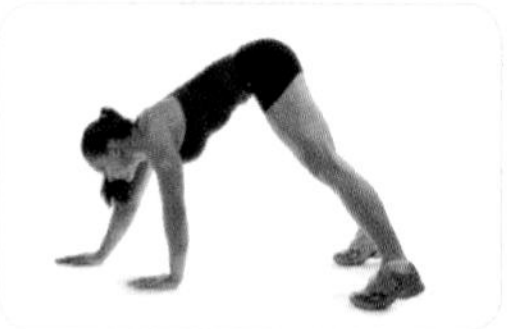
Hand Walk-out
page 124

### D
weeks 1–4

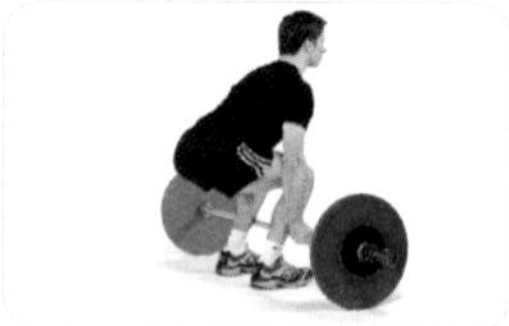
Full with Barbell
page 14

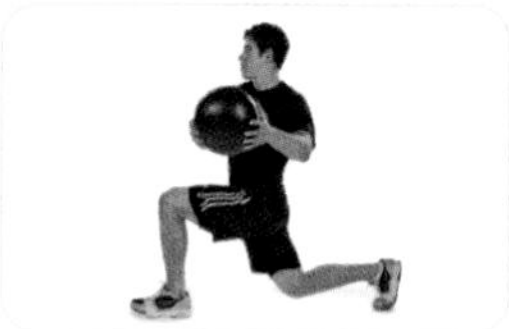
Walking with Rotation
page 40

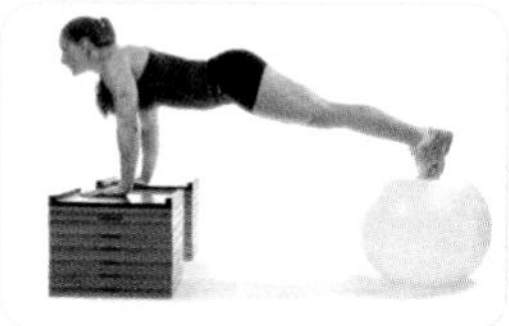
On Physio Ball & Blocks
page 64

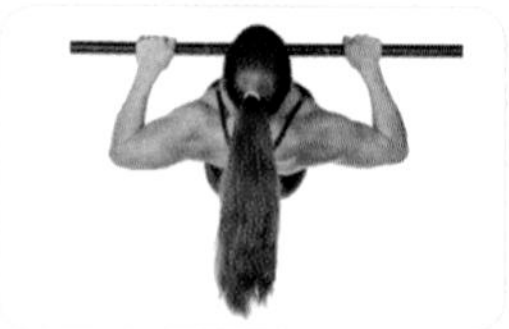
Horizontal Body Row
page 92

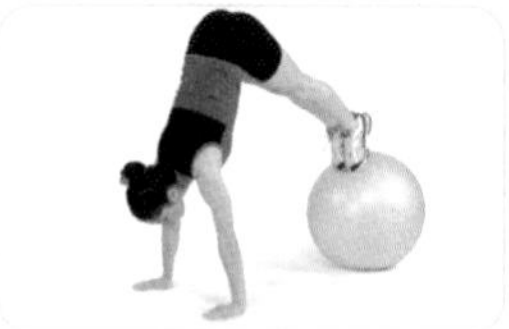
Plank to Pike
page 128

## USER NOTES

## PROGRAM: IX  DURATION: 4 WEEKS

Days per week: 4
Total weeks: 4
Type: Advanced

| Weeks | Days 1 | 2 | 3 | 4 |
|---|---|---|---|---|
| 1 | M | N | O | D |
| 2 | M | N | O | D |
| 3 | M | N | O | D |
| 4 | M | N | O | D |

## PRESCRIPTION

| Week | Sets | Repetitions | Weight/Progression | Rest Set/Exercise |
|---|---|---|---|---|
| 1 | 3 | 8 | TBD | :75 / :75 |
| 2 | 3 | 10 | Same | :75 / :75 |
| 3 | 4 | 8 | Same | :75 / :75 |
| 4 | 4 | 10 | Same | :75 / :75 |

## EXERCISE SEQUENCE

| Order | Workout M | N | O | D |
|---|---|---|---|---|
| 1 | Lunge | Deadlift | Ab Wheel | Deadlift |
| 2 | Push-up | Chin-up | Ab Wheel | Lunge |
| 3 | Lunge | Deadlift | Ab Wheel | Push-up |
| 4 | Push-up | Chin-up | Ab Wheel | Chin-up |
| 5 | Lunge | Deadlift | Ab Wheel | Ab Wheel |
| 6 | Push-up | Chin-up | | |

**Notes:** This sequence is three days on, one or two days off. There are two days that are split, one Ab Wheel–only day and one full-body day. The days before and after full body must be rest days.

# PROGRAM X

**BEGINNER**

## WORKOUTS

| Q | R | S | T |
|---|---|---|---|
| weeks 1–4 | weeks 1–4 | weeks 1–4 | weeks 1–4 |

Full with Barbell
page 14

Backward Towel Slide
page 46

Towel Fly
page 68

Stand-Pull
page 98

Full Single-Leg with Dumbbells
page 20

Lateral Lunge
page 42

Lower Body Rotation
page 72

45-Degree Body Row
page 90

Straight-Leg with Dumbbells
page 22

45-Degree Towel Slide
page 44

Hand Walkover
page 78

Vertical Rope with Alternate Grip
page 102

## U
weeks 1–4

Front Plank
page 126

Hand Walk-out
page 124

V-ups with Physio Ball
page 122

## PROGRAM: X   DURATION: 4 WEEKS

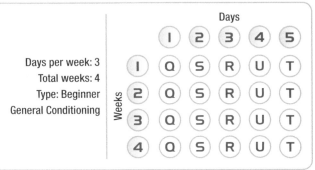

Days per week: 3
Total weeks: 4
Type: Beginner
General Conditioning

| Weeks \ Days | 1 | 2 | 3 | 4 | 5 |
|---|---|---|---|---|---|
| 1 | Q | S | R | U | T |
| 2 | Q | S | R | U | T |
| 3 | Q | S | R | U | T |
| 4 | Q | S | R | U | T |

## PRESCRIPTION

| Week | Sets | Repetitions | Weight/Progression | Rest Set/Exercise |
|---|---|---|---|---|
| 1 | 3 | 6 | TBD | :75 / :90 |
| 2 | 3 | 8 | Same | :75 / :75 |
| 3 | 3 | 10 | Same | :75 / :75 |
| 4 | 3 | 12 | Same | :75 / :90 |

## EXERCISE SEQUENCE

| Order | Q | R | S | T | U |
|---|---|---|---|---|---|
| 1 | Deadlift | Lunge | Push-up | Chin-up | Ab Wheel |
| 2 | Deadlift | Lunge | Push-up | Chin-up | Ab Wheel |
| 3 | Deadlift | Lunge | Push-up | Chin-up | Ab Wheel |

**Notes:** The exercise sequence should be completely rearranged for every workout in weeks 3 and 4.

# PROGRAM XI

INTERMEDIATE

WORKOUTS

| I<br>weeks 1–4 | J<br>weeks 1–4 | K<br>weeks 1–4 | P<br>weeks 1–4 |
|---|---|---|---|
| 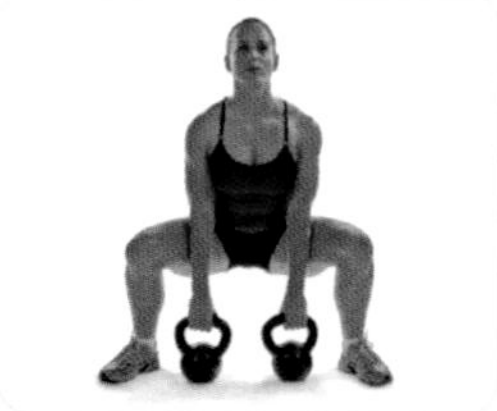<br>Sumo with Two Kettlebells<br>page 19 | 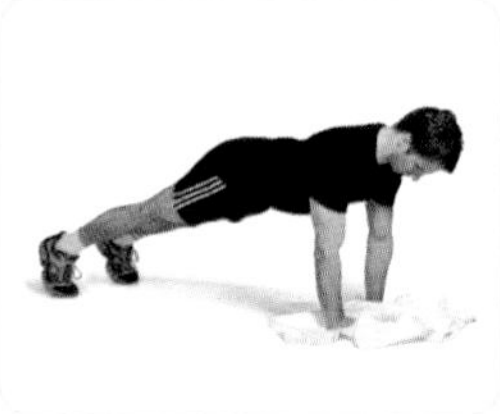<br>Towel Fly<br>page 68 | 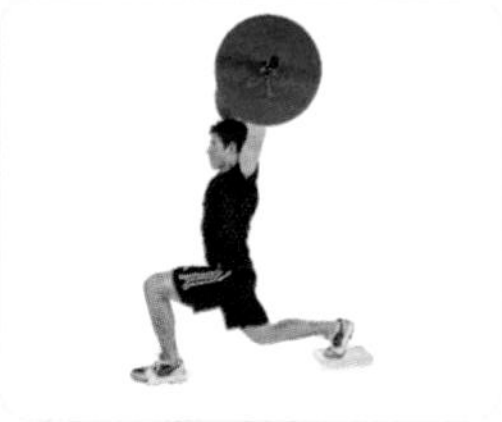<br>Stationary with Barbell<br>page 39 | 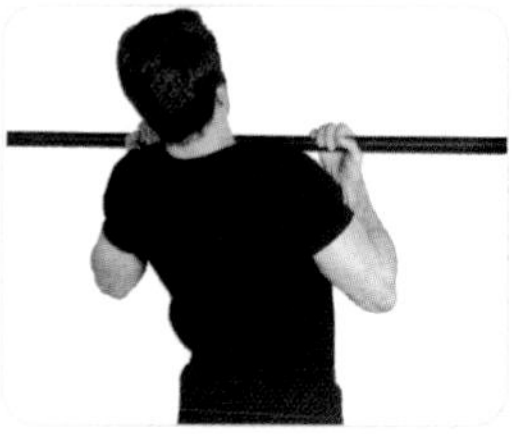<br>Basic Chin-up<br>page 82 |
| 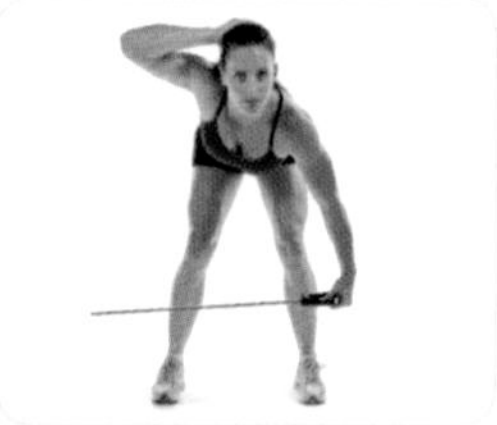<br>Straight-Leg Cable<br>page 30 | 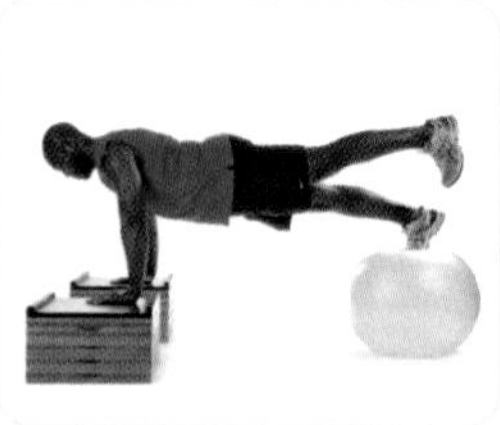<br>On Physio Ball & Blocks<br>page 65 | 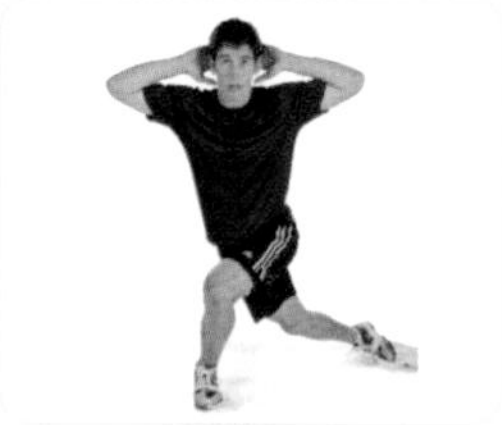<br>Cross-Body Towel Slide<br>page 48 | 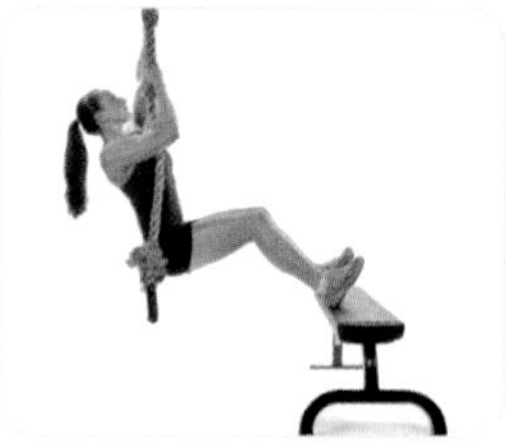<br>Vertical Rope<br>page 102 |
| 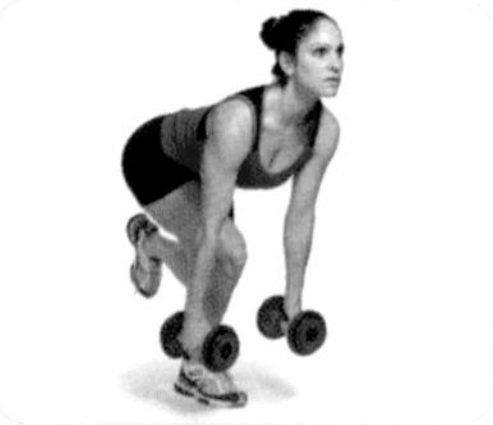<br>Full Single-Leg with Dumbbells<br>page 20 | 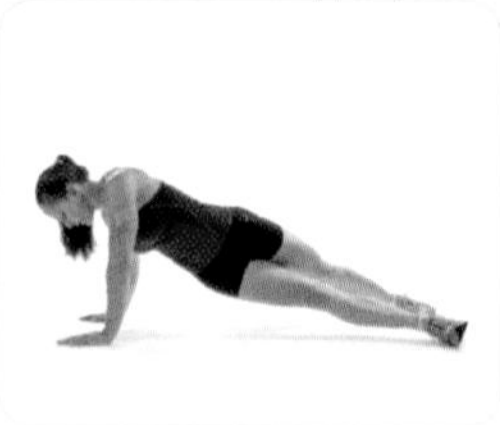<br>Lower Body Rotation<br>page 72 | 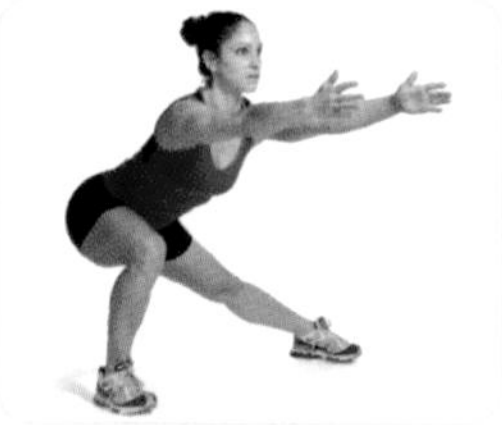<br>Lateral Lunge<br>page 42 | 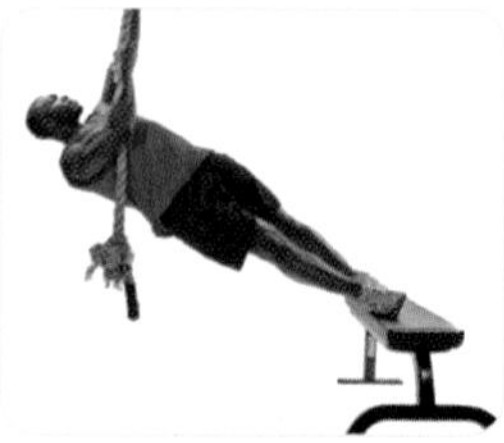<br>Lateral Rope<br>page 94 |
| 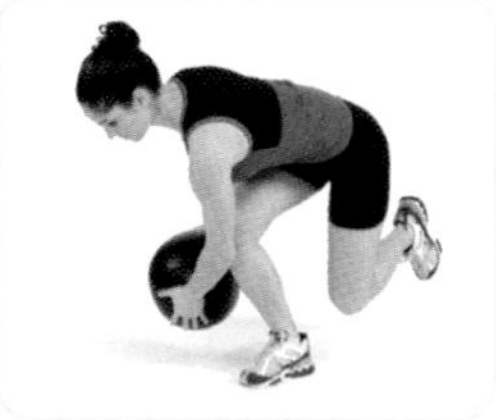<br>Medicine Ball Raise<br>page 26 | 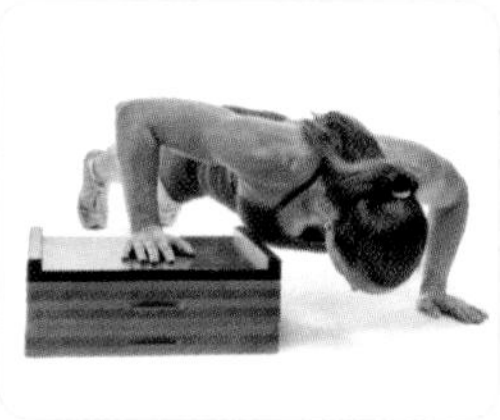<br>Hand Walkover<br>page 78 | 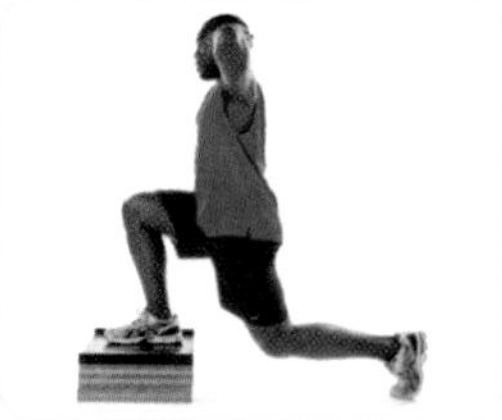<br>Lunge Up to Box<br>page 54 | 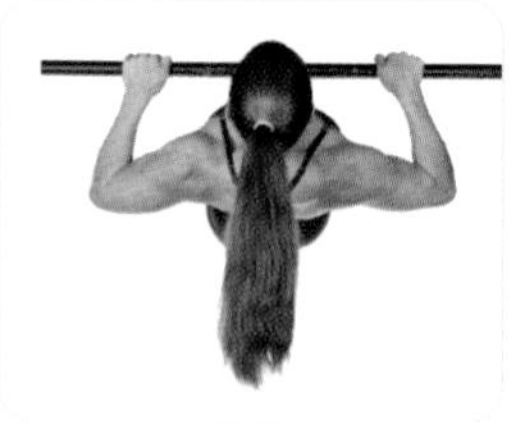<br>Horizontal Body Row<br>page 92 |

## Z
### weeks 1–4

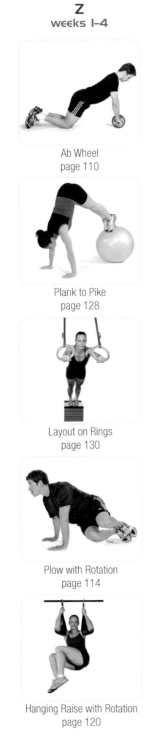

Ab Wheel
page 110

Plank to Pike
page 128

Layout on Rings
page 130

Plow with Rotation
page 114

Hanging Raise with Rotation
page 120

## PROGRAM: XI   DURATION: 4 WEEKS

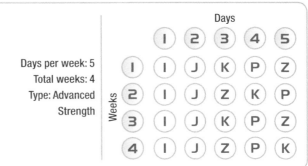

Days per week: 5
Total weeks: 4
Type: Advanced
Strength

| Weeks \ Days | 1 | 2 | 3 | 4 | 5 |
|---|---|---|---|---|---|
| 1 | I | J | K | P | Z |
| 2 | I | J | Z | K | P |
| 3 | I | J | K | P | Z |
| 4 | I | J | Z | P | K |

## PRESCRIPTION

| Week | Sets | Repetitions | Weight/Progression | Rest Set/Exercise |
|---|---|---|---|---|
| 1 | 4 | 8 | TBD | :120 / :120 |
| 2 | 4 | 8 | Increase weight 10% BW (2–5) reps | :120 / :120 |
| 3 | 4 | 8 | Increase weight 15% BW (2–5) reps | :120 / :120 |
| 4 | 4 | 8 | Increase weight 10% BW (2–5) reps | :120 / :180 |

## EXERCISE SEQUENCE

| Order \ Workout | I | J | K | P | Z |
|---|---|---|---|---|---|
| 1 | Deadlift | Push-up | Lunge | Chin-up | Ab Wheel |
| 2 | Deadlift | Push-up | Lunge | Chin-up | Ab Wheel |
| 3 | Deadlift | Push-up | Lunge | Chin-up | Ab Wheel |
| 4 | Deadlift | Push-up | Lunge | Chin-up | Ab Wheel |
| 5 | | | | | Ab Wheel |

**Notes:** For all workouts in this program, the sequence of a given day should never be the same.

# PROGRAM XII

ADVANCED

## WORKOUTS

### V
weeks 1–4

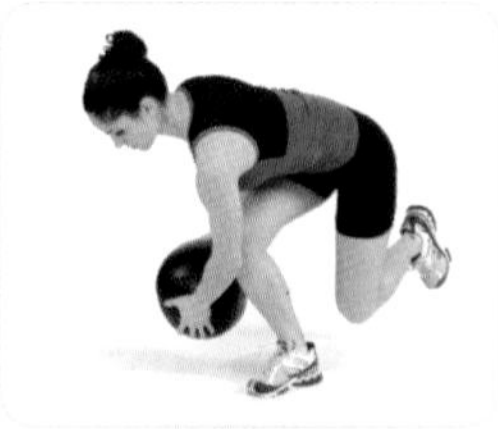

Medicine Ball Raise
page 26

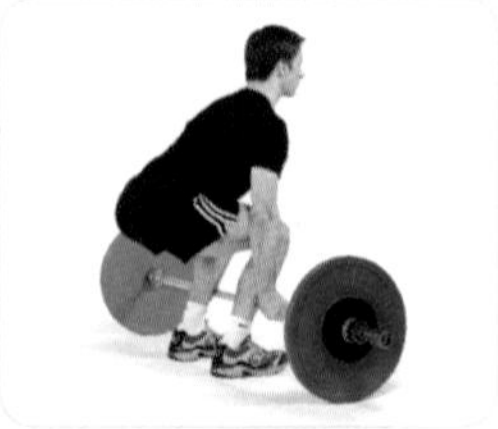

Full with Barbell
page 14

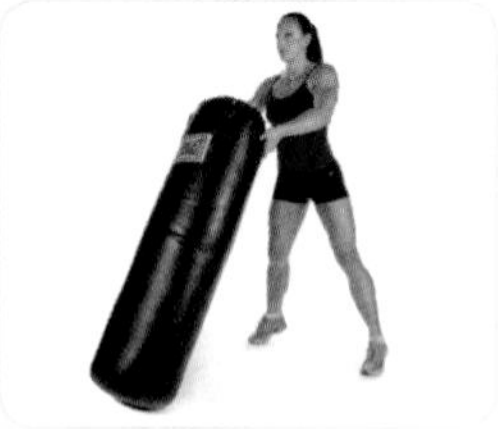

Bag Flip
page 32

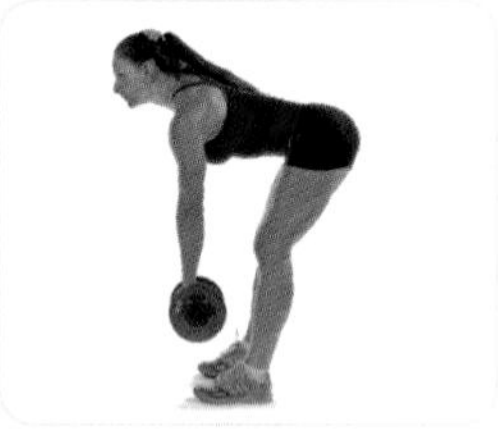

Straight-Leg with Dumbbell
page 22

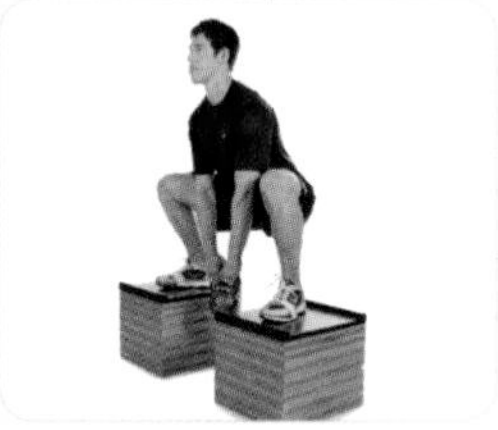

Sumo off Block
page 19

### W
weeks 1–4

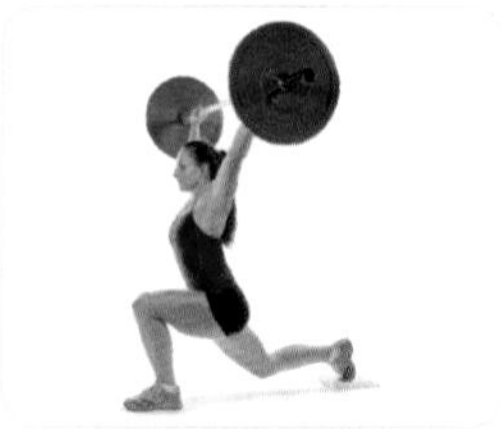

Reverse Barbell Slide
page 50

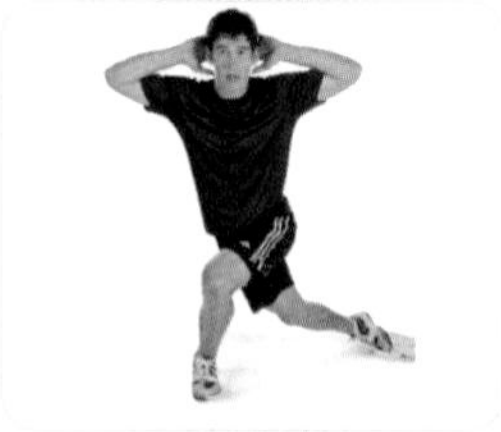

Cross-Body Towel Slide
page 48

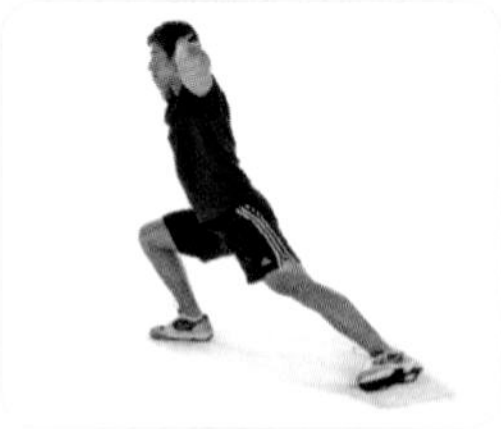

45-Degree Towel Slide
page 44

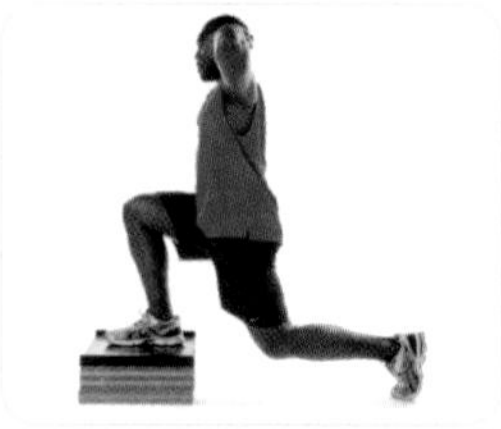

Up to Box
page 54

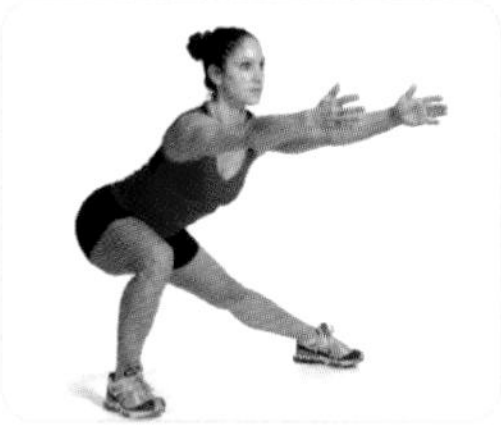

Lateral Lunge
page 42

### X
weeks 1–4

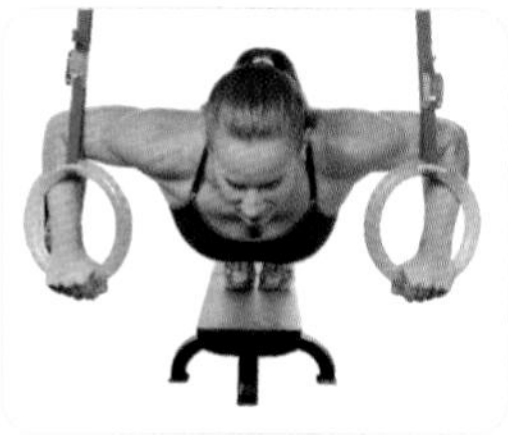

Hands on Rings
page 80

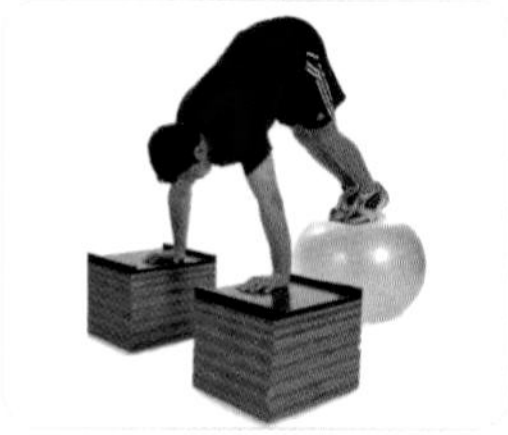

Pike & Press
page 70

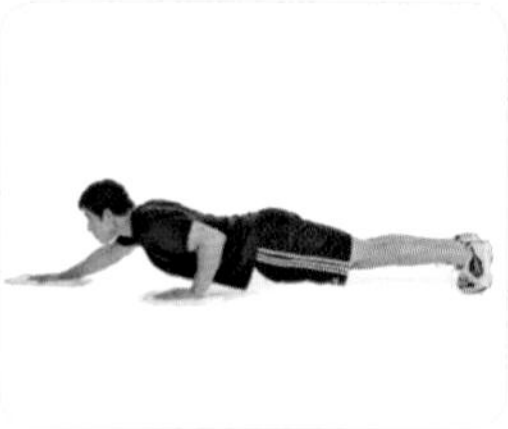

Single-Arm Forward Slide
page 82

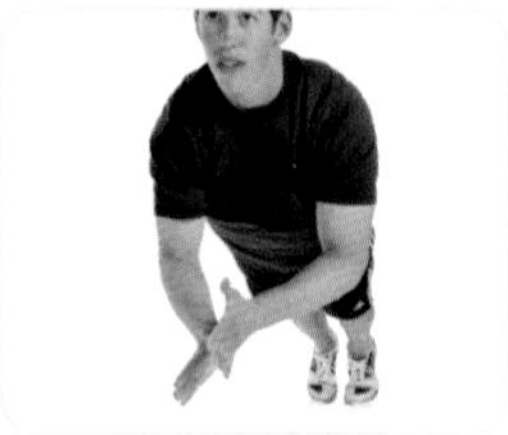

Clap
page 74

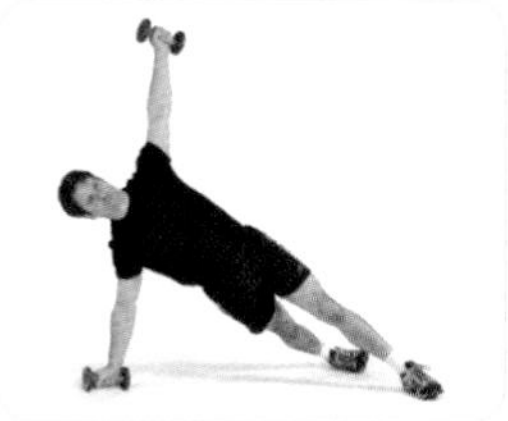

On Dumbbells with Rotation
page 64

### Y
weeks 1–4

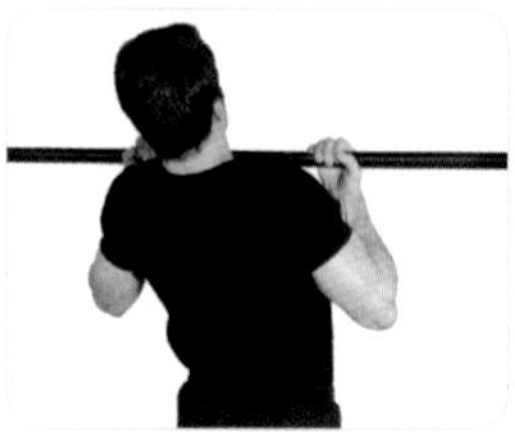

Basic Chin-up
page 86

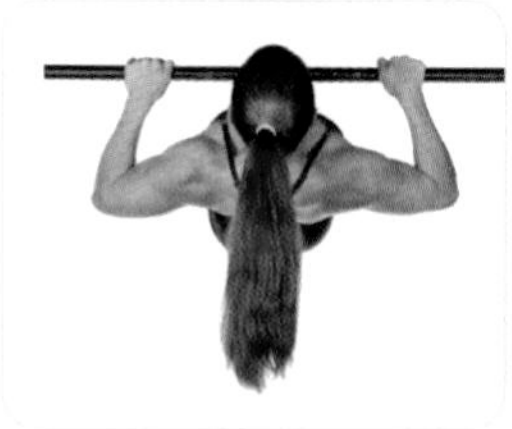

Horizontal Body Row
page 92

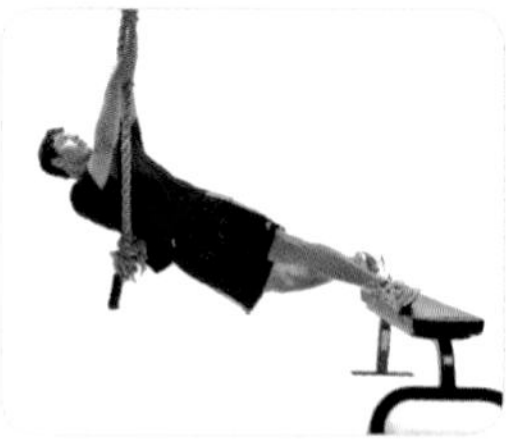

Drop & Pull
page 104

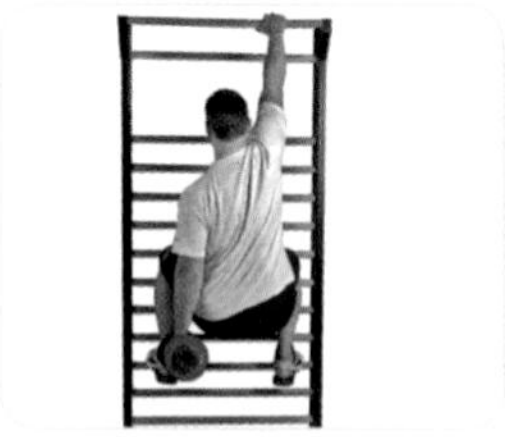

Step Chin with Dumbbell
Page 101

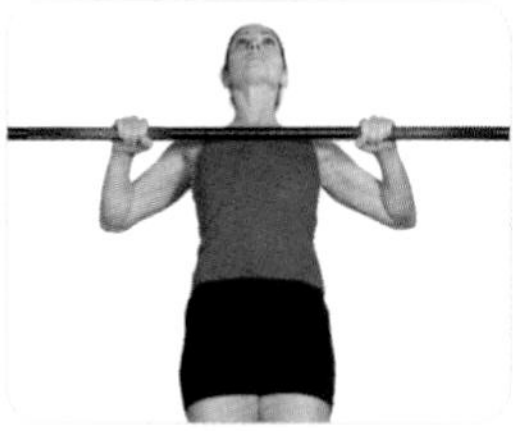

45-Degree Body Row
page 90

## Z
### weeks 1–4

Ab Wheel
page 110

Plank to Pike
page 128

Layout on Rings
page 130

Plow with Rotation
page 114

Hanging Raise with Rotation
page 120

## PROGRAM: XI  DURATION: 4 WEEKS

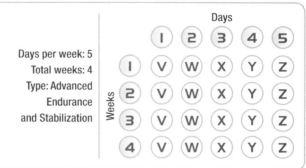

Days per week: 5
Total weeks: 4
Type: Advanced
Endurance
and Stabilization

| Weeks \ Days | 1 | 2 | 3 | 4 | 5 |
|---|---|---|---|---|---|
| 1 | V | W | X | Y | Z |
| 2 | V | W | X | Y | Z |
| 3 | V | W | X | Y | Z |
| 4 | V | W | X | Y | Z |

## PRESCRIPTION

| Week | Sets | Repetitions | Weight/Progression | Rest Set/Exercise |
|---|---|---|---|---|
| 1 | 5 | 6 | TBD | :75 / :75 |
| 2 | 5 | 8 | Weight remains the same throughout the program. | :75 / :90 |
| 3 | 5 | 10 | | :90 / :90 |
| 4 | 5 | 12 | | :90 / :90 |

## EXERCISE SEQUENCE

| Order \ Workout | V | W | X | Y | Z |
|---|---|---|---|---|---|
| 1 | Deadlift | Lunge | Push-up | Chin-up | Ab Wheel |
| 2 | Deadlift | Lunge | Push-up | Chin-up | Ab Wheel |
| 3 | Deadlift | Lunge | Push-up | Chin-up | Ab Wheel |
| 4 | Deadlift | Lunge | Push-up | Chin-up | Ab Wheel |
| 5 | Deadlift | Lunge | Push-up | Chin-up | Ab Wheel |

**Notes:** In this section, training occurs five times per week, so exercises are grouped to one of the 5 Essentials per day, five exercises per Essential. It is not recommended to change the entire order of each group, week to week; however, it is suggested to change the order of two exercises per day, on a weekly basis.

# GLOSSARY

**abduction.** Movement away from the body.

**adduction.** Movement toward the body.

**alternating grip.** One hand grasping with the palm facing toward the body and the other facing away.

**anterior.** Located in the front.

**concentric** (contraction). Occurs when a muscle shortens in length and develops tension, e.g., the upward movement of a dumbbell in a biceps curl.

**curvilinear** (movement path). Moving in a curved path.

**dynamic.** Continuously moving.

**eccentric** (contraction). The development of tension while a muscle is being lengthened, e.g., the downward movement of a dumbbell in a biceps curl.

**extension.** The act of straightening.

**flexion.** The bending of a joint.

**iliotibial band (ITB).** A thick band of fibrous tissue that runs down the outside of the leg, beginning at the hip and extending to the outer side of the tibia just below the knee joint. The band functions in coordination with several of the thigh muscles to provide stability to the outside of the knee joint.

**isometric.** Muscles contracting against an equal resistance, resulting in no movement.

**lateral.** Located on, or extending toward, the outside.

**lordosis.** Forward curvature of the spine and lumbar region.

**medial.** Located on, or extending toward, the middle.

**neutral position** (spine). A spinal position resembling an "S" shape, consisting of a lordosis in the lower back, when viewed in profile.

**posterior.** Located behind.

**proprioceptive neuromuscular facilitation (PNF).** Refers to a neuromuscular pattern of contraction that utilizes the greatest efficiency regarding positional awareness.

**scapula.** The protrusion of bone on the mid to upper back, also known as the shoulder blade.

**static.** No movement; holding a given position.

## LATIN TERMINOLOGY

*The following glossary explains the Latin terminology used to describe the body's musculature. Certain words are derived from Greek, which has been indicated in each instance.*

### NECK

**scalenus.** Greek *skalénós,* "unequal"

**splenius.** Greek *spléníon,* "plaster, patch"

**sternocleidomastoid.** Greek *stérnon,* "chest," Greek *kleís,* "key," and Greek *mastoeidés,* "breastlike"

### CHEST

**coracobrachialis.** Greek *korakoeidés,* "ravenlike," and *brachium,* "arm"

**pectoralis (major and minor).** *pectus,* "breast"

### SHOULDERS

**deltoideus (anterior, medial, and posterior).** Greek *deltoeidés,* "delta-shaped"

**infraspinatus.** *infra,* "under," and *spina,* "thorn"

**levator scapulae.** *levare,* "to raise," and *scapulae,* "shoulder [blades]"

**subscapularis.** *sub,* "below," and *scapulae,* "shoulder [blades]"

**supraspinatus.** *supra,* "above," and *spina,* "thorn"

**teres (major and minor).** *teres,* "rounded"

### UPPER ARM

**biceps brachii.** *biceps,* "two-headed," and *brachium,* "arm"

**brachialis.** *brachium,* "arm"

**triceps brachii.** *triceps,* "three-headed," and *brachium,* "arm"

### LOWER ARM

**brachioradialis.** *brachium,* "arm," and *radius,* "spoke"

**extensor carpi radialis.** *extendere,* "to extend," Greek *karpós,* "wrist," and *radius,* "spoke"

**extensor digitorum.** *extendere,* "to extend," and *digitus,* "finger, toe"

flexor carpi radialis. *flectere*, "to bend," Greek *karpós*, "wrist," and *radius*, "spoke"

flexor digitorum. *flectere*, "to bend," and *digitus*, "finger, toe"

## CORE

obliquus externus. *obliquus*, "slanting," and *externus*, "outward"

obliquus internus. *obliquus*, "slanting," and *internus*, "within"

rectus abdominis. *rego*, "straight, upright," and *abdomen*, "belly"

serratus anterior. *serra*, "saw," and *ante*, "before"

transversus abdominis. *transversus*, "athwart," and *abdomen*, "belly"

## BACK

erector spinae. *erectus*, "straight," and *spina*, "thorn"

latissimus dorsi. *latus*, "wide," and *dorsum*, "back"

quadratus lumborum. *quadratus*, "square, rectangular," and *lumbus*, "loin"

rhomboideus. Greek *rhembesthai*, "to spin"

trapezius. Greek *trapezion*, "small table"

## HIPS

gemellus (inferior and superior). *geminus*, "twin"

gluteus maximus. Greek *gloutós*, "rump," and *maximus*, "largest"

gluteus medius. Greek *gloutós*, "rump," and *medialis*, "middle"

gluteus minimus. Greek *gloutós*, "rump," and *minimus*, "smallest"

iliopsoas. *ilium*, "groin," and Greek *psoa*, "groin muscle"

iliacus. *ilium*, "groin"

obturator externus. *obturare*, "to block," and *externus*, "outward"

obturator internus. *obturare*, "to block," and *internus*, "within"

pectineus. *pectin*, "comb"

piriformis. *pirum*, "pear," and *forma*, "shape"

quadratus femoris. *quadratus*, "square, rectangular," and *femur*, "thigh"

## UPPER LEG

adductor longus. *adducere*, "to contract," and *longus*, "long"

adductor magnus. *adducere*, "to contract," and *magnus*, "major"

biceps femoris. *biceps*, "two-headed," and *femur*, "thigh"

gracilis. *gracilis*, "slim, slender"

rectus femoris. *rego*, "straight, upright," and *femur*, "thigh"

sartorius. *sarcio*, "to patch" or "to repair"

semimembranosus. *semi*, "half," and *membrum*, "limb"

semitendinosus. *semi*, "half," and *tendo*, "tendon"

tensor fasciae latae. *tenere*, "to stretch," *fasciae*, "band," and *latae*, "laid down"

vastus intermedius. *vastus*, "immense, huge," and *intermedius*, "between"

vastus lateralis. *vastus*, "immense, huge," and lateralis, "side"

vastus medialis. *vastus*, "immense, huge," and *medialis*, "middle"

## LOWER LEG

extensor hallucis. *extendere*, "to extend," and *hallex*, "big toe"

flexor hallucis. *flectere*, "to bend," and *hallex*, "big toe"

gastrocnemeus. Greek *gastroknémía*, "calf [of the leg]"

peroneus. *peronei*, "of the fibula"

soleus. *solea*, "sandal"

tibialis anterior. *tibia*, "reed pipe," and *ante*, "before"

tibialis posterior. *tibia*, "reed pipe," and *posterus*, "coming after"

# CREDITS & ACKNOWLEDGMENTS

Photographs: Jonathan Conklin Photography, Inc.
Robert Wright

Retouching: Zoe Campagna
Jonathan Conklin

Models: Mark Tenore, Sydney Foster, Jamie Kovac, Rico Wesley, and Matt Cohen

Poster Illustration by Linda Bucklin/Shutterstock

Anatomical illustrations by 3D4Medical, except insets on pages 10, 11, 15, 19, 21, 25, 29, 31, 33, 35, 39, 43, 45, 47, 49, 51, 53, 55, 57, 65, 71, 73, 75, 79, 81, 89, 91, 93, 95, 97, 99, 103, 105, 111, 115, 117, 119, 121, 123, 127, 131 by Linda Bucklin/Shutterstock

## ACKNOWLEDGMENTS

There are several people who have made very direct and substantial contributions to this book who I want to personally thank. Since I handwrite all of the text in this book (and my handwriting has deteriorated to "barely legible"), I want to recognize Shannon Plumstead, who has again masterfully and expeditiously put my cursive onto the typed page. Greg Cimino for getting the "deal done," as he always seems to be able to do in a way that is agreeable to everyone.

I want to also thank these people for their contributions to the content: Rico Wesley for his help with the text and Gillian Gauthier for her contribution to the development of the sample programs. I would also like to thank Mark Tenore, Sydney Foster, Jamie Kovac, Rico Wesley, and Matt Cohen for their skillful modeling. A huge thanks to Noah Emmerich, a client and friend, and my wife, Deborah, for their immensely helpful contributions of time and advice on how to literally lay the programs out so that they would be both understandable and user-friendly.

I also would like to mention Lisa Purcell at Moseley Road for her patience in helping put this book together, and Sean Moore, who took the idea and ran with it.

Finally, I want to let my family know that without them—Ma, Mary, Jen, Tony, Milena, and Deb—none of this would have meaning. As always, this is for you.